BENEATH THE

CORDELIA FRANCES BIDDLE

SIMON & SCHUSTER

New York London

Toronto Sydney

Tokyo Singapore

SIMON & SCHUSTER
Simon & Schuster Building
Rockefeller Center
1230 Avenue of the Americas
New York, New York 10020

Designed by Pei Loi Koay
Manufactured in the United States of America

10 9 8 7 6 5 4 3 2 1

Library of Congress Cataloging-in-Publication Data

Biddle, Cordelia Frances.
    Beneath the wind / by Cordelia Frances Biddle.
        p.   cm.
    1. Americans—Travel—Borneo—History—20th
century—Fiction.
    2. Women—Pennsylvania—Philadelphia—Fiction.
    3. Yachts and yachting—Fiction. 4. Borneo—History—
Fiction. I. Title.
    PS3552.I333B4   1993
    813'.54—dc20   93-22838
                                                          CIP
ISBN: 0-671-78703-9

ACKNOWLEDGMENTS

I would like to thank my friends Flo Allen and Carol Lanning for their enthusiasm, encouragement, and support; my father, Livingston Biddle, for teaching me poetry; and my husband, Stephen Zettler, for his love and enduring patience.

For my children,
Cordelia, Richard, and Christian

"Alcedo is the Indian word for the kingfisher bird.

A bird who lays her eggs only when the weather is calm,

And the days serene—a time we call the 'Halcyon Days.'

May our ship know only halcyon days,

And may all who sail within her find peace.

I christen thee 'Alcedo.' "

—Excerpt from the diaries of
Eugenia Paine Axthelm

PROLOGUE: THE DIARIES
OF EUGENIA PAINE AXTHELM

DECEMBER 29, 1888
Philadelphia

Dear Diary,

Today is my eighteenth birthday! I am finally a grown-up and very, VERY happy.

Last night was the most lovely "after Christmas" ball at the Axthelms'—George (of all people!!) was terribly attentive and charming—Nell said she was simply dying of jealousy—I said I couldn't believe it myself, and we both started giggling and nearly knocked the tea things onto Mrs. Milbray's lap!

But I do feel sad for poor Philip. It must seem as if I'm deserting him just because George lives such a grand life. Oh, I hope Philip doesn't think I'm frivolous, swayed by wealth and possessions and such like— after all he's been my friend forever. (Since those awful "Tuesday afternoons" and that's certainly a long time!)

Here's what happened: I was talking to Nell by the desserts table, smiling, you know, and gazing about the room, pretending to know everyone there, as if I were having the absolutely best time in the whole world when George sauntered over. He said something to Nell—very shy and sweet—and then just stood there.

Then dear old faithful Philip appeared and asked me for a dance, but I said: "Oh, Philip, you're so kind! But I believe Mr. Axthelm just requested this turn."!!!

Can you imagine anyone as brazen???? Two beaux competing for my hand. Je suis la Belle de la belle Philadelphie!

I'd better go or Father will start grumbling about being late for Gran's (as if we've ever been late).

Oh, these were Father's words on the way home in the carriage:
"Pleasant fellow." (That meant George) "Nice family."
The highest accolades possible! Could anyone ask for more?

Eee.

JANUARY 26, 1889!

My dear, dear Diary,

I am really and truly in love! I know it. I do. George is wonderful. Perfect. He's been reading Mr. Hawthorne's works to me and trying to educate me out of my "schoolgirl ways." Next month we tackle Mr. Melville! George thinks by then I'll be ready. He sits and reads, and I work at my cross-stitch, and Mother's little delft clock tick-tocks away on the mantel and the world becomes cozy and serene.

I've grown extremely fond of the drawing room, and I'm always dressed in my finest for George's "afternoons"—a corset and every-thing—Nell says I'm putting on airs—but she doesn't understand.

I think if Father lets me I'll put my hair up in a swirl, like the pictures in Mrs. Godey's Lady's Book. I need to look as womanly as I feel. A chignon and maybe just a whip of bangs, and then rat it back with a Spanish comb. Tres à la mode, n'est-ce pas?

Must run, and do my "homework" before George comes. I have so very much to learn.

Mademoiselle E.

FEBRUARY 3

. . . Add to the New Year's list:

1. *Don't babble. Be regal.*
2. *Be more mysterious. (One brief glance is sufficient)*
3. *Never, never, never, under any circumstances, giggle. (Not even with poor, dear Nell) Only children giggle.*
4. *STAND UP STRAIGHT. A woman always acts self-assured.*

There's going to be a "the dansante" tonight at the Renny Pauls' house in Chestnut Hill. I know George and I will be the talk of the en-tire crowd! I'm going to wear garnet-colored velvet and shoes to match. Well!

More later—from E.

Actually it's Feb. 15! I couldn't wait till tomorrow. George proposed!

I'm the happiest girl in the entire world and terribly in love. We're to have a house on Chestnut Street, right next to the "Turk's" (can you imagine—all Mr. Axthelm's children use that gruesome name?) Mr. Axthelm will do nicely for me, thank you very much!

Anyway, this is how it happened.

George came over this evening, after supper, but he requested to speak to Father—very serious, you know—as if this were some sort of business endeavor—I could hardly keep from laughing—who says we women don't know anything?

They conferred behind the closed doors of Father's study for what seemed like hours—I in the drawing room, cross-stitching as if my life depended on it. Then Father emerged, with a most formal:

"I'll leave you two young people alone."

Well! That was that. How could George ever have thought I'd turn him down? I knew we were destined for each other from the moment we met! But he was so shy, kneeling there, and so hesitant and wonderfully unsure!

And after he kissed me! I loved that, though I didn't know how to breathe at the same time. I've never been kissed like that before (Philip didn't count). I wasn't sure where my hands were supposed to go or what to do with my neck. I'm sure I'll learn. Fortunately it was just one kiss, so I didn't get too flustered (or look too silly, I hope!) I'm going to experiment with the mirror to get the pose right. I think you're supposed to swoon somehow.

Oh, and I have a ruby engagement ring! A ruby set in a gold triangle with diamonds all around. It's the most beautiful thing I've ever seen. I am never, never, never going to take it off.

I have a thousand more things to say, but I'm far too weary. . . .

Oh, thank you God. Thank you stars and sun and moon and each little cloud that roves the earth.

The future Mrs. A.

FEBRUARY 17

Dear Diary,

I'm sorry I didn't write last night, but I was much too busy. What a whirl this engagement period will be!

We had a perfectly lovely celebratory luncheon yesterday at Mr. Axthelm's. All the family present: Carl, Tony, his wife, Cassandra, Martin Jr. and Isobel, and of course George and I. We were the stars of the show. Many toasts and high, good cheer. The whole group so kind I felt I should burst into tears at any moment.

I looked down that long table at the Axthelm features so similar and strong and was filled with an enormous sense of belonging, of family. It seems amazing to me that they should all look so alike; it's as though they must hold each other dearer than we ordinary Philadelphians do. Gran and Aunt Sally Van and all our crowd are so cold and bland-featured. We're like pieces of suet.

There is Mr. Axthelm with his black hair, pale eyes and that sharp, bony nose (very elegant and Roman) and there is George who has taken those same gray eyes and raven hair and translated them into something poetic and soft. Mr. A. is like a hawk on a precipice and George is like an eaglet peering worriedly down.

"Genie"

FEBRUARY 19

Dear Diary,

I just came from seeing Philip at Frith and Co., the boat builders where he works. I wasn't looking forward to it at all! I felt quite mean—I know we did have sort of a childish "understanding," but that was all so long ago, and no one can be expected to stay in one place forever.

Anyway I did feel bad. I even go cross at poor Tom, who'd gotten into his best livery to take "Mistress Eugenia" down to see "Master Philip." I said we'd never get there if he let Toby loaf along—all the other horses were clipping along at a decent trot—so of course he whipped Toby up and the poor old horse got quite lathered. Then they both had to stand outside shivering in the cold while I went inside and dined on roast beef and Yorkshire pudding!

I am a hateful person, cruel, thoughtless and unkind. Sometimes I just don't understand why I behave the way I do.

Of course Philip was a dear, "overjoyed at my happy news," etc. I told him George wanted him to serve as best man and he was geniunely touched.

And there we were surrounded by all those ghastly paintings of Frith and Co. ships. Philip's so proud of the company's designs, but, I don't know, it all seemed so dull and Philadelphian somehow. Mahogany furniture and tonnage and hull capacity—it all seems so creaky!

FEBRUARY 28

Snowdrops in the garden! The first hint of spring! For the first time in a long, long time I thought about Mother. I think she used to take me out to view the first flowers herself. I have a sharp, but disjointed memory of holding a warm hand and toddling along, trying to keep up, and then being told to kneel down and smell!

"Smell that, Genie, that's the smell of hope," the invisible voice would say.

I got so sad, remembering all of this. I wondered what it would be like to have a mother just now, whether she'd be proud of my match with George, and what she'd say, what we'd talk about or plan.

Then I thought about Gran's house in Maine, and how I stood in that big window under the eaves on the third floor and looked across the bay to the distant blue hills. I remember thinking I was an angel sent to guard the world. I wanted to be someone special.

The lights are being lit all along the street as I write this. I can see people bustling home at the end of the day, and their waiting families busy in their cheery homes. I think I'll break my rule and go down to the kitchen and visit Catherine and Mary. I'm feeling so lonely all of a sudden. I'll work on my Grande Dame role tomorrow.

E

• • •

Dear Diary,

Miss Paine sends her regards and wishes you to know how miserable she is!!!

Poor George. It's just not fair. His father promised him a job at the bank after we were married, and now he won't do it. Says George doesn't have a business head or something. Well, that's not true. He's perfectly wonderful with people. Everyone adores him. (I certainly do) And he can tell marvelous stories, and he loves to read. He's been educating me! My heart breaks for him; he wants so much to have his father's respect—it must be awful being the youngest. I remember when Nicky was alive, sometimes he would tease me and make me feel such a baby. Well, damn the "Turk"! Now, isn't that terrible? But that's how I feel.

Oh, P.S. George says when it's warm he'll take me rowing on the lake in Fairmount Park. Just the two of use together and no chaperone!!!!

Just a small addition—I talked to Father about the "George Question" and he says he's sure Mr. A. will find something for George and that I mustn't worry. I hope so. I do want everyone to be happy.

I must run—my first sitting for my portrait—aren't I the Grand Lady?

Dear Diary,

It is very late. I heard the grandfather clock in the hall strike three. I am creeping around so that Father and the others will not hear me. What could I say? I am so frightened.

And aren't I a silly girl to be afraid just as I'm about to marry the most glamorous, handsome bachelor in all of Philadelphia? Nell would think I was loony and Mary would say I was "daft in the head," but I can't help it.

Here's a poem I wrote:

> *I ask for strength,*
> *Let it not be denied.*
> *I did not think to choose of happiness*
> *Or peace.*
> *I do not ask for love.*
> *I know our lives are filled with crashing seas*
> *And jagged rocks;*
> *I ask for strength,*
> *That I*
> *Might once give mine to those I love.*

Good night diary. This is the morning of my wedding day.

SEPTEMBER 7, 1890

. . . Nurse is cross again; she says that Lizzie's teething has been keeping her awake for days! Really! As if that's my fault. So of course Nurse argued with Cook who took to her room with one of her "back pains" and left the poor little kitchen maid, Anna, to prepare dinner. Then John came in and told me he and the other footmen were not going to stand for an improperly cooked meal. I hate it when George is away; these disasters always seem to occur then. I know he thinks it's my fault the house is not better run.

Oh, he did send word that he's getting us a day sailer for Newport— "big enough for my little family" the letter said. She'll be 60' or so, a decent sized boat for a picnic. He's naming her Akbar, after the Indian king. . . . Must run and see to Miss Cross Patch. . . . E.

• • •

. . . Why we are forced to have these miserable German Fräuleins visited on us, I'll never know. George says they're the most dependable nannies, but I know that's just his father talking. I do hate these women; they're bossy and domineering and they pull Lizzie's hair and scold the baby (who's only a tiny, wee thing) and I feel powerless against them. . . .

. . . Today was the worst of all: Fräulein Dorner argued with Fr. Gertrude and refused to turn the Governess cart round and if it hadn't rained I don't know where they'd have gotten to—probably Camden! Croup kettles again, I suppose. Really! And just when Jinx had gotten over that first beastly cold—she shouldn't have been out at all—but you try telling those Valkyries anything about health!!

Catherine stopped by—not really stopped—her visit had been set up long ago—she's quite overwhelmed by my new surroundings. Her visit cheered me considerably.

As she says, the night is darkest just before the dawn. Just the sight of her was enough to bring back those cozy afternoons in the kitchen, when there was just us and Father was busy (and I had no lessons)— the steam coming off the wood cabinets and the soft sunlight in the windows. Sometimes I miss the old days so much I want to cry.

Well, back to war with the Prussians. Wish me luck. No, wish me strength!

Dear Diary,

It's very late, perhaps one or two in the morning, and the house is fi-nally still. I gave birth to a little boy this morning. It was not a hard la-bor, but George was not with me and I wanted him there. I don't know why. He would have been uncomfortable and awkward, but he would have been there. I don't know where he was. I sent to the Club and to his father's house to no avail. He's home now.

I feel so foolish, weepy and sad when I should be happy. Little Paul is a beautiful baby, quiet and fine, and he's sleeping here beside me. I won out against the Germans (please congratulate me) and the baby is allowed in my room, so I can nurse him myself.

Please, God, watch over my family. Help me to care for my children, and make them strong and kind. And God, please in thy own strength, help them find joy in their lives. Amen.

OCTOBER 20, 1898
Newport

What a heavenly fall day! I feel like a butterfly emerging from her tent. Not one cold, or tooth on the way or poison ivy or twisted ankle or earache or cough, not even a sniffle!! We are as hale and hearty a foursome as you will be likely to find. Cass joked at supper that the three children and I look like an advertisement for Pear's soap! Of course Mr. A. didn't know what Pear's soap was, which set the table laughing—these Axthelms can be pretty amusing when they set their mind to it.

Now it is a lovely fall evening—sea gulls and soft breezes and the gentle lap of beetles asking me to kindly lift the screen and let them in.

Tomorrow George drops anchor and whisks us away for a week on the new boat, Atrippa. We've hardly seen him this summer. This yacht is a Circe, but now we're all off for a ride: one cabin for Papa Bear, one for Mama Bear, one for two little girls and one for a very small boy. . . .

MAY 10, 1899

Dear Diary,

My tenth wedding anniversary! Celebrated with a turn round the park in the new coach and four. George off to Kiel for the yacht races there (he's going to dine with Kaiser Wilhelm and the Vanderbilts!) but I declined the trip to dear, old Allemagne. (I was afraid the accents might make me think I was back with Gertrude and Dorner—heaven help us!—ver ar dze babis, Frau Axthelm?)

I feel quite liberated, an old-hand society matron who celebrates an anniversary on her own. I think I've reached the height of sophistication.

Paul is growing bigger and bigger and naughty as the day is long. He's discovered teasing Lizzie (who hates being the brunt of a joke). Sometimes I feel that having three children is seventy times more difficult than having two. Someone's always in tears; someone's always left out, and mothers do not have the wisdom of Solomon. . . .

SEPTEMBER 14, 1902
Philadelphia

. . . Monsieur Farrier finally told me today (of all times) that he couldn't get enough of the English chintz I wanted for the Alcedo's Main Saloon and that I shall have to use the rose pattern instead—tho' the Famille Rose vases will look magnificent with it. I'm not taking his full advice, however, and am maintaining my plan for the silk cord and tassels on the ottomans.

Some of the embroidered table linens arrived yesterday; they turned out even better than expected—S.Y. (for steam yacht) Alcedo in gold thread and all the burgees embroidered in primary colors—so crisp and nautical. I had George's luncheon served on them as a surprise.

The Turk has insisted on gold spigots for all the yacht's washrooms (well, not crew, naturally) and George and I had a good laugh about washing our hands in gold at teatime. I feel awfully lavish, just ordering one thing after another, but that's what I've been told to do.

Oh, and a set of Hawthorne for George's study. M. Farrier tells me he found a lovely edition, beautifully bound in green Moroccan. I just hope he can keep a secret. He can be such a prattling Frenchman.

Must run . . . John came in to say a box of china has arrived. I sincerely hope they have the yacht's burgee correct this time. . . .

• • •

She is named!

I made my speech, broke the champagne bottle—well, actually I failed my first attempt, which upset George, so he did it—I'd better start at the beginning.

It was a beautiful day. Absolutely perfect. Just starting to grow warm, but with a lovely cool breeze coming off the river. We arrived at 10:00, everyone in their nautical finery—I in a modified sailor's collar embroidered in azure blue, Lizzie, Jinx and Paul all matching.

The ceremony wasn't to begin till 11:00, but George decided on a private toast of champagne, and I thought, "Oh, dear—this doesn't bode well," especially with all the family coming—those can be trying times.

Anyway, then Tony and Cassandra arrived, and Martin and Isobel, and, of course, all the children. (Martin and Isobel's two are such rascals when they're free of their parents—good for them!) And when I think of young Sarah as my flower girl! She's as tall as Cass now and nearly as handsome. Then the ubiquitous Carl who arrived with my father?!

We hemmed and hawed waiting for the Turk (who had to make an entrance) and then submitted to the usual round of newspaper photographs: the Turk with George, with all his sons, with his grandsons, George and I alone—then with the children, etc. etc. and all this time boisterous jokes for the benefit of the photographers.

"Charming wife, George, charming. Better watch out for her!"

A wink, a nod to the audience and everyone laughs. Why, I'll never know. These jokes make me uncomfortable. And George.

Anyway George took my hand, which was lovely, and we had a quiet moment in the midst of the frenzy (you see how potent this Alcedo will be!)

Then the children were all over the Turk, showing off their new sailor costumes and Jinx did her new curtsy (nearly a full "reverence") and Paul pleaded with the Turk to join us which pleased the old man no end. It's strange how the old fox can soften, just like that.

But Lizzie felt her father was being left out, and she reached out her hand to him and asked if she could help steer the boat. To which George replied: "Tell you what, Liz, when Captain Cosby lets me steer, I'll let you help."

And there we were—a family again.
Then it was time for the christening and I said my speech:

> *Alcedo is the Indian word for the kingfisher bird.*
> *A bird who lays her eggs only when the weather is calm,*
> *And the days serene—a time we call the "Halcyon Days."*
> *May our ship know only halcyon days,*
> *And may all who sail within her find peace.*
> *I christen thee "Alcedo."*

I struck the bow with the bottle of champagne, but, of course, it didn't break, so George rushed forward and gave the bottle such a crack that glass and champagne flew all over the place.

Paul, who was standing close, got completely soaked and there were slivers of glass all over him. He was quite startled, but unhurt and very brave about his new suit. While we mopped him up, the Turk joked to George: "There you are! Don't even know your own strength! Ha! Ha!"

We had a magnificent luncheon after: prawns, cold lobster, white asparagus with a lovely green sauce and rhubarb fool for dessert.

Halcyon Days—I hope so!

MAY 15

Dear Diary,

Father has just been to see me with some extraordinary news. It seems the Turk has arranged for him to be appointed to Governor Taft's staff in the Philippine Islands, so he'll be out "that-a-way" when we go to Borneo.

He was so pleased to be "back in harness again, don't you know, Genie." The sight was very touching. It seems he used to know the Ivard family of Borneo—the old diplomacy ties. . . .

Anyway, he's even been assigned a secretary. (Mr. A. can be a most thoughtful fellow—I don't know if I'd trust Father to wander across the Pacific on his own. He's become so absentminded.) The secretary's last name is Ridgeway—Father couldn't remember the first!!

George is out on the Alcedo for "sea trials" and sends word that she is behaving magnificently. I wish July were here already. . . .

JUNE 5

. . . Here's the guest list—Dr. DuPlessis and his wife, of course, so we have a plus and a minus right there.

Then my young cousin, Whitney, as tutor—I hope we don't have to put up with too many silly girls swarming around the boat.

But the surprise to end all surprises! NO NANNIES. Just my dear little Prue. How did I ever win this battle? you're asking. Well, you'll never know. . . .

JULY 1, *near midnight*

. . . George has just visited to tell me that his father wants him to do some business in Borneo—set up a metallurgy operation or something. I couldn't quite make it out, but he is so pleased. He's been discussing it with the Turk and Ogden Beckmann all day. Thank you, God, for making my husband so happy. . . .

JULY 24, 1903
Newport

My last entry from land. Almost everything's been loaded, and we're all set for the festivities tomorrow. Nell's coming up, and Frances and Wynn—we'll be quite a party. But that's not worth discussing now.

I am a-quiver with anticipation. I wonder at my joy at leaving. One would think I was imprisoned in this place, I am so anxious to be gone.

It is a glorious, starry night. I can hear the sea gulls clearly, and through the open window smell the sea.

Dear God, Watch over thy family in foreign lands. Protect and guide us; give us strong and loving hearts. And bring us home again safe, and filled with thy wonder. Amen

It has just struck midnight. July 25. Today we sail!

ONE

*O*GDEN   BECKMANN   WAS
THE TURK'S MAN. It was a title he particularly liked. There was a
threatening scent about it, like wolves near a pasture. "Just remember
who I work for," Beckmann would say quietly, and that would be
enough. Physical force was never necessary. Martin Axthelm, known
in financial circles as the "Turk," could sit in his private railway car;
he could act the model of a sanguine patriarch; he could smoke his cigars and discuss a new marble foyer for the house in Newport; he could
dine with his sons and their wives, throw costumed extravaganzas for
each grandchild; he could be seen at the polo matches at Merion or under the striped awnings of Bailey's Beach; he could appear unencumbered, aristocratic, and forgiving. Beckmann was his man, and
Beckmann had never failed him.

"Not for nearly twenty years, I haven't," Beckmann said aloud. The
thought pleased him, and he pressed his wide, dark face into a smile.
The smile disappeared, then manifested itself as a broadening of his
shoulders and back. Dressed in his habitual black morning coat, Beckmann looked as solid as a bear stretching its claws toward a tree full of
honey.

Beckmann walked on, looked over his shoulder once, then started
up Allyn Street. The sun had barely begun to penetrate Newport's back
alleys, and the refuse littering the cobbled and slimy path squelched
under his shoes. Beckmann pushed his feet down hard; the insistent
slap of leather against stone was the street's only sound. Nearly twenty

years ago, Beckmann thought, that's when I became a "gentleman." Or was turned into a gentleman.

Beckmann remembered the autumn of 1883 perfectly: the Turk moving easily through the various drawing rooms of Philadelphia and Newport with the words:

"You know my secretary, Beckmann, of course. Axthelm and Company relies on his advice. Any problems—he's the man to turn to." The laugh had been relaxed, jovial, almost benign, and the listening ears had been fooled. But then they'd have believed anything the Turk told them, Beckmann thought; that had been the plan.

"They're pompous, Ogden, and they're stupid," the Turk had once confided, "but I've got them where I want them. Axthelm and Company is important to this country. As important as Vanderbilt or Gould or any of those other Johnny-come-latelies. The blue bloods have to grant us a place in the firmament. But we all know a man 'in trade' can't move to the inner circle. And that's where you come in."

So the Turk, with Beckmann in tow, had made the rounds: "You remember my secretary, Ogden Beckmann . . ."; ". . . If there are any questions about Axthelm and Company or the Axthelm Trust, I'm afraid Ogden's the only fellow with intelligent answers. . . ." The same introductory speech and the same easy laugh had been repeated over and over; diamond studs had glistened; starched evening shirts had shone; trays of port and Madeira had made their silent rounds.

"No business at dinnertime, I realize, gentlemen—and ladies"—the Turk had smiled again and again—"but I did want you to make the acquaintance of my right-hand man. The Axthelm family's financial dealings can be difficult to comprehend. Even for me. And I fear they leave me with too little free time for more elevated activities. . . . For instance, this modest proposal of yours to renovate General Washington's headquarters at Valley Forge . . . Now that interests me. . . . Far more than the mechanics of some dreary bank . . ."

The speeches had been greeted with obsequious silence, then the society folk had tittered and given their immediate and goggle-eyed consent. The men's round, rosy faces had nodded studious agreement, while their wives had chattered away over tea and invented a past for the mysterious Mr. Beckmann. He was some sort of German count—perhaps even a distant relative of the great Von Bülow—one woman had ventured (that would explain the accent), whose family had run short of cash (hence his position as a hireling). Though not, as one wag had put it, before his education at Heidelberg had been completed (mystery or no, mingling with the great unwashed and uneducated was unthinkable). The contrived history had been approved, and the snub-nosed, pink-faced ex-Princeton and ex-Yale men had struggled to their feet to raise chummy glasses:

"To our nobleman on hard times . . ." they'd recited, ". . . may he escape the powers that be. . . ."

The remark had been followed by the inevitable laughter. At the turn of the century, in Newport, Saratoga Springs, Boston, or Philadelphia, the "powers that be" were one of two equally evil things: a wealthy father who refused to die or, even worse, a wealthy father-in-law who refused to die. Money, to those living on dwindling amounts of inherited cash, had the insistent pull of gravity. Socialites (who swore they knew better) flung themselves into orbit around the Turk and his sons—and Beckmann.

"May he escape the powers that be," Ogden Beckmann repeated as he picked his way up Allyn Street. On such a simple phrase was my status secured. Now I do what I choose and go where I wish. At the age of forty-eight, I am almost, but not quite, "acceptable," Not yet—at any rate.

Beckmann smiled and moved on. July 25, 1903, he reminded himself. Now the real work begins. The rest was frosting, fluff, illusion. Beckmann glanced over his shoulder one more time before pulling out his pocket watch. The only other creatures on the street were three beggar children who'd followed him from the carriage; Beckmann had been aware of them creeping up the alley, sticking to the shadows, leaping like rats between puddles. They recognized my carriage and my clothes, he thought; they imagine I'm some swell they can either rob or swindle. They're in for a surprise.

Beckmann looked at his watch. Ten to seven: He was early as intended. He snapped the gold case shut, and as he did so the metal collided with the one ray of light that had fought its way into Allyn Street. The explosion was as white as dynamite.

"Coo. Didja see that?" Beckmann heard behind him. "He's a real toff, this one. Didja see that pocket piece? Real gold. And the chain, too. Yards of it, I'd say."

Beckmann didn't bother to turn. Beggars and animals, he thought. Two species exactly alike; they'll lunge toward any piece of meat, maggots or dirt notwithstanding. They spread decay as easily as they do the scraps of refuse they filch from the rubbish bins where the better folk dwell.

Beckmann walked on and flicked aside some stiffened, gritty rags. At least he'd thought they were rags, but the moldy, fetid way in which they broke apart made him wonder whether they weren't the hide and scavenged bones of some small carcass. The smell was too foul to be inanimate.

Beckmann shook his malacca cane free; under his gray kid glove he gave its gold handle a quick caress. It was a reassuring symbol of who he was. Pink gold with a pleasant nub of smoky topaz placed under the palm, he reminded himself: wealth without ostentation. "You must dress the part, Ogden—if we're to be successful." The Turk had dictated, and Beckmann had followed those instructions exactly.

Ever more in awe, the boys crept closer; and all four moved further into the ruined darkness of Allyn Street.

During its days as purveyor to the China trade, the road had been a respectable place of ship chandlers and merchants. It had supplied the clippers that traveled from New England to the Orient, and it had grown fat and lazy with its profits: Cobbles had replaced mud tracks; stone steps led to Greek revival doorways; there were carriage mounts and brass ring tethers, signposts and a countinghouse. But then the day of the steamship had come, and the centers of trade had moved to deeper, wider harbors. Finally, even the dwindling whaling industry had taken its pungent odors elsewhere, and Allyn Street had been deserted to sink into its own sweat-stained despair.

Beckmann looked at the blackened, empty houses. They slumped together as though they'd been blown apart from within, as if the only force that held them upright was their innate sense of loss. One gutted building lurched toward the street; it seemed suspended solely by spit and cardboard. Another had given up the ghost entirely; it was a dusty pile of termite-chewed timbers that blew into ashes with each puff of wind.

They're like aristocracy anywhere, Beckmann decided; they're full of self-pity and dogged repetition. "In the old days we were handsome," they moan; "in the old days we ruled the earth. In the old days we . . ."

"You make me sick," Beckmann said with sudden vehemence, then he realized he'd reached his destination. It was a hastily nailed together pile of boards in a welter of similar creations, but Beckmann recognized it at once. After all, he'd been the one to discover the door and the dank rooms within.

"As discreetly as possible, Ogden," the Turk had ordered, and Beckmann had silently concurred. There'd been no need for the warning. Discretion applied to all Axthelm and Company ventures: Mr. Gould, Mr. Morgan, Mr. Drexel, even Mr. Vanderbilt; partnership demanded special skills, and Beckmann had learned from a master.

"Profits don't come from an overabundant heart," the Turk liked to repeat. "Remember what I tell my sons: 'You take what you want. Let the devil take the rest.' "

"Oh, and don't come running to me with every little problem, Ogden. I trust your judgment."

"You take what you want," Beckmann repeated silently. That's why I'm here. "Don't come running to me" has another translation entirely.

It's time, Beckmann realized. He glanced down the street. The beggar children were still there, creeping as close as they dared. They're adept, Beckmann told himself; they know I'm not here by chance. They're waiting to see what will happen next. But I'm afraid I must disappoint them.

In a sudden move he sprang for them. The speed and viciousness of the attack would have been surprising in a smaller person. In a body as bulky as Beckmann's it was overwhelming. The children leapt backward in terror, but they weren't quick enough. They fell under Beckmann's heavy shoes as his gold-handled, topaz-knobbed cane (that seductive and beautiful cane!) rained blows on their melon-soft heads.

Beckmann didn't stop till the children struggled to all fours and with howls of distress hobbled back down the alley. That'll teach them, Beckmann thought, runts like them, no better than garbage; they should have been drowned at birth. The world's too small a place for misfits and ne'er-do-wells. They're like sponges with nothing to cling to. Cut loose, they fester from within and they stink up anything they touch.

Beckmann straightened himself, dusted off his shoulders and broadcloth-covered chest, pulled down his jacket sleeves, and shook out his cuffs. Now I'm ready, he decided.

At Newport's only deep-water pier the Axthelms' enormous steam yacht, *Alcedo,* was ready to sail. The ship was the largest of the great American-owned yachts, the largest yacht in the world. She'd been built to exacting specifics in the city of Bremerhaven on the North Sea, a place known for the meticulousness of its shipbuilders. The *Alcedo* was nearly three hundred feet in length, as sizable as most ocean-going freighters, with a beam that measured thirty-one feet and a gross tonnage of over eleven hundred. She had a crew of a hundred, saloons and cabins decorated in Louis Quinze furniture, oil paintings, tapestries, Ming vases, Aubusson carpets, and a porcelain service for eighty that had been commissioned in Wedgwood to carry the yacht's own private insignia. She had three kitchens, a radio room, a library, a picture gallery, a dining saloon fitted out with English Chippendale, and a central stair that curved into the main saloon in a slow, showy spiral.

Her mammoth twin engines were imported from Dortmund and Sons. Her electric plant lighted seven thousand bulbs and powered a machine that produced one thousand pounds of ice daily, and all this was kept in ready usage by furnaces powered with coal, which the fireroom gang shoveled into the flames night and day without ceasing.

Decorated with burgees from every yacht club on the east coast of the United States, the ship was also hung with flags from the various nations she would visit. For this was the yacht's maiden voyage, the year-long journey that would carry her off to the farthest reaches of the world. During the past month every shiny inch of her had been painted and repainted with the same glowing white, her brightwork varnished again and again till it looked as though it were encased in rock crystal, and her brasses rubbed with such vigorous spit and polish that they'd grown hot enough to smoke.

The steam yacht *Alcedo:* July 25, 1903, was her day.

Aware of the momentousness of the occasion, running to and fro as if on fire, stevedores, stewards, even boiler room stokers, raced along the dock, from the holding sheds to the ship, from quay-side to the two gangways. Back and forth, back and forth, they ran carrying hatboxes, valises, steamer trunks, wardrobes, sprays of flowers, and the endless supply of kegs and casks, fruits, vegetables and meats that the yacht demanded. Enormous blocks of ice, pulled by dray horses and wagons, rattled and creaked over the wooden pilings and pier. The din was terrific; there was a frenzied tone in every voice. Even the most hardened and leathery seaman shouted words that were both officious and swelled with self-importance. Every man considered his task the only one crucial to the ship's departure.

"Behind you!"

"Watch your step, sport!"

"Going through! Going through! Flowers for milady's cabin. Mind where you put them!"

"Says you!"

"Says I!"

The day was clear and very bright, and everywhere flashes of yellow sunlight glittered down on the foredeck bow and the preparations for the send-off party. Musicians began to tune their instruments; stewards strung awnings of scalloped white canvas that grew hard and tight round the stanchions; they mounded heaps of oysters, littleneck clams, *belons,* and tiny *Marennes blanches* in quivering ice, and placed vats of sevruga caviar within easy reach, then set row after row of champagne flutes on the damask-topped, food-laden tables.

The sunlight smiled on each occupation, leaping from the starched white back of one steward to the Axthelm crest buttons of another, from the hand-carved urns to the Sheffield punch bowls, from the monogrammed borders of the round silver trays to the gold-tined forks and the tortoiseshell knives. The sunlight scampered this way and that, skipping willy nilly as if on its soul's true mission, as if there weren't enough time in this world to show off the lavishness of the ship's new fittings or how enviable her voyage would be.

Then the light grew tired of such opulent splendor and it careened past the bow, blinding weathered faces that struggled along the dock with a bewildering array of luggage. It alighted on pine boxes filled with flannel-wrapped melons, with raspberries, peaches, and Mirabelle plums, before leaping into the sea, which then threw up its own reflection in diamondlike swirls to cover the great hull itself.

A breeze hummed among the guy wires and stiffened momentarily, toppling four buckets of crimson gladioli. Their severed blossoms rolled under the deck ropes, tossing one way, then another till they fell to the dock, scattering over the gray wood and dropping at last with a salty splash into the waiting waves. For a brief second the ship appeared to float in this scarlet pool. Then the breeze moved on, flapped the stewards' high-buttoned coats, slapped the ropes and the halyards against mast and funnel, and lifted aloft the cries of the gulls, the lisp of violins, and the tarry, hot, engine room scent of a ship about to sail.

On Allyn Street, Ogden Beckmann pulled the creaking door shut behind him, and waited for his eyes to become accustomed to the building's dark interior. The door had given way reluctantly with an angry, rasping sound and Beckmann wondered who else had heard it. He stared ahead into blackness, and clenched and unclenched his fists till he saw a wavery glow creep under a second door. He crossed the room, wrenched that door open, then stepped inside and stood near the wall. The stone was damp and uneven; it smelled of mold and brackish water.

A kerosene lantern stood on a plain deal table; there was nothing more. The flame hissed and spluttered; the wick, newly lit, suddenly outlined a man's shadow, and Beckmann spun around. The shadow was tall, lithe; it moved with the ease of a cat in autumn. The light faltered, then grew strong. This time it glowed into a young and tanned face whose eyes were a startling blue. It was the eyes Beckmann noticed first. They looked reckless—insufficient for the task. Beckmann cursed silently; he should have met the man earlier. He should have made sure.

"I didn't expect you yet," Beckmann said. "I'm always early, myself. I'm surprised when others follow my example."

The man didn't answer and Beckmann studied him. At least he was on time, Beckmann told himself, and he's got the proper uniform; he may be more seasoned than he looks. Pratt knew what I needed; he wouldn't have sent someone who couldn't handle the job.

"The uniform's good," Beckmann said. "Did Pratt get it for you?"

"Pratt's never seen me" was the answer. "I use my own suppliers. A face that recognizes you is one face too many. I intend to die when and how I choose."

A cool customer, Beckmann decided, very cool indeed. He looked more closely at the uniform. It fit well; the dark navy serge was pressed and immaculate; the gold braid that signified its wearer's rank as a lieutenant in the United States Navy was shiny from brushing. There seemed nothing wrong, but Beckmann had an uneasy sense of weightlessness. He felt he'd lost control.

"Your name will be Brown," Beckmann said firmly. "Lieutenant James Armand Brown. The United States Naval Academy, class of 1899. That will make you a few years younger than I suspect you really are. But that shouldn't make a difference."

Beckmann waited for a response; when none came he continued. "Other than those facts, nothing more is needed. Any embellishments, ask me first. Problems or questions: likewise." Beckmann glared as he said this; he didn't like the easy assurance in the younger man's shoulders; he didn't like the relaxed hands or the strength he guessed lay below their surface.

"What made you choose Brown?" the man finally asked; his voice was low, almost amused.

"You have a problem with it, mister?" Beckmann snarled, and this time Brown didn't answer.

At precisely 9:00 A.M., while the musicians and stewards stood at attention and the Pinkerton guards were paraded to position at each gangway, the crane and derrick at the farthest end of the dock was at its busiest.

Dozens of white crates, clearly marked *Axthelm & Co* in thick red letters, stood in line to be loaded. Some were high and square, some low and lean; all were heavy. Under the hot July sun, the men struggling with the ropes and cargo net swore at each other in grunts that sounded like blows to the belly. They burned their fingers on the hemp cord and tore skin from their callused hands. Then the crane dipped its neck, squealed its pulleys, and yanked one more box into the ship's dark hold.

Ogden Beckmann appeared among the waiting cases. He moved into the light from an obscuring shadow, his black form growing to solid definition as if the sun were creating its own harsh opposite. Beckmann's face was composed; it held no expression, but he gently touched one of the crates, letting his hand linger there as his eyes followed the activity of the pier.

"Mr. Axthelm on board yet?" Beckmann spoke quietly as the second mate came over to inspect the cargo.

The mate was startled. Beckmann gave him the creeps; he always turned up where you least expected him, and he examined the smallest job like a dog after a bone. You'd like to catch me out, wouldn't you? the mate thought; you'd like to say we was careless with these blasted crates. You'd like to go running off to the old man and say we wasn't doing our best.

But no one could be disrespectful to Ogden Beckmann and keep his job. "Oh, no, sir," the mate answered. "Mr. Axthelm, he doesn't like these early starts. I expect him and the family won't be along till we're near ready to sail."

Then, as Beckmann continued to stare at him, the mate added a hasty: "Sorry, sir. I thought you was talking about Mr. George. The Turk's already on board—" The mate stopped himself. "I mean, Mr. Axthelm senior, sir. No disrespect intended. It's just the name we always . . ."

"Yes, I know." Beckmann stopped the conversation abruptly and turned his steps toward the gangway.

Half an hour later, in his son's study on board, while Beckmann stood at respectful attention, the Turk leaned back within the glossy wings of a high-backed chair. The old man's eyes were sharp as a blackbird's, and his bony nose and chiseled cheekbones twitched and refused to relax. Smoke from his cigar curled lazily round him, but did nothing to soften his features. Without turning his head, the Turk took the room's measure, considered it, and inhaled deeply. If there was one smell he liked as much as the scent of a good cigar, it was the smell of money: the pungent scent of Moroccan bookbindings, leather-topped desks, thick carpets, polished furniture and oak mantels. The Turk nodded his approval; the room was everything he'd wanted: a place of recognized exclusivity, inspiring hushed voices and awed glances. Martin Axthelm, patriarch of the clan and head of Axthelm and Company, was pleased. His son George's boat was just what he'd ordered.

"The best that money can buy, Beckmann," the Turk said quietly. "Another little lesson. Remember it." He raised his cigar and took one final reflexive glance around the room. "Cheating on the details fools no one. Except those who enjoy being fooled."

"Sir," Beckmann responded. He clasped his hands in front of him and planted his feet firmly. No noise from the dock dared intrude on the sanctuary, and Beckmann felt constrained to be equally silent.

The Turk half closed his eyes, then glanced at the curtains draping the windows and motioned for Beckmann to shut them. Once the task was completed, the Turk began in earnest:

"Remember, Beckmann," he said, "I am relying on you solely in this matter. No one else will be out there. No one but George, of course. Which is to say, no one at all. Youngest sons can be a disappointment. You understand my meaning."

Beckmann knew better than to answer. A command was a command.

"Good," the Turk said. "We agree, then. Carl and I can handle that old fool, Paine, from here—though you may hear from him yourself. Or from Ridgeway. He has the yacht's schedule. You'll have the honor of dealing with the Ivards yourself. Father and son. *Père et fils*. A dubious honor, I should add."

The Turk allowed himself a brief chuckle, shifted in his chair and started to relight his cigar. It was his sign that the interview was closed.

"Damn this thing," he said easily. "Why doesn't the boy get some decent Havanas? I'd have sent him some of my own if I'd known. . . ." Then he interrupted his own thoughts, a freedom no one else was permitted.

"Any sign of them yet?" the old man demanded with sudden querulousness. "I've never understood why George must be so infernally late. It's certainly not Eugenia's doing. . . ." The voice relaxed again; the mask slipped back in place.

"What do they say about children, Ogden?" the Turk mused. "And I hope you won't repeat that old saw about an apple not falling too far from the tree. . . ."

Instructions completed, conversation was resumed. It was the kind of chat that allowed the Turk to move among the social spheres of his homes in Newport, Philadelphia, and the Pennsylvania countryside. A light touch was all. A gentleman never said what he truly felt. Even among men he trusted.

"The boy made a good match in Eugenia, at least," the Turk continued with a half-smile, which could have been criticism or pride. "About the only thing he did do right. Those old families can be a hard nut to crack, even if they are poor as church mice. . . .

"They won't marry for money, at least that's what they'd like you to believe. They have, as they say, scruples. And the Paines are the worst of the lot. . . ." The Turk laughed at his private joke. Beckmann didn't join his master. A nod was sufficient. Or the thin-lipped recognition of the Turk's superior wisdom.

"But then, he got her when she was young and impressionable. . . . The best time for women, if you ask me. No, I amend that, Ogden—it's the only time."

The Turk laughed again while Beckmann opened the curtains just in time to witness the arrival of the motorcar containing George, Eugenia, and their three children. The dark green Daimler, one of only three such hand-built automobiles in Newport (the only place in the country able to afford such newfangled luxury) erupted in a flurry of stewards, last-minute packages, overnight cases, hastily grabbed-up toys and four more hatboxes from Miss Gaede's Emporium. Objects flew to waiting fingers, and it took Beckmann a moment to make out George among his possessions.

As the Turk's youngest son stepped from the car, he shielded his pale eyes from the sun, then turned to survey his ship. His face took on a brighter color, as if he were seeing the wonderful thing for the first time. At forty-two, George Axthelm looked eager, almost boyish; his face glowed pink as a teacup. He tugged the visor of his gold-embroidered cap, tweaked it into a jaunty angle, and patted his hair into place. Beckmann wanted to laugh aloud.

A fitting costume, Beckmann told himself. Nautical as a rear admiral come to inspect his fleet. How unalike father and son are—in spite of their similar features; what makes one as conniving as a fox makes the other resemble a field mouse. The three older sons aren't as weak; they don't match their father, it's true. They never will match their father—but they aren't pathetic runts like Master Georgie. But then, he's the baby. The baby with the brand-new toy.

"Your son has arrived" was all Beckmann said while he kept his eyes on the scene below.

Eugenia followed her husband from the car. She was dressed entirely in white, and as she stepped from the running board a breeze found her and caught her in a swirl of dimity, lace, and tulle. Her long skirt billowed about, and her pale hat veil rose to circle her face like a wayward cloud. She was obviously laughing, though Beckmann couldn't hear a word. Her skirts lifted slightly, and he could see the tips of two white shoes: two shoes that seemed never to have touched pavement before. Then Eugenia turned toward her husband's yacht, and a moment passed between the woman and the ship: Eugenia looking upward, smiling, and the *Alcedo,* buoyant on the water, letting her shadow rest where it fell.

The two girls joined their mother then, and Paul, their younger brother, Eugenia's only son. In his white sailor suit, the little boy was nearly obscured by his older sisters. He looked doubtful about his clothes, unhappy in a getup that clearly matched the perfumed excesses of silk stockings and lace slippers and parasols, and he fidgeted, staring dismally at the dock and trying to wrench himself free. Lizzie, the eldest sister, made a teenaged face of disgust that disassociated her from both younger siblings while Jinx, the middle child, shook the wrinkles from her starched pinafore in a decidedly unladylike way as she gave her brother a poke with a secret elbow.

Eugenia shook her head, laughed again, and began to rebutton her gloves. Beckmann could see the blue-white skin of her wrists as she turned one hand then the other, unconsciously finishing her dressing in the open air.

Then Eugenia smoothed Paul's dark hair in a mother's careless gesture, and bent to embrace all three children together. Her face was clear and untroubled and filled with hope.

Beckmann let the curtain fall shut. He didn't move. "Eugenia and the children are here as well," he said.

There was something in his tone that startled the Turk and he looked up, hoping to catch sight of that emotion. The man's got feelings, after all, the Turk told himself. The world is full of surprises.

On the dock, no longer under Beckmann's observant eye, the family started toward the ship. George led the way, nodding to the stewards and seamen who lined the deck. He felt full of importance and pride.

"Nice day for a sail," he repeated over and over, and he even tried out a salute or two. Then he decided the more appropriate pose for the modern yachtsman was one hand thrust casually in his jacket pocket while the other swung rhythmically at his side. But just at that moment Eugenia came up to take his arm, and he was forced to relinquish that posture in favor of the attitude of good husband and family man.

"We're going to have a wonderful time, aren't we, George?" she whispered. "I mean, away from everyone. Family and all. We'll be off on our own. No more business. No more command performances at Linden Lodge . . ."

No more Ogden Beckmann, Eugenia had been about to say, but stopped herself in time. George could be blind when he wanted. If his father approved something, George never asked a question.

"Course we are, my dear," George answered uncomfortably, and he gave her hand a small, stiff pat.

Eugenia pretended not to notice the rebuff. Instead she turned her face full to his and smiled as brightly as she knew how. "Just think," she said, "this is the first time . . . I mean, the first time we've been all alone, George! . . . You and I and the children . . . You know, I was so excited last night I hardly slept. I think I heard the clock strike every hour. I very nearly came into your room. . . ." Eugenia laughed at those words, then squeezed her husband's arm.

". . . And then just about dawn the sea gulls started up, and I thought this is the sound I'm going to hear every morning. I shall come awake to the murmur of waves and the song of gulls. You know, George, I was so happy I wanted to cry!"

"Crying's not necessarily something one does when one's celebrating, my dear," George answered. He felt uneasy with his wife's hand wrapped around his arm; he was certain it looked suggestive and decidedly lower class. Too intimate, by far.

"Where's my Paul? Where's my little Paul?" The shout startled both Eugenia and George, and they looked toward the gangway to see Prue running down as fast as she could, her apron strings flying and her red hair bouncing.

"Where's my best boy? Where're my two favorite girls?" Prue was irrepressible; her nursemaid's cap had come completely unpinned—it danced about in her mop of hair—and her Irish face sparkled.

"All dressed up as a sailor, too! Why I wouldn't have known you, Master Paul! Indeed I wouldn't. I thought you were some toff of a Navy man!" Prue's youthful exuberance filled the dock. For a moment even George's resolute starchiness vanished.

"And no more German nannies! Aren't we the lucky ones?" Eugenia leaned so close to her husband's ear he could feel her breath. It was warm and moist and smelled of strawberries in cream.

George was about to respond that the governesses his father had chosen for the household on Chestnut Street had all been excellent women. Those remarks would have been followed with a reprimand about his wife's lack of gratitude in the face of such generosity, and then a reminder that since he, himself, was of German descent, her attitude was surprising in the extreme. And finally, George was considering a lecture on the benefits of a rigorous upbringing as opposed to the dubious attentions of an uneducated Irish girl when Paul interrupted with a loud:

"You've seen this silly suit before, Prue! Mother forced me to wear it!"

"Paul!" George's voice was too harsh and too loud. "That will be enough."

The group was silenced for only a moment, though. No one was disheartened, because the world was too joyful a place. George's warning fell on deaf ears. Lizzie and Jinx squealed along the dock, yelling their greetings to Prue, to the ship, and to the day, while Lizzie momentarily forgot she was thirteen and a would-be lady, and bounded forward dragging her unopened parasol behind her like a stick down a picket fence.

"We're going to be allowed to join the party, Prue! Mother said so. And I may have a taste of champagne. What do you say to that!"

George glowered at his wife.

"Just a taste, George," she pleaded. "Lizabeth's thirteen, after all, and nearly as tall as I am. It's time she started learning the ways of the world." That hadn't been the right tack to take, Eugenia knew it instantly; it was too full of possible blame. She backed away from her memories, and from her words. "For the celebration, you know, dear. That's all. . . . Just the tiniest sip . . . for fun . . ."

George heard his wife's unspoken accusations. He wanted to reassure her that this time things would be different. He wanted to ask her forgiveness and help, but the words didn't come. If there were words at all. But, this time, he promised himself; this time, I'll make a change.

". . . Still, if you'd rather Lizzie didn't. It's your ship, after all. Your handsome *Alcedo* . . ." Eugenia tried for her very best smile. ". . . You're the master of the vessel."

"I suppose one sip wouldn't do any harm," George answered. He couldn't think of another thing to say.

If the children were aware of any problems between their parents, they made no sign. They whooped along impervious; criticism slipped from their backs like rain; they rolled their eyes and passed secret messages of encouragement. Jinx wanted to know if Prue had unpacked her bug collection and if the bed for her dolls was a hammock like a sailor's; Lizzie wondered if Prue had seen all her new frocks and if the one with the cinnamon-colored sash wasn't the nicest of them all, while Paul resisted, with every ounce of five-year-old might, relinquishing his small hand to Prue's much larger one.

"I'm five," he asserted over and over. "I don't have to hold anyone's hand."

But Prue had either lost her hearing or grown stupid overnight. She clutched Paul's hand tighter as they strode along. "When you're safe on board, Master Paul," she sang out, "you can do as you please. Till then you must do as I please. And what I intend at this moment is to hold you close as a cat."

Paul didn't dare look at the sailors and stewards on deck. He knew every last one of them was watching him and laughing. The march toward the ship became a misery of humiliation.

Suddenly Paul stopped dead in his tracks. "My soldiers!" he wailed, and in spite of Prue's restraining hand, turned and raced back down the dock.

"What is it this time?" George asked. His voice was weary and cross. Taking his family on this trip was proving more difficult than he'd imagined. A day sail with all aboard was all he'd had to cope with before: a few hours, a picnic luncheon and home before bedtime. The rest of his excursions had been strictly nonfamily events: a few men friends, a good crew and some peaceful days or weeks at sea. George began to wonder if this voyage might not be a mistake.

"I think Paul left his lead soldiers in the car, Father," Jinx ventured.

"Thank you, young Eugenia," George answered, and Jinx knew to be quiet. Her father only called her by her full name when he was annoyed.

"Shall I go back and get him, Father?" Lizzie stood straight and tall, and spoke in her sweetest tone, while Jinx decided (for probably the ten thousandth time) that her sister was the most insufferable goody-goody in the world. Jinx would have stuck out her tongue and made a terrible face if she'd dared.

"Thank you, Lizabeth, no." Their father settled the matter. "I'll attend to the problem, myself. Wait here, everyone. After I return with our young truant, we'll proceed aboard. I want us all together. This is a very special day."

When George finally arrived for his meeting with his father, it was from Beckmann's expression that the Turk recognized their visitor. The old man had stayed in his chair with his back to the door. He found it easier to keep control if he forced people to come to him—though he hadn't yet shared that secret with his sons. The Turk looked at Beckmann's face as the study door opened, and registered the expression he saw there. It was disgust, pure and simple. Then the emotion vanished and Beckmann's face quickly resumed its facade of watchful calm.

More and more interesting, the Turk decided as he called out a falsely hearty "George, my boy. Come in. Do come in. Ogden and I were just enjoying the privacy of your library here. Fine set of Hawthorne you've got. Nicely bound. Bit flowery for my taste, though. . . . I'm a Melville man, myself. . . . That is, when I get time to read. . . ." The cordial words fooled no one. "Youth, as they say, Ogden . . . golden youth . . . the envy of all . . . plenty of time for pleasure . . ."

The Turk pulled out his pocket watch, studied it, tapped it, and raised it to his ear in a dramatic gesture of disbelief. "My God, I thought the damned thing had broken! I believe we said you'd be here at . . ." The pleasant tone had vanished completely.

"Yes, Father, I'm sorry, I . . ." George's gray Axthelm eyes glared at Beckmann. Damn it all, he thought, couldn't Father and I be alone just this once?

"Don't apologize, George." The Turk's voice was harsh. "I've told you boys over and over. Never apologize! Even to me." The old man rested his shoulders against the chair. He hated these constant lessons. When would his children ever learn? Tony, Martin, even Carl, his supposed successor: They lacked finesse; they lacked judgment. They lacked ability. But George was the worst of the lot: the baby, the waste of good money and a decent education. At least he was suited for this venture, the old man reminded himself. That was some consolation. George might prove useful for once in his life. With Beckmann at his side, of course.

The Turk allowed himself a sigh, then softened his voice. He couldn't afford to push too hard. "Besides, your delay gave us time to clarify a few details. Come in and sit down, why don't you? We'll go over these Borneo plans one final time."

George hung back near the door; he recognized the invitation for what it was: an order. He felt as if he were back in school. Called to the headmaster's office. Waiting for the ax to fall. But things were going to change when they returned from Borneo, he promised himself. His father would be singing a different tune then. It wouldn't be little Georgie in short pants and a dirty face then.

The Turk ignored his son's hesitation and continued in the same easy mode: "Now, I realize we've been through this before, George, and that you know where you'll meet up with the others . . . where Paine will be . . . and the Ivards, etc. . . . All those . . . those varying groups. . . ." The Turk paused only momentarily. Too much information was never good for business. George should be told what George needed to know; the rest was another man's lookout.

"But I feel it's best to restate our objectives one final time. The satisfactory conclusion of these efforts are vital to the Axthelm interests out there as well as—"

"We've discussed this a hundred times, Father!" The spell was broken. George strode into the room. "I know my job. I'm the right man for it. I . . . I do know what I'm doing. . . ." But the brave words began to desert him, and as his speech grew more hesitant, so did his steps.

"I fail to comprehend why you don't trust me, Father. . . ." George tried to bolster his flagging spirits with this plea, but he ended up shuffling his feet, and standing inconclusively between his father's chair and the chart-laden desk. He was no nearer to wisdom in his father's eyes than he'd ever been.

". . . The crates are being loaded. I saw them myself. Being loaded, that is. When we arrived . . . the family and I . . . Well, they must have at least half of them stowed below decks by now. There are an awful lot of men. . . ."

George paused, waiting for the reprieve that would never come, then hurried on. "I agreed to do this, Father, you know. I agreed to it all. . . . I said, when you told me . . . I said . . ." The carefully rehearsed words failed.

"Besides, it's only, I mean . . . you and Ogden have the thing so well, you know, so well mapped out and . . ." George stopped and looked away. He'd lost; there was no point in continuing. Without meaning to, he lifted his hand and began to pat down his hair.

As usual, it was Beckmann who broke the silence. Interpreting the great man's needs was just one of his tasks. "Now, George," he soothed, "I don't believe your father is questioning your loyalty." But the word had a peculiar emphasis, the consonants so twisted that it did become a question of loyalty, of faith, of knowing good from evil.

George paid no attention to Beckmann. He kept his eyes on his father as the Turk tapped out his cigar. "Damned thing's dead again," he said. "You must get something better, George. Wonder if there's still time."

At his ease, the Turk allowed himself a brief smile. "That report, Ogden?" he said. "The one on the far right corner of the desk? Hand it to me, will you? Sit down, George."

On deck, the children were in the very center of the festivities. Jinx stood near the rail marveling at how beautiful everyone was, especially her mother, who looked just like a queen in a picture book. Eugenia laughed and nodded her head as she talked to the crowd gathered round her, and when she moved the diamonds and pearls at her neck glittered as if a magic wand had touched them. A fairy queen, Jinx thought, that's what Mother is. A fairy queen with invisible wings.

The little girl squinted her eyes, looked across the deck to Lizzie, and waved grandly. Paul, she could only barely see; he was hidden by guests leaning this way and that as they chatted and called out greetings. The ladies' dresses and hat veils and scarves drifted and blew together till they looked like clouds of violet and amber and peach. Or the dresses might have been colored ice creams and raspberry sauce, or nougat frosting, or rose petals scattered on a bridal cake. Paul vanished in this excess of confection while Jinx whispered, "A fairy story; it's a fairy story come to life."

Mother's a queen and I'm a princess, she decided; my name's not Jinx or young Eugenia. It's Delphine. Princess Delphine. That was her favorite name. At least her favorite that day. Princess Delphine closed her magical eyes. Silver and diamond and ruby bracelets, she hummed under her breath, trays of crystal, music and voices, perfume, cologne and peaches in syrup, marzipan candies, sugar biscuits. Around and around and around and around. Above the high and shiny ship, circling and spinning a deathless spell. Sea gulls and salt and the ocean's wind. This is heaven, Princess Delphine told herself, I know it is.

"There you are, Jinx!" burst in her grown-up cousin, Whitney. He was Mother's youngest cousin; he was a Caldwell and he was going to tutor them on the voyage. Mother said Whitney had just graduated from Princeton University and that he knew everything in the world. Cousin Whit was dressed for the bon voyage in his "white hunter" outfit. (That's what Father called it.) He had dun-colored britches, riding boots, a hacking jacket, and an enormous white-chalked solar topee. Although he was older than Lizzie, which meant much older than Paul, he still looked as if he were dressing up; he didn't look like a real grown-up at all. Jinx made a superior face and raised her eyebrows as she'd seen her mother do.

"Putting a kibosh on the boat, Jinx?" Whit teased. The very silly young lady who'd come to see him off giggled. Princess Delphine scowled.

"I'm looking for Paul, but I can't see him in this crowd. You have any idea where I might scare down your brother?" When Cousin Whit was around his college friends (or his girlfriends—he had lots) he sounded extremely foolish. He tweaked Jinx's sleeve, then her nose, then pretended to pull it off and hide it in his hand. Finally he said, "You're looking mighty pretty today, young lady! Even those freckles!" as he and the girl sauntered away.

Princess Delphine sighed deeply and turned her attention to worthier subjects. There was Dr. DuPlessis and his wife, Jane, as well as Mrs. D.'s sister, bossy old Miss Powell. (She was famous, Jinx knew; she'd heard Cook tell Anna, the upstairs maid, that Margaret Powell could divine the future, and that whatever she said came true!)

Luckily Father had not invited Miss Powell on the *Alcedo*'s cruise. It was enough punishment to have Mrs. D. along, even though the doctor was everyone's favorite. He used licorice drops for every cure. And when you got well, you got lemon drops. And he had that funny accent!

"Bruges" was where he said he'd grown up. Lizzie could do a perfect imitation. "Brroooja!" "Leekoreese drropce forgh my leetle pashence." One time Paul had wet his pants he was laughing so hard at his sister's accent. But that had been a year ago, at least.

Now the two DuPlessises and Miss Powell rolled through the crowd toward Eugenia; Mrs. D. gripped both her husband's arm and her sister's, and the three of them looked so wide and roly-poly, like great big beanbags almost, that Jinx decided to forget Princess Delphine and go hear what they had to say.

By the time the little girl reached her mother's side, Miss Powell was already whispering a mournful "Oh, my dear, I hope you'll come back safe to us. Those awful savages . . . I've heard such stories. . . . what they do to women . . ." She left the sentence tantalizingly unfinished. Jinx leaned as close as she dared.

Jane DuPlessis was equally upset. She wheezed above the creak of corset stays (that was always a battle—Mrs. D.'s belly and her whalebone "lady's waist"): "Oh really, Mrs. A., is it true, what Margaret said? Will we be encountering sav . . . ?"

But that last word she couldn't even gasp out. Instead she rolled her eyes in enormous circles. ". . . But of course, not in front of the little one. Oh my. Oh my. Oh my, my, my!"

Jinx saw her mother start to laugh, then stop herself and say, "Now, now, Mrs. DuPlessis, you know George would never allow us to be in any kind of danger. It's kind of your sister to worry, but I trust my husband completely. And Mr. Axthelm senior as well, for that matter. Many of our stops are his doing, you know, and I remember the faith you put in him!"

Dr. DuPlessis patted his wife's plump hand. "You see, my dear," he said, "isn't that what I've been telling you? My little chicken mustn't be afraid. Our schedule calls for only the most scenic excursions. We're not explorers conquering the wild."

Mrs. DuPlessis didn't look completely mollified (Jinx thought she even looked a little disappointed), but she gave her husband a small, brave smile, while Jinx sneaked a poke at her mother. Eugenia had to turn abruptly from her guests to avoid laughing outright. "Jinx!" she said sharply, then to hide her confusion added, "Have you seen your father?"

Jinx recognized the tone: It was the "ladylike voice." Mother's cross, Jinx thought; I haven't been acting like a proper young lady.

Just then Paul, who'd ended up fiddling unhappily behind the two fat sisters, burst in: "Jinx doesn't know where he is, Mother. But I do. He had to go see Grandfather A." And Paul was gone in a flash.

The little boy raced through the ship. He ran as fast as his five-year-old legs could carry him. "Whoosh," he said. "Whoo. Whoo. Whoo." The *Alcedo* was his ship, his trireme, his galleon. The rugs in the corridor were soft and smooth; they muffled the sound of his feet. Muffled oars and a pirate ship, he thought. Or a sloop of the line. Or the *Flying Dutchman* in a bank of gray fog.

"Whoooo," Paul echoed, making the sound of a foggy sea.

Paul raced past the bronze statue of the lady holding her baby. He touched the child's cool forehead as he always did, running by. (The baby's head was shiny with fingerprints.) Then he passed the main saloon, the library, the morning room, and looked up at the paintings of cows and tumbled-down buildings in dark, woodsy fields.

Paul didn't like the pictures; he didn't know why the cows couldn't have proper barns like the ones at Grandfather A.'s country house instead of gloomy places with weeds in the walls. But he liked the tapestry that hung next to the main staircase. It was very old; he wasn't supposed to touch it. The tapestry had a knight on a charging horse; the horse looked fierce and brave and wise.

Then Paul was at the door to his father's study. "Whoosh," he said, one last time. He'd reached his safe harbor.

Inside, George hunched over at his desk while Beckmann stood prodding his elbow. Papers and maps, once neatly arranged, littered the desk top in sliding piles. The Turk watched from the distant sanctuary of his high-backed chair, his eyes were fixed on his son's bent shoulders.

When George finally did turn to his father, his voice was whimpering and small. "Father, I've told you, I do understand this whole business with the Ivards . . . and Mahomet Seh. . . ." He paused while his hands sifted over a toppled stack of letters. ". . . It's going to be fine, Father. . . . Really. . . ."

The Turk stared at his son's hands. Useless, he decided, soft and white and doughy as any mathematician's. Those fingers aren't equal to the task. Then the Turk nodded to Beckmann; the lesson was finished.

Suddenly the door flew open, and there was Paul, full to the brim with the importance of his mission. "Father, Mother's looking for you!" the little boy fairly shouted. For a moment his bright face and brown eyes looked just like Eugenia's.

Then the child spotted his grandfather. "Oh, Grandfather A.! I didn't see you! You were hiding in that big chair. Are you coming on deck with us? We're having a party! There's lots and lots of food. Ice cream, too, and an enormous cake Mother's going to cut. . . .

". . . And you know that very fat lady? . . . Miss . . . ? The one Cook says can tell. . . ."

The Turk took Paul into his lap. "How's my best boy today?" he asked, while his sharp nose softened and his eyes grew hazy and kind. "Getting into mischief out on deck? Making short work of those sweets?"

The old man was transformed; there was nothing mean or impatient about him. He was what every child wants a grandfather to be. "I'll tell you what, young Paul. Let's you and I go up there right now. What do you say? Why, if it weren't for you, we might have been working here forever. You're the lad who saved us!" This was accompanied by a gesture half tickle and half hug, and Paul responded out of long and practiced habit.

"Oh, Grandfather," he said as he twisted happily in the old man's arms, "you always say that. But you couldn't have stayed on board anyway. You have to leave before we sail."

"I wish I were coming with you, Paul," the Turk said. "Linden Lodge won't be the same with you gone." There was real sorrow in his voice. George heard it and stared bleakly at his desk. Then his hand returned to pat down his already immaculate hair.

The Turk rose and walked to the door with his grandson. "One last thing, George," he said, hardly bothering to turn. "A man never discusses business with his wife. I don't want Eugenia bothered with this. Or her father. Paine's there as frosting . . . you understand. Pro forma. The Philippine thing was only . . . You understand . . . little pitchers, as they say."

"Have big ears," Paul sang out, finishing his grandfather's sentence.

George watched his son nestle into the old man's arms. "I understand," he answered.

On deck, a few minutes later, the Turk held court surrounded by his sons with their duplicate features: thin, beaklike noses, and hair as dark and straight as jet. The male members of the Axthelm clan gave the impression of a wall built of quarry-cut stone. One individual member might differ slightly from the next, but the overall effect was one of ordered symmetry—as if the Turk had purchased his family as a group. George and Eugenia were not part of the solid front of Martin, Carl, and Tony, however; they stood removed in a whispered argument. Their faces were taut with anger; they knew they were being watched. Each careful movement showed an effort at control.

"Why didn't you tell me Ogden was coming?" Eugenia was demanding as she tried to maintain her painted-on smile. "How long have you known about this? Or should I say, when did your father . . . ?"

"This has nothing to do with Father."

"Oh, George!" Eugenia felt fury engulf her. She wanted to walk away, give in, give up. This is too much to bear, she thought. I'll take the children and leave. I will. We'll walk straight off this ship, and that will be the end of that!

Instead, she said, "Nothing to do with your father," inadvertently copying her husband's words and tone. All of a sudden she felt as tired and heavy as death. Her shoulders slumped and her brave face began to crumple. Everything she'd worked toward seemed to desert her at once. The voyage was not to be a family event, after all. No, they'd be dragging Ogden Beckmann along with them. They might as well put a towline around the old Turk as well! Or set them up in a longboat like crows in a roost! Memories of every miserable Linden Lodge dinner party crowded in on her. There'd be the same secrets, the same pointed remarks, the same hushed "men-only" conversations. And the result would be George backsliding into drunken incomprehension. Again and again and again. Eugenia thought she might honestly start to scream. Right there on deck—in full view of the world!

". . . I'm the one who asked Ogden to join us . . ." her husband was saying, "not Father. I'm sorry if his inclusion in our little party comes as a surprise, my dear, but I believe he'll be most helpful with this mining business. After all, I know practically nothing about antimony or assaying . . ."

"George!" Eugenia pleaded. "Why do you keep on like that? You know you hate the man as much as I do!" The words were out before Eugenia could stop them. It was the rule of her marriage that she never put words in her husband's mouth. George's affairs were his own. As a dutiful wife, she discussed what affected her own immediate happiness—the well-being of her children and the smooth management of her household. If her husband chose to respond, good. If not, so be it.

Eugenia held her tongue. But, it isn't fair, she told herself over and over. It just isn't fair! Beckmann on the *Alcedo*! A panther would be less odious.

"I don't know what you're talking about, Eugenia," George answered in his stiffest, proper-Philadelphian voice. "I have never evinced the slightest distaste for Ogden. You have an overactive and, if I may add, self-serving imagination."

Eugenia didn't bother to respond. The high-flown phrases meant she was right. George didn't want Ogden along any more than she did. But as usual he had no choice. The decision had been the Turk's.

"Isn't there some way you can reason with your father?" she asked quietly, and then put her hand on her husband's arm with a gesture intended to show compassion and love. But George flinched and drew back as though she'd thrown herself naked out a door.

"My decision's final, Eugenia," George announced. His voice was a monotone and far too loud, like that of a person reciting lines he didn't understand. "And, I repeat, it is my decision. No one else's. I'm sorry if it fails to meet your exacting approval."

Then he added, "It really is for the antimony business, I'm doing this, my dear. . . ." George's words grew softer and more hesitant. "For the success of—because you and I . . ."

Eugenia heard the change in her husband's tone, but it didn't console her; it made the situation worse. Luncheon after luncheon, weekends and dinners, a jumble of years dancing attendance at Linden Lodge rose before her eyes: President Cleveland, Governor Taft, the shoddy little upstart, Gould, with his twitchy fingers and glittering eyes, the International Mercantile Marine, the Hay-Buneau-Varilla Treaty, Roosevelt, and poor, dead President McKinley. There was never a party at the Lodge—never a moment—that wasn't business or politics. Or the politics of business. Not that Eugenia was supposed to notice or care.

". . . the antimony business, and the operation in Borneo . . . This venture's quite a coup. You know that, Genie. Father trusting me with all this new . . ." George didn't continue. He couldn't allow himself to say any more. But things will be different, he promised silently. Things will be different after this.

"Better get back to our guests." George's voice resumed its gruff, patronizing tone, but Eugenia didn't hear it. Her husband had called her Genie. That one small word was a miracle. She nodded her agreement, and then began to smile.

"And there's old Jeff! Haven't seen him in a coon's age. Not since our last reunion." George's troubles were forgotten. This little tiff with Genie will pass, he told himself. It's no more than nerves. This is the first time she's been so far from home. Why, anyone could understand it.

George's face turned happy and untroubled, "We must be pretty special, Genie," he whispered. "We must be pretty darned special to bring old Jeff down from Bar Harbor at this time of year!"

Then he shouted out, "Jeffrey! Good to see you, old man. Bonkser's down at the stern. Lee-side as we nautical folk say . . . How's Susan and the new addition . . . little . . . ?"

As he spoke, George began to remove himself from his wife's side. He brushed her sleeve lightly with his hand, as though smoothing the cloth and nothing more, then he placed that hand in his jacket pocket.

"... Don't know when to quit, do you, my lad ... ?" This was followed by a laugh too boisterous for its own good. The sound turned hollow as air, and finally vanished with a hee-hawing rattle.

"... Good of you to come though ... Just off to the libations table, myself. Let's saunter that way together. Old Bonkser will be ..."

When her husband had gone, Eugenia walked to the railing. She lifted her face to the breeze and looked across the water to trace the sun's path on the waves. The road was clear and straight, like something solid. Eugenia imagined herself out on it, but in her mind she wasn't walking, she was flying. Flying over the waves. She remembered visiting her grandmother's house in Maine when she was child; she was very young, Paul's age, no more, because her mother was still alive. They'd stood on the beach, mother and daughter, with the sun before them and looked at the water in just the same way. Eugenia could feel her mother's hand on her own, evanescent and light, almost nonexistent. "You can fly, Eugenia, if you believe you can," her mother had said. "Like the bird in the poem who sings—knowing it has wings."

On the yacht's forward deck, Dr. DuPlessis was setting up his new "circuit" panoramic camera: the one he'd bought specially for the trip. It demanded his utmost attention, but the crowd, who'd gathered around to watch and give advice, kept distracting him.

"The light's too strong there," someone ventured.

"You'll get nothing but the docks if you set up there."

Amateurs, Dr. DuPlessis thought, though with his Belgian accent it probably would have sounded more like "Amatooorghs".

"The pastel portrait Helleu did of me didn't take nearly as long," one woman laughed to her companion as she reached for the canapé tray. The clink of her jewelry scraping the silver was particularly annoying.

"Why, I believe I will have another," she burbled to a steward. "And tell the boy we'll need more champagne. These photographs may take all day!"

"If you please, ladies and gentlemen!" Dr. DuPlessis ordered. "This is a most delicate operation." His accent grew more guttural by the moment; flustered, Dr. DuPlessis could be nearly unintelligible: "Ve are not havin' ze queek snabshods."

Dr. DuPlessis erected his special tripod, then began to mount the camera. He allotted each action the same precise care while Mrs. Du-Plessis stood officiously at his side, bowing her head one way then another, like a magician's assistant with nothing to do:

"Gustav! Didn't you forget that little piece? ... Gustav! You can't put that there! . . . Oh, all right. All right. . . . I stand corrected. . . . Goodness! You men and your mechanics! What a lot of fussing over nothing. . . ."

Finally everything was ready, and Dr. DuPlessis began to pose his groups. Jinx, Lizzie, and Paul and their older cousins hung back, waiting for the chance to create a small diversion. The older boys, Uncle Martin's and Uncle Tony's sons, egged everyone on, and there were excited whispers about possibly throwing something as the flash exploded. (A few deviled eggs had been reserved for this purpose.) Paul took a noisy part in this conspiracy; he became boisterous and bouncy, shimmying from side to side, as he tried to hold the bigger children's attention.

The first portrait was of Cousin Whit and the three couples who had come to see him off. Two of the young ladies ran out of the photograph at the last minute; one of them snatched at Whit's solar topee as the other girl pretended to pour champagne over her beau's head. These antics caused some of the children to collapse with laughter; the ones remaining upright pointed wobbly fingers and made horrific and embarrassing noises, and upset Dr. DuPlessis so much he decided to attempt private portraits exclusively.

Then Margaret Powell presented herself for a photograph, and the eldest of the Axthelm boys, Uncle Tony's two sons, began making quiet catcalls.

"She's loaded," one of the boys whispered and Paul took up the cry.

But Margaret Powell had, by then, polished off several glasses of champagne, removed her hat, and tossed her long gray hair over her ample shoulders. She was past caring and insisted on being photographed with one of the under stewards. Henry was her chosen victim, a boy of sixteen with his first proud position on the great yacht, *Alcedo*. He looked about in wild-eyed despair as he tried (and failed) to extricate himself from his miserable predicament.

Henry's squirming made the cousins laugh louder; they made faces at the poor under steward till he fled, and Miss Powell, dangerous as a wounded Cape buffalo, bore down on the offenders. She then proceeded to shout prophecies of doom as the children vanished into the crowd.

Paul, Lizzie, and Jinx thought themselves extremely lucky to have escaped with their lives. They'd found a secret corner near the wheelhouse and begun to spread out a stolen feast, including three nearly full flutes of champagne. Lizzie had had her public "sip," but jealousy was jealousy. The glasses had been filched from behind a steward's back and carried by Jinx "very, very slowly" with her fingers deep inside the tall glasses.

Now it was time to share and everyone produced offerings for the feast. Marzipan fruit was highly prized as well as strawberries dipped in chocolate, raspberries and dates rolled in sugar, and five slightly crushed, but very tempting, pink petits fours. Finally the last item to go: a mushroom cap filled with black fish eggs.

"They are not," said Paul.

"Don't you know anything? Each egg is special. I heard Cook say so. Each one is worth a silver dollar." Jinx hated to have her authority questioned. It was hard enough to get the last word with Lizzie around. But a little brother should know better.

"I don't think that's right, Jinx." Sure enough, Lizzie had information the others did not.

"Well, it is," Jinx insisted with a last stab at superiority. "Just because you're thirteen you always . . .

"Anyway, each egg would be a big fish by now if it had been allowed to hatch. That's why they're so valuable." Jinx took a sip of champagne and tried to look as superior as she could.

Paul examined the mushroom doubtfully; he stared at it on its gold-rimmed plate, then suddenly grabbed it and stuffed it in his mouth. His eyes glazed over and his face turned greenish-white, but he managed to keep his teeth closed.

"Paul?" Jinx was immediately sorry. She reached out for her brother and, in her haste, toppled and broke her champagne glass.

"Paul, you can spit it out if you like. I've got a handkerchief." Lizzie decided she'd have to take charge. Jinx could be such a troublemaker.

But Paul was determined; he continued to chew and when the caviar was gone he took up his glass of champagne and drained it in one gulp. The girls watched in horror as Paul's face became shiny with sweat, then red and bone dry, and finally as green as the sea. He dropped to all fours and started to hop down the deck. "I'm a frog," he shouted, "Look, I'm a frog."

"Paul, get up this instant." Lizzie was stern; she tried to sound like Father.

"Paul, what will Mother . . . ?" Jinx was guilty and frightened.

But her brother hopped on. "I drank the whole thing, just like Fath . . . I'm loaded!"

"Hush, Paul," Lizzie hissed. Her voice was sharp and frantic.

"I'm a frog. I'm a . . . loaded!" Paul careened toward the party while his sisters ran to find their mother.

• • •

When George discovered the crowd clustered around his wife and children, his stony silence was enough to quiet even the rowdiest among them. His guests had found the sight of a little boy drunk on champagne the perfect complement to a day of such lavish frivolity, but when their host appeared, even a loud woman, dressed from head to toe in lavender ruffles, had to give up.

She whooped out a parting "Georgie Porgie! Such a party poop! And you used to be so much fun!" Then the group wandered off, searching more food, drink, and easy entertainment, and George, Eugenia, and the children were left alone.

"I was like y . . ." Paul began, trying to rise from his crumpled position in Eugenia's arms. But George didn't hear or even notice his son. His attention was fixed on Eugenia. Jinx and Lizzie watched their parents. They were aware of something, some secret that made the day different, but what that thing was they couldn't say.

George continued to stare at Eugenia. His face was composed and calm; the only hint that there might be stronger emotions at work was a pinched whiteness around his mouth. Eugenia didn't look at her husband; she watched the waves in the harbor. A strand of hair blew across her face, but she didn't move to straighten it. She was aware of feeling only a physical sense of weariness; there seemed no emotion at work at all. So, this is how it feels to be detached, she thought. It's very pleasant, really; it's better than anger or grief or joy.

"Eugenia, I will not have my children behaving like wild Indians. . . ." George began, then stopped.

Something, some shift in position or the sag of his shoulders, made Eugenia turn to face him, but when he continued, "I really fail to comprehend how you can allow these things to happen," the tone in his voice was so empty and meaningless that Eugenia returned to the waves. How happy they look, she decided. Blue and bright and carefree. She imagined herself among them, diving like a mermaid or a dolphin or a bouncy little white duck.

". . . I know that this—" George fumbled along, "that this has been a trying day . . . a trying time." He wished Eugenia would look at him again. They'd get it right this time. If only she'd just . . . what? George couldn't think. Maybe he shouldn't have been so sharp with her. Back there . . . about Ogden and all. . . .

"Genie . . . we've got to . . . We're a team, after all. . . ."

"Anything you say, George," Eugenia answered too quickly. "Shall we return to our guests now?" I'm so angry I could spit, she suddenly realized, but, out of habit, that was as far as the emotion traveled.

George glared at the deck. The day certainly wasn't going as planned!

Well, tomorrow, he told himself, when we're off on our own . . . We'll iron all this out. . . .

"It's just that it looks bad, you know, Genie. Appearances and all . . . We can't be laughingstocks. What with the cream of society here. Newport and all . . . "

"You know how important this is to Father," he almost added, then stopped himself in the nick of time. No point in opening that can of worms again.

George straightened himself and tried for a smile. "Dirty laundry in public, as they say."

"As you say . . ." Eugenia lifted her son to his sleepy feet and in her mind saw a field of stubbly grass. Last year's grass, it looked like, frozen and withered and brown; it broke into pieces when her foot touched it. There was snow, too, or the threat of it, and the sky was leaden and dull; the only sound was the bristling crunch of her steps. She was walking across the fields near Linden Lodge, alone for some reason, putting as much space between herself and the Turk's house as she possibly could. That must have been in the first year of my marriage, she decided. I had no children with me.

Eugenia pulled herself back to the present. "Paul," she said gently. "Paul? Time to wake up, darling. Let's find your friend, Prue, and some nice warm milk."

At the same time, on the dock, in the middle of the few final moments of loading, Brown appeared. He stopped short when he got his first whole view of the ship. Beckmann hadn't been exaggerating. The *Alcedo* was a beauty. Nothing but clean lines and shiny brightwork, and not a speck of rust anywhere. She was fresh as a minted penny.

He put down his canvas bag, unsure where to go next. Lieutenant James Armand Brown wouldn't carry his own gear, he reasoned, but he didn't know whether calling one of the dozens of men who scurried over the dock might be a breach of etiquette. Brown stared at the yacht, giving himself a moment to make up his mind. The important thing, he told himself, is to look like I belong. Gentlemen are never flustered; they learn composure in the cradle.

Watching from the gangway rail, the second mate saw Brown's arrival. There's our "naval attaché," he thought sourly, remembering Captain Cosby's hasty explanation the night before.

"This man has been assigned to our ship as a gesture of courtesy to the Axthelm family. It is not, I repeat, it is not an indication that we will be venturing into waters where a naval escort is required. I expect all hands to give him due respect. He is to be considered a guest, and treated as such."

End of lecture, the mate thought. Case dismissed. Captain Cosby didn't take kindly to questions. The mate looked Brown over again. The bleeding man looks regularly stupefied, he told himself. Be typical of a fancy school like Annapolis to graduate a man who's never seen the ocean. Get on with it, the mate wanted to shout. Move those feet, sailor. You're late! Instead he called the cabin boy, Ned, and told him to hustle his lazy bones dockside.

Ned was twelve; this was his third voyage, but his first on a real live yacht. The mate's anger couldn't dampen his excitement. Not by a long shot. Ned scurried down the gangway. Just imagine, he told himself, some bigwig assigning a naval officer to a civilian boat! Why it might have been President Teddy himself.The old Turk was supposed to be mighty friendly with the Roosevelt clan. And all that stuff in the papers about problems in Panama! Why, maybe they'd get themselves in the middle of an honest to goodness fight. Be held hostage! Then he, Ned, would have to sneak off through the jungle and save the day.

"Welcome aboard, sir," Ned shouted as he stared at the lieutenant's gold braid and beamed. "The second mate told me to fetch you aboard."

But the mate's curiosity had gotten the better of him. He'd crept down the gangway himself. "Morning, Lieutenant," he said. "Captain Cosby was wondering when you'd get here." And he's a man who don't like to be kept waiting, the mate thought meanly, but you'll get a taste of that yourself. Guest or no guest; you're not family. You're no better than us working stiffs.

"Beautiful ship you've got here." Brown smiled. "I've never seen anything like her."

"You're darn right you haven't" would have been the mate's reply, but Brown's sudden candor took him by surprise. So our "naval attaché" isn't one of them snooty, spit and polish types, after all, the mate realized. His anger began to desert him and he felt stranded in sentiments he didn't understand.

"She is that," the mate agreed. "Our *Alcedo*'s a special one, all right. Only the best for this family."

At ten minutes to one, the *Alcedo* was finally ready to sail. The last guests hurried down the gangway, shouting good-byes. They turned back time and again to wave and call advice and, as they turned, they wove themselves into a net of confetti and paper streamers, which

Whit, Jinx, and Lizzie pelted from the rail. Most of the yacht's lines had been cast off, and the ship seemed tied only by those multicolored ribbons, which flew along the ship's sides, tangled themselves in coils, and blew over upturned faces and waving hands. The streamers draped the backs of sailors and stewards, travelers, and those left behind; they spun a web of rose and green, gold and purple, yellow and vermilion, and the ship seemed to shiver within it as though itching to be free.

Lieutenant Brown stood watch near the last bowline, his uniform dark and crisp in the sunlight. He looked smart and official, but he also looked as though he might not have a very important job (at least Jinx decided he didn't). She made up her mind to aim her streamers in his direction. When she'd nearly covered Brown in colored paper, he looked up.

"Caught you," Jinx squealed. The children were as familiar with the *Alcedo* staff as they were with the gardeners and cooks at Linden Lodge or at home on Chestnut Street, but Brown was a new face. Jinx liked him immediately.

"So I see." He smiled up at her.

"What's your name?" She giggled while Lizzie elbowed her hard in the ribs.

"Brown."

"Don't you have a first one? Mine's Jinx."

"I know who you are." Brown smiled again and walked toward the stern.

The crowd on the pier grew silent as it watched the Turk prepare to disembark. He was the last to leave, and the band gathered on the quay ceased playing, waiting his pleasure, while the white doves in their coops and the boys sporting banners, the news photographers and the babes in their mothers' arms, held one communal breath. Without a sound, the crowd surged forward. What a fortunate family, each expectant face said. What strength in unity. How enviable they are. How admirable. How fine.

The Turk acknowledged the moment and tipped his high silk hat. He looked toward shore and pronounced his final farewell. "Good-bye, George," he said as he stared straight at the adoring throng. "Remember what I've told you."

Father and son shook hands and the crowd gave one long moan. The great man leaving his youngest son! it sighed. Sending him forth to discover the earth! There's majesty for you! There's grace and pride.

"And, Eugenia." Eugenia stepped forward on cue.

"Genie . . . if you'll permit me . . ." The Turk's voice sounded warm and caring. "Do give my best to your father when you meet up with him in Sarawak. Please tell him how deeply grateful we are for his help. A man with his brains. A man who knows the East like the back of his hand. He's doing me a great service going to the Philippine Islands. Axthelm and Company is indebted indeed."

"I'll tell him, Mr. Axthelm. I'm sure he'll be pleased." Eugenia moved away from the limelight, leaving father and son together. She motioned for her daughters to join her and circled their shoulders with strong, tight arms. Tomorrow, she promised herself. Tomorrow will be better. In spite of Beckmann. In spite of everything. Surely, I can wait till then.

The crowd moaned louder as it watched both mother and daughters. There's modesty, each heart decided. And beauty, too! If only we could be like that! If only my father, my son, wife or mother, were as handsome or as good. How happy we'd be then!

George tried to smile, but the muscles in his face felt frozen and stiff—as though they belonged to someone else. "You can count on me, Father," he said, then slowly offered his hand, but the Turk didn't notice the gesture. He strolled down the gangway, brandishing his cane like a gold-tipped sword. The crowd went wild with approval, with cheers, with whistles, and with the stomping of hundreds of feet. That was the sign they'd been waiting for.

Then the stairs were rolled back; the band struck up a march entitled "The Great Beyond," and the friends, dockhands, delivery men, fishermen, and children idling away a lazy summer day began to shout:

"Bon voyage! Bon voyage! Safe home! Safe home! . . ."

The Turk looked up at the ship's rail. Ogden Beckmann was there. Standing in the shade of an awning, he slowly raised his hat. It was a simple gesture, deferential yet somehow independent, and Beckmann remained in that pose as the last line was cast off, and the ship's huge bow started to move among the smaller boats of the harbor, drumming her engines and dwarfing everything else by size, intention, and awesome power. Then she reached the mouth of the harbor and turned her face toward the open sea.

A story describing the illustrious day appeared in the social pages of the *Philadelphia Ledger* the following afternoon. It was written by Laurence Sucroft, a man wielding much power in Philadelphia. His description of the *Alcedo*'s departure ran:

> On July the twenty-fifth, in Newport, the Axthelm family's
> newest, and, to date, most spectacular purchase, the steam yacht

Alcedo, departed for her maiden voyage. In true Axthelm style, this will not be one of your run-of-the-mill excursions. Mr. George Axthelm plans to take his family around the world on an expedition that may require as much as one year's time.

George Axthelm is, of course, the youngest son of the patriarch we, in Philadelphia, refer to so admiringly as the "Turk": a man famous as a humanitarian and a philanthropist who has done so much for our city. (Among the many cables received on the day perhaps none was as impressive or appropriate as the message received from President Theodore Roosevelt himself!)

The spectacular "Bon Voyage" extravaganza was attended by the crème de la crème of society, but no one was more beautiful than Mrs. George Axthelm, née Eugenia Paine, the daughter of the Honorable Nicholas and the former Marguerite Toliver (now deceased).

Mrs. Axthelm was dressed completely in white, her dress and chapeau created especially for the occasion by Worth of Paris. Her velvet and moiré slippers were made right here in our "faire towne" and they were covered in seed pearls bound in silver and gold thread. (Our own Miss Gaede had something to do with those elegant shoes, I assure you.) Added to this was the double strand of pearls presented by her generous father-in-law on her wedding day. The pearls were set off to full advantage, and were the envy of all who admired them. (Few can afford a bauble costing close to a million dollars!)

The Axthelm children, the Misses Lizabeth and Eugenia as well as their younger brother, Master Paul, were dressed to match their mother, and the youngsters seemed to enjoy the festivities as much as both parents.

Rumor has it that at least part of the voyage will be business related, as Mr. George Axthelm plans to set up a mining operation on the island of Borneo, certainly a romantic spot, but also one crucial to our navy in Manila Harbor. (The Axthelms are clearly not a family to rest on past laurels!)

We wish the family "Godspeed," and, if we may paraphrase Mrs. Axthelm's speech when she christened her husband's new yacht, halcyon days to all aboard, and a successful and joyous return!

—L. S.

T W O

*E*UGENIA STOOD IN HER
CABIN. Their first shipboard luncheon was finished and she had the whole voluptuous afternoon to herself. She looked at her room, stretched, suppressed a yawn, then kicked off her shoes and began to loosen her shirtwaist belt as she paraded across the floor. Light followed wherever she walked. It was a yellow and blue-white reflection sent from the waves below, and it skittered across the carpet as though it had an urgent message to impart. Eugenia watched the sunlight's movements and reached out her hand to catch it. But the light was too quick. It sped away, jumped to her dressing table, tripping over a gold-handled hairbrush, an enameled button pull, and a row of crystal scent bottles before flinging itself upward. And there amidst the plaster leaves and flowers of the coffered ceiling, the sunlight built a glowing army: Dozens and dozens of diamond-shaped patterns rolled across the room, rollicking with the waves and the rhythm of the ship itself. Eugenia smiled, then laughed. Then she closed her eyes, threw out her arms, and began to dance as well. She swayed to the words of a re-membered tune while around her the ship took up the same lovely song.

I'm ready for anything, the ship sang out, and she plunged through the ocean, breasting waves that rolled in an unbroken line from the coast of Spain or Ireland or Portugal or the dark and misty continent of Africa. The ship flew up, down, sideways; she kicked and twisted in her own happy wake, and shook the stewards clearing the luncheon dishes, the pastry cooks kneading dinner's dough, the *saucier* drying his copper pots, the laundry mangle, and the fireroom gang stoking coal.

"Ta da da rumph, ta da . . ." Eugenia sang along. The sound of a waltz echoing through her brain was as clear as a bell. "Ta da . . . da da . . ." It was lovely whirling through the room; she caught sight of her reflection in the long looking glass as she turned and turned again. The white skirt brushed the peach-colored chaise, brushed the bedposts and the desk's spindly legs.

". . . Da da, ta da . . ." Eugenia danced toward a clothes closet, toward the bathroom door, near a chest on chest, and around a table and chair while the sea light continued to jump through the windows, dart toward her earrings, her necklace, her bracelets, and dazzle them all in pinpoints of silvery gold.

Suddenly Eugenia became aware of her actions, and she stopped and stared about as though caught where she shouldn't have been.

"Goodness!" She laughed to cover her embarrassment. "We'll have no more of that!"

Returned to responsibility, Eugenia undid the rest of her buttons, stepped from her dress, tossed it on the chaise, then walked over to her desk, pulled her diary from its secret niche, and took out her pen and inkwell. I'll be as dutiful as a child, she decided. I'll be circumspect and meek. In her white shift and stockings, Eugenia began to write:

JULY 25, 1903
Somewhere off the coast of New England!

We have sailed! Finally, finally sailed! No more ropes. No more pilings. No more channels. No more piers. No more harbors, and no more you know who!

I thought about so many things as we were leaving! I leaned over the sea and pictured my room on Chestnut Street, the birds I heard every morning, the people I saw coming in to work: the vegetable cart man, his old dog, his horse, the scullery maid next door, the child who couldn't walk.

I thought about being a little girl and standing in the fanlight under the eaves at Gran's house in Maine, staring into the blue and tantalizing distance. Then I remembered the day old Mrs. Reeves spotted me and told Gran I looked like a prisoner trying to escape.

I continued to moon about there in secret, though. I wonder if Gran ever knew. . . . If she did, she never stopped me.

*That's all for now. I must run see to Paul. Poor little fellow
missed our departure—but Prue spoon-fed him warm milk and
put him down for a nap. (I can just imagine the German
fräuleins clucking over that one!) Prue's a dear girl. She has
spunk. Something we all need! Me included!*

*One poem before I close—I hadn't thought of it in years! But
it came to me out on deck.*

> *"Be like the bird, who
> Halting in his flight
> On limb too slight
> Feels it give way beneath him,
> Yet sings
> Knowing he hath wings." V. Hugo*

and E.

Eugenia wrote nothing about George; she wrote nothing about the day
or Beckmann or the Turk. It wasn't so much a decision to hide from
the truth as a fear of confronting it. As her grandmother would have
counseled, "There are some things, Eugenia, that are better left un-
said."

The diary was slipped back into its shelf as Eugenia remembered
with a sudden gasp: "Olive! I nearly forgot about Olive. She can start
unpacking while I see to Paul."

Eugenia pressed the bell by her door and Olive appeared almost in-
stantaneously, knocking on the door while her mistress grabbed for
her wrapper. Where do they hide? Eugenia wondered. It's like magic.
All these servants: a hundred counting the engine gang, but I never see
one unless I ring.

Then orders were given—this part was easy; Eugenia had been mistress of her own house since the grand age of nineteen: "You'd best
start unpacking my cases, Olive. . . . The ones we just brought down.
The evening dresses can wait, though. . . . Except for the one I'll be
wearing tonight.

"But I'll need all the day dresses and straw hats. Leave the silk bonnets in their boxes, however. They won't be required till our first landfall. And, of course, anything woolen must be locked away in the cedar
cupboard."

The devout Olive bowed her head. "I've already taken the liberty,
madam," she whispered. Olive didn't mention that the cabin closets
were smaller than those in her mistress's house on Chestnut Street, nor
that she'd been forced to store some of the finery in her own tiny cabin.

Olive prided herself on being the best lady's maid around. People might say what they wanted about the current rage for French girls, but Olive knew to the bottom of her thrifty Scottish heart that she could outstitch, outpress, and outcurtsy any of that silly foreign baggage.

"Oh, and, Olive." Eugenia hesitated with an afterthought. "The lilac silk for tonight. Let's see it looks extra special. I want my husband to be . . ."

Goodness, Eugenia thought, what am I saying? And to a servant, too! It must be the ocean's doing, she thought. All that riotous company.

". . . . That will be all." Eugenia drew herself back into her grande dame recitation and left the room.

"We had streamers and confetti . . ." Eugenia imagined the next page of her diary as she hurried toward her children's rooms:

> . . . the band played "The Great Beyond," and I stood at the rail till Newport and the whole coast were nothing but a smudgy line which disappeared like a puff of smoke. Then the smaller boats which had followed us fell back, and we were left on our own, and there was nothing to tell us where we'd come from or where we were going.
>
> We are as alone out here as I've been in all my born days and I am happier than I ever dreamed possible!

Shut away in his study, George decided to pour himself just one small brandy before he started working with Beckmann. Damn the man, he thought, why can't this wait until tomorrow? Why ruin our first afternoon at sea? For that matter, why was Beckmann even along? That had been an unpleasant surprise. Trust his father to wait till the last minute to drop that one on him. It had gotten him in a hell of a mess with Genie, too. Nearly spoiled their leave-taking.

George repeated his father's conversation, mimicking the old man's voice like a child sent to bed without supper.

"I think it's best for Ogden to accompany you, George," the Turk had said. "This whole business with the rajah and Mahomet Seh is much too important. And, of course, Ogden knows this new man."

"What new man, Father?" A perfectly reasonable question, George thought irritably. After all, shouldn't he know the names of his "guests," but his father had totally ignored it. He'd even sighed as though it were a mere detail, something already discussed and approved.

"What did you say his name was, Ogden? Brown, was it . . . ?" The Turk had finally given in, though he made it clear this was George's last chance.

He never treated me as any more than a backward child, George realized. Even now. With all I'm doing for him. All that I've promised.

". . . Now, I want this . . . Brown reporting directly to Ogden. He's just the naval attaché to you, nothing more. You should have very little personal contact with him, aside from the usual social obligations. Dinner, a brief stroll on deck, that sort of thing. Treat him as a somewhat lesser guest. His job may not warrant it, but we must keep up appearances: a young man from a decent family. That's the story we're giving out. Ogden assures me Brown knows how to act the part. . . .

"As far as you're concerned, the lieutenant is merely a courtesy extended by our good friend the Secretary of the Navy." A short, hard laugh: discussion concluded. Surely even George wasn't fool enough to miss his father's meaning.

"Now, for a little lunch? Ogden, you'll join us, of course." The Turk had resumed his amiable chat, a tone reserved for public view. And the three had "dined": his father and Beckmann chatting about some damned hybrid lilies the gardeners at the Lodge had developed. The two men had imbued their conversation with all the energy of gentlemen of leisure.

Suddenly George felt immeasurably angry. The whole business looked absurd! A U.S. naval officer on board a private yacht. Couldn't anyone see what was going on? But no one had said a word. Even Eugenia had accepted their new guest's presence without a murmur. How nice, she'd probably decided, a friend for my cousin Whitney. That is, if she'd thought anything at all.

Simple souls, George thought, all of them. Simple and trusting and as dumb as donkeys. He wanted to laugh, but couldn't muster the effort required. He reached for the brandy decanter. Just another little tot, he told himself; then we'll get this infernal meeting over with.

For a moment he thought of confessing everything to Eugenia. He imagined their breathless relief, their laughter at the old Turk and his wily ways.

Genie would say, "Oh, that's all right, George. . . . You did the right thing. . . . It will turn out for the best. . . ." Wouldn't she whisper those comforting things? Wouldn't she welcome his confidence?

But what if she didn't? What if she was upset or angry? Or, worse, what if she cried? What would he do then?

George poured himself another little splash (the last one, he promised) and slumped in his chair, envisioning imaginary acts of defiance and bravery. He was a titan of industry, a medieval prince, a scholar; he was a loving parent risking his life for his family in some heathen desert; he'd been cast ashore on a forgotten isle. . . .

George settled deeper into his chair, staring into the amber-colored liquid that swirled around and around his glass.

At that moment, Beckmann was in the hold, examining the Axthelm and Company crates. Stooping to avoid support beams and rafters, he carried a kerosene lantern at arm's length as he peered at the cases, carefully marking each one. He measured how firmly they'd been lashed down and looked for signs of damage. The crates heaved and sighed; their new wood groaned in their ropes, but they were secure. Quite admirably secure.

He'd been right to be so adamant, Beckmann decided. Special pallets raised each case several inches above floor level. Despite Captain Cosby's repeated assurances that the *Alcedo*'s hold was dry, Beckmann had stuck to his guns:

"We must have wooden pallets, Captain. I assure you, Mr. Axthelm will not allow any harm to come to this equipment. Salt water could be disastrous."

"Mr. George only suggested a good, safe . . ." the captain had protested.

"I am not referring to Mr. George, Captain!" Beckmann had growled. "I am speaking of Mr. Axthelm senior." That had been the end of that. Beckmann swung his lantern into the far corner for one last look.

Behind him, leaning against a curved wall with his arms folded and his face following the swaying light, Brown watched the inspection without moving to help.

"You should spend as much time down here as you can without arousing suspicion." Beckmann didn't bother to turn as he spoke. "I ordered a hammock. Give whatever reasons you choose. You prefer something more in keeping with your military training. . . . A fancy cabin doesn't suit your spartan habits. . . . Civilian beds are too soft. . . . I don't care. Just remember that no one is to touch these crates. You were hired for this job, and I like to see money well spent."

"So you said earlier."

Beckmann stopped his tour, straightened himself slowly, and looked over at Brown. There was something in the man's tone he didn't like. "So I said, Lieutenant," Beckmann sneered the title.

Our "officer's" too insolent, Beckmann decided; I'll have find a way to bring him down to size. And he turned on his heel, strode up the steps, and headed for his meeting with George.

Eugenia had finished dressing for dinner. Olive, protesting but bobbing curtsies up and down, had finally been dismissed, and Eugenia had a few glorious moments alone. Slowly, she pulled a necklace from its velvet box and dangled it in front of her throat. The pigeon's blood rubies and star sapphires went very well with her new lilac dress. Eugenia considered the effect in the mirror. This is the pièce de résistance, she thought as she ran her fingers over the cool, round stones, and pushed the gold clasp into place. The iridescence of the silk perfectly matches the rose, violet, and cobalt blue of the stones.

Eugenia stepped back from the glass to get a more finished view. Thirty-two, she told herself, and three children, but I'm still beautiful. I look almost the same as I did at nineteen. No, better, she told herself; these clothes are far more elegant and flattering than anything I owned when I was young.

Eugenia pictured her aunt Sally Van Rensselaer's garnet necklace; what a treat it had been to borrow that strand of cut stones set in filigree work. And her mother's cameo brooch! Handed to her by her proud father on the eve of her marriage to George!

Poor Mother, Eugenia thought, poor Aunt Sally Van, poor Gran. A stab of pity struck Eugenia's throat, and she felt useless and feeble, unable to help the people who'd once loved her. They're all of them gone now, she thought, but it was her mother who most upset her. "I never gave her anything," Eugenia said aloud. Then she reminded herself: "Don't dwell!" That was always old Catherine's advice.

"Weeping gets you nowhere," she'd say as she stood by the woodburning stove. "It's as good a time as any to learn that." The words were less important than a well-cooked custard. Catherine hardly ever turned to face her young charge as she dished out a steady stream of Irish advice.

Eugenia remembered the kitchen in her father's house as a lovely place, a haven of speckling motes of flour, steam from the kettle, and the hiss-spatter-clink of the cast iron pots. It was a place where the quiet ticking of a clock could be the most comforting sound in the world, or where the smells of nutmeg and ginger and browning butter could drive you to near distraction.

"Don't dwell," Eugenia repeated. "The past is the past."

Anyway, now you have everything you want, she reminded herself. It's what you always dreamed of. Remember those days at school? And the spending money that never quite stretched? The blue blood name let you down time after time, didn't it? You can't buy new gloves with the promise that your great-grandfather was once an important man.

Eugenia looked at her heaped jewelry box; there was a dog collar, stomacher, or diamond rope to match every frock. And I am happy, she told herself. Very happy and very lucky. And tonight will be perfect.

Eugenia tried a seductive smile for the mirror, but the reflection shamed her. She felt self-conscious and silly. I don't even . . . she thought, I really don't know the first thing about . . . because George and I . . . and we never . . . No matter, she told herself. No matter. I ought to be an experienced lady by now and I will be.

Suddenly Jinx and Lizzie burst into their mother's room followed by a smiling Prue. "Mother," Jinx announced, "I told Prue you'd brush my hair. You will, please, won't you?"

"And what's wrong, madam, with Prue brushing it?" Eugenia teased as she dabbed cologne on her wrists; it was easier to fall in with her daughter's game than to wade through self-doubts.

"Oh, she can't do it at all." Jinx grinned at Prue. "She's got that awful fuzzy stuff herself, and doesn't know how to brush hair properly."

"Get on with you, Miss Jinx." Prue pretended outrage.

Lizzie ignored both her sister and the nursemaid. "And, Mother," she said as she wandered to the dressing table, "may I borrow a little face powder?"

"Powder is it, now?" Eugenia said; she felt proud enough to burst. "Why, you're growing into a lady before my very eyes."

"As if no one noticed," retorted Lizzie.

"And a sassy one at that" was Eugenia's happy response.

Before leaving the room Eugenia added a hurried postscript to her diary: "Now it's face powder for Lizzie! Whatever will be next?"

Then underlining, she wrote in large block letters: <u>BANISH SOR-ROW</u>.

Standing in a window seat in the main saloon while he waited for his parents, Paul looked into the ship's bright night. He saw moonlight gleaming on the deck and rail, and for a moment he thought it was snow lying there; it looked so much like a woolly blanket. Then he stared down at the water and saw his own lighted window reflected there. The window bounced orange sparks over the waves, and the other lighted cabins sent out more fiery spots; Paul closed the curtains behind him to stand in the dark and watch the trail leap through the water.

The ship was a wonderful thing, Paul thought, as alive as a whale or dolphin swooshing through the waves. Suddenly he remembered Jonah and wondered what it would be like to live in a whale's belly for a whole year. That's what Father Sparkman said! Back in Philadelphia. When they went to church. When they had to dress up and parade across Rittenhouse Square every Sunday.

But there's no church here, Paul realized, remembering the rest of Jonah's gruesome tale. The ship's a pet, like our own sea serpent. It will protect us from all those rocks and tempests and foes we used to sing about. And from earthquakes, too.

"Jinx," Paul demanded from his hiding place, "Jinx. Come see how bright we are."

Jinx found her brother and then Lizzie discovered them both, and the three children looked out, holding their breath with the wonder of it all, while behind them, muffled through two sets of baize and velvet curtains, the grown-ups chattered away. They made a soothing sound like the hum of bees at the end of Grandfather A.'s garden: Cousin Whit's voice blended with Dr. DuPlessis's while Mrs. D. burst in with snorts that sounded like the gardener's baby donkey.

They could hear their mother, too, the swish of her skirts as she brushed past the chairs and the clink, clink of her bracelets, a sound they knew by heart. And there were exciting smells, too, different from the ones at home. There was the smell of all that delicious food the chef was making for their special party, and then there was the sharp pine-tar smell of the new ship and lastly a more confused scent, which Lizzie identified as the smell of new things: tasseled settees and rosewood tables, celadon jars and marble-topped étagères, and chairs with the funny name of "Louis Quinze," which, if you said it fast enough, sounded a lot like "weekends."

Lizzie knew these names because her father had taught her; he'd said these things were valuable and that some of them had come from castles in France. "Aubusson carpets," her father had said. "Very precious. Very hard to find. Someday these things will be yours, and your sister's and brother's. In England and Europe, one generation passes on its possessions to the next, and just think, Liz, those paintings and things have been in the same family for hundreds of years. The very same family!"

Lizzie knew her father was impressed by this. He was proud of his brothers and his father, and she guessed he thought about Linden Lodge, their grandfather A.'s house in the country, as a sort of castle that would stay in their family for hundreds of years.

"Fountain-blow," Lizzie whispered, but not loud enough for Jinx or Paul to hear her. They were babies; they didn't care about kings and the fancy places they lived. "Ver-sigh," she said. "Mary Ant-wonette."

Lizzie was right as usual; Jinx and Paul didn't care. Their eyes were glued to the waves below while they listened to the grown-up voices and knew for certain this was the best time ever. The happiest days they would have in their whole long lives.

"Whitney. You must not tell that terrible story again!" Eugenia teased. "What will our new guest think!" Eugenia was determined to draw Lieutenant Brown into the dinner conversation. He seemed ill at ease at the elaborate table, with all its forks and spoons, wineglasses, champagne flutes, and that foolish plethora of plates: lay plates, serving plates, soup plates, butter plates, and the Sèvres card holders she'd placed at each person's chair.

"Jane" read one.

"Gustav," seated across the table (as was fitting!) was another.

And "Whitney" with a drawing of three books and an *R* on each cover, and "Lizabeth" with a picture of a lady applying face powder and looking in a mirror.

But Eugenia hadn't known the lieutenant's first name, and she'd been hesitant about asking George. The young man's presence was somehow connected to business, and that was a realm she'd been forbidden to enter. Now Eugenia regretted her timidity. There was nothing to say but "Lieutenant" or "Our guest."

"Whitney, you can't tell stories about when I was a little girl. What will the children think?" Eugenia waved aside a second serving of Lady Curzon soup, and looked toward the door. She wondered what was keeping George. She'd waited the first course as long as possible, and now here was Higgins passing the tureen round a second time and still no sign of her husband or Beckmann. "Anyway, Whit," she added, forcing her thoughts to return to her guests, "you're eleven years younger than I am. What you know is pure hearsay."

"Yes, he can so tell stories, Mother!" Paul shrieked, overexcited at sitting at the grown-up table, and as full of himself as a five-year-old could be. He bit off a huge chunk of his second roll, and then committed the great sin of speaking with his mouth full. "Cousin Whitney tells it funny!"

"Cousin Whitney is funny when he tells the story," Eugenia corrected her son absently. "And, Paul, you know the rule about speaking when your mouth is full. You're eating far too much bread. It will spoil your appetite." The words came out by themselves.

Then Eugenia turned to Higgins, the head butler, and said, "We'll hold the fish course a moment longer, Higgins. Mr. Axthelm wouldn't want to miss it." While the butler transmitted this order to the other servants, Eugenia looked back at the table, resumed her party face, and told herself that business came before pleasure and that a good wife should be happy with whatever her husband did.

"Well, Cousin Whit never tells it correctly, Paul." Eugenia tried to laugh. "And anyway, I didn't exactly fall out of the canoe. Really, Whitney, you see what you've started." Her eyes strayed to the door again. This is supposed to be our festive first night out, she thought. And here we are finished with the soup course, and there's still no sign of George.

"Paul," Eugenia said more harshly than she'd intended, "save some room for your dinner."

But Paul was not to be daunted. "Tell about the canoe, Cousin Whit, and how Mother fell in the duckweed and how everyone on the dock . . ."

"You did say my husband promised to be down in just a few moments, didn't you, Lieutenant?" Eugenia interrupted, then smiled in what she thought was a lighthearted manner. Oh, these forgetful men, she wanted her face to say. What we wives must put up with!

But Lieutenant Brown's blue eyes were too much for her; they looked through her to something hidden. It was as if he saw all those other times: the birthday parties with a wilting cake, the visits to the zoological gardens that never happened, the kite-flying excursions postponed again and again because her husband was shut away in his darkened study, too "tired" for his children's noise and bouncing pleasure. Eugenia felt her face grow red and she lowered her eyes. It's not just because he's a stranger, she told herself. It's something else entirely.

"Yes, ma'am. Mr. Beckmann said they'd be down directly," Brown managed. Then he, too, looked away.

"Tell the parasol part, Cousin Whit," Paul burst in, "and how Mother chased Mr. Harris and tried to beat him on the head for laughing and how you . . ."

"That's enough, Paul!" Eugenia's voice was sharper than before. Lizzie and Jinx looked across the table at each other and shared a private communication no one could interpret. Mrs. DuPlessis studied the grape leaf design of the silver candelabra and her husband muttered something about "Lady Curzon soup being a lovely potage. . . ." Only Paul seemed impervious to the change in his mother's mood.

Of course it is Beckmann's fault, Eugenia decided angrily. I should have known. George would have been on time if it weren't for that awful man. She raised her eyes, met Brown's again, and looked quickly away.

"Oh, well, Mr. Beckmann!" she sang out to cover her thoughts. "We may as well persuade a ferret to quit a rabbit's nest as Mr. Beckmann to leave off worrying about business." Then she turned to Dr. DuPlessis, the dinner partner to her left. Her grandmother's litany would save her.

"If all else fails, Eugenia," her grandmother had repeated too many times to count, "turn the table. Unpleasantness can be masked by a maidenly shrug." But her grandmother had also told her the way to "survive difficult conjugal nights" was to "rework the week's menus in your mind."

Now, why am I thinking about that? Eugenia wondered. Then she put the idea out of her mind.

"I think we'll have to teach our new guest a thing or two about Mr. Ogden Beckmann, wouldn't you say, Doctor?" Eugenia laughed. "The first one being that he's the most determined man on earth."

"Not above my Gustav," Mrs. DuPlessis chimed in. Peace seemed to be restored. Now perhaps we'll get on with our supper, she thought. She was as hungry as a bear.

Jinx read Mrs. D.'s thoughts. The lady's appetite was a source of constant amusement for each child, and Jinx tried to kick Lizzie under the table to remind her of their joke, but the blow landed right in the center of Mrs. DuPlessis's well-padded ankle. Jinx looked up in alarm, and Mrs. DuPlessis glared.

Really, she thought, their father is correct in calling them hooligans! He allows his wife too much sway; he's far, far too kind, that man, too decent for his own good.

"Well, now, I happen to know a very good story. . . ." Dr. DuPlessis interjected with his careful English. He was well aware of his wife's feelings regarding the Axthelm children, and he recognized a potentially dangerous situation when he saw one. He also knew his wife could turn a blind eye when she wanted, that she'd excuse George's absence with all sorts of reasons but the true one.

Dr. DuPlessis decided he'd have to take charge of the table. Kindly, deliberately, showing a side of himself he rarely exposed, he spread his short, stubby fingers on the tablecloth as if preparing for a magic trick.

"Now, I'll tell you a little secret," he began, nodding to each guest. "It is a professional secret that must never leave this room."

The children were enraptured; Eugenia was grateful. I will never make fun of this good man again, she promised herself. He really is the gentlest soul on earth, as well as the most discerning.

"And the little secret is . . ." Paul and Jinx opened their eyes as wide as they could. They didn't make a sound.

". . . that I cure my patients only with threats to visit them again. . . ."

"And long, long, really long, stories!" Jinx whooped, nearly choking on her own laughter.

Mrs. DuPlessis was incensed. The very idea that a mere child should make fun of her husband. She wanted to say: "You ungrateful little wretch!" and box her impudent ears, but decided on the more diplomatic:

"You mustn't say that about your anecdotes, Gustav. I, for one, always find them most entertaining and enlightening. Perhaps childish minds are not . . ."

"A mind is a mind, my dear," Dr. DuPlessis cut short what he recognized as the beginning of a full-blown lecture. He did it so gently not even his wife noticed. "Remember what our Lord said: 'Suffer the little children . . .' "

But at that moment, George appeared in the doorway. He lurched forward, walking unsteadily as he tried to calculate the distance and steps required to make it to his chair.

"So shorry . . . sorry," George corrected himself, forming the words with difficulty as if they were arcane phrases in a foreign tongue.

"Sorry, ma dear. Unavoidably detained . . . Old Beck . . ." George leaned backward, searching for his ally. "Beckmann and I . . . Unavoidable . . . I'm"—George straightened his tongue around the impossible vowels again—". . . afraid. Unav . . . Where's old Beck? You here, Beck . . . ?" George peered around the room, blinking resolutely as he tried to bring his family into focus.

"Why don't you sit down and join us, George." Eugenia wanted to sound welcoming, but she knew her voice was tight and hard. Damn Beckmann, she thought. Damn them both!

"Exshellent shug . . . suggestion, Genie. Don't mine if I do. Take my ease. Take a load off the old . . . " George staggered toward his chair. Higgins was immediately there.

Good God! Eugenia thought. It's worse than ever. Why, George? she wondered. Why must you do this to me? Anger overcame her; it flushed her face, knocked the breath from her lungs, till she thought for one horrible moment she might cry.

"What's this? Old Higgins? Creeping out of the blue to hold the chair for Master Georgie? Don't you think he can get up in his chair by his lonesome?"

"George." Eugenia tried to divert her husband's attention. It was disgraceful that the servants hear this, she thought. She waved her hand as a sign of immediate dismissal. When the stewards had filed through the pantry door, she began again.

"You missed some lovely soup, dear! We had Lady Curzon, your favorite. . . ."

"Soup? Soup?" George stared at her with barren incomprehension. He reached for the back of his chair, but mistook its distance from the table, and suddenly man and chair came crashing forward. But George remained on his feet, poised delicately and glaring at the chair as if it had purposely moved out from under him.

With the reproachful dignity of a man deceived, he lunged at the crafty table again, grabbing the lace cloth with such force that the lay plates and silver, the gold dishes filled with oranges and grapes and pears, clattered together and sent purple, orange, and green shot flying across the clear white field.

George sank down. "Sorry, sorry . . . my dear," he repeated. "Late and all. Couldn't be . . ." George stumbled over the rest of his prepared speech "Ogden? You here?" He needed his best friend's help.

Beckmann materialized then; he stepped into the room with a cool and businesslike smile. "Right behind you, George," he said easily.

"Got to explain . . ." George turned and blinked at Eugenia, leering a crooked smile as if he were trying to place this new and charming face. Then all of a sudden his attention jumped to Paul. The little boy stiffened, but tried to look happy; the grin fixed on his face didn't waver.

"Paul . . . my boy!" George's smile contorted into sorrow. "Nice, Genie, I forgot . . . the children . . . here . . ." For a moment, George seemed about to weep; he slumped in his seat and stared at his hands and the crumpled linen. His head fell forward and Eugenia didn't know if he was about to be sick or burst into wails of recrimination. Instead he staggered back to his feet.

"Well, by God, you'd think this were a goddamn funeral. Let's have some champagne. Higgins! Another round, by God. Fill 'em up!"

With calm dignity, Higgins took on this task alone. He didn't allow the other servants to return to the room. He'd seen his master like this before, and he knew it was behavior one could expect in a true gentleman. They just couldn't hold their liquor. One little tot set them reeling. Why, back at the establishment on Chestnut Street, there'd been more than one occasion. . . . But Higgins didn't finish that thought. Instead he returned his attention to the swinish group in the kitchens. A fat lot they know, he cursed silently. They'll be tittering over this, or my name is mud. Why, they wouldn't know a gentleman from a cigar store Indian, not even if he came up and punched them in the nose. I'll have to set the record straight on that score. That I will.

George watched Higgins with fascinated wonderment. The precision in the man's hands was a marvel. I'll bet he never spills so much as a drop, George thought. I'll bet he just sits in those kitchens of his and practices the livelong day; it's enough to make anyone sick! With that, George swayed so suddenly and violently that Eugenia thought: This is it. She wanted him to fall then, wanted him to crash to the floor within full sight of his adoring guests, drunk, dirty, and unconscious, but she kept her thin smile set.

Paul couldn't watch his father any longer. Instead he glared at his knife, three forks, and two spoons, and whispered miserably, "I think Father's tired again. You know, the way he gets at home." Paul said these words to Jinx, but he didn't look at her. He knew he wouldn't like what he saw in her face. She'd be looking at him as if he were the stupidest creature alive.

Paul decided to take matters into his own hands. Father should take a nice nap, Paul decided. I'll tell everyone, and then he can go back to his room and lie down.

"Father's tired," the little boy declared loudly. "He should have a rest."

"Shhh," Lizzie whispered. Her voice sounded like a snake's, and Paul was completely silenced while Jinx stared in remorse at the plate in front of her. The yachting flags painted on it seemed to be swimming in a pretty pond, but then she realized it was tears that made them move. Jinx closed her eyes and felt them slip down her cheeks.

"Well, George, we had wondered where you'd . . ." Eugenia tried again, but she knew her smile had stuck and that her bland, cheerless chatter couldn't fool a fly. And why is it so important to fool them? she thought. Why can't I let them see the truth? But she didn't. And she hadn't. Not ever. She'd kept up her practiced role: good wife, good mother, good woman. Perfect. Good.

She felt as tired as if she were struggling up a long, arid hill full of rocks and boulders and inescapable heat. "Well, everyone, shall we—" Eugenia trudged on—"shall we . . . I believe the chef . . . some roast lamb . . ."

But poor little Paul, at that moment, whether by accident or design, dropped his spoon and fork. They'd been engaged in a silent battle: the spoon, knife, and fork; they'd been knights in silver armor. But when the knife won, the others crashed to the floor. Paul stared at the soldiers lying dead on the carpet. This was serious, he knew—Mother liked good manners.

"Paul!" Eugenia spun on her son. Her voice was so shrill it reminded him of lightning crackling. "Don't play with your silver! These things wouldn't happen if you didn't continually fidget."

Fury carried Eugenia forward. In a flash it was all Paul's fault. The spoiled evening and her husband's inattentions. If we'd had a romantic evening alone, none of this would have happened, she told herself. But even as the words formed in her mind, she recognized them as a sad delusion.

"Perhaps you should have eaten earlier with Prue, after all," Eugenia insisted, clinging to the thing that had aroused her anger. But the cruel words stung her as much as they did her child. How can I be so unkind, Eugenia thought. He's so very little; it's not his fault. But she felt incapable of turning back. She looked at Paul; his head was bent, and his bony shoulders were rigid as wire. Her heart moved out to him, but she felt incapable of forgiveness.

"Genie, Genie . . ." George tried to soothe, "the little chap's just . . ." but his voice sounded as if he were talking in his sleep, repeating a worn-out phrase he'd heard long ago. George looked up from the pitch and toss of the table. Shouldn't be all this fuss, he thought. Dinner, table manners . . . poor little fellow . . . Genie was always lashing out at the kiddies. . . . You had to be . . . had to be . . . But George couldn't quite remember what word you used with children.

He pictured his own father, but that memory became confused with Beckmann and Borneo and all the wretched business that should never see the light of day. Rajah Ivard, Mahomet Seh, Brown, the whole money-grubbing plan.

George rose unsteadily to his feet. " 'I'm the master of my fate,' " he misquoted as he surveyed the room and his guests' upturned faces. " 'Beyond this place of wrath and tears . . . my head is bloody but unbowed.' Invictus— there's a poet for you!" But instead of continuing the speech, George blurted a sudden "Rough sea, my dear . . ."

The room seemed awash in evil-smelling fumes. George's lips became green and he clamped them together. "Rough sea . . . have to . . . have to see Captain . . ." And he dashed from the room.

For a moment after her husband had gone, Eugenia sat bent over, studying the napkin on her lap. She examined the lace border, so delicately stitched by an unknown and dedicated hand, and she put her finger through the largest space and ripped the border in two. The threads tore in half like wet paper, and crumpled into a soggy ball.

Then Eugenia forced herself to look up at her guests: at Mrs. Du-Plessis's fat and astonished face, at the doctor's, at Whitney's, even dared herself to stare at Lieutenant Brown, while she said with her best party smile, "Well, I hope you're all still hungry. The chef promised us quite a dinner tonight."

When she was finally alone in her cabin with the terrible dinner and each polite "good night" and "sleep well" behind her, Eugenia walked through the room. She didn't turn on a single lamp. The darkness seemed comforting somehow, like a presence that loved her. She pressed her body into the wall, and stood so still she might have been a piece of the wall itself. Then she leaned her head against the port-hole's cold glass. The sea was black, and she watched the ship push forward in the icy Atlantic night. She wanted to cry, expected to cry, but no tears came.

I should have gone out on deck, she thought, but I was afraid. I was afraid Lieutenant Brown might be there. Or someone. It didn't have to be Lieutenant Brown. It could have been anyone seeing me like that. It's just because he's a stranger, Eugenia reasoned; that's why I feel so shy. Because I don't know him.

But I'm not sad, she told herself harshly, I'm something, but I'm not sad. I just wanted to go out on deck, that's all. I wanted to feel the wind on my legs. I'd have turned my face right into the storm and opened my mouth, and no one would have heard me at all. Not the DuPlessises or Whitney. Or Beckmann or anyone. My problems with George are my own.

Eugenia walked to her desk and took out her diary, but there were no words to describe what she felt.

> *We had Lady Curzon soup, a lovely blancmange, some glazed onions in sherry cream. . . . George was a bit late for the proceedings, poor dear, working late again, but his arrival and hasty departure did nothing to dampen the festivities. . . .*

Eugenia's thoughts stopped there. She wouldn't let them go on. Instead the lacquered wheels of George's phaeton coach sprang into her mind. Her wedding day: May 10, 1889. Black wheels and the glossy flanks of a new Morgan gelding: They seemed all she could remember suddenly. Not the waltzes swelling from the tent, not George's niece

Sarah proffering a stolen red rose, not the boys' stunts or the photographers' shouts or her veil covering her face as she turned and turned and turned and turned.

It was the wheel she saw; a black wheel on a spiky lawn amid shadows cast by countless trousered legs. There was something about the carriage brake that George hadn't understood. So they'd waited, just married, shy and hesitant among the rice and flying streamers, till the brake was finally mastered with a loud masculine bluster. It was Philip who did it, Eugenia realized suddenly. Philip, my first beau. The only boy I ever kissed.

Eugenia lifted her hand and looked at her fingers. A shiny wheel on May-green grass, how fine it had seemed on that spring day fourteen years before, but there was something about it that seemed to call from the past, as if it were a matter of dire need, as if someone were whispering, "This. You must never forget this moment."

"I feel something," Eugenia said aloud. "But I won't let myself be sad."

In the now quiet ship, Beckmann sat in George's study and composed a message to the Turk. A steward stood at attention nearby.

"Take this to the telegraph room," Beckmann said, without glancing at the man. "It must get through to Newport as soon as possible."

"Yes, sir."

When the steward left, Beckmann didn't move from the desk. His concentration was completely on the paper before him. Beckmann took up his pen and continued a more detailed report to his master. He was a keen observer; nothing that had happened during the day had escaped his notice. It wasn't a bad day, either, Beckmann reflected. Not bad at all. He dangled his pen over the clean page. His instructions were to send reports at every stop, and to keep his own personal log of the voyage as well. The Turk liked to be informed. "George drunk at dinner," Beckmann wrote.

> Started drinking before our meeting.
> Eugenia handled it fairly well. She may prove more valuable
> than previously thought.
> Checked on Brown. Gave further instructions.
> Shipment riding well.

No need to mention Brown's insolence, Beckmann concluded. What was a problem if not an obstacle in search of removal?

So, we settle in for our first night, Beckmann thought. Our happy group. This is going to be a pleasant trip. Very pleasant, indeed. He pulled a cigar from George's humidor, sniffed it, and broke off its tip. I like these cigars, he decided and smiled, in spite of what the old Turk says. There's one more thing George and I have in common.

The *Alcedo* pushed through the night. Her engines churned, and the fire that kept up the steam and the coal that kept up the fire continued a relentless rhythm. On she went: past midnight, past one, past two, past four. While the stewards dozed in their cots, and the passengers rocked in their downy beds, the ship rolled them all into dreamland. Her staircases sighed, her cupboards groaned, and her wardrobes and doorways set up a nighttime whine. The *Alcedo* didn't listen; she had work to do. Quirky or vigilant, lazy or proud, whatever this ship was, she was her passengers' only home. She was their haven, their shelter, their salvation. From rock and tempest, fire and foe, hers was the arm, hers the unending and mother-sung voice.

T H R E E

"WHERE DOES BECK-
MANN'S cable put them, Carl?" The Turk spoke to his son from the depths of his chair. The great man's study in Newport was almost dark; the only light came from a waning fire. It had been ordered to take the chill out of the stone-walled room, but by the time the Turk spoke, the fire had burned so low only a few rough embers remained. They shone out of an ashy sea and there was nothing cheery or heartening about their light. The tall clock in the corner was equally hushed, and the deep windows with their wine-colored drapes, the tables, footstools, hassocks, and Persian carpet stretching wall to wall to wall: None of these things intruded on the men's watchful silence.

"Carl?" the Turk repeated. But it was Anson, the Turk's major-domo, who answered:

"Just past the *Ambrose* lightship, sir."

Carl closed his own mouth with a quiet snap, and stared into what was left of the fire. Only one half of his face was illuminated, and that half gave nothing away.

"On course and on time," Anson continued in a soothing and sanctimonious tone, bending forward as he spoke, his white gloves ready to jump to his master's bidding. "Shall I wheel the globe closer, sir? Light the lamps? Revive the fire?"

Although it was well past midnight, the faithful Anson still wore the starched shirt and tailcoat in which he'd presided over dinner. Instructed to wait for the cable and deliver it immediately, he'd been told to entrust no one else with the task. A mere formality, Anson knew; he'd served the Turk long enough to recognize which duties demanded his undivided attention—and which must never be repeated backstairs.

"No, that will be all, Anson. You may go."

"Sir." The majordomo withdrew as stiffly as any adjutant hoping to further a military career; he looked momentarily as though he might click his heels together and bow before he turned and pulled close the double doors that led to the Turk's inner sanctum. A lifetime of service to one family had made Anson proud; if he'd grown old in the Turk's houses, he'd also become regal. The master need never concern himself with an unruly staff as long as Anson's stern presence was felt. There was not a housemaid, footman, stable boy, or under gardener who didn't fear him.

Carl's jaw twitched, and his eyes darted from the fire to the floor and back again. Pompous ass, he thought. Thinks he's got hold of Beckmann's job. Thinks he's going to shed that swallowtail coat and quit the pantry stairs. Thinks he'll mingle with us better folk. Instead of letting those thoughts slip out, though, Carl feigned indifference, settled back in his chair, and said, "This isn't too much for him, Father?"

Carl drew out the words "too much" until they circled the two men's heads with an echo of mistrust. "At his age, I mean?" The studied subtlety took on an aristocratic tone. It was Carl's latest weapon.

"Too much?" the Turk asked. "For Anson? No, I trust him completely." The father laughed at his son's effort. He's too obvious, the old man thought; he hasn't learned the trick yet. He's still wobbly as a pup.

"After all, Carl, you must remember I've been acquainted with Anson longer than I have with you." The Turk matched his son's slow drawl, but he upped the ante. He went one step further. "Anson is what we, in the business world, refer to as a 'known commodity.'"

"So you are fond of reminding me, Father." Bested, Carl turned petulant and mean. He stretched in his chair seat till the leather crackled. A "known commodity," he told himself, unsure whether the comparison pleased or irked him.

Neither man spoke after that. They continued to sit, hidden from each other, staring at the fire grate, engrossed in their private thoughts. This was not a social occasion; there were no inviting cigars, no decanter of port left within easy reach. Father and son had finished with the family dinner, announced hale and hearty good nights to Tony and his wife, Cassandra, to Martin and Isobel, and to all the various grandchildren, nephews, and nieces who gathered by command or desire in the Turk's many houses.

Then, after the last hall light had been dimmed and the last footman scurried past bearing the last serving of warm milk and biscuits, the Turk and his third son had encamped in private to await Beckmann's cable.

It was Carl who finally broke the silence. "I wish I had your confidence, Father—that everything was as simple as you present it. The yacht will be a long way off, remember, when they—"

"Youth, Carl, youth," the Turk interrupted with an easy laugh. "Don't rush things, boy. Learn patience. This is no more than a child's waiting game. Enjoy it while you can."

Then the voice grew serious; it took on a distinct edge: "Don't make demands, Carl. And never use threats. For your information—I do remember. I remember everything."

The Turk stopped speaking, and Carl waited, not daring to move, knowing that any shift in his chair would be regarded as weakness. Threats, his mind argued, threats! Look who's calling the kettle black.

Carl listened for his father's breath, but the sound was too measured to trust; he had no way of knowing when it might be safe to speak again. The clock kept to its unobtrusive pattern, and a few spent embers scattered on the hearth: Their noise was nothing; they might have been mice on a closet floor. Then a sudden summer gust rustled outside, picked up the ocean spray from the garden's long seawall, and pitted it against the glass. Sand and salt speckled the window. There's a storm coming, Carl told himself; that's a wind from the northeast. The sound was refreshing; it reminded him that a world existed outside his father's door. Carl decided to try his question again:

"And what is it that you want me to do, Father?"

Good, the Turk thought; the boy's learning something, after all. He may be easily whipped into place, but he'll never be cowed.

"What I want you to do, Carl," the Turk answered, "is keep an accurate record of the yacht's whereabouts. I want—as nearly as can be estimated, given changing tides, winds, currents, etc.—an up-to-date account of her position.

"The necessary charts and equipment are in the cupboard nearest my desk. You may start tomorrow. This is not to interfere with your other work, however. I want that understood. It will be a sort of hobby—if you will. That's what you'll tell the others. . . . You're worried about your dear brother, and so forth. Brotherly love's an acceptable excuse for keeping tabs on anyone."

There was a pause in which neither man moved, then the Turk

turned in his chair, reached out his hand for a book close by, and ended his instructions with a perfunctory "Good night."

Anger carried Carl to the door. The old fox thinks he's put me in my place, does he? Carl fumed. He thinks he's dealing with an underling: Anson or some servant! He forgets I'm his son; he forgets I've been in on this from the beginning. He forgets how much I know.

"At least Beckmann's with them," Carl announced from the door. It was his parting shot and it was intended to wound. "In case this carefully constructed scheme should spring an unforeseen leak."

The effect was instantaneous. "Is that the best you can do?" the Turk demanded. "Beckmann? I don't take advice from Beckmann!" The old man's voice rose, and his face became mottled and livid. In spite of the darkness, Carl watched purple patches bloom over his father's cheeks and throat.

"Don't you forget what we've come from, Carl," the Turk struggled. "And don't ever forget why we're here!" The voice was furious, thunderous. Carl couldn't remember when he'd last seen his father so riled. The abrupt change took him by surprise. He dropped his hand from the doorknob and stared. "No, Father, I haven't forgotten why I'm here," he was about to answer, but the Turk's speech cut him off.

"You think your fancy education makes you smarter than me, is that it?" the old man continued. "Makes you shrewd. Makes you ruthless. That's what you think, isn't it? You . . . Tony . . . Martin. You think you're better than me."

Carl stood his ground. He didn't speak. Then, with the slightest of movements, he put both hands in his pockets, and in doing so stood straighter and taller.

The Turk noticed the defiant stance. It was everything he hated— this collegiate, upper-crust pretension. It made his blood boil. Damn them all, he thought: Damn their clans and their snobbery; damn their sheltered, shallow souls. In his anger, the Turk forgot who had ordered his sons to copy the elite.

"But your fine books don't count, Carl, and your fancy speech won't save you when you're down. You have to get your hands dirty to rise to the top. And that's what I've done. That's why I'm no German peasant, scraping a few coins together, nodding to Von this, Von that, begging for a day's work and servile till I die."

Rage propelled the Turk from his chair, and he clawed at the armrests as he jostled himself to his feet. Carl watched the entire performance. He didn't make a sound.

"Why do you think I came to this country, boy? Why do you think you've got your big house, your gentlemen's club, your tailored suits and your motorcars? Because you deserve it? Because the old man wants what's best for his children? Because it's your right as an heir? That's blue blood bunk, that's what that is!" The Turk paused here, but only for a moment; he wanted to make sure his words were hitting home.

"No, you've got the best because it is the best. No one's impressed with less. We're not a bunch of socialists here, all talk and no plan; democracy was invented for the man with balls. That's lunacy about men being created equal, that's all it is."

Carl considered responding, but stopped himself. He listened to the breeze pick up: This time the windows were pelted with more than salt and sand; this time there was rain as well.

". . . But I'm proud of who I am," his father was continuing. The voice had lost none of its fury, but it began to rail randomly, as if the speaker were wrestling with some private fear. "And you know why, boy? Because it allows me to be king of the heap. People kowtow when I walk into a room. And I visit with presidents. I give them advice. And it's listened to, I tell you, because business is business; it rules the goddamned world."

The Turk started to pace the room; he moved from table to bookcase, from window to fire screen, and his steps grew quicker with every turn. Desk to chair, door to desk. The crunch of his shoes rattled the carpet and shook the floor. Carl was almost entirely forgotten:

"Where do you think we'd be if it weren't for those Jew Rothschilds, or that conniving bastard Morgan, or that cretin in New York, your illustrious Mr. Gould?" the Turk continued to shout. "Trust them? Not with a penny. But that's the beauty part. That's the game. We play for the highest stakes; we knife each other in the back without blinking an eye. But that's why we rule the world. Power's invincible. And don't you forget it." The Turk laughed once; it was a hollow sound, like a bell with a crack. The noise seemed to startle him, and he looked around as if confused by his surroundings. "This is my room," his face appeared to say, "my study in my house, on Bellevue Avenue, in Newport, in nineteen and three. . . ."

Then he looked toward the door, saw Carl there, and struggled to regain momentum. ". . . You and Tony and Martin . . ." the Turk stated, ". . . the three of you brothers . . . You sit back; you watch. You wait. . . ."

The voice grew stronger; it became didactic and calm. "You wait, Carl. Don't deny it; you're holding out for your chance. And you should. You should!" This was better. The old man was back on track and he knew it.

"If you learned anything watching me, it's that you take what you want. Forget the little guy. He's small because he's afraid. He's nobody and he deserves it. But I'm somebody. I'm the biggest somebody this country's got. And if you're a thief, you'd better be the best, because the second best dies. . . ."

Carl walked out the door on that. Then he stood in the silent hallway and wondered if he'd gone too far.

But now it was dawn, the twenty-sixth of July, the day after the greatest yacht in the world had moved her condescending bulk through the harbor and out to sea. She was only a memory to the city's laborers, a squib in a newspaper someone else read, a land apart like a priest's come-on description of the pearly gates. The laborers had their own fish to fry.

In the side streets and alleys of Newport, they began their sullen gray scuttle: men and women and children passing each other in silence, moving toward an appointed place at a steady, wordless pace. There was the jangle of a lunch pail here and there, but more often there was nothing. Fists in pockets, hands under shawls, fingers wrapped around bony arms and still thinner stomachs: people whose only concern was another meal.

Lofty decisions, plans to mold a better or even a different future, were as far from their minds as visions of themselves setting sail on a white ship on a sunny day. It was laughable. Lunatic. Stuff for the idle rich. Let them have their games, the working folk thought; they'll only harm each other. Let them play at being princes; it's got nothing to do with us. The slow turn of the wheel and the complex machinations that had put it in motion were ignored or misunderstood.

Then morning came at last as it always did, and the laborers hurried faster. There was work to be done, jobs to be reached, positions found and money scrounged, before the sun was risen. Pink rays began their finger-slip upward through disappearing clouds, and the landscape was shadowy no longer. Then the milkman's horse and cart appeared and the coalie-oilie man's voice was found, and they started their distinct clatter down the cobbled streets toward the fine houses where the rich folk dwelled. And inside, the upstairs maids, the downstairs maids, the boot-blacking boy, the scullery girl, and the cook began their tiptoed preparations for another wearying day.

While about 150 nautical miles east-southeast of the *Ambrose* lightship, in the midst of the green-gray North Atlantic, the sun was long up to claim the ocean as its own. It turned the *Alcedo* into a gleaming object that hovered on the water, moving without seeming to move, pushing forward as a swan glides, the strength and power of its thrust completely hidden. The white ship and bright sunlight combined to create their own insular vision. The world at peace, the picture said, the world of confidence and enviable ease; heaven established right here on earth. The turmoil of the engines, the reverberating shout, the sweat on the firemen who shoveled the coal, the heaped fires, oiled pistons, and curses from the boss screaming, "Faster! Faster!" were masked in this facade of outward calm. Then the sun turned hard yellow and the sea took on its familiar veiny and bottle-dark froth. It was morning of the second day.

Eugenia was already up and at her window; all reveries, melancholy, fury, or confusion were banished by the view before her. The sky's brilliant blue streaked straight down to meet the water. There was no insipid haze at the horizon, no blurring of heaven and earth, and definitely none of the sulky gray heat waves that shrouded every land-locked Pennsylvania summer.

Eugenia thought she'd never seen anything so fine. *Walk out, walk out,* the ocean called her. *I'm solid as stone; I'm a dancing floor, halls of marble, a palace of glass, and I'm always and always and forever yours.* Salt spray splattered the round porthole and Eugenia reached out the tips of her fingers as if she might magically touch it.

Then she replaced her breakfast tray on its pink wicker table. Coffee and French toast with cinnamon sugar, *fraises des bois* and Devonshire cream: The beckoning scent lingered in the air. And I'm still hungry, Eugenia realized. That thought lifted her spirits beyond all reason, and she walked to her wardrobe door and tossed dress after dress on the floor till she made the perfect choice. Then a petticoat, a camisole, a sash of pale blue, and slippers to match.

As her mother finished dressing, Jinx raced into the cabin; her face was pink and shiny and her words tumbled out as quickly as her panting breath:

"Where've you been, Mother? We've already had breakfast and everything. Prue said to let you sleep, but I was sure you couldn't still be in bed. Besides, I saw Olive bring in your breakfast things!" The little girl ran to a window without bothering to wait for a reply.

"Did you see where we are? Captain Cosby says we're more than a hundred miles out. Just think! Miles and miles and miles, and all while we slept in our beds. We're like Wynken, Blynken, and Nod.

" 'Wynken, Blynken and Nod one night / Sailed off in a wooden shoe. . . .'

"Do you remember singing that to us, Mother? You used to make up the funniest tunes!"

Eugenia took up the familiar song:

". . . So shut your eyes while Mother sings
Of wonderful sights that be,
And you shall see the beautiful things
As you rock in the misty sea . . ."

"And that's us!" Jinx shouted. "The fishermen three: Paul and Lizzie and me!"

"And 'I,' darling," Eugenia corrected her daughter softly, "not 'me.' And I believe Wynken and Blynken are two little eyes and that Nod is the little head. . . ."

"Well, mine makes more sense," Jinx countered with complete assurance. "Besides, it rhymes."

Then Eugenia's youngest daughter grew tired of poetry, stretched her head inside the porthole as far as it could go, and tried to look down into the waves. "You can't see any land at all, Mother. Not a mountain or anything!

"Oh, did I tell you Paul woke up crying? He said it was like being the only people on the earth, but Prue made it all right. He's with Cousin Whitney now, watching him eat breakfast. He's having kippered herring. Ugh!" The little girl didn't stop for a moment. She had too much to say, too much to think about!

"We're going to play ring toss, 'deck quoits,' Cousin Whit calls it. You're on my team. We've got to beat Lizzie and Whit. Paul's on their team, too; what a baby. He's boasting he and Whit are going to be ship champions. I think Lieutenant Brown might play, too." Jinx stopped her recitation and turned suddenly coy. If Paul could have a hero, then so could she.

"Well, hurry up, Mother. Or they'll start without us!" And Jinx rushed out as quickly as she'd come in. "What about today's lessons?" Eugenia was about to ask, then decided: Lessons be damned. She picked up her hairbrush and began to untangle her dark brown curls, then sweep them up into what she considered was a breezy, nautical style.

Then cast your nets wherever you wish—
Never afraid are we!

No more Turk, she thought suddenly, no more Carl, or Martin, or Tony, no more whispered conversations as we wives pour coffee. And no more, "Remember, Eugenia, the governor's very important to me just now. I seated him beside you because he went to school with your father. You'll know what to say. . . ."

"No more of that nonsense, ever!" Eugenia slapped her brush back in place on the dressing table with a movement so hasty and rash that the scent bottles jumped and the button hooks collided with two pots of face cream and knocked them rolling till they covered the linen cloth in a lemony swathe.

Well, Beckmann, Eugenia realized abruptly. There's still Beckmann to contend with. But we'll get around him. Push him overboard if he gets too nasty. Eugenia's exuberance carried her into the corridor and up the stairs, as she envisioned acts of childish revenge: salt in sugar bowls, trouser legs stitched together, and shoelaces hopelessly knotted. I'll win Beckmann over, she vowed, or I'll eat worms on hot buttered toast.

They lined the deck; Eugenia, Jinx, and Dr. DuPlessis against Whitney, Lizabeth, and Paul. True to her word, Jinx had persuaded Lieutenant Brown to join them. But he was odd man out; he kept score and cheered both sides equally, something Jinx had not particularly envisioned. She shot him a pleading glance, but he failed to see it. Then the players closed ranks and another match started.

The deck chairs and chaises had been shifted under the awnings to clear a place for the all-important game and a net strung up between the wheelhouse steps and the service companionway, separating the two areas into equal war zones. Tea couldn't be served without disrupting the game, and Mrs. DuPlessis considered this as she rested uneasily on a shaded chaise. A little plain toast would do me a world of good, she thought, or one of the butter biscuits the pastry chef makes, or the tiniest sugar cookie; sugar always aids an edgy stomach. Mrs. DuPlessis was not sure she liked the sea; it spoiled her appreciation of food completely.

Don't watch the horizon, she told herself, but her eyes were drawn there again and again. "Oh . . ." she sighed, and pulled her hat veil closer, then she shrouded her feet, hands, and round body in a blanket one of the stewards had provided till she looked like a mummy waiting for burial. Only her lips were visible and they were as motley green as the waves. "Oh . . ." Mrs. DuPlessis moaned louder, but her husband failed to hear her; he was caught up in something more important than she.

The second match was fast and frantic; tricks had been learned and strategies plotted. Dr. DuPlessis made a sudden and spectacular leap; his legs slid out from under him, and he grabbed the hard rubber quoit before it hit the deck. Pride and effort quivered across his body. He stood up, brushed salt dust from his knees (an effort requiring several grunts), and took an elaborate bow.

There were shouts all around: whoops of joy or fierce disappointment, encouraging words, and growls of despair. Everyone was out of breath; everyone had turned pink in the face and glowed with a competitive gleam. The Sand Pirates (that was Whitney's team) was in close lead over the Winged Beetles, which was captained by the rapidly rising star, Dr. DuPlessis. Paul began to wonder if he'd chosen the wrong side.

Twice a ring was thrown overboard and everyone raced pell-mell to the rail to watch the thing plummet from sight. But then the under steward Henry was summoned and another rubber quoit produced. Henry trundled back and forth to the games chest so many times that he became convinced Higgins would take the price of the quoits out of his wages. With each trip Henry's steps grew slower; beans could have sprouted under his feet.

"Next person loses one overboard, goes after it," Whit yelled as he prepared to flip a quoit into the air.

"What if it's you, Cousin Whit?" Paul shouted back.

"It's Captain Whit to you, laddie . . . and anyway, I don't count."

"That's not fair!" shrieked the children in unison.

Then they were back at the game, heaving the ring high over the net or dropping it like a secret stone into the corner. Lizzie dived for one toss and tore her skirt; Paul managed to get off a shot while lying on his back. Eugenia ended up on her knees, heaving the ring frantically into the air where Whit (unkindly) caught it, then flipped it to skim the net and drop, with a wiggling plop, just inside the boundary.

"That's not fair, Whitney." Eugenia had struggled to her feet too late. "We were all so far back from that last throw. And besides, two on our side are in long skirts."

"That didn't stop me!" Lizzie yelled. She forgot she was supposed to be a young lady of the world.

"I guess your team is just not as organized as we are," Whitney called back. "We have defensive and offensive players. We're professionals over here."

Then both sides shook hands, laughed, and apologized to Henry while Dr. DuPlessis ran to get his camera. They posed for the official photographs dutifully: winners and losers (the Sand Pirates had taken the championship) arranging themselves under and beside the net, while Paul was lifted high on Whit's shoulders and Lieutenant Brown held aloft the improvised flag they'd made from Eugenia's scarf.

Finally the group disbanded (much to Mrs. DuPlessis's pained relief) and the doctor went to look after his wife while Lizabeth, Jinx, and Whit decided to hunt up the domino set, and Eugenia settled herself in a chaise to read to Paul.

George appeared in the sunlight then. The bright light startled him and he jerked back, screwing his eyes shut; then he opened them wide, pulled himself up ramrod straight, and walked straight to Eugenia's chair. He was meticulously dressed in his yachting outfit: his blue cap square on his head and his brass buttons gleaming

Eugenia had seen her husband come out on deck, but she didn't stop reading.

"Morning, Eugenia, Paul," George interrupted in what he hoped was a hearty manner. "Having a good time out here, are you, son? Decide you like the sea, after all?"

"Oh yes, Father. I love it!" The little boy smiled at this sudden attention. "We were playing ring toss—Whit caught one when it—"

"That's fine, son. Fine," George spoke too quickly. "Why don't you run along now, and find your sisters. I have to talk to your mother."

Paul looked uncertainly at Eugenia.

"That's a good idea, Paul," she said to soothe him, then she rubbed his bony shoulders and patted his small back. "See if you can find Whit and those dominoes. Maybe Prue knows where they are . . . and I promise later we'll read about the pirates. . . ."

When Paul had trotted away, Eugenia and George looked at each other. George saw that his wife's dress was wrinkled from the game, and that her hair had come loose from its pins to curl freely around her face. He liked to see Eugenia properly dressed . . . properly attired, but she looked so happy sitting there in the sunlight that what he saw, in an instant, was the eighteen-year-old he had married. The years in between vanished and he was alone with his bride, in love and hesitant, waiting for her smile.

And the breeze is the same as it was on our wedding day, George decided: A southerly wind and a cloudless sky . . . The atmospheric conditions must be almost identical. . . . George saw his wedding day all over again: the square white tents and the teeming greenery, the violins sawing away, the lace-topped groaning boards covered with every imaginable treat. And talk about champagne! . . . Made a real splash in the papers, his marriage:

". . . Youngest Axthelm heir . . . daughter of one of America's most distinguished families . . . Eugenia Axthelm, née Paine, was married this afternoon in Grace Church. . . ." How pleased Father had been!

"Marry into them, my boy. That's the only way," the Turk had said over and over, and he, George, had done just what he'd been told.

Eugenia looked at her husband's face, saw his faraway smile, and then noted coldly that he'd cut himself several times while shaving. She realized his tie wasn't quite straight, but that his perfect blue jacket with its shiny buttons was as correct as ever. He must have cursed that tie, she told herself.

George cleared his throat and began: "Eugenia." The voice was quiet and precise; it belied its intention. "Genie . . . my dear . . . A few words before luncheon . . . I . . . I have something to . . ." Damn it, George thought, I had this all worked out in my mind; and here I am stammering away like a schoolboy.

". . . My dear . . . I . . . I want you to know that what happened last night will not happen again. You have my word." There! George told himself. That wasn't so hard.

Eugenia hadn't turned her head throughout the whole of her husband's speech. She'd concentrated on the waves, and how they surged together and pushed themselves upward. They glowed with life. For miles and miles and miles they continued, swelling into each other, becoming one enormous wave family: brothers and sisters, mothers, fathers, cousins and aunts, great-grandparents, and babies newly born and topped with pearly foam. Eugenia closed her eyes to the sight, then quickly opened them again and looked at her husband.

"Yes," she said. "All right." It was an action accomplished in a second, and, like a habit, shrugged off without examination.

George noticed how dull his bride's eyes had become. May the tenth, he repeated to bolster his spirits. May the tenth, 1889. But the vision of that glorious day had already begun to fade; there was no swell of orchestra, no hum of guests, no perfume in the trees. Nothing.

"Very good, my dear," he agreed in his most formal manner. "Then we have . . . we have everything settled between us. Set straight, so to speak." With that, George drew his mouth into the proper expression for a preluncheon stroll, and retreated to the welcoming shade of the awning.

It was Paul who broke his mother's silence when he came running back. "What did Father say, Mother? Was he angry?" The little boy had to repeat his questions, then he touched his mother's arm to remind her, and his dark eyes, so similar to Eugenia's, were wide and fearful.

"Mother?"

Eugenia turned, saw her child standing there, smiled automatically, and lifted her hand to touch his shoulder. This too shall pass, she told herself. Don't cry over spilled milk. . . . Night is darkest just before the dawn. . . . Where are those fine old, empty sayings when I need them?

And here is Paul, and soon the girls will come out: each one of them clamoring for some piece of me I no longer remember possessing. But that's not what Eugenia said; what she said was:

"Paul, I didn't see you there, darling. Are you ready to read again?" She didn't say those comforting words because she was a martyr or a saint; she said them because they'd become routine, because anything different might halt the accustomed motion of her life. And thus we roll on, she thought. On and on.

"Let's see," she added, "what chapter did we start . . . ?"

But Paul was still unhappy; his mother's smile wasn't reassuring enough and her words had a peculiar sound. "Mother, was Father mad about my drinking the champagne yesterday? And . . . the . . . the frog?" The frog imitation seemed almost too awful to mention. Even Jinx and Lizzie wouldn't tease him about that!

Eugenia saw her child's fear and it struck her heart so fast she thought she might cry. "Of course not, darling," she answered as she smoothed the wavy brown hair on his forehead; the curls were soft and warm—baby hair still, Eugenia thought.

"Your father just needed to talk to me about business, that's all. That's all. Now, no more long faces!" Eugenia touched her child's small chin, pulled it up to the light, and smiled as she looked in his eyes. "Shall we read? We'd just gotten to that exciting part. What was it? Pirates? And the ship becalmed . . . ?"

"May I listen, too, Mrs. Axthelm?" Lieutenant Brown appeared beside the chair. "Paul's been telling me all about the story." He hesitated. He felt suddenly out of place. A stroll down the deck had seemed so natural, but then there'd been George and Eugenia and no way to pass without intruding, and no way to retreat without looking as if he'd overheard their argument. Social behavior was confusing, to say the least.

"Paul told me all about the story you're reading. He assumes I'm the world authority on the South China Sea. . . ." The words sounded phonier and phonier. Brown couldn't even remember why he'd come forward at all. Eugenia and her problems had nothing to do with him.

"Well, yes, of course . . ." Eugenia hesitated. "If you'd like. . . ." She felt horribly confused, and then frightened of her own reaction. What is it? she thought. Why can't I just treat this young man the way I do

Dr. DuPlessis or Captain Cosby or even Whitney? She looked up at him, at his dark uniform and bright blue eyes. Even under his Navy cap she could see their brilliance.

"It's just a child's story, though, Lieutenant Brown, and I can't imagine you'd be—"

"No, it's not, Mother! I told Lieutenant Brown he'd like it. And he said he would, so there!" This was going to be fun. The little boy settled happily in his mother's long chair.

"—and I'm not a very good reader, really. . . ." Eugenia rattled on.

"Some other time, then," Brown imagined himself saying: "Of course. Don't let me interrupt." Brown rehearsed all those phrases in his mind and rejected them all. Instead he pulled a chair close to Eugenia's and sat down.

Oh dear, Eugenia thought, I wonder what Mrs. DuPlessis is making of all this. Grist for the mill, I should imagine, something to write to that wretched sister of hers. The picture Eugenia had of the two fat sisters and their pursed, disapproving lips and very beady eyes made her suddenly smile. She felt reckless and happy, like a child learning how to cheat a nanny.

"You know what I imagined this morning, Lieutenant?" she asked as she turned her face toward the sun. "I imagined that the ocean was a dancing floor. All white and green marble you could waltz across for days.

"Have you ever thought that?"

Mrs. DuPlessis (lesser sister of Eugenia's famous censorious pair) sat in the library nibbling a digestive biscuit she'd stolen from the teatime sweet tray. She wanted to eat one of the pralines she'd taken as well, but didn't know if she could risk it. Not with her stomach at sixes and sevens.

And Gustav's certainly no help, she reflected bitterly; he's having the time of his life! Engaged in all these childish activities! Why, I might as well not exist! I might as well be back in Philadelphia!

Mrs. DuPlessis sighed a long, dramatic sigh, rummaged in a reticule she kept for embroidery, and found the pralines. I don't care, she thought. I might as well die as I am.

And when I finish the pralines, I'll start on the macaroons, Mrs. DuPlessis decided as she fished them from another satchel. She hadn't wanted to be caught with so many goodies, so she'd concealed them in two separate bags. And all to avoid that little minx, Mistress Jinx, and her suspicious watchful eyes. What an absurd nickname, Mrs. Du-

Plessis told herself, not appropriate at all. With that the grand lady closed her contemplation of young Jinx. To be inappropriate, in her book, was to be worse than dead.

"My dearest Margaret," Mrs. DuPlessis began the letter to her sister. The writing was faint but even; the first impression it gave was of looping fragility, but on closer inspection, the words marched across the page in large, regular lines and an obviously solid determination:

> I have weathered the first night, Praise God; I didn't think I should. Mr. Axthelm insisted that we were having perfect weather, but the ship does roll horribly even when one cannot see a single wave.
>
> Of course you must know (he) did not behave at all well our first night out, and I almost felt some sympathy with Mrs. A. and the children till the little boy disrupted the entire meal. Playing at table, my dear! What can one add? A spanking would have been in order, but, of course, you know the mother is much too indulgent.
>
> (He) has been the very model of decorum since then. As I knew he would. A perfect host, though we hardly ever see him; I imagine he must be working very hard.
>
> (His) worries about business must be very trying. One can only forgive the occasional slip.

Mrs. DuPlessis hunched forward over the table and stared disconsolately out the window. The last macaroon was gone and the tea she'd brought with her had become a greasy yellow puddle at the bottom of the cup. Should I ring for more? she wondered, then reminded herself: No, Gustav says it's unhealthy to eat between meals. And he always discovers my little weaknesses.

Mrs. DuPlessis looked ruefully at the accumulated crumbs on her ample chest. Unsuccessfully she tried to brush away the flakes of sugar, coconut, and pecan icing before she picked up her pen again.

> And, though I wouldn't mention it to anyone in the world but you, dear Margaret, I have begun to have some very tiny suspicions. I won't divulge them now. Heaven knows I should be the very last person in the world to ever wish to spread a rumor.
>
> After all, a space as confined as ours is bound to create some unnatural friendships and animosities. We cannot all be as blessed, dear Margaret, as you and I and the sainted Doctor with our own inner peace and sanctity.
>
> All I will say is that I hope Mrs. A. knows enough to count her blessings. After all, she has everything the world has to offer, and

her husband merely behaves the way most men do. We all know that we must carry on Godly lives in spite of the burdens our husbands place upon us.

I am not speaking of my own husband, of course.

Soon we will be in Madeira and I shall endeavor to find you some fine lace, though the Doctor described the women who make it, and how they are blinded by such close work.

Such a terrible tragedy, but life goes on. Life goes on.

I remain, as ever, your loving sister,

Jane

FOUR

AT TWO-THIRTY IN THE AFTERNOON of July the twenty-ninth, luncheon was nearly finished—at least the serving part of it. What remained on the table were a few half-finished bowls of floating island, the silver basket of almond meringues and lemon-zest ladyfingers, the fruit and cheeses tray and, of course, the finger bowls, cake plates, various water glasses and wineglasses, and an endless stream of cutlery: a spoon for this, another for that, a fruit fork, a cheese fork, a cake fork—to say nothing of the knives. Henry thought the meal would never end. By his own count he'd picked up Master Paul's serviette sixteen times. He wasn't assigned to Miss Jinx—that was the job of young Robertson (footman-in-training, Robertson, if you wanted to be a stickler about titles)—but Henry had seen Robertson fetch clean linen nearly as many times as himself. There was some consolation in that fact, at least. Even the high and mighty had to scrape serviettes from the floor.

Henry looked across the dining saloon to see if the other servants felt as put upon, but he was met by uniform stoniness. They looked like a ring of plaster saints placed behind each chair. White high-buttoned jackets, white starchy sleeves, white gloves, white wing collars, and faces to match: they didn't look like real people at all. If they counted the amount of custard remaining in each dessert bowl, their perfect eyes didn't flicker.

Henry sighed (in his mind only) and held in a yawn till it burned the back of his throat. Six o'clock in the morning, he recited to himself, till whenever dinner's done, or whenever the fun and games inside and out are over: quoits on the deck, sets of checkers fetched then forgotten, a Parcheesi board launched like a kite in the wind, then sucked down the smokestack till it gave up the ghost, not to mention the arranging and rearranging of those cumbersome deck chairs themselves! No wonder I'm always yawning, Henry told himself. Get this. Get that. Up. Down. Back and forth to the kitchens a hundred times a day.

"Move it just the teensiest bit forward." (Mrs. DuPlessis had the most cantankerous—and persistent—demands.) "No, not that far! Now my feet are exposed to the sun! I distinctly said teensy, didn't I? Though perhaps that is too difficult a word. . . ." Every day Henry tried to shut out her whiny complaints, but it was hard; it was hard.

"And this tea, Steward, why, it's stone, frozen cold! When I asked for a fresh cup, I certainly didn't mean clean china and the same old tea. Run down to the kitchens and fetch some more. . . ."

At least Mrs. Axthelm's pleasant, Henry decided. She knows my name at any rate, and she doesn't order me around too much. She even gets up and helps herself when I bring the morning broth and biscuits out on deck. And the youngsters aren't so bad either, when you think about it—leastwise when they're away from the dinner table.

Henry returned to the clink of glasses and the scrape of spoons over near-empty china. It was an easy chattery sound, like squirrels nesting in a leafy tree; it had a faraway, summery sound that would be comforting if you weren't standing on your blessed feet. It would be very comforting indeed.

". . . But, really, that's fascinating Gustav, isn't it, Mrs. Axthelm? . . ."

". . . And what sort of big game do you suppose we'll be . . . ?"

". . . I've heard British East Africa . . ."

". . . Dolphins? Really? This morning? Why didn't you children call me? . . ."

Henry listened to the noise of the words and the noise of the plates— the clatter of spoons, the creaking of chairs, the sugar bowl crunch, and the splash in each finger bowl like a fish in a pond—and tried to remember which particular sound signaled his release. It's Mrs. Axthelm's chair, he told himself, the little squeak the legs give when she pushes back from the table. That's when I know I'm done.

With that bright hope before him, Henry retrieved Paul's napkin one final time, but this time did not return it. Paul looked up; his face showing surprise, then a trace of fear, a momentary crossness at the failure of his prank, then sheepishness at being discovered. Poor wee mite's bored, that's all, Henry realized, just plain bored. He's only a kid. He shouldn't have to sit palavering with all these grown-ups. I wouldn't like it and I'm sixteen; I couldn't have stuck it when I was five!

Henry remembered his own haphazard dinnertimes. Lucky to have any meal at all, he'd been, with one baby constantly squalling and then those fights between his parents, leastwise when his dad was there at all. The other times his mum just screamed at the kids. But I never had to stick out no social chitchat, Henry reminded himself: Me and my brothers, we just hopped it as soon as we could.

Henry gave Paul's shoulder a small nudge to show sympathy and solidarity, though he hoped Higgins wouldn't notice.

"Invisible, my boy!" Henry could imagine Higgins ranting while his ferret face turned splotchy and snappish. "We are invisible to these people. Which is just as it should be. Your task is to serve, not make a spectacle of yourself!"

Henry didn't think he'd ever made a spectacle of himself, but that was Higgins all over—a bunch of five-dollar words and a manner to match. Higgins liked to lecture on the "differences between a gentleman and a common laborer"; Higgins liked to imagine he'd received some holy dispensation that had raised him from the class he'd been born to and dropped him, floating like some tailcoated angel, just beneath the admirable souls he adored.

It's like being in Limbo, Henry often said to himself. Like that place my old mum said naughty folks go, where you fly around in the pitch dark for years and years and years, hoping for word that all your sins are forgiven. It's a lot of cold mush, if you ask me.

Henry shook his brain out of the past and back to the dining saloon. Dr. DuPlessis was in the middle of a story, and his wife was following along with her chirrupy laugh to show everyone how much she appreciated intelligence.

Now there's a "spectacle," Henry decided as he coaxed his tired, prickly feet to work a while longer. A fat old behemoth like her pretending she's a schoolgirl in the Sisters' College. And she ain't no lady, neither—not the way she stuffs her mouth.

Fearing those thoughts would appear on his face, Henry bent forward to scrape the crumbs from Master Paul's place. The silver brush made a whiskery sound on the lace cloth, then tapped against the flat receiver with the small plink Higgins insisted on. "Just to let the lady or gentleman know you're done," Higgins had warned. "Our objective is: Never intrude. Our objective is to serve and wait."

Henry stretched his toes as far as he could, then rubbed one ankle discreetly against the other. It was a trick he'd practiced; his shoulders never moved. He was as smooth as melted wax.

"... And what do you think the most interesting sight will be on Madeira, Doctor? Aside from the island being our first landfall, I mean; that will be exciting enough. ... What do you recommend we see first? ..."

That was Mrs. Axthelm speaking. Henry woke up. He'd signed on to see the world, hadn't he? He'd better start concentrating. But then Dr. DuPlessis started rambling on about something called "cog roads" and ladies who made lace, and how bad it was for the heart to carry heavy loads in the mountains, and Henry's brain started to snooze again.

"Just a trace more cream ..." was the last thing he heard. "One final meringue, and that's absolutely and positively all I'll ever eat again. ..."

While the diners began what Dr. DuPlessis referred to as the "vital postprandial rest period," and the stewards, under stewards, chefs, pastry cooks, and ever-alert Higgins enjoyed a moment of unharried peace, George sat in his study in the middle of another conference with Beckmann.

The recently deserted desk was littered with maps, with charts, geological reports, and letters, which slid together in slippery piles, obstructing each other and confusing each issue. George and Beckmann ignored those heaps of paper. They faced each other in their leather chairs—a reasonable but unfriendly distance apart—while the afternoon sunlight, streaking in bold and determined shafts through the windows, fell across their faces. It was bright, the sunlight, happy and alive as it burst into the room, but where it collided with the men it became no more than yellow stripes. They could have been anything, those stripes: light beams from an electric torch, a naked bulb swaying in a black room, lines of forgotten paint. The stripes hesitated on each face, then moved on in search of a happier home.

George was the first to break the silence. "But really, Ogden," he began, "I still fail to understand why this fellow Ivard is so important to our interests in Borneo. He's a white man, after all, and I don't see how ..." George was tired; a whine like a child's had begun to creep round his words. He leaned his head against the chair back and wished this interview would end.

Beckmann stared at the striped study wall. I'll have to go over the whole thing again, he realized angrily. I might as well be talking to the

engine room stokers as Master Georgie Axthelm. Better the stokers—
at least they understand dollars and cents.

"As I just explained"—Beckmann's voice was level and precise—
"the present rajah, Sir Charles Ivard, is an acquaintance of your father-
in-law. You do remember this much, don't you, George?"

Beckmann didn't bother to wait for a reply. It's like talking to myself, he thought, or very near.

"Ivard may seem exotic to the rest of the world . . . the only white rajah, and all that rubbish, controls most of North Borneo, etc. . . . . But
he's really old school. It was his uncle who started the whole thing.
Went out by way of Singapore, then hopped across the water to Borneo,
grabbed a sizable chunk of land in the usual tribal battles, made himself
rich, went home, was knighted by the old queen for his efforts, and left
the title to his nephew, Charles. Or Sir Charles, Rajah Ivard, as he's better known. He's younger than your esteemed father-in-law but of the
same generation."

George is either with me or he's not, Beckmann told himself, and
he's either concentrating or his mind has drifted off in the usual fog.
Most likely, it's the latter; then he'll be up the proverbial creek without
that famous paddle when the time comes. Beckmann continued without a second thought:

"Sir Charles is an interesting specimen, however. He had the education and upbringing of an English gentleman, but he's still a newcomer
in British social circles, a gate-crasher, a titled nobody. He doesn't fit
in England; he's considered colonial in the most rigid sense of the
word.

"So he'd got to stick it out in Borneo and make some kind of life
there. In other words, he's the kind of snob only an educated and cast-
adrift Briton can be."

Beckmann paused, waiting for the response he didn't expect.
"Please pay attention, George," he said finally. His voice was annoyed
and curt; he sounded like a schoolmaster speaking to a particularly
stupid new boy—a tone guaranteed to produce tears. "We've been over
this before."

But George wasn't a new boy; he might not be a sixth-former, but he
wasn't a bloody first-year boy either. "I realize that, Ogden," he answered. If there was one thing he'd learned it was how to parry these
little jabs.

"I realize that. I just don't know why all this ancient history is so
bloody important. We're not dealing with the dear departed uncle now,
are we? We just have to worry about Sir Charles."

That got him, George thought, that got the nasty old goat. In truth, he couldn't remember half of what Beckmann had been saying. And it wasn't that he thought it unimportant; it was just that Beckmann had a way of talking that was terribly confusing. It made him feel as if he were failing in his classes or had been caught in some horrendous lie. The words went round and round, but they ended up sounding the same.

Beckmann ignored George's efforts. He'd watched the Turk use the same technique year after year; there was never any of that "wisdom in youth" nonsense about the old man. When he spoke, his sons shut their mouths and listened. They listened or they lost out.

"But," Beckmann began again, "and this is important, Sir Charles is not our man. Yes, he is titular head. Yes, he looks good . . . knows Eugenia's father, will welcome us with open arms, and so on. . . ." Beckmann paused momentarily as George shifted in his chair. He's like an insect, Beckmann decided with disgust. He's as unfocused as a flea. A waste of good money and a decent education—as his father's so fond of repeating.

Beckmann gripped the chair arm and continued the lesson. If I could handle this myself, he thought, how much easier life would be.

"No, Sir Charles is not our man. It's the son, Laneer, we want—the rajah muda—which I gather is a term like crown prince. Laneer Kinloch Ivard: the usual spectacular name. He's been after the old man to get off his duff for years, kick out the Dutch, and take over all of Sabah."

"And Sabah is?" George's flaccid voice attempted what he thought was a pertinent question. He imagined himself in his father's shoes, letting the other fellow do the talking, speaking only the words that hit home. For the first time in the long afternoon, George felt himself an equal.

But George's brief pleasure was immediately broken. Beckmann jumped to his feet with a snarl. "Jesus, George, we've been through all that!"

Beckmann's thick teeth hissed, "Sabah is British North Borneo. Laneer wants to extend to the basin of the Labas River. Get rid of the native sultan, who sides with the Dutch. Don't you remember any of this? We went over and over it at Linden Lodge! Ivartown, don't you remember? The coal seams at Ivartown and Sadong? The Samuel brothers' Shell Company and its incursion into the trade . . . ?"

Beckmann calmed himself, walked to the window, and looked out. The sea returned his stare and moved on, shrugging its shoulders, unconcerned.

Yelling does no good, he reminded himself. George requires manipulation. A loud voice is liable to make him slink away with his tail between his legs, and a kicked dog will bite when you least expect it.

Beckmann returned to the desk, leaned against it in a relaxed manner, crossed his arms over his chest, and forced his lips into a smile.

"Now, as you know, your father feels we can control Laneer. I'm not sure. And that's where you come in. We'll both have to make that decision when we get there." Flattery, Beckmann told himself, flattery. I'm saddled with George and he's saddled with me, but we'll get nowhere if he takes it into his head to pout.

"My concern with Laneer, George, and I'll let you in on a little secret I never told your father, is that Laneer may be too close to his native friends. You catch my drift."

George didn't, but by then he felt so suffused with good-natured warmth that he didn't care. A secret Father doesn't know, he thought. Imagine that!

"Indeed," George said. "Yes, indeed. That could be a concern. Yes, I see your point."

Beckmann smiled again. It was an ugly smile; his big teeth clenched and his jaw shut tight. Then his left hand jerked up, and his forefinger and thumb slowly squeezed together.

George looked up and imagined he saw a tiny person in Beckmann's hand. No bigger than one of Jinx's small dolls, it looked glassy-eyed with fear as it felt Beckmann's mealy thumb push harder and harder. Then all at once blood, brains, and bits of fraying tissue squirted over the heavy hand. George rose abruptly. He had a taste in his mouth like bile or something more bitter, something metallic; it flattened his tongue like a doctor's spoon.

"Good. Yes. Ivard, *père et fils* . . . Fine . . . Laneer . . . Charles. Fine. Yes." George ticked off the names like a litany. The recitation allowed him to relegate those people to history.

"Laneer . . . Sir Charles . . . Sabah . . . Borneo." There'd be no more visions of Beckmann crushing the life out of some poor soft-headed native-lover. "Fine. Yes. Fine."

George forced himself to banish all thoughts of Beckmann's huge hands or yellowing teeth; he rose, looked once at his desk, then moved to his bookshelves. He attempted an unconcerned air, pacing over the carpet as if taking a stroll.

"Now, Ogden, something else we need to discuss. You know, of course, that the children have made quite a friend of our Lieutenant Brown, and I gather they spend . . . well, quite a bit of time with him." George stumbled on the words, silently cursed the repetition, but pushed on.

"Quite a bit of time, in fact." George stressed the mistake; he glanced at Beckmann, daring criticism, but the bland face gave nothing away.

"Well, they, the children, I mean, are making regular visits to the man, have made something of a pet of him. You know the stories and all that nonsense. Why, the other day I heard Paul . . . but . . . never mind. . . .

". . . but . . . what I mean is . . . Well, dash it, Ogden! Surely you can see the danger? My children traipsing around all those boxes and crates . . . with what we have there . . . what the fellow knows?" George tried to make the appeal sound reasonable, but he knew Beckmann would see through these poor excuses, would see him for what he was, a man who'd lost control, a father who saw, moment by moment, his children's love departing.

"I mean, you know, these stories . . . pirates in the South China Sea . . . that kind of thing, and you know how children are . . . They get all heated up . . . imagine things. . . . We're on some kind of secret and desperate mission . . . or, well . . . just children's talk, mind you, but . . ."

George stopped. Everything was slipping out from under him. It reminded him of sawdust. Sawdust innards in an old plush lion, a toy he'd loved too much as a child. Just one hole, that's all it had needed, just one small hole, and he'd been left with nothing but a torn and empty sack.

George looked at Beckmann, but Beckmann might have been made of sticks and stones. There was no evidence he'd heard anything at all.

". . . Well, you see the dilemma. Have a word with him about it. I mean, Father wouldn't have wanted . . ." George's words trailed off on their own. Why can't I say what's on my mind? he wondered. Why do I have to hide the truth?

"I see your dilemma, George." Beckmann's tone was quiet, but it had no hint of sympathy. He paused, as if thinking, as if considering his next move, but George knew the hesitation was a sham. He knew, in his heart of hearts, that his fate had been sealed.

"However"—Beckmann drew out the word, savoring his power—"I don't think you should . . . disallow this, George. To do so would only cast suspicion. It is, as you say, only children's talk and Brown does have a legitimate reason for accompanying us. Your father saw to that, you may remember—with Secretary Hay.

"Besides," Beckmann concluded in a falsely offhand tone, "I gather the children rather like him. And you wouldn't want them disappointed, would you?" A nail in the coffin! Beckmann positively beamed.

George looked at the smiling face, at the well-fed body, and the wide and too powerful hands, then he turned away toward the desk. His shoulders sagged and his back slumped out of its rigid line. "Why don't we discuss the rest later," he said. "Mahomet Seh, and all that other . . . No point putting all our eggs in one basket. You know how these native things go."

George attempted one of his father's dismissals: the great man leaning over his desk, weighing matters too complex for mere mortals. Then he considered heaving every single paper to the floor, and imagined the lovely mess they would make—white papers, colored maps, black words, scattered over every inch of carpet. Finally he realized he was too tired to move, too tired to lift a finger.

"As you wish, George," Beckmann answered. "As you say, our plans for Mr. Seh will wait." Beckmann started from the room, but turned for his one parting shot: "And I'm sure, after you take time to consider it, you'll understand the reason for this decision on Brown."

George heard Beckmann leave. His first reaction was to put his head down and take a little nap, but then he decided: No, no. I've got to keep busy, got to keep going. Nothing gets done by sitting around and stewing.

George began to organize his papers. First he built several small and orderly stacks, then he made two larger ones, then he wrote neat, triangular notes on the upper corners of four pages in a notebook; and finally, on the lower right-hand corner of the map of Sabah, he penciled in: "Brown. Beckmann. Seh. Children?" The words were faint, but block-letter clear, and he read them over and over, complimenting himself on his astuteness and honesty.

The most entertaining job he saved for last. On a scrap of paper torn from his monogrammed stationery, George drew a caricature of Beckmann's face and beside it a huge hand gripping a wriggling figure he labeled: LANEER KINLOCH IVARD. The sketch pleased him; George added himself, a small face peering out from behind many flying papers. He labeled that one: ME. The sketch was then folded into thirds and hidden behind the center drawer of the desk: his secret compartment. George chuckled when he did this; he felt as free as a child.

Then he took out a fresh piece of paper and began a letter to his brother, Tony:

July 29

Antonio:
Well, here we are! Under way on the Briny! Blue skies, fair days, fair food, fair nights . . . as they say in Tibet!!!

All aboard hale and hearty, good grog, good women . . . you know the old song.

Powwows with O. (As in "Gr-Ogden") He had the cheek to explain the whole Ivard-Paine connection again and REMIND me. The old "classroom trick." Har. har. har. (As if I could ever forget)

Seriously don't understand why we're trusting a fellow like "His Royal Highness, the Rajah Muda." Sounds a bit of a pirate. Gone native, d'you think?

Weather continues lubberly (as in land!!!). Raised sails this a.m. and cut engines. What a sight! What a sound! Or absence thereof.

Kiddies said they saw dolphins along about noon. But yrs. truly was by then mired in ye olde salt mines. Worse luck!

Give regards to Father. Tell him I'm working my tail off, and not to worry about a thing. On second thought, I'll write myself. Don't want YOU taking all the credit, you ol' debil, you. Har. har. har.

Best to Cass and all at home.

Giorgio

Eugenia's cabin was nearly dark. Only two lamps beside her chaise longue were lighted, and she lay reading in their warm light, propped up by many lace-bordered pillows. Her satin robe had been discarded on a nearby chair and her loosened hair was tossed willy-nilly over the back of the chaise. Eugenia looked up, groaned aloud, then forced her eyes to return to the book, but the words leapt about; they wouldn't settle down and she kept losing their meaning altogether. Finally she gave up and dropped the slim volume on the floor. It fell with a thud; there had been more force in her hand than she'd intended.

"Damn," Eugenia said. "*The Head-Hunters of Borneo*, now who could've guessed that subject would be dull?" Eugenia glanced back at the book; her small silver marker was nearly to the end page. "And I was almost done, too. Damn. George would have been so pleased."

Eugenia smiled and closed her eyes. My secret cache of books, she thought, my little surprise. The political, geographical, and financial education of one Mrs. George Axthelm, née Paine—of the famous Paines of Philadelphia. Eugenia made a face that was part disgust and part humor. I'm free of all that folderol, she reminded herself; I'm free as a bird.

Eugenia stretched her hands over her head, stared at the ceiling, and considered getting up from the chaise, even thought (briefly) about walking on deck in her nightdress and robe (in her mind she saw shadows scudding across deserted chairs and a wind that turned her dressing gown into a togalike shroud). "Like Lot's wife," she said aloud. "A pillar of salt . . . a pillar of society!"

The image brought a happy laugh; Eugenia sank further into her pillows, kicked a silk throw till it slipped from the chaise and slithered to a heap on the floor. "That's what you get for one backward glance!" Eugenia laughed again. "You're turned into a Philadelphia matron!"

The picture seemed funnier than anything; Eugenia gave in to it, then reminded herself (as firmly as she could) that she had work to do. She placed her hands at her sides, sat upright and proper, grabbed the book from the floor, and promised, this time, this time, to finish it.

"*The Head-Hunters of Borneo: A Narrative of Travel up the Mahakam and down the Barito.* Carl Alfred Bock. Samson, Low, Marston, Searle and Rivington, London, 1881."

Eugenia glared at the musty pages and tried to envision what Mr. Carl Alfred Bock had actually seen on his trip along the Mahakam River, whether there'd been pirates or pagan rites or wanton women in bare-breasted sarongs or men with no clothing at all. Probably, she told herself, but either Mr. Carl Alfred Bock failed to notice those outrageous things, or else he deemed them "overly suggestive"—"unsuitable for the reading public." Passion and lust and greed and sin: We alter the truth to suit our Protestant sensibilities; we wash everything and make it oh, so easy, safe, and nice.

Eugenia rolled her head against the pillows till she felt each strand of hair drag slowly over the chaise. She listened to the sea, and the night sounds of a ship whose body rolled ever forward. Then she thought about her husband and their two separate bedrooms, and wondered how such a thing could have come about. That's not how married couples should behave, she told herself; we're missing something, but maybe we never had it. Or we never knew what it was.

"The best thing, dear," her grandmother had told her with the delicate cough that signaled a subject was taboo and would never be discussed again, "the best thing for those difficult, ah, conjugal evenings, is to simply lie still and make up the week's menus in your head. That always worked for me, at any rate. You may have other household concerns. Whatever they are: I definitely suggest a list. A list always keeps one going. It's something definite to concentrate on. And then, of course, you have the one chore out of the way."

Nice and neat, Eugenia thought, but you should have said two "chores," Gran. You've got two "chores" out of the way. Love in Philadelphia, Eugenia reminded herself, passion among the pilgrims. No wonder George and I have reached this sad impasse.

Eugenia lifted her arms and stared at them in the milky light. Their pale skin reminded her of a baby's arms: unused and searching for warmth. Then she dropped her arms and gave in to the movement of the ship: the sea rising and the boat bearing back down. One wave shivered under the bow, then the hold, then the stern. It was followed by another and another and another; they swept the ship with daring devotion. Eugenia closed her eyes. The arms of the chaise embraced her and her dressing gown skirt slipped round her ankles like hands.

All at once Eugenia was aware of someone knocking at her door. She didn't know how long the person had been there; she was afraid it had been some time.

"Yes?" she called, springing up. Habit was habit, after all. "George? Is that you?"

"Eugenia? May I come in?" Eugenia recognized Beckmann's voice, though his inexplicable visit stunned her. What on earth can he want at this time of night? she thought as she spun around looking for some less flimsy covering than a pink nightdress. Her robe seemed to have vanished from sight.

"I'll be with you in a moment. I just have to find my . . ." Eugenia scrambled aside the pillows, shook the chair cushions, and looked under the skirted seat. She didn't have time to consider her surprise, and it wouldn't have occurred to her to refuse Beckmann's request.

Finally finding the dressing gown and yanking it on, she ran barefoot to the door.

In the sudden, harsh light of the hall, Beckmann looked like a specter instead of a man. There was only the outline of a person in a dinner suit: a swallowtail coat with a high, tight waist, two wide shoulders, and two straight arms. Eugenia couldn't see a face at all.

"I'm not disturbing you, I trust," Beckmann said. He didn't wait for her reply. He was in the room in a flash.

"Not at all," Eugenia answered as she tugged the sashes of her robe tighter. "Pleasant of you to drop by. Though it is a bit late."

Now that's not what I meant to say, Eugenia thought. Why can't I speak my mind? Why must I be so polite?

"The reason I came, Eugenia—" Beckmann stopped himself; the words were cut off in midair as if the sentence were finished. He looked down at Eugenia. He knew what he wanted lay within easy reach; words were a convention that no longer mattered.

Eugenia felt Beckmann staring at her. She ran her fingers through her hair, wishing she could move away. She felt exposed with her hair unpinned; she felt girlish and unsteady.

"I'm afraid you've caught me at a rather bad time," Eugenia began.

"I was about to retire for the evening. . . ." Then she forced herself to return to the chaise, and placed herself square in its middle.

"Won't you sit down, Ogden?" she said, pointing to a distant chair.

Beckmann obeyed. He sat as faithfully as a dog. He breathed in the smells of the room: a perfumed female scent of a closed place and a thin, sharp odor of silk on warm skin.

"Your feet are bare," he finally said. "They must be cold. Let me get your slippers."

Eugenia nearly jumped out of her skin. For a moment she thought she had; she thought she'd bolted for the closet and her velvet shoes. My feet, she thought in desperation, he can see my feet. She tried to curl them under her robe, but the robe slipped open and the sheer hem of her nightdress was no hiding place at all.

"Let me get your slippers," Beckmann repeated. His voice was thick. The words he wanted to say lay like iron in his throat. Wait, he told himself. Wait. The time will come.

"Is something wrong, Ogden?" Eugenia watched Beckmann's hands tremble on the chair; she sensed danger, but didn't know where it lurked. "Is . . . ? Is anything the matter with my husband?"

Before the question was fully formed, before it was even finished, Eugenia knew the visit had nothing to do with George. And she also guessed, though she couldn't say why, that her husband's name would not be mentioned again.

"You are very beautiful, Eugenia." There, Beckmann thought; I've said it.

Eugenia couldn't think where to look or what to say. "You're very kind," she managed, then cursed the unconscious repetition. "But I'm afraid you're being overgallant."

Drawing room phrases, she hissed to herself. This isn't a dinner party, Eugenia; this isn't a tea dance. Why do you think that behavior will save you?

But there was nothing to do but continue. The path had already been chosen. "As I said, I was just about to retire. And . . . well . . . I'm afraid you find me at a rather awkward moment. I'm rather dishabille. . . ."

"I like seeing you this way."

There's no going back now, Beckmann told himself. He leaned forward heavily; his lips felt as dry as dust.

"It's getting late. . . ." The words fell out of their own accord. "I'm sure we've all had a long day. . . ." Eugenia retreated to the familiar, but the familiar shrugged its dainty shoulders and turned the other coy cheek. There was nothing in the lexicon of euphemism and Victorian advice that proved any worth at all. For the first time in her life Eugenia recognized that she was defenseless and utterly alone. Make a list? she wanted to scream. Make a list? You never said anything about this! "Conjugal" nights! You never told me about this!

"I can't leave," Beckmann said. "Not yet." And Eugenia felt her heart fall through the pit of her stomach.

"I . . . I beg your pardon?"

"You know what I want," Beckmann imagined saying. "You know why I'm here. This debutante act doesn't wash with me." The brutality of the onslaught would be interesting to watch, Beckmann thought. He saw it all, saw her shrink before him, cry and cringe, then he recognized the sham of his response. What he wanted was her delicacy: her sexuality hidden from view, waiting for him alone.

"I know who you are," he said finally. "Underneath."

Eugenia looked at her toes, at her pink hands, the dressing gown edged in lace, the satin chaise with its row of pillows. They were every one of them an invitation; they dragged her forward and held her up under the light.

She listened for a footstep in the hall. If only someone would pass by, she thought. It doesn't matter who. I could call out, say I need water, tea, a blanket, something. But even as she imagined the routine and prosaic interruption, she knew she'd never risk it. Not even if the passerby were George. To call out was to admit her own secret guilt. Beckmann had discovered the truth.

Eugenia stared at her wrists; the skin was blue as candytuft. The gauzy sleeves could never disguise it. How have I come to this place? she thought. George and I? I, alone? Our separate bedrooms. The polite conversation we pretend is love.

Suddenly Beckmann lunged to his feet. His body felt swollen, his shoulders and legs stiff with inaction. The visit wasn't going as he'd planned. He'd pictured himself debonair, relaxed, romantic, a man-about-town, a man accustomed to pleasure. A gentle hint was all he'd meant to drop. Just the suggestion there was someone to turn to. Should the need arise. Should Eugenia seek more solace than the comfort of a solitary bed.

But things had gone wrong and he'd said too much. He'd shown his hand, and there was nothing for it but to soldier on. If I can't win her by wooing, Beckmann told himself, then I'll win her by fear.

"I've watched you, Eugenia," he said. "I've watched you since you were eighteen, and first came to the Axthelm house. I've watched the girl become a woman. There is nothing that's escaped me.

"I know who you are and I know what you want. You can pretend, hesitate, close the door and promise yourself this was only a dream, but you know, and I know, that I will not wait forever."

Beckmann had finally gone. He'd said what he'd said and then left. Eugenia studied her hands on her knees; it seemed amazing that she hadn't moved at all. Or maybe she had and couldn't remember. Maybe she had given in, thrown herself backward, ripped off her clothes, felt the rasp of his coat and the grip of his legs.

But there were the pillows; there were the books; there was her dressing gown and her ten naked toes. The room had taken no notice; the room had closed blind eyes.

Eugenia heard the next knock before it had time to echo.

"Yes?" She bolted upright, thinking to bar the door, then deciding in a sudden hot flush of bravado to confront what she knew would be waiting. She grabbed the door with such force that the wood shuddered under her hand.

"George?" Her husband's appearance took her completely by surprise. "George?"

"Expecting Santy Claus, Genie?" George shambled past his wife. Eugenia could see he'd been drinking; his walk was uneven and his shirt was rumpled and stained with red-brown spots. None of it mattered, though. None of it mattered at all. Relief sparkled through the door.

"I thought it was . . ."

"Shouldn't be calling up the servants this late, Genie," George chided, but his voice was gentle and soft. "I could fetch anything you want, you know. Like I used to . . . remember . . . when . . ."

Eugenia looked at her husband. No jacket, she realized; he's not wearing a jacket. He's walked through the ship without the one thing he holds dear as faith. Why, any stray person might have seen him! Eugenia felt like laughing aloud.

"Oh, I didn't send for anything, George," she said, and her voice sounded light as air. "It was just a strange noise I heard. Or maybe I imagined it."

There's no turning back now, Eugenia told herself. I let the moment slip; I lied. But the problem seemed unimportant somehow, easily banished and forgotten. I'm going to go on, Eugenia decided. I'm going to continue as though nothing happened. Tomorrow morning I won't remember a thing. I'll tell myself Ogden's visit never happened.

George walked into the center of the room and Eugenia followed him. She lit another lamp, straightened her dressing table, picked up a shawl. The room that had deserted her to her solitary panic was suffused with warmth and joy.

"My, it was awfully dark in here," Eugenia laughed. "I apologize, George. I was reading over there, sitting . . ." "Alone," she was about to say, then changed her mind.

". . . I didn't realize how dark it had become. . . . We'll turn the lamps on. Every single one!"

"Genie, I need to talk to you." George's interruption was startling. Eugenia stopped her recitation cold.

George looked at his wife's eyes; they were so innocent sometimes, large and brown and as guileless as a baby's. And what he had to say would cloud them, or possibly make them cry. George couldn't face that fact; he retreated to safety, to the phrases as familiar as his name.

"Forgive my, ah . . . my appearance, Genie . . ." he blustered. ". . . Working late . . . going over . . . Ogden and I . . ."

"You were working with Ogden? Just now?" Hope spread across Eugenia's face, turning it as pink and round as a pearl. Maybe none of that awful business happened, she told herself. Maybe I dreamed the whole sordid story. It was a wonderful thought, worth clinging to as long she could.

"No . . . No . . . not now . . . earlier . . . evening . . . afternoon . . . some . . ." George was aware of losing his grip. The alcohol he'd used as fuel before visiting his wife was in danger of undermining the mission itself. George clenched his fists, gritted his teeth, and plunged forward.

"Damn it, Genie . . . that's not . . . that's not what I wanted to . . . not what I came in to . . . And yes! Yes, I have been drinking!" George burst out at last, but the words were no more defiant than those of a small and frightened child.

"I didn't say anything, George," Eugenia answered. She raised her hand and placed it on his sleeve. The touch was light, unsure, but it was there.

George's face softened; he stared down at his wife's hand. "No, no you didn't, my dear. I'm sorry, I didn't mean . . ."

Neither of them spoke; they looked at each other, then at the room, at the walls, at the bed, the dresser, the still rumpled chaise. Eugenia tried to smile; she wanted to look encouraging—the wise and helpful wife—but George frowned and stared at the floor. If they'd heard the clock ticking, that moment would have sounded like an hour.

Finally George caught sight of something tangible, something to discuss. He picked up the book Eugenia had left on the floor.

"What's this, my dear? *The Head-Hunters of Borneo*?" George pretended to weigh the slim volume in his hand. "Pretty racy title for my young bride . . . Let me see now . . . published in London . . . What do these Roman numerals mean? . . . 1881? . . . Why, Genie, you've got yourself a veritable antique."

"Oh yes, George," Eugenia burst in. "I've been studying up on the places we'll visit. . . . I thought . . . I thought it would be helpful with your work there and . . ." A shadow flickered across her husband's eyes and Eugenia told herself: Go faster, faster; you'll lose him if you don't. He'll go back to his own room, and that will be that.

"And Dr. DuPlessis has been teaching us such interesting things about the island. . . . You know, about the trees and birds and animals. 'The flora and fauna, Madame Axthelm . . .'" Eugenia tried and failed at an imitation of Dr. DuPlessis's carefully groomed accent.

". . . Anyway, there are huge mangrove swamps that nearly block-ade the coastline, and proboscis monkeys or something. . . . Well, the natives call them 'Dutchmen' because of their big red noses. Isn't that funny?" Eugenia saw George frown again. That was the wrong thing to say, she told herself with fury. When will you ever learn? He'll leave again, and you'll deserve it.

Anger at her own shortcomings, her lack of finesse, her lack of any seductive charm, rocketed her forward at a ridiculous rate.

"Oh, but this book!" Eugenia babbled. "Well, perhaps you'd care to read it. It describes various customs and tribes and their feuds, though I suppose they think of them as wars. . . . And I should say wars, too, shouldn't I, George?"

Eugenia stopped all of a sudden; she stopped and let the night air and the stillness of the ship envelop her. I've failed, she thought. I've failed again. Propriety and a history of women making lists have finally won out.

"And I guess you thought I'd forgotten the white rajah—Mr. Charles Ivard! . . . And how he knows Father and . . . and . . . and all those chats at Linden Lodge when . . ." But there was no excitement left. The words had the emptiness of a catechism prayer.

George sat wearily on the chaise. He hefted the little book in his hand and stared at its faded gold title, and because Eugenia had no way of knowing how her words affected her husband, or revived the secrets he'd come to confess, she blamed herself. There was no one else at fault.

"I had thought . . ." George began, ". . . I had decided tonight . . ." The healing words were stuck in his bowels. Nothing would bring them forth.

"Yes, George?" Eugenia perched beside her husband. "Yes?"

"Perhaps some other time, Genie . . . I . . . I didn't realize it was so late."

"Oh, but I want you to confide in me, George!" The words jumped out like a shout.

"I know you've been unhappy and the trip isn't turning out to be all you'd hoped, and . . . and I want to help if I can, want you to talk to me. I think that together . . . I mean, at one time . . . because the business end of it . . . that ore-smelting business or mining or whatever your father calls it . . . why, that's not important. . . .

"And we don't have to go to Borneo. It might not be such a wonderful place. We could just sail off and go wherever we choose. The only thing that matters is that we're together!"

"It's Beckmann, isn't it?" Eugenia suddenly asked, and the brave words ceased. Not even the smallest trace was left echoing in the air.

George didn't have the words to comfort his wife. It was all too complicated: Beckmann, his father, Ivard, Brown. The crates in the hold, the last-minute changes, Laneer, Paine, and "machinery" that wasn't designed for work in any mine.

"No, Genie," George said, "it's all right. Just sit here beside me a minute. Let's just be quiet for a minute."

Their faces were dark in the lamp's yellow shadow. Only their knees, nearly touching, were lighted—and Eugenia's bare feet. They looked like a child's toes to George, a child on a summer day.

"Aren't your feet cold, Genie?" he asked.

"No!" Eugenia's voice was too loud, too sudden. "No . . . no, they're not. . . . I forgot them really. Forgot my slippers . . . But no . . . no, they're not cold."

George looked at his wife's leg. It was clearly defined under her dressing gown. He looked at her thighs and her hands lying loose in her lap, and moved his own hand slightly. He imagined himself touching her fingers or her leg, but he didn't seem to have the strength. Forty-two, old boy, he thought. You're not getting younger. George kept his hand where it was.

"Ah, well, my dear," he said, "I see you're tired. I'm sorry to have disturbed you." And he rose and walked to the door.

Eugenia stared at the floor. She saw light from the hall streak into the room in a quick triangle when the door was opened. She saw it hesitate a second, then run out. It left only the faintest glimmer of itself, a thin yellow line. Eugenia watched the strip of light and willed herself to stay seated, stay quiet, and still.

And it's not even as though I expected him to stay, she reasoned. I just . . . I just don't know what I'm doing wrong. What do other wives do? . . . There must be something I don't know. . . . We have three children. . . . We did that. . . . But that can't be all there is to it. . . .

But that was too complicated a question. She and George were not an easy family at the best of times. That couldn't be the answer.

But then maybe it's not me, Eugenia decided. Maybe these problems have traveled with us. . . . Maybe it's still the Turk, after all . . . and George is drinking because of . . . what? . . . what?

Eugenia struggled under the weight of unformed questions; they were heavy, dark, and slippery as eels and she felt them slithering over her head and face and shoulders. Borneo? . . . she wondered briefly and looked at the book in her hand. In spite of sitting so rigidly still, she'd ripped five pages from the spine. They slid apart, limp and wafer-thin. *The Head-Hunters of Borneo* . . . Eugenia tried to push the pages back into the stitching, matching the small holes with the even white thread. She concentrated on this task as if desire alone could make the book whole again. But the pages kept slipping; they had nothing to secure them and no sooner had she repositioned one page than another would fall out, crumpling with the pressure of her hand.

"Damn!" she said fiercely. "Damn! Damn! Damn!" And she took the covers of *The Head-Hunters of Borneo* and wrenched them apart. She ripped the pages from their stitching and the stitching from the spine, then began on the paper itself. She tore handful after handful till her fingers were raw and red, and the paper, mounded insensibly in her lap, scattered on the floor.

Eugenia watched it go; she watched the tattered mess drift toward the grate, the dustbin, the furnace, and the sea. "Oh, I'm so sorry," she said suddenly. "I'm so sorry. I'm so sorry."

In her dreams, Eugenia saw a wedge of light. It ran across an earthen floor in a golden streak, then darted toward a dusty corner, up a table leg, and down a copper kettle. A door opened, a door closed, and the light kept rapid pace; it was as lively as a tongue of fire.

Then somewhere a wind blew, kicked up the noise of shutters banging, storm doors rattling, and rusted hinges on creaky wood frames, and the light, the happy, bright light, retreated, flew off, ran away. Eugenia stared at the floor. It was mired in dirt, caked, pounded with dung and with mud. There was a line in her memory, but the line was dark as night.

After that, she was standing in the sunlight on a summer day. She was ten or eleven years old, a girl in a pinafore without shoes or socks, and her toes tickled a tuft of warm grass. She heard bees overhead and looked up. The sky was dark with movement. Bees swarm in the air, made a noise like a cyclone in a neighbor's barn, then plunged under the eaves of her grandmother's house.

"They're coming in!" she shouted, but no sound came out. She turned her body homeward, but her feet wouldn't move.

In every window, in every open door, under each green awning, within every arch of the blue-white colonnade, were the angry black bodies of a hundred million bees.

"They took the house!" Eugenia screamed, but the words went nowhere. "They have the house, Gran. We can't go in! We can't go back."

"There, there," her grandmother answered, "It will all be right as rain. It was an accident, my dear. A sudden squall . . . they said. . . . There was nothing to be done. The boat tipped over, they said. . . . And the boy was underneath. . . ."

"No!" Eugenia cried. "You don't understand. There are bees in the house!"

"Nothing to be done. And nothing to do but wait."

*I*N *1903*, the island of Borneo was divided in half: the south was controlled by the Dutch, the north by the English, though the Dutch had a far firmer grasp. Their ports, built for the spice trade in the late seventeenth century, opened onto the Java Sea and Macassar Strait; the next areas of civilization lay across the water in Batavia or the trading village of Soerabaija.

Along the northern coast, it was the same story: There was no town of any decent size unless the traveler left the island, sailed east by northeast across the South China Sea to reach the newly established city of Singapore, a place with definite British sympathies. Voyaging north and to the west from the precarious little outposts of Sabah and Billiton, there stretched the Sulu Sea and finally the fertile Philippine Islands where a handful of Spaniards fought the overwhelming and mighty hand of the United States of America. Manifest destiny clothed in twentieth-century jargon. Imperialism run amok.

Inland Borneo was nothing; there were no tea or rubber plantations as there were in Ceylon or Annam; there was no sudden clearing of jungly mists and a view of a white house with a whitewashed veranda. There was no village of friendly or unfriendly natives whom one could persuade or coerce to work the fields; there was no open land, no cultivated crop, no neighbors with whom to hold dance evenings or shooting parties. So, for the westerner, Borneo had no interior; it was a blank on the map, a green place marked: "jungle," "possible river," "mountain range—undetermined height."

The life of the island existed solely by water. It was dependent on the large and small ships that plied the coast: the monthly packet from Singapore, an unscheduled steamer from Java, the native boats from Billiton. Borneo was a wild and unexplored place; but for the men intent on making a fresh start, the men who'd drifted apprehensively through the Strait of Malacca seeking a fortune or an easy mark—the cashiered career men, ex-convicts, countinghouse clerks with a price on their heads, the hardened souls who'd found no breathing space in India or Burma or Penang, the shysters, tricksters, card-playing hucksters, who'd deemed colonial justice far too strict—Borneo was just the place.

Seen from the sea in a dusky predawn light, Sarawak, North Borneo, is a black and mountainous mass. There is nothing illusory in its darkness; it is a thick, heavy presence, and as the sun begins to rise and heat the air with fragile color, the land remains unchanged and ominously black. Morning light filters over the water; flying fish take their morning sunbath; they shimmer pink and silvery-gray, flash in rivulets of rainbow hue. The sky glows red, then lavender, and then a bright cerulean blue, but the mountains loom dark and fearsome, as though they were covered with a billion hungry ants.

The monthly packet from Singapore or the native boat skirting the coast must take caution here. The islands near Sarawak are filled with pirates. There are hundreds of secret coves hidden under banana leaves; fronds of nipa and sago palm, camouflaged by snaky vines that twine through the mangrove swamps, slither from tree to tree and bay to bay till they suck away a harbor's safe passage. The coves are transitory; they shift with the monsoon; they shift with the tide; they are a wonderful refuge for any creature too vile or evil for the open air of a sunny town.

At low tide, the exposed coastal mud is alive with hairy fish that jump like frogs and flip-flop through steamy muck to burrow among the roots of the mangrove and casuarina trees or leap in their branches. Crabs scuttle up and down their slimy holes, and fire-red ants crawl over every branch and twig. The ants devour everything in sight; spiders and shiny-shelled beetles, tree frogs and shrews, are wasted in their path. Everywhere the black ooze swarms with life. It is the beginning of the earth, a testing ground where only the fittest survive. The noise of chewing, crunching, cawing, slipslopping tide pools, and violent battles can be deafening.

A boat, traveling to a trading post or the sultan's residence in Kuching, must pass those dark islands in order to enter the mouth of the river. Then it's the Sunghai Sarawak, the river at last, safety again, treacherous winds avoided, sea-Dayaks and pirates outwitted or out-run. But the river is long and narrow; it turns round and round; it pulls the boat deeper and deeper and deeper into the jungle. There are set-tlements here and there: empty, ramshackle houses on stilts near the water's edge, the thin smoke from a hastily deserted fire, and some-times though very seldom a person in the undergrowth: a woman pass-ing out of sight, a man dragging a dugout canoe into the reeds.

The tramp steamer ghosts on. For a moment it creates the only sound in the riverine world: the slipshod thud of a single, rusty engine. The Sunghai Sarawak becomes narrower; the banks grow closer; croc-odiles slither into the water with the merest splash; kingfishers, birds with wings as blue as lapis, disappear among the heavy leaves, and somewhere something crashes through the canes of bamboo, shaking the topmost green and calling forth a thousand shouts of protest or of terror. The spell has been broken. The steamer has lost her will; leafy branches scrape her bow, crack against her wheelhouse; she is no longer an ocean-going vessel; she is a part of the jungle.

No town yet. The river winds around another bend, then another, and surely, the captain thinks as he dodges that thickening greenery, surely we'll find the town at the next turning or the one after that. It's been two hours of arduous maneuvering—snags where there should be deep water, currents washing backward—how far must we travel be-fore we find Kuching?

The sultan of Sarawak's position as ruler was weak. The coastal vil-lages near his royal residence at Kuching were constantly under siege from pirates while marauding Dayak tribes paddled up every estuary and attacked the few inland habitations. Little by little, to protect him-self and to maintain the appearance, if not the substance, of his reign, the sultan had come to rely on European aid. The present sultan's fa-ther had been courted by both the English and the Dutch, but he'd died without giving his true allegiance to one country or the other.

A complex system of receiving special ambassadors with their lavish tokens of goodwill had suited the old man. He'd been fond of showy things and fond of his place in the world's hierarchy. "A sultan," he liked to say, "is every bit the equal to the king of the Dutchmen."

His son, the present sultan, was his father's match. The only differ-ence in the two rulers was that the old man had remembered a time when there were no gifts and no foreigners vying for his hand. His son had no such memories: If varying groups of men wanted his coal fields, his mineral deposits, antimony, or whatever foolish thing their West-ern hearts clamored for, why, then, let them pay for it.

But, ah dear, which nation was a ruler to choose? Which one had the prettiest gifts? Which would bow (or stoop) the lowest? Which could fill the royal coffers with his weight in precious stones? Lolling on silken pillows in the Victorian hodgepodge of a palace that island labor had built to the glory of their king, the present sultan considered these weighty problems. Dutch. English. English. Dutch. The nations went round in his head like the spinning tops in the game of *Main Gasing*. It was enough to make anyone dizzy.

Then the sultan turned his attention to a pet lizard perched beside him and whispered a self-pitying: "Dear, wrinkly little Patti. Whatever shall we do? Two suitors! Not one, but two. How can anyone be so burdened?" As he spoke, he tugged the length of silken cord that chained the lizard to its wooden prison. The sultan did this lazily, the way a child might drag a stick through sand, but the lizard didn't move, didn't open its red mouth, didn't blink its grainy eyes. It looked bored, peevish, even angry, so His Highness, the Supreme Ruler of Sarawak, yanked the cord with a decisive, wrenching snap that forced the animal to twist its bunchy neck, open its jaws, and gasp until its tongue slipped out.

"Dear, dear Patti," the sultan sighed again, "I must always be sending you these smallest of reminders. You are such a naughty girl. You forget I am master here." Then His Highness released the rope, flicked it aside, rolled onto his fat stomach, kicked a few more pillows from his bedlike throne, and resumed his contemplation of the Dutch-English dilemma. Which one? he thought. Which one? Whom must I choose this time?

The Dutch perhaps? Those beer-drinking, cheese-chewing men with their strawberry noses and ears as hairy as a common ape's? Or the English with their genteel ways, their Oxfordshire and Eton School, their high teas and their queen? The sultan moaned inwardly. Such a terrible sorrow, he mused, that I was never educated in England. What a good little British schoolboy I would have made, and then what a reluctant and regal ruler! Loyal to my queen and country beneath all my pearl-encrusted jackets, my jeweled turbans, and gossamer-thin sarongs.

"Ah dear," the sultan groaned aloud as he toyed with a star sapphire on his fat third finger (such a pretty gem!) and wept (in his tormented soul) over this terrible quandary—or the need for action at all. The lizard, momentarily forgotten, backed away and tested the strength of its chain.

The noise of the sultan's sudden wail shook the rajah, Sir Charles Ivard, out of the near stupor he found himself in after sitting motionless in the airless, steam-bath heat of the royal audience chamber.

"Anything wrong, Your Highness?" Ivard asked as he stretched his weary muscles and leaned forward. Sweat prickled along the back of his correct and knife-white tropical suit; his starched collar had turned to mush and his cravat felt as warm as a knotted wool scarf.

"Or may we proceed with our . . . our little chat? . . ." Ivard felt his way slowly; the sultan's brooding silence had lasted a long time, and Sir Charles wasn't altogether sure His Royal Highness remembered what the original discussion had been about. ". . . the position the Axthelm family will occupy . . . and though I don't mean to insist, there is also the matter of this man, Mahomet Seh . . ."

Sir Charles, Rajah Ivard, the ruler of Ivartown, Sarawak, the only white man with the title of rajah in the world, knew better than to dictate policy to his immediate superior, the sultan, but diplomacy only went so far. Even for a Briton of the old school. The outward display of courtesy and obedience required to maintain his lucrative toehold in Borneo could only be borne so long. And (as he liked to remind himself) an hour of sitting in silence while some fat, greasy Hoogli rolled around in bed and tortured a hapless pet was time enough. Past time, if you asked Sir Charles Ivard.

To think my uncle had to endure this as well, Ivard thought, as he stared at the floor and a small regiment of termites that had begun to scout the tiled surface. That was way back in the forties, Ivard remembered, in the early days of Queen Victoria, when this fellow's father was nothing but a loutish youth, and this overwrought palace no more than a native hut built on rotting stilts. I'll bet there were days when the old man wished he'd stayed put in Scotland. Days when he wished he'd never heard of Sanford Raffles and Singapore and the fabulous north coast of Borneo. But then, of course, there would have been no Ivartown. And without Ivartown there would be no further need for a rajah and his dynasty. I'd be a purblind bloke on a pension, and my son, Laneer, a young man with no expectations. Though, in truth, the title of rajah's no better than prince when you come to it—and no better than charwoman if the sultan of Sarawak's your boss.

The termites spread out, seeking any furniture leg not set in a protective saucer of kerosene, while Ivard stifled a yawn, then masked it with the slight stiffening of jaw muscles that was the exclusive trait of British (and Scottish) restraint. It was a trick he'd found extremely useful in his fifty-odd years in the tropics, like going to sleep with his eyes open when the gamelan players squawked out their unmusical, miserable medleys, or remaining upright as the shadow puppet masters spun out one more endless tale of Malaysian blood and gore.

I may be viewed as an exotic figure, Sir Charles Ivard told himself, I may be described as a white king in a brown man's world, but in reality I'm no better than any time-serving bureaucrat dancing attendance on a petty tyrant. And I can't say who's worse to deal with: this man or his long-dead father.

"We had been discussing the Axthelms, Your Highness . . . and Mahomet Seh . . . his continued raids along the coast . . . which I realize are most unpleasant subjects . . ." Ivard let the sentence die off; he tried to be as nonchalant as he could, though he knew Mahomet Seh held the key to his future. There was nothing like fear to send a small kingdom scurrying into the protective arms of a larger one.

". . . But perhaps we should continue another time . . . when you're feeling more energetic. . . ."

"Oh, it is not a want of energy, my dear Ivard," the sultan wheezed. "It is not lack of desire that mars my concentration. It is the burden of leadership—as I'm sure you can comprehend—it is the weight of responsibility to so many hundreds of people that fatigues me. My poor, unsuspecting subjects! What would their lives be with no ruler of vision? What terrible fate would befall them if my decisions faltered?

"Should I run to the Dutch, for instance—or to the British, as you keep pressing me to do? It is such a confusing choice, dear Ivard. Such a delicate issue . . . and I fear . . . I fear that some of our would-be wooers lack . . . how can I put this gracefully . . . I fear they lack altruism . . . that they toy with our royal personage for monetary gain. . . .

"Look at your English countryman, Mr. Marcus Samuel, and his Shell Transport and Trading Company . . . or Royal Dutch—how do you call that commercial venture . . . ?" The sultan paused to let this new criticism sink in, then continued with an abrupt change of mood:

"But . . ." he announced, and his voice grew playful—a tone Ivard didn't like at all. There was no talking sense when the sultan decided to have fun. ". . . At this moment, my dear Sir Charles, I am considering no such lofty melancholics." (A favorite word—as sweet as honey on the tongue!) "At this moment, I am recounting my past sins."

The sultan smiled indulgently; he knew Sir Charles Ivard would never permit himself to acknowledge that the sultan of Sarawak was less than a perfect man. The little speech was a trap, a way to catch courtiers and foreigners alike in a tangle of duplicity and ill-concealed doubt.

Ivard didn't respond; his face was a practiced blank. The fellow's no better than suet in a currant pudding, the sultan decided with a noisy wheeze; he's a lump of British clay, and no pleasure to toy with at all.

"But what were we talking of," the sultan continued with as much world-weariness as his voice could muster, "when I fell into this little reverie? . . . And don't tell me it was that silly pirate you keep bringing up. . . ."

Without bothering to glance at Ivard, the sultan turned his head toward a shuttered window and made a grimace of exaggerated displeasure. The shriek of macaws bubbled through the rattan and bamboo shades of the audience chamber. Whup! Whup! they called with the persistence of a baby cursed with colic. Whup! Whup! came the grating reply. Whup! Whup! Caw. Caw. Caw. The sultan covered his ears with his hands. The nice taste of his words; the pleasure he took in their syrupy gloss, dried up like yesterday's cake.

"We were talking, Sir Charles . . . We were talking about . . . ?" the sultan demanded.

"Yes." Ivard's pragmatic voice jumped into the breach. "I realize it's an unpleasant subject, Your Highness, but we were discussing the rebels and the rebel prisoners. . . . Seh's followers. Unless properly dealt with, his men may . . ." Ivard knew the effect caused by using Mahomet Seh's name, but it was a calculated risk. The screws had to be tight enough to feel. "I need say no more, surely, Your Highness. But British protection could aid in these internal struggles."

Suddenly Ivard wished more than anything that he could stand, throw open the louvers, and sweep some air into the fetid place. The floor smelled of mongoose piss, his chair like a rotting cabbage. The currents that eddied between the walls and the throne, around the arched doors and the blockaded windows, were as nauseating as fish balls baking in the noonday sun. Ivard tried to sit up straighter, but nothing helped. Heat and rancid sweat trickled past his nose. He pulled out his handkerchief, but the thing was already drenched.

"Ah, yes, dear Ivard . . . the prisoners . . . always the prisoners . . . always the rebels . . . Filthy fellows. Filthy, absolutely! You should see them! Perhaps you will. . . ." The possibility of an excursion to his prisons pleased the sultan so much that he heaved his body upward, straining his embroidered jacket till the shoulder stitches gave way with a creak like a falling tree.

"Would you like that, Ivard? Would you like to walk to the stockade and see the wretches—the captured rebels? . . . No, it is too much to ask. It is too far to travel in this heat. We must stay put. We must rest. We will wait till we've caught the leader himself. If, as you keep insisting, they have such a thing as a leader. I tend to believe the devils acted on their own. And if on their own, then they are mere ragamuffins not worth discussing, and certainly not worth the esteemed presence of the British navy—or the faithful Dutch."

With that calculated jibe, the sultan sank further into his nest of pillows. He appeared to have eliminated all affairs of state, all concerns excepting those that dealt with his physical well-being. The platform throne (which Ivard referred to in private as "the old heathen's bed") was littered with half-empty trays and silk-covered salvers containing *gula melaka, gado gado, ketupat, tahu goreng,* and all other sorts of Malay temptations. The sultan opened one container, peeked inside, made a face, and pushed the offending food away. Coconut meat and nangka fruit in syrup spilled across the already stained mattress. Suddenly the sultan lunged sideways and clapped his pudgy brown hands.

A young bearer darted forward to whisk away the offending crumbs, but the sultan pushed the boy away with a wide, unwholesome foot:

"No, it is too late! You didn't see this in time! Am I to wallow in filth like some disgusting animal? And look now! Look! You've frightened my little Patti! My dearest, dearest Patti!"

The sultan grabbed the lizard, which in terror had leapt from its perch and now swung in the air at the end of its purple noose. "See, see! You might have killed her! Now go!"

While the sultan cooed loving whispers to Patti's horny head, the bearer withdrew, bowing and miserable, while another (and hopefully more favored boy) moved in to take his place. The sultan took no notice; all palace servants were slaves; you put them to death, then went into the jungle and brought back some more.

"It is the only way, after all, my dear Ivard, to teach these devils any manners. My country must not be a backward place, after all. We must move into the new century. And, alas, my people do not have the long history of education and so forth as you British people do. Punishment to fit the crime, and so forth . . ."

The sultan's voice left off its whiny tone and became insinuatingly gracious again as he reeled Patti back up to her perch. The lizard made a noise like a strangled cat, and clear liquid belched from its mouth.

"No, no, my mind is made up! I've done with those absurd prisoners. I will not discuss them. I will be like your dear, dead queen. I will not compromise. A great statesman is ever thus!

"So, no more about British might, Dutch duplicity, syndicates from around the globe—such an ill-omened name, don't you agree? It begins with the word *sin*! Did you never notice that unfortunate connection?" The sultan never paused for a response; one was not expected. He and Ivard recognized the difference between question and rhetoric. And position.

"And I won't hear a word about rebels, either, Ivard—or your so-called rebels who, in my mind . . . in my esteemed estimation, are the merest bits of wasted flesh. Those men no longer amuse me; they grow daily more filthy and wretched. They have ceased to be entertaining. They are apathetic. They are deeply, deeply disappointing."

If the sultan could have produced a tiny tear at that moment, he would have. It was a shame how his countrymen had let him down, he reminded himself; they refused to make good enemies. They were fatalistic soldiers and as useless as mud. They cowered when threatened; torture proved hopeless. The sultan dangled a piece of colored coconut to the frozen Patti, but the lizard wouldn't be coaxed; its tongue had turned purple, and its sides heaved like bellows.

"So, we change subjects—I do admire that word! We speak of cheerier things!" the sultan announced, brightening measurably. "Tell me again, my dear Ivard, when is this young Mr. Axthelm coming? Mr. George, is it? Our savior? When does he come to turn the tide and save us from both Britannia's rule and dour Dutch reform?"

But that opening proved dreary as well. The question was no sooner asked than the sultan grew tired of it; he rolled monumentally to his feet and stretched out an arm in a gesture worthy of the most flea-bitten actor.

"Ah, but my little leopard cubs!" he sang out, on firm ground again, with a chattering speech needing no interruption. "Did I tell you about the sweet darlings? Snow white, like their mother—" The sultan stopped his hymn of praise momentarily:

"Whatever villain killed my Gurda will suffer for it."

And Ivard was sure the culprit would. If he'd been an imaginative man or one given to seeing beyond the immediate present, a picture of that "villain's" demise might have flashed into his mind. But Ivard was neither imaginative nor inventive; he was a Britisher born and bred, and he was in Sarawak—as he'd been all his adult life—with a specific mission set before him.

That mission was the quintessence of colonial rule; it had sequential and easily plotted tasks. One year led into another: False liberty granted was true liberty withheld; a few coins displayed in the sunlight stole riches no heathen could possibly envision or attain; a very few village elders grew fatter; a few more princelings grew rounder. But the real wealth, the mind-boggling and vast slice of this very large pie, went to the men with the ruler-straight minds and the steel-encased stomachs who lay siege to every foreign shore. Thus the British Empire, he reminded himself, thus German rule in Africa, Belgian in the Congo, and the bloody Dutch nibbling at the coast of bloody North Borneo when they should stay perfectly satisfied with their holdings in the south.

As if divining Ivard's thoughts and judging himself no match in the game of overseas properties, the sultan decided on another form of conversation. One he knew would garner a certain response. It was important always to keep these suitors on the tips of their itching toes.

"And how is my dear Laneer, our treasured rajah muda, your handsome son? Our incomparable and fickle youth?"

The sultan could almost hear Ivard groan. The sound was all the more gratifying for being hidden. "We have not seen him in many days, Sir Charles. Not a good sign, not a good sign indeed. We hope he is not at more of his naughty games."

Ivard sighed aloud. He hadn't meant to. He didn't even realize he had. Laneer was someone Ivard didn't like to consider. His only son (his only child), was a complicated entanglement the white rajah would have preferred to forget. "No saying whence that seed had sprung," he liked to say, as if the phrase could explain his son's behavior. "A bit of a fish out of water," he tried to bluff when questioned by the few foreigners who made their way to Borneo. "A bit of an odd duck." One didn't like to admit that one's son had "tendencies" considered inappropriate in a gentleman, but there it was. Laneer was Laneer.

Ivard sighed again.

The sultan had won, though he couldn't show his hand. "My dear Ivard," he teased, "you are certainly looking most unwell! Shall I send for my physician. A new one. . . . ."

The sultan lowered his voice and shifted his body in order to be closer to Ivard. ". . . The other was trying to poison me!" The whisper smelled like snake bait, the quivering flesh like mouse droppings in glue.

"Oh, no, Your Highness," Ivard stammered. "You are most kind. A passing . . . I am quite recovered."

"Ah, you English and your indigestion. You English and your countryside." The sultan smiled and returned to his throne. How he relished these discussions! "Your dear, dead queen, your Prince of Wales, your Windsor Castle, your kippers on toast! So much nicer than those smelly Dutch beers . . ."

The opening went unnoticed. "As you say, Your Highness," Ivard answered, and suddenly realized how tired he was. I'm not a young man, he told himself. I've grown weary with these games.

"If you'll permit me, I think I shall return to my own . . ." Ivard stood. His legs felt wobbly; pins and needles rushed toward his ankles and feet.

"Sit, Ivard!" the sultan shouted. "I gave you no permission to rise."

Ivard sat heavily; this was going to be a long afternoon. Even Scotland seemed preferable. A quiet retirement, a few old friends, a game of chess that lasted for years. He looked toward the windows. What were the birds like in Scotland? he wondered. The only ones he could remember were the birds of the jungle; he had almost no memory of grassy knolls or uncluttered hills or farmyard gates. Sheep dotting pastures, pine trees and oaks, the spire of a village church, a smithy's anvil, a market square. What was it like to hear the silence on a wintry heath? Ivard wondered, or the hum and dash of a dragonfly on an August-warmed lake?

Perhaps," the sultan said, "I should have called in your dear son, Laneer. Perhaps he could have helped me."

Ivard recognized the threat in the sultan's words, but somehow didn't care.

"And what do you think, my precious?" the sultan said as he grabbed the reluctant Patti. "Shall we wait for our friend, the rajah muda, Mr. Laneer Ivard? Shall we share our troubles with more sympathetic ears? Younger ears, too!

"Yes? No? Oh! Here is Patti saying 'Wait. Wait for Laneer.' See how her eyes begin to blink?"

"As you wish, Your Highness," Ivard answered. "You may discuss this with my son, Laneer, although there is no mystery to the . . . ah, arrangement with the Axthelm family . . . if that's what you're referring to. . . . I have explained what they . . ." Ivard stood again, but made no further move.

The sultan didn't bother to turn his head; Ivard could have been doing handstands for all he cared.

"Yes, the Axthelms!" the sultan sang out. "That's what I want to talk about next."

The sultan felt revived and happy. It was so much more pleasant to ponder a person than a nation. And in the ruler of Sarawak's short sight, George Axthelm was like the former Prince of Wales—a jolly smiling fellow with no interests in policy of affairs of state. "You say this George Axthelm has a son. And the same age as my perfect young heir? Five or six, you said?"

"You have a very good memory, Your Highness," Ivard answered. The endless afternoon grew longer by the moment.

"Bring my chief son to me!" the sultan shouted with a voice so loud it shook the silent palace. Ivard could hear feet scurry from every different corner. Men ran to do their master's bidding like people awakened by the clang of a gong; they raced one way and then another, not sure where they were headed, but rushing there just the same. They crashed into each other; they caromed into walls; they banged into doors, and bumped down the stairs.

"My boy!" the sultan screamed. "I must have my son!"

Then the palace erupted in oaths and cruel words as one servant yelled at another, and each royal retainer screamed at the man less important. *"Ke mana?"* ("Where is he?")

"Siapa!" ("Who!")

"The sultan's son! Bring forth the sultan's son!"

And the bearers carrying baskets of food were kicked, and the porters sleeping in corners were kicked, and the ayahs and amahs, dodging blows, started to wail. Then the birds in their wicker-wrapped love nests took up the squawking shout. Squealing with excited rage, mynahs, crested hornbills, and crimson-winged parrots added a hundred shrill warnings while the sultan closed his (oh, so sleepy) eyes and awaited the arrival of his child.

Sir Charles, Rajah Ivard was correct in assuming that the sultan of Sarawak did not care to mention Mahomet Seh by name. Seh was a thorn in the sultan's side, a prickly reminder that all was not right at home—a nagging voice that said, "Clean up your own country or someone else will come in and do it for you."

There had always been pirate raids, of course; the town of Api Api had been burned to the ground so many times it had been given the Malay term meaning "Fire! Fire!"

But in the past the pirates had always gone away; they'd taken what they wanted, burned the rest, and then returned to their sly, hidden coves.

Not so, Mahomet Seh.

Seh was a man with a god, a man with a mission, a man with a hungry mob of disgruntled villagers, tribesmen, and fisher folk following his path, a leader of something Sarawak and all of Borneo had not seen before: a rebellion. He and his men were of the Dayak tribe, but Seh had started his career as a pirate, a *perempak,* moving back and forth along the coast, setting fire to whatever villages were unprotected and destroying the small warehouses owned by Chinese shopkeepers. But then the British navy had arrived in full force from Singapore (at the insistence of the rajah) and the Dutch had come up from Java, and Seh had been forced to move inland after raiding the town of Kudat on Maruda Bay, just west of Kuching.

That raid had been the last straw for the Chinese, and for the few English as well. Trade, and the sultan's desire to move into the modern-day world, were disrupted; Mahomet Seh was officially declared an outlaw. But the terms *rebel* and *rebellion* were Seh's own choosing; they were not ideas that found favor in the sultan's sight.

Now Seh lived where he could, sustained by some settlements while overrunning those that had remained loyal to the Crown, picking off any misguided village too slovenly or slow to run their livestock into a jungle shelter or hide their food in a secret cave. And all this time the sultan promised on his deepest honor, swore, wheedled, and whined to the English, the Dutch, and his own unimportant race that he would have the man's head. The problem was that Seh had promised the same thing.

The Dayak kampong of Saratok was a typical Malay village. Just east of Kuching on the coast of North Borneo, it was a small, uneven grouping of the typical tribal dwellings called longhouses. The longhouses were narrow buildings, set on pilings near the water's edge, and they consisted of one-room apartments connected to a communal great room and an open air veranda that stretched its entire length.

This bamboo-floored porch was often connected to another longhouse veranda or to a rickety bridge, so that in times of flood or monsoon it was possible to walk from one dwelling to another without stepping on the muddy, turbulent ground. Each family unit—mother, father, children—was allotted one room in its clan's longhouse; uncles, aunts, grandparents, and cousins took the others. Privacy was unknown; love affairs, infidelities, political leanings, and the all-important interpretation of each and every dream were discussed and gossiped over from morning till night.

But the kampong of Saratok, because it was so close to the royal residence in Kuching, also had a small garrison of the sultan's soldiers. They were housed in a longhouse like the others, though this particular dwelling was set apart. A tribesman needed to walk through mud and rotting vegetation to reach it. This was seldom done, however; the clans and the soldiers maintained an uneasy peace at best. And the skulls and shrunken heads that hung from each roof like so many braided onions attested to the Dayak proclivity for taking their victims' heads. The Dayak, as well as the Kayan and Bajua tribes, were renowned headhunters.

On this particular day, several mornings after Sir Charles Ivard's tedious interview with the sultan, the problem confronting both soldiers and villagers was the recent capture and subsequent dispatch of one of Mahomet Seh's rebel gang. Separated from his clan, perhaps even a deserter, the man had been caught stealing, but the local official (with an eye on the glory of palace life) had decided to make an example of the thief. His hands were not to be cut off; he was not to be branded or his tongue cut out: he was to be killed. And better yet, he would be hanged: English style. It would be justice and a good example.

The problem was that had happened the day before and the body, still hanging by the neck and covered with dirt from being dragged to the improvised gibbet, had now begun to bloat and stink. It looked all right from a distance; it looked no different than the swollen carcass of a babirusa pig or an orangutan, but it smelled terrible. The stench blew through the village, carried by the river's breeze, and seemed to settle everywhere, sticking to whatever it touched as if it would never leave again. Even the bamboo slats joining one dwelling to another seemed permeated by the reek of rotting flesh, even the roofs baking in the sun, even the pilings that raised each building above the swirl of tide and refuse.

The official didn't know what to do. Clearly, the body must be cut down, but who would do this? There was enough danger of reprisal from Seh and his band of cutthroats as it was. Insult should not be added to injury. Yesterday had been easy; he'd simply ordered the five scraggly soldiers assigned to the village to string the man up. They'd added a few refinements of their own to the task, of course. (It had not been the official's order to drag the prisoner through the mud, bound only at his feet and toes.) But now these same guards balked at further implication. They complained it was bad luck to cut the man down. They said Seh must come back for his own. They grumbled and glared and spit on the ground and the official was afraid he might soon face a mutiny. And there would go his chance of promotion; his removal to the godly home of their great and glorious ruler.

So the body hung there, swaying slightly with the wind, putrefying the air, the town, and the souls of its unhappy inhabitants. Mothers turned their babies' faces to their breasts, cupping hands around tiny noses and mouths, while the older children ran along the slippery notched logs that served as kampong stairs and twisted leaves over their mouths and bulged their eyes as if the smell might burst through the tops of their heads.

Night came and the people of Saratok retreated to the farthest interior of their communal homes. The great rooms were deserted and every veranda was silent. Each family hid in its own cubicle, hoping that by morning the rebel's body would have disappeared, carried off in the darkness by kites with huge black wings, or by a crocodile that would somehow slither up the gibbet to drag the fat prize away. No one dared mention Mahomet Seh by name.

But Seh did come in the night; the old men were the first to hear the stealthy noise. They remembered proud days of creeping out before dawn to raid another village, they remembered returning home with their trophy heads, and they remembered the women's smiles. The old men, covered only in loincloths made from vines and leaves, rose from their reed sleeping mats and moved into the shadowed doorways.

"How many heads have you taken?" they murmured their Dayak prayer. "How many lovers have you had?"

Then the young men heard the whispering and shook off sleep as well; they congregated in corners and under the edge of each roof, tensing shoulder muscles and thighs, and the young women, feeling their beds go cold, followed, then clung in nervous bunches and wouldn't venture outside. They twisted their sarongs around their nervous hips, and crossed their hands over their breasts. But the old women refused to move; they turned stony faces to the wall and waited without breathing. Their days of welcoming heroes were long past.

The soldiers heard the whispering and were on their feet immediately. Or perhaps they hadn't heard a thing and were roused from their dreams by the stomping fury of the frightened official. However it happened, the soldiers also appeared, and soon the night-lit kampong looked like a shadowy garden infested with rats. The movement was so slight it was barely discernible, but then there, in that corner, something moved. And then over there. And over there. The whole kampong shuddered, shifted itself, and stirred.

Seh's men found the body and began to cut it down, but the soldiers, counting the rebels, felt it was time for promotion and decided to advance. No shots were fired; there were only three old flintlock guns among the two opposing forces (in 1903 guns were rare among the tribesmen of Borneo) and besides no one had learned how to use them properly. The fight became a silent tug-of-war, the rebels at the head of the body, the soldiers grabbing the feet, and the villagers tensing forward to choose sides or scurry home to their longhouse cells.

The rebels grasped their dead companion's shoulders, but the body was naked, as well as slippery, so they pulled his arms instead. They pulled hard and gained some ground; the soldiers were left with the swollen toes. Then one soldier grabbed an ankle while a rebel lunged for the chest and the corpse came apart: legs and arms and stomach in a sudden rush of decomposed skin. The opponents fell back; a soldier vomited; a rebel sprawled against his dead friend's split-apart face; and the people of the town made a noise like a gale in the masthead wires of a ship at sea.

The body dropped from the gibbet; it fell piecemeal, slopping over the steps, then it slid or was kicked or simply tumbled, unraveling, into the black mud below. No one saw it land, but they all heard its soft and final plop. Then the old women, still staring at the walls of their quiet rooms, began to wail. They made a sound so mournful and lonely and bereft, so full of longing for past lives, past glory, past hopes, that everyone, the sick soldier and the fallen rebel, stepped back. Then the old men took up the sound and the young women and the young men; but no one could have said what the sound meant. It was just a sound of the night and the jungle, like the song of the rhinoceros beetle, or the squeal of a fallen deer.

But by now the mail packet or the steamer or the freighter from Billiton or Buitenzorg or Soerabaija that had advanced upon Sarawak begins to retrace slow steps down the river. The captain breathes a sigh of relief as he calls out orders to the Malays standing watch at the bow. He'll be glad to get back to civilization, he tells himself. Glad to be among people instead of naked savages. Glad to speak a few words in a European tongue.

How simple it is, the captain thinks, to have only current and tide to contend with. There's something odd going on in Kuching. The captain's quite sure of it. First there was the trouble taking on fresh coal, then the company chit that was mysteriously refused. The superintendent paid off on last month's visit was no longer in charge, and his successor hadn't any idea where the man could be found. Something fishy is going on for certain.

So the captain turns his face to the clear wind blowing in from the sea, happy to risk pirates and typhoons, happy to watch the Sunghai Sarawak disappear in the salt waves of the South China Sea. He promises himself not to think of this place till another month goes by. Anything can happen before then: He might strike it rich and retire in splendor; he might move on to Penang or the Macassar Strait.

And the musty-looking European passenger who'd hoped to find some opportunity in Kuching, something to sink his teeth into, make his name from, or just scrape by, leaves, too. He'll try the British community in Billiton or Sadong, perhaps even tiny Brunei, though he's heard it's terribly primitive. But this place, this Kuching town, well, the Ivard family has it all sewed up. No point in staying here.

And there's something going on; the traveler knows. He's seen the East. He knows the signs. So he smiles and nods to the captain as both men turn back briefly to watch the last of the town disappear behind a bend in the river.

S I X

*T*HE ALCEDO REACHED
THE ISLAND OF MADEIRA early in the morning of August the
eighth. It was a rocky place, one of the first outcroppings of inhabit-
able soil in the eastern Atlantic Ocean, and it was tall and craggy, but
blanketed with an incredible emerald-bright green. Steep inland
mountains disappeared into clouds, and seemed to rattle them till they
swirled wet fog over the whole of the jagged terrain. The mountains
stood taller, yawned, knocked their heads in the air, and more water
spewed forth.

Then the lush, lilting color of the foothills was changed into a sodden brown mass while, at the water's edge, the new day's sun battled
and lost, and finally and miraculously won. Quirky and imperious, the
sunbeams raced across each strip of sand, turning them bright gold,
ocher, silver, saffron, and white. Coves and tiny bays leapt forward,
sparkling, dazzled as if granted, at long last, a life all their own. As if,
waiting in humble darkness, they had finally been blessed.

In the wheelhouse, Captain Cosby and the first mate took their eyes
off the hills and inviting greenery. The sight of the yacht's first landfall
was all very well, they told themselves, but what they needed was a
safe harbor. The cove in which the ship had been scheduled to anchor
was shallow and hazardous, so the captain had been forced to stand
off, test his ship's lines and try to discern which way the prevailing
winds and tides would move the huge vessel. Normally a ship of her
size would have been berthed in the port of Funchal, but the Axthelms

had wanted "to experience the simple people, to live in the wild." Embracing nature could be filled with vicissitudes.

The captain eyed his compass and read and reread the depths his charts measured while a mist-filled cloud began to cover the yacht's bow and envelop her in a clammy embrace. Soon the whole deck was slippery wet; the funnel-sluiced water and beady drops slid from the rail, the steps, the lighters and longboats, or clung heavy and pearly-pale inside every entryway door. The foghorn bellowed and the smoke-stack belched leaves of black soot as the engines churned in their own frothy wake, and with each new motion, each new noise, more water rained down on the boat.

Captain Cosby gave a few orders to the helmsman, but except for his well-chosen words, the rest of the bridge hands and watching crowd were silent. All crew members unoccupied with breakfast trays, arrival procedures, coal bins, or laundry tubs had rushed on deck as soon as they could. Stokers crowded against cooks, sailors lounged beside scullery boys; stewards and mates leaned into the fore and aft ropes as eagerly as the Axthelms and their guests pressed the wooden "family" rail. The entire ship was ringed with people gazing at the newfound country, the ship's first and wondrous landfall. It didn't matter that most of the men had seen these sights before, or that one island could look exactly like another; if you ringed the globe ten times and ten times again, this moment would remain: the *Alcedo*'s arrival in the great world.

"Hard to port," Captain Cosby might say or: "Starboard, one quarter." There was a murmured order from the bridge, a responding shout from the port bow, another from midships, and another from the stern, but the sounds seemed to have no bearing on the ship's movement; they were gratuitous, as if the men were merely following the yacht's own lilting call. The *Alcedo* ghosted on, a magic thing, bearing herself forward with willful pride.

"Starboard. Hold," Captain Cosby said at last, and George, who stood at his side, nodded studious agreement.

"Fine job, Captain. First-rate. Tricky passage . . . that bit back a ways. Tricky maneuver. . . ."

"I'll go tell everyone we've made it safe and sound, shall I?" George nodded again; his expression indicated that history had been made. He looked round the wheelhouse and graced all present with the largess of his command. His eyes had the unfocused gaze of a king's.

"Thank you, sir," Captain Cosby said. He didn't have time for pleasantries; there was plenty of work ahead, but the boss was the boss.

"I believe I'll bring the kiddies up here," George announced, unwilling to relinquish the moment. "Show them how this kind of thing is done."

"As you wish, sir. Though there's not much to see at the moment. Just the anchor cables letting out."

"Do them a world of good," George said, "a world of good. This is history we're witnessing, Captain. I need not remind you."

Captain Cosby doubted that one yacht traversing the Atlantic could be called historic, but he nodded brief agreement while he kept his eyes glued to the foredeck and bow and the anchor's releasing winch.

"A good lesson to be learned," George pontificated as he straightened his shoulders and observed the deck rail. "It's not an easy thing sailing a ship, Captain. And there are metaphors in that, I need not tell you. There are metaphors in that."

"Sir," Captain Cosby answered.

"Fine job, men. You're to be commended. Every one of you." George faced the navigation officer, mate, and helmsman in turn.

"Yes, indeed. My compliments." Then he left the bridge to convey the good news: The *Alcedo* had reached Madeira. His ship, his realm, his mandate, had been brought to safe harbor again.

After the ship dropped anchor, Eugenia, the children, Prue, and the DuPlessises had retreated to the main saloon. The wet, blowing air, the water pelting from rails and walls, the sodden flakes of soot that rained from the fog-covered smokestack, had descended in such a sudden deluge, that they'd been forced, laughing and unreasonably happy, to return to the warmth and protection of the saloon fire.

A tea tray was immediately produced (Higgins was ever vigilant) and Turkish towels carried forth in great clumps. Stewards stood ready with dry shoes, clothes brushes, and chamois skin nappers; Olive had her mistress's hairpins, a fine-toothed silver comb, and her silver brush. Such repairs should not take place in public, she thought, but there it was. You could never tell with the gentry. What was considered "coarse" for common folk was "picnicking" for the well-to-do.

A weekend camp atmosphere pervaded the room. Clothes had been ruined, the starch in every shirtfront and pinafore turned limp and worthless; faces, collars, and shiny cuffs were streaked with black; but the travelers danced about like children caught in a summer squall. The fire was inviting, the snap and cozy hiss of it delightful. The saloon was a haven, the ship an enchanted world.

"Oh, look!" Eugenia said as she bent over the carpet and shook water from her hair. "It might as well have been raining goats and mares! My hair is . . . My skirt is . . . Oh, well. . . . Oh, well. Who need worry?"

She unpinned her hair and tossed it over her head. Shiny drops of moisture leapt toward the lamp shades and velvet pillows. "We can't very well go ashore like this!"

"And my best dress, too!" wailed Mrs. DuPlessis, but her complaint had the sound of operatic comedy: an age-old excuse for a new dress. "I can't very well go ashore at all. Why, even my curls are a-tangle!" And Mrs. DuPlessis did look ridiculous; her elaborate, if old-fashioned, pile of graying curls had slipped lopsided toward one ear. She resembled a rather large twelve-year-old girl who'd found an ancient wig in an attic, tried it on, and was in the process of pretending she was the lady of the manor.

The children stared but said nothing. Teasing was a waste of time when everyone was having so much fun. And besides, Mrs. DuPlessis looked just like them. Jinx smiled at her new friend and Mrs. DuPlessis smiled in return.

"Aren't you two men concerned?" Eugenia asked both Dr. DuPlessis and Paul. "But what's an old shirt or collar to you. You never have to think about what you wear."

Paul was thrilled with this inclusion. "You two men!" He stretched to his full five-year-old height, brushed off his knickers, and scraped one shoe clean on an already soggy sock.

Whit wandered in, and then Lieutenant Brown, and the room seemed more festive than ever.

"And here are our two dandies!" Eugenia laughed. "Dry and clean and freshly pressed. I suppose the ladies of Madeira are more important than showing your faces on deck first thing in the morning."

"Now that's not fair, Cousin Eugenia." Whit pretended dismay. "It's true, I've put a lot of thought into my. . . ."

"Wardrobe!" Paul couldn't stand still any longer. "Wardrobe! Wardrobe!" he whooped.

"I need another towel, Prue." Jinx twisted her skirt, pooling a little puddle onto the flowery floor, but nobody cared. A fresh towel covered the spot and that was enough of that.

"Wardrobe! Wardrobe!" her brother shrieked. The word was as fine as warm toffee. As fine as a day at the beach.

"Wardrobe is exactly what I mean, Whitney!" Eugenia teased. "Now that we're on land. Why, there might just be some young lady here who'd—."

"Catch your eye!" Paul bubbled, finishing the sentence the way it was supposed to be, the way it had been night after night after night, while he and Jinx played checkers or charades or "Simon Says" or "I Packed My Grandmother's Trunk" during the joyous hour after dinner before the dreaded "Bedtime, children" banished them from the bright lights forever. Paul couldn't wait to meet this young lady who his mother said would catch his cousin's eye; he knew she'd be as beautiful as Christmas candy.

Eugenia smiled at her children; even grown-up Lizzie was in on the joke. She suddenly looked no more mature than a very young child. The superior thirteen-year-old tinge had been washed away by wet cheeks, wet hair, and fingernails gone grimy from grasping a sooty deck rail. Eugenia handed her daughter her hairbrush and comb. The gesture was gentle, a simple expression of sharing, and Lizzie took both silver things as though they'd been made of the sheerest glass. Neither mother nor daughter spoke.

"And what about you, Lieutenant Brown?" Eugenia resumed her joke. "Did you spend hours at your toilette in preparation for this great morning?"

Brown was startled at his inclusion in the family group. He'd come to the saloon pro forma; he considered it polite and his duty to be present when all went ashore, but the intimate scene that had greeted him had made him wish he'd stayed below. Uncomfortable, feeling a great deal less than the well-heeled officer he'd been told to represent, Brown couldn't think of a word in reply.

Eugenia sensed Brown's embarrassment, but his hesitation made her draw back as well. She felt her words were shallow and the joke had gone too far. She looked at herself and saw a silly society bauble, a lady with time on her hands, a person of no value.

"You young men! You young men," she tried, but her efforts fell with a thud.

George saved the day. He strode into the room, blustery and bright with accomplishment. "I just came down to let everyone know we've made a safe landfall," he said. Authority and self-importance emblazoned every word.

"Oh, we know, George. We know!" Eugenia ran to her husband, safe again, on track again, the little wife, the charming knickknack, the ornament all men desired.

"Why do you think we're all so drowned looking?" she laughed. And this seemed so amusing that Paul and Jinx skittered onto the floor while Mrs. DuPlessis clasped her hand to her breast, sucked in her breath, and tried to keep her corset from bursting its seams. Whit clapped George's shoulder, Dr. DuPlessis bobbed his head with hiccups, Lizzie flopped on a chair, and Eugenia beamed at the room. Land, they all thought. We've reached land! We are strong; we are safe; we have crossed the great Atlantic; it is nothing from now on!

"Well, at any rate, I came to reiterate Captain Cosby's invitation to join him on the bridge." George's superior tone would never be shaken again, and Eugenia looked at her husband in wonderment and pleasure. The morning was everything she'd hoped it would be. For the first time since the trip began, she felt they'd left the Turk and the whole conniving Axthelm family behind forever. "I am the master of my fate," she told herself. "I am the captain of my soul." She took her husband's hand; the movement was impulsive and exuberant. Hang convention, she thought; we'll do as we please.

Their parents' obvious happiness infused the children as well. "Oh, me, me, Father!" they shouted in unison. "We want to go, too."

"Of course, we'll all go. Won't we?" Eugenia said. "We're wet enough already. Let's all go up to the bridge!" And she took her husband's arm and then, as a quick and generous afterthought, Lieutenant Brown's, and said, "I am completely happy!"

Henry, the under steward, and Ned, the cabin boy, stood side by side, watching the ship swing on her twin cables. Even with two anchors set, the huge ship still moved to the rhythm of current and tide. Ned's eyes were fixed to the sight; Henry feigned bored indifference as befitted his advanced age and superior position.

"You going ashore?" Ned asked excitedly. Drops of fog beaded up in his hair and began to run down his forehead and cheeks. He shook free the way a puppy would, first to get rid of the water and then for the pure joy of it.

"Not a chance of it," Henry said. "Old Higgins will have something for me to do every infernal minute. Just you wait."

The words "just you wait" were a reference to Henry's superior age and experience. He might be new to ocean travel, but he'd been around, Henry had, and he'd seen plenty of fellows like old Higgins. Henry wasn't a young whippersnapper like Ned.

"Anyway, like as not, there won't be much to look at. These places is all pretty much the same. When I was a kid like you, I liked them all right. But I'm sixteen now. I'm grown up." Henry sounded as if he were trying to persuade himself; he squared his raw, bony shoulders and tried to pull his jacket sleeves over his very red and very long wrists. "And anyway, nothing's as good as home."

Ned was impressed in spite of himself. He knew he was being conned, but curiosity got the better of him.

"You live on a farm then, Henry?" he said. "I've never seen a farm. D'you have cows and all? Pigs, chickens, and things? Crops and a barn with hay? I had an aunt that kept chickens once, but she died."

Henry didn't answer. He studied the green island, and didn't know what to think.

"D'you have a horse, too? There's a boy I know—back on the streets. He can ride a horse. I asked him if I could try it, but he said he'd catch hell if he let me. It was one of them livery horses, black, you know, and sort of brown. I bet your horse's nicer than that."

"I'm going in," Henry said abruptly. "It's too damned wet out here. If you want to catch your death, I won't stop you." Henry removed his cloth cap, shook it firmly, then plastered it back on his head. His wrists jumped out of his sleeves again, and he yanked at his cuffs as if ready to tear them right off.

"See ya," he said, and walked away.

Ned was impervious to the snub. He gazed at the green island and lowering clouds as if he'd never seen anything so wonderful before, as if this were a paradise he alone had discovered. "The other end of the earth," Ned whispered.

"Who on earth are you?" Jinx's voice made Ned nearly leap out of his skin. He spun around and caught his trouser leg on the rail stanchion. One leg was stuck fast; the other pawed at the air.

"The cabin boy, miss." Ned wrestled with the rail, till he heard a heartrending rip. He didn't dare look down. It occurred to him he might have no pants left at all.

"Well, I've never seen you." If Jinx was aware of her companion's awkwardness, she didn't show it. "And I know everyone on this ship. It belongs to my father," she added as an afterthought, just in case the boy was not who he claimed.

"I know that, miss." Ned sneaked a look at his leg.

"I thought you might be a boy from town," Jinx said. Her voice sounded imperious and scolding, and Ned didn't dare glance up.

"The boats haven't been lowered yet, miss. And we haven't had no visitors, neither." Ned was barely able to get this information out. It seemed unbelievably bold. He hung his head lower and held his breath.

Jinx ran to the rail and tottered against it, leaning as far as she could over the waves. Ned was right: There were no boats alongside. Criticism turned to chagrin, then to the slightest smattering of remorse, and finally ended as full-fledged admiration.

"How old are you?" Jinx asked, and swung on the rail, as if meeting a new friend on the first day of school.

"Twelve," Ned answered. He forgot to say "miss," but realized his mistake too late. "Miss," he whispered, though Jinx didn't hear.

"I'm nine," Jinx answered. "But I'm going to be ten soon. This

month. On the seventeenth of August. I was born when the hot bird
sings. That's what Mother says.

"She's going to give me a big party. She always does. She likes parties. My mother's a very festive person. As well as very beautiful. They
write about her in the newspapers."

"Is that right, miss?" Ned knew his social skills had failed him. He
felt ugly and awkward: His pants were ripped, he had no cap, his fingers were dirty, and his hobnailed shoes looked as though something
big and muddy had rolled over them in the night.

"Maybe you can come," Jinx said, and then, as if Lizzie were whispering warnings or Mrs. DuPlessis were rolling her eyes, Jinx realized
how outrageous her words must sound. But there was nothing to do
but go forward. There was no such thing as turning back.

"I think I hear our nursemaid, Prue," Jinx lied. "We're probably
ready to go ashore." And Jinx turned and ran for the door.

George's deserted beach, the place he could "live in the wild" had been
strewn with bullock carts, wagons, men, mules, and horses since just
past dawn. They'd drawn slowly up the dirt track leading to the cove,
following a rumor, like an instinct for migration, that had insisted a
wealthy American on a huge white ship wanted to travel inland,
wanted to see the sights. The rumor spread as rumors do, and the road
had become packed with carts till they finally burst forth with a noisy
rush to the beach. Like a dam collapsing, the results were scattered and
wide. There was no order in the crowd; they grabbed what position
they could and stuck fast.

The men had whiled away the hours rebraiding manes and tails,
flicking water from wet ribbons, finding dry ones and then tying them
to brightly painted wheels and decorated bridles, or alternately polishing harness bells or protecting them from the infernal rain with bits of
fraying calico. They'd worked silently, looking over the competition,
calculating who could beat out whom, which cart was jauntiest, which
the most colorful, who had a chance and who had none.

A bow was applied, but it turned soft and greasy with the interlop-
ing drizzle. The bow was removed; bells were repolished: a third time,
a fourth, a sixteenth, a twentieth; the beach chimed like a carillon, but
still the long-expected ship did not appear. Yellow and red seat covers
were wiped clean, carriage sides rubbed down, but still there was no
ship. Horses stroked the soft sand with hesitant hooves; waves rolled
in; waves receded, a cart jounced against a hidden rock. But still there
was no yacht.

It was a game of musical chairs played in fearsome earnest; the prize was a week's wages, a month's, a year's. Take the bows off, put them on, spit on the bridles and rub till they gleam; cover the seats or dash the cloth on the ground. Hurry! Hurry! Don't waste a second! Any minute now we'll see her rounding the point. Any moment now she'll be here.

Finally, someone a long way down the beach had shouted through the mist and the huge ship had loomed forward. First the men saw the bow, then the midsection; then little by little the ship had become real as the fog parted before her. She was a goddess from the sea; she was a ghost ship; she was an omen, a miracle; she was bigger, more magnificent, than anyone could have ever imagined.

The men and animals stood stone-still and stared until one driver shook himself of the spell, whistled under his breath to a friend, and jogged his startled animal toward what he hoped was the landing place.

By the time George, Eugenia, the DuPlessises, Whitney, Beckmann, Lizzie, Jinx, Paul, and Lieutenant Brown had been set ashore, and the hampers of food baskets, table linens, silver, and blankets had been safely unloaded, there were close to twenty carts, all trying to outdo the others with the brilliance of their decoration, the sublime comfort of their cushions, and the docile, sweet natures of their lovable and perfect beasts.

The British ambassador to Portugal (and therefore to the island of Madeira) was Sir Randall Jeffries, and he arrived in the midst of the confusion over the carts and animals. He'd been delayed on the road from Funchal, not because his driver was confused or lost (Sir Randall would never have permitted that) but because of the crush of traffic on the one-lane track.

"Looks as though you've summoned everything on wheels, old man. Not even visiting royalty gets this kind of treatment," he shouted as welcome as he jumped down from his phaeton-type coach. Sir Randall was an easy man to talk to; he'd been in foreign service all his life. He could make the most mundane chitchat seem invigorating; he knew when to discuss politics and when to leave it alone.

Lady Jeffries was his equal. A tall, handsome woman in her fifties, she had the equine stature and rippling gait of other English ladies of her social class. As long as her hat was straight and her kid gloves matched, nothing else really mattered. She smiled pleasantly to Eugenia, tried to call out a greeting, but, finding her words drowned by the din around her, gave up and pantomimed: "Welcome. So glad you could come." Her eldest daughter, Marina, seated beside her in the coach, immediately stood, made a polite bob, then sat again, smiling as warmly as her mother.

Whitney turned around and mouthed an astonished "Catch my eye!" to Eugenia, which Jinx intercepted and transmitted to Paul by means of a swift poke in the ribs. Then Paul also noticed the Lady Marina and her parasol and her wide lacy bonnet, and he went as goggle-eyed as his older cousin. Eugenia raised her eyebrows, gave a small, private laugh, then realized Ogden Beckmann was staring at her. She turned sudden and studied attention to Lizzie's wind-blown hair, and didn't hear another word. Beckmann, she told herself, we might as well invite a weasel into a dovecote.

Sir Randall Jeffries was trying to dissuade George from hiring every cart in sight; with the grace and humor of a born diplomat, he was explaining that so many vehicles could not possibly make the trip inland to the village of Chopina. The mountain road was too narrow for such a long caravan, he reasoned as he pointed toward the summit of Pico Ruivo, the island's tallest peak. There wouldn't be enough room to turn round when they reached the top. And besides, he himself had already engaged the best drivers. They and their animals stood at the ready; their carts were comfortable; there was plenty of room for the luggage.

But George was determined. He described the need for stewards to serve luncheon, extra clothes in case of inclement weather, and Dr. DuPlessis's panoramic camera, which would fill half of one cart all by itself. George walked back and forth along the stretch of sand and rock, looking over his potential procession, while he talked with the ambassador and, by means of an interpreter, with the drivers themselves. He studied the carts, stroked each beast, gauged the worth of each and every master. He was in his element. He was a prince inspecting his troops, a patriarch attending his family's needs; he could talk with crowds, walk with kings. His was the earth, his the birthright. He was George Axthelm of Philadelphia.

The children happily trailed their father, admiring the glossy, warm animals, the bright yellow, red, and purple paint that glowed on each cart and made every spoke on every wheel jump to giddy attention. They tested the spongy seaweed-strewn ground, slipping down tiny hillocks and dunes. Paul threw clumps of dry sand, which exploded in whiffs of fine, grainy smoke; Jinx stooped to hunt seashells and Lizzie was beset, over and over, by one little voice that said, "You're a young lady now; you should go say your how-do-you-do's," and another that said, "Phooey on that. Let's play!"

After a long inspection tour, and many unintelligible entreaties

(George had never heard Portuguese spoken before—it sounded to his confused ears like a mixture of German and something infinitely exotic and strange), he made up his mind to take all the carts. Lieutenant Brown was given the task of organizing the lighter's return to the yacht, detailing the departure of the stewards, and remaining on board himself to await the party's reappearance that afternoon. Paul was disappointed when his hero was left behind, but he soon forgot his troubles. He watched the lighter pull back toward the ship. Six sailors tugged on the oars, and the boat bumped through the waves, lifted from the burden of passengers and packages, which had nearly swamped her white gunwales. She looked like a baby porpoise swimming home to her much bigger mother.

Then the sun appeared, breaking through and banishing the clouds, the mist, and the threat of rain. It was splendid, the sun, huge as if clothed in ceremonial armor, and it gazed down at the crowd, the deferential waves lazing from ship to shore, and the palm frond trees waving their spiky leaves in the brightening sky as if to say: "Follow me. I am master here."

The Axthelm family and their servants, the DuPlessis, Ogden Beckmann, and the Randall Jeffries settled themselves into rugs and cushions, springy-backed chairs and cariole seats, and began their journey in a blaze of light.

Paul looked back on the long procession. Not even the crusader knights could have been so impossibly grand.

"Dear Father," George wrote late that afternoon. He sat in his study, in a quiet ship. The excursion, the arrival, the novel experience of resting at anchor again, seemed to have worn everyone out, and George considered he might be the only soul left still awake. He leaned back in his chair, tipped his feet on his desk, and contemplated the day (and his accomplishments) with growing pride.

Very well planned, he decided, even if I do say so myself. . . . Very well planned indeed. . . . Pleasant people . . . pleasant little excursion up the mountains . . . what travel should be . . . a nice luncheon on a pretty hillside. Rosy-cheeked, smiling natives. And the drivers so grateful for that little something extra . . . Unspoiled . . . Good we came . . . good for the wife . . . good for the kiddies. George's thought's circled his head like the aroma of a good cigar. He put his feet on the floor and took up his pen again:

Dear Father,
Pleasant first stop. Jeffries on hand as expected . . .

No, that wasn't how to begin at all. It didn't convey the arrival, the scene at the beach, the awestruck manner with which the drivers had studied the yacht. George ripped up the letter and began anew.

Dear Father, Greetings from *Funchal!*

But that wasn't it either. George reached for another sheet of paper, rubbed his finger over the gold-tipped crest, and gazed out his study window. What was it Genie had said? he wondered. He tried to picture the spot where she'd stood. It had been the edge of a hillside halfway to the village of Chopina, and they'd stopped for the view and then decided, on a sudden whim, to take their picnic luncheon there. Higgins was immediately bustling over the ground, giving orders, spreading rugs, setting foldaway tables under the trees. And as they'd waited for luncheon to be called, Genie had turned to him and said . . . What? Something about the sea . . . something about . . . George racked his brain, but he couldn't remember.

And that hat looked damned good on her too, he thought. I must remember to tell her. He made himself a mental note. . . . Now, where was I? he wondered. . . . Ah, yes . . . Genie.

"Look, George! Look how silver the sea is!" That's what she'd said. "It's like something solid, like something you could walk on."

And then Jeffries had said, "Pretty little thing, your wife." And his aristocratic face had opened in a languid smile.

Pretty little thing! Just imagine old Jeffries saying that! George was almost beside himself with pleasure. Genie, noticed by an English nobleman!

"Walking on the sea," she'd said. Why she was poetic as well as pretty. It had definitely been Genie's day, all around. Even Beckmann had forgotten to be dour.

"Dear Father . . ." George began again.

. . . And little Lizzie in that Spanish shawl! The picture of her wrapping herself up for a photograph suddenly jumped into George's eyes. She'll be a beauty, too, he told himself, or I'll eat my hat. George shook his head, imagining himself discouraging local swains. Someone like that rascal Whitney, no doubt, he thought, or our young Lieutenant Brown.

George smiled, then nearly laughed aloud when he remembered Whitney and the Lady Marina. The poor fellow had asked for the drubbing he got; he nearly slipped down the entire mountainside trying to retrieve that girl's scarf. Heroics can take their toll!

There he'd been, clinging to the edge of the cliff, clawing at what remained of a good-sized shrubbery, while his feet dusted off all the loose soil and he called out a frantic, "I say, I say up there. Oh, I say! I say, can anyone hear me?"

What a laugh they'd all had! Beckmann and Jeffries hoisting the dangling fellow back to terra firma while the women clustered around, giggling and cooing: "Whitney, you might have been killed." . . . "How can you men go on like that?" . . . "Shame on you." . . . "Don't you listen to them, Whit; they're insensitive brutes."

It had been like the good old days at Princeton, George thought. Picnics near Lawrenceville . . . the time rain had driven them into a deserted barn, the stolen kisses in the dark. What had been the names of those girls? he wondered. Mona had been one . . . then a Nancy something. . . . Before Genie's time, of course . . . way, way before . . .

George returned to the letter. Won't get very far with all this lollygagging, he told himself. Time to knuckle under, old man. No more daydreams! He reached for the pen. His body felt healthier than it had in a long time, fit, robust and full of vigor.

> Dear Father, Greetings from Madeira!
> A happy arrival. Our fair Alcedo did an admirable job with her first ocean crossing. Thanks also to some fancy footwork from Capt. Cosby & crew. Was present throughout the anchoring process, and I can tell you it was a most impressive performance. MOST impressive.
> M. Jeffries et al. on hand to meet us. Thank you for the intro. Patrician family, but very reasonable. Everything I'd hoped. As is the island.
> Picked up a little book entitled *The Land of Wine* written by a fellow Philadelphian!!! and published in '01. Thought it might bring some amusement to the dear old Lodge and its stay-at-home denizens. Might plan the same sort of treatise when I get home.
> Governor's Ball in two days' time (in honor of self and wife), so we'll move on to Funchal proper, and get a chance to see more of the coast. We expect to receive visitors on board all day prior to the festivities. The ship is *much* wondered at here. Think we'll have to beat the curious off with a stick! Don't know if the city docks will take the crush.
> Ogden well, and the fellow, Brown, seems to know his stuff.
> Eugenia sends fond regards. The children are well, and have become real little sailors.
>
> *With best wishes,*
> *Your son, George*

That's enough for now, George thought as he leaned back in his chair once more. He listened for the roar of the engines, then remembered the ship was resting at anchor. The only noise was the far-off hum of the furnaces gobbling coal; it gave the place an incredibly cozy feel, like listening to a heart beat.

Hard to describe, really, George told himself. The pomp and ceremony. My position here . . . Father'd never understand. Or maybe he wouldn't believe me. George felt his eyes growing heavy. Long day, he thought, long day. His shoulders felt like lead and his finger no longer moved. A little snooze before dinnertime, he told himself, a little shut-eye before I put on my old bib and tucker.

Youngest and ne'er-do-well son! George thought as his eyes closed completely. Won't the old devil be surprised. Astonished, I'd say. Yes, indeedy. Yes, indeedy!

On the afternoon of the Governor's Ball in the Axthelms' honor, the girls fluttered in and out of their mother's cabin, helping her dress, running errands for Prue, who knelt on the carpet beside the billowing ball gown, armed with needle and thread while a flatiron warmed nearby on the hearth. The docile Olive had been reduced from lady's maid to assistant lady's maid. It seemed that Prue could fix anything, even a lost line of jet beads. Pins in her mouth, she motioned to Olive, who swiftly obeyed. Another measure of wide hem was stitched into a rolling loop.

"Oh, I think just the pearls, Mother," Lizzie said, standing back and appraising her mother's appearance. "They're really more . . . more . . . *comme il faut.*"

Lizzie had become almost insufferably upper-class since her introduction to the Lady Marina Jeffries. Lady "Nina" was exactly who Lizzie wanted to be like when she was nineteen. Lizzie tilted her head to one side in a perfect imitation of her idol and said, "And I like your hair better that way—off your forehead. May I borrow a little face powder?"

"Yes, you may, darling, but don't sprinkle it all over the dresser the way you did last time." Eugenia tossed the words over her shoulder and watched the work on her gown progress.

"Mother! I am not a child!" Lizzie's tone was reproachful and hurt, and Eugenia half turned to trade a look with Jinx, who was busy fastening a ruby brooch to her pinafore. Jinx made a face, copying the imperious Lizzie, and Eugenia smiled, then returned to the ministrations of Olive and Prue.

"No, let's keep the hem the same length all along the front," she said. "And then sweeping down into the train. Or perhaps the loops should start only on the right side. I don't know. Why don't you pin it and we'll see," she added as an afterthought.

While Prue and Olive worked their silent fingers, Eugenia studied herself in the glass. Am I really as beautiful as everyone says? she wondered. I've certainly been catching some admiring glances. Even some from my own husband! The thought made her blush, and her cheeks turned crimson and the color spread to her throat and naked shoulders.

"Lady Nina says ladies should be as tranquil and modest as possible," Lizzie observed. "She says only common folk show emotion."

Paul wandered in at that moment. He stood in the doorway, his hands holding him in place, and he swung back and forth as he watched the activity of the room. He was clearly torn by extreme curiosity as well as an equally potent disgust at the whole silly scene. He balanced himself in the door and advanced no farther.

"Well, Paul, have you come to see how grand ladies prepare for a ball?" Lizzie scarcely gave her brother a glance.

"He's got his 'Oh, girls' expression on again, Mother," she said as she uncorked a vial of perfume, held the stopper to her nose, closed her eyes, and disappeared into some distant realm where she was the center of everyone's enthusiastic attention, where her dress was the loveliest and her beau the most handsome and gallant and brave.

"Girls!" Paul repeated inadvertently, glaring at the room in general. "Girls and parties." The 'girls' of his criticism shared a look of amused indulgence. Jinx affected Lizzie's style, Lizzie took on her mother's, and Eugenia looked at her two very different daughters and felt herself the luckiest woman in the world.

"I've been talking to Lieutenant Brown," Paul declared, it being understood that such a man-to-man talk far outweighed the frittering foolishness going on here. "He's been telling me all about pirates in the South China Sea. We're going there, you know." When that most important information failed to bring a response, Paul continued with a swagger:

"I went down in the hold and helped him inspect those big crates, and everything. You know, the ones that belong to Father."

Paul left off his swinging and stepped into the room; he was irritated by his sisters' superior ways and he glared at them, defying the warning glances they shot back. "You like hearing his stories, too," he insisted.

The room was silent for a moment. Only Prue and Olive, intent on their tasks, were unaware of the impending confrontation. Eugenia couldn't move, pinned, as she was, by their efforts, so she called out gently, "I know you love hearing those stories, Paul, but I think it hurts your father's feelings that you spend so much time with Lieutenant Brown. I think your father would rather tell you stories himself."

"But he's always busy!"

This was the last thing Eugenia wanted to hear. It brought to the fore all her doubts about her marriage, about herself and her efforts to create a family, but they were fleeting fancies and her mind banished them as quickly as it could. Then it chased away the pity she felt for her son and left her with irritation. The emotion seemed irrational, but there it was.

Controlling her voice, trying to be a reasonable and wise mother, Eugenia said, "Yes, dear, I know. But your father has a lot on his mind just now. You mustn't . . ."

She hesitated, unsure how to proceed or what it was exactly that Paul should not be doing. Why am I protecting this man? she thought. Why are we pretending? But those words were buried as quickly as they appeared.

"You mustn't disturb Lieutenant Brown, Paul. He was assigned to our ship by some very important men, and I'm sure he has work to do." That seemed a good way to tidy things up. Eugenia was satisfied. She returned her attention to her dress.

"Oh, that's lovely, Olive!" she said. "You two are certainly the most creative ladies I know. I'll definitely be the belle of the ball tonight."

"He doesn't have to do anything at all, Mother!" Paul was determined to have this out. "Sometimes he just sits down there and watches those big boxes. The ones with Father's machines. That can't be very important work. Watching boxes! And he likes to tell us stories! He's been everywhere; he knows a lot of things Father . . ."

"Don't be impertinent, Paul!" Eugenia's voice was sharp in spite of Prue and Olive, in spite of the cardinal rule of never arguing in front of the servants. "You know your father and I have a very important party to attend tonight. Why don't we discuss this little matter another—"

"You don't understand, Mother!" Paul burst out. "Just because I'm—"

"Paul!" Eugenia spun around, ripped the hem of her dress out of Olive's startled hands, then stopped her tirade on the tip of her tongue. What am I doing? she thought. Why should this matter?

She began again, in a slow, careful voice. It was a sound none of the children liked: It meant no arguing; it meant watch your step; it meant Mother's really mad.

"Your father has asked that you not visit Lieutenant Brown," Eugenia said. "I know you will be a good boy and obey him." Eugenia turned back to Olive and Prue; her hands shook; her lungs felt full enough to burst; she imagined herself running up a hill. There were no trees, no bushes, no birds; the winter wheat had turned yellow; the sky was snow-heavy gray. She was running, stumbling, nearly falling. Her desire to reach the hilltop was astounding.

"Why don't we try this diamond circlet on the ruching," Eugenia told Prue, and that was that.

Paul saw his sisters' self-satisfied expressions. Behind his mother's back he stuck his tongue out at those miserable, craven creatures, but they only looked at each other, shook their heads, and batted their eyelids in female dismay and returned to their ladylike play. Jinx lifted a bracelet from her mother's jewel box and Lizzie sampled another perfume. Paul was forgotten, eliminated, relegated to the ranks of lowest-of-the-low.

Stupid girls, Paul thought. He wanted to run over and pull their silly hair. That would fix them. They always got the best of him, twisted his words around, made him seem like a baby. It just wasn't fair!

Well, he'd show them. He'd sneak off to the hold if he had to.... He'd become a ... what was that word Prue read yesterday? ... desperado ... He'd be a desperado! Paul glowered at the floor, caught between heaven and hell while the preparations for the Governor's Ball continued unimpeded.

The children ran to the rail just as the sun was beginning to set. On the dock below, their parents, Cousin Whitney, the DuPlessis, Lieutenant Brown, and Mr. Beckmann were preparing to leave for the party. There were two carriages waiting: a cabriolet for the two honored guests and a four-in-hand for the others. The horses stamped their shiny hooves on the wooden pier. It was a nice sound; it reminded the children of the stables at home. One horse whinnied and jangled its bridle, then another sneezed and shook the cabriolet. Its leather harness made a creaky sound and it reminded all three children suddenly of Christmas at Linden Lodge and sleigh bells and rides in the snow.

When their mother and father had finally settled themselves, the ball gown tucked under a rug, and their father's tailcoat and top hat neatly in place, Lizzie said, "Father and Mother look just like a fairy prince and princess." Her voice was dreamy; she'd forgotten to be a lady of the world.

"They do," agreed Jinx. She rested her cheek on the rail and gazed at the magnificent spectacle. The rail felt as cool and smooth as gooseberry ice, and Jinx thought about peach ice cream and the kitchens at home, and the pump and the salt and the kitten who once fell into the leftover milk.

"When I grow up, I'm going to have a gun and be like Lieutenant Brown," Paul declared. He hadn't forgotten his sisters' cruelty and he wouldn't be wooed by their smarmy talk. Fairy princesses were stupid. "I'm going to have a uniform, too."

"Oh, hush, Paul, you'll get us in trouble again," Lizzie said crossly, and the little boy was silent, nursing his anger and praying for revenge until a light on the shore caught his eye and he began to imagine pots of buried gold. They were heaped under a musty old oaken board, and only he, Paul, would discover them. And he wouldn't share a thing. He wouldn't even tell!

His sisters' fecklessness was forgotten, and he stayed contentedly at their side. The children swung on the rail together and watched the sky grow red behind the mountains, and the mountains become darker and darker until they were black as ink and lumpy as coal: the most fearsome forest in a fiery sky.

The Governor's Ball in honor of Mr. and Mrs. George Axthelm, Esq., was magnificent. If it was possible to outshine the newly rich of Philadelphia, New York, or Newport, the ball on the island of Madeira that took place on August 10, 1903, did just that. It was as though this small dot of green that lay near the coast of Portugal had decided to create a competition: its nation's antique wealth and history impressing a newer and more prosperous cousin.

Folly, the weathered, regal buildings muttered. *Your upstart ways are folly. Do not overreach yourself. You cannot conquer the world in a day. You must learn from our example.* The brightly lit, wide-open doors and windows creaked and hummed as the island's grandees, officials, foreign aristocracy, and ministers of trade stepped out of a steady line of glossy coaches. From the gravel drive and pebble paths, the rooms sounded like matrons gossiping behind their fans. Dance music rose; dance music drifted away; the insistent words never faltered.

Inside the main house, the ballroom was draped with heavy loops of greenery intertwined with roses. Some of the roses were in bud, some full-petaled and round, and their loose abundance was reflected in an endless array of silver goblets and epergnes, candelabra, and deeply chased ewers. Silver and gilt, silver and gold, candlelight and tumbling flowers. Red and summer-pink, orange and lemon-yellow, and every conceivable shade of green: olive green, forest green, and a tint as pale as falling snow. The colors rose to the rafters, raced toward the gods and goddesses carved there in fabulous disarray, then flung down into every crevice of every arched and welcoming door.

There were cellos in the wind and violins, and from some interior sitting room, the sound of a mandolin. There were canopies of palm fronds and fiddle leaf fig, sconces shaded in velvet and mother-of-pearl, bull's-eye glass mirrors with frames as curlicued as cathedral spires, and a row of looking glasses that stretched the length of one entire wall. Back and forth, a hundred times, a thousand, the room repeated itself: lace and satin and taffeta and tulle; mauve, cerise, celadon, and ivory; diamond stud pins and gray baroque pearls; powdered cheeks, pomaded hair, and layers and layers of lacquered curls. It was as if everyone of any importance in the world were in this one place, as if they'd all convened here, at this moment, to dance before the Americans.

"Beautiful," Eugenia murmured. "It is beautiful." She sat at a table near the dance floor and looked across the room to her cousin Whitney. He was with the Jeffries family, and although Eugenia could see him force his attention on the ambassador's story and nod in accommodating agreement, Eugenia knew it was the young Lady Marina that her cousin sought to impress.

And she is a pretty girl, Eugenia reflected. So nice the family was along for the ride up the mountain. That was where this all started. On the way to the village of Chopina. Eugenia wished she could hear what they were saying. The ambassador shook his head as he spoke; he looked serious and thoughtful, and his wife tilted her neck slightly in conjugal concurrence. Then Whitney smiled in a glazed and foolish way and tried to send covert glances through a barricade of parental propriety to the Lady Marina, his newfound love. Eugenia closed her eyes and listened to the music.

What's the harm of Whitney having a romantic interest in Madeira? she wondered. It wouldn't be a bad place for him to end up. After all, anything's better than Philadelphia. The only thing that holds us back is our own lack of imagination.

Marcus Aurelius, she remembered suddenly, Father's Latin quotations! How did they go? Eugenia opened her eyes and stared at a chandelier. I should certainly remember those "Meditations," she told herself. I heard them nearly every day of my life:

"Either you go on living here" ... What was the exact translation? ... "Either you go on living here, to which custom has sufficiently seasoned you by now; or you move elsewhere, which you do of your own free election; or you die ..."

Eugenia smiled. Something as succinct as that! "Which you do of your own free election."

Eugenia looked at Whit's bravado and the girl's shy glances and her smile grew broader. And why not? she considered. Why not? The Jeffries family is attractive, well-connected; the ambassador, intelligent. After all, he paid me enormous attention on our little excursion, didn't he? That surely proves his worth!

"A pleasant party, Mrs. Axthelm." Eugenia hadn't realized there was anyone near her; she'd forgotten for a moment that she was even visible. Her shoulders jumped as she dropped back to earth.

"Oh, Lieutenant Brown!" she gasped. "You startled me." Her face turned pink, and she stared at the floor in dismay. How awful, Eugenia thought, I might as well be back in Miss Hall's School for young ladies. Eugenia clasped her long gloves together, and stared at her fingertips.

"I seem to have caught you with some guilty secrets, Mrs. Axthelm." Brown sounded quite different all of a sudden; he sounded controlled, mature, a handsome gentleman at a dance, and Eugenia looked up, wondering if the change was visible. Perhaps it's his dress uniform, she told herself, or the room, or then again, perhaps it's only my imagination.

"Nothing of the kind!" Eugenia tried to retrieve her bantering air. "I was just lost in some serious daydreams about a possible match between Marina Jeffries and my cousin. You see how we dowagers spend our time!"

Eugenia forced herself to look away from Brown's clear blue eyes and easy smile. A dowager, Eugenia thought, is that how I picture myself?

"And then, I didn't know I was being observed. I thought I was alone, in my little corner. Finally sitting out one dance." Eugenia didn't dare glance at Brown's face again; she gazed across the room as if it were the most fascinating place on earth.

"Well, I won't pry, Mrs. Axthelm," Brown said quietly. But he didn't walk away.

"Lovely party, isn't it?" Eugenia finally managed. "I hope you're not having too dull a time. We should have found you a young lady like Whitney's." After that, neither of them spoke. The music continued and the party continued while Brown cursed his dress uniform, his white gloves, and the voice or the instinct that had dragged him across the ballroom, and Eugenia repeated: Dowager, matron, is that how I see myself? Is that what I am? Her ball gown seemed too tight, her shoulders too bare and the amount of jewelry dripping from her throat, ears, arms, and hands felt heavy enough to sink a ship.

" 'Which you do of your own free election . . .' " Eugenia murmured without thinking.

"Ma'am?" Brown burst in, glad for conversation again, glad for any sound—no matter how incomprehensible.

"Yes, Lieutenant?" Eugenia answered in an equal rush; she had no idea she'd spoken aloud. She looked up in confusion, pasted on a smile, and decided she felt as awkward as she had in all her born days.

"You were saying?" Lieutenant Brown asked; he couldn't tell if Eugenia was making fun of him or not, but words were better than silence.

"I was saying?" Eugenia repeated. Worse and worse and worse, she told herself.

"Elections?" Brown prompted. "You said something about a free election." He knew he was in over his head. He didn't understand politics at all. With a casualness he didn't feel, Lieutenant Brown rested his white-gloved hands on the back of a chair, while Eugenia simultaneously babbled:

"I must have been talking in my sleep again." But that effort was more gruesome than imaginable, and Eugenia desperately tried to right herself. "Something we all do, I suppose . . . or talk without thinking, I should have said . . .

"Actually, it was Marcus Aurelius I was thinking about," Eugenia corrected, but that sentence turned as inconsequential as dust. I might as well be discussing lady's hairstyles, she thought, or peony beds, or how to train a new upstairs maid.

"He was a stoic. . . . A Roman emperor, I think. Or a general . . ." The little speech began to falter; in Eugenia's ears it became didactic, prissy, and as plain as a post.

". . . Or maybe all three . . . I forget . . . Anyway, it's just an old saying my father liked to repeat . . .

". . . . It's not worth consideration . . . Lieutenant . . ." Eugenia stopped her recitation and forced another smile. Safe ground at last, she told herself. Thank God! Oh, thank God! Charming wife, good mother, pleasant hostess, grateful guest. Eugenia tossed back her head and said with the warmest voice she owned:

"But, Lieutenant, did you come to do your 'duty dance'? Because if you did, I am simply dying for a dance."

"No, ma'am, I came to ask if you would do me the great honor of giving me this dance" was what Brown answered, and his tone was so quiet and so heartfelt that Eugenia was at a complete loss. There was no answer that wasn't flippant, and no words with any meaning. Then the room disappeared and the orchestra disappeared and the night air lost its wind.

• • •

George didn't notice his wife's discomfort; he only saw that Lieutenant Brown had marched across the room and asked her to dance. Good, George told himself, the lad's got manners, no matter what Beckmann says. And, after all, "Manners maketh the man."

George returned to his conversation with the governor. "You were asking me, I believe, sir, about my father's feelings on the Hay-Buneau-Varilla Treaty? As you know, Secretary of State Hay is a close friend of the family. In fact, it was Secretary Hay who—" George stopped himself. No point letting that cat out of the bag, he thought.

In the momentary, but awkward, lull, George, the Governor, and Ogden Beckmann moved closer to the punch table. George thought the enormous monteith was one of the most magnificent things he'd ever seen. It looked like a miniature castle keep worked in silver, all crenellated walls and spirals. He made a mental note to try to order one like it.

"Yes. Secretary Hay. A most interesting dilemma, that treaty," the governor answered. "Before your fortuitous arrival, Mr. Axthelm, we, these gentlemen and I"—the governor indicated a small and somber group of men standing nearby—"had been discussing this problem of the chargé d'affaires from Colombia."

"Ah, yes, the chargé d'affaires . . ." George repeated. He tried to remember where he'd heard that title before. "Mmm, yes . . ." he said, buying time.

Ogden Beckmann, who stood between George and the governor, had lost interest in the conversation's slow and painful progress. The United States Congress and the treaty with Colombia and the chargé d'affaires; it seemed a ridiculous discussion for a backwater place like Madeira. Portugal's days of greatness were over and done. It was nothing but a sleepy little country full of superstitious fishermen. What the United States did in South America and Panama was of no concern to Portugal. It could never profit by using the proposed canal.

Beckmann's eyes followed Eugenia and Brown as they waltzed across the room. George might not have noticed his wife's face as she got up to dance, but Beckmann had. It had filled him with fury, like a surprise blow to the gut, and he'd had to force himself to remain where he was. In his mind he saw himself stride across the dance floor and punch the damned fellow in his square, honest jaw. But Beckmann was nothing if not a man of restraint, so he watched Eugenia's dancing grow less and less constrained as he began to plan his attack. Yes, he told himself. Yes. Yes, indeed. That might do nicely. That might be just the thing I need.

George was laughing heartily by then; he was back where he belonged. Politics were not his forte; he was better with a quip or an ir-reverent anecdote.

"Oh, I don't think Father's got any quibbles with the two hundred fifty thousand dollars per . . ." George chortled. ". . . It's the ten mil-lion that got his goat. What did he say, Ogden? You were there during that famous . . . I should say infamous . . . tirade. . . . Morgan was there, too . . . you know. . . ." George turned to Beckmann.

"I really do not remember, George," Beckmann said coldly, "I have never known your father to say anything ill-advised."

George ignored the warning. "Ill-advised!" he guffawed. "To that pirate, Morgan? Now there's a five-dollar word for you! 'Ill-advised.' I'll remember that one! . . .

"Anyway, Governor, it was something about: 'that bunch of spics aren't worth ten million.' . . . Don't know how he thought we'd get the province down there otherwise. . . . Force, I guess. Wouldn't you say, Ogden?" George smiled briefly at the stony Beckmann, then returned to the governor.

Just think of it, George thought. Little Georgie Axthelm . . . kow-towed to like royalty! Everything I do or say approved of and admired. And on top of it, being able to nettle Beckmann so easily! George handed his punch glass to the waiter hovering at his side.

"This time, lad, make sure there's some 'punch' to it!" He laughed loudly at his own joke. "Punnnch!" he said, drawing out the word to indicate just how far his wit could travel.

"I believe, George," Beckmann said in an icy voice, "the kind of phrase you're drawn to could have an unfortunate effect here. Madeira, when I last heard, was still part of Portugal."

"Punnnch?" George asked. "What's wrong with saying 'punnnch'? "Oh, you mean . . . 'spics'!" George shook his head to indicate how foolish anyone would be to take offense, then he grabbed his refilled glass and drained it down in one gulp. "We were talking about Panama and Colombia . . . not Portugal."

"Yes, George, I understood. But when you refer to a nationality . . ." Beckmann seethed. To think all the Turk's efforts could be undone by one drunken sot. If he could have plunged a knife in George's foppish heart, he would gladly have done so.

George cut off Beckmann's reprimand. "What do you say to that, Governor? Beckmann, here, thinks we're talking about building a canal through the streets of Lisbon or Madrid or someplace." As he laughed heartily again, George's whole body seemed to swell with pride; his fat diamond studs twinkled and his shiny face and hair glistened. He looked as sleek as a well-fed beaver surveying its own sunny lake.

The governor smiled politely at both Beckmann and George and made a necessary decision. "It looks to me as though that glass has a leak in it, George," he said. "I may call you George?"

The governor motioned to the waiter and indicated that the glass must never go empty again. It was his political responsibility to anticipate the needs and desires of his illustrious guests and, surely, the son of the great Martin Axthelm of Philadelphia should take precedence over all others.

"No, indeed, George," the governor continued smoothly, "as you so cleverly put it, you are not building a canal through Lisboa! And, if I may add, whatever Martin Axthelm decides . . . I need say no more, surely . . . Panama is no concern of ours. . . ."

This wasn't the only political talk in the room. The Portuguese grandees, the Englishmen, and the Frenchmen whose social and financial affairs rested on the goodwill of America carefully watched George and Eugenia and rated them accordingly. Their varying needs of Americans and of Axthelm dollars in particular dictated the verdict. The Catholic grandees and their ladies were apt to be cool, the women decidedly so, but some of the men, watching the effervescent Eugenia, became increasingly forgiving.

Besides, families and fortunes stuck on the tiny islands that made up Madeira had no desire to appear uninformed. The shifting alliances of countries greater than their own were a matter of grave importance. One man—one family, one group—sought to best his neighbor in discussions of Manila, or the blockade of the Venezuelan ports, or Cuba's agreement to release Guantánamo and Bahía Honda to the United States Navy (and Presidente "Roosse-felt"), or the ramifications of Anglo-French *entente cordiale,* or just what imperial Germany (and Count Bernhard von Bülow) might mean by the term *weltmacht*—or world power.

But if those men (and their ever-fickle fortunes) were needy enough, they agreed (with all due humility) on the immeasurable charm of the brash Americans whose arrival had caused such consternation.

"Señora Axthelm," they said, "Señora Axthelm is the feather in her husband's cap."

While the women, in their distant corners, hissed behind painted fans, "It is not à la mode."

"Bare shoulders!" one wailed, then "Bare shoulders!" became the group's rallying cry.

Eugenia had decided not to follow the current fashion set by King Edward VII's consort, Queen Alexandra. The queen had a scar running across her neck, so she favored high-necked dresses set off with a triple-strand choker of diamonds or pearls, and after the enormous celebrations (culminating in the great durbar at Delhi on January the first of that year) that had transformed her husband from lowly Prince of Wales to "king-emperor" and protector of the vast British Empire, the new queen's preference had been adopted worldwide. The dowdy, stay-at-home fashions of Queen Victoria's time that had fought, tooth and claw, against the wanton "Edwardian" styles worn by her son's many mistresses had been supplanted by regal reticence. Bare shoulders were a thing of the past.

But Eugenia did not have a scar on her neck and she'd chosen to show off her neck and bosom in a lavish nest of lilac satin, and this, the ladies of Funchal could not, would not, forgive. As well as the outlandish and inappropriate display of wealth evinced by the huge yacht's arrival! ("American excess," they muttered again.)

But the ladies were only the ladies, after all. They didn't decide the fate of the world; they had almost no knowledge of it. Gauging the high winds of politics was a thing only men understood. So the ladies retreated to angry glances at the interlopers while their husbands prepared to keep watch.

"Martin Axthelm . . ." the men echoed.

"The Bank of . . ."

"The yacht . . ."

And: "Did you know there are gold . . . ?"

"You don't say! Gold! In all the washrooms? Really!" Then the men nodded at George across the room and were flattered, even elevated in their companions' eyes, by his slightest and most flimsy response.

"And what year was it that you graduated from the Naval Academy?" Eugenia asked as she and Brown whirled by the long wall of mirrors. "I know you told us at dinner that one time . . . but I'm so bad at dates. . . ." Eugenia had thought this conversation would be as easy, but she still felt tongue-tied and inept.

". . . Anyway, it's good of our Navy to give you leave to escort us." She wished her partner would answer. She felt his arm around her waist and his hand guiding their steps, and she tried, and failed, and tried again to ignore that pressure. "Always look at the gentleman with whom you are dancing, Eugenia," her grandmother had warned, but Lieutenant Brown was holding her too close. And she didn't want to pull away.

"I hope . . . I hope you're happy with us." Eugenia leaned back just enough to look up into his face. "On our ship. Yacht, I should say. Or is there another . . . term . . . ?

"No . . . yacht will do fine," Lieutenant Brown said. "And yes, I'm very happy," he wanted to add, but couldn't. Instead he pressed his hand to the small of her back and led her through the crowd.

Marina Jeffries was waltzing with Whitney. Her quick and innocent smile was matched by his bashfulness. He felt clumsy as a heifer. And, hang it; he couldn't think of a clever thing to say. He stepped on his own feet and then on her toes and, at one awful moment, came down full weight on a corner of her train, threatening to send them both crashing to the floor. But she was sweet, and he felt, in spite of his hopeless inarticulateness and boorish behavior, that he was somehow manly and strong.

While Lady Marina danced with young Mr. Caldwell—". . . such a well-brought-up young gentleman," Lady Jeffries had noted pointedly to her husband—Mrs. DuPlessis shifted wheezily in her chair and regaled the ambassador and his wife with the lurid tales she and her sister had spent a lifetime collecting.

No story, from the lesson of a schoolboy nearly whipped to death for stealing a penny, to the grisly details of her sister's gangrenous toe, to the ladies' present aches and pains and their varied and tortuous remedies, had gone unchronicled. Each was a catalog of grim despair: "From which we must heed a warning, my dear. From which we must heed the knell. . . ."

Now Mrs. DuPlessis was preparing to launch into her current favorite topic: ". . . the cannibals of the South Sea Islands. A most interesting account! Written by a man named Ranie or Rennie or some such. Scottish, you understand. . . ." Her lowered voice and the insinuating emphasis on the poor writer's origins damned both him and his country.

"But in spite of his probable lack of education, my dear Lady Jeffries, it's such a stirring account! I mean, they actually cut off the unfortunate victim's head and *impale* it, gore and all, on the bowsprit of the canoe! And this was a woman, my dear! A woman's blood sanctifying the birth of a war canoe!"

"Well, perhaps, Mrs. DuPlessis," Sir Randall remarked sleepily, "that's where we get our term, *masthead*."

"Oh, Sir Randall. That is too, too awful." But Mrs. DuPlessis didn't gasp with dismay; she giggled, rapped his wrist with her fan, and said, "Really, Your Lordship, you are much, much too naughty!"

Then she leapt from her chair with such surprising speed that the chair nearly toppled backward. Both Sir Randall and Lady Jeffries pulled away in reflexive horror.

"Oh, goodness!" Mrs. DuPlessis gasped in annoyance. "There's my Gustav waylaid by another miserable little bookish type! He'll be there all night, discussing some paltry scientific scheme. And glasses, too!" Mrs. DuPlessis moaned. "The man's actually wearing glasses and not pince-nez. To a formal party like this! I must go shake Gustav loose at once. You'll excuse me, of course." Mrs. DuPlessis hardly bothered to turn around.

"So pleasant chatting with you and hearing all your exciting tales," she called as she hurried off in pursuit of her wayward husband.

"Hearing tales?" Sir Randall said laconically. "I should have said it was the other way round." And Lady Jeffries quietly smiled.

"I suppose it's not what you're used to, our little vessel." Eugenia rushed ahead with this new train of thought. The yacht! A safe subject for conversation at last! Her shoulders and neck were warm and pink with the speed of the dance. A polonaise had been followed by a polka-mazurka before the room had settled into the more sedate rhythm of a waltz. She'd told herself over and over that she should seek another partner, but she couldn't tear herself away somehow. She thought they could both go on dancing all night.

"But do you find it has, what's the term, a good helm? Isn't that nautical?" Eugenia laughed, and the nervousness of the sound nearly gave her away.

"Excellent, Mrs. Axthelm." Lieutenant Brown smiled down at her. What are we talking about? he wondered. Ships? Life at sea? Something neither of us cares about?

"And yes, or rather, no. No, she's not what I've been used to," Brown said. "Your *Alcedo,* I mean. I've never . . ."

There was nothing else to add. Eugenia felt like a bird in his hand; one moment she was gone, the next she was back settling into his fingers.

"Well, I do think, Lieutenant," Eugenia said, "that you and I will have to stay dancing partners forever. We certainly outshine everyone in the room." Her words seemed so bold, she couldn't believe she'd said them. Oh, I am damned forever, Eugenia thought, surely and irrevocably consigned to waste in hell.

She stared into the bristly blue of his jacket and suddenly imagined laying her cheek there. How rough the coat would feel and how warm. It smelled of tobacco and eau de cologne and something bitter but surprisingly pleasant. "Let's dance all night," she said. "Out into the moonlight and away across the lawn! Do you know, Lieutenant, dancing is my absolutely favorite thing!"

"I don't think its right, Gustav. Three dances is too much. It isn't seemly. Especially in that dress." Mrs. DuPlessis's words were muted but vehement. "Bare shoulders indeed!"

"Well, my dear," Dr. DuPlessis began while he tried to edge his way onto the ballroom floor. Dancing with his wife was never easy; even a deserted room would provide too many obstacles. "Isn't it the latest—?"

"Fashion indeed!" Mrs. DuPlessis spit. Out of habit, she finished her husband's sentences for him. "No, it is not! I am not disporting myself half-naked and I'm fashionably turned out."

Dr. DuPlessis smiled at his wife's fierce assumption. Her one great vanity was still her figure. She rigorously followed the advice of *Mrs. Godey's Lady's Book* or its current incarnation and then found dressmakers who'd adapt the latest styles. Mrs. DuPlessis would never (perish the thought) admit she was fat. Corsets were invented for the likes of Mrs. DuPlessis.

"You are, my dear. You always are." Dr. DuPlessis maneuvered his wife through the jostling bodies. He'd always protected his wife's vanity, even if some of her sartorial efforts made him uneasy. But what were a few extra flounces or a tight bodice when the intentions were good?

"A lovely—" he began, hoping to draw his wife's attention away from her preoccupation with Eugenia's behavior.

"I do not want to talk about the evening, Gustav. You know perfectly well I don't. Now you know what you must do. You must go over there immediately and cut in. I can't bear to think of poor Mr. A. . . .'"

"Oh, my dear, I don't think it's my—"

"Of course it's your place, Gustav. Anyway, I insist upon it."

"But, my dear Jane, if Mr. Axthelm felt—"

"No, he wouldn't, Gustav. He'd do just what he's doing. Pretending not to notice. Behaving like a gentleman. Carrying on with his conversation."

"But he seems—"

"Well, he isn't content. I'm sure he feels mortified."

"But, I couldn't presume—"

"Gustav! You know I'm always right in these matters. You do remember, I'm sure, that my dear sister is a renowned psychic. And I myself have often been lauded for my second sight!"

Dr. DuPlessis sighed. That was his wife's favorite argument, her family's predilection for divining the future and unmasking the torment in another's soul. It also meant that Jane DuPlessis had made up her mind. "And what would you like me to do, my dear?" he said.

"Well, cut in, cut in, of course. Goodness, Gustav, how dense you men can be."

Ogden Beckmann had also kept count. But that's exactly what I want, he tried to tell himself, exactly what I'd planned. What do I care? This means nothing. Let her have her little fling. She'll be mine in the end. Tonight doesn't matter.

Beckmann brought himself back to the conversation around him. He forced himself to concentrate, forced himself to forget Eugenia, forget Brown. I control them all, he reasoned. I'm the one who calls the shots. The phrase made Beckmann smile suddenly; he liked puns, and especially unintentional ones. His smiled grew broader and he turned a bemused ear to a small man standing at his side:

"... la compagnie de Monsieur Ford en Deerborn ... Monsieur Morgan et la compagnie Mercantile Marine Internationale ... ?"

Beckmann recognized the names Ford and Morgan, Deerborn and Mercantile Marine, and he felt his back go up like a cat in a corner. The reaction was reflexive; Beckmann didn't stop to wonder whether he was being pumped for information or whether the questions were merely idle island gossip.

The names had brought Beckmann a brief whiff of danger; they'd dragged him away from the autonomous safety of his ocean-going kingdom. Ford and Morgan were reminders of the Turk's presence, and the Turk shoved Beckmann back into place.

"I'm not at liberty to say, gentlemen," Beckmann answered brusquely. "Mr. Axthelm may have had some dealings with Mr. Morgan as far as the Mercantile Marine is concerned, but I wouldn't have that information. And as for the Ford automotive factory at Deerborn, your guess is as good as mine. Though I believe the initial investment was a mere three thousand dollars—American."

Then Beckmann decided to change his tactics. Tit for tat, he told himself. You take what you want. Let the devil take the rest. And, who can tell, these idiots may know something I don't.

"Perhaps though, gentlemen," he began, "you could enlighten me on this new Krupp business in Germany." Beckmann waited while a ripple of muddled translation raced through the group. A Frenchman spoke to a Swede, who asked a Russian, who turned to an Italian, who then questioned a Hungarian. French was the unifying tongue, the language of diplomats and therefore of businessmen, but the varying accents made the words as unintelligible as the builders' shouts in Babel.

"Allemagne! Von Bülow! Admiral Tirpitz!" Beckmann shouted, and wished he could add: "Don't play dumb with me!" But language failed him and he was reduced to shouting names alone: "Krupp. Essen. Munition works. . . ." Beckmann's voice rose and his throat went tight. He looked toward the mirrored wall, saw Eugenia and Brown reflected there, and dragged his eyes away. This isn't how the great Turk would behave, a voice in Beckmann's brain warned, he has self-control; he's strong; he's better than you. But Beckmann hated criticism and he hated the oily voice that whispered in his own head. He shut it off by making his own words louder.

"Friedrich Alfred Krupp!" he snarled. "In Essen . . . forty thousand goddamn workers housed in a goddamned 'model of proletarian living' . . . You can't tell me it's possible to build an entire city of workers that the rest of the world pretends isn't there!"

"Kiel . . . Germania . . . 'sheepyard' . . . ?" One frightened Frenchman finally gathered the courage to ask, but Beckmann yelped, "Not the shipyards, you idiot. I don't care two figs about the shipyards! I want to know what the Krupp family's up to with those fancy new buildings in Essen."

The downcast eyes and bovine stares that greeted the question made Beckmann nearly implode with rage. He wanted to get away from Madeira, off the yacht, and out of the Turk's wily grasp. He wanted to be somewhere else and any other person in the world. You stupid, foolish, fops, Beckmann raged. I hope Krupp's cannons blow you all to kingdom come.

While Beckmann dealt with the business interests of the island, and its political gossipmongers and muckrakers, George was surrounded by a more genteel but equally curious crowd. He tried to concentrate on their polite questions (they seemed stuck on Roosevelt's 'trustbusting' campaign) as he watched his wife spin effortlessly throughout the long room.

He had a lovely, floating sense of well-being brought on by an excess of alcohol and flattery. The aristocratic accents around him seemed charming; his wife was dazzling, his ship one of the world's great wonders, and he himself born to rule.

". . . the Expedition Act, Mr. Axthelm . . . How can you explain President Roosevelt's position in regard to . . . ?"

". . . and this problem with the coal miners . . . the Anthracite Coal Commission . . . ?"

"Because, really, sir, if we allow the workers to have a say in . . ."

"I quite agree, gentlemen. I quite agree. Couldn't be more in agreement." Social and political convictions created an instant bond. George unwittingly copied his father. "After all, we are not socialists here," he said, and his words drew forth the soft, sated laughter of inherited wealth.

Three dances, George thought lazily, why, Genie's danced with the same fellow three times in a row. In his syrupy brain, the revelation brought a conflicting muddle of emotions. First was jealousy—his wife seemed to be having a bang-up time. Second came pride—why, everyone wanted to be with Genie—he must be the most envied man in the room. And finally there appeared the all-protective, sugar-coated voice of reason:

Genie shouldn't be "stuck" with some "antique type" doing a "duty dance," it said. He and his wife weren't newlyweds. He didn't like to dance and she did. He'd never wanted her to be a wallflower. On and on; the excuses could have lasted all night. George returned to the futile conversation around him.

The ball continued. Some dancers stopped to eat and clustered together at the long buffet tables, choosing between supper or breakfast foods as they filled gold-painted plates. Some dancers lingered at tables on their way from the floor; they greeted friends and acquaintances with equal enthusiasm, the men nodding sleepily as the women grouped themselves in the bright plumage of self-admiration and pride. Older couples received younger couples; the entrenched condescended (if only briefly) to the less fortunate: while the really important people, the state officials, demiroyalty, the ranking men of the town, drew an anxious crowd wherever they went. And they moved constantly. They strode across the room, appeared to hesitate, and then hurried on again as if there weren't enough attention or flattery to be found in any one place.

The Lady Marina danced with Whitney, who grew less bashful and began to be the man of his imagination. He stopped stepping on his partner's feet; he stopped counting each dance's measure before leaping in at the middle; he stopped holding the young lady stiffly at a distance, because as he looked down at her pretty, smiling face he saw only admiration there. The manly, self-possessed lover, the sophisticated boulevardier: Those images were his inspiration and slowly that is what Whit became.

Mrs. DuPlessis continued her various tirades; her audiences shifted and murmured excuses, but she plowed on undeterred while her husband drifted off to seek the "bookish" conversations that caused her so much pain. Of course, that was well after the doctor had cut in on Eugenia and Brown. And after Eugenia had smiled and said, "What an unexpected pleasure."

She'd placed her hand in Dr. DuPlessis's, appeared utterly grateful, and whispered, "For the sake of propriety . . . I am thirty-two, after all . . . But then I don't suppose the young man feels as comfortable as we do here . . ." Eugenia nearly convinced herself.

But then that dance had led to one with Ogden Beckmann. And that had been too awful to consider. Eugenia had closed her heart and mind and soul to memory. She moved in Beckmann's arms as if she'd left her body behind and gone visiting elsewhere. She couldn't have said if he'd spoken or not; she heard every word around their dance but his:

"Mr. Morgan . . ."

"Lord Delamere . . ."

". . . King Edward . . ."

". . . the Congo Free State . . . the Baghdad Railway . . . Imperial Germany certainly had her hands full that time. . . ."

". . . German East Africa . . . British East Africa . . . King Leopold . . . and the Congo scandal . . ."

Finally the hated dance was over, and Eugenia quietly returned home; she didn't question her whereabouts; she didn't even think. She just came in and pulled the key from the door.

Then she turned her smile on bright, put her hand on another partner's shoulder, and began all over again. The piano played a solo; the violins kept time; the timpani moved forward; Eugenia danced with one muzzy face after another.

"Manchuria . . . the Russian position . . . Isn't it true that your Secretary Hay is going to force . . . ?" The scent of stale salmon mousse breathed across her neck. Eugenia beamed.

"Don't you agree, Mrs. Axthelm . . . ?" Someone's sweaty palm grasped her back and Eugenia shifted course instantly. ". . . this preoccupation with Macedonia . . . ?"

". . . at the durbar, I was told . . . the report mentioned several thousand . . . No wonder they rioted . . ." This one smelled of cigar smoke; Eugenia saw imaginary clouds of gray rising from his shoulders. She touched an ashy buttonhole and was met with a simpering shrug.

". . . and Plekhanov . . . it is Plekhanov, surely, not Trotsky or Lenin . . . you know, at that little 'do' they're having in London . . . the 'Social Democratic Workers' or whatever they call themselves. . . . Mensheviks against Bolsheviks . . . Your husband believes . . . and rightly so! Bloody cheek, if you ask me! Bloody cheek to think a piddling bunch of serfs should tell us how to run the world . . . !"

Perhaps two or three times Eugenia was aware of a word she'd heard before: a name from the Turk's drawing room, a place discussed in an undertone, and she found herself paying attention as if deciphering a secret code. She had a sensation like fear, but it quickly vanished, washed aside by other phrases.

"Manila, I hear . . . the Moros and that leader of theirs—Aguinaldo . . ."; "Lord Landsdowne . . ."; "General Luther von Trotha . . ."; ". . . the Gulf of Persia . . ."; ". . . the Czar . . ."; "Mr. Axthelm, your father in law, that is . . . the Republic of Panama . . ."

The words tumbled on to the rhythm of a polonaise, a rondo, a waltz. Eugenia caught Brown's eyes on her and glanced away; she brushed his jacket sleeve inadvertently and drew back; she saw his straight open brow and redoubled her efforts with the men at her side.

No, Eugenia, she told herself. It is the night; it is the warmth of the room. It is anything I can name, but it's not for me.

George had had enough. He'd watched his pretty little wife dancing with every other man at the party, and he was getting hopping mad. The only problem was what to do. There were a number of possibilities, he reminded himself as he prowled the edge of the party, paying little or no attention to his surroundings, the question was which one to choose.

I can't very well walk over and cut in, George reasoned. That would look terrible. And I can't stand on the sidelines like some heartsick antelope. George glowered and moved on.

There was something in the way his wife glittered that made him uneasy; he was afraid to approach her—as if she'd become someone else. He watched the transformation with fascination; he was drawn to her, but knew he'd never measure up. He felt insignificant and foolish, so he shambled into the banquet table, bumped against ladies holding dishes of cakes, lurched into waiters carrying champagne in crystal goblets.

"S'cuse me . . ." he mumbled. "S'cuse me . . . s'cuse me." He grabbed one glass after another and marched on.

Ogden Beckmann was aware of George's progress and so, increasingly, was the governor. That excellent host covered his concern with an extravagant smile as he motioned to two aides to keep a look-out for their illustrious guest. Beckmann's response was the thinnest of smiles.

George wobbled farther and farther afield. If only for propriety's sake, he muttered silently. I mean, Genie should want to dance with me. . . . It looks better for a wife to be . . .

Damn, George told himself suddenly, I can't remember anything anymore. What was that word? . . . Attentive! That's it! . . . She should seem more attentive. After all, I'm the most important man here. . . . We should be together . . . Genie's hand on my arm, gazing up. . . . George frowned; even the thoughts were painful to form. I'm not jealous, he told himself. Certainly not! . . . Decidedly not. No sirree.

"Not jealous!" he hissed through his teeth.

"Pardon, sir?" said the waiter guarding the punch bowl. A fresh batch of amber-pink liquid, fresh and compellingly icy, swirled within its merry sides.

"Sir?" the waiter repeated.

"Punnnch," George said. "Punnnnch, goddammit! Don't you know who I am?"

Eugenia stood talking to a man whose name she hadn't quite heard, discussing world affairs she couldn't really follow, so when George rushed over, throwing his arm around her shoulder, she felt at a terrible disadvantage. Foremost in her thoughts was the impossibility of a proper introduction and then, to make matters worse, there was her husband's clumsy and far too public and intimate embrace. Eugenia stared at the plate of tea sandwiches she'd been handed; they tottered in her hand and the awkward moment seemed to last forever.

"Where you been, Genie? Didn't see you out . . . Didn't . . ." The words collapsed into each other and George looked startled, as if he were watching them fall. He opened his mouth wide, popping his eyes in surprise. "Lovely party . . ." he finally managed.

And Eugenia knew that not only was George drunk, but that his mood had shifted momentously, that it blew from a southern and dangerous climate: a hurricane, a tornado, a typhoon. Damn him, Eugenia thought. Damn him to eternal hell.

She put down the plate of tea sandwiches, concentrating on the task as if it were the most important one in the world.

"Well, George, here I am," she said. "You found me at last." Then she smiled and slid out of her husband's grasp, hoping the words sounded like an old and charming game.

"Mr. . . . ah . . . Mr. . . ."—Eugenia mumbled an attempt at a name—"and I were just talking about Lord Delamere's most interesting new experiment in . . . in . . ."

Eugenia paused; she hadn't understood a word. "But here you are,

George! And just in time!" she added brightly, her words as glittery as glass Christmas balls. "This is much more in your league! You did say Delamere?" She turned back to her nameless companion. "And British East Africa?"

But George was in no mood for pleasantries. "You gonna introduce me to your little friend, Genie?" he mumbled. "George Axthelm, Philadelphia."

George grabbed the man's hand and pumped it up and down. "Lovely party . . ." he said, then trailed off, blinking across the bright and spinning room.

"British East Africa?" he mumbled finally. ". . . That what you said? . . . Old B.E.A? We're headed in that direction . . . Genie tell you? . . . Little shooting . . . black buck and . . ."

"Glad to meet you again, sir." The other man came to the rescue, "We only just passed in the receiving line. Ships in the night . . . as they say. . . ." The man tried to laugh. "I'm William Townsend—"

"William! Will! You don't say! My oldest . . . dearest friend! How are you, Willy?" George bellowed out affection. "Genie, this is Will, my best, my oldest . . . School was it? . . . Princeton? . . ." George peered at Townsend as he tried to place the smooth, pink face. "Coming on to Kenya with us, are you, old boy? . . ."

"I've already met Mr. Townsend, George," Eugenia said. Her words were as firm as she dared; they had only the slightest hint of warning.

"I've been talking to Mr. Townsend for the past several minutes. And, no, I don't believe he'll be joining our little excursion." Why tonight, Eugenia thought. Why now? Everything was going so well. Why did this have to happen? Eugenia raised her eyes but saw only Ogden Beckmann standing close by, watching.

"Once to every man and nation . . ." she thought, then tried to eliminate the hymn from her mind. A lot of good that's done me, she argued. "New occasions teach new duties." . . . "And the choice goes by forever." . . . What absolute rot, she decided.

"We're going off on safari, Mr. Townsend," Eugenia said with her best party smile, "as you must have gathered from my husband's remarks. So this discussion of Lord Delamere is extremely . . ."

"Who?" George interrupted. "Who d'ya say?" He'd seen his wife glance at Beckmann and he'd seen some sort of signal pass between them, and he wasn't about to allow any secrets here. No sirree. They weren't going to hog-tie him! Not on your life.

"What's Delamere got to do with Father and the business in Borneo?" George demanded.

"I don't believe we were discussing your father, George." Eugenia tried to keep her voice pleasant. "Or Borneo."

George wasn't paying attention to his wife, however. He was thinking about his father, then Beckmann, then Brown. Brown and Beckmann and the old man at home. No sir, George promised himself, they're not going to hog-tie me.

"I saw you with Mr. Townsend, Genie . . ." George began his attack, ". . . and I saw you with Brown—and with Beckmann." He leered at her, then pointed to his head and grinned at Townsend, croaking in a lugubrious stage whisper, "I know everything there is to know! Don't think I don't."

The comedic act grew spiteful. Despair, rejection and grief spilled out in George's words.

"Don't think I don't, Genie," he said. "Don't think I'll stand idly back while some . . . some lightweight . . . some ne'er-do-well . . . There are secrets here, Genie . . . things you'll never understand. . . ."

Suddenly George rounded on Townsend, throwing an arm over the startled man's shoulder. "The little ladies . . . eh, Willy, old man? God bless 'em. That's what I say.

"And look at this one, will you?" George squeezed his wife's arm. "Great little gal. . . . Eyes? Shoot daggers straight through you, if you're not careful! . . . And knows her own mind . . . I'll say! . . . You married, Willy?"

"No, sir. I haven't had the pleasure yet." Townsend watched George drag Eugenia back and forth in a shambling embrace. The firm of Dalcott and Lustrow would be proud of him, he knew. Here he was a junior officer engaged in the most informal of conversations with Mr. George Axthelm of Philadelphia! Old man Dalcott would give him a special commendation, Townsend was sure of that.

"Not married, Willy? . . . No? . . . That's too bad. . . ." George continued his dreamy rocking, then swayed and pulled Eugenia so far off balance she almost fell. George grinned. "See that, Will? Graceful little thing, my wife . . . Loves to dance, too . . . Do anything for a dance, won't you, Genie? Anything!" George started to caress his wife's cheek, but his hand was so clumsy and brutal, she drew back as if she'd been mauled.

"I think it's time to go, George." Eugenia's voice was firm. It's no time for a confrontation, she thought angrily. But then it never is. Ever.

"Go, Genie . . . but the night is young! Not past the shank of the . . . and I haven't had my turn at dancing with you. . . ." George stressed the word *my,* leaning over his wife. He reeked of alcohol, hot wool, and laundry starch gone sour and Eugenia flinched instinctively.

Left alone, standing on his own two feet, with all support gone,

George felt the room suddenly begin to swim. The perfume, the candles, the greenery and linen cloths, the silver bowls heaped with oranges, reminded him of something he'd once seen, and he gazed at the spinning mass trying to remember where that distant place had been. There was a high, thin smell of cinnamon and nutmeg from a hundred buttery cakes, and all of a sudden George knew exactly where he was; he was a very little, very naughty, boy, and he'd been banished upstairs to the musicians' gallery, while below him in Linden Lodge's great hall, his father and brothers moved slowly around the base of a giant Christmas tree.

George's face puckered at the memory. "Got to take the li'l lady home, Will," he said. "Wants to go home. Otherwise, I'd stay on. . . . You know I would. . . . I'm the man for it! Show me a party and I'll show you George Axthelm, by God! . . . Don't you do it, Will. . . . That's the ticket. Don't you marry. . . . Trapped forever!"

George became dramatic again; he rolled his eyes and shook his head in an impersonation of tragic loss. Then he ended the speech beaming down at Eugenia's bare shoulders as if he'd forgotten her entirely. He stared at her necklace. "Rubies . . . ?" he finally mumbled.

"George?" Eugenia knew the moment for reason had passed. "George?" she repeated. For a moment she imagined leaping out of her skin. She'd be free then, a silvery thing like a lean, long fish slipping through the air. She'd be invisible; she'd escape.

"George," Eugenia said. "Dear? It's time to go now."

But Eugenia didn't have to struggle long; while she stood in her husband's grip, trying to plan the next move, the governor appeared. "So this is where you've gotten to, Mr. Axthelm!" His voice bounced across the room. He might have been saying: "What a beautiful day"; "What a lovely view"; or "Another enchanting dinner." The governor was a consummate politician.

"Ah, Mrs. Axthelm!" he continued. "I see your husband's found you at last." Even those words were no more than society banter. "Ah, well, well . . ." he continued, "a late night . . . I think we're all weary. . . . And you both must be especially so. So many new faces!"

He motioned to his aides and they positioned themselves on either side of George's sagging body, then the governor placed a hand on his guest's arm as if he were deep in fascinated conversation, and in that fashion they paraded from the room.

Eugenia was glad she didn't have time to think. She followed the procession to the carriage, nodding farewells and I'm-so-sorry-we-must-leave's and reluctant summonses to the DuPlessises, to Beckmann, to Whitney, and finally to Lieutenant Brown.

And after all, she told herself, it's not so very hard. It's what I was born to do, how I was raised, why I and my mother, my grandmother, my great-aunts, and my whole long family line were bred.

The *Alcedo* was resting quietly when the carriages rolled up and the passengers departed. Beckmann, Brown, Whitney, the doctor and his wife, George (with some assistance), and Eugenia hurried quietly inside the dimly lit ship. There were only the most perfunctory of good nights, a smattering of "lovely-party/lovely evening's," and then the ship was quiet again, left to the sailors who watched the night and the officer on the bridge.

Nothing more was said. Nothing more could be said. The party-goers, the honored guests, retired to their private beds and soon they were dreaming like children, rising with the rhythms of a remembered dance and then falling and falling and falling.

While at the same time, many thousands of miles away, in the Sulu Sea, near the Strait of Tablas, an eight-hour sail from Manila Harbor, Eugenia's father, the Honorable (and venerable) Nicholas Paine, was sweltering out another airless afternoon in the cabin of the Pacific and Orient steamer he'd taken from San Francisco Bay.

This day was different from all previous days, however; this was the packet's last night at sea. Tomorrow the long transpacific crossing would be over. Tomorrow they were due to reach the Philippine Islands. Paine had decided to use his hours wisely; he'd decided to box up his beloved books.

Ridgeway, "the infernal Ridgeway," as the Honorable Nicholas referred to the weedy, blond scarecrow of a secretary Turk Axthelm had assigned him, had already sorted through the old man's letters and papers, his lovingly thumbed copies of the *London Times,* and the stray scraps that comprised the Honorable Nicholas's cryptic notes to himself.

Ridgeway, "the infernal Ridgeway," had shaken his yellow locks, stroked his beardless chin, and then had the gall to suggest getting rid of those bits of yellowed paper altogether:

". . . There doesn't seem much point in keeping them, sir, if you ask me," he'd said, smelling prissily of eau de cologne, camphor, and righteous acts.

But the Honorable Nicholas had shouted, "I didn't ask you, you young whelp! We're not in Philadelphia. So leave me be!"

And now here he was, Paine thought, alone, admirably, and most blessedly alone, with the books that were to sustain him through the next several hotter-than-Hades months. Reverently the Honorable Nicholas picked up a slim volume of Richard Hovey's works. "Sea Gipsey" was really, he stopped momentarily to formulate a decision, one of the world's great poems:

> I am weary with the sunset,
> I am fretful of the bay. . . .

"The islands of desire," that's where they were headed . . . and all thanks to the munificence of Mr. Martin Axthelm, Sr., the "Turk."

" 'The islands of desire,' " the Honorable Nicholas said aloud as he placed the book in a crate next to his copy of *The Meditations of Marcus Aurelius*. There won't be time for this tomorrow, he reasoned, what with meeting with Governor Taft's aide and all . . . getting my feet wet . . . setting up the new digs. . . . Good to be back in harness again, Paine decided, surveying the turmoil of his half-packed stateroom.

But now where is that little note to Martin Axthelm? he wondered, where could I have . . . ?

Paine peered into the box and then across the dresser top and finally over to his barracks-cornered, glassy-topped bed. These Malays and Filipinos, he thought warmly, teach them just once; they're like finely trained retrievers, always at your heels, always eager . . . A bagged grouse or a well-made bed . . . The same thing, really . . . In actual fact . . .

Now, now, now, that wasn't what I . . . Paine dragged himself slowly back to the present. "Ridgeway!" he bellowed suddenly. "Ridgeway! Ridgeway, I need . . ."

But there was no answering scurry of feet; Paine listened a minute, then two, then five. "Damn," he said with a weary sigh. "I've got to teach that boy some manners. I've got to show him who's boss. We're not back in Philadelphia."

With that Paine flipped an entire box topsy-turvy, scattering its contents over the rolling floor while he hunted frantically for something whose importance he'd already forgotten, because it would never do, no, it would never, never do to be seen as a scattered or a careless old man.

SEVEN

*E*UGENIA DREAMED SHE
WAS IN A CART, a buckboard, something that rattled and groaned
with each creak of its wobbly wood wheels, and everywhere there was
fire: huts burning, sheds burning, and thatching and dried haystacks
catching the sparks and bursting into flame as if of their own free will.

It was the plague, she knew; they were escaping the plague: she and
the children fleeing a dying city in the dark of night. She didn't know
what year it was: thirteen something, fourteen something. And the
place? She couldn't remember: Dresden? Toulon? Aix-la-Chapelle?
The place didn't matter. "Ring around a rosy . . ." she sang under her
breath, ". . . ashes, ashes, we all fall down. . . ." Rosy rings on her babies' white bodies: 1412. Anno Domini: fourteen hundred and twelve.

There was a driver for a time, a surly peasant with a broad, sweaty
back who wouldn't speak but who planted his boots so far apart on the
footboard she had no room for her legs. The man's body was hot and
smelled of singed skin and hair; he cursed the ancient horse and shook
massive shoulders that seemed, for a moment, to sob.

The children were huddled in the back of the cart under a black velvet cloak. After settling them, Eugenia had thrown dirty straw over
the cloak so no one could see the fineness of the cloth or the brightness
of its ermine hood. She'd had a momentary pang of fear as she'd scattered the straw; the hood was a temptation. Would it be noticed?
Would her children be discovered? After what seemed a very long time,
hours instead of seconds, she'd decided to leave the hood attached: the

only remnant of her former life. She'd stroked three little heads, said, "I love you. Keep quiet," and they were off.

Eugenia was dressed in black as well; she saw herself clearly, as if part of herself sat in a tree, looking down. She was swaddled from head to toe in greasy sacking. She might have been a man, a woman, a specter or death itself. Eugenia wrapped herself tightly in her own arms and stared at the driver's boots. They were fine boots. Green calf-skin with a deep red lip. She wondered how he'd come to own them.

Then the driver disappeared, taken from one dream into another, and Eugenia was the one flailing the tortured horse. They raced over the cobbles, shrieked at by thieves who broke through charred and smoldering doors at a jerking run.

The thieves were women or men or children and they were all of them, all, as irrepressibly evil as anything Eugenia had ever seen. Long and fraying hairs of squandered cloth blew about them as they darted through the smoke and ash; they screamed at each other and waved batlike arms; they hooked their heads to one side and yelled at the horse and at Eugenia. The words fell out of the gassy air like cinders, like soot; in the end they were only words. With each crackling oath, Eugenia and the children were farther from town, farther and farther from home.

The horse stumbled, then righted itself. The carriage shafts slatted against the animal's bony sides; its skin was festered and raw, rubbed red by the harness, by the whip, but Eugenia had no pity for the horse. She yanked the reins and cursed as eagerly as the driver had. And her children? Did they sleep? Did they cry? Did they bang their soft heads together under the cloak? Were they even alive?

Nearer and nearer Eugenia and the children came; the air began to smell sweeter; the burning houses pulled apart. There were fields and then woods. The woods rose cool and damp, scented with pine bark, safety, and immeasurable peace, and oh, Eugenia thought, soon we will be there.

Suddenly men swarmed from the trees; they poured like vomit from the gnarly trunks. Like moss-colored bile. They wore hoods; they car-ried torches; they surrounded the carriage. Eugenia was thrown to the ground and the children were tossed like lumps of hot lead onto the spongy turf and the cart, the knocked-apart, splintery cart was over-turned. Trapped by the long shafts, the horse was powerless to protest; it collapsed onto its weak, old back, still moving feeble legs in the air as if a few more steps, only a very few, could pull it to safety.

The men set fire to the cart. Flames licked the driver's box and the floor, hesitating as if unsure what to sample first; they tested the age and sweetness of the wood and roared a decision. Soon fire engulfed the whole of the upturned cart, then sped in a single spectacular leap across the reins to the struggling, upside-down horse. The fetlocks and hooves were the first to go. Against the black sky, they made a vision of pure fire.

Eugenia woke up, looked at her room, at the curtains blocking the early light, and at the white rims with which the sun had encircled each one. The sun wanted to get in; it wasn't about to let something as insignificant as a piece of fabric deter it. Eugenia studied that small battle of wills—morning and practicality against the slothful indulgence of a darkened bedroom—and resolutely swung her feet to the floor.

The silk threads in the Kashmiri carpet felt cool; she let her toes play among them, then stood up. If you don't want to think, Eugenia told herself, move forward. She walked to her dressing table, to her washstand, turned on the taps, and watched a swirl of clear liquid spill over the porcelain. The spigots were two gold swans, the hot and cold taps two cygnets; the water bobbed beneath the family and cast its reflection to their outstretched wings.

Eugenia touched the cygnets, touched the swans. Why? she thought. Why today? The seventeenth of August . . . Jinx is ten years old today. I have a party planned, a cake, games, presents, costumes, a pantomime. Where did that awful dream come from? What does it mean?

A plague, escaping with the children and a horse burning alive . . . Eugenia lowered her head, gripped the washstand, stared at the water, stared at the hand towels, at the soap in its pink and gold shell. Without realizing it, she had begun to cry.

"Anson, I'm afraid this is most urgent." Carl leaned forward in the dark upstairs hall of Linden Lodge; he hated this devout waiting, these tired-out rituals before the Great Man's door. He even hated the smell filling the long corridor; it was always the same: clipped boxwood lanes and the damp limestone that had created the Lodge's confused replication of a Norman or a Gothic or a Moorish citadel. "Make up your mind," Carl wanted to shout down the corridor. "You can't be a castle in Spain if you're a fortress on the Irish coast."

"My father is expecting me," Carl repeated firmly and considered pushing his way inside. The picture of himself barging into his father's study brought brief and unexpected pleasure.

"Mr. Axthelm left word, Master Carl, that he was not to be disturbed." Anson was immovable. He would never forsake his master.

He would fight to the death. He'd stood his ground against Master Carl before.

"So I understand." Carl tried to control his temper; he measured his words, giving equal weight to each one:

"However, this information is vital to my father's business interests in the East. It is of the utmost importance that I see him immediately.

"And do try, Anson," Carl reminded the majordomo with a rise in tone that sounded like steam escaping a radiator vent, "to call me Mr. Axthelm and not Master Carl. Or perhaps you hadn't noticed that I am no longer a child."

Carl brushed past the sentry, determined to reach the black door. August the seventeenth, he thought angrily, the "dog days" in lush and lovely Pennsylvania, that bountiful, green-gardened state so extolled by its happy natives. All day and all week there'd been the threat or the promise of rain, but the storm wouldn't come; the grass turned stiff and yellow; the sycamore leaves withered to wax paper while the "hot bird," the locust, rattled like death under a fierce morning sun. While he, Carl, the brains and power behind the great family, cooled his heels outside his father's locked door. It was enough to make anyone lose patience.

Carl looked down the Lodge's dark hall. It was lined with bronze and marble warriors; they stood at fixed attention on matched and even stands; they fitted each alcove, loomed from every shadow: swords, shields, clubs, and bare arms and shoulders catching what little light dripped from the parchment-shaded sconces. Carl stared at the figures, but no longer saw them. If only it would rain, he thought. Anything to wipe away this heat, the stupor of too many flowers, too many swollen trees, too much black earth, corn, tomatoes, dahlias, lilies gone on a rampage.

"I insist you open this door immediately, Anson," Carl said. His voice was loud, certain, as energetic as a dive in a freshwater pond. "I won't be held responsible if this message fails to get through in time."

In honor of Jinx's special day, the foredeck of the *Alcedo* had been turned into a medieval fairground. There were bright banners and ribbons, fanciful shields and crests with animals nature could never duplicate. There was a banquet table filled with more food than the birthday guests could eat in a week, and there were bells and wind whistles and chimes that jangled and jounced under every flag and ribbon till the colors seemed to take on their own sound: something high and tinkly for yellow, something misty and remote for blue; green was a crash like cymbals, and orange-red made a noise like oboes in a crowded street.

And then there were the costumes! At Jinx's command, everyone had appeared in fancy dress: Jinx herself was Neptuna, queen of the waves. She wore a lavender mantle with wings that her mother and Prue had stitched from blue gauze and wire, and she carried a scepter, which she banged against her halo by mistake. Mother and Lizzie were the queen's handmaidens. Paul was supposed to be a henchman, but he'd refused to wear the necessary purple tunic; he just wore a gold paper hat, which, in Jinx's considered (and well-aged) opinion, looked extremely silly with knickers and a sailor's blouse. Paul also waved an enormous crimson and silver cardboard sword.

The sword had been the creation of Cousin Whitney, who hadn't had the same luck with his own costume. He'd decided to attend the party dressed as a Barbary ape—a fitting choice, he thought, since the *Alcedo* was on its approach to Gibraltar—but the papier-mâché nose hadn't dried properly and when he'd tried to pull it off, the thing collapsed.

To make up for "this serious lack of a simian nose," as he called it, Cousin Whit grunted and waddled around, trying, at least, to act like an ape while he stole food and clambered onto the table—Jinx knew she'd get into terrible trouble if she'd started behaving like that!

Then there was Father dressed as a Roman senator with a toga and laurel leaves in his hair, and Mr. Beckmann as the "Great Atlantic" in a huge blue cape, but his scepter wasn't as grand as Jinx's; it was just his regular walking stick with ribbons tied round the knob. Lieutenant Brown was a medieval soldier with leggings and a leathery shield. Mrs. DuPlessis was Martha Washington in a cotton wool wig stuck with thirteen miniature American flags, but the best costume of all belonged to Dr. DuPlessis.

He was a moth, and he'd made giant green and black wings that actually moved. "The Rajah Ivard Birdwing," he called himself. "The 'Lepidoptera Ivardiana' from 'The Land Below The Wind.' A recent discovery and very famous in scientific circles. I thought my replica might be appropriate, considering the place is part of our agenda."

Dr. DuPlessis couldn't sit at the table with everyone else (his wings wouldn't allow it), so he made mothy noises and mothy motions and waved around humming mothlike songs while he pulled a secret string that made his wings flap in the breeze.

Mrs. DuPlessis hated her husband's impersonation, of course. "That's enough, Gustav," she hissed, till all her thirteen flags shook. "Our guest of honor has seen enough." She said that over and over, but Dr. DuPlessis pretended not to hear; he danced a mothy jig and swooshed around the table, eyeing his wife's wig.

"Cotton wool!" he said. "One of my favorites! And serge and flannel and woolen leggings! Oh, my goodness, but I'm hungry." Jinx thought this was the funniest thing she had ever seen. She almost swallowed a spoon filled with ice cream and caramelized syrup.

"Speech from the birthday girl's mother," Whit shouted in his furry monkey suit. "Speech from Cousin Genie!"

Eugenia reluctantly stood and looked down the long table. Mounds of meringues had spilled over lemon tartlets; baskets of petits fours, chocolate almonds, and marzipan berries lay on their sides, picked over or picked clean; the table was buried under a sea of half-eaten sweets. Perfect, Eugenia promised herself, it's perfect. It's exactly what I would have wanted when I turned ten. It's exactly what I needed to make today. A fairy tale setting for a fairy tale life.

"Happy birthday, angel," Eugenia began, then stopped abruptly. Her dream wouldn't leave her alone. Against the black sky, the hooves were a vision of pure fire, she told herself. But why the plague? And people with arms like bats?

All morning long Eugenia had worked to dispel those memories. I won't think about this, she'd told herself over and over. It was just a dream. Too much rich food. Too much excitement. An "overactive imagination," as my grandmother used to say. Horses dying, thieves and babies with the plague have nothing to do with me.

"Ten years old . . ." Eugenia began again. She felt on firmer ground momentarily.

"1893 . . . you were born in the last century, Jinx. Just think of that . . ." But saying the date had been a mistake; it reminded her of another. 1412, Eugenia thought, why did I pick that year?

"Hear! Hear!" Whitney jumped into the breach. "Ten years old today! Bravo, Jinx!" Whit grabbed a plate full of cookies and pretended to swallow it whole.

"More stories!" yelled Paul. "More stories! Tell about when Jinx was little and ate all the paper ducks!

"Or the time you found her fingerpainting the nursery wall . . ."

Jinx glowered at her brother and brandished her scepter. "You don't even count, Paul!" she said. "You came to my party without a costume!"

"I've got my hat and sword," Paul parried. "And anyway, I didn't want to be one of your dumb old henchmen." Paul stabbed the air with his magnificent sword and caused Henry to nearly drop a tray of tea sandwiches.

"Oh, I don't think we'll have any wicked baby stories today, Paul,"

Eugenia laughed. "After all, your sister's nearly a grown lady now."

Lizzie looked up at her mother and gave a self-satisfied glance that meant "Aren't little children amusing?" and Eugenia smiled in return. Concentrate, she told herself. You are here. That other thing, that was nothing. It was a dream; it wasn't even real.

"I don't really have a speech, I'm afraid. But I did want to give you my own small present, darling. . . . Before we cut the cake, and you get on to your other gifts." Eugenia pulled a small box from her pocket. She'd wrapped it in green silk and then tied it with a jonquil-colored bow. The present looked like a meadow in springtime, as warm and innocent and fresh as May. Eugenia felt her hand tremble slightly and her eyes gloss over. As innocent as May, she thought.

"Don't cry, Mother," Jinx said softly. She reached out to touch her mother's hand.

"It's just that I'm so happy," Eugenia said firmly. "So happy and so proud . . ." She tried to smile, but it was a failed attempt; instead she stared at the table and felt utterly exposed. There was a driver for a time, she told herself, looking at Beckmann inadvertently; he had green boots with a wide red band.

"I wanted you to have this, Jinx . . ." Eugenia continued, promising herself that she'd seen the last of her dream.

"It belonged to your great-great-aunt Sally . . . someone you never knew. . . . It was her garnet necklace. I used to borrow it as a special treat. I'm sure your father remembers when he first saw it. . . ." Eugenia pulled the necklace from its box. How insignificant it seemed suddenly: seven tiny stones on a filigree wire. I gave such credence to this necklace, Eugenia thought. It was a talisman, a good luck charm; I knew it would never fail me.

"Anyway, it was one of my favorite things, growing up," Eugenia said, hurrying faster, "and I always hoped I could own it. And now . . . and now, I give it to you!" Eugenia finished with a flourish, though she felt tears approaching again. Foolish, foolish, foolish, she told herself, and sat down as quickly as she could.

"And a lovely present it is, my dear," George said, rising ponderously as he folded his toga draperies over one arm. George was afraid his wife wasn't feeling quite up to par, quite up to snuff, so he'd decided it was his duty to come to her rescue. All morning she'd had a pale, strained expression. At first George had thought it might have been the result of his little overindulgence in Madeira—his wife could harbor grudges—but he'd quickly eliminated that worry from his mind. Too much work on the party, he'd told himself, too many late nights stitching Jinx's little costume, too much painting and papering and overseeing Olive and Prue. Not to mention Higgins and the pastry chef! George's excuses were convincing; he believed them completely.

"A lovely sentiment, I'm sure, my dear . . ." George's voice boomed over the waves as if he were addressing a session of Parliament. The words had the same contrived and silky tone. ". . . A gift our young lady will treasure forever. . . ."

Eugenia looked at her husband and the long table, at the happy faces of her family and her friends, and felt something change within her, as if a wind had blown through her, and blown her clean. Sorrow disappeared, and confusion vanished. A May meadow, she remembered: a tent filled with gardenias, bridesmaids, and bouquets of white roses. Dreams are only dreams, after all: good or bad. Eugenia reached for her ten-year-old's hand and smiled.

". . . Speech from the birthday girl!" George was tapping his wineglass with a silver spoon.

"Speech from the birthday girl!" Whit joined in.

"Speech! Speech!" The tablecloth shivered with the guests' demands. Bowls of powdered sugar jostled and spilled, and mounds of this play snow began to cover everything in sight. Cutlery trains were lost in distant wastes; napkins looked like mountains in the grip of a blizzard. Plates became lakes and saltcellars were huddled men with their backs to the wind.

Jinx was thrilled with this Christmastime effect. The table looked exactly like a toy emporium's holiday display, where they had wind-up railroads crossing wintry bridges, dolls with fur muffs propped up in sleighs, and maybe a family of stuffed bears wearing big red bows. Jinx stood up, beamed at her father and then at her mother, tried to shape some words into what she imagined a birthday party speech should be, but ended with a simple: "Thank you, everyone! This has been my best birthday ever. And I love my new necklace!"

". . . And to our safe passage past the Rock of Gibraltar and our arrival in the great and historic Mediterranean Sea. Ladies and gentlemen, I give you the Pillars of Hercules . . . !" George continued his oration as if there'd been no interruption. He was overcome with his own grandeur. ". . . The fabled home of Hannibal on the one side; the mountains of Andalusia on the other. Spain and the great, stretching continent of Africa. . . ."

"What about the Barbary apes!" Whit sprang forward, setting Jinx's plate flying as he screamed with a high monkeylike shriek: "Can't have speeches about birthdays and the Rock of Gibraltar without mentioning the Barbary ape!"

This was followed by whoops of laughter and loud applause. The somber or troublesome or mournful mood had passed. Paul stamped his feet on the floor and banged his sword on the present-strewn table with so much force that the tinsel-wrapped packages bounced into a plate of cinnamon puffs and tipped over two trays of mincemeat tarts. Stewards rushed into service, but they couldn't move fast enough.

"Speeches! Speeches!" everyone shouted, then: "Let's tell jokes!"; "No, let's tell stories!"

Only Eugenia sat back, watching. An enormous sense of peace infused her. Out of the blue, it had appeared. Out of the blue, doubt, confusion, and worry had vanished. My children are fine, Eugenia told herself; they're strong and good and true. That's all that matters in the end.

"Speeches! Speeches!" was quickly followed by Dr. DuPlessis's singing a moth mating song: "My ears are green. My antennae are sharp . . ." while Mrs. DuPlessis slapped down her teacup and ordered, "Stop that at once, Gustav," and Paul (heedless as ever) shouted:

"The Barbary apes! The Barbary apes! The monkeys in the zoo . . ."

The words became a chant that turned into a song, which Dr. DuPlessis, Lizzie, Jinx, and George roared in unison:

". . . Hi ho the dairy-o . . . the monkeys in the zoo . . ."

". . . The rat takes the cheese . . . the cow jumps over the moon . . ."

". . . And the fish ran away with the spoon . . ."

"Not 'fish'! you idiot! 'Dish'! Every year you get dumber and dumber, Paul." But both Jinx and her brother were laughing so hard they were crying. Insults were insignificant when they were part of a game.

". . . And the fish ran away with the spoon . . . !" Paul sang louder.

Then "Fun and frolic!" became the cry as Whitney leapt from the table, yelling, "Who's ready for the festivities to continue? Lizzie, Paul, and the birthday girl? Who can keep up with your old Cousin Whit? 'Red Rover,' 'Stop and Go,' who can beat me?"

My children are happy, Eugenia repeated; I have everything I wanted. The mind only travels so far.

Inside his study at Linden Lodge, the Turk listened to the clamor in the hall and wondered how long Carl would put up with Anson's protective insubordination. If Beckmann had been there, they might have had a nice little bet going; Beckmann's pocket watch could be remarkably efficient, though in wagers, as in all financial dealings, the master beat out the man.

The Turk sighed and looked around the room; it was good to be home again, he thought. The season at Newport was fine for Tony and

Martin, Junior and their wives; they had their "set," their parties, their picnics, their "evenings at home." They'd been "received" in the glittering social whirl because he, "The Old Man," the "Turk," had made it his business.

But the truth was that he hated Newport. He hated Bellevue Avenue, the casino, the snobbish Cliffwalk Lane. He hated the people and their softness; he hated their lambent leniency and simpering pretension. What they said had no weight. The Turk leaned into the arms of his chair, wrapped his white fingers around the damp, cool leather, and smiled as he remembered his sudden departure from the seaside resort: the feigned regret he'd expressed at leaving so unexpectedly, then the "intime little ball" the Rhinelanders had thrown in his honor, the three dull-as-dirt dinners and five luncheons he'd forced himself to attend before he'd finally allowed himself to pack up and leave. His private railway car pulling into the station had been a wonderful sight.

The Turk had known there'd be rumors all right; he'd anticipated them, looked forward to them really, but it was Carl who'd brought in the first report. It was urgent business calling the great man away:

"Government"; "Foreign policy"; "Some Hottentot in the Philippines" (or was it Léopoldville? and someone hot under the collar?). Whatever the actual facts, the summer crowd had unanimously agreed: "It's all very hush-hush."

Carl had carried the first report home, imitating the privileged accents to a tee, and both father and son had shared a long, satisfying laugh.

"Isn't young George headed that way?" Carl had described one particularly well-connected woman drawling at Bailey's Beach.

"Which way?" Another had giggled while the men exchanged indulgent smiles. The Turk had done nothing to stop the gossip.

It's certainly good to be home again, the old man thought, resting his head on his chair back. The room had the strong earthy smell of walls covered in ivy or of wool rugs dampened by a summer rain. Pleasant place, Pennsylvania, the Turk decided. Picturesque but solid.

The voices outside the room grew louder; now and then one clear word or phrase wormed its way through the keyhole or under the door. They're not the first threats this room's heard, the Turk chuckled to himself as he reached for a cigar. And they won't be the last either. If you were to poke a hole in that desk, the Turk thought, oaths would ooze out like sap.

Suddenly the old man's good mood deserted him. "You don't get anywhere by being polite," he said aloud as if Carl had already entered the room.

"And you're a failure if you're kind. How many times do I have to remind you, my boy? Strategy's what you need. Learn to use other people. Twist the screws.

"You think it makes a difference that we're family, but you take my word: there are no worse enemies than your own kin."

Drying slices of *boeuf en daube,* Scotch salmon in melting jelly, smoked pheasant turning dry as paper, tea sandwiches wrinkled as rocks, peaches floating belly-up in Nellie Melba syrup—the long party was over. Even the cake, the magnificent replica of the Rock of Gibraltar that both the pastry and sous-chefs had lovingly carved in angel food, marzipan, and white chocolate cream, was deserted, discarded, left for the sea gulls or the breeze.

Eugenia stared at the table. There was nowhere to go, and nothing to think or feel that hadn't been explored over and over and over again. "Have this cleared completely," she ordered Higgins's busy hands. "The cake as well. And then the table. There'll be more room for games without all these mahogany legs and posts." If you lose your way, fall back on the day to day, she quoted silently; now, there's a maxim worthy of my grandmother's coaching. I'll have to remember it. Though perhaps it was never forgotten.

Eugenia tossed her napkin into the middle of the mess and stood, but remained close to the table as if the work there demanded a mother's devoted eye. "Leave the presents on the chaise, however, Higgins. My daughter likes to admire her hoard."

Eugenia studied the gifts lying in their ripped paper and ribbon: *Rebecca of Sunnybrook Farm; Little Lays for Little Folk*; a six-inch doll with a blue-eyed porcelain face, a lead model of a lancer's carriage (this was from Paul); a diary with a key (Lizzie, of course); a mother-of-pearl locket hanging on a pin (Ogden Beckmann); and an illustrated volume inscribed by Dr. DuPlessis and entitled *Lepidoptera of the World*. Eugenia's own small gift was lost among them.

"Your children sent me to ask if you'd join in our game."

Eugenia wasn't surprised to see Lieutenant Brown standing near the empty table. She hadn't seen his approach, but it seemed absolutely fitting that he should appear. Another problem to deal with.

"What game are you at now?" she asked. Her voice was measured and cool. There will be no more foolishness, she tried to convey. What happened in Madeira was an aberration, a mistake. It will not happen again.

"We're throwing berries to the gulls. It was your son's idea." Brown's voice sounded far too intimate; it gave Eugenia a moment's panic.

"I don't think I'd be much good at games today." Eugenia forced a laugh. "I'm afraid I'd spoil all your fun." But the joke didn't work; it sounded desperate and full of longing, like a spinster's protestations.

"I think I owe you an apology, Mrs. Axthelm . . ." Brown began. He moved forward slightly as Eugenia retreated. The mechanics of dismantling the table continued—mahogany leaves and chair backs darted by, a silver candelabra, an epergne full of roses—but Eugenia and Brown took no notice; they might have stood on an empty deck.

"Nonsense, Lieutenant. Nonsense." Eugenia walked over to a deck chair, picked up her hat and shawl, and said in a loud, cheery voice:

"It's a bit cooler this afternoon, don't you think? It must be because we're nearing the Atlas Mountains. Though one would think the Mediterranean would be warmer than the Atlantic. At least that's always been my uneducated perception. I've never traveled this far from home. My father did, of course, but that was way before my time. And George, as well; he's traveled as well. And you, too, I should imagine. If the stories Paul carries forth from your lair are all true."

Eugenia put her straw hat firmly on her head and tied the ribbons under her chin. She gave every moment deliberate attention, as if putting on a hat were her only concern. "As for me, I'm really a stay-at-home, content with domesticity." Finished, Eugenia turned and faced Brown.

Don't come near me, her eyes said, *don't talk to me. You frighten me. You make me forget who I am—what I want. But I have everything I've dreamed of: a happy family, a pleasant home, nice things. Don't make me challenge that; don't make me question it. Because I won't do it. I won't.*

Brown looked at Eugenia's face and saw stubbornness as well as fear. She was trying to overcome emotion with the strength of her will. Brown understood that trick; he'd used it himself. First you look at a problem, he told himself, and you learn where the danger lies. Then you bring that difficulty down to size, make it simple, make it small. You go on your way. You never look back. The rule's the same for every game. And that's why I'm here, he realized, a man without a past whose future's in his own two hands.

"All the more reason for you to join the children's game, then" was all Brown said.

George had kept his eye on the young lieutenant. His attraction to Eugenia was obvious and George didn't like it. He didn't like it one bit. Though he understood it. Genie's a damned attractive woman, he told himself, a bit emotional now and then, but what woman isn't?

George studied his wife and Lieutenant Brown, and forgot to concentrate on his children's game.

"You're up, Father," Lizzie announced. George could hear pride and pleasure mixed in her voice. She'd been so happy to have him join the fun; she'd run to fetch more fruit, more bread, so he'd have plenty of food to toss to the gulls. She'd been so attentive and smiling, it had almost broken his heart.

"You take my turn. There's a good girl." George didn't look at his eldest daughter, but he could feel her pull back, dismayed, hurt, immediately defensive. Where do they learn these tricks? George wondered. Men don't behave like that.

He returned to his perusal of Brown. That damned fellow better not say anything unseemly, George decided, recognizing the set of his wife's jaw and her overbright eyes. If he does, I'll just go over and knock his block off. Shouldn't have been at our little family get-together, anyhow. That was all Jinx's idea, but then she'd also wanted to invite that cabin boy, Ned. Children can be so naive, George thought; they think everyone's got the same set of values, that they want the same things out of life. George felt the sun on his back, but it did nothing to calm him. I'll have to be more specific, he told himself; I'll have to take a firmer hand in the kiddies' upbringing. I can't have them mistaking compassion for friendship. Human beings are not born equal, after all.

George glowered at Brown. He had half a mind to walk right over there and set things straight. Damn Beckmann, he recited silently, returning to his favorite culprit; this is his doing. That lieutenant, or whoever he really is, is here to do a piece of work; he's no guest. I should have taken control earlier. It's Father I'm responsible to. This little exercise is between the two of us. Beckmann has nothing to do with it. He's here to help if I need him; that's all.

While George concentrated on "correcting the record," "taking stock," and "accepting the fallen mantle of leadership," his children, Whitney, and Dr. DuPlessis continued their game of "feed the sea gulls."

Tempted by an endless barrage of goodies, and braced for fierce competition, the birds swooped close to the ship's rail and grew louder and more demanding as bread, strawberries, raspberries, pieces of peach and melon, were tossed in the air. The gulls grew shrill and insistent; their wings whirred together with a rush as they fought and cawed and cackled and screeched.

While the players, heaving one treat after another, shouted back: "Good catch!"; "Did you see that one? And he's the smallest, too!"

They called out encouraging words as each child and each adult attempted to throw further and higher, and they laughed when food dropped or slipped, by accident, into the sea. They shrieked and they joked and they teased; their voices were loud, bossy, and hungry for attention.

George was oblivious; he'd forgotten the game, Jinx's birthday, Lizzie's smiles. His mind focused on Beckmann and Brown to the exclusion of everything else. They're no friends of mine, he promised himself. They're along for the ride, because Father thought it "wise," because Father likes "safety nets" and "backup plans." But I can't let a couple of lightweights push me around. This is my ship; this is my family; I'm going to have to take more control.

"It has to do with the Russians in Manchuria, Father." Carl had finally penetrated the inner sanctum. He felt weary from the effort, as if he'd run full tilt up the stairs. "The news just came in. Though I believe the date of this diplomatic debacle was five days ago on August the twelfth."

The Turk didn't move, didn't shift his hands or even blink. Of course, his expression said, *I've been expecting this.*

"What news would that be, Carl?" he asked; his voice was soft and deceptively friendly. "But before you tell me, why don't you close the door. I think I feel a slight draft."

In August? Carl thought. Why, it's hotter than Hades in here. Then he remembered who he was dealing with and recognized the reprimand. His face grew red, but he marched to the door as ordered.

"Much better," the Turk cooed.

You don't fool me one bit, you old lizard, Carl thought, butter wouldn't melt in your mouth. Or ice, for that matter.

"Now, Carl, you were saying?" As expected, the Turk's tone had changed; there was nothing kindly about it; it took pleasure in cruelty. It said: I know every weakness you have; don't try to cross me.

"The Russians in Manchuria . . ." Carl began again; he wouldn't allow himself to rise to the bait; he kept his voice level: business as usual. "On August the twelfth, the Japanese minister, under instructions from his government—"

"I thought you said Russians, Carl," the Turk interrupted with a condescending laugh. "Now you're telling me a Japanese minister . . . make up your mind, my boy. Which one is it?"

Carl continued as though his father hadn't spoken. "On August the twelfth, in Saint Petersburg, the Japanese minister, under instructions from his government, presented a note to the Czar protesting the Russian failure to relinquish their hold on the Chinese state of Manchuria."

"Yes?" the Turk said. "What's that got to do with us?"

"Let me finish, Father." Carl's words were unexpectedly harsh; the Turk accepted them in pleased silence.

"Underlying this ostensibly altruistic gesture, Father—one Oriental nation standing up for another in the face of a much larger bully, et cetera—was the overt suggestion that should Japan receive a free hand in Korea, she would, in return, turn a blind eye to the Czar's effort in Manchuria!" Carl paused momentarily to allow the enormity of this disaster to sink in. "Between them Russia and Japan mean to divide up the East."

"As I said, Carl, how does this affect us? The Americans have the Philippines; the British control Singapore. Let the devil take the hindmost."

"But don't you see, Father? The Russian fleet in Port Arthur . . ." Carl was beginning to see holes in his logic. The extraordinary piece of news he'd hoped would win him favor seemed no more enlightening than a description of yesterday's luncheon.

"Port Arthur's all the way up in Manchuria, Carl. It's a long, long way from Borneo. And as for the Hottentots, let them eat each other whole; they're unimportant. Japan, Korea, Seoul, who cares?"

"But I'm thinking of the munitions, Father. There'll be a lot of weapons floating around out there. They could jeopardize our . . ."

"I doubt it." The Turk was growing tired of the history lesson. "Our only concern is the stability of our leadership in Manila, William Henry Taft et al. Ownership of the Philippines is key. Although, in the end, it may not be as vital as I'd once believed." The Turk's voice became reflective; he seemed to be pondering a recent discovery, mulling it over as he spoke, turning it inside and out.

"Deals are created equally by enemies and by friends . . ." he continued, ". . . and sometimes enemies are easier to trust."

"Well, I still feel George is not up to that kind of international . . ."

"And who should I have sent in his place, Carl? You?" Carl mistook his father's tone and quiet laugh, thinking what he heard was an opening for discussion, a frank exchange of ideas, an appraisal of Axthelm and Company's position in the East.

"But, the whole issue of those guns, Father . . . that's what makes me nervous. I never thought George was equipped to . . ."

"Sit down, Carl," the Turk ordered, and Carl instantly dropped into a chair. "We needn't discuss the reason your brother was assigned this little task. It was my decision, and, as such, not open to criticism. If you don't know my methods by now, you never will."

Imperceptibly the Turk's voice grew warmer. "There's an expression Imperial Germany's been playing around with lately, Carl. The word is *weltmacht,* which means world power. As irresistible as a law of nature, they say . . . so don't you worry about Manchuria or the yellow-skinned devils . . . let them waste their time fighting over pieces of rock. We've got more attractive fish to fry. . . .

"Besides, my boy, as you like to point out, Beckmann's with George. And Beckmann never fails."

Eugenia wanted to join her husband and children. She watched them at their game near the aft rail and imagined being part of the fun: Jinx and Paul crowding close while Lizzie looked proudly from parent to parent. Eugenia pictured herself shouting: "Bravo, Paul!"; "Well done, Jinx!"; "Lizzie, my dear!" And then she pictured George's approval and how their doting and parental eyes would linger on each other.

But every time Eugenia started down the deck toward the happy group she'd catch sight of something that kept her away. There'd be Paul's proud, little back and the way he took his father's hand; there'd be Jinx's pleased smile, or Lizzie's laugh and the fluid, womanly dip of her shoulders as she turned to give her father a compliment.

I've failed, haven't I? Eugenia thought. I've been self-centered and unkind, and I've driven everyone away. I'm a foolish woman in a party dress, and I don't have one decent goal in the world.

Eugenia leaned her full weight against the rail and stared into the water. She had the impression she was standing on a great height; if she leaned out to look down, she would fall forever.

I must shake myself out of these doldrums, she told herself, and stretched out her hands. The wood rail felt as smooth as a glass plate, as warm as summer sand; she could hear the ocean and the gulls, and smell the salt foam.

It's going to be all right, Eugenia promised. I'm just a little over-wrought; it's an emotional time, after all: my daughter's tenth birthday. It brings back memories I'd rather not have: George disappeared to God knows where . . . Lizzie assigned to some awful Prussian nurse . . . and a midwife with eyes like a fish . . .

"It's that damned dream," Eugenia said vehemently, as if the act of speaking aloud could save her.

"Mrs. Axthelm, are you quite all right? Can I get you . . . ?"

"Oh, Ogden! I didn't see you!" Eugenia leapt back from the rail. "No. No, I don't need anything. No, thank you." Why didn't I notice him, she thought. How long has he been watching me?

"I thought you seemed worried . . . or ill. . . ." Beckmann reached out as if to aid her. She felt his hand on her wrist and her arm turned to stone.

"I'm fine, Ogden. Really." Eugenia tried to cover her surprise. "I was . . . I was just coming back to join the game. 'Red Rover,' is it now? Or 'Stop and Go' . . . I'm afraid I haven't . . . ?" Against the black sky, she thought, the hooves were a vision of pure flame.

"Eugenia," Beckmann said quietly, and stepped closer.

Eugenia could feel the warmth of his breath, the stillness of his body; she could smell the heat in his jacket and the sun on his face, but she was unable to pull away.

"This is the first time I've had alone with you since . . ." Beckmann didn't have any idea what he was going to say.

"We should return to the festivities, don't you think, Ogden?" Eugenia forced the words and her best smile. "We shouldn't be away too long."

The game of "feed the sea gulls" continued; the excitement was terrific. Everyone got into the act and they lined the rail, armed with bread and berries, bits of pocketed cake, or the stray sliver of smoked pheasant that had slipped from the table. Henry was sent down to the kitchens for more ammunition: What remained of the birthday feast was tossed to the wind.

Even Eugenia tried her best to get into the spirit of the afternoon. She was determined to put her worries behind her and she reached her arm as far out over the water as she could, aimed at one seemingly desperate bird, and threw. The treat crashed into the water.

"Come teach Mother, Lieutenant Brown!" Paul demanded. "She's awful! She throws just like a girl."

"Paul!" his sisters protested in unison.

"That's because she is a girl, Paul," Lieutenant Brown said, brushing a nest of bread crumbs from the little boy's hair. Brown looked at Eugenia and smiled, and she forgot to look away. I don't care, she told herself. I feel nothing. She held out her hand for the bread or the fruit or the piece of discarded ham, and that was that. I don't care, she repeated, and almost believed it.

Ogden Beckmann watched Eugenia and Brown, and George watched them as well. It's a children's game, they promised themselves—Lizzie's playing, and Jinx, and there's young Paul taking his turn. A charming family scene, where could be the harm in that? And Whitney's joining them now, and Dr. DuPlessis. What could be more innocent than that?

"You did it, Mother!" Paul shouted. "That was the best shot yet.

You're almost as good as Jinx and she's almost as good as me!"

"As good as I am," Eugenia nearly corrected, but instead laughed and said nothing. She leaned against Brown and let his hand guide her arm. A children's game of catch, she reassured herself. What can be more innocent than that?

But at that moment George decided to intervene. He couldn't have said why he did it. His feet seemed to carry him forward by themselves.

"Doing well there, my dear," he heard himself say. "I've been caught up by your performance. Very impressive. Quite an improvement. You're to be complimented, Lieutenant Brown." The words rolled forth of their own volition. "My wife's certainly looking happier about her skills."

Eugenia looked at her husband and suddenly frowned. "There's no need to be unkind, George," she said. But she knew he had every reason, just as she recognized what he'd truly wanted to say.

"Why, Genie, I didn't mean . . ." Taken off guard, George was helpless.

All of a sudden Lizzie decided she was furious with her mother. First there was her mopey behavior at the birthday luncheon, and now she was being unbelievably selfish and mean; she was excluding Father from all the fun, taking a longer turn than anyone else, and getting far too much attention.

"Have you come for another turn, Father?" Lizzie asked as defiantly as she dared. "Because you can have my place if you want."

But Jinx was not to be outdone nor Paul. They couldn't shove each other out of the way fast enough.

"Stand here, Father! Come over here!" They crowded close, full of elaborate joy and gratitude. *See, Mother!* their tight little shoulders and bobbing heads declared. *See how it's supposed to be?* Jinx's eyes narrowed into glittering strips of possession and pride; Paul kept a hand on George's blue jacket or a foot against his father's white trouser leg; Lizzie seemed ready to burst with joy, and Eugenia felt like an intruder.

"If you're all going to gang up on me . . ." she began; her voice was edgy and sharp; she couldn't think what came next. The piece of bread she'd held in her hand felt as heavy as cannon shot and she dropped it in the water.

"Genie . . . Genie . . ." George soothed. "I certainly never meant . . . Why it's only a game, my dear . . . you needn't . . ."

"You've all been having this wonderful time while I was . . . while I had to . . . had to organize the party . . . get your mess cleared away . . . make sure everyone was . . . everyone was . . ." Eugenia was filled with regret; every cruel word or deed she'd ever said or done rushed in to jeer at her, but the words kept tumbling out. Blame and anger fought in a void.

The children didn't answer, and George didn't answer. They looked at the deck and shuffled their feet: Paul and Lizzie and Jinx because they were young, and had been so very often in the wrong, and George because an argument was—well—an argument. Best to withdraw, he cautioned himself. Give Genie her head for the moment. Let her blow off a little steam. Anyone can have a bad day. Anyone can get up on the wrong side of the bed.

But Eugenia wasn't finished yet. Her husband's cowed expression and her children's sheepish glances only filled her with more rage. She was a child in a tantrum, hating herself for losing control, but flying forward at full throttle.

Then, as if unable to stop herself, or perhaps it was out of spite, or maybe even high, good spirits; whatever the cause, at that moment Eugenia did a very strange thing. She snatched off her gray straw hat and gripped it in one hand like a torch. The hat was broad-brimmed and banded with a single wide row of pink silk peonies gathered on a damask ribbon—a lovely thing, as pretty as a spring morning—and Eugenia frowned as she began to spin it in her hand, studying the delicate petals and pearly straw as each took to the breeze and light. Then, as quickly as she'd removed the hat, she threw it, threw it high above her head in an arc that headed straight for the sun.

The silvery disk sailed across the sky. It seemed as though it would fly forever. "Whizzer!" Paul said under his breath. "Oh, Mother!" the girls whispered and touched her skirt, while Mrs. DuPlessis bent close enough to mutter, "What an extraordinary gesture!"

Eugenia didn't hear any of it; she followed the path of her hat as it chose its course toward heaven. She watched it turn and turn, and it seemed as if her heart were in it, and her soul, and she leaned out over the waves to watch it disappear up into the clouds.

But suddenly the hat fell. Caught by the wind or the cold, wavy spray of the ocean, it faltered and then crashed, bobbed once, twice, spilled feathery petals over the disruptive foam, and sank.

"Oh!" Eugenia gasped. She looked at the waves for a sign of struggle, or a death-defying return, but there was nothing. The hat was gone.

"Don't worry, Genie," George said quietly. "We'll get you another one, won't we, children? We'll . . ."

"That's right, Mother," Paul and Jinx piped in. "We can . . . because Olive's got tons of . . ." Their little bodies clustered close in sympathy and love. "Remember when I made that rabbit out of feathers stuck in a box and the cat at home . . ."

But Eugenia paid no attention; her family might have been the breeze stirring in her ears; they might have been the ghosts of her dream. She stared at the sea and saw her hat falling. Over and over and over again she saw it sink. Without hope, without recourse, it vanished from her longing sight.

"Manila . . . you were saying, Carl?" The clock in the Turk's study ticked a reassuring cadence. He took up a cigar, held it between his finger and thumb, and studied how the leaf wrapped the whole and made a cylinder as smooth as whittled wood. Finally he snipped the end and lit a match. The comforting aroma of sulfur and tobacco were as close to heaven as he'd care to come.

"So, you heard from Paine . . . or rather, from Ridgeway. The old fellow writes me himself . . . in his own hand . . . Quite extraordinary. . . ." The Turk chuckled at a private joke. "Of course, I never read them. You can, if you think they'd help." The Turk laughed again. It was a confident sound, as satisfied as the yawn of a cat.

Carl didn't answer. I was the one Father chose to succeed him, Carl thought angrily. It wasn't Tony; it wasn't Martin. It was me. I'm the boy at his beck and call, not them. They can have their fancy houses and fancier friends, I'm the son he needs.

"We'll be leaving leaving Newport tomorrrow, Carl. . . ." he tells me. "Have the late train meet our carriage at Grand Central"; "Then delay the six o'clock to Pittsburgh . . ." or the "eleven o'clock to Marblehead" or the "afternoon connector to Washington." It's do this, do that. And I hop to, don't I? I'm on my feet and out the door before the ink is dry. If it's results the old goat wants, he gets them every time.

Carl glowered at the carpet, then at the footstool near his father's chair. What's the point of going on about Manila now? he wondered. Who cares about old Paine or General Woods or any of those geezers? Who cares about the Philippines?

"No more exciting news items then, Carl? No more problems with the Czar annexing Manchuria?" the Turk chided, then indulged himself in another delightful pull on his cigar. Smoke encircled his face and he was lost to the world.

Carl heard nothing.

And that situation with Carnegie, he recited to himself, heaping fuel on the fire, that event Father referred to as "the sorry little spectacle in Altoona . . ." I'm the one who remembers all those lectures: labor, management, that damnable "open shop," 10 percent wage increases, all that bunkum. I'm the one who's sat drooling at the great man's feet, waiting for a handout, a kind word. And what do I get for my efforts? What's my reward in the end? A kick in the rear. That's what he gives me!

Carl hunched forward suddenly; a decision had sprung into his mind, and he felt like a new man. He felt strong and determined. Let my brothers waste themselves on families and wives, he told himself; let them waste their energy; let them waste their lives. That's not the road for me.

The Turk lazily flicked the ash from his cigar as he studied his son. In its crystal tray, the ash shifted, then crumbled; individual strands of burned tobacco slid into their neighbors, tumbling down like metal chips without a magnet. "What do you think of our chances for rain?" he asked, meaning by that sociable remark that all discussion was closed, that matters had been settled according to schedule.

The Turk gazed at the windows and their heavy copper screens. There were the sounds of jackdaws in the nearby trees. They quarreled with a lusty squawk, and shook leaves and branches, hopping about in trumped-up, yellow-beaked rage. The Turk listened to their feud. August in Pennsylvania, he thought, feeling contentment roll along his back; one of my favorite times of the year. A time to settle in, anticipate the end of summer, look back on the fruits of the season.

The birds grew bolder; one sounded as it were tapping on a screen. Then a breeze kicked up and swirled into the room. What was left of the ash went flying. The Turk turned his head and sniffed the wind.

"Rain on the way, wouldn't you say, Carl?" he asked, but took no notice of Carl's silence. The Turk had his own agenda. He looked out the window. The sky had become dirt gray, and the few remnants of sunlight left mustard-colored splotches on the undersides of the nearby leaves, while across the wide lawn, the weighted boughs of the sycamores and elms turned belly white as their greenery blew upward. Along the drive, it was the same thing, and beside the reflecting pool and rose walk: everywhere leaves in commotion, everywhere the wonderful anticipation of water on dry and dusty faces.

The Turk closed his eyes and tried to imagine how that water would feel. "I'd welcome a summer shower myself," he said. "I do love the sound of rain in this house."

*T*UNIS, TUNISIA. The French pilot sent out from the capital's official port of Tunis-la-Goulette inched the *Alcedo* forward, taking soundings every few feet as he tried to navigate the ship up the long, narrow channel that separated the city from the Mediterranean Sea. In the wheelhouse, Captain Cosby stood to one side, watching another man bring his boat to harbor. This was the first time the *Alcedo* had required a local pilot and Cosby didn't enjoy the sensation. He stared at his deckhouse, his charts, his logbook, his sextant, his calipers, his ship's wheel, and silently cursed the Arab port, the Arabs, the Frenchmen who called this benighted place home, and especially the man who controlled the *Alcedo*'s fate: the pilot.

Shouts in a frenzied garble of French and Arabic raced back and forth from the deckhouse to a small rusty tug that waited at the ship's starboard side. Ostensibly, the purpose of the tug was to aid the much larger *Alcedo,* though, in reality, one swipe from the yacht's bow would have reduced the tug to a few sheets of crinkled metal. Captain Cosby gave a quiet order to the mate, who transmitted the order to the ship's starboard bow. Extra lengths of knotted rope were let out; in case of collision, Cosby did not want the paint on his white ship marred.

The problem with Tunis, of course, was the famous sandbar. It shifted daily; no pilot could tell exactly where the thing might lurk; one morning it would heave onto its side and slit the bow off an English frigate, the next it would rumble under a local freighter. The sandbar had no conscience, no national pride; it didn't care where its victims came from or who their fathers might be.

"Yes, effendi," the pilot muttered to Cosby or no one at all. "No, effendi."

"Who can say for certain, *mon capitain,* sir, in these unhappy times?" The pilot rocked on his heels, shrugged his shoulders, and waved his head slowly from side to side as if he'd forgotten what nationality he was. "We must feel our way here, *Capitain,* effendi, sir. *Capitain.*"

The apology did nothing to reassure Cosby, especially since it was accompanied by more than one sudden dash to the deckhouse door and shrieks and screams that echoed in a terrible mixture of language and intention from the ship to the tug and back again.

With the *Alcedo* slowed to a crawl, beggar boys from canoes began the time-honored tradition of clambering aboard while families in feluccas sailed too close squalling for handouts as their pot-bellied children either plunged or were pushed into the greasy bay. Boats were swamped: grappling hooks were wrenched from bony elbows; grimy hands clutching the *Alcedo*'s hold were driven off. The yacht's sailors were kept busy; just when they thought they'd driven off one band of marauders, another appeared. The men raced from the stern to the bow, from starboard to port, shouting every oath they knew; their stiff blue shirts, their white caps and trousers, were the epitome of righteous, stiff-shouldered, American contempt:

"Tell it to your mother, sonny!"; "One on port side! Elbow him in the ribs!"; "I got that kick right where I wanted it!"

In the deckhouse, Captain Cosby looked down on the maelstrom and forced himself to maintain an outward calm. He thought he saw chips of paint flying, or heard metal bending or wood cracking, and he definitely smelled the biting open-sewer scent of harbor water on slimy bodies. The deck will have to be washed, he told himself, the entire ship scrubbed clean after this, the rails revarnished, gouges removed, and all the brasses brushed and repolished.

Meanwhile the pilot's ingratiating whispers rose to a shout. "These people, effendi . . ." he yelled above the din, ". . . these are not my people. These are the dregs of our once great city. . . . These people do not matter, *mon capitain.* . . . We French people . . ."

At that moment, George climbed up to the deckhouse; he'd decided it was time for action. He couldn't have his sailors wasting their time on beggars, after all, soiling their uniforms or, worse, tearing them. Enough was enough. One couldn't be the entire world's breadbasket, he'd told himself. One was not responsible for every wretch who cried for help.

"The hoses, Captain," George yelled as he walked through the deckhouse door.

"Sir?" Cosby's voice was equally loud. They might as well have been standing on opposite ends of a very large field.

"The fire hoses, Captain! Have them manned! We have to knock these creatures from the rigging. We can't carry them all the way into Tunis-la-Goulette. Think of the danger!"

Captain Cosby doubted that the beggars, no matter how profuse or noisy, posed any real threat, and he hated to turn fire hoses on people, even on people he imagined might dismantle his ship.

"They're awfully strong, sir!" Captain Cosby screamed over the orders from the pilot, the answers from the tug, and the kick-scream-curse variations on deck.

"Exactly!" George answered.

Cosby couldn't hear the word, but he saw the enthusiastic nod of George's head.

So the fire hoses were unwound and turned on the invaders. The decks were doused, and the rigging, and, lastly, the *Alcedo*'s sides. Men and boys in the midst of climbing the ropes were the easiest to hit; the harder the water pressure, the higher they scrambled; then there'd be one shout or fifteen or twenty-five when the wet hands were torn loose and the brown bodies plummeted into the harbor. Then the sailors turned their attention on the native craft: feluccas were swamped; children were washed from their tiny prows; faces appearing beneath the ship's rails were squirted so hard their owners lost their breath and finally their bearing.

Eugenia came out on deck with the children. This is an Arab world, she'd instructed; it's noisy because people express themselves more freely here than they do at home; the Arab people love to argue and shout; fighting is a form of entertainment. Eugenia had herded her children outside to watch the yacht's arrival; she'd thought they'd see charming little boats hawking charming native wares: bright colors, happy smiles, pretty trinkets to welcome the Americans.

But the sight and sound of so many collapsing bodies was too horrible to bear. Eugenia bustled her babies back inside and closed the saloon door with so much force that it nearly made Tunisia and the beggars and the sandbar and the French-Arab pilot vanish like yesterday's bad dream.

"Chinese checkers, anyone?" Eugenia announced as breezily as possible while she shook out her skirts, rearranged her cuffs, found her handkerchief, forgot it in her hand, and reminded herself to breathe.

"Lizzie," Eugenia added with a determined smile, "will you be a good girl and fetch the board?"

The children were too startled to argue. Lizzie didn't say, "I'm not a baby, Mother. I can't be placated by a child's game." Instead she pulled out the board and colored marbles, set them on a table, and blocked out all other sound.

And Paul didn't pipe in, "We haven't played this in forever! Not since Lizzie got too big for games." And he didn't demand the yellows or the blues; he stared at the color his sister allotted him, and watched the marbles take their familiar wedgelike shape. While Jinx tried not to look at the windows, and found she couldn't help herself.

She'd see the outline of a naked body, there one moment and then gone; she'd hear the sound like something soft dropping onto something hard, and she'd hear words that might have been children moaning before a witch turned them into stone. Jinx gasped and lost all concentration in the game.

But her mother had a remedy for that; she called Higgins and told him to draw the drapes.

"Very bright in here, don't you think?" Eugenia remarked as the chief steward entered the room. "I suppose we'll have to take care in this African sun, but no point in starting too early. We're not in port yet. We can have a little respite before it's too late."

"Very good, madam," Higgins answered as he pulled the drapes to with a bang. And that was the last Eugenia and the children saw of their arrival in Tunis.

Lieutenant Brown looked out across the harbor. They were all one and the same to him: Bombay, Penang, Calcutta, the smells and the noise, the wharf and the customs house, the bribery, the native-born "gentlemen" in their dirty coats, the racket of ricksha drivers, the "guides," beggars, and boys dancing forward and back beside any open cart. Arab, Malay, or Hindu, Lieutenant Brown had never known it to vary. Not since he'd first shipped out.

But there was something different in Tunis; it wasn't the confusion along the pier or the uneasy way the yacht had been delivered to her berth. It wasn't the narrow channel or his own careful habit of marking an escape route. It was none of the things Lieutenant Brown had trained himself to notice; it was a feeling only, a sense of something about to happen.

Standing at the bow rail, Brown suddenly remembered a childhood morning in September or October. It could have been either month,

Brown thought, but he knew it was after summer and before harvest-time, the quiet days when the scrambling fight against too much rain, too much drought, weevil, or budworm was over for another year.

Fog had covered the valley where his family lived; he could see it as he'd seen it then—through the dirty glass of a single window. The fog hung in the treetops and sifted down amongst the rows of tobacco and feed corn, lying there like an old dog, too sad, too tired, or too wise to move. He'd heard crows fighting, too, squabbling over some squirrel's wrung-out carcass or merely having their own idea of a raucous good time, though their screeches were noisier than usual. And there were faces in the window beside his own: younger, most of them, wide-eyed and scared. They'd stared at the sheeted fields; no one blinked and no one spoke. They'd watched the morning and the fog and waited.

Tunis, Tunisia. Lieutenant Brown brought his thoughts back to the present. Time for another jostle through the crowd, he reminded himself, another little session of reverent sightseeing: "The Mosques and the Splendors of Ancient Carthage," and all of us starched up and polite enough to burst.

Suddenly Brown wished they could get on with it, get the job done. Maybe that's why I'm uneasy, he reasoned. It's not the place; it's the waiting.

And it's not that I have to lie, he promised himself. I'm used to that. It doesn't matter what they think of me later. Eugenia or her children. I wasn't part of their life once and I won't be when this is over. Tunisia, Egypt, Brown silently recited the ship's stops, the Red Sea, Africa, the Seychelles, and finally Borneo. I'll do my job and move on.

Eugenia came out on deck. It was hot and stuffy inside, and it seemed as though the whole ship smelled of the lamb cutlets they'd had for luncheon. Lamb cutlets, slivered potatoes, *haricots financière,* baked tomatoes in cream, mint sorbet, and ladyfingers: They might as well have stayed in Philadelphia. After that chaotic arrival, "good solid food" was, as George had put it, "just what the doctor ordered," but Eugenia didn't agree.

"We didn't come to Africa to pretend it was Chestnut Street," she'd argued. "We can't drive people into the water, tell ourselves the 'natives' do this kind of thing for sport, and then sit down for tea!" But George had only smiled indulgently and glanced over her head with a complaisant look she'd guessed was intended for Ogden Beckmann.

Just what the doctor ordered, Eugenia repeated inwardly as she walked to the rail and leaned her body into its steadying hand. She didn't know what she was thinking. The morning had been supposed to be full of wonder: the first taste of Africa, the first sense of the ship's headlong tumble into an enchanted and mysterious world, but instead it had been merely startling. First the ship had lurched one way and then another as if that strange little man, the pilot, were trying to follow a bread crumb trail into the woods, then George had ordered men swept away like leaves on a tennis green, and now he was apparently in the most robust of spirits, having planted his opinions, his desires, his Philadelphian sensibilities, on foreign soil.

Eugenia stared at the city spread out below her. The docks pointed inland toward the native town, and the European sector: one collecting dust at the base of the Bir-Kassa hills, the other emblazoned with trees and gardens and named with the impressive-sounding Avenue de Carthage and Avenue de la Marine. But Eugenia couldn't see where one distinct township ended and the other began. Carthage, she reminded herself, this is ancient Carthage, where they sacrificed babies and brooded on the day they'd finally defeat Rome. But even those drastic tales were no more than words. They conjured up nothing, and answered no questions.

A thousand smells and sounds wafted up to the ship: something that sounded like the bleat of a goat, something that might have been a camel, a call to prayer, a rattle of bells, and one long note that was keening and splintery cruel. Then there were the acrid smells of spice and urine, scents like lime flowers and juniper boughs and the reek of cesspool water. The combinations danced around, displaying one partner, then another, eliciting a desire to travel further—or a sense of gulping revulsion. The place was as foreign as anything Eugenia had known; it made her feel as though she'd been dropped on the moon.

She held the rail in her hands. So this is how we arrive on our great adventure, she told herself, with tomatoes in cream, mint sorbet, and fire hoses at the ready. " 'Where ignorant armies clash by night,' " Eugenia said aloud.

"I hope that won't be the case, Mrs. Axthelm," Brown answered. He hadn't meant to disturb her; he realized she believed she was alone, but it was either speak or sneak away.

"Oh!" Eugenia said in surprise. "Lieutenant Brown!" She'd recognized his voice immediately, but she was buying time to hide her embarrassment.

"I didn't see you there! You must have escaped the DuPlessises' lecture as well." Eugenia straightened the gauzy jacket of her afternoon dress, trying to create crisp regimentation where none existed.

"I know they mean well," she continued, paying no attention to her words, "at least, I hope they mean well. . . ." Her private joke began to lift the spell.

". . . I'm sure they must . . . and what they've discovered about these countries is always so . . . well . . . so, informative . . ." Eugenia laughed. "Oh, listen to me making excuses! I sound just like my husband!"

She looked up into Lieutenant Brown's face. "Truthfully I am heartily glad to desert the whole tedious crowd. And the lectures about the Carthaginians and their unfortunate children. And the lamb cutlets. And the *haricots financière!* The *haricots* especially."

Eugenia laughed again, then leaned forward, balancing herself on the rail, and it seemed to Brown that she was capable of anything, of flying off or recklessly leaping into the waves.

"So where are we now, Lieutenant?" she rushed ahead. "I think . . . it's just a guess really . . . that you've been here before. . . .

"I don't know what makes me say that. Woman's intuition, I suppose. So, tell me what wonders await us here? In Tunis, Tunisia. In La Goulette . . ." Eugenia gazed at the hazy city, and felt relief and laughter spin around inside her like water in a well. It's so good to be out on deck, she thought; it will be even better on the streets. Away from the boat and the fire hoses, and the safety of looking down on an ancient and very dead civilization from the unapproachable confines of our majestic tower.

Lieutenant Brown didn't understand the change in Eugenia or why she needed to pretend she'd never met him before, but it suited his decision; it made his role easier.

"I haven't been here before, ma'am. I wouldn't know," he answered as he kept his eyes fixed on the pier and stood as upright and stiff as he imagined a Lieutenant James Armand Brown might stand.

The words sounded so strange that Eugenia spun around for a closer look, and as she did she flung out a hand as though she were dancing or falling. "Oh," she cried out, "I didn't mean to—"

"Pry," she'd been about to add, but stopped herself in time.

"I see," she added after a moment. "Of course. As you wish. So . . . we are both newcomers here."

Brown didn't speak. He stared at the wharf, and cursed himself for hiding the truth, then for being forced to hide it and, finally, for the pain that story would inflict. And just when I believed it didn't matter, he told himself. Just when I'd convinced myself that a lie was nothing at all.

"I have traveled to other places, though . . ." he said, starting up another speech entirely. "Exotic places, like this, some of them. At least"—Brown attempted a smile—"they looked exotic to me. . . ."

"Oh, yes?" Eugenia's voice was eager; for a moment she sounded so much like Jinx that it would have been difficult to tell them apart:

"As exotic as this? With as many, oh, what would you call them? . . . odd sounds and smells and colors . . . and . . . and music . . . ?"

All of a sudden, Eugenia laughed again. "You know, Lieutenant," she nearly sang out, "I'm very happy.

"I am!" And Eugenia realized what she'd said was true; she was strong and brave and full of hope. And it had come as such a surprise! It was as if someone had been trying to tell her something for a very long time, had been shouting or whispering the good news, but what she'd heard had been no more than noise. And then the noise took the form of words, and the words became thoughts, and the thoughts were real.

"But tell me all your adventures!" Eugenia said. "Paul says you've been in the South China Sea and attacked by pirates. But you know Paul! A 'lively imagination,' as we mothers say when a child tends to invent things!

"So . . . are these stories made up or are they true? . . . Do we have a hero in our midst? . . . And where else have you been? Tell me anything at all! Just talk. . . .

"We're going to have a wonderful time here." Eugenia stopped the rush of words. "I feel it, don't you? I feel this city is just the beginning. We have the whole world before us. . . ."

As she rattled on, Eugenia disengaged herself from Brown; she smoothed her dress, shook the lace at her cuffs, and pushed back wisps of hair that had fallen into her face. She was all movement, switching the wrinkles from her skirt or straightening her embroidered belt, and she was unaware of the effect these gestures had.

Lieutenant Brown felt his resolve desert him. It melted away as if made of no sterner stuff than day-old ice, and he was left holding nothing but his uniform, his rank, and his good name. Lieutenant James Armand Brown, he recited, the United States Naval Academy, class of 1899. Lieutenant Brown.

"Well, I'm ready," Eugenia announced joyfully, and hurried down the deck. "I'll go get the children and George and the DuPlessises and everyone and we'll start off.

"North Africa! Just think of it. Even the name is wonderful! And guess what else? No Ogden Beckmann. Isn't that the best news? He's staying on board. And for our whole stay, too." Eugenia didn't know why she'd added that information. The words were out of her mouth before she could retrieve them.

The excursion to the Moslem holy city of Kairouan was to be the focal point of the yacht's stay in the country of Tunisia; George had determined this all the way back in the snowy depths of Philadelphia: Kairouan by caravan, and the children dressed up as little Arabs. It would be a parade to end all parades.

To accomplish this transformation the family first had to visit the souk in the way station town of Enphida. There they were pounced on by every sort of charlatan, mountebank, pickpocket, beggar, faith healer, soothsayer, snake charmer, sleight-of-hand artist, and "honest merchant" an Arab bazaar could uncover. But George was equal to the challenge; he merely bought everything in sight.

"This way, kind sir . . ."

"If you would be so gracious, honored sire . . ."

"My humble shop is just along the path, effendi . . ." The stench of heat and greed were equal and palpable.

"And a very good price. Only for you. Because I like to see a man of art with a work of art . . ." Or a saddlebag. Or a six-foot brass urn. Or a bolt of embroidered wool. Or a child's vest, a fez, ten fezzes, twenty, what did it matter? The goods of the country tumbled in front of George's ever-moving feet. Tiny shop fronts burst open to display their luscious wares: a camel saddle inlaid with mother-of-pearl, a scimitar of Damascus steel, a robe encrusted with silver braid. Shoes of velvet, slippers of gold. A lance found deep in the Atlas Mountains. Its owner swore to its authenticity.

"Roman, honored sire. From Carthage. From the times of the Crusades."

"The Crusades were . . ." George had started to correct this quite obvious error, then had the good sense to stop himself. "What do you think, Genie?" he'd asked finally, shaking his head as he chuckled. "Shall we buy it? . . . Roman? . . . From Carthage? . . . From the times of the Crusades?"

Sometimes Eugenia answered, but more often she did not. There was something repellent in the quantity of goods displayed before her. They reminded her of overripe fruit: papayas or mangosteens; they exploded from thin shells; they split apart with steamy color and a terrible stench. They enticed you for a look, then drove you back, panting for air and cool water.

Pigeon's-blood purple, vermilion, and cinnabar; sandalwood, jasmine, attar of rose. Beads of amber, ropes of silver, hoops of gold and brass and copper; pots of cardamom, aniseed, fenugreek; Bedouin anklets and rings and amulets. Eugenia stared and felt her skin grow colder, while her children cavorted down the street and her husband ordered everything, everything, carted off to the ship.

"And mind it's carefully wrapped! Can't have a thing like that broken!"

"Yes, effendi." Offended, the merchant booted his boy out of the path.

Soon boys were flying all over the street; they collided with camels and monkeys in cages, with pyramids of green eggs and baby goats on tethers. Carts were tipped; merchants screamed.

"Yes, effendi . . ."; "Yes, effendi . . ." Salaam, salaam, salaam. Boys and dust and boxes of cockatiels went screaming through the air.

An adventure, Eugenia kept reminding herself; this is an adventure. But the riot of sound and smell and color was too much to comprehend. It didn't feel as much like an adventure as a rout. Eugenia was reminded of the sheep they'd seen the day before. Driven along a rocky mountain ridge, the animals, shepherds, and wolflike dogs moved at the same pace. They hurried as if from disaster, a fire or flood, but they fled without sound. The sheep didn't bleat and the dogs neither whined nor barked. The only sound above the muffled stumble of hooves on stone was an intermittent, high-pitched whistle the shepherds forced through their blackened teeth: a thin, prolonged hiss that cut through the scorched, hot hills.

"A little tired, madame?" The voice startled Eugenia back to the present. "Perhaps you would care for a small rest?" Mr. Suravy approached her, gasping. Mr. Suravy was the guide, the native-born "Englishman" who spoke with a strange accent and smelled of last week's curry.

"A little tea?" he wheezed again. But Mr. Suravy, for all his Somerset pretensions, liked the tea they served in the tiny shops. Hot tea in glasses and laced with so much sugar and mint it was impossible to taste anything else.

"No thank you, Mr. Suravy," Eugenia said, backing away from the dirty suit and sweat-streaked solar topee. "I think I'll just go up the street and find my husband."

"Of course, madame. I will accompany you." Mr. Suravy leaned forward on his plump but nimble toes. Nothing was too much for him. No discomfort too great in the service of his honored guests.

"Whatever you wish, madame," Mr. Suravy puffed, and thought how pleasant life would be after these rich Americans left, when he was alone again in his beloved bazaar. Tobacco, he thought; he'd buy a tin of really fine tobacco. The best money could produce, because he'd have the cash then. He'd have a lot of it. Enough for a year or more.

George Axthelm hadn't even blinked when he'd been told what the services of a good guide would cost; he hadn't even moved. And now here he was, the great voyager, purchasing everything in sight, never questioning the price, never learning the steps to that careful and elegant dance called negotiation. What was he paying? Five times the amount, fifty, a hundred? Mr. Suravy shook his head in hurt dismay.

And maybe some potted English cheese, he thought, returning to his reverie, from the Cheddar Gorge. And perhaps Havana cigars. He'd sit on the veranda, after dinner, looking like a real Englishman. He might even entertain! But suddenly Mr. Suravy realized he didn't know anyone who could appreciate a fine cigar or a crumbling slice of blue-ringed cheese.

He didn't know anyone but Arabs or the other men like himself who'd made a life out of pretending to be something they were not. French, English, or German, they got themselves up to look like their namesakes; they studied *Burke's Peerage;* they learned the names of the schools and the titles of the masters; they memorized bloodlines (horse and human) and recited, like catechism, all the latest gossip. They were frauds, but they got by.

"Of course I must accompany you, Mrs. Axthelm," Suravy repeated heavily. "I am your host, after all." He breathed garlic and mutton chop all over Eugenia's face; he smelled hot and greasy and unwell and she couldn't help flinching. Is this the sort of Englishman we'll be meeting from now on, she thought, remembering Ambassador Jeffries' elegant manner. Do even the English alter when they arrive in this strange country? Is it the climate or the place or something more insidious than that? And what about me? Will I retreat to haricots and tomatoes in cream or will I start making "allowances" for the natives and then for myself, saying, "One must break with tradition" as I let my hair fall loose and sleep in a shuttered room long after morning is past?

"You know Sir Randall Jeffries, then?" Eugenia returned to the social banter she understood as she strolled up the street at Suravy's side. "I believe I heard you mention that fact to my husband. We met him, you know, when we stopped in Madeira. A beautiful place . . ." Was it? Eugenia wondered. All of a sudden she couldn't remember much about Madeira at all. It had been green, European; Eugenia had an image like something Swiss, a picnic in a mountain meadow, wildflowers, pine needles, the sound of tree branches bending. She didn't allow her thoughts to continue to the Governor's Ball.

"Sir Randall Jeffries? Indeed, madame," Suravy said, mopping his very wet brow, then he turned aside further scrutiny with carefully re-hearsed patter: "Shall we look at the necklaces, the *qiladeh* as they are called, in this shop? They are particularly fine. See the half-moon, the *nasf al qamar,* and the crescent, the *hilal;* they are perfect examples of Bedouin jewelry. If you'd care to . . ." Mr. Suravy babbled on and on as he pressed her into the recesses of the street's largest shop.

Eugenia tried to smile gratitude and courteous attention while the men lounging at the shop entrance stared. Unveiled, dressed in obvi-ously wanton wiles with a tight waist, a fitted jacket, and a curving, suggestive skirt, Eugenia felt naked and foolishly afraid. She felt as if she were the one on display, not the jewelry mounded before her.

"No, please, Mr. Suravy . . ." she murmured, finally able to stop the mechanized sales pitch and stream of information, " . . . I'd like to find my husband." She could feel eyes on the small of her back, on her arms, her hips, and the nape of her neck. Her skin prickled, and she was reminded of a feeling she had whenever she stood at the edge of a precipice. It wasn't a fear of heights that made her hands go cold and clammy, it was the knowledge that at any moment she might jump.

"How romantic you Americans are! The inseparable couple," Suravy quipped as he swiftly changed course. "How I envy you!" The hungry-eyed men and disappointed shopkeeper were deserted with the snap of Mr. Suravy's deft fingers.

George had decided to drape his two daughters in Arab burnooses. They peered through the crocheted veils and giggled. It was as hot as anything inside the black dresses; it was like hiding in a tent. But it was fun, and it was even better fun watching Father have such a good time.

Paul stepped forward, the last to be equipped. "What do you think, Lieutenant Brown?" George asked loudly, turning his son around for a better display. "A scimitar at the waist to complete the picture?" George's voice demanded attention and everyone clustered together to see what wonder he'd accomplish next.

"Or Whitney, what about you? Or Dr. DuPlessis? A scimitar for you, too? Or Prudence, Prudentia . . . What for the nursemaid of child-hood years?" George turned to his audience. He'd paraded them up and down the street and they'd oohed and aahed and made all the right noises: a compliment for one decision, envious astonishment at an-other. Duplicate purchases, triplicate purchases, another djellaba, six more scarves: praise and flattery flowed without ceasing.

"Or you, Mrs. D.? A scimitar for a lovely lady? You never know when it might come in handy! Dr. D. looks like a man who needs a threat once in a while."

"Oh, Mr. A., you do say such awful things!" Mrs. DuPlessis twittered. Or tried to twitter. She was feeling horribly hot and out of breath; her pulse felt uneasy, and were those palpitations she noticed in her chest?

Mrs. DuPlessis wanted to sit in the shade and have a servant fetch a cool glass of lemonade. Then she decided: No. What she wanted was to be back on the ship, lying comfortably in a chaise under the awning. And she'd have hot tea, she changed her mind again, hot tea and sugar biscuits or maybe macaroons! Mrs. DuPlessis's stomach grumbled loudly at the heavenly thought of macaroons. Their lovely almond scent and crumbly sweetness nearly made her swoon.

"My goodness!" she said. "It must be getting close on to luncheon time!"

But Mrs. DuPlessis's delicate reminder did no good; George was impervious to anything but his own plans. "What do you think, son?" he asked, stepping back to admire his handiwork. "A white headdress? And then perhaps these rope things . . . What do you call them?" George asked over his shoulder. No one answered, but he plowed ahead without noticing.

". . . these rope things in crimson like a real Bedouin! . . . We'll wrap them around your head"—he spun Paul around, "and voilà . . . as they say in Paris . . . a real, live Arab sheikh! The Thousand and One Knights! . . ." K-nights, George pronounced the word. "Or is it 'Nights'?" He laughed loudly at his own joke. "Whoever can answer that question wins the prize!"

" 'Nights,' Father!" The children jumped up and down while everyone else stood about foolishly, trying to keep in the spirit of the game as their interest flagged and they grew hotter, wearier, and more and more anxious to be done with the souk, the shopping spree, and the whole turbulent day itself.

"Perhaps we might consider . . . a light repast of some sort . . ." Mrs. DuPlessis began again.

"Never!" George roared delightedly. "We can't leave until everyone has collected a prize! Now, I want each of you to search out the most expensive, most outrageous thing he or she can find so I can buy it for you.

"Hurry up!" he bellowed. "The first one to find his . . . or her prize wins—an extra one!"

The group began to scatter through the square, Dr. DuPlessis supporting his unhappy wife while the children tore ahead. The shopkeepers, in response to the onslaught, spilled more wares into the street. Allah is good, they told themselves; Allah is wise. He has sent these foolish folk as a lesson, as an aid in times of trouble. With each prayer of thanks, they added to their stockpiles, dangling one embroidered slipper here, a beaded jacket there, a Sudan short sword near a pile of carpets, a fiendishly shiny firelock beside it or a saddlebag studded with azure blue beads. It was nearly impossible to walk without stepping on some delectable object. Silver and gold and sparkling gems seemed to glint in every corner. Jinx, Lizzie, and Paul decided this was like Christmas or a dream come true, and they'd been set free in the largest toy emporium in the world where everything, everything, was theirs.

"Whoo-whooo-whoooo!" shouted Paul.

"Here! This one! . . . I've found mine! . . . No, this one . . . This is better . . . Here, Father! I've won! . . . I've won! Me . . . me . . . me . . . !" yelped the girls at another market stall, while Lieutenant Brown interrupted George's spree with a quiet:

"If you'll excuse me, sir. Perhaps I'd better go back down the path and see if I can find Mrs. Axthelm and the guide. He didn't look as if he . . ."

"Nonsense, my boy! She can look out for herself. She shouldn't have dawdled!" George kept his eyes glued to his busy guests. Nothing would cheat him out of his joyful mood. This was his day, his night on the town, his royal parade, his coronation.

"But perhaps Suravy couldn't . . ." Brown began.

"Nonsense!" George said; his voice for all its boisterous bravado was steely and mean. "She'll find her own way. I do make myself clear, Lieutenant? A chain is only as weak as its weakest link." Then, as if he'd exposed too much, George added:

"Genie's all right, old boy. Wives need time to themselves. All this fretting over the kiddies, proper food, protective clothing . . . all that mother stuff . . . I know my wife, Lieutenant. I know what's best for her."

After that there was the small incident of the trained monkey. It was an insignificant, white-faced beast that turned somersaults at the end of a chain and the children found it during their rampage through the souk. The monkey's owner, knowing God's hand when he saw it, persuaded the creature to spin faster than it ever had. This was accomplished with the aid of a small, but very sharp, stick that the owner, being a sensible man as well as a merchant, had learned to apply in secret.

The monkey leapt backward, leapt forward, till the iron collar that clasped its scrawny neck drew splotchy drops of blood. The children laughed, encouraged by the merchant, encouraged by the noise of the place and the dust and the smells they couldn't understand. They were given cinnamon-coated nuts by someone who grinned and bowed, and were urged to make use of the merchant's stick. It was like Punch and Judy or the make-believe battles of circus clowns.

That was how Eugenia found her children. She didn't stop to think: How cruel they've become. She didn't say: "What are you doing? That poor thing's a creature just like you." Eugenia never hesitated because she knew, with sudden certainty, that her family had been caught in a spell. And she reached out her hand to break it.

She meant to take the monkey in her arms; she meant to show Paul and Lizzie and Jinx how the tiny thing had been hurt, and return them to their fine and loving senses, but the monkey had no knowledge of her motive. It saw sleeves, gloves, and two straight, demanding arms, and it hurled itself into a suicidal leap and bit Eugenia's hand.

What a hue and cry rose up then! The bazaar erupted in oaths and accusations. The merchants screamed that the "filthy peddlers of animal antics" had ruined their business, and the snake charmer and the man with the muzzled, hairless bear and the vendors of birds in boxes shrieked back.

"I'm all right," Eugenia shouted above the din. "Really. It's all right! I had on my glove. He didn't break the skin . . ." And she started to remove her glove to prove that, yes indeed, she was safe, that the day was not ruined, and that everyone could return to their business. ". . . It was my fault, honestly . . ."

But the monkey was already dead, strangled by a wild-eyed shopkeeper while its owner howled in the bloody dust, and Eugenia's naked hand and snow-white fingers did nothing but incite the crowd to further fury. The lady was wounded; the lady-wife of the generous and honored gentleman!

It was George who saved the day, George dispersing coins to each outstretched hand as if they were Communion wafers. "That's the show for today," his voice boomed out; "nothing more to see here! Off you go, now!" while Mr. Suravy sought out the injured parties and made generous restitution.

When all was done, George looked at his wife. "I don't know why you do these things!" he said, studying her as if trying to choose which crime to list first. "It's not Rittenhouse Square, you know. You can't parade around, mixing in other people's lives, doing whatever you want." His voice was genuinely angry; even the children knew to stay silent.

• • •

Finally peace was restored and the journey to Kairouan was begun in splendor. A pasha's retinue couldn't have done better. There were camels for everyone, extra beasts for those that might pull up lame (as if their drivers would ever let them); there were donkeys or mules for the weak-stomached and there were Arabian horses ("Excellent stock—very fast, effendi") for those who needed a bit more sport. George perched himself on the largest camel and posed for Dr. Du-Plessis's camera. He tossed an Arab scarf rakishly over his head and demanded that two drivers stand in nervous attention near the forelegs of his mountainous beast, then he threw out his arms as if he'd decided to embrace not only the entire crowd before him but the whole world as well. The great George Axthelm on top of the world.

"An adventurer!" he shouted. "What do you think, Genie? Or an old-time explorer?"

"Yes, George." Eugenia's answer was inaudible through her wisps of sun-veil. Her little Arabian mare pranced about, anxious to be off. Eugenia felt out of practice; her sidesaddle didn't quite fit, but the effort of controlling her horse had the soothing effect of allowing no other thought.

"Can't hear you, my dear," George called down. He'd decided to be magnanimous again; he could afford it, after all, with everything going so swimmingly. George considered how pleasant it was without Beckmann. It's like a real vacation, he told himself. Like a schoolboy's lark.

"Nice to be off on our own isn't it, Genie?" George said. "Out from under the glowering eye . . . Why, who knows what might happen with us on our own . . ."

But Eugenia missed not only the words, but her husband's attempt at a suggestive leer.

"One more photo as the mighty warrior, Mr. A.!" Dr. DuPlessis's voice rose above the growl of camels and the angry cackle of their drivers.

"Us, too, Doctor!" Jinx and Paul and Lizzie demanded, shrieking.

"Of course! Of course. Everyone in their finery and on their chosen mount! . . . Paul, don't cross your eyes like that! . . . Jinx, my dear young lady, you must sit still!"

"Gustav!" wailed Mrs. DuPlessis. "I can't get up!"

Mrs. DuPlessis was indeed stuck. Even though her camel had obediently folded its knees and crouched as low as possible for the lady to mount, either one of the drivers or the animal itself had decided enough was enough and, as Mrs. DuPlessis's right foot dangled in the air, trying to swing to safety, the camel had begun to rise. It was an ungainly and slow movement, full of bumps and thumps, and with each gulping lurch, Mrs. DuPlessis was carried farther and farther from the earth. Her free foot switched wildly; her skirts and wide body shivered in despair. She looked like a quilt tossed on a bed; she shifted and seemed to settle, then all at once began the inexorable slide to the ground.

"Gustav! Help!"

Dr. DuPlessis spun around with his camera; the tripod tipped, but he pulled it back in time.

"Gustav!" Mrs. DuPlessis's wail rang through the square.

Dr. DuPlessis waved his arms; he looked terribly distressed; he opened his mouth to call for aid, but no sound came. Then he did a most unusual thing. While his wife clung to the saddle, slipping gradually from sight, he took a picture.

Later that day and indeed for many days, for the rest of the voyage, whenever the pilgrimage to Kairouan was mentioned, Dr. DuPlessis would be teased about that photograph. He'd always answer the same thing: "But I'd been taking portraits, you see, and I don't know . . . Why, there was my wife, and all I could think was to take her portrait." Then he'd look around whatever room the group had gathered in and wait for signs of support, but the image of Mrs. DuPlessis's plight would always remain: a wide backside without head or arms, an acre of gabardine skirts, and a camel steadily pointing its woolly rump toward the sky.

But for now, with her husband apologetically bumbling words of regret, Mrs. DuPlessis was righted. She was pushed and pummeled and soothed into place. The animal's reins were placed in her hands (for show only—she had a driver on either side of her camel's head) and they were off.

"Gustav . . . !" she called out loudly. "I don't think I like this. . . . I think I'd rather ride a . . ." But her words were drowned by a shout that echoed and reechoed the length of the bazaar; the crowd had been satisfactorily entertained.

It wasn't a sound Eugenia recognized; it wasn't the happy cheer of the crowd at a Maryland steeplechase or the college boys in eight-man shells racing on the Schuylkill. It was more like the wail of a hurricane or the imagined scream of banshees.

Eugenia moved her horse close to Lieutenant Brown's. He seemed, fortunately, to be moving at the same speed she was and with equal distance from the rest of the crowd. She felt a brief pang about her children's well-being, but then realized they were with George. And as long as George had money they were safe. Safe and apparently very happy.

"What a terrible noise, Lieutenant," Eugenia called over the shriek and clamor. "Have you ever . . . ?"

"Yes!" he shouted back, and trotted nearer. He was determined not to lose Eugenia again. He'd lost her once that day, and that once had been enough. "It's just their way of saying 'Godspeed.' Kairouan is . . ."

"What?" Eugenia stretched sideways in her saddle to hear him.

". . . It's a holy city . . ." he said, but the words kept flying off in the clanging wind. ". . . Like Mecca . . ."

"But it's an awful sound," Eugenia said, and lifted herself to look back. "It doesn't seem like Godspeed or anything like it. It sounds too angry for that." And I wouldn't blame them, Eugenia realized, not with our behavior here today.

The mob began to close ranks behind them, and Eugenia imagined the human faces and bodies becoming demons, djinns or afriti. Their cloaked bodies would sway together, growing in size and number till they stretched across the sun: a malevolent, howling mass.

". . . It's a tradition . . ." Brown was saying, ". . . a kind of song or warble they make with their tongues and the backs of their throats . . . a sort of all-purpose noise . . . the Arabs use it for greeting friends, heralding victory, jeering defeat. Almost anything. . . ."

"What do you suppose they mean now?" Eugenia asked with her eyes on the crowd.

"God knows. But it's nothing to worry over. Your future's definitely safe in this country," Lieutenant Brown laughed. He thought to say something else, then changed his mind.

"I'm glad you're here," Eugenia said. "With us, I mean."

The two horses trotted together at the back of the line while in front, like a picture from a fairy tale, stretched George's caravan. Squinting her eyes, Eugenia could almost see palanquins there, palanquins and tasseled umbrellas and banners of damask and silvery silk. And she thought she could hear the sound of trumpets and *tabourets* calling forth the songs of war, but it was probably only the wind, she reminded herself. The wind and the sand and the voices of man and beast.

Eugenia's children were mounted on camels; at each camel's head ran two drivers, two more raced at the tail, and at each flank galloped or pranced the extra horses, and the donkeys and mules. They paraded through the mist of a million particles of flying sand. The caravan loosened itself and separated according to each camel driver's private whim, and the afternoon grew hot and silent: the peace broken only by some animal shaking itself or trying to bite a rider's dangling foot. At intervals and seemingly from nowhere, men appeared. Guides, they said they were, and they presented the usual stream of goods: bits of brass, rugs or blankets, and now and then tiny bones that looked too human to be otherwise. "A young Pharaoh, effendi!" George was told. "A tiny prince. The price for you, sire, very good."

Eugenia rolled along and took it all in, but part of her remained aloof. There was the placid picture of her face, and then there was her mind, and she wondered, wandering up one sand dune and then another, if those two beings could ever be the same: if, in turning a bland and lovely smile to the world, she could become that careless woman.

The caravan dispersed, regrouped, and the day wore on. Sometimes they were hampered by fellow pilgrims, and at other times they broke upon a vista so serene that they'd stop as one mass to admire it. Eugenia watched her children cluster near their father as his determined excitement drew them in, but she saw it from a distance; she and her little horse kept apart.

Forever she would keep that image with her. It would rise up when the ship was again at sea and she stood alone on deck; it would appear before her in the midst of another city or another market square. She would see the caravan to Kairouan stretched across the desert. She would see it as though she hovered above it on an angel's invisible wings: the horses and camels and mules wavering over the white expanse of sand. From her vantage point, so high in the air, the desert looked like a broad back of a velvety beach. The animals kicked up whiffs of smoke as they paced their steady way toward the holy city. Up the dunes, down the dunes, crossing and recrossing the rippled road to Kairouan.

And it was quiet in this vision, perfectly and absolutely silent. No driver reprimanded a recalcitrant camel; no child whispered; no adult struggled for words. No insect buzzed; no bird sang. Muffled in veils and turbans and scarves, the procession stared straight ahead and didn't dare speak. It was that silence Eugenia would always remember. The silence of a stone in the desert's deep heart.

*O*GDEN BECKMANN fought to stay awake. He'd gone down to the ship's hold to check on the crates and make sure no one tampered with them while the *Alcedo* was stuck in the pestilential hole of Tunisia, but the heat had grown too much for him and he'd decided to stretch out in the hammock that had been fitted for Lieutenant Brown's guard duty. Only for a moment, Beckmann told himself. Only till I regain my strength. He felt burdened by his own girth; what was considered powerful in Philadelphia seemed bulky and unwieldy under the burning North African sky.

Beckmann breathed deeply and hoisted himself into the rope net. The hold was hot and airless and the hammock swayed slightly, though the ship did not. The *Alcedo* lay on her keel as though stuck in sand or cement. Why Tunis? Beckmann thought. Why waste time like this? We should be getting on to our destination, not frittering away precious days sightseeing!

Besides, Beckmann reminded himself, there's no need for pretension now. What could our illustrious doctor and his waddling wife do if they found out? Jump ship? Head home in a huff? Or that fool Whitney? Or even Eugenia? They've got no choice but to continue: The Turk owns them all. And, damn it, he should have been stricter. He should have told George exactly what the rules were. "Refuel," he should have said, "take on whatever provisions you need, but keep moving."

Beckmann glared at the dark beams above his head. They glittered as if they were alive; they looked like shiny black skin, and Beckmann realized they were swarming with ants. Ants and beetles and every variety of winged insect paraded up and down the wood. He felt a sudden urge to crush them all. It wouldn't take much, just a neatly aimed blow with his foot, but Beckmann didn't attempt it. Instead he studied the procession. He watched the outriders at work and the mavericks; he watched the huddled mass of families and the timid laborings of the abject and the lowly. He watched them spread their dogged path over the wood, disappearing, each one, to their own determined end.

Even Eugenia, Beckmann decided suddenly. The Turk pulls her strings the same as he does the rest of us. She should take better care. But as Beckmann tried to reassure himself on that count, doubt began to trickle back into his mind. Perhaps no one controls her, he realized, perhaps she doesn't know the meaning of the word. Maybe she floats along because she doesn't care what the Turk does or what George has; maybe none of it much matters. You can't reason with a person who doesn't speak the same language.

The discovery made Beckmann uneasy and, at the same time, sad. He lashed out with his foot and sent a hundred little black things flying. Crushed, battered, wings torn, backs broken, they fell in dumb confusion on the floor. Beckmann got up and walked over the squirming bodies to the crates. Shells and wings snapped beneath his feet. No, the Turk doesn't own Eugenia and neither do I. For the first time in his life Beckmann felt helpless and old.

He stared at the Axthelm and Company crates. Stacked and orderly, resting coolly on their wood pallets, they stared back, found him guilty of sentiment and emotion and then damned him. Beckmann yanked himself back to reality: he'd come down to check on the crates not moon over Eugenia. When the time came, he'd do what he needed. And you can always fall back on fear when all else fails, he reminded himself. Fear's an excellent weapon.

Beckmann walked to one of the low, oblong boxes and began to pry it apart with a crowbar; the new wood split and cracked and slivers of pine fell on his jacket as he worked his way around the box. When the whole top had been loosened, Beckmann began to raise it. Buried nails appeared and he watched each shiny point find the light as if he were performing a private ritual. He was surprised to see how clean the metal was; it was silvery and bright and very sharp.

Then Beckmann carefully lifted the lid and laid it on the floor. Inside their cradle, a dozen Springfield rifles slept peacefully. They nestled into each other like babies, shiny stocks and barrels swaddled in layers of oilskin and parchment. Straw pillows protected them from any injury the ship or their own careless selves might inflict. Beckmann drew in his breath and stared. The rifles were as beautiful as any living thing.

He lifted one and unwrapped it. "The Springfield 'short,' " he said, unaware that he'd spoken aloud.

"The A3, .30 caliber, brand new this year, and destined to become the foot soldier's favorite weapon. Or so the people at the factory in Massachusetts insisted."

Beckmann was inclined to believe them; they were pragmatic men—arms manufacturers, not bleeding poets—and if they'd told him that what he held in his hands was history in the making, well, maybe they were right.

"This new model will change the face of the world forever, sir," Beckmann had been told. "It will become the sharpshooter's pride, the sniper's ally; no army will be able to do without it. It's light, small, quickly loaded, but, above all, deadly accurate. We, in Springfield, are rightfully proud; all our tests have shown this new rifle superior in every way."

"Try it on, sir," Beckmann had been urged. "I'm sure you didn't imagine anything as powerful and potentially lethal could be so comfortable on the arm. The size is the innovation, you see; we've always made good rifles at the factory here, but it's the abbreviated overall length that will win this beauty a prize. From what I understand, it will suit your needs to a tee. And you will notice the way the bayonet retreats into its own sheath. Nice bit of craftsmanship, that."

Beckmann raised the pristine barrel, savoring its heft and the way it balanced on his palms, ready for anything.

Yes indeed, he told himself; this is the weapon we need. If only Brown can carry out his part of the bargain and teach those bloody savages to use it. A plan's only a plan till it's tested, Beckmann silently repeated the Turk's dictum as he slipped the A3 back into its oilcloth wrapping and returned it to its waiting brothers. Machinery for an ore-smelting operation, he told himself, surveying the rest of the red-lettered crates: Antimony and mining and young Georgie Axthelm founding a new business on Borneo's shores, now there's a laugh. Now there's a good, long laugh.

The city of Kairouan was suffocating and filled with noise. Any idea the Axthelms or their guests might have had of a religious retreat, a quiet shelter where the faithful might pray and give private thanks, was soon dispelled. Hotter and dustier than the souk in Enphida, spilling with fanatical crowds, the bazaars and alleyways of Kairouan jostled and jumped with human sound and the crush of warm, brown skin. There was nowhere to move without being mauled, no place on the body not accosted by hands, fingers, shoulders, legs. Beggars reached up; pilgrims, on their 'hajj,' pushed forward; and vendors clutched at every sleeve or dangling hand. The pandemonium took the sightseers by surprise, and Eugenia and the children, Mrs. DuPlessis, Dr. DuPlessis, and Prue huddled together, as if by remaining small and inconspicuous, they could disappear.

Only George was truly game. He rallied his troops, called for order, and dispatched the panting Mr. Suravy for sedan chairs and carts.

"It's a showplace!" George insisted. "We must see it. The Moslem faithful, the devout, the sinners. It's a spectacle! You won't see its like back home on the Main Line or at the Merion Cricket Club!" he chortled. "Am I right, Brown? You must know a thing or two about these Johnnies! Seven trips to Kairouan worth one to Mecca and all that. At least, that's what Suravy told me."

After the lieutenant's near mutiny in the souk, George had made sure the fellow knew who was boss. There was no moment when he failed to demand the young man's full attention. It was like levying a tithe; habit made it easier.

"Paul, lad!" George roared, rubbing his hands together, as if about to produce the greatest treat in the world. "You'll come with Father. We'll leave these ladies to their whimpering. We'll see the sights. We'll be men!"

"No, George, please," Eugenia protested. "You'll lose him in this crowd. He's too little for all this buffeting about." Eugenia looked up in dismay at the hordes of people trampling past them. "Leave Paul here. Please. We'll sit on this little wall, and we'll wait . . ."

"Listen to your mother, son! She thinks she can always get her own way. Sorry, Genie," George said with a short, mean laugh, "this time I really must insist. Can't have any more monkey bites.

"So. So." George clapped his hands, the camp counselor with another trick, "Anyone else ready for adventure? Lizzie? Jinx? Anyone else brave enough to come with Father, or are the lot of you going to sit there cowering in the shade?"

It was a difficult decision. Each person had a different motive in choosing George over Eugenia. Mrs. DuPlessis's was obvious—though the lure of sitting under some pleasant awning almost made her renege on her promise to herself. She would never have admitted it was personal gain that kept her on the winning side; it was just that George was her host. And really, she reasoned, a very generous and good-hearted man. "I'll come, of course," she added her quavering voice to the crowd.

For the children, the choice was more complex. It had to do with: standing up for Father, which was Lizzie's criterion; not disappointing him, which was Jinx's hope; and showing how grown-up I am, and how much I love him, which was Paul's golden rule. Whenever the children had a chance to take sides, George's was the one they chose. Mother was always there, they reasoned; but their father was often too busy or too something to notice them. So they grasped any opportunity to prove themselves worthy.

George got what he wanted. He and his children, the DuPlessises, Whitney, and Prue went off with the sweating Mr. Suravy to "admire the admirable sights" while Eugenia and Lieutenant Brown were left behind.

"Are you sure it's not too much trouble?" George jeered as the group divided. He made up his mind about Brown on the spot. The boy's a bit soft, he told himself, a bit of a Parlor Peach. George wondered how Brown would survive in Borneo, but he didn't give the question any more consideration than the time it took to ask.

"No, sir. Not at all." Brown had decided it wasn't worth arguing, though he'd felt like it. He felt like telling the lordly Mr. Axthelm just what he thought of a man dragging his family into this hellhole. He couldn't figure George out, that was certain. Did he enjoy making everyone suffer or did he only think about himself? Lieutenant Brown watched the children troop off after their father and tried to reassure himself: Suravy's with them, he repeated inwardly; Suravy's good name is on the line. Suravy won't let anything happen. And I'd be a fool if I thought I could intervene.

It's Eugenia who needs care, Brown decided; he sensed she couldn't move another step. He didn't know what was wrong; it wasn't sunstroke or heat or anything as simple as that. She was docile and quiet, as if she'd just stepped out of a boxing ring. Brown had seen men punch-drunk like that; you only needed one well-aimed blow to bring them down. It was a time to be most careful.

All of a sudden, Brown realized that he despised George. True, he was only a small-time bully, but he'd sold his soul to the devil. I mustn't forget what this voyage is all about, Brown reminded himself. What he didn't understand was Eugenia's part in the thing. Was she here because she was his wife, because someone suggested a "grand tour" might do the "young George Axthelms" a world of good? Because she wanted to be a good mother and helpmeet, or because she knew no other way?

As if she could hear his thoughts, Eugenia turned to look at Brown. "Well," she said. "Here we are." Then she stared at the valley below them. It was dun-colored and gray; there was no tree, no leaf, no green, as far as she could see. Everything must be dead out there, she thought. How could anything survive where there is no water, where the sand boils like a pot of lentils and there's never time to be still? You must hurry on and hurry on or the sand will bury you alive.

Then a bird that looked like a kite or a vulture flew overhead and passed back to circle the long valley. Something is living, Eugenia thought. Or was. A hot wind blew in her face and she took off her hat, shaking out the mosquito netting and then carefully rewrapping it around the brim. Her movements were studied and exact. She believed if she were precise enough—devoted enough attention to this small task—she would be saved. But she was wrong.

Wrong. The word rolled itself into a huge black ball and jostled her brain. So many mistakes, she thought. A long line of them. Year after futile year. But how did you learn to pick and choose? Was it something you were born with, or was it developed, like a skill? Where was the moment you stood on your own and said, "I will do this. From henceforth, this shall be my life."

Eugenia squinted into the hard light and tried to think, but all she saw was a sand-choked plain, a dark bird wheeling within its leaden shadow, and all she could think was: How can anything exist without water?

"Would you like to go inside, Eugenia? Mrs. Axthelm . . . Find some shade?" Lieutenant Brown asked quietly.

Eugenia heard the correction in her name and smiled but didn't turn; she kept her eyes on the horizon. "Stand by me," she said.

"So you see," Mr. Suravy repeated in a singsong cadence, "seven pilgrimages to the city of Kairouan is the equal of one to Mecca."

"But that's just arithmetic!" Mrs. DuPlessis burst out. "That's no way to worship God!"

"It is their God, madame," Suravy said pointedly, though he tried to retain his professional poise. "I suppose they may worship Him however they choose."

"Well, I never," Mrs. DuPlessis was about to snort when her husband gently interrupted. "I believe we're going on to Mecca as well, Mr. Suravy. Does that grant us a special place in the Moslem firmament?"

"Ha-ha," George laughed, "only if we convert, old man! And I don't think I fancy becoming a follower of the Prophet! Even if they do get an extra quota of wives." George performed an elaborate, ogling wink for the benefit of his audience.

They stood outside the mosque, unable to go in, and the steps around them were packed with so many beggars they might have been flies on a piece of meat. Mrs. DuPlessis kept raising her arm as if to wave them off, but the gesture was ineffectual; the beggars continued to buzz noisily about their heads and feet. The children were especially oppressed by this; they leaned into their father and slowly closed and opened their eyes as if, in the time it took to blink, the whole place might vanish without a trace.

Paul stared, and started to put his thumb in his mouth, but a glance at Prue made him change his mind. He watched the crippled boys, no bigger than himself, twist their tortured bodies through the crowd and longed to go back to the safety of the ship. "Why does God do that?" he wanted to ask his father. "If He loves us, why does He hurt us?" There was a little boy with no legs who slid himself along on what looked like a tiny sled; his arms were strong and as long as an ape's, but his body was thin and puny. "Why would God make a baby like that?" Paul wanted to say. He looked at Lizzie and saw her watching the boy, too, but her face seemed as perplexed as his own.

". . . onto the next stop then?" Mr. Suravy was saying. "Or does anyone need a short rest stop?"

"I'd like—" Mrs. DuPlessis began.

"By all means!" George overrode her. "On to another viewing! What do you say, children? As good as the circus, isn't it?" George's boisterous voice filled the small square. "Exotic animals and costumes . . . dwarfs . . . now we just need some dancing girls and a few clowns . . . ha-ha . . ." George laughed at his own joke.

"What do you say, Suravy? Do you think a few clowns could be arranged?"

"Perhaps back at the ship, Mr. Axthelm," Suravy answered testily and wondered for perhaps the hundredth time that day whether George Axthelm's money was worth this anguish. Tunisia was his home, after all; it wasn't a joke or freak show set up to convince wealthy Americans of their superiority. The Koran was being studied and interpreted long before the ruffians sent to populate the New World had been released from their clammy prisons.

Suravy tried to soothe away his anger. He willed himself to think about good cigars and crumbling cheese lying on a crystal plate; he told himself the Axthelms wouldn't stay forever, but his unforgiving brain refused to be fooled. What if I were to tell them I'm a convert? he wondered suddenly. What if I said that I am a follower of Mohammed? Would they be shamed? Would they murmur, "Oh, Mr. Suravy, we're so sorry if we offended, but how interesting, please tell us more . . ."?

Or would they scoff at him, return to their floating palace, sail away, and say, "Quite dotty . . . gone native . . . but then what do you expect when they're born out here . . ."?

Those were the phrases Suravy expected, the words that would blow away his lifetime of work, his friendships and triumphs, as if they were no more than thistledown in a child's imperious hand. Suravy decided to say nothing. These are my guests, he told himself, these are my brothers. *Insha'Allah.*

"Just stand by me," Eugenia repeated as she leaned against the low stone wall and watched a distant arc of sputtering sand move over the desert; it was like a miniature tempest or a whirlwind spinning in one square foot of space. Riders, she guessed; the sand spout must belong to pilgrims like ourselves. People journeying in search of something they'll never understand. As far before as we have come into this bright, burning world, she thought. The words sounded like the refrain of a poem, but she couldn't remember which one. As far as we have come . . . we are, what? . . . at peace? . . . at rest? The line ended there; if there was more, she'd forgotten it.

". . . So, Suravy, old sport," George repeated, clapping the guide on the shoulder, ". . . off into the fray!" Then he bellowed loudly, "What do you say, boys and girls? One more portrait of the group before we set off? . . . Doctor? If you would be so kind."

While Dr. DuPlessis hurried to his task, Suravy tried to shoo the beggars away. *"Imshi!"* he said wearily. *"Imshi!"* But the beggars only droned away a few short steps before resettling in a cluster thicker than before. It was useless and Suravy felt sudden despair for his awkward country; he knew it hadn't created a favorable impression; he felt betrayed and defeated.

"What's that you're spouting, Suravy?" George's voice was loud above the square.

"It means, 'Go away.' " Suravy answered reluctantly.

"Imshi! I like it!" George shouted, *"Imshi, Imshi!* It has a good ring to it! What do you think, Mrs. D.? . . . Prue?" Suddenly he came up behind them. *"Imshi!"* he yelled in their ears, as if saying "Boo!" or "I caught you!"

Both Mrs. DuPlessis and Prue spun around and George was so gratified he started to laugh uncontrollably. "See that, Whitney?" he shouted. "Scared the socks off the little ladies!"

• • •

As far before as I have come into this bright, burning world . . . , Eugenia thought again. The refrain wouldn't leave her alone; the words circled around and around while she stood at the wall, letting the dust of the street settle and rise and then settle again. The pilgrims in the distance moved nearer, at least their sand squall moved nearer, and Eugenia felt suddenly bereft, as if she and all the people wandering the earth were children deserted. She wanted to turn to Brown for comfort, but knew that was plain foolishness.

I am a wealthy woman, she tried to convince herself; I have children and a place in society. I will return to Philadelphia and my only recollection of this time will be photographs and names. None of these feelings will matter because I will have ceased to trust them. I shall go home, and come back to my senses. But the poem reappeared of its own volition: As far before as I have come . . .

Whitney hadn't been paying attention to George's antics; he'd been studying the stylized calligraphy that spread across a nearby wall, trying to remember, from his brief encounter with Islamic art in Princeton, what the design meant. It wasn't just a pretty picture, he knew that much; there were words within the scrolling forms and he was about to question Mr. Suravy when George bounded over, infinitely pleased by his success in scaring the ladies, and, in fact, pleased by the whole day.

"Not thinking of taking the veil, are you, old man? Or whatever they call it? Converting?" George shouted in a boisterous but dramatic tone. On the word *converting* he dropped his voice and rolled his eyes meaningfully toward Suravy.

Whitney stared at him. "Taking the veil?" he asked in confusion. "Converting?" Whit seemed surprised to see George there at all.

"Converting . . . old man . . . becoming a bloody A-rab, a Mussulman."

"But I thought 'taking the veil' was a term for . . ." Whit looked genuinely perplexed.

"And it is! It is, old thing . . ." George blustered on, "that's why I don't want to see you mooning about over this religion nonsense. We've got enough bleeding hearts for one ship already!"

Whitney was taken aback by George's vehemence. He decided there'd been something he'd missed, but couldn't imagine what. He looked across at Prue and Mrs. DuPlessis; it couldn't be them, he thought. George couldn't be angry at them. Was it the children? Whit wondered. The doctor? Or could it be Mr. Suravy? Had he caused this burst of anger?

"Bleeding heart?" Whitney repeated slowly.

But George had already scampered off to get his troops moving; he'd decided enough time had been wasted with photographs. It was time to get on with it. Get the show on the road.

Neither Lieutenant Brown nor Eugenia said a word. They watched one kite flap its languid way across the dull sky until it was joined by another, then another. The birds circled nearer, then farther: one so high you could scarcely see it. It was a dark speck, lost in the blink of an eye.

There were so many things Eugenia wanted to say; she wanted to ask what it was like to live in a country like this one, or anyplace where the heart of the day was not what you saw, but who you were. She wanted to ask how it felt to go wherever you chose, and to know, in the midst of your travels, that the very center of your being contained peace and strength. That no matter where you were, or what accident or good fortune might occur, that you would have yourself. She wanted to say, "What is it like to trust that person—yourself? What is it like to know no limits?"

Instead she watched the high, bitter birds and the distant desert; she watched the buttery haze of sand and air where the land touched the sky; she watched the dunes ripple as more riders drew close. She thought: He is standing at my side and that is enough.

By late afternoon of the following day, the *Alcedo* had worked her way back along the passage and into the Gulf of Tunis. The sandbar had shifted, of course, and the pilots had demanded more *buqshas* for their difficult and, as they'd insisted, terrifying task, but the captain had paid without grumbling. He was glad to be rid of the harbor, glad to be rid of the smells and caterwauling along the quay, and glad, finally, to call off the extra watch Ogden Beckmann had ordered to protect the crates that filled the yacht's hold.

What a handful of uneducated Moslems would want with ore-smelting equipment was beyond Captain Cosby. But Beckmann had been adamant. And if he'd set a lieutenant in the United States Navy to guard those crates when the yacht was at sea, then who was the captain to grumble? Besides, old Turk Axthelm had masterminded the whole thing; he'd sent his henchman on the voyage, dictated where the ore-smelting machinery should be stowed; he was the one they really worked for. If he said boxes of chicken feathers were important, they'd all have to agree.

Captain Cosby breathed a tremendous sigh of relief as he watched the ship's bow clear the breakwater and bounce into the choppy sea. The Mediterranean again. How blue it looked after the foggy murk of the harbor. How fresh and clean, like something you could scoop up and drink. Captain Cosby remembered stories of shipwrecked sailors going mad with drinking salt water, but he could see the desire. The water did look inviting. It looked as tempting as anything.

The reed boats were the first to fall away, then the feluccas; then the pilots were put (shouting and gesticulating to the end) into their own launches and sent packing. Finally the last of the curious local freighters and tramp steamers drifted off as well, and the *Alcedo* was left on her own. Captain Cosby settled to the routine of the bridge; he was in charge again; there would be no more special watches (not until they reached another port) and there'd be no more special demands.

The ship would nose her easy way along the African coast while the engines hummed a steady hymn. The firemen would shovel coal as the cooks warmed the ovens; the beds would be made, slept in, and made again; the draperies would be closed and opened, the tables cleared, then reset, and the deck chairs gently turned as their inhabitants yawned or gossiped, fell asleep or gazed vacantly at the ocean's tantalizing expanse. That view was what had made Captain Cosby a sailor; it was the most seductive thing in the world.

"This heading all right, sir?" the mate asked; he was a man of few words.

"Fine," Captain Cosby answered. The wheelhouse was silent; not for anything would either man disturb the other's thoughts, or the peace that settles on a ship at sea like snow over a meadow.

Eugenia stood near the companionway door, her head and shoulders thrown backward and her skirt and shawl sifting around her in the evening breeze. Gray light flickered on the water; it whined over the waves like a cranky child packed off to bed. Then darkness came and the wind picked up, and Eugenia pulled her shawl closer round her shoulders. In the main saloon, they'll be gathering before dinner, she told herself; they'll be discussing the charming sights in Tunis and Enphida and Kairouan while they suck down cheese straws and pigs in blankets and marinated herring on toast. Then they'll begin the jesting thrusts that turn words into a facsimile of feeling—into something recognizable and safe. While I stand in the night wind waiting for something to happen.

Eugenia had a sudden memory of a childhood illness, and of being forced to eat only boiled potatoes and water for three long weeks. How voluptuous soup had sounded, or boiled eggs in a cup! She smiled, remembering that first glorious meal after the potato regimen. What did I ask for? Eugenia wondered. Old Catherine's creamed tomato soup and sardines on toast. I can still taste that meal, Eugenia realized. It was better than anything I'd known.

And who was it, she wondered, who'd hidden peppermint drops in a bedroom drawer? My mother, perhaps? Could I have been that young? Eugenia pictured herself, a very small child, standing in someone's bedroom waiting for the tantalizing smell of mint and sugar to waft over her before climbing up the dresser, the armoire, turning drawers into stairs as she worked her way toward the forbidden treasure.

Peppermint creams, soups made of tomatoes, tiny fishes on toast: Where were those simple desires now? Eugenia thought. They'd been so easy to satisfy. You couldn't crave what you'd never known.

The wind blew stronger; it kicked at her skirts and brushed past her face. There was a fine mist in it, like a drizzle of rain or fog, but when Eugenia tasted it, it was salt. She licked her lips, then walked to the rail and scooped the spray from the wood and put her fingers in her mouth. Salt, as pungent as memory, as demanding as faith: The taste was wonderful.

T E N

*I*N THE ALCEDO'S HOLD,
Lieutenant Brown stared straight ahead and kept up his mask of
grudging attention. A lantern, hanging from one of the beams, rocked
to the ship's steady rhythm, but the light it cast and recast on Brown's
face showed no change or movement. He might as well have been made
of lead.

"... you're gone all day ..." Ogden Beckmann's voice rose until it
was close to a shout. "I suppose you think you're getting pretty
fancy ... that you can desert your post whenever you please ... that
you're one of the rich folk now ..."

The lecture had gone on for some time; Brown wasn't sure how long.
He watched his hammock drift back and forth, and wondered how
many knots the ship was doing and where along the coast of North
Africa they were at the moment. Then he wondered if he'd still recognize any of it.

"... Well, let me tell you, mister, you're not ...!" Beckmann's
voice sounded like broken machinery; it clinked and hissed, but you
got used to it. You learned to recognize the problems. You lived with it.

"... And you never will be! No matter how friendly you get with
the madam. ..." Beckmann put an ugly connotation in the word
friendly; he made it sound like the worst sin imaginable. He did the
same with *madam.* But the effort was too obvious; it was a joke.

"... You've got a job to do ... or had you forgotten that? Answer
me, God damn you!"

"No, I hadn't forgotten." The words were quiet, almost bored. Brown shifted his gaze to the lantern.

"And what did you think when you finally sauntered back down here? Didn't you notice one of the crates had been tampered with?"

"I didn't look," Brown answered.

"Didn't . . . Didn't . . ." Beckmann sounded as if he were choking on his own words.

"Look." Brown prompted.

Beckmann couldn't speak for a moment; he wanted to kill this man; he wanted to wrap his fingers around that insolent neck until the cheeks puffed out and the eyes bulged and the skin turned blotchy blue. The image calmed him enough to continue:

"I thought that was what I'd hired you to do." Beckmann enunciated every word.

"A crate was disturbed. You saw it obviously . . ." Lieutenant Brown interrupted, but his eyes didn't flicker; they stared into the dark hold as though watching something only they had noticed.

"I saw it because I was here!" Beckmann exploded. "Because I did not go off on the Axthelms' little sight-seeing adventure. Because I remember why we're on this delightful holiday. Because I don't pretend to be either George's or Eugenia's . . ."

"Were any of the rifles disturbed?" Brown asked, though he knew the answer already.

"Look, Lieutenant"—Beckmann decided on a new approach. He'd be more controlled than his opponent: the "lieutenant" was a pointed jibe—"the question is not whether the rifles were tampered with, but that you didn't notice anything. That you failed to do your job."

Beckmann heard himself, and wondered for a moment what power he held over Brown. Not much, he realized, and then had a queasy feeling as if he'd climbed the face of a rock and found, too late, that there was no way down. Beckmann clung to the surface and surveyed the world below. He could use the Turk's position as a threat, he reminded himself, but what good would a mere name do—especially on a boat in the middle of nowhere? He could threaten Brown with dismissal, but where would he find a replacement?

"You checked the rifles," Brown stated. "Nothing's missing." It wasn't a question; Brown was running down a list. Beckmann felt anger singe his throat.

"Why don't you look for yourself," he snarled.

As Brown shifted the lantern nearer the open crate, its flame threw out a protesting surge, and greasy smoke seemed to settle over everything, burning the tongue, clouding the eyes. It reminded Brown of the stink of slave ships working the South Sea Islands. "Willing workers" for the "labor trade" in New South Wales: natives rounded up, bartered, then transported to work the farms of the new colonials—with the emphasis on "willing." Moment by moment, Brown felt himself pulled backward into his own past. He thought of the low wall in Kairouan where he'd stood with Eugenia, but that time seemed as faraway and phony as a dream. The hold was the only real thing.

"You opened this crate yourself," Brown observed wearily; he didn't bother to inspect the splintered wood.

"Of course I opened it myself," Beckmann answered; his voice was the teeth-gnashing snap of a badger. "Who else do you think has access to this room?"

Brown slid off the lid and stared at the rifles as the lantern swung its lullaby: back and forth, to and fro, rolling to the groan of timbers and the rattle of waves, uncovering and recovering its babies again and again. Brown lifted one of the Springfields from its bed, unwrapped the oilskin blanket, and held it in his arms. Beautiful, he thought, the rifle was beautiful; it made him forget the dark hold and the reek of remembered ships. What he held in his hands was perfect.

Neither man spoke. Beckmann wanted to say: "Fine piece of workmanship, isn't it?" But he didn't. He wanted to discuss the future and allay his fears, but he couldn't allow himself that fraternity. Brown must be taught a lesson.

"Well, what do you think?" Beckmann finally asked.

"I think they'll do us proud," Brown answered. "Who else has . . . ?"

"No one." Beckmann was all business again.

". . . Not even seen them?" Brown continued as if Beckmann hadn't spoken.

"No one," Beckmann repeated.

"But George?" Brown asked.

"No, not even our fine host, Mr. George Axthelm," Beckmann said with a hard crunch on the family name.

"But he knows they're . . . ?"

"Of course he does. This is his ship, Lieutenant. Or had you forgotten that, too? Along with everything else. Including where I found you. And how you came to have this cushy little job . . ."

Brown didn't hear the rest of Beckmann's lecture. Eugenia, he told himself, aware suddenly that what he wanted was to take her in his arms. He could feel her standing near him in Kairouan; he could feel her hand on his arm and the quick warmth of her body as she turned to look at his face. Eugenia, he realized, Eugenia doesn't know.

". . . No one else . . ." Beckmann was continuing expansively,

"... not the captain ... not the mate. The crates contain machinery for the antimony works in Borneo as far as the crew's concerned. Nothing more. That's what they were told, and apparently that was enough." Beckmann chuckled over Captain Cosby's stupidity.

"Mind you, I wouldn't trust a captain who didn't inspect his cargo. Why, that one box has enough powder in it to blow the entire ship to kingdom come. Properly ignited, of course." Beckmann laughed again, then continued with an easy "Ah, well, when you pay them enough, they never ask questions. The Turk sees to that."

And neither should I, Brown interpreted. I should toe the line like everyone else. The great Turk Axthelm owns us all. Even his own son. Suddenly the ship's hold felt unbearably hot, the air suffocatingly sweet, as if some creature had crawled into the creosote beams and died. There was a smell of flesh gone bloated and foul.

"I'll seal these rifles back up, then" was all Brown could answer.

"Yes, do that." Beckmann was surprised at the change in the younger man's behavior. Maybe I do have the upper hand, he thought; maybe I hold all the aces, after all. Beckmann decided to press his advantage. "And, Brown," he added firmly, "as I've mentioned before, no one is to enter this room. No one on any pretext whatsoever. Is that clear?"

"Yes, sir." The words were thrown away; Brown's thoughts were on other matters.

But if Beckmann thought he could impress Brown with his talk of the Turk and his power, he was wrong. Brown might have been bought at one time—he might have come on the voyage for no more than the promise of a fat fee at the end—but something inside him had changed. He was beginning to see the world differently. He was beginning to see Beckmann as no more than a neighborhood strongman and the Turk as a bagful of air. Eugenia, Brown repeated, Eugenia doesn't know.

Eugenia's father, the Honorable Nicholas Paine, sat ramrod straight and as still as a stick at his desk in Manila. As a member of Governor William Howard Taft's special staff in the Philippine Islands, he'd been supplied with a handsome set of offices overlooking the Pasig River. A reception room opened onto Ridgeway's office, but the larger corner room with its double windows and fine view had been reserved for Paine. Why he needed such a grandiose space, the old man couldn't understand. No one came to visit him, and he found his role on the governor's staff elusive and confusing. But, he reasoned as he surveyed his new home, the rooms were pleasant; they had nice mahogany paneling, nice appointments ... "Why this desk alone must have cost a pretty penny," Paine said aloud, touching it with hesitant fingers.

"Georgian, from the looks of it . . . a campaign-type affair with a leather top . . . The old Turk never does anything by half measure . . . no, indeed."

Paine looked around for something else to concentrate on. He was certain, given a little time, that he'd be told why he was here.

"Surely Governor Taft wouldn't have taken me on if there wasn't sufficient need . . ." he reassured himself, unaware of the sound of his voice. Paine's thoughts had a way of turning vocal when he least expected it. ". . . Even as a favor for his old friend Turk Axthelm. . . ."

Paine contented himself with that promise as he lapsed into momentary silence. He strummed his fingers on the desk and felt the comforting cushion of expensive leather. "And I'm a damned sight better qualified than most of the young whippersnappers out here." The words bubbled out again, and the Honorable Nicholas sighed, stared at his hands, his shirt cuffs, and then the expanse of desk top that lay beyond them. The empty hours of rereading his favorite books or writing the occasional letter were trying. Especially now with monsoon season coming on.

"And it's even hotter today," Paine announced, and his words were irritable and high-pitched; they matched his starched collar and cardboard-straight tie.

The louvered shutters had been pulled against the oppressive midday heat, but the sun crept over the wooden slats, trying to find a chink in the armor. Inside it felt like an oven while outside the tropical rains threatened and threatened but never came. Getting a little old for this weather, Paine told himself. Used to be my cup of tea, the tropics. . . . the trick was to look cool, outfinagle the other fellow . . . make him believe you were as icy as a cucumber sandwich on a silver platter . . .

Paine's thoughts returned to his various triumphs: the time in Aden when he'd staged that little tea party, the day in Cairo . . . or perhaps it'd been Alex . . . when Lord Erlich had noticed him. . . . Made a special point of coming over, too, Paine remembered gleefully. . . . Dragged his assistant, Rennell Rodd, along as well . . .

"That set the other chaps on their ears, I tell you!" Paine's voice filled the room again, creating an echo of itself as if drumming up approval or support, before finally drifting into silence.

It's all a thing of the past now, the old man realized. There's no one to share these triumphs with . . . wife dead, son Nicky, too—gone in that boating accident—and Genie off and married into a family who could buy and sell any of these petty exploits. Government service doesn't mean a hill of beans to them—and neither does tradition.

The Honorable Nicholas slumped in his chair and stared at the few damp pieces of paper that lay curling on his desk top. What were all those scribbled pages? he wondered as he watched them blow about. The fan fluttered overhead and gave the papers a false appearance of activity, but Paine knew the stir was only from the punkah fan and the punkah wallah boy squatting silently in the corner, raising and dropping his arm with the stolid movement of someone fast asleep.

"I could have made a place for myself once," Paine mumbled. "Time was when . . . well, no use crying over spilled milk. Got to soldier on . . . stiff upper lip and all that . . . show these fellows what a 'blue blood' can do . . ."

A large black beetle began to cross Paine's desk; it trudged over a packet of letters, two books, a fountain pen, an eyeglass case, and several sheets of letter paper.

"Got to soldier on . . ." The old man's voice grew even quieter; he bent his head to watch the beetle till his chin nearly rested on his chest. ". . . Nose to the grindstone . . . shoulder to the wheel . . ." The Honorable Nicholas stared at the insect until he forgot who was who and what was what—or why he'd sat down at his desk in the first place.

Glasses? . . . Paine felt the bridge of his nose. No, got them on. . . . Maps? . . . No, looked at them earlier today. . . . Forget my own name, next thing, he told himself. As if anyone would care . . .

The beetle collided with the inkwell and flipped helplessly onto its back. Paine's eyes opened wide, and he glared at the creature as if he'd never seen it before.

"Ha!" he announced in an outraged voice. "That'll teach you to come crawling around here! Stuck upside down, are you? Well, bully for you!"

The struggling insect waved its feeble legs, clawing the air in futile supplication. "You won't come clambering over my desk again!" Paine shouted. "Not on your life!

"Now, where was I? . . . Where . . . ?" The Honorable Nicholas's nerves were beginning to tell on him. He felt burdened by confusion as if it were something he wore: a coat several sizes too large or a hat that slipped down over his eyes. "Where was . . . ? Ah, yes! . . . Writing to Genie! . . . That's it, by God! . . . Writing to . . ."

It's that infernal Ridgeway, the Honorable Nicholas remembered suddenly, returning to his pet peeve, the secretary Martin Axthelm had sent with him, the weasely fellow he considered no more than a squinty-eyed spy.

"That infernal Ridgeway!" he said out loud. "He's the one who gets me all mixed up! Doesn't mail my letters! Holds up the ones Genie sends, and never relays the missives Martin Axthelm writes!"

Paine concentrated on his wrath over the spineless, miserable Ridge-way as he watched the weary weavings of the doomed beetle, which tried and failed, and then failed again to pull its body upright. You got yours! Paine gloated, and he considered giving the dying creature a jab with his pen, then reminded himself that the beetle had probably been wallowing in filth somewhere. It would make his pen dirty and un-pleasant.

". . . Letter to Genie . . ." Paine remembered, and he dragged his eyes back to the empty paper. ". . . Letter to . . ?" A look of fierce con-centration came over the old man's face. "The antimony trade? Old Ivard? . . . George's metallurgy business?" The Honorable Nicholas ticked off the words as though one of them held a clue, while his body took on the thin military stiffness it wore in public.

"The sultan? Should I be writing to . . . or old Ivard, was it?" Paine repeated, glowering at the desk as though he expected to see an answer there.

"Sterling family, the Axthelms. True blue . . ." When all else failed, that litany could be depended on to pull the Honorable Nicholas back from the brink. He said the words and waited for them to take effect. "Red-blooded Americans. All the way."

Suddenly Paine plunged his pen into the inkwell, and the beetle be-side it shuddered once, twice, then lay still while its legs slowly folded. Paine watched the spectacle, wondering where he'd seen the insect be-fore, then he dashed his pen to the page:

"Genie—Hope you and the children are well," he wrote.

> It sounds as though they've become real travelers. I trust that life at sea is proving harmonious and restorative. There's nothing like a dose of salt water to cure the ills of the world. You may not remember your grandmother's house in Maine or how you and your brother, Nicky, used to love to leap through those cold, salty waves . . .

But this wasn't the right direction to take; it was too fraught with maudlin nostalgia; it wasn't the cheery tone Paine wanted. Genie shouldn't have to worry her pretty head about a thing . . . not a thing. . . . Her father would take care of it all. Why, when this was over, just see if her life wasn't better! Just see if it wasn't! The Honor-able Nicholas smiled to himself, and took up his pen again.

> Do take care to have all fresh water boiled thoroughly, Genie. You don't want a bout of "Gypy tummy" and I know how careless

these nursemaids can be. Someone Paul's age would be especially susceptible.

And Genie, when you get on to Aden (or down Zanzibar way— if George decides to do a bit of shooting in good old B.E.A.) be sure to ask if anyone remembers Lord Erlich's staff (Rennell Rodd was his chief man). Your old pa cut quite a figure in those parts. Long before your time, my dear. Still and all, might be one or two old-timers left who'd show you a good time.

Just mention my name—you can say I was in Alex, as well. (Alexandria, for the uninitiated) But, for heaven's sakes, if you run into Buffy Turcotte, don't listen to *his* stories.

And remember the water. Gypy tummy's bad, but cholera's endemic out here. Epidemic, really. Don't know how the Alcedo takes on her drinking water, but you take care. Don't want any misfortune befalling my favorite daughter . . .

Paine paused and looked at the letter. What else did I mean to tell her? he wondered. She knows about the sun . . . heatstroke . . . ? he asked himself: No, that's not it. . . . Ivard . . . ? The plans to meet the yacht in Sarawak and the big celebration in Kuching . . . ?

Paine stared across the room at the invading spears of sunshine; he tried to think, but his brain moved with the speed of chilling jelly. "Oh, my heavens!" he shouted suddenly. "The luncheon with General Woods!"

Paine shot backward in his chair and tried to struggle out of its grasp. "Ridgeway!" he shouted. "Ridgeway! You forgot to remind me of the time. Ridgeway, damn you!"

Ridgeway appeared in the doorway; he was the picture of unhurried calm. His hair and face were the same pale color; he looked like a pickled yellow squash. "Sir?" he asked innocently.

"You didn't tell me what time it was, man!" Paine kicked and clawed at the unmoving chair; it wouldn't release him for anything in this world. "Isn't that your job here? To . . ."

"But, sir . . ." Ridgeway soothed, "it's only twenty minutes to one. You're not due there until half past." Ridgeway's mouth formed itself into a neat half circle of smug perfection.

Paine felt his own face go scarlet with rage. "I know what time I'm due, Ridgeway," he spluttered. "I know what time luncheon is."

With a sudden gasp, the Honorable Nicholas stood and glared defiance and vengeance at his secretary as he tried to rid himself of the chair, which continued to cling to his legs. Paine glanced down, gave one well-aimed kick, and sent the chair flying.

"And, Ridgeway," Paine continued evenly, straightening his waistcoat and watch fob, "have this place cleaned up while I'm off at H.Q.

Can't have this . . . Can't have this . . . Why, look here, man . . . insects everywhere. . . ." Paine jabbed the dead beetle with his pen point. "Vermin! Never this way in Alex! Indeed not. I had a staff back then!"

Before dining with Nicholas Paine, General Woods had spent the morning inspecting his troops at Fort McKinley on the outskirts of Manila. That dawn there had been a problem with a native Moro tribesman who had gone, as the local population called it, *juramentado*. He'd run amok, single-handedly charging a group of American troops, and was stopped only when a bullet from a .45-caliber revolver hit him squarely in the neck. By then he was only twenty-five yards from his intended victims and so full of holes it had been a wonder he could have moved the last few feet at all.

One of Aguinaldo's stragglers, Woods knew, thinking over the incident as his orderly laid out the clean dress uniform appropriate for a formal luncheon. This Philippine problem was difficult all around. General Emilio Aguinaldo had been a good native ally at one time, or so Woods had been told when he took command. Aguinaldo had been supplied with arms for his war against the Spanish by the great Admiral Dewey himself, but that was long before Dewey had destroyed the Spanish fleet and successfully "freed" Manila into the care of its wise American uncles.

It hadn't taken Aguinaldo long to become dissatisfied with his benefactors, and he'd finally turned rebel. Following his capture in March of 1901, his followers had retreated to the hills, where they executed guerrilla raids, and created crises like the one this morning.

Juramentado, Woods repeated to himself as he submitted to the painful buttoning of his tight white mess jacket. How he hated these damned things; his neck felt like a balloon about to pop. "I'll finish it myself," Woods ordered curtly.

Then, to top off the rest of the miserable morning, the camp historian had insisted on a photograph of the Moro rebel and the "brave lads who shot him down." Woods had found the men's euphoria astonishing; he'd looked at the body swelling in the hot sun and thought: What is the world coming to? A group of American soldiers gloating over the death of some poor misguided bugger while his cohorts lurk in the hills, calling down their gods to drive us from the face of the earth?

Woods didn't usually concern himself with government decisions. He hadn't questioned what had caused Aguinaldo to turn against his mentors: He was here to do his job. But he realized that if they failed to capture the rebels soon, news of this particular man's exploits would make matters worse. So General Woods had ended the morning commending the men who'd dropped the Moro and exhorting them to "bag a few more." Then he'd saddled up and ridden back to headquarters just in time to allow himself to be pinched and squeezed into some miserable excuse of a too-tight jacket.

Of all the times for formality! Woods had been surprised when it was suggested by someone close to Taft that it would be "fitting for the general to entertain old Paine." "Fitting to entertain" a man who's appearance in Manila had nothing to do with government or the military and everything to do with business!

These damned politicians, Woods decided angrily. Craven cowards, every last one of them. But, why should I have to kowtow to the Axthelms as well? I don't owe them a goddamn thing.

"Leave it, Orderly." Woods barked out his command. "If I can't dress myself, I might as well pack up and go home."

". . . But what was so amusing, General . . ." the Honorable Nicholas chortled as the orderly ladled a second helping of soup into his gold-rimmed plate, ". . . is that my son-in-law had completely forgotten to release the brake!" The old man laughed with an expectant, high-pitched noise that sounded to Woods's inattentive ears like a horse's impatient whinny.

"Sorry, sir. I didn't quite hear . . ." Woods began while he tried to catch the eye of an adjutant standing at attention near the window. Perhaps there might be a way of ending this interminable meal a little earlier, Woods told himself. The room was stifling, after all; the shutters on the window served to baffle the breeze but failed horribly with the sun; and Woods was unused to these endless, idle lunches. He had men waiting. Matters of consequence to be decided. The Moro rebel had been the least of his worries.

". . . I said he hadn't remembered the brake!" Paine guffawed again, nearly slopping soup out of his open mouth. He swiped at his lips with a wide, starchy napkin. "George, I mean. My son-in-law. George! Of course, you don't know him, do you, General? . . . George, that is. . . . You know his father, of course," the Honorable Nicholas added with a toothy smile.

"No, I've never had the pleasure," Woods answered. So this was going to be one of those "do you know" interviews. General Woods stared grimly at the yellow-white lines burning across the wall. A patrol boat must be moving up the Pasig, he realized as he watched the streaks of light shift with a sudden staccato rhythm. Even in the general's second-floor apartments, the quick passage of a boat on the river was noticeable. Glinting metal and glass sent messages tapping over the walls.

"Ah," Paine continued, "I thought . . . well, I just assumed that because Martin . . ." The old man felt completely safe using the Turk's first name now; Woods was obviously a social inferior.

". . . I just assumed . . . because Martin asked me to look you up . . . that you were friends."

"How do you like Manila, sir?" Woods asked, turning from his contemplation of the semaphores on the wall to his guest; Woods was going to put a stop to these antics.

"Very nice, very nice . . ." Paine mumbled, fazed by the general's cool response. Then he suddenly noticed the orderly standing beside him holding a plate of steaming food. "Ah, veal chops!" He grinned as he attacked the plate with childish pleasure. "How lovely! Haven't had chops for ages!"

Paine cut up his meat with such rapt absorption that Woods softened for a moment. He returned to his perusal of the wall and the reflecting sparks, and when he continued, his voice was gentle: "You were telling me, sir, about your daughter's wedding?"

"Eh?" Paine mumbled, his mouth full of white-gray chop. "How's that?" Paine blinked and chewed and blinked again. For the life of him, he couldn't imagine what the man was talking about.

"Your daughter's wedding," Woods repeated.

"Ah, Genie. Yes, Genie . . . Genie's wedding! Well!" Paine felt the whole picture come back into focus. His daughter's wedding. His only living child! A day in May more years ago than he cared to admit. Philadelphia in springtime, lilacs and green grass, music in the breeze, a lovely time.

Paine warmed to the story all over again. "Of course the phaeton wouldn't budge!" he began, and his voice bubbled with pleasure. "The carriage, don't you know . . ." he explained with a deprecating wave of his hand, ". . . and George was terribly upset, don't you know . . . Bridegroom's nerves, I should suppose. . . .

"Of course, I stepped in. Did I explain that I held the title of master coachman with the Chestnut Hill Club for six years running?"

"You did, sir." Woods's answer was polite and kind, but he felt his determination slipping. The luncheon was dragging on far too long.

"I did?" Paine hesitated, momentarily squelched. "Against much younger men, too . . . I tell you that?" The old man paused again.

"Did I mention how grateful Martin was for my intervention with the phaeton? . . . We went up to his office just after and had a nice long jaw. . . . He's an extremely busy man, don't you know. Very flattering . . . his taking such an interest . . .

"The families have become terribly close, of course, since that day. . . . Then when this business with Sir Charles Ivard came up, naturally I offered my services. . . . We were at the school together, old Ivard and I . . . Did I mention that?"

"You did, sir. Very interesting." General Woods hadn't been put in this difficult position for a long time; the hours in his quarters in the old fort seemed to slip futilely away while down on the river there was bustle and life, the squalling of boat people, the answering shouts from their women on shore. A new nation in the making. Work to be done.

"I tell you about George's new business out there?" Paine asked quietly, studying his empty plate. "New metallurgy company . . . ? Antimony . . . ?"

"Yes, sir, you did. Before luncheon." The general made one last attempt at cheerful encouragement. "Very interesting, antimony." He wanted to be accommodating if only out of respect for this old man's fierce but faded aristocracy. He tried to remember the rules of polite conversation.

"I suppose there's a great deal of profit to be made from these newly discovered mineral deposits?" Woods asked.

"Oh yes, indeed, General!" Paine looked up and smiled again. Returned to his former glory, he positively beamed, "As I told Martin . . . 'Martin' . . . I said . . . 'There's profit out there!' . . . Then I recommended George for the job! . . . My son-in-law!" But Paine stopped himself suddenly and stared down at the white tablecloth.

"Nice place, Manila," he managed after a moment, then came to a halt again. "I suppose I told you why I'm here."

But the Honorable Nicholas Paine knew in his heart he'd already told that story. Had repeated it over and over and over and over. He stared at the tablecloth and its intricate weave. It looked like a checkerboard or a Parcheesi set, but he couldn't follow the strands to any conclusive end; they wound into each other; one stopped and another took its place; they twisted around and around and around.

"I love my daughter a great deal, General," the old man finally said. "I'd do anything to see her happy."

"Dear Lord and Father of mankind,
Forgive our foolish ways,
Reclothe us in our rightful mind,
In purer lives thy service find,
In deeper reverence, praise. . . ."

*T*HE AIR INSIDE THE MAIN SALOON was hot and impatient; Eugenia could feel it as though it were a person beside her. It wanted to be outside. It wanted to have done with sermons, lessons, and pretending to be at Grace Church in Rittenhouse Square. It wanted to be on deck watching for sight of land or hunting for the blue back of a dolphin or inventing a distant home for the foam-covered logs and branches passing through the *Alcedo*'s wake. It wanted to be skimming along the rail singing its heart out, not searching for meaning in the Ninth Sunday after Trinity.

". . . In simple trust like theirs who heard,
Beside the Syrian sea,
The gracious calling of the Lord,
Let us, like them, without a word,
Rise up and follow thee. . . ."

While Eugenia sang, she pushed her shoulders into one of the high-backed chairs the stewards had set in a row for Sunday service and wondered where the ship was. Toward what ancient kingdom were the engines carrying them? She had a notion that the waters of the Mediterranean were alive with souls, that everything that had gone before still breathed in the water: Biblical purges or the simple yearnings of one unnoticed woman, the slaughter of babies or a monthlong feast in celebration of a birth or a harvest or a kingly marriage. You had only to look down through the brown-speckled waves to catch a glimpse of beckoning faces. Phoenicians, Assyrians, Minoans: Their lives called you from the past. They said, *Come back to us; you and I; we are one and the same.*

> ". . . *Drop thy still dews of quietness,*
> *Till all our strivings cease:*
> *Take from our souls the strain and stress,*
> *And let our ordered lives confess*
> *The beauty of the peace. . . ."*

The chair was as disapproving as a corseted chaperone; it hampered all freedom. Eugenia pressed the small of her back into it and the calves of her legs, but the thing wouldn't budge. It reminded her of every Sunday morning in her life. "Religion was never meant to be like this," she wanted to leap up and shout. "Religion should set your mind to wandering, not pin it like a moth in a box." And then she involuntarily recalled the Shelley poem: "The desire of the moth for the star, Of the night for the morrow . . ." Eugenia forced her memory back to her singing. No more romantic poets for me, she decided. Shelley and Keats and Byron and Browning, they stand for everything this facsimile of a straight-laced Protestant service is trying to ignore.

> ". . . *Breathe through the heats of our desire*
> *Thy coolness and thy balm,*
> *Let sense be numb, let flesh retire,*
> *Breathe through the earthquake, wind and fire,*
> *O still small voice of calm."*

"A-men," Eugenia trailed after the rest of the congregation. Finally, she thought, one more part of the service completed; she closed her hymnal with a slap, and the children, lined neatly beside her, closed theirs as well. Then the stewards standing near the wall and Whitney and Brown and Ogden Beckmann and the DuPlessises shut theirs, too. The bang of books sounded like relief, but it wasn't. Whether you liked to sing or you didn't, whether you could carry a tune or the noise was like cats in a fight, any hymn was preferable to George's ponderous gospel readings and sermons. At least that's what Eugenia felt. Thebes, she thought. Ariadne and Pasiphaë and the Minotaur. *Daedalus, interea, Creten longumque perosus* . . . I wonder when Father taught me that Latin passage if he'd ever guessed I'd be here myself.

"Dearly Beloved . . ." George began while Eugenia suddenly remembered: No, first comes the Suez Canal, then the Red Sea. The name seemed twice as compelling because it had never been part of a

Latin lesson or a dutiful recitation of Greek mythology.

". . . we are gathered once more, in this safe and perfect haven . . ." George's voice droned on and the children started to shift in their seats, but Eugenia didn't bother to correct them. The Red Sea, she decided, is a stream carrying us inexorably toward the unknown. We'll slip along it and we'll slip along it, and before you know it we'll find ourselves another world.

". . . And from First Corinthians, our epistle for today . . ."

That world will be the Indian Ocean, where everything is wild and nothing's been tamed. Eugenia listened to the rumble of the engines, then felt it move through her spine. *Get up and dance, it said. Get up and shout. Throw out your hands. Lift up your heart.*

> ". . . *and all did eat the same spiritual meat; and all did drink the same spiritual drink . . .*
> ". . . *But with many of them God was not well pleased: for they were overthrown in the wilderness. . . .*"

Beside his mother, Paul jounced miserably in his chair and tried to make sense out of his father's words. How could anyone drink out of a rock, he thought, and how could a rock be Jesus? A rock was a rock; it wasn't water and it wasn't a person. Paul thought the Bible and his father's sermons were awfully confusing. Mother always said if he paid attention, he'd understand, but it seemed the harder he listened, the worse it got. Paul looked over at Lieutenant Brown and then at Cousin Whit, but Whitney had his "tutor manners" on; he looked as though he were trying to make up a test for a lesson. Lieutenant Brown was no help either. Even though his eyes were open, Paul thought he looked asleep.

> ". . . *Neither let us tempt Christ, as some of them also tempted, and were destroyed of serpents . . .*"

Paul's shoulders slumped; he knew about temptation: temptation was nougat candy after you'd already brushed your teeth for the night; it was sticking out your tongue at your sisters; it was eating rolls before dinner was served. Paul started to swing his short legs back and forth; he tried terribly hard to concentrate and not think about how hot the room was or how much nicer it would be out on deck. If we were at Grandfather A.'s, he thought, we could go swimming in the big stone pool. Then he remembered it was Sunday. We'd be at church, he told himself, even if we were still at home.

And now there was another story about a good son who stayed

home with his father, and a bad son who went away, but the father liked the bad son more; he was so happy to have him come home that he gave a great big party and killed a fatted calf. Paul swung his legs harder; his knickerbockers scratched the chair: up, down, back and forth, high, low. The buttons on the seat pinched his skin, but Paul didn't care. He felt sorry for the good son working in the fields. He wondered if his own father would have forgiven the bad boy. And if he did, then why did you have to be good all the time, like Father and Mother said? Could you do all those naughty things and still have people love you? Paul's little legs went flying and Eugenia reached out a gentle, reminding hand. She didn't need to turn her head; the touch was enough. Paul sighed and tried to sit still again.

Then they were kneeling:

> *"Almighty God, Father of all mercies, we, thine unworthy servants, do give thee most humble and hearty thanks . . ."*

Then they were standing. Then they were sitting. Dr. DuPlessis started to read something; Mrs. DuPlessis blew her nose loudly, and Paul suddenly remembered his soldiers. He wondered if he could pull his two favorites from his pocket without being seen. They'd been having a tremendous fight before church started and Paul knew they wanted to continue it. He could feel them jumping around in his pockets. Very slowly he reached in one hand and pulled out Major Brown, named after his hero, Lieutenant Brown, and then he reached for the major's enemy, the Infidel Ali. Ali was cruel; he had slaves and carried a knife in his teeth. He was a Turkish Saracen.

> *". . . A thousand shall fall beside thee, and ten thousand at thy right hand . . .*
> *". . . Thou shalt go upon the lion and the adder: the young lion and the dragon shalt thou tread under thy feet. . . ."*

Dr. DuPlessis's pronunciation made "thy feet" sound like "ziii feeeed," and "dragon" sounded even scarier than it did in English. Paul decided the Infidel Ali rode a "drrragoon" and it breathed fire and ate five-year-old children for breakfast.

It was Jinx who spotted Paul's inattention to the service. She watched her brother pull the toys from his pocket, and her eyes became slits of self-righteous envy. It just wasn't fair, she decided. Mother let Paul get away with everything; now he was playing during church!

"Paul!" Jinx whispered.

Paul didn't move, but his body became stiff and wary, then obstinate and determined.

"Paul!" Jinx whispered louder; she recognized that game of his—when he faked deafness and then turned around with a baby's smile and an innocent "What?"

"Paul!" Jinx was determined to have her brother answer; she nudged him in the ribs. Hard.

Paul sat like a lump; he knew he couldn't move; he couldn't put his soldiers away, and he couldn't hide them. He also knew he hated his sister with all his might; she was a "meddlesome female." That's what Father had called Mrs. DuPlessis late one night and Paul had never forgotten it; he liked the way the words clanged together.

"Meddlesome female," Paul whispered back.

"You're not going to get away with it!" Jinx gloated under her breath, but her words had become louder and Paul looked sideways at their mother to see if she'd heard.

Good, he thought; she hasn't. Yet. The little boy began to hide Major Brown and the Turk, Ali; he rolled the two figures into his hot, wet palms, but Jinx had the final say: She stuck out her tongue in sneaky but triumphant glee.

That was it for Paul. Down crashed the soldiers and up jumped Paul, kicking at his sister and trying with all his might to lay a blow on her freshly chalked white shoes.

Eugenia's mind was far away when her children started to squabble; no matter what mythic and visionary properties they granted her, she didn't always see what they did. Sometimes she just didn't care or sometimes she was merely wrapped up in her own distant thoughts. At that moment Eugenia was listening to the noise of the ship's engines, and the soothing hum had led her to reflect on how comforting a life so circumscribed must feel: You did your job; you turned over and over and over again, and in return you were bathed in oil, polished, talked to (at least that's what the chief engineer did), and nurtured like a newborn baby. The clatter and crash of Paul's two fallen warriors snapped her back to reality.

George had been aware of growing discontent among his two younger children, even in the midst of explaining to his congregation the most edifying of the gospel stories. While Dr. DuPlessis read the psalm, George had realized disaster was imminent. He'd been irritated at Eugenia for not taking a firmer stand; he'd believed she saw Paul and Jinx's impending row and didn't care. He'd thought she was trying to disrupt the service on purpose, just as she sometimes sang too loudly and other times wept during prayer.

Bohemians, he'd raged silently: My children will become worthless, foppish artists and live in a garret with no running water. Or they'll be Marxists and rant about unions and "open shops"; they'll stand on soapboxes down near Delancey Street for all the world to see, and I'll be known as the father of idiots. George, sitting alone near the makeshift altar, at the head of the slapdash and grudging congregation, had let himself grow more and more angry.

And then everything had come apart at the seams just as he'd predicted it would: Paul and Jinx were fighting. And in the middle of this holy time.

"Paul!" George jumped to his feet at nearly the same moment as his son.

"Jinx!" Eugenia said, not a second later, knowing as definitively as her husband just who the true culprit was.

"You mustn't . . ." George said loudly as Eugenia scolded, "Leave your brother alone," while Jinx and Paul, caught in everyone's sudden stare, were as still as marauding rabbits trapped in a farmer's light.

Mrs. DuPlessis was aghast and said so; her husband hadn't the faintest idea what had happened; he stared at the prayer book in his hand as though it had sprouted horns. Whit clucked what was intended as a teasing remark to Paul, and Prue sprang to her feet, intending to drag both children from the room. Lizzie pretended not to know either offender while her parents fed their anger at each other by taking irrational and unyielding sides.

"If you'd only . . ." George said.

"How can you ask them to sit still when . . . ?" Eugenia answered.

"I don't believe anyone's asking anything! In my day, you did—"

" 'What you were told.' I know!"

"Well, that certainly makes sense to me . . ." Mrs. DuPlessis huffed as she got up enough steam for the rest of her argument.

"But what happened, my dear? Was it my reading of the . . . ?" Dr. DuPlessis gazed sadly at the warring faces around him.

"Oh, Gustav! Sometimes you can be so obtuse!"

The room, the hopefully reverent room, was in complete turmoil. There was no one in agreement; there was everyone to blame. It was as if some malevolent soul among them had deliberately let loose a snake. Then a terrible thing happened. It took a minute or two, a long, long time, for anyone to recognize the sound. The ship had become absolutely still.

The children looked at each other and bolted for the deck while Eugenia walked purposefully behind. Mrs. DuPlessis said, "What's this?

What's this? What's this? Another disaster?" and George blustered, "I'm sure if we all just sit tight . . . there must be some excellent . . . the captain . . . why don't we . . . Eugenia!"

But he'd lost her, and the rest of his audience. They were on deck, lining the rail, looking at the listless ripples gurgling like yesterday's soup near the motionless hull. The ship was dead in the water.

Suddenly there was a shuddering explosion and the ship began to stir again, drawing in and then spitting back out the brown muck that had begun to cake her sides. The explosion was followed by a whine and a sigh, as if the ship had, at long last, groaned aloud. Then the *Alcedo* was quiet again.

"I'm sure there must be some reasonable . . ." George began, "I'll just go find . . ."

"Of course, Mr. A.! Whatever you think best. I'm sure you'll . . ." Mrs. DuPlessis lulled while she glared at Eugenia's rigid back. If there hadn't been such a rampage during the service, none of this would have happened, Mrs. DuPlessis was certain of that.

"Dead in the water!" Whit whispered. "Deader than a door nail."

"Oh, my . . . oh, my . . . oh, my . . . " Dr. DuPlessis mumbled over and over; he turned first to Ogden Beckmann and then to Lieutenant Brown, but neither man had any words of comfort.

"The desire of the moth for the star . . ." Eugenia recited silently. She felt a nearly uncontrollable urge to laugh aloud.

The children watched as strands of blackened seaweed, sodden twigs, and ancient blistered foam blew past their ocean home. It was as if those dark things of the deep were looking for a way in, a crack, a crevice, and the children were reminded of all sorts of evil tales: the wolf and the pigs, the troll under the bridge, the brother and sister whose bread crumbs were stolen by greedy birds. Their minds flew around those terrors and they didn't dare speak. They heard Mrs. DuPlessis's strident questions and they heard Dr. DuPlessis's awkward answers; they heard their cousin, Whitney, their father, and Mr. Beckmann, and they heard their mother say nothing at all. She seemed separate, as if she weren't on the ship at all.

Where are we? the children wondered. Are we going to die? Is the ship going to sink and carry us down to the bottom of the ocean? Will we turn green? Will starfish eat out our eyes? Will an octopus make a home in our bedrooms; will he grow and grow and grow till he bursts through the walls and his tentacles sweep out the bookshelves and beds? Will barnacles cover us all? The children looked at the horizon;

they stared and stared, but there was nothing to be seen. No sail in the distance, no puff of far-off smoke. The *Alcedo* was alone on the water, and they were alone as well.

Then they heard Captain Cosby's hearty voice. He said, "Sorry about all that, sir. Thought we could make it into Port Said before the thing caught, but as you see, I wasn't calculating on the power of these engines of yours." Captain Cosby sounded gruff but cheerful. The children decided to pay attention.

". . . Yes, sir, I did know she was in a bit of trouble, but as I said, I thought we'd make it into port, rest up awhile, replace the propeller if we could or else just knock some sense back into it. And you folks could take in the sights.

"As I mentioned, I didn't want to bother you with these details, and a stop in Port Said would have been a necessary precaution anyway. I thought the old girl could make it across the Med—"

Captain Cosby tried to laugh and the children heard their father interrupt him angrily. "This is not an 'old' ship, Captain," he said.

As with the many times Jinx, Paul, and Lizzie had heard the adults arguing, they decided to close their ears. So they didn't hear their father's furious questions or Mrs. DuPlessis's indignant agreement; they heard only the tone in those voices and that was enough.

". . . That would have left the propeller at the bottom of the sea, I'm afraid, sir. At the bottom of the deep, blue sea," Captain Cosby laughed, "which, fortunately, is not the case . . ."

Lizzie, Paul, and Jinx looked at each other and with one accord peered over the rail and stared into the water as if they could see the wayward propeller lying there. There it might sit, shiny and gold, half-buried like sunken treasure, just beyond mortal reach.

". . . nor do I intend to let that happen. So my suggestion, sir, is that we take her in under sail. Shouldn't take much longer, a day or two—three at most. Fortunately we're pretty close. And the sails raised would be a novel experience. For the kiddies, especially," Captain Cosby added easily, then ruffled Paul's hair. It was a comforting gesture and Paul felt immensely relieved.

"It's either that, sir, or wait out here for an east-bound freighter. I wouldn't suggest risking that, though. We're an awfully large vessel to ask for a towline."

"Thank you for your suggestions, Captain," the children heard their father answer, and they knew from the snakelike way he said it that the "suggestions" had come too late.

"I'll let you know what I decide. And, Captain"—George's voice sounded angrier than it had before; it sucked the breath out of each child's lungs, and they were grateful beyond measure that they weren't Captain Cosby—"I believe I'm capable of deciding what's best for my family. In the future you will be so kind as to keep me informed of any malfunction."

Rebuffed, Captain Cosby started for the companionway door, but before he could reach it George called, "Port Said, you say?"

"Yes, sir. Or Bur Sayed, as the natives call it. At the entrance of the Suez Canal. We shouldn't have too much trouble in repairing the *Alcedo* there. The Suez Canal company maintains a pretty good facility, and the inner harbor is protected by a breakwater. There's also a British army barracks, so the place is safe from privateers. Not an easy thing to find in the Arab States."

"And a day or two sail, you say?"

"God willing, sir. And with the wind on our side." Captain Cosby tried for an affable chuckle, but George cut him short:

"I realize you cannot be held responsible for the wind, Captain." He looked at the group around him and at Ogden Beckmann standing near the door, a disapproving presence. What can he report to Father this time? George thought rebelliously. I didn't sabotage the propeller myself; I didn't plan for this delay. And it suddenly occurred to George that Beckmann was no more in charge of the progress of the boat than his father was. That the almighty Turk, sitting in Linden Lodge, was as powerless as any of them.

The discovery was an epiphany; it was a sudden light in the brain like a photographer's flash. I'm in charge here, George thought; I'm the one they're all looking up to. George felt like jumping up and down, like pulling off his clothes and diving headfirst into the water, like yelping with joy. It was the happiest he could remember being. It was bliss incarnate.

"Very good then, Captain." George tried to sound dignified. "Port Said it is. And under sail. No point sitting out here, waiting for one of the big fellows. We'll do just fine on our own.

"And ... ah, Captain"—George felt joy begin to bubble in his voice—"before we start out on this ... ah ... cruise of yours, we might take this providential opportunity to do some target shooting from the stern. That is, if you have no objections."

George didn't wait for the captain's reply. He reached an encouraging arm around his son's small shoulder. "What do you say, Paul, would you like Father to teach you how to shoot?"

The little boy was startled; first he'd expected a lecture about his behavior in church, then he thought they were all going to drown, then his father had yelled at Captain Cosby, and now, here he was, offering the best game imaginable. Target shooting! With clay birds and noisy guns and the grown-up smells of hot metal and smoke. "Would I, Father! That'd be whizzer!"

"Then we'll do it, Paul. You're the boss!" George was in seventh heaven. That'll show you, Ogden, he told himself. It's my game now; I'm the one calling the shots. Not you, and not Father. And not some mysterious place in the mist. We'll get to Borneo when I say so. So put that in your pipe and smoke it.

"Set up the targets on the aft deck!" the proud man called, and his commandments echoed the length of the whole long ship.

All this time Eugenia had stared at the sea and held back her laughter. Dead in the water, she repeated to her self over and over. There was something that sounded like voices rising around her: They chanted in Latin, moaned duets in Italian, shouted boisterous hymns of Anglican faith, or quieted babies or crooned to their flocks. A choir was stirring around her and stirring her on, but all Eugenia could think to add was a song she'd learned as a child:

> As I was out walking for pleasure one day,
> All by my lonesome to pass time away . . .
>
> Together we wandered. Together we roamed
> Till we came to the place she called her home. . . .
> She said if you'll marry, and stay here with me,
> I'll teach you the language of the little Mo-hi . . .

She wished she could sing it aloud.

"Pull!" George sighted along his shotgun, leading the clay pigeon that hurtled into the air. The shot was successful; the thing burst into a hundred fragments that spewed across the sky then plunged like hot cinders into the water. As good as the Fourth of July any day, George decided. "Pull!" he shouted again, while a steward hastened to reload the firing apparatus. The aft deck of the *Alcedo* had taken on a medieval appearance, as if the ship were fending off marauders with a giant crossbow. The machine that hurled the clay pigeons into the air was a silvery object on fat legs with a long, lethal neck and an internal spring capable of propelling a target several hundred feet into the air. Stewards moved back and forth behind and beside it, supplying weapons and lead shot and dragging out extra crates of clay "birds." Their serious bustle and the shiny importance of the machine itself made the deck look like a fortress under siege. All that was missing were helmets, chain mail, and vats of boiling oil.

"Pull!" George shouted louder, and the firing apparatus hurled another target into the air.

A second perfect shot. If the bird had been real, there wouldn't have been much left but a heap of feathers bouncing in the foam. George chuckled at the image and turned to Whitney: "Beat that, my lad. If you dare."

While Whit nervously took his stance, George held his Purdy shotgun close, pretending to look it over for hidden damage. But there was only love in his face as he gazed along the barrel and stock and touched the trigger and firing pin. His shotgun. His Purdy. Made to measure in London. The way shoes were ordered, or suits. No wonder the thing fit like a glove, George thought. Oh, he'd lend out the other shotguns or rifles, do all manner of things with them. But not this Purdy. George stroked the smooth barrel. What a day, he told himself. What a day. What a lucky chance about the propeller.

"May I try now, Father?" Paul reached up to touch the gun.

"Oh . . . ah, you there, Paul?" George said with surprise. He hadn't forgotten the promise he'd made his son; he'd just kept putting it off. It was men's work, shooting, and even though his intention to teach Paul had been founded in a true, warmhearted feeling, its accomplishment was tricky. It was easier to be boisterous among your peers—easier to lose yourself in the spirit of play—when you weren't looking after someone else. Fatherhood wasn't always what it was cracked up to be.

"Didn't see you there, Paul, son . . ." George stammered, ". . . and . . . well, no . . . You can't try yet, my boy. Not yet . . . In a minute, though. In a minute.

"Why don't you, ah . . . why don't you go . . . No, that's fine . . . you just stand right there." And George placed Paul squarely out of the way.

Paul stood fast, as if this position were part of a ritual. If his father had told him to stretch out both arms or balance on one foot, he would have done that, too. Anything for a chance to be with the men.

"Too bad. Too bad, old man," George bellowed as Whitney's clay target fell unharmed into the water. Paul was completely forgotten; his father brushed past him to give Whit a consoling slap on the back. "You win some. You lose some." George's laugh was smug, almost coy. "No one can blame you for trying, old man."

By the time he called the next contestant George was guffawing loudly over another private joke. "Lieutenant? Care for a go? See if you can save the reputation of the young bucks here. I believe you're our resident marksman . . . If Ogden's word can be trusted. . . ."

George's voice boomed over the still ocean; it pounded along the deck and silenced even the sea gulls. It was the only noise for miles around. That's my father, Paul thought proudly. That's my father we can hear. And I bet if there was a ship nearby, it'd hear him, too. "May I try now?" Paul quietly tugged his father's sleeve.

"What? Paul? Still standing here? There's a sport! . . . No, no, not yet, laddie. In a minute, though . . . After the gents." George passed a shotgun to Lieutenant Brown, winked broadly, and signaled a steward to reload and prepare to fire.

"Paul! Come over here," Whitney called, noticing the child's disappointment. "I'll show you how to hold the gun if you'd like."

"I'm waiting for Father. He promised to teach me," Paul answered staunchly and he continued to stand, rooted to the spot, the spot where his father had put him. Father was going to show him how to shoot. Father was going to help him. What did he need anyone else for? Father was the best shot around. Everyone knew that.

Eugenia hadn't been able to get near the complex proceedings. With all the movement of sailors, stewards, and contestants, and what George termed "the hazardous equipment" near the aft rail, mother and daughters had been politely refused entrance to the exclusive shooting club. But Eugenia wasn't content with the snail's-eye view the girls had been allotted, and she didn't want to curl into a corner of the floor and gaze up adoringly as each combatant blew balls of clay into a powdery mist. She only wanted to watch Paul, see the joy on her child's face as he finally did something to make his father proud, but she couldn't get close enough. So she stood near a side rail, listening to the proceedings as she stared at the ocean and wondered why the ship didn't shift with the breeze or why the water stayed so still.

It sucked around the hull, dull brown and sluggish, like water washing near the pilings of a pier. There were bits of chewed-up things floating languidly past: a soggy palm frond, bark from an unknown tree, submerged and irretrievable twigs—things that had once had a home, a place in the sun and rain. A storm must have carried them off, Eugenia decided, tossed them to the wind, condemning them to drift with the tide, with today's fancy, yesterday's dream. Just like us, she realized, just like this ship. The discovery made her surprisingly happy.

The palm fronds passed on. Twigs bobbed under an eddy, then reemerged slowly, as if their purpose in life were a delicate reminder of what the world would be without direction. The tree bark waved off; the brown water returned to its opaque, oily sheen; a clump of seaweed poked its nose around the ship's bow then disappeared.

"Pull!" Eugenia heard again. The excited shout was followed by her husband's raucous laughter.

"Dammit, Whit! That one was fine! You blew it to bloody-well smithereens!" That was George taking charge. Eugenia recognized the swagger in his words. She stared at the water; her husband's game took on the trancelike pace of memory.

"Next up? Ogden? Brown? Who'll do the honors? Got to keep this game a-rolling!"

It must have been Brown who stepped in then. No one spoke when he took his place and no one spoke when he finished. Even to Eugenia, the shot sounded different; it wasn't sport any longer. She shrugged her shoulders; she closed her mind.

Then there was Ogden, then Dr. DuPlessis, then Paul's small voice repeating his request, ". . . Could I, please? . . . now, Father? . . ."

Must men behave this way when they're together? Eugenia wondered. Or is it that we're adrift with no place to bind us? Have the rules changed, or have we? Eugenia decided to leave George to his carnage. The deck could be littered with fragments of clay for all she cared; it could look like a garden bed devoid of flowers, or a potting shed invaded by ravaging raccoons. Eugenia would go down to her cabin and write in her diary. She'd describe the way the sea looked when the ship no longer thrust herself forward. She'd try to comprehend what it meant to remain upright and balanced on something as intangible as water.

So Eugenia didn't witness her son's triumph when he was allowed to take his turn.

"Father," he'd finally found courage to say, "you promised."

Then George had answered, "Oh, all right, Paul. All right." His voice had been brusque, and he'd demanded the array of weaponry hurriedly and with as little enthusiasm as possible.

Henry, who'd been called up in the thick of the game and whose task had been to keep the men and shotguns well supplied while his fellow stewards and under stewards produced liquid refreshment and meat, egg, and onion sandwiches, had been given the unfortunate job of holding the gun rack for George's inspection.

"I can't see if you twist and turn like that, blast it!" George had bellowed at the under steward. "How can I find . . . ? There isn't a thing that might . . ."

"What about that one?" Paul had asked, then glanced at Henry and wondered if the under steward minded being yelled at. Henry looked like a boy to Paul, not as young as Ned, the service cabin boy, but young all the same. Then Paul wondered for probably the hundredth time why Henry and Ned weren't allowed to join in their games. He knew better than to ask Father; he knew he'd already been told the reason, but either he'd forgotten or the answer hadn't seemed quite right. It was like a lie no one bothered to hide.

"What about that one, Father?" Paul asked again, and pointed to a gun that looked smaller than the others, one that seemed to be waiting for him alone.

"Want to try that one, do you, son?" George chuckled suddenly; his voice sounded angry and mean. "That's no shotgun, son; that's a Holland and Holland rifle! I would have said it had too much kick for a tyke like you, but you're the boss! You know best. Take it away. Take it away." And George laughed for the benefit of the crowd.

Paul wasn't sure what his father meant; he didn't know what a "Holland and Holland" was; he thought it was the name of a place that had a lot of water and people with silver skates, but he took the rifle anyway. It was heavier than he'd expected and he had a hard time lifting it from the rack, but he managed. He'd show his father he wasn't a "tyke." He wasn't a "baby" and he wasn't a "mama's boy"; he was Paul Axthelm and he was going to learn to shoot like a grown-up. Paul took his determined stance.

George watched his son struggle with the heavy rifle; he saw the boy's face show doubt, then fear, then resolve, and he was reminded suddenly of his own self-discovery: that he was master of this place, and that anything that happened here was of his doing. For good or evil.

George suddenly realized that his son's arms were too small and his body too weak and that, in his pleasure and pride, he'd forgotten to do the thing he'd most wanted. He'd forgotten to be a father. George moved close to Paul and said, "That's too much of a weapon for you, son. We'll find you another . . . Henry, come back here and . . ."

But Paul was wise to that ploy. "I want to shoot, Father. I've watched you. I know how." And Paul raised the awkward, heavy thing to his shoulder and began to squint along the barrel. He felt so good and strong standing there with everyone watching! Even his sisters were quiet, even Mr. Beckmann and Captain Cosby and all the loitering crew.

"No, son, that Holland and Holland is just too big for a child your size," George reasoned gently, as he reached for the rifle. "Let me take . . ."

But Paul's grasp was firmer than George had anticipated; while he tugged at the barrel his son wrenched it free and swung it in a violent arc toward the sky. "Pull!" the little boy yelled, his high, thin voice full of bossy pride.

The steward in charge of targets was too startled to think; he let fly a clay bird just as Paul's small fingers squeezed the trigger.

The blast was terrific. It shook the ship; it rose to the sky and drove the sea gulls mad; it echoed over the shaken waves. It was a noise to end all noises. It reverberated in the halyards, the masthead, the stanchions and every metal nail, then grew silent, and the lack of sound left in its place was as startling as the rifle's retort.

"Bravo!" someone finally shouted.

"That's the lad," said another bright voice, and each man stared at the sky for a sign of that miracle: the lucky first shot.

No one saw Paul sprawled on the deck, the rifle flung to one side. Even George, concerned father that he'd suddenly become, scanned the horizon like everyone else. He hadn't seen his son fall and he hadn't watched the look of terror spread over the small face.

It was only when the captain laughed, "Bit of a stiff one, that rifle," that George looked back. For a moment he thought his son was dead, he was so terribly still. Then George recognized the look on Paul's face. It was mortal, hopeless humiliation. Paul wasn't dead; he only wished he were. And the bumps and bruises he felt after being so cruelly flattened were nothing compared to the boy's heartsick chagrin.

"That's all right, son," George soothed. "It happens to the best of us. No one here is . . ."

But by then the group was clustering close, chuckling heartily and nodding sage encouragement. This was a rite of passage, the way it would always be done, they assured each other. There'd always be a greenhorn and there'd always be stout men like themselves to cheer that newcomer on. The bluster of recounted exploits filled the deck as the captain, Whit, Lieutenant Brown, even Ogden Beckmann, stooped over Paul. The little boy was raised by many arms and planted firmly on his feet. Even the stewards and sailors joined in the jamboree. For that moment, there was no difference in class or age or intention.

"Nearly blew you away, that one . . ."

"Clear off your feet . . ."

"Knocked flat . . . Why, I remember the first time I . . ."

"They weren't so easy on me! I had to . . ." And the sympathetic mob turned to more important things: their own shaggy stories. Paul was forgotten. He brushed off his clothes, made his shoes and trousers and sailor's blouse neat and tidy while he frowned and frowned at his inept little hands.

"Paul!" George called once from the midst of the cheery crowd. But if the child heard his father, he didn't answer. He went about his business; he didn't look at his sisters; and he didn't look for his mother. He knew he'd failed; he didn't need anyone to remind him.

"We'll try it again, son . . ." George shouted while the admiring throng surrounded him. "Next time we'll . . ." But the encouraging words were lost in the crowd.

When Lizzie and Jinx hurried into their mother's cabin to tell her about the fiasco at the shooting match, she handed them over to Prue and the comforting lights of their own cozy cabin, then tried to console Paul. But her son wouldn't speak to her or open his door, so Eugenia ran up on deck alone. Darkness had fallen and it surprised her; she felt as though she'd been asleep and forgotten to eat dinner or go to bed. The ship seemed different altogether and it wasn't merely the lack of motion or engine noise. There was no one below decks, no one in the main saloon, no smell of supper in the passageway. For a moment Eugenia wondered if she and her children and Prue were the only souls left on earth.

The aft deck was shadowed with damp nighttime clouds, and fog rolled over the rail and down onto the teak floor when Eugenia walked through the companionway door. Only two lanterns had been lit and they stood on two tables, casting a sheepish yellow light over what was left of a celebration feast. There were overturned bottles and platters of sandwiches gone flyblown and stale. George and almost everyone else seemed drunk beyond comprehension. Even the sailors and stewards were tippling. The shooting lodge atmosphere that had pervaded the afternoon had continued way past dusk. Eugenia could hardly believe what she saw.

"What's the matter, Genie?" George slurred the simple words as he advanced on her, spewing the vicious stench of whiskey mixed with beer. "Little fellow couldn't take a joke? Gone running to Mummy?" George leered and lurched into the bulky body of Ogden Beckmann. "See that, Beck? Little lady's mad as a hornet. Thinks I wanted to . . ."

Then some memory of the afternoon made him stop his bluster. "Paul shouldn't have . . . it was his own fault," George complained. "I told him not to, didn't I, Beck? Told him . . ."

"Yes, George. You did." Beckmann steadied an arm momentarily, then let go and George crashed forward. Beckmann didn't stop him. George was on his own that time.

Eugenia looked around her; Beckmann appeared to be the only one sober, and Lieutenant Brown wasn't there at all. Men staggered through the darkness, weaving in and out of an unsteady light; one of the lanterns was set swinging and groups of unrecognizable, sweaty faces sprang from the black night. There was a cry of "Long live, Mr. A.! . . . The best . . . the fairest boss a . . ." The rest of the words were swallowed by cheers while someone, somewhere, very noisily vomited and began to sob.

Dr. DuPlessis and Whitney were among the bodies that careened through the dark. Eugenia heard their voices but no words. Bottles littered the deck and rolled against her feet. Something was thrown overboard; someone dived in after it; there was a scream of "Watch out for sharks!" followed by more laughter as other bodies were pushed or collapsed into the black waste below. There wasn't a breath of air; Eugenia watched men shamble across the deck, pulling down the tables of food and ale till the refuse ran in sloppy streams across the planks and gathered in puddles under the rail.

"Is Captain Cosby . . . ?" Eugenia began.

"Great night, Genie! Great night!" George moved to embrace his wife. "Gone to hell in a hand basket, we have. Dead in the water! Dead drunk, too, if you want the truth, eh, Ogden?"

Eugenia slipped out of her husband's grasp. "Didn't the captain say . . . ?"

"Can't sail now, Genie. No bloody wind!" George guffawed. "Hear that, Beck? Little woman doesn't know beans . . . no wind, Genie! No wind! We're stuck here, my dear. Stuck here forever. Now, how about a little kiss?" George barged into his wife, stepping on her feet and bruising her arms, but she didn't give in.

"Did Captain Cosby . . . ?"

"Damn it all to hell, Eugenia! I told you we're stuck. And even if we weren't. . . . even if we weren't. . . . You know what I learned today? Do you, Genie? Do you? Do you?" George started a jig; he grabbed his wife's waist and pulled her with him. "Made a wonderful discovery. You'll like it. All about Father and old Beck here. . . . All about the big mystery . . ."

Eugenia would have looked to Beckmann for help, but she knew that was useless. There was no possible way to forget his appearance in her cabin that one night or what he'd said, and George seemed to be playing directly into his hands. Eugenia had a sense of being alone for the first time in her life. There was no protection against injustice or cruelty, no home to retreat to, no person or name or position to slip behind. She couldn't say, "I'm Mrs. George Axthelm. Remember your manners!"; she couldn't fume, "My husband will be most upset when he hears about this!" or "my father" or "my grandmother" or "my father-in-law." Those rules no longer applied. Eugenia looked at Beckmann; she looked at George; she thought: I am completely on my own.

Eugenia pulled out of her husband's grasp again. It's useless to talk when George is drunk, she reminded herself. He says things he doesn't remember and things he doesn't mean. Or he makes promises he has no intention of keeping. And the ship can't be in danger, because Captain Cosby would never allow that to happen. Eugenia decided to return to her cabin.

George began to whimper as soon as he felt his wife slip away from him. "Aw, Genie . . ." he muttered, "give us a little kiss. . . . If you do, I'll tell you my secret . . . what I figured out today . . ."

"Not now, George." Eugenia pushed him away, intending to gently indicate the inappropriateness of his behavior, but her arms were stronger than she realized, and with no effort at all she was on her own. Opening the main saloon draperies was more difficult, or up-ending cushions for a yearly cleaning. "I've got to say good night to the children. They're worried, I'm sure."

George hated to have his wife patronize him. "It's always the children!" he exploded. "Always the damned children. That's all you care about. It's never me or what I feel. Every time . . . every time I get the least bit romantic, you say you've got to check on the children. The goddamn . . ."

". . . 'Is that Lizzie with a bad dream?'; 'Did I hear Paul coughing?' " George imitated in falsetto. "Not now, not now, that's all you ever say! Ever since Paul was born. No, before. Way before. Paul's just an excuse. He'll grow up as weak as his mother. Look at his performance today if you doubt me. Fell over like a goddamn stack of . . ."

"How can you say that about your own son?" Eugenia considered asking, but the words weren't worth the effort. She stared at her husband and drew herself into her newfound person. I am completely on my own, she thought. The gift of freedom felt wonderful.

". . . You don't give a damn about me, and you never have," George was continuing, his voice a childish wail of woe. "But don't think I wasn't wise to you from the first, Miss Eugenia Paine. Carriages and sable rugs, that's all you cared for. Who my father was—not me. You don't give two figs about me!

"Where do you think you'd have been if it weren't for me and my money? Do you think anyone'd give a damn what you did? Think they'd have given you the time of day?" Done. Said. But blaming Eugenia didn't bring George any relief; if anything, he felt angrier and definitely more alone. The words had only stirred up memories he hated to confront; he felt sorrier for himself than he had in all his born days.

"Your father. Your money," Eugenia repeated. The words were detached, dispassionate; she set them out as if for examination. Five months before, one week, or even yesterday, she wouldn't have been able to behave as she did. She would have felt cornered and at fault, but that was then and this was now. What had changed within her was undefinable, but Eugenia knew it was there.

"You'll throw that in my face till the day I die, won't you, George?" she added. Her words were as reasonable as a geography lesson. "But what about why you married me? What about your part of the bargain? The wonderful pact made between us, your money for my name? If you want to be mercenary, why not mention that?"

It's all so easy, Eugenia told herself, there's no need for tantrums or tears or self-recrimination. George and I, Beckmann, the Turk, the whole web of our existence has lost its pull.

I was eighteen, she realized; I loved this man and I believed we'd be happy. I wanted to be a good wife and mother, and all I needed was to be loved in return. But now we've gone as far as we can go. The phrase brought Eugenia enormous solace.

"You spoil everything I try to do. . . ." George fell back on his final weapon; he started to whine. George's drunken sobs were a sham of self-indulgence. When he cried, he only made himself feel better; no improvements came from his grief.

Eugenia didn't look at her husband. Her eyes began to wander the sky and she discovered that above the lanterns' smoke, the heavens had cleared; they'd become bright and filled with stars. If the sky had been turned into a pond or a lake or a well, she could have seen straight through to the bottom.

"I'm going in," she said quietly and began to walk down the deck.

". . . We shouldn't have come. We shouldn't have come on this trip. We should have sat tight at home. Nice and cozy. Nice and quiet. But oh, no. Father says, and then you say, and then someone else throws in their two-cents' worth . . . and off little Georgie Porgie trots, good as gold . . ."

Eugenia didn't hear the rest of her husband's practiced complaint. She closed the companionway door behind her.

"Going in" had meant her cabin and a bedtime chat with her children; it had meant stories and prayers and three blankets tucked close to three sleepy heads, then a safe little book, a shawl round her shoulders, and two pillows at her back. It had meant brushed hair, a washed face, and troubles put high on the shelf. But the night and the day had been too strange for that. We've gone as far as we can go, Eugenia told herself.

• • •

In the hold of the ship, Lieutenant Brown watched Eugenia step into the circle of light.

"I didn't know where you were," she said, then looked through the porthole at the starry night. "I was up on deck. But you'd already gone." She didn't know what else to say. The explanation seemed sufficient. She stood where she was and waited.

"Eugenia," Lieutenant Brown said. Then he was beside her and holding her. His arms felt warm and tremendously strong and his face smelled of brine and soap and something as comforting as tobacco or toast. She lifted her face to his and put her hands on his shoulders and then on his back.

"I'm here," she said. "I'm here." She opened her eyes, and was amazed all over again at how clear the night sky had become.

TWELVE

SOMETIME DURING THE NIGHT, the ship had begun to sail. Eugenia woke to the creak and roll of its timbers. Brown was still asleep, his face turned toward her, his cheek nearly touching her shoulder.

"James," she whispered. The name was new; she felt strange and rebellious using it, as if it were a secret she shouldn't have guessed, "James," she whispered again, "wake up." But he was not to be wakened; he stirred, brushed her arm with his lips, but he didn't open his eyes.

"We're sailing," she said, and turned her head to look up through the porthole. The night was still bright, though the moon had gone. It must have set, Eugenia realized. It must be very late. But the discovery didn't trouble her. In one night, she'd become a person unconcerned with mundane things. She shifted the pillow made of her chemise and his shirt and kicked off the blanket that had once been her dress. She had no other thought than her immediate comfort.

"We're sailing!" she said again, and lay on her side to look at her lover's body. The hair on his chest and legs shone like heat and Eugenia could feel warmth all along her own body, all the way into her toes and fingers. "James," she said, kissing him. "James. James. James." Over and over she kissed him—his eyes and nose and lips, the hollow of his chest, the flat of his stomach and his wonderful hands—till he woke up, smiled, slipped his arms around the small of her back, and they began all over again.

• • •

"Where are they now, God damn it?" the Turk thundered as he sat bolt upright in his chair. His body was so stiff he looked as though he might fly off toward the ceiling at any moment.

"Port Said, sir," Anson answered evenly. He didn't move or proffer the accustomed globe.

"And what the hell are they doing there? Carl!" the Turk shouted without moving or looking in his son's direction. "What the hell are they doing in Port Said? It's not on their scheduled route! They were supposed to pass down into the Red Sea without stopping in Egypt. Just provisions, water, coal, that sort of thing. And now you tell me they're lying about in some hotel. Not even on the ship. Next thing you know, George will take it into his head to visit the pyramids. My God!" The old man was apoplectic with rage; his thin face was red and mottled, even his hair stood on end as if a fire crackled inside it.

"Repairing a propeller, Father. At least that's what the cable said. That's what you just read . . ."

"But what about Beckmann? How did he allow . . . ? How can he . . . ? My God! My God! We're ruined now!" The old man collapsed backward into his cushion. His body went limp; even his starched shirt, gabardine jacket, and knife-creased trousers sagged in a heap. There seemed nothing left of the Turk but a pile of empty rags on his chair's leather seat.

Anson and Carl looked at each other across the dark room. It was the first time they'd admitted a mutual concern. Neither knew what to do next. They'd brought Beckmann's wire into the study expecting nothing more than the usual report, but the Turk hadn't even finished reading it when he'd sprung upward like a scalded cat. His gestures had been stiff and jerky and he'd harangued them like a mean old man with seventy-odd years worth of pent-up resentment.

Now here he was, slumped into silence, staring at the floor and dragging a shawl round his creaking shoulders. It wasn't a reassuring sight. Not reassuring at all, Carl decided. How would they ever set things straight if anything happened now? If the Turk collapsed or his heart gave out? None of Martin Axthelm's sons had ever imagined their father as anything less than the potent wielder of power, the patriarch to whom the world shuffled forward on bended knee. And the old man had never shared a thing with his children; he was the only person privy to the complex and myriad dealings of Axthelm and Company.

Carl had a sudden picture of Linden Lodge as a wooden box stuffed with papers. There were so many scraps of this and that—yellowing titles and deeds and deals, all the slippery things that build an empire of money and greed—that the house was in danger of bursting its seams. In his vision, it began to split apart; it spewed out yards of paper, which he, poor Carl, ran to retrieve. A lease in perpetuity for this, a lien on that, stocks in companies long ago liquidated, mortgages, foreclosures, false histories of failed businesses. The seemingly inconsequential documents that people sign and forget until it's too late. "I didn't realize . . ." they beg with a moan; "I thought that meant . . ." But Carl didn't know those stories. Only his father did. That tired old man's mind held the future.

"But Captain . . . ah . . . Captain . . ." the Turk began slowly. He sounded as if he'd just wakened up, as if he were talking to someone in dreamland. "Captain . . . ah . . ."

"Cosby," Carl and Anson answered in immediate and grateful unison.

The Turk looked up at them and scowled. Idiots, he was surrounded by idiots. He sighed and began again. Very slowly.

"Cosby," the Turk enunciated clearly. "What I said . . . Captain Cosby . . . Didn't he have any warning? Couldn't Cosby have saved the propeller? Couldn't he have . . . ?" Then the Turk began to laugh; it was a mirthless, hollow sound and it terrified his already frightened audience.

"And I thought I'd hired the best when I hired Cosby," the Turk continued bitterly. " 'He'll do anything to save his ship,' I was told. 'He's like a bulldog bitch with a litter of pups. Nothing will shake him.' Well, they lied to me when they told me that. You can't trust anyone. Not even your friends, Carl. Remember that. Not even your friends. . . ."

"But, Father . . ." Carl interrupted.

"What? What . . . What!" The Turk's rage bubbled over again. "What do you have to add to the present confusion? Are you going to tell me Cosby's a nice man, or that I should wait for Beckmann or, worse, put my confidence in your dear, departed brother? What pearls of wisdom are you going to produce for us now, Carl? . . ." The Turk's words grew unintelligible again as he sank back in a sea of oaths and mumbled recrimination.

Carl felt Anson's eyes appraising him. He shouldn't be here, Carl reflected; he shouldn't be a witness to this collapse. "Why don't we discuss this alone, Father," Carl said pointedly.

"What for?" the Turk snapped. "Anson knows everything there is to know. At least as much as you do." The old man laughed again, but this time it was his accustomed laugh, cruel and quick. "Besides, you were damned pleased to have him here a moment ago, weren't you, Mr. Fine Ideas? When you thought I was about to pop off. When you thought the old man had gone off his nut," the Turk taunted, and waved a bony finger at his son.

Carl wondered what had happened to his father. Perhaps he's ill, he thought. Or perhaps he's finally getting too old for this. "What I meant, Father . . ." Carl began again in the patient voice of a weary teacher with a recalcitrant child.

"What . . . what!" the Turk shouted. "Idiots! Every last one of you! Nincompoops! Idiots! Fools!" The old man leapt from his chair and hurled his shawl on the floor.

"What I meant," the son continued methodically, "is that this little accident won't mean much of a delay. Certainly a few extra days or even weeks can't alter the course of events in Borneo. . . ."

"You don't know anything, Carl! Anything! Now get out of here. Out!" the Turk shrieked. "And don't show your face in this room again!"

September 1, '03
Port Said

Dear Father,
By now you will be in possession of my cable as to our where-abouts . . .

George put down his pen, stared at the page and then out the windows to the bustling street below the Hotel Belle Ville. A marine mist blew through the open panes; it was salty and damp, but it carried with it the unmistakable smell of humanity cramped into city living. Next came the noise of street vendors and cart wheels, animals bellowing and belching, and all the varied accents of the town's French and Arabic residents. There could be no doubt that the room and the desk were on land, and that the easy (perhaps too easy) routine of life at sea was over.

From his bedroom windows (on the second floor—with a fine corner view and plenty of cross ventilation) George could see the town's lighthouse and one vast shoulder of the monumental statue of Ferdinand de Lesseps, the creator and architect of the Suez Canal. The statue gave George courage; it was a reminder, on foreign, Moslem soil, of the supremacy of the Christian approach to life. It brought with it order, the ability to separate right from wrong, and the power that clear-thinking men would always have over the heathen unwashed. George sat up a little straighter, knowing that he was a representative of the master race. He took comfort in his jacket and boiled shirtfront (even in the trickle of sweat that had begun to work its way under his collar) and he positively reveled in his necktie's choke-hold knot.

We'll be here for the next week or two. Jonathan Clive assures me it won't be longer, and Captain Cosby is undertaking necessary precautions against future problems. He's proven himself a most knowledgeable man. I believe I found the ideal captain when I took on Cosby. Your recommendation was impeccable, as usual, Father.

And I mean that, George decided, Cosby's all right. Got us here in one piece—and gave us a nice little run before bringing us safely to rest. Father should be pleased with the compliment. (George either noticed—or he didn't—that the use of the word *I* had superseded his habitual *we*.)

Clive's boat yard is quite the place. Near the British barracks and full of the spit and polish of the "auld" sod. It's good to see that kind of hustle and bustle going on out here. One does get weary of the Arab way of life. So much is directionless; so much is left to fate and Allah, that ambition and the proper ethics of a good upbringing become subservient to expediency or desire. I don't believe you'd find the place your cup of tea, Father.

I will let you know how the yacht proceeds. In the meantime, best wishes to all at home.

The dutiful son signed his name, then chuckled to himself as he tucked the letter into its envelope. What will Father say when he sees this? he wondered. George indulged a picture of the Turk's vehemence—and Tony and Martin and Carl dodging about and waving ineffectual arms as if the threats and oaths were hurled brickbats. Cosby's all right, George repeated happily. This stop has proved providential. Destiny or whatever the soothsayers call it. Bur Sayed—Port Said—even the name suits my mood. We take something Levantine and as unruly as a flock of chickens, and presto! magico! it becomes a European port with a most sensible appellation. George smiled and turned his attention to more immediate matters. He stood, straightened his cuffs, looked at himself in the mirror, slicked back his hair, picked up his straw fedora, and left his hotel room for a visit to Jonathan Clive, the ship chandler.

What a decent fellow, George reflected as he strolled along the quay-side. Clive finds us decent lodgings, looks after the captain's and crew's needs, and then makes certain we're never at a loss for entertainment: carriages for a picnic, a sloop to view the bay, games for the children, a Punch and Judy show in the hotel lobby. And the way he does business, too. Nothing ruffled about him. Calm in the midst of this Arabic turmoil. "It will keep, Mr. Axthelm." (That's what he tells me in that thick Scottish brogue of his.) "It will keep."

George considered his new friend's advice while he passed beyond the Hotel Belle Ville's pleasant grounds and continued along the harbor's edge. Jonathan Clive's words had taken on a meaning that had nothing to do with their literal translation. "It will keep" had become George's catchphrase, his totem, his rune. It represented his hopes and unspoken dreams. Because George had finally allowed himself to plan for the future: what he'd do for Genie when all this was over, what he'd be to Paul and Lizzie and little Jinx. What he'd build of their lost family. It will keep, George told himself again, because I have the time and the wisdom to keep it.

Several times he'd thought about describing this new self to Eugenia. Pictured what he'd say and how. First about his discovery on the *Alcedo,* the day of the shooting match, when he'd realized it was he, not his father and certainly not Ogden Beckmann, who controlled their future. And then about this recent revelation: Jonathan Clive's magic words. But George didn't want to risk confiding in her yet. He wanted this person, this new George Axthelm, to come as a wonderful surprise. He decided not to tell her, but to show her. A picture's worth a thousand words, he reminded himself.

"And it will keep. It will keep." George smiled as he walked down the esplanade. The port town, despite its Arab leanings, had a decidedly sophisticated and French air (to George's way of thinking, at any rate). It reminded him of Deauville or Lausanne, with its outdoor restaurants, its strolling gentry, its unhurried air. From the cool protection of one of the town's many café awnings, George could sip his absinthe and coffee and watch the world go by. Now, he decided to do just that. The visit to Jonathan Clive's shipping store would wait. George sat at a table and glanced happily at the world around him.

A seawall, built of rectangular-cut quarry stone, protected the wide esplanade. There were trees in stone-capped wells and benches, and here and there a pot of ridiculously bright Egyptian flowers. But in spite of those vivid colors and the quick swirl of a burnoose or djellaba, the town, or at any rate this part of it, looked comfortingly European. Like the places he'd visited during his youthful "grand tour."

Too bad Genie didn't know me then, George reminisced. What fun we would have had. And he remembered leaving unnamed ladies snoring in rumpled beds while he rose and opened heavy, green shutters to stare at fabled streets. I should have had Genie with me then, George reflected; she would have liked all those places, those picture-perfect towns and hillsides. But George's thoughts didn't make him sad, and they didn't make him feel like reaching for a whiskey or a brandy and soda; he believed his life was about to change. And he'd make sure that it did.

Paul and Jinx raced along the street toward their father. They'd spotted him a long way off, then shouted back to Prue, Cousin Whit, and Lizzie (who'd decided, for some unfathomable reason, to become a grown-up): "Hurry up! Hurry up! We're going to surprise Father!" Paul and Jinx didn't wait for a reply, however; they pelted down the esplanade to the café where their father had just perched himself (as he did most afternoons) "to watch the world go by."

The children had been on land a week and they loved it. They were staying at a hotel! Eating dinner in a restaurant at a table d'hôte (whatever that was!) and every minute was exciting and full of exuberant fun. They didn't see much of Mother, it was true; she was always "resting" or had a headache or was too tired to join their outings or games. But they had Father! And what's more, he'd given them a wonderful surprise!

In the beginning of the voyage, he'd said they didn't have to keep up with their lessons while they were in port, so when they'd pointed out that this town was a port like the others he'd had to relent and say, "Well, all right, kiddies. You win. No lessons till we're at sea again."

So, no lessons the whole of the glorious stay in Port Said! No lessons and a Punch and Judy show and a picnic and visits to the wharf to see Mr. Clive. No lessons! And games with Henry and Ned in the hotel garden where Father gave them a tetherball and bow and arrow set! Henry and Ned, who worked on the yacht. Imagine! Jinx thought this inclusion of their two new friends more than made up for Ned's not being allowed to join her birthday party, and Paul decided he was going to be just like Henry when he grew up. He said so, too, and he promised never, ever to drop his serviette again.

"And if I do, Henry," Paul had stated in the cooling shade of the Hotel Belle Ville garden, "you know, when we're at sea again, and you have to stand up while we're all sitting there eating, why, I'll jump right off the chair and get it myself."

Henry hadn't answered anything to that, and Lizzie hadn't said anything either. But then Lizzie had become awfully strange since they'd been in Port Said. Sometimes she was impossibly ladylike and bossy, and sometimes she was downright quiet.

Actually the victory over lessons had been won by Paul. It had occurred on the morning they'd arrived (after a two-day rolling sail when everyone had been a little seasick—even Mother). The children had gone to visit their father in his study and Paul had been the one to pipe up, "Isn't Port Said considered a port, Father?"

Jinx had held her breath; she hadn't dared ask such a bold question. She knew their father would see through the ploy right away, that he'd get angry and use the stern, formal voice he saved for lectures. "Don't try to duck responsibility," he'd say. "You won't get anywhere being lazy." Then he'd give some example the children couldn't follow, like the Phoenicians and Abyssinians, and they'd be dismissed to return to their "timely" studies.

But he hadn't said any of those things. He'd been talking to Mr. Beckmann when the children had burst into the room with the all-important question, and he hadn't even guessed what they were up to:

"How long are we going to be in Port Said, Father?" Jinx had asked as guilelessly as she could.

"Till the propeller's repaired." Their father hadn't looked up; he was still working with Mr. Beckmann.

"And how long will that be?" Lizzie had joined in then as she strolled toward the desk. "Oh, maps," she'd added, "I adore maps. May I join you, Father?" The voice she'd used had been sugary enough to catch flies. Jinx and Paul had shared a disgusted look behind her back.

"I don't know, sweetheart." Their father still hadn't taken full notice of his children's presence or their questions. "Maybe two weeks."

"But what about our lessons?" Paul had drawled (as if the question had just occurred to him!).

"Lessons?"

"Yes, Father, our lessons. The ones we have to work at every day with Cousin Whitney. Our 'tutorials.'" Jinx had made a sour face; she hated the arithmetic drills most of all.

"Now, children. Did you come in here to interrupt me with something as unimportant as that?" For a moment Lizzie and Jinx and Paul had thought their father was angry. Then he'd teased, "You know the rule. Lessons at sea. No lessons in port."

That had been when Paul's inspired query had made its appearance.

"But isn't Port Said a port?" he'd asked, and all three children had held their breath at the daring brilliance of the question.

"Is it considered a . . . ? Oh, I see what you're getting at! . . . You're scoundrels, every last one of you!

"Yes, it is 'considered' to be a port, Master Paul . . . and no, neither you nor your two accomplices have to do a lick of work as long as we're there!" Their father's laugh had been proud and happy. "You win," he'd said. "No lessons till we're at sea again."

Whooping with delight, Jinx and Paul had dashed from the room.
Lizzie had been as pleased, but she'd sworn she'd never race around like
a wild Indian, so she'd sauntered slowly into the passageway, where
she'd been grabbed by the hot, excited hands of her little sister.

"No lessons, Liz! Just think! For the whole time we're in Port Said.
Two weeks or maybe more!"

"Very nice, I'm sure." Lizzie had covered her mouth to hide the tiny
yawn she thought approximated bored, adult behavior, but the effort
was lost on the two younger children.

"No lessons!" they'd giggled and shrieked, and their loud, hiccupy
excitement had drowned out the words hidden behind the study door:
Mr. Beckmann's curt remark and their father's irritable answer. But all
three children had known from the disapproving, angry tone that
something was wrong, and they'd rolled their eyes at each other,
knowing for certain that they and their father, in secret consort, had
won some fabulous game.

Eugenia's hotel room was hot. With the thick, louvered shutters closed
and barred, the sea breeze could only creep in at the cracks and the air
smuggled in was wet and warm like deserted water standing in a tidal
pool. The bed was wet as well; Eugenia imagined she could slide from
it as if it were a sluice slipping into a lake. Everything—the sheets, the
tumbled mosquito netting, the bedstead, even her own long hair—
smelled of salt and hazy, breathless heat.

But she was so happy! She moved her face on the pillow and gazed
across the floor. Where a shaft of sunlight crept in, the tiles shone like
fire. Eugenia was reminded of farmers burning the autumn earth. The
brakes were white-hot; heat rose in thin and wavery lines and from
where she'd stood, in that far-off time, the men bending over the
flames looked as if they were the most fortunate people in the world.
They looked as though they walked in fire.

The rest of Eugenia's room, the rest of the third-floor room at the
Hotel Belle Ville, was blue. Blue from the shutters, blue from the sea,
blue from the flickering paint that shimmered on the ceiling. It was an
ocean cave. Neptune's home. A palace for mermaids and nymphs and
gods. It was everything she'd been born to know. Eugenia turned and
dragged her slow hair across the rumpled bed.

"James, are you awake?" she asked.

"Yes."

"I am too."

"I would have guessed that, Eugenia, if you'd given me another moment. Or if you'd talked a little more." Brown laughed and raised him-

self on his elbow. "That's usually a good indication that you're awake. If you're talking."

"Oh, you're so wretchedly unfair!" Eugenia's voice was filled with delight. "You love to tease me, don't you?" She pushed the pillow into his chest.

"That's because you're so—"

"Easy to tease. I know." Eugenia laughed and sat up.

They looked at each other across the mound of sheets. His face and body were in shadow, but she could see him clearly; when he moved the shadow moved and Eugenia reached out her hand to trace its path across his cheek.

"How long have we been here?" she asked.

"Two hours or three. I don't know."

"No, I mean days. In this city."

"Five maybe. Or six . . . or seven . . . I've lost all track of time." Lieutenant Brown recognized suddenly how true that statement was. And it wasn't just time; Brown knew he'd forgotten something more important than the date.

"All I think about is when I'll be able to be with you," he said as he lifted his hand to hers and tried to block out the warning voice whispering in his ear. He told himself, I should get up and leave. But he didn't.

"I love everything you say to me, James," Eugenia said. "And everything you do." Then she kissed his forehead and eyes, moved her head so close to his that it felt like being hidden from the world.

"Everything?" He laughed as the voice disappeared in the pillow.

"Oh, you are so wicked!" Eugenia's body tumbled over his. "What I meant was . . ." But the rest of her words were lost in the sheets and the bedding and their tangling joyful limbs. I am completely happy, Eugenia thought. I am overwhelmed with love.

After the pleasant little respite with his children, George went on to visit Jonathan Clive. He liked the stroll down to Clive's office almost as much as the hours he spent there. There'd be tea spread out immediately, and a new tin of Walker's biscuits unwrapped as ceremoniously as if it were the Grail itself.

"We must cleave to the old ways, Mr. Axthelm," Jonathan Clive would say and go back to stirring the pot, turning it slowly in his hands till the black stuff was ready to be poured through a battered but glossy strainer.

George liked the Scotsman's practiced regimen. No words were spoken while the tea was prepared, and no words were spoken until the first swallow of the potent brew had been ruminated over, accepted, and understood. Only then was conversation permitted.

There'd be talk of the port, talk of the freighters and their various cargoes, talk of the way the city had changed from its first days as a creation of the Suez Canal company to its glory years when the French, hoping for another Alexandria, had poured money into it. So forth and so forth, on and on—good men, bad men, dreamers, fools—down to Port Said's present incarnation as workhorse of the eastern Mediterranean. The Gateway to the Great Canal. Ferdinand de Lesseps' dream come true: a dazzlingly white city standing on the verge of the long Red Sea.

Clive was convinced there was no other city like it. He was convinced that anyone, with decent determination and a willingness to work, could make a livelihood in Port Said. And not only a livelihood. With enough luck and elbow grease, there were profits to be made here as well.

"Profits" was as far as Jonathan Clive would go. He never said "a fortune" or "a killing"; he said nothing about "establishing an empire." It was enough for him to discuss the matters of the day, sip his tea, and ponder the strange and marvelous workings of the universe. For nearly fifty years he'd watched his fellowman arrive on these shores full of hope and a bagful of money or full of schemes and empty pockets. He'd seen every kind of get-rich-quick plot; he'd seen family fortunes hacked to bits and he'd seen hard-working men struggle and succeed. Those were the men Jonathan Clive liked to dwell on, the good folk who found their reward; those were the stories he liked to spin.

George decided, listening to Clive's quiet and steady words, that this was as close to true religion as he would ever be. Forget all that bunk they preach in church, he'd tell himself. (The bunk he was guilty of himself.) Those ladies with ostrich-plume hats who sauntered weekly into Grace Church or those men with their ivory-handled canes, would they even recognize honesty or loyalty or truthfulness? Even if it rose up and poked them in the nose with a stick? Had they ever tried to make the world a better place?

"There was a man, came out here once . . ." Jonathan Clive might begin, and a wealth of mystical wisdom would tumble into George's mind like a treasure box spilling open on the sand.

". . . not a farthing to his name and a suit so worn and shiny you could nearly see your reflection in it . . ."

Then the room would grow even more silent, till the sea gulls, passing their careless way by the open windows, became no more than fretful shadows.

A steamer might sound a blast, but the blast would fade to nothing. There'd be only the ticking of the ship's bell and the rattle of the ancient silver tea strainer.

". . . but he was an honest fellow and you know what he told me before he packed up for home? . . . And mind, he'd made a fair penny in his day, set his son up in that office across the jetty, made good marriages for all his daughters . . ."

Jonathan Clive's homilies were the best part of George's day. Leaving the quay-side shops, he'd feel strengthened and full of resolve. He'd set this thing right, he'd promise himself, have it out with Father and with that damned Beckmann. Write to Paine, Ivard, whoever . . . and set everything straight. He wasn't ready yet, he knew, but he would be soon . . . . Just a week or two, maybe a little longer . . . . Then he'd send off the letters and cables, take on the whole Axthelm clan if need be . . . Martin, Carl, any and all. . . . Just see if he didn't, he'd promise himself. Just see if he didn't.

George would walk through the evening streets, trying to rekindle the determination he'd felt in the ship chandler's office. It will keep, he'd say to himself. It will keep. And he'd hurry back to his wife and children, repeating the phrase he knew could save him.

Eugenia flung her hand upward and hit the iron post of the bed, but it didn't stop her. The bedstead, the twisted sheets, the darkening room, might not have even existed; she took so little notice of them. All she felt was Brown's body beside hers, on top of her, inside her. She thought, We are the same person, and she moved her legs against his and her hands over his back as if it were her own body she touched.

Everything was wet; their chests and stomachs sucked together and their knees slid open and apart and Eugenia thought, We will drown in all this wetness, and then all of a sudden she realized something else. Under the weight of his hot body, with her hands enfolding his shoulders, back, and shivering thighs, Eugenia thought, I am slipping away completely. Then the room became night through which they were falling and falling while a black and distant sky opened like a gift above them.

In her dream, Eugenia pictured herself passing George on the stairs. They were dressed for dinner: she and James and the DuPlessises and Whitney, making their entrance into the hotel dining room. George was walking up the stairs while she and the others were on their way down. They were laughing as they strolled the circular steps; Mrs. DuPlessis had a large feathered fan, which she used to tickle her husband,

and his response was so eager and flirtatious that they'd all begun to laugh. Then Mrs. DuPlessis said something even bolder, though Eugenia couldn't remember what, and they laughed harder still.

George was on his way up; he was in his street clothes, not his evening clothes, and when he saw the group, from the foot of the stairs, he smiled and mimed words of surprise but didn't speak. Mrs. DuPlessis mouthed something in response, though Eugenia couldn't hear that either, and then she waved her fan and winked and shook a fat wrist that was covered with sapphires and pigeon's blood rubies. Mrs. DuPlessis's whole arm dripped bracelets and loops of pearls; there were coronets intertwined in diamond ropes and eardrops and enameled lockets which popped open to show miniatures of silver and gold. Mrs. DuPlessis opened her mouth wide and Eugenia could see that even her teeth and tongue glittered.

George walked up the stairs while Eugenia walked down. The Du-Plessises waved and pointed; George waved and pointed back, but when he passed his wife and Lieutenant Brown he looked at them as if he couldn't see them. They passed each other in silence while George stared through their faces as if he saw no one at all.

In the garden of the Hotel Belle Ville, the waiter was clearing away afternoon tea. There'd been sweets and lime squashes served to the three young people from the American yacht as well as their two companions, boys the waiter felt were overreaching their station. He recognized the older one as a servant like himself. Henry, his name was. The younger one, Ned, was probably only a deck boy. A waiter at a first-class establishment like the Belle Ville shouldn't have to attend riffraff, the man told himself, but Americans were funny creatures. They believed in equality—at least they said they did.

So the children and their two friends had been allowed to order whatever they liked while a shockingly poor example of a nanny had lounged in the shade and talked to an equally poor example of a tutor. The waiter guessed the tutor was some kind of relative from the overly friendly way he talked to the three Axthelm children, but he also heard the young man mention lessons, which caused each child to make a face of exaggerated disgust.

Les enfants Américains, the waiter thought as he swept colored sugar into a silver-handled crumb receiver, *quel dommage. Ils n'ont pas la politesse. Ils sont des petits sauvages.* The waiter missed Marseilles and the proper manners of French children. He looked at what remained of a plate of cream cakes that had been decorated with pink and blue icing and miniature American flags. Each cake had a bite taken out of it, as though ferrets had been gnawing there. *Bêtes,* the waiter decided, *ils sont des bêtes, certainement.* The waiter set his black cummerbund straight, flicked crumbs from his equally strict jacket sleeves, and drew his shoulders into Napoleonic rectitude as he began to tackle the tossed and discarded napery, the iced drink spoons, tea spoons, dessert forks, and the remnants of a meal that had contained every indulgence and nothing of healthful living.

I hope I do not die in this place, the waiter recited to himself. I hope before long that I may return to my homeland, and to people who know the value of a meal well prepared, well served, and well enjoyed. Americans are no better than Arabs, the waiter grumbled silently as he retrieved limes that had been rolled across the table like cannon shot. They eat anything put in front of them; they insist on coffee that tastes like bathwater and order for their breakfasts meat and eggs and hot, gelatinous gruels. Serving these horrors is enough to turn anyone's stomach. *Quelle horreur! Un brisement de coeur, vraiment!*

The waiter replaced the bowl of limes on a side table, building a pyramid of green that looked as precarious as a plateful of uncut emeralds. Each lime displayed the best side of its shiny and fragrant skin and then climbed to the top: four, five, six tiers high. Satisfied, the waiter stepped back, plucked two branches from a bougainvillea vine, and placed them, like an emperor's crown, at the base of the bowl. Presentation is all, he told himself. *La beauté, la sainteté, nous voulons créer quelque chose durable et fort.*

Henry watched the waiter, recognized judgment passing over his superior French face, then leaned his shoulders as unobtrusively as he could against the garden wall and crossed his arms in a poor imitation of relaxed unconcern. Henry didn't know whether to sit or stand. He'd felt awkward being included in the Axthelm children's sudden feast (a feeling obviously Ned hadn't shared) and he felt tall, ungainly, and ugly now. His clothes weren't right, his hat was a disaster, and his chin either needed to be shaved or left alone. There was nothing Henry could do that felt right. He put his hands on his forearms, noticed his chewed, black nails, and dropped his fingers to his sides, then he shifted his posture again, waiting for someone to address him so he could reply with the clever, witty words he'd practiced. At that moment Henry looked death square in the face, and death was the definite master.

Miss Prudence was laughing, and Mr. Whitney alternately joining in the joke or returning to the flimsy pages of some dog-eared periodical; Miss Jinx was playing a child's game with her brother and the unobservant Ned; while the source of Henry's misery, Miss Lizbeth Axthelm, sat staring at the ground. Henry felt pinned to the spot; he couldn't speak to Miss Lizzie with everyone milling around, and he couldn't leave either. The reason he'd invented for coming to the hotel began to sound contrived even to his own sixteen-year-old ears, but he knew he couldn't very well leave before Mr. Axthelm returned. Not after all the fuss he'd made about an important message from Captain Cosby.

Damn, Henry thought, and the word *Girls* slipped involuntarily from his nearly shut lips.

"Having trouble with the ladies, Henry?" Whitney said with a distant chuckle.

"Sir?" Henry was startled enough to jump straight away from the wall. Without being aware, he stood at attention, as if Higgins had caught him snickering in the pantry.

"Did a fair young miss catch your eye here in Bur Sayed?" Whitney repeated.

"No, sir. No, no. Nothing like that, sir," Henry promised loudly, and he felt Miss Lizzie shrink inside of herself as though she'd come face to face with a blizzardy wind. The little white lawn chaise she'd hidden herself in might as well have been on the North Pole.

"It's been my experience that when a young man starts talking to himself, it's because he'd rather be talking to a young lady," Whitney drawled, then returned to an ancient edition of *Sporting Life*.

The magazine was over a year old and yellowed with many mossy thumbprints, while the photographic essays describing grouse shooting in Scotland and fishing the weirs and tarns of Wales seemed foolish and inappropriate to the sultry heat of Arabia; but sport was sport, and Whitney was determined that a safari in Africa was only the beginning of his newly chosen career. There were alpine goats to be tracked down near the Matterhorn, he'd promised himself: caribou in Newfoundland, tarpon off the coast of Florida, duck migrations in the Punjab—not to mention the vast wilderness of the Canadian Rockies where every species of fish, fowl, and mammal was simply waiting to meet its maker.

"Paul," Whitney called, "do you want to see a picture of a very large salmon that a man named the Honorable Sir Patrick McGrath caught last year? It was hooked in something called a tarn on a river in Wales I couldn't pronounce if I tried. But it's got a lot of *l*'s in it and a lot of *r*'s, and we could make up a proper American name if you'd like."

But Paul was too busy playing with Ned and Jinx to listen, and Whitney returned to his publication.

"Dirty plates left too long breed crime," Henry vowed silently, repeating the safe litany of shipboard days, where everything and every-one was kept in its appointed place. He made certain no words escaped this time. "The tines of a fork need polishing three times"; "Close your ears to all around you and save your eyes for the divine." They were Higgins's phrases, rules drummed into each steward and under steward, and they represented a point of view toward life and a life-time of service that no one could question. They were Henry's prayer when he felt in doubt. ". . . Save your eyes for the divine," Henry re-peated to himself as he glanced toward Miss Lizzie.

Then he announced, "Well, I guess I'd better be getting back to the ship. Captain Cosby's probably found Mr. Axthelm by now any-way . . ." With each word, Henry saw Miss Lizzie grow more rigid. Her arms looked as though they had fire pokers for bones, and she stared so hard at the ground, Henry expected it to open up as though a hole had been bored in it.

". . . It probably wasn't all that important anyway . . . you know how the captain is. . . ."

"That's fine, Henry," Whitney answered; his voice was a million miles away. "You do whatever you think best."

Henry looked at Ned, who was shooting arrows into a target, and at Master Paul, who was running to collect them, and then at Miss Jinx, who was shouting, "Me next. Me next," and he shuffled his feet into the loamy garden soil and didn't move.

He thought about home and how the Massachusetts pastureland looked on a September afternoon when the sun was beginning to slant so low and yellow that everything—saplings, hedges, thorns in a thicket, even blades of grass—cast a shadow three times its size. He thought about milk cows coming down the lane: the smell of flies and dusty hides, the twitching, viny scent of bramble and chewed cud, and the woolly slap of tails switching against knees and rumps and warm, moist backs.

". . . If you don't think Mr. Axthelm's due back for a while . . ." Henry tried again. ". . . I think Ned and me, we've intruded on your afternoon long enough . . . and I could go down to Mr. Clive's and see if Mr. Axthelm's there . . . that is . . . there's probably not much point in me taking up any more of your time. . . ."

Henry looked at Miss Lizzie the whole time he said this. He felt free to because everyone, including Miss Lizzie herself, was absorbed in some other activity. But as he watched her, he saw her throw her feet to the ground, jump up, grab her hat and unopened book, and hurry toward the hotel door.

"Lizabeth Axthelm!" Henry heard Prue say. "Whatever are you

thinking? Now come right back here and say a proper good-bye to Henry. He's been your guest this afternoon, after all. Nice enough to walk all this way in the heat of the day, too. You should be grateful that someone entrusted with a message for your father would be so diligent. Most young men his age would be off mooning about, not doing their duty. Most boys Henry's age have only one thing on their mind."

But Miss Lizzie didn't come back, and she didn't turn. Instead she did a terrible thing; she burst into tears, ran inside, and banged the door after her. Henry knew the crashing sound of the wood and the racketing of the metal hinges would remain in his heart as long as he lived.

"Girls!" was Paul's astonished reaction.

"My dear Diary," Eugenia began, then stopped. How to explain what she felt? What senses were traveling through her body? What her heart had discovered? She stared at the words again. Nothing ventured, nothing gained, she reminded herself, but her hand wouldn't move.

My dear Diary,

It seemed such a schoolgirl conceit, a letter to oneself, a record of events, as if the parties, guests, food, anecdotes, costumes, or sights observed were a genuine measure of the soul's long life.

Eugenia gazed across her room. The shutters were closed but the louvers open; what remained of the afternoon sun wandered in with the sleepy cadence of a portside town. There were voices rising from the street below: the genteel clip of a European couple strolling the esplanade, the demanding splutter of beggar children trailing in their wake, before giving up and returning to their raucous play. The children reminded Eugenia of young dogs; they rose with the sun, slept with the dark, and spent their days in search of food and pleasure. Each day saw the same routine: The hot afternoons were spent sprawled under benches, the early mornings rolling in the dust or jumping in the water, and the evenings cadging scraps and coins. It seemed an admirable life, as carefree as dust.

My dear Diary,

The words were a reminder to get to work. Instead Eugenia glanced at her bed, unmade and molded to James's vanished body, and wished she could call him back and forget the formalities of evening meals and dressing for dinner and polite conversation. She wished she could nestle into the crook of his arm, smell the comforting scent of sweat, damp sheets, and morning's perfumed soap. She wished she could close out all memory except falling asleep with his arms around her breasts—so close together that not even the drops trickling from their two wet bodies could find a way to slip between them.

My dear Diary,

We are in Port Said, where we've been for nearly a week. The Hotel Belle Ville is very pleasant, the nicest place I've ever stayed, though I realize that's not saying much.

No, it isn't, Eugenia realized. My innocence of the world up until now has been acute, to say the least. And think what would have happened if I'd stayed wedded to Philadelphia. I would have died—pure and simple. The image of herself as a middle-aged matron surrounded by her growing brood was horrific: she'd have needlepoint scissors in one hand, pince-nez for failing eyesight in the other, a family pew for Sunday matins, roast beef with Yorkshire pudding at dinner immediately after, then there would be ladies' literary afternoons and turkeys distributed to the needy on Christmas morning. A list of sensible activities as long as one frightened woman could make it.

Port Said is quite an amazing place. I don't think I can do it justice but I'll try. It is European—well not so much European as French, and because of that, it is wonderfully languid with a forgiving eye to all human foibles. I've never been in a place so "worldly." You have the feeling that everything that happens in the complex dealings of one human being with another has been seen before—and accepted. (Someone recently told me—I don't remember who—that it is rumored to be the wickedest place on earth!)

The other half of the town is Arab, of course—desert Arab, the voyagers over the Great Nefud, the Hamad wastes, and the sand peaks of the Dahna: These people are as wild as starlight. If they once knew what it was to shoulder human responsibility and waver between doubt and remorse, they have forgotten it. As we may also—being here. As we may become imbued with these strange and foreign sensations . . .

Eugenia paused and put down her pen; a ship's whistle blew in the harbor. It was answered by another. They were bossy voices, full of matronly advice; they admired the sounds of their own reputations. A tug responded—or Eugenia believed it was a tug; it had the high-pitched, ingratiating squeak of a smaller vessel. Then a third matriarchal shout followed. Then a fourth, and a fifth. Port Said was full of ships that considered their passengers priority; they were like so many mothers ensuring that their children be first in line at dancing class, at prize day, at the swimming races, egg hunts, and fancy dress parties. The hoots and bellowing calls were polite, but just barely. One ship gave way to another out of practicality, not courtesy.

Eugenia returned to her diary, but the moment of exposing her secret life had passed. The ships brought back too many memories. The room had been invaded by every convention she wanted to escape. Her grandmother's house in Maine came into her mind: the painted porch, the ruler-straight row of wicker chairs that faced the sea and remained empty most of the day, the hydrangea bushes clipped into a neat, rectangular hedge, the rules of when to enter the water and when to avoid it, the reminders not to wet your hair after three o'clock in the afternoon—lest it stay damp until dinnertime.

Then she remembered her own adult bedroom at her husband's house on Chestnut Street and the little delft clock that sometimes sounded as regular as a metronome and sometimes ticked crazily: louder, softer, faster, slower—as uneven and full of panic as a bat caught in an attic. She'd hated that clock when it misbehaved, simply hated it, considered dashing it to the floor, against a wall, or out the window. It was a palpable note of dismay in an ordered and well-managed day.

As we may, also, find ourselves pulled into behavior that would have seemed inconceivable at home, that would have been beyond all imagination.

Eugenia reread the page, and wondered if the hints were too broad for safety's sake, then realized: This is my private book; why can't I say what I choose? Eugenia dipped her pen into the inkwell again, determined to write about James: how it felt to lie together in a lazy bed, half awake, half asleep, half in some distant country of dreams, but totally consumed—one being with another.

A knock on the door stopped her.

"Yes?" she called without moving. "Come in." Eugenia didn't bother to straighten the bed or tie up the strings of her dressing gown; she'd forgotten everything but the pictures her mind had begun to draw.

"Ah . . . ah . . . ah, Genie . . ." George fumbled, standing in the doorway, staring at his wife, at her unpinned hair, her open dressing gown, her unmade bed. "Just . . . ah . . . just came up to make sure you were all right . . . bit worried, you know . . . all this Arab food . . . and when you weren't up and around. . . ."

The word *Arab*, George pronounced as "A-rab" with a long, hard *a*. It was a small stab at Philadelphian condescension, but it sounded forced, like behavior once spontaneous that can no longer be duplicated.

George will cling to the old ways, Eugenia told herself. It was the first time she'd thought about her husband in days, and she stared at him as though he'd appeared suddenly after a long absence.

"Got a bit of a feverish look, too, Genie . . . Shall I fetch Dr. D.? Wouldn't want my little wife coming down with some tropical ague . . . Shouldn't you get back in . . . ?" George glanced at the bed again and fluttered his doughy hands. The movement was a vague imitation of helping his wife from her chair. To anyone else the restless fingers would have looked useless, unsympathetic, self-centered, and lazy, and Eugenia decided that was exactly how they did look; they were as flaccid as a nest of sun-baked toads.

". . . The kiddies said you took to your bed directly after luncheon. I must have already left for Clive's office . . . don't take much to this siesta sort of stuff, myself, never have . . . guess I have too much of the Yankee in me . . . and anyway the bustle of the boat yard is refreshing . . . none of this Middle Eastern 'next week,' 'next year' mentality. If you want something done, it's done. . . ."

Eugenia didn't answer. She let her husband talk. She didn't think: How fortunate George didn't burst in sooner, James and I might have been caught. She didn't chastise herself by saying: My children must wonder what's become of me. She didn't feel guilt for any of her actions or a moment's hesitation, she merely sat where she was and realized she'd learned a very important lesson. I can hide my feelings, she told herself; I have mastered the art of deceit.

"I'm feeling much better, thank you, George," Eugenia said, and her face opened into a pleasant, polite smile. "It was nice of you to come up and check. I was about to start dressing for dinner. I'll be down to join you all shortly. On your way out, could you ring for Olive . . . ?"

Eugenia stood and wrapped the sashes of her dressing gown crisply round her waist, then looked across at her rumpled bed as though she'd forgotten its existence.

"Goodness!" she laughed. "On second thought, I'd better ring for the hotel maid first. I must have had a spot of fever or something to make a mess like that. Can't have Olive in here before things are a bit more tidy. She'd lose all respect for a mistress she deems infallible."

The sound of Eugenia's laughter and her easy manner were completely convincing.

She walked across the tile floor and pulled the shutters wide open. Sunlight, as practical as a starchy nurse, pushed its way into the room.

"Oh, my!" Eugenia protested again as the light glared down on a tossed lace blouse, one shoe, a chemise, a pair of pantalets. "I've become as irresponsible as a child. Please do excuse me, George, while I set things right."

Good, Eugenia thought, as her eyes searched the piles of clothing, there's no trace of James to be found. But there was nothing thrilling about this discovery; it was plain common sense. She might have been setting place cards at the dinner table or surveying a bowl of cut flowers: Practice makes perfect, she told herself.

George watched his wife; he was about to speak, then thought better of it. She seemed to be behaving strangely—bustling about too quickly, shoving clothing into corners, tidying up for all she was worth—but he decided it was probably just a touch of fever, after all. And the change wasn't incompatible with how he felt himself; he liked to see Genie active; he liked the return to American ways. Lately she'd become elusive, a bit mysterious, a bit caught up in the mores of the East. It's nice to see her coming round, he told himself. It's nice to see her correcting her own behavior.

If any other thought had entered George's mind, he would have dismissed it out of hand. Eugenia was his wife, he would have countered; she was raised in Philadelphia, came from a good family, went to the right schools; she'd memorized all the codes of social conduct. She would never do less than her duty; it was what she'd been taught.

"We'll be in the garden then, Eugenia," George said, withdrawing with hesitant but dignified formality, "having an aperitif before dinner . . ."

"Fine," Eugenia answered. "I'll be there."

She heard the door close, and gazed at her bed again. ". . . I met a lady in the Meads . . ." she recited, partly to herself and partly to the room. Her voice wove around the bed and tumbled clothes, around the sea smell and human smell, and a sharp earthy scent like unfired clay:

> *"Full beautiful, a faery's child,*
> *Her hair was long, her foot was light,*
> *And her eyes were wild."*

Eugenia curved the pillows into something round and respectable, pulled the coverlet into a straighter line, and as a last touch fluttered the top sheet so it appeared as if no one had disturbed it.

"I made a Garland for her head,
And bracelets too, and fragrant Zone;
She looked at me as she did love
And made sweet moan."

Eugenia passed into the cool alabaster of her bathroom, rang the bell for water, then walked back to her dressing table and took up a vial of perfume and a jar of bath salts.

"I set her on my pacing steed
And nothing else saw all day long,
For sidelong would she bend and sing
A faery's song. . . ."

The rest of the Keats poem was then dismissed to the farthest and most inaccessible corner of her mind. So, Eugenia told herself, I have taught myself to lie.

"Are you sure?" Lizzie asked Henry. They stood on the quay-side, as removed from the rest of the family as Lizzie had dared.

"I heard Mr. Clive telling Captain Cosby."

Lizzie didn't answer. She had a picture of the dining table on the yacht, of Henry serving, of Higgins lurking in the background, of Mrs. DuPlessis grousing, and of her father and Mr. Beckmann exchanging glances that could mean anything. Lizzie shut out the terrible sight.

"When?" she demanded.

"Less than a week, I guess. The new piece has already arrived. It shouldn't take too long to repair the damage now." Henry dragged his eyes off Lizzie's face, glared at the water, and wondered why the sea gulls sounded so different from the ones back home. The sea gulls in Port Said had a complainy-sounding cackle, as if they were making noise to be disagreeable and nothing more. In fact, the whole of the harbor was disagreeable; the waves were a yellowish green-gray, not the welcoming blue of the North Atlantic that kept calling: *Come jump in us; come swim with us.* And the Port Said waves smelled terrible, too; they reminded Henry of outhouses and old fish heads.

"Does Father know?" Lizzie asked, then immediately corrected herself. I should have said "Mr. Axthelm." Henry's a servant: I keep forgetting.

But that was the heart of the problem. Lizzie hung her head and stared at the pebbles and dust of the quay, and then down at the water. She kicked a few loose stones and they fell with a plink into the greasy sea. They didn't leave a mark or a circle to grow into another and another. They just vanished from sight. Lizzie felt lonelier than she had in her entire life. She wished she were home; she wished she'd never set foot on the *Alcedo;* she wished she and Jinx were in their nice, safe rooms on the third floor of their house on Chestnut Street and that Paul were across the hall, and their day nursery was full of sunlight, and that it was springtime and the cherry trees were in bloom, or maybe Christmas holiday after a big blue-white snowstorm with icicles hanging from the eaves, and the bright light of shiny snow-crust reflecting up onto the walls, and turning everything a pale silvery color that looked cool but cozy at the very same moment. There was no end to Lizzie's wishes.

"I'm sure Mr. Axthelm must know, Miss Lizabeth," Henry managed to answer.

Lizzie winced at the return to formality. It's not fair, she raged to herself, other girls have beaus; if Mother and Father hadn't dragged me off, if we'd stayed put where we belonged, I'd have had one, too.

Lizzie glanced momentarily at Henry, and Henry decided it was his turn to kick pebbles into the waves. He realized he was a miserable failure, that Miss Lizzie was way beyond his reach, and that if news of his "walking out" with her ever reached Higgins, he'd be horsewhipped for sure.

Henry closed his eyes, and Lizzie promised herself: He's only a serving boy; I can do better. Besides, what would Mother think? What would Father say! Don't be a goose, Lizzie. Go off and play with your sister. Pretend you don't care. But none of those encouraging phrases helped. Lizzie and Henry continued to stand where they were, and the waves continued to make slurping, drooly noises against the mossy quay steps, and the birds continued to waver overhead, mocking or berating everything in sight.

It was Paul who broke the impasse, as he often did, just by being himself. Paul saw only what he wanted to see. And at that moment, it was that his new friend, Henry, was stuck talking to his sister.

"Henry!" he shouted, running down the esplanade. "Guess what Ned said?"

Lizzie steeled her heart. I don't care, she told herself. I don't care in the least.

"Ned said that Father said that we're going to start sailing soon! Ned said that Father said that Mr. Clive's ready to fix the propeller. Ned said he heard Captain Cosby tell the mate. That's how he found out. Isn't it exciting?" By then Paul had reached his sister.

"Isn't it, Liz?" he asked; he was breathless, and the bare legs that stuck out from his white shorts, high socks, and chalked-up shoes were speckled with dust and flecks of translucent gravel.

"Do you want to wake up the entire town?" Lizzie snapped.

Paul opened his eyes so wide a sea serpent might have dropped in his path. "But it's almost lunchtime," he protested. "Nobody sleeps during lunch." His goggle-eyed expression never wavered. "Prue says . . ."

"You don't know anything," Lizzie insisted.

Henry hated to see a little kid like Paul mistreated, but he didn't know what to say. He couldn't take sides and he felt awful standing silent, but there was his dilemma in a nutshell: Miss Lizzie—who was about as perfect and beautiful and smart and clever as any young lady could be—against Paul, who was harmless as a fly.

"Ned says we can still be friends, though," Paul blithered on, unaware of the misery he was creating.

"Jinx thought maybe you and he wouldn't have to go back to work, on account of being our friends and all. But Ned said the captain would 'tan his hide' if he didn't.

"Is that true, Henry? I thought that was just something they did to camel skins to keep them from smelling so awful. Tanning, you know . . . Isn't that what they told us, Liz . . . when we were in that last place . . . ?"

Lizzie made up her mind that her brother was probably the stupidest person on the face of the earth.

Paul gave up with worrying over words, or where the *Alcedo* had or hadn't been, and continued as if he'd never hesitated: "Ned called Captain Cosby 'the old man,' but I thought he meant Father, so I said I'd ask Father not to tan his hide. But then Ned said I shouldn't interfere in 'crew' business . . ." Paul's voice carried out over the waves. His speech seemed to last all day.

". . . and I said that Father's got those targets set up on the stern and that we could all take turns shooting at . . ." Paul faltered in his steady stream of words. ". . . Course I'm not very good . . ." he added sheepishly.

"We all know that, Paul!" Lizzie's sudden, mirthless laugh ended all further talk.

Everyone heard the news finally. George had been hoping for a big surprise—an announcement at dinner, wonder and pleasure on each listening face—but things hadn't turned out as he'd planned. First there were the rumors, spread by the unhappy Ned and miserable Henry, then the point-blank questions from the children; then there was Eugenia's puzzling reaction, as if she weren't all that pleased to leave Port Said, and finally Mrs. DuPlessis's: "Well, it's about time, dearie!"

George felt a tide of events swoosh by and knock him off his feet; he didn't feel in charge at all. "It will keep," he told himself, but one thing led to another and the secret didn't keep, and there was no managing anyone's response just as there was no orchestrating a perfect Christmas morning when each present is opened in awed and grateful silence.

Eugenia's hesitation about leaving the hotel had been the most confusing, George decided. Not that his wife had said anything—she'd just seemed unenthusiastic. But when he'd timidly pointed out this tiny fault, she'd mumbled something about shipboard life being constraining and too much like life in Philadelphia! Imagine that! George couldn't fathom how anything as free-roving as the ocean could ever be considered a hindrance to imagination or an adventurous spirit.

So the secret of the repaired propeller was out, and the group prepared for another departure while the captain, cooks, provisions officer, and inboard and outboard crews scurried around to get the ship in apple pie order.

Eugenia was on her way down the hallway that led from her bedroom at the Hotel Belle Ville. It was the last night on shore, and she dreaded the dinner she was walking toward: the mindless toasts, the witticisms that were flat as mud pancakes, and Mrs. DuPlessis's stagey whispers about the "A-rabs and Frenchies" that only a brick wall would have been deaf enough to miss. And Eugenia felt strangely out of step with her children, too; the intense love she was experiencing for James seemed to bathe them in an odd glow, as if she'd become incapable of behaving like an ordinary, pleasant person.

Her children's response was equally puzzling; they obviously recognized the power of their mother's new emotion, but instead of drawing closer, they withdrew, puzzled, silent, uncertain. Eugenia had thought that opening her heart would make her a better mother, that she could wrap her children, herself, and the man she loved in a web of warmth, but she hadn't learned the trick yet. She didn't know how to temper emotions or how to carry them with her from place to place.

Now she walked down the long hall of the Hotel Belle Ville as if she were walking past walls of mirrors. Everything was a reflection and a judgment. With each step she felt more awkward and self-conscious.

"Eugenia, a word please, before we join the others."

Without turning, Eugenia shut her ears to Beckmann's voice, and stiffened her back. It was a confrontation she'd been dreading for a long time. She didn't speak, but she finally looked at the doorway where he stood.

Beckmann's body seemed even more massive in shadow, and the black wool cloth of his dress suit gave off the acrid odor of wet sheep in a panic.

"Yes, Ogden?" Eugenia answered in a noncommittal, almost pleasant, tone. She wasn't about to let a disaster like his visit to her cabin occur again. I'm stronger now, she promised herself; I know what I'm doing. It was the first time she'd put that thought into words. The discovery made her smile.

"You're looking lovely this evening, Eugenia," Beckmann said, but Eugenia could hear the effort each breath cost the man; he seemed to be strangling on unspoken intentions. She listened to the rasp and gurgle as his chest rose and fell and his thoughts bubbled to the surface only to be rejected without voice:

"What I wanted to say . . . that is . . . if I may be permitted—"

"I would rather not endure a scene like your last one, Ogden," Eugenia interrupted. Power made her bold, and boldness built its own success. For a moment Eugenia felt immensely desirable, a female lusted after by many men. She felt as capable of picking and choosing among her lovesick conquests as a lioness stretching in the sun. Everywhere she turned there were growls as one male drove away a rival; Eugenia didn't care. She spread her claws in the sand and leaned her wide, yellow head on her paws; the earth was warm; it smelled of smooth stones and heat.

"What I wanted to say . . . I mean . . . I've seen . . ."

Eugenia felt her heart stop, then creep forward. Beckmann didn't elaborate and Eugenia didn't answer, but she examined every word and nuance for a sign that she and James had been discovered. She listened to Beckmann's gargled breaths, smelled his fear, and watched his shoulders maintain their compulsive line. He doesn't know, Eugenia told herself, he doesn't know.

"I really should be getting downstairs, Ogden," she said. "My husband's waiting for me, and I don't want to spoil his party. If you're not ready, I suggest you hurry." The blow that proves the combatants equal, Eugenia decided. She felt light enough to lift off her feet and fly.

THIRTEEN

*L*ANEER IVARD GLARED
AT THE WATER. Sunghai Sarawak, he recited viciously, what a stupid name for a river. And while I'm at it, what about Kuching or Ivartown itself? Who's ever heard of those places in the real world? The world that counts, the world of Harrow and Surrey and a "small place in the lake district"?

"You know my good friend, the 'rajah muda,' Mother?" Laneer remembered all the soothing little phrases that had echoed through the common room or the tea shops in the public school's town of Harrow-on-the-Hill. "I thought I'd invite him to join us up in Lochcarron."

Or Inverurie or Kirkby Stephen or the summer house in Torquay. Laneer Ivard's schooling in England had been filled with such invitations; he was the only son of the world's only white rajah; he was the good joke that you could beat "the bloody Hottentots" at their own game. That you could, being a son of the Empire, take over the whole of some backwater place *and* crown yourself its supreme head. He was the embodiment of all that Victorian England desired.

"Rajah muda!" the swells at Harrow had shrieked during his first days there. "What the bloody hell is that? You don't look like a darkie."

And Laneer had explained, holding back the dismal truth about his pestilential home in Sarawak, who his great-uncle had been and how it had come about that his father was a rajah and that he lived in a palace in Ivartown in a faraway land called Borneo.

"Rajah muda, the crown prince—like the Prince of Wales!" A wit among the "right" set had jested, and from then on Laneer had had to compete with the excesses of his namesake, Edward, Prince of Wales, denizen of Marlborough House and patron of the very racy Marlborough Club.

But competing with a future king of England (even on an insignificant scale) cost more than Laneer's monthly stipend could support. Finally, either the purse in Borneo had grown thin or his father had gotten wind of his son's escapades, and Laneer had been recalled, sullen and spiteful, to Ivartown, to the bosom of the family, to be the comfort and aid of the aging Sir Charles, rajah of Sarawak. Any pretensions about being English, about being "proper," about "belonging," disappeared in the wake of a Pacific and Orient steamer as Laneer left Southampton and Britain forever.

Sunghai Sarawak. Laneer watched the water swirl below the jetty. It was muddy and thick, like something left too long in a peasant's pot, and Laneer decided he hated the river and the land more than he'd hated anything in his life. He needed to get back to England, he told himself; he needed to return in triumphant nonchalance. And he imagined arriving in heavy-lidded splendor, with stories of uprisings, severed limbs, and blood-splattered walls he was just too weary or too jaded to repeat. He'd be the toast of the town. He'd be the apple of every hungry eye.

Sitting as still as dirt and just as unsettled, the Honorable Nicholas Paine glanced up at his secretary and blinked. "But why didn't he write me himself?" Paine demanded; his eyes felt dry, as grainy as an old camel's. He closed and opened them again; the lids dragged up and down; it was a most uncomfortable feeling.

"He should have written me himself," the Honorable Nicholas insisted as he tested his eyelids and squinted until his vision was reduced to two thin slits. This was quite an experiment, he decided. Snap! went his eyelids; squeak! went his eyes.

"I'm sure Mr. Axthelm didn't want to trouble you with such mundane details, sir." Ridgeway recited the standard answer, calling as little attention as possible to his own communications with the Turk. "I'm sure Mr. Axthelm is aware you have far weightier concerns." Ridgeway considered moving from his spot near the old man's desk, then realized the shift in position might confuse his employer. Paine was capable of imagining a stranger had pushed his way into the room, or that his secretary had sneaked off on a secret mission, that he'd been gone for hours or mere moments, when the reverse was always true.

"However, in response to Mr. Axthelm's desires, I've booked passage for us both on the next steamer to Singapore. From there we can ... " Ridgeway put himself through the motions of an explanation, but his mind was as far from the activity as a spectator at a croquet match.

"But why didn't he let me know himself ... ?" Paine's tone was becoming increasingly querulous. " ... Hmm? ... Ridgeway? ... I've got a letter from him in my hand! Right here in my hand! A recent one, too! Axthelm never mentioned leaving for Borneo immediately. He only asked to be remembered to General Woods. And Woods doesn't even know the man! Doesn't move in those circles at all! Why, when we had luncheon that day, Woods told me he never ... "

But before the Honorable Nicholas could immerse himself in that favorite topic—who knew whom and when and where—Ridgeway interrupted with a cool: "Will you need me to pack your papers or would you like to do them yourself this time?"

" ... It seems Woods ... What? ... What? ... Would I like to what?" In spite of the chair's determined grip, the old man felt he was pinwheeling in circles. He felt like one of those wind-up things his grandchildren had. What did they call those toys? he wondered. What did the children ... ? Tops! ... That was the name. He was spinning like a top.

"Pack your papers yourself." Ridgeway was not about to be chastised; he smiled, but his voice didn't match his demeanor.

"What? ... What? ... Papers, you say?" Paine looked around the room, the office in Manila, his new home, his sanctuary; the Honorable Nicholas touched his desk. That's right, he told himself; I'm in Manila. I'm in my corner apartment overlooking the Pasig River. I have a nice leather-topped desk and I'm here to join Governor Taft's staff ... I think.

Paine glanced about him, unsure momentarily what he was doing in Manila at all. "Papers?" he asked. "Pack up my papers? Whatever for?"

"For the trip to Kuching, sir. To meet with the rajah, Sir Charles Ivard, and the sultan of Sarawak. ... And your son-in-law eventually ... and your daughter, Eugenia." Ridgeway enunciated each name, but none of them seemed to catch the old man's fancy; even Eugenia's slipped by without remark. This is going to be harder than I thought, Ridgeway realized.

"Of course. Of course. Sultan ... Ivard ... know all about them ... Absolutely necessary. Whatever ... " Paine bluffed, then continued with a persistent whine. "But I just got a letter from Axthelm.

One from Carl, too . . . most unusual . . . he said his father was under the weather . . . been ill, don't you know . . . or something . . . and that I shouldn't . . . no, never mind."

The Honorable Nicholas stopped himself and stared at the desk top. "We're leaving right away?" he asked as he studied the inkwell and row of neat and unused pens. He felt horribly confused. His thoughts swirled around like newsprint caught in the wind; just when he thought he had a glimpse of one page, it spun off, unread, unreadable. Whoosh! There went a headline. Whish! An editorial blew past. And there was a photograph. And didn't that look like the society page? "We're sailing right away?"

"Yes, sir," Ridgeway answered as he watched Paine's untidy back slump, straighten itself, and slump again. Ridgeway wondered just how far he could push the old man. "What did the letter from Mr. Carl say, sir? I should send a response before we . . ."

"Never you mind, Mr. Nosy! Never you mind. I can keep a secret as well as the next man!" Paine's voice was filled with spite, and he suddenly hunched over the desk, jutting out his elbows and resting his cheek on the leather top as if hiding a scribbled message from a strict headmaster.

"Of course, sir," Ridgeway replied easily, but he thought: A letter from Carl. And who else? What else does my dear employer know?

"God damn it, Beckmann, can't you understand English? I said we won't be going to Borneo yet!" The air in the study on board the *Alcedo* was rank with steam and smoke. George wanted to get outside and away from Beckmann, but he was the one who'd insisted on the meeting, rehearsed and rehearsed the words till they were letter perfect. What George hadn't counted on was Beckmann questioning his judgment.

"I said we'd be sailing down the coast of Africa. I intend to do a little shooting while I'm here, Ogden. And I don't mean the kind of feeble half-day excursion you and Father had obviously envisioned. So, you might as well get used to the idea.

"Oh, and while you're at it," George added as if this were only an afterthought, "you might as well get used to the idea that this is my ship.

"Not yours. Not Father's. Mine. . . ." George was feeling the results of the brandy he'd used as fuel; he leaned against one of the side tables that bracketed the long chesterfield sofa; the wood felt pleasantly cool under his hand; it renewed his courage. ". . . And I'll do what I wish with her. . . ."

While George continued to rant, Beckmann stared at the room impassively. What's happened here? he wondered. What brought about this change? Beckmann's mind began to flip through the hundreds of pictures it saw every day: the large and small vignettes of daily life. Beckmann saw George strutting out of Jonathan Clive's office in Port Said, he saw Lizzie, Jinx, and Paul run to greet their father; he watched Whitney boasting and the DuPlessises' simpering and Lieutenant Brown appearing late for dinner. Beckmann remembered Brown's surly self-confidence during their stay in Port Said and looked at George again. It couldn't be that Brown and George were in league? That they'd made some sort of pact? But the thought was too absurd. Not Brown with his history. And surely not George with his. Those two could never conspire against the Turk.

Beckmann went back to his file of pictures. The clue was there, he knew; it was something he'd already seen. Eugenia, Beckmann decided suddenly. This has something to do with Eugenia. That's what this swagger is all about.

Beckmann remembered Eugenia in the Hotel Belle Ville. Each time he'd watched her, either hidden or not, she'd lingered too long or else passed too quickly, and there'd been something in the deliberate way she'd moved that had let him know she was there for the taking. And George, for all his oxlike stupidity, had obviously gotten the same message. He was going to lay claim to his wife before anyone else could. Beckmann felt like laughing aloud. Strange, what this climate does to us all, he decided. No wonder people behave like animals out here. I'd do the same myself given half a chance.

But we can't have a piece of skirt ruining our plans, Beckmann told himself, focusing his thoughts again. Eugenia's the treat that comes when the job is done. George will have to be set straight on that account. This is no honeymoon, after all. Recreation comes later, and only to those who deserve it.

"If you're concerned about your wife," Beckmann answered George's unspoken thoughts, "I don't think traipsing off to Africa will . . ."

"Concerned about Genie! Don't make me laugh, Ogden. This has nothing to do with Genie." George was nonplussed by Beckmann's astuteness. Got to be careful here, old boy, he told himself. You're dealing with a fox in a henhouse, remember that. Ogden Beckmann's probably got reasons to be on this little voyage that even Father couldn't guess. But the notion of Beckmann finding Eugenia attractive only elated George further. He felt triumphant; he'd already won that prize.

"Nothing to do with Genie," George blustered again. "And I won't tell you what's made me change my mind!"

George was a child with a wondrous secret; he was bursting to tell it. He crowed with confidence. "But I will tell you we're not going across the Indian Ocean. Not yet, at any rate. We're going to Africa. And we're going on safari to hunt big game. Because, as you will eventually learn, my dear Ogden, every last one of the world's little plots will wait till the time is right. It will keep, Ogden. It will keep."

"But I'd really become quite fond of the place," the Honorable Nicholas complained as Ridgeway led him through the crowds that spilled out on both sides of the long open-sided custom house sheds. "Manila, that is. Don't know why we have to leave in such a deuced hurry. I had that nice dinner all scheduled for next week, and then Harry Fellowes said he'd take me down to . . . down to . . . the place with the pink pearls. . . . What was . . . ?" Paine's voice broke into a teary sniffle as he tried to come up with the name.

"This way, sir. Down here." Ridgeway felt his position was becoming increasingly untenable. I might as well be dressed in a starched white cap and apron, pushing a pram, he told himself. I'm no secretary; I'm a bloody nanny. Ridgeway shouldered aside the other passengers as he moved himself and his human cargo beyond the reflected heat of what seemed like miles and miles of speckled tin roofs. The two men were on the city wharf, but the steamer gangway continued to look as remote as the Russian steppes.

" . . . Cebu, that's the spot Fellowes mentioned! . . . Down to Cebu Island . . . If you wouldn't interrupt me, Ridgeway, we'd get on much better," Paine announced as firmly as possible given the noise, heat, confusion, and constant buffeting he was taking. He put the blame for his forgetfulness entirely on his underling.

"The hell we would," Ridgeway whispered under his breath. The old goat's impossible; he'll ruin everything. Even if the *Alcedo* does get to Kuching in time, there'll still be a week or two for Paine to prance about the sultan's palace, and he'll talk his head off or my name is mud. I'll have to write to Beckmann, the secretary decided; he'll know what to do.

With his hand firmly gripping his charge's arm, Ridgeway hustled Paine closer and closer to the ship. "Right this way, sir," Ridgeway soothed, determined to continue his task in the safest manner possible. "The gangway's just along here. We have two nice staterooms on the starboard side. . . . 'Port out, starboard home,' you must remember that saying, sir, from your earlier visits to the East. . . . And we'll be back in Manila before you know it. . . ."

• • •

". . . So you see, Mr. Beckmann, the situation here has turned increasingly difficult . . ." Laneer Ivard wrote, then stared at the words and the way they waved over the cream-colored page.

> . . . My father cannot hope to understand the workings of the Oriental mind. (For all his years in the East, he remains a man from Leeds, which confidence, my dear Beckmann, I trust you will keep to yourself. Leeds, as you may be aware, is not a city "comme il faut.") And, as such (under-educated and so forth), my father fails to comprehend the Sultan's designs or, as we gentlemen liked to say at University, his "little foibles." . . .

How perfectly worded the message was! How impressed Beckmann would be! Laneer Kinloch Ivard, rajah muda of Sarawak, preened himself as he glanced over the letter. Training could transcend breeding, determination, the bend sinister; Laneer Ivard would yet return to England. And when he did, it would be with his weight in rubies and an ocean of witty and scandalous stories. (Some, of course, hinting at an evil no Westerner could ever comprehend.)

> . . . Please do all you can to hasten your arrival! I will do what I can, in the meantime, to keep the gentlemen in question occupied. And out of harm's and each other's bumbling way!
> I remain, your most humble and obedient, etc. . . .

> *Laneer Kinloch Ivard*

"Sinen," Laneer called softly. The houseboy was immediately at his side, materializing out of the dusky air like a spirit in a lamp. "Sinen." Laneer took the boy's hand and grazed it with the letter as if it were a feather or a piece of magician's silk.

"This must go to Labuan," he whispered in Malay as he continued to stroke the boy's soft hand and softer arm, "and then very far away. Over a big ocean to a place you have never seen. But don't worry, Sinen, when I leave here I will take you with me. You will always be with me."

But Sinen, though he understood the Malay words, had not the foggiest idea what his master was saying. He looked at the letter floating up and down his arm and heard only Labuan. It was the farthest place he could imagine. Maybe it was like heaven, as the rajah muda said. Or maybe like hell.

"We're going to stay in Africa, then. For a while."

"We are." Eugenia lay back in her deck chair while Lieutenant

Brown stood beside her. It was as close as they dared come and all they dared say, but the meaning behind the words was as full as an afternoon at the Hotel Belle Ville. The Red Sea had been outdistanced, with its dangerous middle passage: Jiddah, Mecca, and Suakin, the port for Sudan. Soon the *Alcedo* would pass beyond the Gulf of Aden as well. She'd reach the Indian Ocean, and be free of every constraining native craft that scuttled to catch up, crisscrossing the waterways as if the white ship were a magnet and every metal thing that floated on the surface of the waves must leap to her side.

"I'm not sure how long we'll be there. George wants to do some shooting. . . . I don't even know if we'll all be going on safari, or if . . ." Eugenia yearned to take Brown's hand and whisper: "Or if you and I can be alone together."

She shifted suddenly in her chair and let herself look up into his eyes. I've become reckless, she told herself. Anyone could see what I'm thinking. But at the same moment she realized she didn't care who saw her or what they thought. She felt giddy enough to laugh out loud. The rattan of her chaise creaked with a breathy rush as if it had become her voice.

"Shooting," Brown repeated slowly.

The remark was confused with memories of their stolen hours together and the nagging voice that kept pestering him about the job ahead. In Port Said, away from the ship, it had been relatively easy to forget the rifles in the hold and forget that the woman beside him was Axthelm's wife. The afternoons were all that counted, and Brown wished they could return to those peaceful times. Maybe in Africa, Brown tried to convince himself. Or maybe we're only postponing disaster.

Eugenia didn't hear any of the hesitation in Brown's voice. She heard what she wanted: an echo of her own thoughts. "We'll stay a week or two, I should imagine. Maybe longer. It will depend on the game, I suppose. . . ." Eugenia stopped her explanation and added a quiet: "Will you be going out with them, Lieutenant? On safari, I mean?"

"I don't know. I don't much trust guns, Eugenia . . . Mrs. Axthelm. . . . As you remember." The lie again. Brown hated himself instantly, but when he looked at Eugenia's ready smile, he made a decision. And the lie was no longer a lie, he realized; it was part of a necessary role, part of what she believed him to be. Eugenia doesn't know, Brown told himself. And I must never let her guess.

"I suppose the children and I will be spending most of our time in camp, Lieutenant. Near Nairobi or someplace like that." Eugenia spoke quickly and quietly, then leaned her cheek into the canvas cushion and watched Brown's face. How good the pillow feels, she thought, how warm and filled with sunlight.

Eugenia looked down the sleeping deck at the other chairs and pillows, each arranged invitingly, as if dropped from the sky by a loving hand. Except for a sailor scraping varnish before reapplying a fresh coat to the wooden rail, she and James were the only souls on deck. The heat blowing over the Arabian desert had driven everyone else below.

Why should I care what happens next, Eugenia thought, what I'll have to say and do when we return to Philadelphia. What censure I'll meet. The present is all that matters.

Brown looked at Eugenia and saw a similar picture: the two of them on a empty hillside and all the time in the world on their hands. He forced himself to forget Beckmann and the job, Newport and all the other back-room, back-alley deals. This time was all that mattered.

Africa then. The voyage past the city of Aden and down the coast when the days blew by like the wind, when the water hugging the shore was any water and the land, when it appeared, any land. None of the passengers pulled out the atlas; no one mentioned interesting pieces of history; no one leaned against the rail and shouted: "That must be Ras Mabber!"; or "Iddan!"; or "Ataleh!"; or "Port Durnford!" No one cared.

The simple and circular pleasures of shipboard life were resumed. There were games on deck, games in the main saloon, books to be read, letters written; there were conversations around the dining table and interrupted stories told in the lolling shade of striped awnings. There were teatimes and evenings by the fire; there were lazy breakfasts and sleepy "good nights"; there were dreams remembered and dreams forgotten. But none of it mattered. Mombasa was the word on every tongue. When would the ship reach Mombasa?

FOURTEEN

*T*HE THIRD OF OCTOBER. British East Africa and Kilindini Harbor at the end of Mombasa Island. The deep-water port that served Nairobi, the highland farmlands, and the rest of the colony's broad and empty interior. The wharf was packed with porters shifting baskets of bursting and overripe fruit, bearers bundling rolls of raggedy-tailed cloth, old women hawking chickens whose screams echoed over the flap and flurry of their own scrawny wings. There were boxes of this, boxes of that, salt-stained, sea-spoiled cargo from halfway around the world, from places no one could even remember. A customs official stood in the midst of the melee, yelling and waving tight-sleeved arms as two men shifted in front of him, shrugging and stammering as their eyes darted out looks of encouragement and embarrassment at the growing crowd. Good. Good, the crowd nodded back. Maybe some excitement this time. Maybe handcuffs and the stick. But the official's complaints were too ponderous or too difficult to follow, so the crowd surged on, a streaming hot mass, black mostly, dark as oil oozing from muddy ground, but here and there a turban and yellow face, and everywhere and on everyone some patch of brilliant color—cobalt, cerise, heliotrope, purple, gold and as shiny as cream.

Little boys darted through the crowd, a hand in this, an arm under that, while their older brothers danced backward, wheedling, persuading, talking fast, unwilling to let go: They could do anything! Porter? Sure! See the city? Sure! Just give them a chance. Cook? The best! The best! And when finally turned down, when impatiently waved aside, they ran on to the next prospective employer and the next and the next.

Lizzie, Jinx, and Paul watched the maelstrom from the deck of the yacht. They dashed from side to side, from one rail to another, peering down at the pier and then out to the irresistible hubbub beyond. Was that a fort on the hill above town? Were those tumbling stones near the water's edge part of a Turkish ruin or a Portuguese plantation from hundreds and hundreds and hundreds of years ago? And what about all the jungly parts of the island itself? What secrets did they hide? Or those funny, narrow streets that looked no bigger than ant trails disappearing in the grass? The children raced back and forth, from the port rail to the starboard, from the bow to the stern, full of questions, wonder, and longing. "Africa," they repeated, forgetting age, appearance, and the decision to present themselves in a chosen light. They were finally in Africa!

George was in the midst of organizing equipment for the journey inland. The big game safari was his major concern at the moment, and to stock it he'd ordered his three Winchester repeating muskets, nine repeating rifles, four repeating carbines, two Mannlicher-Schoenauer sporting rifles, four W. and C. Scott hammerless shotguns, two Holland and Holland .450 Nitro Expresses, and three Woodward "over-and-unders" laid out for close inspection on the sunny teakwood floor of the foredeck.

Satisfied that his sporting weapons were in perfect working order, George nodded his approval to Higgins, who in turn gave a brisk nod to Henry, who yanked himself back to reality and stopped watching Lizzie pelt across the open deck. Under Higgins's eagle eye, Henry carefully rewrapped each weapon. First came the fitted felt bags, then parchment wraps and oilskin sheets designed to keep out dampness and dust, but before each was returned to the individual case that would carry it the several hundred miles up to the open plains, George took up one of the Mannlicher-Schoenauers. He weighed it with both hands, testing its heft and balance, the butt end, the barrel, the beautiful, burnished curve.

"Good," George announced. "We'll take them all."

Jinx, Lizzie, and Paul flew around the ship. Everything was new. Everything was wonderful. There were men from the King's African Rifles come to escort them to the train. There was a tall man named Mr. Oliver Smythe-Barrows who Father said knew everything there was to know about hunting wild animals on the veldt. He had long mustaches and wore shiny boots polished with stag's horn, and he promised Paul he'd see a rhino. There were black porters jostling their way through the crowd and hoisting everything in sight onto enormous shoulders and wide backs, and there was the sound of a hundred or a thousand or maybe a million voices beckoning them on, off the boat and up into the distant country beyond. The words were strange and exciting: foreign, sharp, and pungent as aniseed or sassafras leaf.

"... The Victoria-Nyanza Spur ... the final leg of the rail can carry its travelers in something approximating modern-day comfort ..." Lizzie and Paul and Jinx heard in the main saloon. "... Oh, yes! The railway goes nearly to the Falls itself ... Quite a marvel of technological ..."

"... Uganda Rail ... just completed this past March. The view of the Great Rift Valley ..." This was overheard outside the deckhouse, while at the stern was the low-voiced and quickly hushed warning:

"... Spot of bother with the Nandi tribe, but I wouldn't worry if I was you .... Them naked savages is always up to some sort of ... But remember what happened the last time ... them Mau Mau ...? We made short work of them. ..."

The names raced over the children's heads as they tore along, taking it all in. Lions and treks and British East Africa. The Kikuyu Escarpment, the Mau Escarpment. The "Lunatic Line" and old Tippu Tip. They were going on a train that would take them to all those places! They would cross a bridge half a mile long! They would climb and climb and climb and climb; they'd leave Kilindini and the ocean behind forever. There'd be jungle and grass, scorpions in their boots and cheetahs lolling in the trees. There'd be puff adders under their beds and green mamba snakes lying in wait on every path. What could be more dangerous? What could be more exciting?

The "Somali in Jubaland," the "Masai," the "Nandi" ("Nandi" was repeated again and again). Lizzie and Paul and Jinx practiced the names as if memorizing a magician's spell while they brushed past Whit, ran into Higgins, nearly bowled over Mrs. DuPlessis, and bumped full force into the doctor.

"I'm sorry. ... We're sorry. ... Sorry. ... Excuse us!" they sang out, racing through the ship, while around their heads flew a new secret language: Somali, the King's Rifles, Kavirondo, Wakamba, Wankikuyu. Africa.

"D'yes, Buus," the head porter answered as he stared stoically at the weathered planks of the wharf. The rest of the porters waited in a knot behind him.

"Scotsman teach you English, porter?" George tried the jest again. His solar topee felt unbelievably hot; sweat trickled behind his ears and dripped into his collar. He wished he could remove the wretched hat, but that didn't appear to be the white man's dress code. Only the natives left their heads unprotected.

"Scartsmaan?" The porter made an attempt at George's accent.

"Teach you English? You know, Scotsman? . . . Scotland? Scotch?" George was getting nowhere. His foray into native humor had fallen flat; he glanced up at the yacht behind him and frowned. He'd wanted to handle this little shoreline task himself. Show Smythe-Barrows and those blokes from the King's Rifles that he knew a thing or two himself.

"We take bags railway, porter. Ourselves," George continued doggedly, determined to get the job done.

No answer. The porter glanced back at his minions and their all-appraising grins.

"In carriage. With us. Not now." George pointed at his feet and raised his voice in order to be better understood. "With us. When we go, baggage goes."

"D'yes, Buus." The head porter glared at his smirking assistants. They'd live to regret this insolence, he promised himself. It was the headman's job to understand the white man's strange demands, not theirs. The porter indicated a heavy trunk lying near the gangway stairs and shouted in Swahili, "Railway!"

"No! No, porter!" George guessed the destination. "We take bags railway. Same carriage. With us. . . . Not now. . . . We're not ready to leave yet . . ." George added limply, knowing there was no translation for that civilized and fickle emotion.

Beckmann decided to send a telegraph from Zanzibar, the German protectorate that was the next civilized town along the coast. Zanzibar had direct communication with the rest of the world, if he could get a cable down there from Mombasa. That "if" was the problem. A cable from Mombasa south to Zanzibar. One hundred and fifty miles could be more difficult to traverse than several thousand. Mombasa was British; Zanzibar belonged to the kaiser. In dividing Africa, the European nations had created islands of nationalism that were as zealously guarded as fortresses under siege.

But the Turk had to be told, Beckmann realized. He had to hear about this new delay. An extended safari in Nairobi. Several weeks, maybe a month, in the interior, a vacation hunting useless beasts on the open veldt. Jesus. What would George come up with next? Beckmann walked the length of his darkened cabin, and decided it was safer to circumnavigate the ship's radio officer and go into town himself to send the cable. There'd be a British residency, he knew. A lieutenant governor or an aide. Or a German consulate.

Better the German, Beckmann decided as he pushed past an absurdly delicate fruit wood armchair and a spindly desk with a stag and doe inlaid in rosewood and tulip poplar. A German will recognize the importance of the Axthelm name, Beckmann told himself. After all, these men out here are ambitious. If they're any good.

Of course, there was the danger of George's finding out. That was Beckmann's deepest concern: the offhand remark, the sociable banter as local dignitaries came to "pay their respects." "So glad we could be of help ... when Mr. ... ah ... Beckmann, is it? When Mr. Beckmann came in with his request. ... Naturally we did all we could. ... It's not easy getting a cable through to our neighbor on the south, you know. ... British East Africa and German East Africa aren't always ..." Then there'd be another of George's trumped-up scenes when he'd succeed in humiliating only himself.

Beckmann paced back and forth, crisscrossing the carpet as if he were a tiger in a box. He walked on the rims of his feet, letting his weight sink evenly as if he were flattening leaves and broken branches; each footstep carried its own concern; each one spread a separate desire.

Beckmann wished he could be done with George. The "youngest son" was nothing but a stone around his neck, a dead albatross on a fraying rope. Name and family connection notwithstanding. Beckmann strode to his porthole and looked at the confused hysterics of the crowd below. At least there's still slavery in some parts of this continent, he reminded himself. They know what's what in Zanzibar. At least down there people understand their purpose on this planet.

God damn George Axthelm, Beckmann thought suddenly. God damn him to eternal hell. Beckmann glared at the porthole and then pictured Eugenia. She was drifting along a shadowy hall, draped in something white and diaphanous, and she turned once to grace him with a perfect, languid smile. Damn them all, Beckmann repeated. Damn every living one of them.

"... Freretown?" George repeated hopefully, trying to stall for time until the lieutenant governor's men arrived to escort the Axthelms and their belongings through the crowds. Freretown was the name of the village opposite Mombasa where the freed slaves lived. Oliver Smythe-Barrows had pointed it out earlier, when he'd described the black men's hero, the Englishman Sir Bartle Frere, and his magnanimous exploits. George was determined to prove himself a man of equal stature.

"From Freretown?" he asked again. "You live Sir Bartle village?" George made the words simplistic, and invented an all-purpose accent that sounded like a mixture of minstrel show and nasally African pidgin.

But the head porter and his cohorts just stood there, looking for all the world, George decided, like a bunch of woolly sheep. Their faces had the same fatuous expressions and they glanced at each other as idiotically.

"Jesus," George swore under his breath. "From . . . Living in . . . ?" The sheep just stared. "Frere . . . Sir Bartle . . . .?"

A smile began to creep over the chief sheep's face. The dawn of civilization, George realized, and repeated very slowly and very loudly, "Sir Bartle Frere." He accented the letter *r* for reasons only he understood.

"*Kisaoni!*" the sheep shouted back as they pointed eagerly toward land.

"*Kisaoni!*" the rest of the flock bleated, and they dropped the trunks and hatboxes and baskets of linen and began to chant wildly, "*Kisaoni! Kisaoni!* Freretown, same *Kisaoni.*"

While at that moment Oliver Smythe-Barrows, accompanied by a member of the King's African Rifles, strode through the group. "Doesn't do much good to get these Johnnies stirred up, old man," he said quietly, and nodded a curt order to the guard. "I know you Americans enjoy your little rebellions, but out here we tend to frown on—"

"Just a meeting of the minds, old chap." George cut short the criticism. "My small contribution to cultural exchange."

"*Kisaoni.*" George returned to the head porter, playing with the syllables, as if they were a strange but pleasant taste on his tongue. "*Kisaoni.*"

The family's departure from the *Alcedo* was as tumultuous as the ship's earlier arrival had been. The crowd filling the wharf sighed and shouted every time a member of the Axthelm party or one of the red-and-white-uniformed officers appeared on deck; soon a noise flowed through the expectant mob that was as steady as the howl of a hurricane.

There was Mrs. DuPlessis in a pale lavender frock with a matching lace-encrusted parasol. The crowd sighed, then shrieked, then sighed again and created a communal shiver that resembled a jelly mold being shaken.

Then Whitney marched toward the rail, dressed to the nines in full hunting regalia: his solar topee freshly chalked and a "Sam Browne" belt strung across his chest. He was greeted by shouts of encouragement—and a few that sounded alarmingly close to derision.

Then George and Captain Cosby appeared, chatting as they strolled the length of the deck. Howl. Yelp. Yelp. Yelp. The clamor was stupendous. Hands clapped; dress cloth flapped; tin containers clanged together.

While the children, peering one at a time over the pearly rail, jumped back from the moans that threatened to rip open the entire wharf. They ducked down and hid and waited for the noise to subside before showing their faces again. It was as frighteningly compelling as a game of ghosts played in a pitch-dark room.

More calf-hide trunks appeared, more baskets, more wicker hampers, collapsible tables, walking sticks, shooting sticks, a campaign desk with glowing brass pulls, shoe boxes, hatboxes, a medical chest fitted out with what looked like a thousand tiny drawers. As each object made its bow, the crowd stamped its collective feet and clapped joyous hands high in the air. This was better than King "Ed-ward's" birthday, better than old Queen Vicky's death march, better than a hanging.

"We'd best get you off to the station as soon as possible, sir," the lieutenant governor's aide said to George, "before we have a full-scale riot on our hands. These blighters are simple souls. They'd trample you as soon as their own."

So carriages were brought round, the horses dancing and nervous in the swirling dust, and the boxes, desks, traveling trunks, and camp beds were settled and sent roaring away to the station. But the crowd was not to be tricked; it stood its ground and waited for the Bwana Khubwas, the white masters, and their perfect white babies to set foot on the pier.

From the draped shelter of an awning, Eugenia looked down at the whole enormous spectacle. *Yes*, her eyes said, *I am home. I have found my place at last.* She watched His Majesty's finest struggle to contain the crowd; she saw the way their jaws jutted as their hands checked and rechecked fixed bayonets, and she studied the crowd spilling happily around them and thought: They have as little concern as a cloud of newborn chicks. It was a giddy discovery and it made her feel weightless, as though she'd suddenly left the ground.

Here and there she saw a cast-off uniform, an old serge coat, a peaked hat, a braided cap. These objects were too tight, too loose, too stoop-shouldered, too faded, but none of it mattered. Their owners could not be humbled by impermanent things. They surged toward the soldiers and then backed away; they could have been swimming in a lake or dancing in the dark, Eugenia realized. They wanted a closer look at the Bwana Khubwas; that was all that counted.

Eugenia knew that Brown was beside her. She felt him close but couldn't take her eyes off the crowd; it was as if she and this swirling mob had become one, as if they were all part of some wonderful spiraling ascent toward heaven. She watched more carriages race down the wharf, bellowing out wind and dirt and driving the crowd to a frenzy. She watched Mrs. DuPlessis rush bullheadedly down the gangway to thunderous applause and she watched that lady's good husband hurrying behind. She saw Whitney and Smythe-Barrows and her own three children and Prue scurry into a four-in-hand and she saw it stream away in a hail of pebbles and gritty dirt and shouts so joyous they had no translation.

"We must be next," Eugenia whispered, but the words sounded as if they'd been ordered by someone else. Eugenia spoke the way a foreigner might, because she'd been told the phrase was correct for the situation.

"I'm glad we're going," she added.

Brown didn't answer. He scarcely heard; his thoughts were on Beckmann, where he'd gone and why. He's up to no good, Brown told himself. Beckmann has a secret of his own. He's gone up into Mombasa town while I'm sent off inland. There's something Beckmann knows. There's something he's holding back.

FIFTEEN

HE AXTHELMS' PRIVATE RAILWAY CARRIAGE was waiting patiently in Mombasa station, but the competition between the local porters and those who'd followed the family and their luggage from the pier was anything but patient and anything but gentle. Under waves of heat billowing from the building's new tin roof, Wakamba tribesmen fought Wankikuyu, and Swahili fought them all. It was a tribal war waged over steamer trunks and twine-wrapped boxes. If the baggage could have been divided as simply as a bloodied gazelle, victory would have been clear: One tribe would profit; one would be covered in shame. Grunts and snarls echoed through the station as each citified warrior tried to wrest a prize from another. The object of stowing the luggage safely on board was nearly forgotten.

"Let's do away with the lot of them," a red-faced sergeant major in His Majesty, King Edward's, Rifles muttered to a cohort.

"It's these Americans. The sooner we pack them off, the better." His companion scratched the sweat from his neck.

"Never seen anything like it," Red Face spit disgustedly. "The kaffirs must think these foreigners are the second bloody coming."

"God, I miss Delhi," the neck-scratching corporal sighed.

"Not me. It's Brighton for me. A chair on the bloomin' esplanade and milk-toast at a quarter till," Red Face swore.

"You won't like it."

"You bloody wait."

Paul crept up on the soldiers as quiet as a mouse. He'd dodged out of sight of his mother, sisters, Prue, and even hawk-eyed old Mrs. D. to wander the length of the shiny, new train. The Uganda Rail had two steam engines that were bright as pennies, and a special car, painted dark green and yellow, that had tables and pillowy chairs and long settees and windows as big as a house's just to make his family comfy!

"Will we be leaving soon?" Paul swaggered into the open, trying to sound as grown-up as his father.

"Where the bloody H. did you come from?" Red Face's eyes popped out.

"I was just . . ." Paul began.

"Well, you'd better 'just' get along back, then, laddie." The sergeant major bent down to Paul.

He looked very grand to the little boy, like one of the lead soldiers his Grandfather Axthelm had given him before they left Philadelphia. He had gold on his blue jacket and a crimson stripe on his trousers.

"I have a soldier just like you," Paul said magnanimously.

"Do you now?" Red Face winked at his companion.

"Only his face is painted white."

Red Face scowled.

"And his hat's different," Paul continued on, unaware of his gaffe. "But he's got the same purplish stripes as you. Only smaller, of course, because he is smaller. He looks frightfully smart."

Frightfully was Paul's new word. He'd heard it over and over this morning while he and his sisters darted through the ship. The soldiers on Father's yacht had said it, and the lieutenant governor's men, and even Mr. Oliver Smythe-Barrows.

" 'Frightfully', eh?" the red-faced soldier asked.

"Oh, yes, sir." Paul smiled, sure now that he was recognized as a man of the world and not a baby to be left with his mother.

"Well, Mr. 'Frightfully,' I think you'd be 'frightfully smart' if you'd get along back to your mum," Red Face growled.

"Better take him, Chapman," the neck scratcher complained. "I'll watch over this lot here."

"Just make sure you're here when I get back, Daniels. I don't want to hear you've shipped for bloody Brighton."

"Fat chance of that!" Daniels was indignant. "You're the bloke wants a bleedin' bath chair in bleedin' Brighton! It's Delhi for me, and don't you forget it."

Paul and his sullen escort walked along the platform, dodging crates and boxes and people everywhere. There was shouting all around and, what seemed to Paul, mindless running about, as if something were on fire and no one knew where the water buckets were hidden. Steam from the two engines gushed in sudden spurts of foam and the porters got lost in them, like people lost in the snow, but Paul found the sight and especially the smell of the big engines comforting. It was like the smell of the laundry room at home and Paul suddenly realized he missed that large, homey place. He decided to walk closer to his guard.

Sergeant Major Chapman wasn't used to children. Oh, he'd wanted a family once, but most English women didn't fare well in the places he'd been stationed, so he'd put off the wedding bells once, then a second time, and now, as he liked to boast, who would have him? But the grizzled veteran sensed the child's fear in spite of his efforts at soldierly disapproval. "Better take your hand here. There's a good lad," he said gruffly, then clasped Paul's fingers and scowled, as if daring any observer to find him less than professional.

Paul and Chapman walked through a cloud of steam. "It's like a blizzard," Paul said, holding fast to the big hand and at the same time pretending that such caution was beneath him. "We had a blizzard last winter. I think it was last winter. I heard Father talking about it. The streets were all snowbanked. . . . I think that's what Father said. . . . In Philadelphia," Paul added to give credence to his story. "That's where we're from, you know."

"Are you now?" Chapman pretended to listen as he steered his small charge through the raucous melee. His face looked very stern, but Paul was too small to notice.

"Oh, yes. Our whole family," the little boy continued proudly. "But you know, when it snowed, me and my sisters . . . Should I say 'I' or 'me'? . . ."

When Chapman didn't answer, Paul continued, ". . . Anyway, me and my sisters went out sledding right in the middle of Chestnut Street. Right where the carriages usually go! And you couldn't see where the street ended and the gardens began!"

"Couldn't you now?" Chapman turned abruptly to avoid a mass of beggars huddled near the train's kitchen car. But he was too late; the young prince had been spotted. Men without noses, men without hands, indiscernible forms dragging bodies without legs or arms, tumbled toward them. Chapman picked Paul up in his thick arms and strode resolutely away.

"Do you . . . do you like snow, sir?" Paul said as he looked over the sergeant major's shoulder to watch the bodies disappear in a cloud of white-gray smoke. The raggedy figures howled and whined and rattled empty pots that sounded to Paul like the chains around a ghost's hollow leg. He stared and stared while the ghosts became fainter, then quieter. Better to talk about the snow, Paul decided. "Do you, sir?" he repeated. "Like snow, I mean?"

"Well, I can't say, laddie," Chapman answered roughly. "I haven't seen it in a long time." The sergeant major wanted to put the little boy down but decided not to risk it. Not with that bloody lot mewling about. He didn't know how much Paul had seen, but he knew even a glimpse was too much. Africa was no place for a white child.

"But in England?" Paul persisted.

"I haven't been in England for a long time."

"But it's your home!" Paul was horrified. Imagine not going home! The idea was too awful to consider.

"This is my home," Chapman said. His voice was quiet, and Paul wasn't sure he'd heard correctly.

"This?" the little boy asked as he looked at the bubbling confusion of the station—the noise, the heat, the violent and choking smells—and at the beggars who trailed through the steam like demons in a dream. He expected a giant to walk in at any second. A giant with a seventy-foot club who would bash open the tinny roof and shout, "Fee-fie-fo-fum. I smell the blood of an English-MUN."

"Not the station, laddie," Chapman chuckled, mistaking Paul's dismay. "I didn't mean I live in the station. I mean Africa. Africa's my home now."

"It is?" Paul said, and suddenly the whole of the continent seemed as terrifying as the train station. Even more, because it was a bigger and more monstrous giant. Its gnarled back was blistered with mountains, its hands dangled lifelessly under the sea, and where its nose or eyes should have been there were deep and icy lakes.

"Well, you might at least tell them to shut down the damn steam!" Eugenia snapped, using words she never would have allowed in front of her children. "No one can see more than two feet in this mess!"

Eugenia tried to control the edge in her voice, tried to tell herself that panic would never find her son, that cool heads must prevail, that Paul would come to no harm; but a mother's fear is irrational, and Eugenia saw demons nearly as large as her child had, and she had no large and grown-up hand to cling to.

"I do fail to understand, Eugenia, how the three of you could have lost him." George, in his own fear and anger, had reverted to the tool he knew best: condescending sarcasm.

"So you keep repeating!" Eugenia shouted back. "As if that could help us find Paul! Next I suppose you'll say this experience will help 'toughen him up.' Like that wonderful little 'experience' when you taught him how to shoot a rifle." Eugenia ran full tilt at her opponent; she didn't care who saw her or what anyone thought. "That was certainly a worthwhile endeavor."

The rest of the group of Dr. and Mrs. DuPlessis, Lizzie, Jinx, Whitney, Brown, and Smythe-Barrows dashed in and out of the carriage, called along the platform, and gave orders to anyone who'd help find the little boy. They were too busy to stop. Eugenia and George's fight went unnoticed.

"If you didn't mollycoddle him all the time, he wouldn't have decided to wander off. He'd know that you don't just . . ."

"Jesus God, George!" Eugenia exploded. "Do you hear what you're saying?"

"Excuse me, sir . . . ma'am." Sergeant Major Chapman coughed and stepped into the carriage holding Paul. He tried to doff his cap, but his arms were full, and he was left staring at husband and wife as if he'd blundered into the wrong room and found two people naked in bed.

"Paul!" both Eugenia and George cried in unison, and Eugenia ran toward her son.

"The little fellow was just"—Chapman felt Paul's arms tighten around his neck—"just having a bit of a jaw with Corporal Daniels and me. He's been in good company," he added, setting the child down as if he were a crystal figurine found in an empty shed. "So . . . here he is. Right as rain! Eh, laddie?"

"Yes, sir," Paul answered. He was mortified by the sergeant major's attentions, and he hated to have anyone see his mother and father argue, and he also hated Father to see him carried like a tiny baby.

"Paul!" shrieked Mrs. DuPlessis, trumpeting her way into the carriage. "I just heard you'd been rescued from the heathens . . . ."

"Paul, lad!" blustered the returning Whit and Dr. DuPlessis in noisy unison while Lizzie ran up the carriage steps and burst into loud, long sobs.

Worse and worse, Paul thought, and he fidgeted in his high-buttoned shoes, while his father did an unforgivable thing: He pulled a billfold from his jacket.

"Let me thank you, Sergeant. . . ."

"Chapman, sir . . . Sergeant Major." Chapman's eyes bulged as he watched the bills George lifted from the wallet. "But I couldn't . . . it's all in a day's work. . . . I couldn't accept. . . . His Majesty's own, sir . . ." The sergeant major pulled up a knife-tight salute and turned on his stamping heel.

• • •

Back in the safety of Daniels' comfortable presence, Sergeant Major Chapman stared at the porters, who'd finally begun to settle about the station like sleepy flies who've exhausted all possible food sources. This is no place for a white family, Chapman thought as he glared at the floor. No place for high-strung thoroughbreds like that woman especially. Why, that Mrs. Axthelm, she's no better than a brood mare. All excitable prancing about and no substance whatsoever. And her husband! Wouldn't like to rely on him in a lion hunt, Chapman told himself. Those people should have stayed home where they belong. This continent's no bloody afternoon picnic. They should leave it to people who know what they're about. They should leave it to people with common sense and good working-class brains.

The sergeant major stirred up the dust with his boot and watched it swirl, then drift across the station floor. That's what you get for marrying, Chapman reminded himself, you end up with some piece of fluff who knows more about bonnets than babies. And you can't trust them either. Not a one. They'll bat their eyelashes at any subaltern in a new dress jacket, and before you know it you're home on leave and the cupboards are bare.

Chapman scuffed the dust again and the dirt rose higher, coating his trouser legs up to the knee. Ordinarily Sergeant Major Chapman would have considered such dereliction a sin, now he let it go, almost enjoying the grime and the heat and the dank air, which stank of unwashed bodies and garbagy food. Good thing I never married, he repeated to himself. Marriage isn't for serious men; it's for the weak, for the spongy, for stay-at-home schoolboys with soap on their noses. The words were very nearly convincing.

Corporal Daniels shifted his weight from one foot to the other and considered knocking the dirt from his cuffs, then realized his sergeant major would probably stir it up all over again. Daniels decided discretion was the better part of valor. "Get the chappie back in one piece?" he asked for the sake of conversation.

Chapman only grunted, then added out of the blue and so ferociously Daniels had to turn sideways to be sure he'd heard right: "He's got a tough row to hoe, that wee lad. A tough row, all the long way."

When the train finally left the station in a hiccup and hiss and swoosh of steam, Paul had become a celebrity. The train stewards and the cooks winked at him with hearty smiles while his sisters smiled their devoted awe. Paul had been awarded the best seat by the best window, and if that wasn't good enough, Jinx had promised to change with him or Lizzie. Anything their brother wanted! Any little thing at all.

The train jostled and wheezed past the huddling knots of porters, past the posts and platforms and train sheds, and leapt onto the bridge that separated Mombasa Island from the mainland. It rolled slowly at first, then gathered speed as the coal fed the engines, and the engines persuaded the wooden boxcars and passenger cars to come along for the ride. Colors began to fly past the Axthelm carriage: the ocean's blue at first, changing shape and shade with each rattle of the wheels, bright blue like a sapphire, then paler, palest, till it was almost white; then the white of shallow water turned to yellow, to tan, then brown, the murky chocolate color of mud and silt slime.

The train bustled on. The harbor was deserted, the fishermen's huts and the shoreline warehouses were left behind. The mud became dusty dirt, then rutted roads. Bullock carts waddled along weaving paths; native huts were replaced by an imitation of European houses, gingerbread on the roofs, a coach and driver out front. There was something made of orange brick! Something made of stone! The train hurtled by them all. Faces turned to watch, but they were quickly left behind; there was the blur of a smile, the flash of a jaunty cap, the sheen of copper buttons in a tall shop window, and then nothing as the train sped ever faster. *Good-bye! Good-bye! Good-bye!* sang the rails and the racing wheels. *We're going to places you'll never know. We'll see sights you'd never imagine. Not in a million, zillion years!*

Then the fancy houses and tree-lined streets of Mombasa town disappeared in a final burst of one long, luxuriant, and recklessly British garden. "Cultivated," Mrs. DuPlessis exclaimed, though as she turned to speak, the garden was already past. "Did you see? . . . Rose of Sharon and English ivy!"

And suddenly there was grass. Grass everywhere, spiking along the walls of huts, running in determined lines down the crooked cart tracks, blooming and blossoming into every deserted place. It was green; it was yellow; it was red, silver, blue. It was tall or flat, thick, thin, clumped like a bush or mounded in a high and lavish bed. Then the grass and final huts of Freretown (*"Kisaoni! Kisaoni!"*) whipped out of sudden sight and the Uganda Rail began to climb in earnest.

It jounced from side to side, rattling teacups, upsetting the sugar dish, brushing the trees, and snagging branches and leaves as the children flew from seat to seat.

"Look! What's that?"

"Where?"

"By the big tree. Oh, now it's gone! It might have been a panther, though."

"I caught a leaf in my window!"

"It looks like silver!"

"It's olive, dopey. It's an olive leaf."

Soon the train was in a forest of olive and juniper, flying along through a gray and shining tunnel: the color like tarnished silver, like mercury, like steel.

". . . another cup of *chai,* Jane? As they say in the bush . . ."

"Thank you, Gustav, but I believe I'll wait until dinner. You might ask, however, if there is just the tiniest of those lovely cucumber and tomato sandwiches remaining. I'd . . . ."

". . . Coming out on safari with us, Lieutenant?" Whitney bellied up to the train window as if it were a barroom rail.

"I don't know, Whitney. Mr. Axthelm hasn't—"

"But you two young bucks certainly will. . . ." George's laugh bounded through the car. ". . . The more the merrier, I always say. Isn't that right, Dr. D.?"

"Couldn't put it better. There's a little proverb we use in Belgium . . ."

"And, of course, Oliver will be along to guide us all. Won't you, Ollie, old man? . . ."

"Whatever you say, Mr. Axthelm. You're the boss, as you Americans say. . . ." Smythe-Barrows was quick to join in the spirit of the afternoon.

"It's George to you, old man! We'll have no British formality out in the bush. . . ."

George walked the length of the carriage, receiving accolades and grateful smiles and bandying quips like a general sent to encourage his troops. Mombasa station was behind them, and the disruptive complication of transferring from one safe haven to another accomplished with only minor discomfort, at least that's how George would have put it. He strode through his new dominion, soothed by the European paneling on the walls and ceilings, cosseted by the reassuring smell of plush-covered armchairs, mahogany tables, and a decent carpet on a polished wood floor. A touch of Chestnut Street in a distant realm.

"After all," he said, "all's well that end's well. . . ." The matter of Paul's disappearance and rescue was reduced to cliché. George was back where he belonged.

"You're right there, George. Absolutely . . ."

". . . A miss is as good as a mile, I always say . . ."

"Ha-ha. . . ."

"Ha-ha. . . ."

"Quite an adventure for a small laddie. . . ." The dominant male voices washed through the carriage like the smell of brandy and cigars swilling through an opera box.

Eugenia turned her face to the window. All's well? she thought. All's well? Tears started to her eyes and she moved her head so no one could see her cry. The sounds of pleasure and self-congratulation swelled around her and Eugenia looked at the window and felt her tears roll like rain, like a flood down a drainpipe, like a spiraling pool.

". . . Mackinnon Road's the first town we'll pass, and yes, it is the correct name . . ." George shouted to his guests. ". . . Its namesake is old Mackinnon who chartered the Imperial British East Africa Company . . . shipping magnate, I heard . . . had a yacht he christened *Cornelia* . . . liked to entertain the royals . . . Then after Mackinnon Road comes Ndara, then Voi. . . ." The memorized names were ticked off in triumph. George was in his own field of clover:

". . . Then we'll pass Ndi and Manyan and finally cross the Tsavo River. . . . But hang on to your hats there! They don't call this the 'Lunatic Line' for nothing . . . I expect we'll find the pepper and salt have been shaken up together . . . ha . . . ha . . . ha."

As the train climbed higher and higher, George's voice rose with it. "After that it's up the Chyulu Range, past Darajani and. . . . You all keeping up with me? Places not too difficult to remember, are they? . . ."

Eugenia tried to hide from her thoughts and she tried not to listen to her husband. Paul was nearly lost, she told herself. Can't anyone see where this folly might lead? She stared at the shifting glass until her own eyes turned it black and iridescent, and it began to reflect all those things she wanted to avoid: a mother's grief and a mountain of tears. We are as evanescent as rain, she thought. Our lives don't matter in this place; we're at the whim of any flying, creeping thing: tsetse flies, adders, ants, wasps, panthers. How can I protect my babies? What have I failed to see?

Eugenia glared at the window with such fierceness that if such things had been possible, it would surely have broken. It would have splintered its hundred fragmented selves over the trees and grasses and dust of Kibwezi, Emali, Kima, and Kiu; it would have spewed glass and fear on and on and on while the train moved deeper into Africa.

What have I failed to see? What have I failed to do?

"*O*H, REALLY, CARL. Do you take me for a complete simpleton? We're not after the coal seams at Ivartown or Sadong. In spite of what our illustrious president says about the Philippine situation and the need for safe American coaling stations in the South China Sea. . . ." The Turk paused and glanced left and right along the wide stone veranda at Linden Lodge; the attitude was one of dramatic secrecy, but Carl didn't take the proffered bait. He let his father play the part. Enough rope, Carl reminded himself, with enough rope the old man may hang himself yet. Being the Turk's constant companion since the *Alcedo*'s departure had taught Carl a few unexpected tricks. The latest was to keep his mouth shut and his eyes glued to some object his father prized. It was amazing what feigned concentration could inspire. Greed, selfishness, a terror at being bested, at losing: Carl had seen his father run the entire gamut. Not that he'd admit it. Not in a million years. But Carl had learned to recognize the signs.

Finally the Turk decided it was safe to proceed with his lecture; there seemed to be no gardeners or other time-serving loiterers about. The privileged information was secure at least a few moments longer. "It's oil, my boy," the Turk whispered. "There's oil along the northern shore of Borneo!

"And when we take complete control of the Philippines, as we're sure to do, and when our ships no longer run on coal and steam—and mark me, they won't forever—why, who do your think will rule the world then? Hmmm? The Filipinos? The Malays? Our brothers, the ring-tailed monkey-men . . . ?" The Turk allowed himself a gigantic cackle. ". . . Oil!" he giggled again. "Oil!

"You feeble-minded young idiots don't know the first thing about vision! You think oil's used only for lighting the bloody streets. . . . Oil's for lamps, you tell yourself; and coal's for heat . . . for ships . . . for trains . . . No point tampering with something that works. . . . No point asking too many questions . . .

"So you believed me! You thought I was sending a ship full of people halfway round the world for coal! . . .Off to Borneo for a few lumps of coal! . . . A handful of rocks we could dig out of any old lumpy earth! . . ." The words were a mockery of a coal miner's accent, a clownish composite of rural Wales and the deepest interior of Virginia.

Carl let the words run on while his glance drifted across the veranda with its carved balustrades, its cloistered benches, ivied columns and its ornamental fountains either pilfered or purchased from castles all over Europe. He studied everything in turn, as if appraising its worth, while his mind kept pace with its own plans.

". . . I feel sorry for you, Carl," his father continued. "You and hundreds like you. You'll never succeed. You'll never create an empire like mine or Morgan's—or Vanderbilt's—and you'll never put together a machine with a few pieces of scrap metal and start a company like that one in Dearborn.

"That's vision, my lad. That's vision! And do you know how much it cost Mr. Henry Ford to get that plant of his going? Three thousand puny little dollars! You wait and see what it's worth in another fifteen years. You talk about your wise investments . . ." The Turk felt his eyes begin to follow his son's. Wherever Carl's concentrated stare landed, the old man's was right behind. Carl gazed at a garden urn pulled out of a French chateau, then at an obelisk reputed to be Egyptian; next came a pair of Chinese stone lions and lastly a carved marble bench from a Roman villa. The Turk's face flickered over each one. If he could have ordered his possessions covered and hidden from view, he would have done so on the spot.

"Off to Borneo for coal!" the Turk insisted, and his voice rose with the effort to recapture his son's respect. "And you believed me! Like Marcus Samuel! Hunting up seashells for the ladies back home! The Shell Transport and Trading Company—purveyors of maritime curios! That ship of his—the *Cowrie*—that's a tanker, my lad. A tanker, not a freighter. A tanker that travels on liquid fuel! . . . That sailed all the way from Borneo to the Thames river on liquid fuel. Ten thousand miles, my lad. A trip of ten thousand miles without so much as a speck of coal!. . . .'She sells seashells by the seashore'. . . ." The Turk shrieked with pleasure; for a moment his son's mysterious motives were forgotten.

" . . . 'she sells seashells . . .' " the Turk repeated. The words seemed the funniest he'd ever spoken; they left him gasping for breath. Carl listened to the laughter and wondered how much longer he'd have to endure the old man's ravings. It seemed as if his father had grown senile overnight. Senile, erratic, and full of crazy spite.

" . . . You and the others like you, Carl, you'll spawn fools for children and all of this glory and wealth will be squandered in blood gone thin and squeamish and green as a rotten cheese!" The old man doubled over with a long and loud guffaw. Carl could hear throaty wheezes and gurgles, but he didn't turn his head.

Instead he stared at a fountain of Nereids disporting themselves in the waves, then at twin pedestals that had once graced the Parthenon steps. Everything is perfect, Carl told himself. Everything as ordered. Even the day—the gold and blue and violet-green of Indian summer. But early October becomes late October, and summer is swallowed by winter. You can't stop the inevitable. And you can't hide from the truth.

Oil, Carl repeated silently. Which rock does my dear father think I've been hiding under? I could tell him more about that precious commodity than he'd ever care to know. I could recite stories of foreign alliances that would make his ancient hair stand on end. There are enough names and enough new investors to make his heart stop beating.

But Carl didn't allude to any of those facts. When he finally spoke it was with a polite "Liquid fuel. An interesting concept. And as far out as Borneo. Quite astonishing."

Then Carl decided the moment had come to deliver Beckmann's cable, the one routed from the German protectorate of Zanzibar. The timing is perfect, Carl told himself. Beckmann's cable might just drive Father round the bend.

At the shooting lodge, or *ketito*, in the veldt somewhere near Nairobi, the Turk's favorite grandson tiptoed to his bedroom window and whispered into the night: "Yes, Father, I'm up."

The dark compound had just begun to stir in the predawn glow and Paul could see men scurrying about. Lights, like the flares of medieval torches, jumped and spluttered and made the men look as if they were preparing for battle, as if an enemy waited at the gates or they were going off to lay siege to a distant fort.

The "Big Trek." The safari! Paul knew that soon the lorry would be arriving, and the pack animals and the carts. They were the same ones that had brought them in from the train station in Nairobi, but this was going to be bigger and better. This would be a caravan stretching for miles across the open plain. Paul had heard Mr. Palmer and Mr. Smythe-Barrows describing it: All the black men would sing and chant, and the animals would whinny and stomp on the grass. It would be just like the Crusades! And he, Paul, was going along!

"I got dressed last night," Paul whispered to the screened door, "so I wouldn't keep you or the other men waiting."

The other men! Paul had really said it! He was going to be like "the other men," like Mr. Davies and Mr. Palmer and Mr. Smythe-Barrows. He was going to hunt and kill things just like Father! And it seemed so long ago (though it had only been last night) that his father had wakened him to say, yes, he could go on the trek; he could go on the "shoot."

Jinx had wakened up, too (what a baby!), and she'd started to snivel and whine about its not being fair. But Father had been firm. "Only men on safari!" he'd ordered, then he'd given Paul his very own "Sam Browne" belt, told him to go back to sleep, and left the room Paul and his sister shared. (Lizzie had her own room because Mother said she was nearly a lady—which was fine with Paul except when Jinx acted like a girl and cried.)

"Well, get a move on then, son," George called again from the dew-speckled porch. "We'd best be off before your mother wakes. We don't want to incur any more of the tiger's wrath." George tried to laugh at his own joke, but it didn't work. He ran a nervous hand over the back of his neck and wondered if he'd been too loud. The boxlike house with its encircling wood and screen porch reminded him of an echo chamber, and, Jesus, if there was one thing he didn't need, it was another scene with Eugenia.

"He's just a baby, George!" she'd screamed yesterday afternoon, and her voice had been loud and uncontrolled, as if they were the only people in the whole of Africa. "I absolutely refuse to let . . ."

"And a baby is all he'll stay, my dear. If you have your way!" Remembering his answer, George wiped the sweat from his face. My wife might as well be a fishwife, he thought. That's where her fine upbringing has led her. Shouting matches with her husband—what's worse than that?

"You don't care if Paul lives or dies! You're only thinking about yourself!" The picture of Eugenia's face contorted in rage was too much to consider. George closed out the rest of the memory.

Damn her eyes, he told himself as his shaking and clammy fingers clutched a wet chair back. Damn her to eternal hell . . . . As if I don't care about my own son! . . . . Haven't I proved just that? . . . Bringing the *Alcedo* to Africa instead of following Father's orders, taking this nice little family detour instead of . . .

And there was my little subterfuge with Beckmann as well, George reminded himself suddenly, bolstering his anger. But Eugenia's too stupid to realize how I masterminded that one. . . . Left Beckmann on the goddamned boat . . .

And instead of thanking me, instead of saying, "Oh, George, however did you manage it?" instead of saying, "Oh, you're so wonderful and brave," what does the wretched woman shriek? "You only think about yourself."

You only think about your bloody self! The memory of Eugenia's accusations made George so angry that he whipped the dew from the veranda rail with a sudden, jerky motion and bawled in a voice loud enough to wake the whole of the sleeping compound: "Paul! Old man! Get a bloody move on!"

By the time the expedition was actually mounted, the sun had appeared in the sky. The Big Trek. The Big Day. George's new friends, the white hunters, Palmer, Davies, and Sir Harold Chalmondely, moved along the line on horseback, as did Lieutenant Brown and Whitney, while Oliver Smythe-Barrows walked back and forth on foot, checking and rechecking the bearers' loads, the cases of supplies, the weapons and cartridges. Even a fortnight's safari required an impressive list of necessities. There'd have to be a decent dinner served each evening, and a bottle of claret couldn't replace a Riesling or a Riesling a Bordeaux.

But the wines, tinned fruit, and potted shrimp took far less space on the bearers' backs than the cook tent, the wash tent, and the several sleeping tents bundled into their well-wrapped khaki mounds. Paul looked around in awe, then leaned down to speak to the *syce*, the groom, who held the bridle of his broad-backed pony.

"We look like an army, don't we, Vadyaji?" the little boy asked, while the *syce* merely shook his turbaned head in agreement: What the small American boy might or might not have said was of no concern to him.

Eugenia arrived at the scene just as Dr. DuPlessis was finishing up his photographic record of the historic event. She stood apart, trying to gather reason and argument. George can't take Paul, she told herself, he can't. But she had no idea how to stop her husband. Mrs. DuPlessis flapped near, then huffed off toward the men; Jinx and Lizzie rushed over, said something their mother didn't comprehend, and then also rushed away. Eugenia's thoughts were focused completely on her son. George cannot do this, she promised herself. I won't let him. I won't.

For the first time in her life Eugenia knew she hated her husband. Even during his drinking escapades with the ruined children's parties and sad Christmas mornings, she'd found a reason to forgive him. She'd covered them both in excuses till the excuses had turned to truth. Convenience won out, because, as Eugenia reasoned, life goes on. And too, there was so much at stake: her children's well-being, their pleasant home, her own comfortable existence. It was easier to gloss over the bad times. It was easier to look the other way.

But something had changed, and now she hated her husband. Let him go out there and blow himself to kingdom come, if that's what he wants, she told herself. He can't take my son. The thoughts were rational and calm; Eugenia had passed judgment on a man she no longer knew.

George sidestepped his roan gelding toward the shadowy place where his wife waited. He'd seen her arrive, and her composed expression had given him a moment's pause, but he was too buoyed up by camaraderie and the knowledge that among his peers he was justified, to give Eugenia's anger a second thought. A man's home should be his castle, George recited inwardly. I shouldn't have to put up with this nonsense, no indeedy. The other fellows wouldn't, and they know a thing or two.

"See you made it out of bed to wave good-bye, Genie," George blustered, then let his horse prance so close its hooves nearly trampled Eugenia's dress. Might is right, he told himself; familiarity breeds contempt; never submit or yield; never give in. The stirring phrases bolstered his courage.

"You can't take Paul," Eugenia answered. Her voice was quiet; her body didn't move and her face was untroubled and serene. She looked straight into her husband's eyes as if his agitation and the nearness of his horse were obvious ploys, impressive to him alone.

"And how, my dear, do you propose to stop me?" George decided on a smile and a smirking tilt to his head. Take it easy on the little lady, he warned himself, you're the master here. George added a complacent grin.

That passive good humor did the trick. Eugenia grabbed for the stirrup, the girth, the bridle, the blanket—anything to sink her fingers into. "You can't take him, George," she managed, feeling certainty desert her. "He's too small. . . . He doesn't know the first thing about guns . . ." Stop, Eugenia told herself. If you're not careful, you'll cry. And then he'll have won.

But reminders are only as strong as the habits they serve. The husband is master; the wife is weak: Those were the rules of Eugenia's marriage. "Paul's only a little boy . . . ," she repeated, ". . . he . . . look what happened on the *Alcedo* . . ." Eugenia hesitated. The memory of the shooting match was indelibly bound with another, and she found herself face to face with guilt and blame and an unforgiving sin. Eugenia backed away and put down her arms, defeated by her own condemnation.

"And I repeat, Eugenia, how do you propose to stop me?" A laugh proved George knew exactly where he stood.

Unwillingly the other hunters witnessed this domestic quarrel, and they moved off, rolling their eyes and shaking their heads over the foolishness of the scene. Sir Harold whispered to Palmer: "That old saw about women in the bush just about sums it up, doesn't it?"

"They'd better sort this out quick, though," Palmer agreed. "We don't want to start out much later. The sun's moving higher, and you know where that puts us come noontime."

Only Lieutenant Brown remained nearby, letting his horse nose the ground while he kept his eyes on Eugenia and George. Jesus Christ, man, he thought; you're letting your goddamn horse trample your wife's feet. He yanked the reins and wheeled toward George.

At the same time Eugenia was trying to decide between what seemed a myriad of choices: Do I cry? she wondered. Or scream? I could scream, I think. I'm sure I could; it's not very hard. Or I could beg. Eugenia looked at each emotion as if it were clothing on a rack: You choose the right one, and your son is safe; you make the wrong choice, and you forfeit everything.

"Perhaps, sir, it might help if I stayed behind." Lieutenant Brown's voice startled both George and Eugenia. "With Mrs. Axthelm and the girls, sir."

"What's that, Brown?" George demanded harshly, unwilling to give up his private confrontation with Eugenia.

"If Mrs. Axthelm's concerned about being here on her own with the girls and Dr. and Mrs. DuPlessis, I wouldn't mind remaining in camp as well . . ." Brown couldn't think what else to say.

No, Eugenia's eyes said. *That's not it. Can't you see, James? It's Paul I'm frightened for, not myself,* while George chuckled, "Just so, Lieutenant. That's the very thing my wife's worried over . . . these little feminine concerns . . . . Safe as rain here in the compound, but she won't listen . . . well, you know women . . . " Finding Brown a sudden ally made George smug and cocky.

" . . . Won't listen at all, will you, Genie?" George smiled down benignly. "Can't bear to see all the menfolk leave. Thinks lions and tigers lurk around every bend . . . you know how it is, Lieutenant . . ."

It's not me, James, Eugenia's eyes pleaded. *Please, I want you to stay with Paul. You must stay with Paul.* But Brown didn't dare look at her face and Eugenia couldn't allow herself the words she was thinking, and they found themselves quite easily trapped.

George turned his horse abruptly. "Fine, Brown," he announced, "you stay behind." The decision made him surprisingly happy. He didn't like Brown, he realized. He was a constant reminder of the *Alcedo*'s true task. It would be good to be rid of him for a while. In fact he'd be glad to be rid of them all, George decided. Beckmann, Brown—and Eugenia. The trek into the bush need have no displays of his own incompetence.

"Good of you to volunteer," George called over his shoulder. "I'm sure you'll be a great comfort to the faint of heart here at home." If there was any other motive for his action, George would have been the last person to admit it.

So it was settled: Paul was to leave with his father and Brown was to remain behind. The train of riders, bearers, carts, porters, and Aspari guards started forward in a cloud of dust and noise. The horses nuzzled each other and whinnied, the lathered leather of their saddles, stirrups, and girths creaked together while the wagon whips snapped and all manner of birds, startled out of their grassy homes, clapped frantic wings in the air. Legs of men, legs of horses, bellies of mules, and spokes of wheels rustled through the brittle grass with a sound that carried the jounce of springs and a bounce of communal delight. Paul turned back to wave to his mother and sisters, the DuPlessises, and Lieutenant Brown, but they were hidden first by the weaving line itself and then by the hundreds of crickets, grasshoppers, and flying ants that billowed like sparks from the sun-burned ground.

"Couldn't you have . . . ?"

"Stopped him," Eugenia wanted to say, but knew she couldn't. She held the words back and stared at the dusk creeping into her bedroom. The long day was finally ending. *I mustn't worry,* Eugenia told herself. *I've got to learn a little faith. This isn't the last time my child will be in danger. I'll have to trust in wisdom or kindness or something human at least.*

"No." Brown answered the unfinished question, then sat silently in his straight camp chair while the evening light continued to settle. It slid around the table legs and the washstand; it wrapped itself in the cretonne folds of an easy chair and then slipped unnoticed toward the bedstead, the curtained dresser, and the unlit lamp. The African night moves quickly; soon the room was completely dark.

"Well," Eugenia said, "we're finally alone. We got what we wanted."

They waited, out of private hesitation or mutual consent, through the last of a long, long dinner when Dr. DuPlessis expounded (over two cigars) on his theories of elephant behavior, and Mrs. DuPlessis nearly fell asleep in the honey-colored trifle. Then the girls were finally put to bed by Prue, and Eugenia went in to hear their prayers while Lieutenant Brown sat on the veranda with the doctor. And just when it seemed as though it would never happen, a formal and gentle good night was said by both the doctor and his wife, and Eugenia and Brown were left alone.

It wasn't the same as the hours at the Hotel Belle Ville, Eugenia realized as she slowly removed her clothes and placed them on the chair by her dresser and washstand. After all the anticipation, she felt suddenly awkward and shy, but there seemed nothing for it but to get into bed. She pulled back the sheet and slipped in as quickly as she could.

They made love as quickly. Their bodies found each other, their arms and hands discovered what they sought, but their minds stayed apart, as if each were listening to something far away and different. It will be better next time, they both promised. It's the strangeness of the day . . . or this place . . . or this room. When we know each other better, they told themselves. When we feel truly safe.

Eugenia stroked Brown's back and the curve of his shoulder; she turned her face to his and whispered, "My dearest." And Brown kissed her neck and held her shivering breast and murmured, "Eugenia." But their thoughts flew around like the nightjars and cuckoos, like the squealing beetles and terrified frogs who raised such a racket in the hovering night.

Beckmann . . . rifles . . . cartridges . . . Borneo, Brown's thoughts repeated in careful order, while Eugenia's rose and sank with each faraway sound, each wail or grunt or ear-piercing yelp: Paul, James, Lizzie, Jinx . . . James and Paul and . . . James alone.

"You know we French stormed Ratisbon . . ." Eugenia wrote in her diary the next morning. The sun was already high in the sky, but she was still in her robe, huddled over her desk, trying to puzzle out the words to the poem she'd suddenly remembered. Or hadn't remembered.

A mile or so away,
On a little mound, Napoleon
Stood on our storming day;
With neck out-thrust, you fancy how,
Legs wide, arms locked behind,

Eugenia put down her pen. There was more to the poem, and obviously a reason for its coming to mind, but the connection eluded her. " 'You know we French stormed Ratisbon . . .' " she repeated aloud.

"What are you doing still in bed, Mother?" Jinx burst into the room.

"Don't you know to knock first, young lady?" Eugenia reprimanded carelessly, then added: "Good morning, angel. And I'm not in bed. I'm trying to figure out the words of a poem. It's by Robert Browning, I think, and it came to me in the middle of the night. I can't remember the ending and it's making me crazy." Eugenia had told herself that life must return to its usual mode, that her outward behavior mustn't change, and that all worries should be shelved. She was determined to create a happy and insular world.

"Maybe Dr. DuPlessis knows," Jinx said over her shoulder as she prowled around the room, wholly uninterested in her mother's problem.

" 'As if to balance that prone brow,' " Eugenia recited half to herself. " 'Oppressive with its mind.' "

"Mother!" Jinx wailed.

" 'My plans that soar," Eugenia teased, "to earth may fall, / Let once my army-leader Lannes, / Waver at yonder wall . . .' " Then she looked at her daughter. "No, Dr. DuPlessis wouldn't know. I don't think his head's been filled with romantic poetry."

"Maybe Mrs. D. then. She's flighty. I bet she's read gobs of that stuff. Maybe even more than you." Jinx draped herself in her mother's hat veil, and Eugenia felt happiness suffuse her. Everything's going to be all right, she promised. The important thing is not to create difficulties where none exist. We are a family here. This is my daughter.

"Oh, I'm sure! Mrs. DuPlessis is the very one!" Eugenia responded to the joke, and both mother and daughter began to laugh together. Don't mope, Eugenia told herself, and don't "dwell," as old Catherine used to say.

"Oh, Mother . . ." Jinx burst out, suddenly recalling her mission. ". . . I was sent to tell you Dr. and Mrs. DuPlessis are leaving for the village in an hour. They want to know if you're going."

"Are you and Liz?" Eugenia remembered Mrs. DuPlessis's plan, but she couldn't bring herself to go alone.

"No, we're going riding with Lieutenant Brown."

"Oh." Eugenia sighed, and the picture she saw was as bright as the day: the three of them riding by a stream under a small copse of trees, and sunlight filtering through in bands of hazy yellow that looked as strong as garden walls, that looked as if you could climb up till you reached the treetops, the sky, and finally the sun itself.

"I wish I could go," Eugenia said without thinking, and her voice reminded Jinx of a gloomy old dog.

"You can, Mother! Just tell Dr. . . . ."

"No, darling." Eugenia caught herself and forced a bustling smile. She couldn't risk being seen alone with James just yet. They'd give too much away. It was nearly impossible for them to pass each other without involuntarily touching or holding out their hands.

"You and Liz go. I'll do my duty here." Eugenia made a face in imitation of Mrs. DuPlessis's disapproval and started to dress.

As Jinx left the room, her mother asked casually, and as if she'd only just this minute thought of it, "Any word from Father?"

"I don't think so," Jinx answered as she closed the door.

" 'You know we French stormed Ratisbon . . .' " Eugenia repeated when she'd been left alone. " 'A mile or so away . . .' "

The "visit to the village" was Mrs. DuPlessis's idea of a dream come true. She was to play Lady Bountiful at long last; her husband would minister to the medical needs of the "poor, pathetic little Wankikuyu," as she referred to the natives, while she, the good, kind lady from Philadelphia, would stroll about their huts, dispensing homilies and lemon drops.

Mrs. DuPlessis had already described the outing in detail in a letter to her sister. But she hadn't alluded to the fact that Joseph, the number-one boy at the *ketito,* had tried to discourage her, nor to the fact that the Swahili house servants and Somali outdoor boys had stared firmly at the dirt each time she sauntered up to discuss her plans. A visit to the village was what she wanted and a visit to the village was what she'd get!

Mrs. DuPlessis closed the letter to her sister with a fervent:

> We shall soon see, my dear Margaret, just how unfortunate these people are. I hope God may grant us equanimity with which to witness their sorrow, though I must confide that we have al-

ready been apprised of the most dreadful situation among the Belgian-ruled heathen in the "Congo." I cannot bear to mention the atrocities committed there—other than to tell you they include baskets full of body parts!

Thank all who dwell in Heaven for the creation of The Aborigines Protection Society. (You do recall Mr. Richard Fox Bourne, don't you dear?) I am duty bound to do my part as well.

Your loving sister, etc.

With that, Mrs. DuPlessis hurried out to find Mrs. Axthelm and the good doctor and hasten them both toward the task at hand.

" 'Pickaninnies,' my great-aunt used to call them," Mrs. DuPlessis burbled as the cart bounced through the rutted grass. "Of course," she whispered as if the cart boy cared or even understood, "that was in the South and a great many years ago. Before the war and that misguided Mr. Lincoln."

The South: Mrs. DuPlessis's famous ancestral homeland. The South encompassed Richmond, Atlanta, Charleston, West Virginia, Delaware, and even parts of Pennsylvania; wherever Mrs. DuPlessis's numerous first and second cousins "once removed" or aunts or nieces had made their way was "southern." Eugenia sometimes wondered if Maine might be next. "Those lovely antebellum houses in Wiscasset and Kennebunk," she could imagine the lady sighing. "The War" had put an end to "The South," of course. In spite of Mrs. DuPlessis's avowal that slavery was a sin, anyone listening to her recitation about the "old days" might wonder whether the "sin" was in slavery or its abolition.

"But this isn't the South, Jane," Dr. DuPlessis murmured gently while the cart whished through the long grass and the cart boy slapped the reins against the horse's sweaty back.

"I know that, Gustav. Don't you think I do?" Mrs. DuPlessis's voice started to waver dangerously, and she sat up even straighter than she had before.

On the narrow seat beside Mrs. DuPlessis, Eugenia wondered whether corset stays kept the lady so erect or whether it was an innate sense of leading by example. Everything Mrs. DuPlessis did had a holier-than-thou attitude; she was self-righteous in the extreme.

Then Eugenia left her considerations of Mrs. DuPlessis and began to wonder where James and her daughters were. She pictured the three of them with the grooms and horses ambling through the scrub grass, unfettered by the necessity of performing good deeds or bad, and her body unconsciously slumped in languid imitation.

"You'll ruin your back if you sit like that," Mrs. DuPlessis's cross words brought Eugenia back to the cart and the reason for the expedition. "Sometimes I wonder how your generation can be so lax. In my day a lady . . ."

"Pickaninnies, was it, Jane?" Dr. DuPlessis asked as he tried to assuage his wife's hurt feelings, and temper what sounded like an imminent lecture.

"Well, that's what my great-aunt Sadie used to say." Mrs. DuPlessis reverted to type immediately, and began to preen herself in her words.

"When dear Margaret and I went down to Lambert Hall to visit, there were always a bunch of them who'd race up to the carriage. And oh, such happy faces! You should have seen the pleasure they took in our fancy 'Yankee' clothes! It was 'Missy' this, 'Missy' that . . . and those perfect little cherub smiles . . . Why, I remember my great-aunt Sadie telling me . . ."

Mollified and comforted, secure in her peculiar vision of the world, Mrs. DuPlessis's reminiscences about oyster roasts and turkey shoots spilled without interruption all the way to the Wankikuyu village, all the wide breadth of the African landscape and the far reach of its white-hot sky.

The "chief's chief son" and the chief's eldest daughter and her retinue met the goodwill envoy. Their skin was the color of polished copper pots; they'd been painted with oil and ocher-hued earth, and Eugenia thought they were the most extraordinarily proud people she'd ever seen. The women surrounding the chief's daughter were covered with row after circular row of shiny copper wire; the metal flashed in the sun and they stood as still as statues while they watched the "Mercans" descend from the carriage. Eugenia thought her own clothing looked shoddy and ephemeral in comparison, and, as if to prove the point, her shoe caught the hem of her dress and she nearly fell flat on her face as she stepped from the cart. We're the primitive people, she realized, we're the ones who need to hide our flaws under skirts and coats and hats and ties. And corsets

". . . They haven't been known to bathe up until this present time . . ." Mrs. DuPlessis was rasping from behind her handkerchief. ". . . Joseph told me . . . and such a dear he is . . . I'm simply entranced by the Old Testament names they like to use out here . . . He says that they'll wash their hair in, oh, how can I put this delicately? . . . It's a liquid that serves a biological . . ."

Eugenia turned away from the rest of Mrs. DuPlessis's remarks and watched as the doctor's traveling table and portable medical box was assembled and set in place. The work was given great care, as if the table and box were sorcerer's totems, and by the time the impromptu clinic was ready, the whole of the village had appeared to watch the spectacle.

Dr. DuPlessis strode forward to his chair, but none of the crowd stirred. "Any injuries? . . . Illnesses? . . ." The doctor cleared his throat. "Dropsy? . . . Stomach complaints? . . ."

No one stepped into the magic ring; they continued to stare the way cattle, surprised near a stream, warily watch an intruder and try to decide, first singly and then as a clannish group, just what the stranger is up to. Is it a wolf, a badger, a bee? Should they run away? Should they snort and stand their ground? Or should they simply return to the study of their own superior grasses, and wait till the thing disappears?

"Tell the chief you want to see the children first," Mrs. DuPlessis prompted loudly, and then graced the group with a wide, vacuous smile.

"If any children would like . . ." Dr. DuPlessis announced, then began to pull from his pockets what looked like an endless ribbon of lemon, licorice, vanilla, and currant drops wrapped in shiny wax paper. Dr. DuPlessis's act was as studied and deft as a conjurer pulling silks from a ring.

"Ohhhh . . ." Both the crowd and Mrs. DuPlessis murmured in unison, and Eugenia decided to sneak away before that lady had a chance to vent her disappointment at not being the first to win the hearts of the "little dears" with a roll of sugar. She knew without being told that this was a moment Mrs. DuPlessis had claimed as her own. Membership in the much vaunted Aborigines Protection Society demanded superhuman goodness.

Four women trailed Eugenia as she strolled the perimeter of the village, and numerous children picked at her skirts, but when she stopped to speak or touch a small hand, the world became as still as morning air and her audience drew back into themselves. Eugenia felt she'd stepped into a painting that didn't include her white-parasoled figure; she felt she'd become invisible. The women might have followed a shadow or nothing at all, and the children might have been clutching motes of speckled dust instead of a white linen skirt. Eugenia shaded her eyes and stared at the far hills, the bunchy line of fever trees, and then at the cart tracks, which had folded under the grass like a hand print settled in a mound of warm dough. She thought about Paul and George, then about the girls and James.

She pictured her daughters riding near trees as spotty as birches, then she saw Paul and a cloud of yellow-green smoke. She saw the girls again; she saw James with them; she saw sunlight streaming over his handsome face. But her son had vanished. Eugenia pulled her hand down from her eyes and walked quickly back to the center of the village. Common sense is what I need, she told herself, common sense and practicality and my share of elbow grease. Don't be dramatic; don't invent disasters; Paul is fine; he's well and happy and I am a foolish and overwrought mother.

While Dr. DuPlessis and Eugenia finished the last of the bandaging Mrs. DuPlessis moaned from a distance, "It's just awful what they allow their children. . . . . Why, my goodness, they have more than they can possibly feed, . . .

"And I feel so sorry for . . . Why, imagine! In this heat, too. . . . Wouldn't you think someone, missionaries or someone, would have? . . . . After all, what good are these protection societies if they fail to . . . ?"

The singsong litany flowed unabated. Dr. DuPlessis knew better than to interrupt; he nodded his head slowly and several times punctuated his wife's complaints with an inconclusive "Mmmm" or "Yes, I would, my dear."

Eugenia tried not to listen, though she did what she could to help the doctor's work. She held a length of gauze while Dr. DuPlessis tried to clean a child's ulcerated arm. "Just hold this bit, Eugenia," the doctor said, placing cotton wool on the infected wound. "Then try to see if you can explain to his mother. She must keep the opening clean and dry. I'll give them some more lengths of gauze and more salve, but cleanliness is vital."

The little boy tried to be brave, but tears poured down his dusty cheeks as he stared first at Eugenia's hands and then up at her face. Eugenia felt her stomach turn over and her cheeks grow hot; the reaction was instantaneous. She looked around for the boy's mother, but she was cowering near a hut wall, afraid to watch.

". . . And see that little girl . . ." Mrs. DuPlessis whispered hoarsely, ". . . not a day over eleven, I'll warrant, and a baby already on her hip. . . ." Mrs. DuPlessis's whisper became a moan; then the moan turned into a sudden, gulping sob. The intensity of the noise startled both Eugenia and the doctor.

"Ah, now, Jane, Jane . . ." Dr. DuPlessis said, jumping up to help his wife.

"But we couldn't . . ." she wailed, and her tears grew as loud as those of a small child frightened by a nightmare, ". . . not in all that time . . . God can be so cruel!"

". . . Now, now, Jane. . . ." Dr. DuPlessis was at a loss; his words dripped uselessly, like water from a rusty pipe.

"Yes, He can! Downright cruel!" Mrs. DuPlessis's vehemence did nothing to lessen her tears. Anger spurred them on.

"I know I shouldn't say that. But they told us, Gustav . . . when we . . ."

"I know, dear. I know."

"But that last time . . ."

"I know, dear."

"It's not fair!"

"I know, dear. I know."

Eugenia turned away from the DuPlessises' private grief and busied herself rolling bandages. The emotion had taken her by surprise; she hadn't imagined Mrs. DuPlessis ever desiring any more than a second helping of dessert. And it suddenly occurred to Eugenia, clearing away the doctor's bottles of tonic and salve, his silver nitrate for the eyes and cod-liver oil for strong bones, that everyone has within them two people: One is an adult growing older and one remains a child. And when the child inside is frightened and lonely and afraid, then the adult must reach down to that being, to himself, and comfort and cradle it till the dark night has passed.

*I*T WAS VERY LATE. Perhaps two or three or even four in the morning. Lieutenant Brown didn't know. He only knew that it was dark outside, and that he and Eugenia had slept for a long time. He turned to look at her as she faced him, deep asleep and unaware of his movement. In the faint light that slipped through the shutters she seemed to be smiling. Fast asleep and smiling. Her hand cradled her cheek and Brown bent down to kiss them both. Eugenia stirred, tried to say something, but the words were the words of a dream, spoken in one world, incomprehensible in another.

Brown knew it was time to go. He knew he couldn't trust himself to lie beside her any longer. It would be getting light soon and he'd have to be safely back in his own room by them. "I'm leaving, Eugenia," he whispered, and pulled himself from the bed.

The floor was cold, the night air was cold, but before he dressed, Brown reached down to tuck the sheet and blanket into a warm nest so Eugenia wouldn't have to wake up both cold and alone. He slid the blanket over her shoulder and moved the pillow till it sheltered her back and neck. Perhaps she won't realize I'm gone till the sun comes up, he thought as he found his boots and jacket. Perhaps she'll curve into this hollow of warmth and protection the same way she curves into me.

Lieutenant Brown walked carefully to the door, aware of every creak in every board, then stood for a moment, waiting and listening. When he'd decided it was safe enough he opened the door quickly and stepped purposefully across the veranda and out into the night.

This was the fourth day at the *ketito* after George's departure and Lieutenant Brown had already established a routine for leaving Eugenia's room. He circled the entire lodge, walking about twenty feet from the veranda as if on a nightly patrol. This was his ready excuse: He was there to watch over the family, and it seemed a logical explanation, given his supposed military training, that he tour the compound every night.

The ground was wet. The African dew fell as heavy as rain and the grass and dirt of the camp were soaked, as if a storm had drenched them. By the time the sun was only halfway to its midday mark, the land would be parched again, but for now it was sodden as marsh grass beside a swollen stream. Water squelched under Brown's boots as he walked his course. It reminded him of the flatland where his father and uncle had tried to grow corn. Every time it rained, the hollow had flooded. Every damned time. The corn grew up spindly and stunted, if it grew at all.

Armand, Brown thought suddenly. I wonder where Beckmann found that name. The Brown was understandable. Anyone could be named Brown; anyone could be named Jim, but the Armand was confusing. Brown wondered if the name had belonged to someone long dead. If there'd been a real James Armand Brown or if Beckmann had pulled the name from the air as a display of his own quirky power and guile.

James Armand Brown, Naval Academy, class of '99 . . . or was it '98 . . . ? Brown stopped and stared into the night, trying to remember the story Beckmann had recited back in Newport. The dates seemed irrelevant, but the carefully constructed history began to elude him— his biography, his pedigree, his bloodline, the reason he'd been allowed on the *Alcedo* as an equal, allowed to join the family, play with the children, talk to Eugenia. James Armand Brown, a fine southern heritage, orphaned as a young man, a commission to Annapolis, and relatives with clout but distant enough to leave him on his own: Brown could imagine the type of young man James Armand would be. He'd seen enough of them riding past that damned waterlogged cornfield.

Brown shook the dew from his boots and walked on. Bitterness gets you nowhere, he told himself. Bitterness makes you drink and forget to sow the seed. Bitterness beats your children till they take to the road and scatter like coal dust in a winter wind. Bitterness rails about the "old country," the soldiers, the strikes; it smashes tables and windows and breaks down doors. Then it kills you.

Eugenia, Brown wondered, all of a sudden. The picture he had of her sleeping was so vivid he might have been lying beside her. She'd reach her hand to his shoulder or maybe stroke his leg with her foot. She'd be asleep at first, unconscious of her movements till they both woke up. Then she'd laugh in that low, quiet way and say, "I am so very happy. You make me so happy." Or she might sit bolt upright, not caring that she was completely naked, and demand: "Tell me about the others, James. Please?" Brown loved that in her: her unquenchable, childish jealousy. She wanted them to belong only to each other.

And that's what we've created during the past days, Brown realized. The loving couple, the loving family. I've taught Jinx and Lizzie how to ride bareback, how to hobble their ponies on the open veldt, and why they should always walk them home to the kraal. I've taught them to look out for snakes and to watch the way a mother bird wavers near her nest. I've shown them what it means when she drags her wing and why no one must ever, no matter the temptation, disturb her precious babies. While in the evening, in the quiet hour after dinner, as Joseph fusses over the sitting room fire, and our little group looks like God's idea of a perfect family inside a perfect home, I've smiled above both girls' heads and tried to teach Eugenia how to win at gin rummy.

In the gully below the *ketito,* there was a sudden thrashing noise, then a quick high whine followed by silence. Brown was instantly alert. It wasn't the sound that disturbed him; he knew there were enough native eyes and Snider rifles guarding the compound to prevent any animal from breaking through to the houses and huts. It was his own slowness that bothered him. Brown was aware of losing his edge, of becoming lazy and forgetful, a dreamer with nothing more on his mind than the comforts of hearth and home. George, he remembered quickly. George will be back before you know it. This time is a reprieve; it isn't real.

Brown continued his patrol. The *ketito*'s roof swelled in the darkness behind him and cast a long shadow knifing over the ground. It looked like the prow of a boat or the peaked roof of a Chinese temple, while the veranda supports stuck out at angles like punji stakes in a tiger pit. Lieutenant James Armand Brown looked at the shadow and tried to remember where he'd seen its like before.

While Beckmann, back in the port of Kilindini, on Mombasa Island, paced the *Alcedo*'s deserted deck and cursed himself for letting Brown leave. George's suggestion, of course. And as idiotic as always.

"It will look better, don't you think, Ogden, if Brown comes along inland with us?" George had babbled. "Besides, you're the one who's really in charge of those Springfield rifles. Brown's here just for . . . just for . . ." George had faltered, ". . . well, the actual event in Kuching . . . you know . . . Mahomet Seh and all that . . . just for that one day when we . . ."

The spoiled youngest son had stumbled so much that Beckmann had wondered if perhaps the old Turk was more wily than anyone knew. Whatever whitewashed story he'd fed his son was apparently enough. "Yes, George," Beckmann had wanted to say, "you're right; Brown's along for that one day. Just to hand off some brand-new, extremely accurate and extremely expensive Springfield A3s to a bunch of woolly-haired savages in a jungle no one will ever see again. Believe what you want, George. Make things easy on yourself. Swallow your father's lie; look the other way."

But Brown was a loose cannon, and Beckmann knew it; he was a problem, not an answer. A man with a new identity and new name. An invention of his masters. And, in spite of his true history, an unrelenting romantic. Beckmann had discovered that early on, perhaps even the day the *Alcedo* had left Newport; there'd been a hint of weakness in the way Brown had looked over the ship. Its size and grandeur had taken him by complete surprise and Beckmann had caught the man out, found him guilty of daydreams and wishful thinking.

It would be like Brown to discover chivalry all of a sudden, Beckmann realized; it would be like him to create a cause out of this adventure, start spluttering, "We can't supply both sides; it's too dangerous a proposition. I should have been informed," and other equally useless drivel. But he'd better keep those emotions to himself, Beckmann told himself. There's nothing Brown can do to help Eugenia or the children or even poor old George except get the job done and get it done in time. And then disappear.

"No one will get hurt if they do what they're told, Ogden," the Turk had cautioned all those months before. "The plan is foolproof. Just make sure there's profit for everyone, and nothing can go wrong. Remember that. We're none of us altruistic or kind. Pander to a need and you'll get your result. It's a very simple maxim. So simple, it's often overlooked. The sultan wants something, old Paine wants something. Likewise Rajah Ivard and Mahomet Seh.

"What are their desires, Ogden, do you think? And George's? And this man, your mercenary? Get to the heart of the matter, Ogden, and you'll never fail. And a mercenary's the easiest of the lot. He wants money, pure and simple. You feed him a line, tell him the rifles are earmarked for a rebel chief, and you're home scot-free. He doesn't need to know about any other deals, and, believe me, it's better for him and for us if he doesn't."

The conversation had ended there with a stubbed-out cigar and a curt dismissal, and Beckmann had been satisfied, even inspired, by the message, but now, wandering the dark ship, he began to wonder just how you discover a person's true need. And when you know it, what do you use as bait?

George was in his element. The "Bwana Khubwa," the great master, as he was called, had just brought down a large bull eland, and he stood beside it, resting one boot on its motionless side while the other hunters kept their respectful distance.

"Horns twenty-eight inches in length with an eleven-inch circumference," Oliver Smythe-Barrows dictated to Davies, the official score-keeper. "Nice work, old man. You've got an impressive list of kills to cart home to Philadelphia."

"Think I'll have the fellow's head mounted, Oliver, if you can arrange it. Be an attractive addition to the collection."

"Where do you plan to put all these beasts, George?" Whitney strode forward to examine the eland. Tradition kept the competing hunters at bay till the one responsible had a chance to examine his prize alone. The only exception had been the day they'd shot the Thompson gazelles; the group had brought down twenty-nine in a single morning and no one knew who'd shot which. The carcasses had been divvied up with the larger share going to George, the Bwana Khubwa, as even his companions occasionally called him. No one had needed the meat—although gazelle cutlets were considered a delicacy, so the heads had been severed, and the "Tommies'" bodies left for the natives or the jackals: whichever arrived first.

"I'm going to build my own trophy room," George boasted. "In spite of what my dear little wife may say. Take over part of the garden. Dig up some of those infernal rosebushes."

"Better watch yourself, old man," Palmer joked as he examined the eland's carcass himself. "That's the sound of a man too long in the bush. You start dispensing with the niceties and pretty soon you'll be giving up Philadelphia altogether, packing your kit and joining the rest of us gypsies."

"You think we Americans are all tied to apron strings," George laughed. "You swim across the Atlantic and I'll show you a trophy room that will rival President Roosevelt's! What do you say, Sir Harold? You've been up to his place in New York State. Think we can start a gentlemen's competition?"

Without waiting for an answer, George continued the directions to Smythe-Barrows. "Tell the *neapora* to cut off the head, Oliver, and we'll have eland steak tonight. A treat for all.

"How would you like that, son?" George suddenly remembered Paul's existence and turned to the child, indicating that the Aspari release his young charge. The native guard moved but didn't change expression; the only sign he gave of having heard his master was that Paul suddenly found himself propelled into the circle of his father's new friends.

"Fine, Father," Paul answered quietly as he stared at the animal's clouded eyes. Flies had begun to gather there and around the distended, drying tongue. Paul's instinct was to touch the dead eland, try to comfort it, tell it about angels and heaven and God, but he knew he shouldn't. "He's big, Father," Paul said without looking up.

"You bet he is, son," George chuckled, mistaking his child's words for admiration. "Now, just to refresh the memory of these very forgetful gentlemen"—George winked over Paul's head—"let's see if you can recite the names of all the animals we've killed."

Paul hated this task. It seemed every time they stopped he was called on to perform. He couldn't get all the names right and even if he did, or almost did, his father was sure to interrupt with some new demand. "How many impala, son?" he might say, or "Where did we get that rhino?" Then he'd laugh with the other men and say, "Just a hunter-in-training, after all, but he's got to learn sometime! And we'll keep one of those rhino feet to hold his school pencils. It will be a good souvenir." Mr. Palmer and Mr. Davies found that a very good joke.

"Springbok," Paul began quietly, "and hartebeeste, wildebeeste, elephant . . ."

"How many?" George interrupted.

"How many what?" Paul was afraid the interruption would make him lose his place.

"Why, elephant, of course."

"One. A bull," the little boy recited dutifully, "eight yards long."

"Eight yards, was it! Oliver, what kind of measure were you using?"

Paul could hear laughter growing all around. ". . . And oryx," he continued, "and dik-dik, buffalo, sable, warthog . . ."

"And which tastes the best?" George quizzed.

"Oryx."

"And which tastes like beef and makes you think you'd like a little Yorkshire pudding and some cranberry preserve and horseradish sauce?"

"Eland. . . . Like this one."

"Good lad. What do you say, gents?" George called. "A hand for the youngest member of the team."

Paul listened to the applause and guffaws and stared at the eland's face and its long, ridged horns. He tried to imagine what its head would look like at home, hanging on a wall. Or the tiny dik-diks or the springbok, which had leapt out of the bush like a flock of birds. They'd been caught midair, mid-leap, and then dashed to the ground. Some had died immediately, some had not, but Paul had been amazed, standing in that treeless space near his father, how easily a bullet could kill. And with such a very little hole, hardly visible at all. Sir Harold had shown him the wounds; he'd been very proud. "A nice, clean death," he'd said. "The only way to go, lad. Remember that. But don't hit the head or you'll have no trophy for your efforts. Not much point to the exercise, then."

But, of course, those were different rifles and ammunition than the ones used for rhino and elephant, "big game," as Mr. Palmer called them; each species required a different weapon. That had been another of Paul's lessons: the .450 Nitro Express, the Holland and Holland "double," the Winchester repeating . . . it was hard to keep track of them all.

Paul glanced at the flies that had begun to crawl from the eland to his trouser leg. He shook them off, but they came back, as sly as ink. He knew he had to sneak away before his father began another quiz or he was asked to help Mr. Smythe-Barrows with the measuring, and then he'd have to put his hands on the poor animal's stomach or watch while they cut off its poor, trembly feet.

"Well, gentlemen, I guess that's it. . . ." George signaled to the *neapora*.

Good, Paul told himself, I'm safe; it's time to leave.

". . . But before we head back to camp, I have one more question for our young apprentice. . . ."

Paul's shoulders stiffened. He braced himself; he'd get it right this time, he promised.

". . . What's the most extraordinary sight we've seen this past week? And no fair helping, anyone. That goes for you especially, Whitney."

Paul thought of a hundred things; he thought about having breakfast by candlelight so as to be a mile from camp by sunrise; he thought about the dew that covered the high grass like foam and wet you through like a wave turning you upside down at the beach. He remembered the sounds he heard in his tent at night—guinea fowl and bullfrogs, low-pitched growls, roars and whimpers—and he saw a picture of the camp, which was a circle of tents around a cook fire. Sparks flew up and out like the fireflies at home in summer.

He thought about washing in a canvas basin and being allowed to drink black coffee. He thought about sitting close to the camp fire after dinner and dozing while the men told stories, and then waking in his own cot to listen to the natives' far-off singing and the tok-tok-tok of their wood-and-bamboo drums. But he knew none of those answers was what his father wanted to hear.

"The time we saw the python swallow the waterbuck calf," Paul recited carefully.

"Good work, son. Excellent. A quick study," George chortled. "You'll have to write your grandfather about that. He'd like to hear all about it."

"Yes, Father," Paul said. He'd been told to write Grandfather Axthelm about the python and waterbuck every day since they'd seen it. "I will."

"And a picture, too! Your Grandfather A. likes pictures."

"Yes, Father." No one would like to see that poor waterbuck, Paul decided. Even in a picture.

"And now, everyone," George shouted eagerly, "back to camp. Double rations at the bar for the first man there."

Yessirree, George decided, looking around his tent; this is my world. This is the place for me. His contented gaze fell on the neat camp chest and immaculately made bed. He flopped into a chair and let the bearer pull off his hunting boots. This is the life, George thought. Out roughing it with my son, teaching him about life, death, good and evil, comradeship, and self-reliance. Things a man must know.

George remembered Jonathan Clive's words of wisdom and chortled softly.

"Sir?" The native was immediately attentive, but as a mere camp bearer he wasn't allowed to use George's title. "Bwana Khubwa" was reserved for the *neapora* headman or the beaters—not for a lowly bearer or porter. "Sir?" he repeated in his best spit-and-polish British voice.

"Nothing, nothing," George answered brusquely. No point getting into a discussion. "Just finish and get out."

"Sir." The bearer gathered the boots, holster, and "Sam Browne" for a rubdown and shine with a bit of well-worn horn.

It will keep, George thought, it will keep; it will keep. Yes, indeed. And as long as I damned well want it to. "Whiskey soda," he shouted at the retreating bearer, and threw his grass-stained, dusty legs over the white-sheeted bed and stared contentedly up at the tent's peaked roof.

Everything would keep: Eugenia, his marriage, the war against his father. George had the feeling he could close up those parts of his life as if they were possessions to be stored in a closet. They might have been rare books or ivory miniatures too fragile to expose to daily use. Treasures meant for a museum or church vault. George would lock them away till he wanted them, until the day when desire or loneliness made him need to touch the things he owned.

"It will keep," George said aloud, and involuntarily saw his father. The wily old "Turk" and his double, Master Carl; George could imagine them plotting together in Philadelphia, moving their pawns in Borneo and Manila—the figures of Beckmann, Brown, and George himself—as if they were no more than carved blocks on a square wooden board.

"Check," Carl might say.

"Mate," his father would answer. And the game would begin again.

"You must learn finesse," the Turk would murmur as he shifted the pieces. "You must learn the rules of the game, and how to use them to advantage. Remember, Carl, no one is looking over your shoulder. You have only yourself to answer to." George could imagine the conversation; he'd heard hundreds like it. Even as a young child in school, deceit had never been the issue. Achievement was all.

But what does Father, Carl, or even Beckmann know about the world? George wondered. They're old men before their time. They're numb to their senses. What do they know about setting out before dawn and walking through grass so high and wet, it soaks you to the waist? Or stalking a herd of antelope or sable, staying down low, downwind, and keeping so quiet you hardly dare breathe?

Or the thrill of bringing down a lion? How could they understand the first wide shot, the sudden charge, and the calm, almost trancelike, reloading? What would two shopworn men in a musty house overlooking the Wissahickon say about that animal's paws? Could they comprehend their size and shape or the thick, seductive claws? Could they feel the communion of staring into two dying, yellow eyes? The necessary sacrament of one life yielding to another?

George remembered his first lion. He'd been a beauty, a young male, not fully bearded but fierce as a tornado. The hunters had startled him as he'd lunched on a warthog haunch; they'd come round a stand of thorn trees and there he was, by himself, enjoying his meal as if nothing in the world held greater concern.

Oliver Smythe-Barrows had stepped aside so George could take the first shot, but he'd missed. The lion had charged while George had begun the slow, painstaking job of reloading. That one task had seemed to take all day: the bullet dropping into the chamber, the bolt thrown home, the rifle repositioned on the shoulder, and the eternity that had passed before he'd squeezed the trigger. George had felt he'd been swimming through terribly cold water, as though he'd capsized in an icy lake. And all the time the lion was roaring. It was a sound so loud, George had imagined it resounding all the way up Kilimanjaro and all the long way down.

The lion was still roaring when it fell. The earth thudded as it received the full and furious weight; the thorn trees shook; what birds had squatted there flew off squalling; and the lion had died. But not like a fish does, George thought proudly. Mammals don't lose their color and go lifeless the way marlin or tarpon do. Those creatures may look magnificent hauled up on deck, but they're very definitely dead. They give up and then they die. When you reel them in they're cold as stone.

Not a lion, though; a lion looks at you. Its pale eyes measure their final foe, and there's a moment that exists between hunter and hunted, a passing of courage and wisdom from one soul to another. I've met my match, the eyes say; all that I had is yours.

Night had fallen by the time dinner was served. With a day as busy as a safari day and the necessity of whiskey sodas and long-winded reminiscences, dinner was never announced till daylight had vanished completely. The table had been spread under the stars, though that was the only and very slight concession to camp living. Two silver candelabra tilted on a white damask cloth and pyramids of Cape oranges and apricots were mounded on filigreed plates. Enormous fruit bats raced overhead. Their movement was so marked they might have been penny rockets or shooting stars, but they had no light about them; they were as black as charcoal. Their wingspan was vast and when they swooped down, following the trail of some doomed insect, the blots they made against the bright and starry sky looked like dark holes punched there.

". . . that sable . . ."; "My bongo . . ."; ". . . the big buck we caught at the water hole . . ." The conversation never varied from night to night, though its participants would swear it did. Each animal differed from another: the way it charged, the way it ran, the way it fell, or the clever way it eluded defeat.

". . . Cape buffalo. Nothing more dangerous when you wound them, Davies. Give me a green mamba any day."

"You won't say that, Palmer, when one makes a beeline for you. Look at what happened to the cook's boy. Attacked on his way for more flour for the breakfast biscuits. Chased by a snake! What an ignominious demise. . . . At least it was quick. . . ."

"Well, you can't convince me." That was Sir Harold's voice. "A wounded lion will circle back, you know. You'll swear he's ahead and suddenly he's snapping at your heels. . . ."

"When I was in Jubaland one time . . ."

". . . the trek that took us almost to the coast . . ."

"Down near the Masai-Mara when we were tracking that old bull elephant and I didn't have . . ."

Stories told over and over, expanded, embellished, the heart of the tale as elusive as truth, as fleeting as bravery, as hard to instill as trust. Hunting stories, tracking tales, accounts of survival, cleverness, and need. George listened to them all and recounted his own while the bats zoomed through the darkness, making a mockery of any winged or beetlelike thing that moved. Tomorrow morning they'd be lodged in the trees; they'd hang upside down like desiccated leaves, but for tonight the firmament was theirs.

"But, why, James?"

"Because I don't think it's wise, Eugenia."

"But it's not so very far . . . they're only near Lake Victoria or somewhere . . . and besides, Joseph could get a top-notch guide. He told me that one of the Masai would . . . they're excellent trackers, you know . . . it wouldn't take any time at all. . . ." Eugenia rushed ahead with her argument, but she didn't dare meet Brown's eyes. She kept her head bent and studied her bed and pillow, as if she could find an answer there. Am I being unreasonable? she wondered. Is it wrong to worry about my son? Or do my fears bring problems of their own?

"Oh, Eugenia . . ." Brown said. His voice was gentle and quiet, but he couldn't comfort her, and he couldn't make her change her mind. He knew she worried about Paul, thought about him almost constantly, but it was something they could never discuss. " . . . Just imagine the difficulty of trekking all the way . . ." he began.

The difficulty, Eugenia told herself angrily. As if everything we've done in this past five days has been easy. Or wise. But she knew she could never say those words; her life with Brown was too tenuous to risk confrontation. She moved her hand to smooth the sheet. In the semidarkness her fingers looked blue.

"I only meant that, with a good guide and, well . . . it's just that he's so very little," Eugenia tried again, then hesitated. Why does this have to be a decision between two people, she thought. Why can't I have both James and my son? Why must I give up one for the other?

" . . . You know . . . with all the proper paraphernalia . . . it shouldn't take so very long . . ." Eugenia let the words trail off and stared at the copper screen shimmering in the late-night air. She wanted to return the argument to practicality; it should have nothing to do with emotion.

"I know why you want to go, Eugenia. I know how worried you are," Brown said quietly, and touched her arm. "But Smythe-Barrows is with them and he's the best there is. Besides"—Brown tried for offhanded levity—"British East Africa's a big place, and the shooting safari could be anywhere. I don't know how we'd ever find them."

Brown knew better than to mention Paul by name; he'd done it once before and the look of hurt and sorrow that had come over Eugenia's face made him wish he hadn't spoken at all.

"Remember, Victoria-Nyanza's a long way away; trekking in would be hard on the girls . . . and on you. . . . And unless I've learned nothing about you at all"—Brown tried to laugh and lifted Eugenia's hand in the air—"you'd race us all the way up to the lake only to find Smythe-Barrows, Palmer, Davies, and the whole lot cooling their heels and stacking ivory." The playful gesture failed. Brown replaced Eugenia's hand and continued in a quieter voice:

"I can't let you go, Eugenia. You know that. I'd never forgive myself if anything happened. You mean everything to me."

There it was. Said. The one thing she most wanted to hear. And the one thing that held her back. Eugenia shifted her gaze to the floor. There was something she was remembering, something a long time ago, and the way the uneven lamplight spiraled along the wooden boards almost brought it back. She was reminded of her grandmother's house back in Philadelphia and an early September day. The sycamore and poplar leaves had begun to turn yellow and the world to embark on its slow, stately drift toward winter and sleep, and each blade of ripening wheat, each seeded stalk, gave off a sense of life fulfilled, accomplished and replete. But they were waiting for something to happen, and that's what Eugenia remembered.

"I know I'm being irrational about this, James," Eugenia began again, "and I don't want to put anyone in jeopardy. . . ." The words were serious; they took a long time to form. " . . . But I thought we could make it a trek for all of us . . . you and I and the girls . . . the Du-Plessises needn't come . . . and we'd have a wonderful few days off on our own. . . .

"We could have fun at the same time as . . ." Even as she was saying it, Eugenia knew what the end of their search would find. Her greatest hope was to have Paul home, safe and sound, but that meant George, and that would put an end to her time with James.

Suddenly one of her father's warnings came into Eugenia's mind.

She couldn't remember why he'd said it or when, whether he'd been prompted by his own need or a misguided concern for her, but she remembered how horrible the words had seemed at the time. "No one's that happy, Genie," he'd said. "We mustn't expect too much out of life."

No one's that happy. Don't expect too much.

Why do our lives have to be so complicated? Eugenia wondered. She remembered how angry her father's advice had made her, how she'd railed inwardly and refused to listen. Why can't people be happy? she'd asked herself. Why can't they fall in love, have children, love them and each other, too? Why can't families be whole and strong? But as she pondered those questions in her room in the *ketito,* she realized it wasn't that simple. Whether you liked it or not, life was filled with decisions: "If you are unhappy here, you can either remain here, or you can move to a new place, which you do of your own free election. . . ."

"It's not that I don't love you," Eugenia said finally. And it's not that I love my son more; those words hung in the air between them, unspoken and far more potent for being denied.

Lieutenant Brown didn't answer. He knew what she was thinking, but there was nothing to say. He wasn't the father of her children; he wasn't her husband. He knew Eugenia had to struggle with her fears and hopes alone, that no amount of care or love should lift that power from her. "Why don't we go to sleep," he said. "Morning will be here before you know it."

"Well, what shall we do today?" Eugenia was determined to put aside last night's confusion; she forced a cheery voice as she rolled back the mosquito netting and looked at the streaks the red sun had shot into the sky.

"Red sky at night . . ." she added as she turned to look at Brown's face. "I suppose in the Navy you follow more technical weather predictions." She traced a shadow across his shoulder and down his arm and tried to smile.

"Red sky at night," Brown repeated, "sailor's delight."

They both smiled at that, though neither laughed. At another time, they might have, but they still felt a strain from the night before.

"Red sky in morning—" Brown recited.

"I suppose you'd better go," Eugenia interrupted; her voice was quiet. She hated to have him leave. If just once, she told herself angrily, if just once he could stay till the sun is in the sky. We could scramble out of bed, wash, talk about nothing, find our clothes and laugh and try to set the bed aright. Nothing's fair, Eugenia decided. I can't have

Paul and now here I am spoiling my few moments alone with James. "Sailors take warning," she announced bitterly, and turned her face to the pillow.

But Brown was already up, already dressing. He was late this morning and he knew it. Time was wasting; he couldn't risk being seen. And his discussion with Eugenia would go no further. There were parts of their lives no one could change.

Eugenia heard the careful rustle of Brown pulling on his clothes, but she didn't look up. His self-discipline filled her with jealous fury. It seemed so easy for him to turn away and leave. So easy to jump out of bed and close the door. I suppose this is what our love-making finally comes to, she decided, fueling her anger: Familiarity breeds contempt.

"I'll see you at breakfast," Brown whispered from the door, and Eugenia told herself: I'll call him back, tell him how much I love him. We'll lie in this bed and forget the world. I won't worry and I won't be mean. But Brown was already gone.

By the time Eugenia, Brown, and the girls arrived at the kraal that morning, the *syces* were already saddling the horses. Nero, the fat little pony who was Jinx's mount, was the first ready. Jinx jumped up without waiting for the others; her *syce* looked dismayed, but she could tell this was only a game. She knew all the servants liked her family; she heard it in the way they shouted, "Yah, missy!" when she walked the compound with Lizzie, and she saw it in their smiles.

To Jinx, living at the *ketito* was like having your favorite dream come true. Everyone was happy; nothing went wrong, and no single foolhardy or forgetful person ever got cross. Jinx wished Paul were with them to share the good time; she would have liked to watch his pranks and listen to his stories, but she also sensed, somewhere deep inside her, that her mother was happier with Father away. Or maybe it was just because Lieutenant Brown was with them, and he was so much fun.

"I'm up first!" Jinx shouted at the top of her lungs. "I win the prize. Too bad, Liz! You'll have to be my vassal today."

"Now, I thought, Miss Jinx, that the prize had something to do with helping saddle Nero yourself. It seems to me he was already dressed when we got down." Lieutenant Brown tightened the girth of his own mount and looked over at Eugenia. Nothing would spoil his pleasure in the moment. Life was built on such small things; you had to take them where you found them. He watched Eugenia and smiled. They couldn't change the way the world worked, but they could be happy today.

"Oh," Jinx laughed, "you changed the rules again." But she knew he
hadn't. It was just so much fun to tease. She spun her pony in a preen-
ing circle to show off how very smart she looked. And how well, in this
one week, she'd learned to ride. And it wasn't even sidesaddle like
they'd been supposed to learn at home. What a treat!

Eugenia stood beside the kraal gate and watched James and her
daughter. She forgot the "I wishes" and the "what ifs," and allowed
herself to feel the sun on her arms and face and back. Be happy for the
moment, she told herself; this time is all you have. And her smile grew
so strong and sure it could have encompassed the whole earth.

Then Mrs. DuPlessis rolled down the hill toward them. It was the
same routine every morning: Mrs. DuPlessis with the faithful Joseph
dogging her heels.

"Eugenia," she'd wheeze, weaving toward them, "I don't know why
you have to start out so early. Why, the children have barely enough
time to digest their porridge before you all go jouncing off. . ."

And Eugenia would try not to laugh; she'd try to show attentive concern. "But it's not early. The sun's already high in the sky."

But every morning, Mrs. DuPlessis's response would be the same: "I
just don't think it's safe. And I feel responsible to your husband. I know
you've faith in Lieutenant Brown, but I think an older and wiser . . ."

It was at that moment that Dr. DuPlessis invariably arrived on the
scene. "Morning, Eugenia! Brown!" he'd call from the hilltop.

"Morning" was always the enthusiastic response from the kraal. It
was the closest thing to family happiness Eugenia had ever known.

Every morning she and Brown and the girls set out for their ride
while the older couple fussed and worried: Mrs. DuPlessis, an old
mother hen whose yard has suddenly emptied, and Dr. DuPlessis, the
good husband and kind man he'd always been.

"I only wanted to make certain . . ." Mrs. DuPlessis would murmur,
finally puffing back up the hill to sit beside her husband. "I didn't
mean to intrude . . ."

"I know, dear, I know," Dr. DuPlessis would repeat over and over as
they settled themselves to watch the expedition depart.

"We'll bring you back some swamp mallows," Eugenia might call.
"The pink ones, Mrs. D."

Or the girls might shout, "And an orange butterfly if we can catch
it." Morning after slow-paced morning.

"Take care of them, my lad" were always the doctor's final words.

What magic times those were. Jinx knew she'd remember them forever.
And what a lot of things she saw and learned! There were baobob trees

whose trunks were thick enough to hide a mother elephant, mimosa trees with spiky branches, kangaroo grasses, and Mann's heath, and each day brought a new discovery. Kangaroo grass could mean lions nearby; Mann's heath hid puff adder snakes.

There were secretary birds and bustards, weavers and guinea fowl; Lieutenant Brown taught Jinx and Lizzie what to look for as they rode along. There were Thompson gazelles that quivered like water spaniels, dik-dik that jumped like crickets, and oryx with wavy, black horns. The birds and animals of the place seemed like brothers and sisters to Jinx. Stretching high in her saddle, she watched their unhurried flight as if she were racing with them, as if she had tiny hooves that bounded over the plain, or as if she'd taken wing and were circling above, beyond, and away, calling: "Farewell. I am leaving you. Farewell."

"Are you happy, my darling?" Eugenia asked as she pulled at a fig stem with her teeth. The picnic lunch was finished and the big rug empty except for Brown and Eugenia. The girls were off climbing a small outcrop of rocks under the watchful eyes of their *syces;* Eugenia could see them, but they were too far away to hear. She waved happily, then looked back at Brown, dangling the fig the way a puppy would a toy.

"Yes. I am," he said. "Very happy." And he snatched at the fruit.

"Too slow," Eugenia laughed, and rolled away. It felt so wonderful to be alive. The sun and blue sky, the brown grass, green grass, thorn trees, and brambles, even the hot midday wind, felt full of joy. "Do you know why I like figs so much, James?" Eugenia teased as she lay on the rug. "I like the way the seeds feel on my tongue."

Brown laughed. "That's quite a remark for a well-brought-up lady," he said. "I guess I haven't been a very good influence. And you've finished the whole plateful on top of it!"

"So I have." Eugenia laughed again and picked up the plate. There were drops of water where the figs had stood; the drops glistened in the light, each one its own complete world. When Eugenia tilted the plate the drops ran together, but when she put it down they separated and turned as round as moons.

"Tell me about Harlan Parish again," she said. "Where you grew up. Tell me about the plantation and what happened after the old slavery days. I love to hear you talk. I love how your face moves and the way the sun circles your head and how your eyes go back and forth, seeing something near and then very far away."

"It sounds as if you're doing a lot of looking and not much listening." If they'd been alone and there'd been no bearers, *syces,* or children, he would have stretched out beside her on the rug. He would have had one hand under her jacket and another under her back. That picture was all he could think of now.

"Oh, but I am, James. I remember everything you tell me. Now, go on. I'm all ready. Comfy and lying down." Eugenia laughed again. "Just where you'd like to be, I'll bet." Her words and laughter were low in her throat. It hardly mattered what she said. Eugenia turned her head; if only his face were next to mine, she thought, how happy I'd be.

The stories Eugenia loved were the ones Brown dreaded: the fabricated history of his imagined past. All he could do was recite events in other people's lives. He'd talk about the boy who'd ridden by his own father's dusty farm, and he'd become that other boy. He'd feel the smooth leather of the English saddle; he'd feel the thoroughbred's neck muscles as it took one jump, then another, and he'd imagine what it must have been like to be that young man arriving home, carelessly handing his horse to one liveried servant while he called for another to wipe down his boots and another to bring a glass of chilled punch.

His invented years at the Naval Academy were more difficult. When Eugenia asked those questions Brown turned them aside saying it was a time he didn't like to remember. Whatever Eugenia inferred from those remarks made her thoughtful and often sad. Brown didn't like to see her unhappy; he didn't know what she was imagining, but he felt he had no other choice.

"Tell me about your aunt and uncle again and your tutor and how unhappy all the servants were to see you leave for Annapolis. And how your old black mammy cried," Eugenia said now, and pulled out a long grass stem and waved it in the spattering light, turning it around and around till it seemed to glow with heat. Then she suddenly looked into Brown's eyes. "I'm so sorry, you know, James, thinking about your real mother. I wish . . . I . . . ."

Eugenia stared up through the acacia branches at the flashing sky. There was something about children losing mothers and mothers losing children that was too painful to mention. "No," she said, forcing a smile, "not how everyone cried. Tell about the nights. When you were little. When you'd creep out of your window and climb over the roof and shimmy down the white oak to listen to the darkies singing. I love those stories."

Every day the stories followed a different path and Eugenia memorized them all, as if she could make up in concentration and desire what she'd lost in time. And every day, they'd be interrupted; Jinx or Lizzie would come running back to demand they come quick. Some new wonder had been discovered; there was something marvelous to see. But the interruptions were part of being a family; they only brought Eugenia and Brown closer.

"Aren't you two ready to leave yet?" Jinx might demand, throwing herself onto the rug, while the once reserved Lizzie would shriek with delight: "Don't tickle me. I won't sit still if you do!"

The long mornings and afternoons grew together, but each moment was as complete and easily remembered as a moment in a dream.

Then they were in the saddle again, traveling the long way home, watching the shadows stretch before them like taffy pulled out warm and wet. Jinx listened to the gentle swish-swish of her pony's tail slapping flies; she listened to the tap, whistle, tap of grass grazing Nero's wide belly and she listened to the slow, whinnying breaths that were each horse's language. She wondered what they were saying: if they were discussing the day or their riders, if one was commenting on a particularly fine patch of greenery while another complained about the size of the shardlike stones.

"Well, she's not so bad," Nero might be saying. "She's light, but forgetful. Sometimes my mouth goes all . . .'"

"Pay her no mind, that's what I do." That would be Lizzie's pony interrupting in its usual bossy manner: "Doze off, daydream. . . . Think about oats and barley. . . ."

"Who's going to watch out for lions then, smarty?" Mother's mare was a terrible worrier; its whinny wavered with concern. "That's what I'd like to know. . . ."

Then Lieutenant Brown's gelding would answer with an assertive: "Stop all the bellyaching! People watch out for lions!"

And that remark, repeated over and over like the tale end of a joke, would draw such a guffaw from all the animals that they'd stop right where they were, shake themselves, wiggle their heads, and snort and neigh as if nothing in the world had ever been so absurdly funny. At least that was what Jinx imagined as they plodded their way homeward.

And there was music, too; Jinx heard it singing in the long grass:

Schlaf, Kindlein, schlaf,
Der Vater hütt die Schaf,
Die Mutter schüttelt's Baumelein,
da fallt herab ein Traümelein,
Schlaf, Kindlein, schlaf. . . .

It was a nursery song from Jinx's baby days, and the tune was repeated by the wind, by her pony's feet and the gentle creak of her stirrups. Over and over and over again, clear as anything, clear as iced water, or dewdrops sitting in the sunlight: *"Schlaf, Kindlein, schlaf . . ."*

> Sleep, baby, sleep,
> Thy father watches the sheep,
> Thy mother shakes the dreamland tree,
> And down fall little dreams to thee . . .

Jinx sang along while the animals on the distant plains grew big as buttons, then small as pinpricks. A cloud would scud over a hilltop and the grazing zebra or impala in its path would become dark as night, then the cloud would move on and the grass and striped bodies would appear brighter, shinier, and happier than ever before.

Those were the days at the *ketito* near Nairobi when Eugenia and the girls, Lieutenant Brown, and the DuPlessises waited for George's return. They were routine and simple: each person with a life all his own, and they seemed, each one, to have lived within their small world forever. The mornings existed within the family of Eugenia and Brown; the afternoons and evenings belonged to the DuPlessises, the new-crowned grandparents, those specialists at games and stories. Dr. Du-Plessis remembered everything, Mrs. DuPlessis, nothing. Lizzie and Jinx vied with each other over who would follow her lead at "Kitty-on-the-Corner" or "Memory," while Dr. DuPlessis sat by the fire and told tales that took their breath away.

Those were the days when time hesitated, drew back, and finally blew away altogether. The nights were a different thing; the nights belonged to Eugenia and Brown.

"Did you ever memorize any poetry at the Academy?" Eugenia was serious and quiet. She watched James take off his jacket, but her thoughts were a long way away.

"Not that I remember," he answered, trying to toss aside the question. He moved to turn down the wick in the dressing table lamp, then slid off his trousers and folded them carefully over the bench.

"No, really? None at all?" Eugenia was horrified. She unloosed her sash and skirt band without thinking, then started on the buttons of her blouse. "What did you learn?"

"It's a naval academy, Eugenia. Not a school for poets."

"Hmm," Eugenia said, frowning. She dropped her blouse on a chair, "None at all?"

Brown laughed and walked toward her. "None," he said, and untied the ribbons on her chemise. "I know some limericks, but I don't think they're what you're looking for." The chemise fell on the floor.

"Oh, it's driving me batty," Eugenia burst out suddenly, back in the room, aware of James beside her and how comforting and warm his hands felt. "It's a poem by Robert Browning . . ." she admitted, ". . . and I know this is no time . . . that I'm not being a bit romantic, but . . ."

"Well, you might as well tell me what it is," he said, kissing her neck. "We can't have you concentrating on the wrong things."

But Eugenia hardly heard him; her thoughts had started to wander again. She ran her fingers along Brown's shoulders and chest, but her fingers moved of their own volition and the messages of love and safety they sent to her brain were nearly overlooked. Her mind was busy; romance would have to wait.

"It's about Napoleon," Eugenia said finally, "and a battle at a place called Ratisbon."

"You're right." Brown was smiling down at her, watching the streaks of concern spread across her face. "That's not romantic—"

"It's not the war part I'm worrying over, James," Eugenia interrupted. "It's a line somewhere . . . near the end, I suppose . . . and I can't remember . . . something. . . . Something about this boy who came to report on the battle . . . and he was . . . or he said . . . But that's the part I've lost. . . .

"Oh, really"—Eugenia stopped herself and laughed—"how do you put up with me, James?" And she wrapped her hands around his neck and held his shoulders tight and looked up into his bright blue eyes.

"There's something in the end of the poem that seems like an omen or a warning and I feel . . . well . . . I knew the ending once, but now I've forgotten it. . . .

"You know. It's like waking up from a dream in which you were a different person, living in another place, speaking a different language. And in that moment before you come fully awake, you say to yourself: 'I knew I could speak Urdu all along.' "

"Urdu, Eugenia?" Brown laughed and pushed her hair back from her neck.

"Swahili, Farsi. You know what I mean. Something tremendously exotic and difficult."

"I don't suppose Farsi is that difficult for Farsi babies." Brown stroked Eugenia's hair from her forehead in a rhythmic, gentle gesture. "Or for Farsi mothers, either."

Brown's hands made Eugenia feel warm and peaceful. "You never take me seriously." She tried to protest, though her worries seemed suddenly far away, as unimportant as specks of dust curling in a sunny corner. "I love the way you do that," she said finally, while he continued to caress her face, her throat, her shoulders, and gently untie the strings of her cambric petticoat.

Eugenia leaned into his body; she kissed his neck, his fingertips, his ears, his lips, lingering over each with a silent breath as if there were a tiny being there, someone to keep warm and alive and safe. And it seemed to her, standing on the fire-lit floor, that their two bodies, hers and Brown's, had created a new life together and that they moved as one creature like the water, sweeping aside fear or confusion as if it was no more than chaff riding the tides.

Your skin is warm, one body said. *And yours is hard,* the other answered: *Here where I stroke my hand, it's as hot as a heated stone.* The bodies grew slippery and wet; they slipped though the sheets, slid apart and around, over and in, again and again, and Eugenia thought that everything she did, that everything she tasted or felt, were new and quite different than before. There was no hesitation, because this person was no stranger but a part of herself, and she knew that she and James had created something strong and inviolable. They'd become one soul.

"Touch me here," Eugenia said. "And here and here." Salt water seemed to pour from every part of her and her breasts grew as full and heavy as breasts filled with milk.

"And here," she said, "and I will . . . Oh, James." Eugenia sighed and threw her head back and then up. The bedstead made a dark bridge on the wall while above it, streaking upward in strips of thin gold, were the reflecting and shadowy lights of the lamp. They danced like djinns and afriti toward the ceiling and beams. They circled the room like the drawings in a nursery tale. They were silver and copper; they were all shine and gloss and they flew above her head as lightly as down. "James," Eugenia murmured. "Oh, James."

E I G H T E E N

INX NEVER FORGOT the sight of her mother falling. It happened so quick. They'd been riding along, happy as punch, pulling pranks on each other, waving foxtail grass over each other's heads, when her mother had suddenly asked, "Who wants to race to the top or the hill. James? Liz? Jinx?" And before anyone could answer she was off, laughing back over her shoulder, as she whipped her horse to a canter and then into a full gallop.

She scrambled up the hill, leaning forward so she looked as if she'd become part of the horse, while her skirt swept back in a swirl like rain down a mountainside. It was a beautiful sight and Jinx would remember, through the rest of her long life, how envious she'd been, how she'd thought there'd never be anyone to equal her mother, and how unfair that had seemed on a cloudless, African day.

But then the terrible thing happened—a loose stone or the rustle of a snake, a whir of two tiny wings—something frightened the horse, made it leap sideways, while her mother, as if she had wings, blew on toward the crest of the hill. The fall took forever; it seemed as if Eugenia would not, or could not, come down, but would fly on and on till she reached a soft and welcoming patch of sun-strewn ground.

Jinx and Lizzie and Lieutenant Brown watched; they were glued to the spot. Then Lieutenant Brown kicked up his horse, told the girls to stay put, and raced across the plain. First Lizzie and then Jinx ignored the order, and they whipped their horses and bent low in the saddle while their mother continued to dance through the air.

She looked like a bath towel tossed from a seawall or a sheet tangling on a windy line. She looked anything but real. But Jinx knew as she pushed her pony faster and faster again that her mother was real, that it hurt to fall, and, with each breath of her small, panting body, she remembered that people can die when they fall from horses or that their bodies can be so badly broken they never move again.

"Mother! Oh, Mother. Oh, Mother," Jinx cried, but her words disappeared in the thudding of hooves and the warnings whistled by the sinister wind.

Eugenia's eyes were fixed on the crest of the hill, so when the horse stumbled and she started to slip from the saddle she couldn't, at first, understand what had happened. They'd been going along so well, racing toward a grassy spot of open ground, but then, suddenly, here she was flying on alone. It took a long time for her to realize she'd been thrown. The thorn trees dotting the ridge looked the same; the scrub brush still stood in a clumpy circle, and the sunlight still glared through the spindly leaves.

Then the shadows began to look different, slanted at a different angle, and Eugenia knew she was falling. I must tuck in my head, she told herself. I must roll when I hit. I must avoid that stone and that bush. The ground came nearer and nearer, and in spite of her good intentions, she stretched out her arms and threw her head back as if waiting for a loving embrace.

Lieutenant Brown watched Eugenia hit the ground. His horse was already climbing the ridge and the girls were right behind him. "Mother!" he heard one of them scream, but he didn't have time to stop. Eugenia fell in a heap like a sack full of rags tossed in an alley and then lay completely still.

The sound was the loudest Eugenia had ever heard. She expected swallows to start up in screeching black clouds or for rocks to tumble from the distant hills; she expected the earth to shake. But it was only the noise of her own body striking the ground, after all.

She lay huddled and motionless, and at first the air was quiet; not an ant crept through the grass, and then, all of a sudden, there was commotion everywhere. James stood beside her. She saw his boots; they were streaked with dust and horse spittle. He knelt close and she saw his face. She felt his hands on her neck. Please don't move me, she wanted to say, but couldn't.

Then she saw Lizzie throw herself on the grass; her riding skirt rose like a meringue gone lopsided and tough. "She'll be all right, won't she, Lieutenant Brown?" Lizzie shouted. "She won't die?"

"She can't!" Jinx screamed, and started to race back and forth at her mother's feet. Eugenia couldn't see her daughter's skirt, but she could feel it swishing against her boots. Jinx ran one way, then another, worrying the ground with each step as if fierceness alone were enough to raise the dead.

"Memsahib is . . . ?" the head *syce* asked while the two bearers began to wail. The sounds they made were like notes played on a reedy flute and Eugenia wondered as she lay there, listening, where they'd found the instruments. They hadn't been in the packs, but this was Africa, she reminded herself. Mysteries lurk behind every bush; one must always be prepared to meet a devil or an angel.

"Eugenia?" James asked. "Can you hear me?" He looked into her eyes and lightly touched her brow.

"Yes," she wanted to answer. "I can. I'm fine." But she couldn't. It was like being in a dream she couldn't escape.

"*Syce*, fetch the doctor and the wagon. Tell him the Memsahib may have broken her neck."

"No, no, no," Eugenia wanted to shout. "You mustn't say that. I'm fine . . . I couldn't have . . . Really . . . I'm fine . . ." But her neck couldn't or wouldn't turn and her body refused to budge; it lay where it was, numb and dull as stone. Eugenia closed her eyes; she felt sleepy all of a sudden, as sleepy as a baby; she couldn't stay awake one second longer.

"Look! She's dying!" Lizzie shrieked. The bearers' noise grew frenzied and frantic. The grass rattled and seemed to pop, the dirt creaked, and the stones sounded as if they'd snapped in two.

"Mother, oh, Mother!" Jinx cried out.

Eugenia lay at rest in the midst of her dream. She was a very small child standing in a dark hall. There were bunches of flowers everywhere, pink ones and yellow, white and a ghoulish purple. The clock was striking and the curtains were drawn, and from behind the closed door of her father's study, she heard voices huddling and whispering together. They belonged to her aunts and grandmother, to her distant uncles and elderly cousins, but her father's was not among them. Her father was still upstairs. Then the door opened and her aunt Louisa', not Sally Van, came out to fetch her. Aunt Sally Van sat inside next to Grandmother Paine. They wore tall black hats with shiny feathers, which they'd wrapped in musty veils, and Eugenia could hardly tell which lady was which.

"Come here, dear," Grandmother Paine finally said. "I have some rather unfortunate news."

George came awake with a start. They'd been shooting all morning without bothering to return to camp. Their picnic luncheon had been late, and he and the others had slid from their saddles and collapsed on their rugs and blankets without even bothering to remove their kits or wash up. Poor show, George told himself as he looked at the remnants of drying cheese rinds and an overturned bottle of claret.

Smythe-Barrows was stretched out with his helmet covering his head; Sir Harold's pink face had slipped into a patch of sunlight while his mouth gaped wide open and snored. Whitney had attempted a comfortable position but had only succeeded in looking more dead to the world, and Paul was curled at his father's feet like a puppy.

Got to get a move on, George decided as he struggled to sit up. Got to get back to the *ketito*. "*Neapora!*" he shouted, then reminded himself: No, no. We're not going back to the *ketito* yet. We've got a couple of days still on safari. No point in racing back to Beckmann's infernal schedule. We'll hang about Victoria-Nyanza a while longer. I promised myself we'd bag another rhino, not jump on to Borneo or wherever this little game of Father's is to be played out.

"*Neapora!*" George shouted again. Below the small rise the bearers were moving about like a steady stream of ants, each proceeding with its own appointed task. The pack animals were ready, the boxes and baskets stowed. The lunch things had been washed up and repacked. George had only to wake his companions and they'd set off again. They might continue toward the spring they'd seen yesterday. There'd been a multitude of tracks visible in the mud, but it had been the wrong time of day. If they hurried, they'd make it just before dusk.

"*Neapora!*"

"What's up, old man?" a sleepy voice asked.

"George?" called another.

"Father?" Paul twitched and hid his face in his hands.

"Yes, Bwana Khubwa?" The *neapora* stood near George's shoulder. "We are ready for the sirs," he said slowly and distinctly. "We travel to Victoria Falls?"

"I've changed my mind," George announced, without realizing he had. "We'll go back to the *ketito*. To Nairobi," he added loudly because the *neapora* only stood and stared.

"Nairobi!" the others groaned, stirring themselves into action.

"But, I thought . . ." Sir Harold began.

"Isn't . . . ?" Whitney faltered.

Smythe-Barrows didn't say another word. He watched George and sat very still.

"I've changed my mind," George answered gruffly. He couldn't have begun to say why. He could never say the idea came in his sleep; omens and portents were patently absurd.

"I've changed my mind," he repeated evenly. "It's as simple as that. Now let's get a bloody move on."

When she woke again Eugenia was in her own bed in the *ketito* and both Dr. and Mrs. DuPlessis were bending anxiously over her. Eugenia could tell Mrs. DuPlessis was very frightened; her breath came in short, irregular gasps.

"Sit down, my dear" were the first words Eugenia heard. "You'll do her no good if you faint."

Mrs. DuPlessis sat without a murmur; this was no time to argue.

"Can you hear me, Eugenia?" Dr. DuPlessis said.

"Yes," Eugenia wanted to answer, but the word seemed too long and difficult to form. She had time to think as she worked on the sound. She thought about Paul's bedroom at home and the way morning light filled the room. She could see a row of velveteen animals on the windowsill; they looked like people taking the air on a summer's porch. She could see a tiny refraction in a bubbly windowpane; it made a thin rainbow that leapt over the chair and onto the bed. Then she heard birds singing and saw a swallow attempting to build a nest under the eaves. The room was bright, and the children were what? Two and seven and . . . or three and eight or . . . ?

"Mmmm . . ." Eugenia finally managed, and opened her eyes.

"Praise God!" Mrs. DuPlessis gasped. "She's alive."

"We always knew she was alive, Jane," Dr. DuPlessis gently reminded his wife. "Didn't we, Eugenia?" He patted her hand. "How are we feeling? Any broken bones?"

"Mmmm . . ." Eugenia tried to shake her head.

"Just a joke, my dear. There's nothing broken. How's the head feeling?"

"Awful!" Eugenia laughed suddenly. The sound of her own voice was strange; it was as if someone else had spoken. But she knew it was hers and that the comforting, silent world was a thing of the past.

"That was quite a nasty fall you took. You gave us all a scare." Dr. DuPlessis smiled while his wife sang out, "I just knew you'd pull through! Praise God!" Then she bustled, "I'll get the girls. They'll be so pleased!"

"Why don't you wait a bit, Jane," Dr. DuPlessis warned quietly. "Give Eugenia a chance to get her strength." But hearing the disappointment in his wife's creaking corset, he added, "No, tell them their mother's fine, if you'd like. That she'll be up and around in no time. And then you can all break into that last tin of licorice whips.

"Jane will have your girls spoiled for good if you're not up soon, Eugenia," Dr. DuPlessis added, winking at his patient.

"I don't spoil them, Gustav. You know I don't. The poor little things were just so frightened about their mother that I just had to . . ."

"I know, dear. I know. Hurry along now. The girls are waiting."

Dr. DuPlessis watched his wife leave. Eugenia thought he was about to say something else, but he stood up and said only, "A mild concussion, that's all. That and the wind knocked out of you."

"Where's James," Eugenia wanted to ask but couldn't. Her eyes wandered the room; she saw everything, saw the chair on which James had dropped his jacket and the bench where he'd left his boots. She moved her hand slowly across the sheet, searching for comfort.

As if Dr. DuPlessis had read her mind, he said, "Your Lieutenant Brown's gone to Nairobi to find out about the train. He feels it would be better to have you back on the yacht as soon as possible." Then Dr. DuPlessis looked down at her, picked up his bag from the table, and started slowly from the room.

"Call me if you need me, Eugenia," he said finally. "I'm always nearby. Whatever you want to tell me."

Eugenia watched him leave. She wanted to return to her silent world; she wanted James with her; she wanted him in bed beside her; and then she wanted to be off on a gallop with the children. All the children, not just the girls. All of them. Eugenia turned her head to the pillow. It hurt to move, but the pillow smelled comforting and warm; it smelled of James's body and her own. It smelled of grass and fields and yellow wheat.

"I have something rather sad to tell you, Eugenia," her grandmother had said. "But I want you to be a brave girl."

Eugenia awoke with a start. The dream was too awful to remember, too awful to consider. She reached for the lamp at her bedside, but the thing wouldn't light. The punk was too wet or the wick too short. She dashed her hand against the table with her efforts, and then stared into the dark night lying at her feet.

Something so cruel she couldn't even name it had been in the room. Something with a pointed face and eyes as dead as wet stones. Eugenia wanted to cry, but she knew the thing was still watching. She pulled the sheet around her shoulders, stretched her legs as stiff as two sticks, and waited.

What was it? she wondered. She'd been dreaming about Paul. But Paul had been a rabbit or a kitten, something white and small that mewed pitifully and lay curled on a forest path. She'd bent down to pick it up, the kitten or rabbit, but its mouth was filled with blood, and she knew there was nothing she could do. Then she'd become a small white thing herself, lying on a city ledge, clawing at a window. Then she'd fallen to her death.

It was the fall that woke her. But as she was landing or waking or dying she had another clear vision of Paul. Paul in his little serge sailor suit, surrounded by natives, gunbearers, porters. They were in a clearing somewhere and the vegetation was the green of a deep jungle. There was banana frond and bird of paradise and Paul had started to run when he'd caught sight of his mother. They were the last steps he took.

Eugenia shut her eyes tight. I will make this terrible thing happen, she warned herself. It was only a dream; it was nothing more. Eugenia struggled to sit up, but her head hurt mightily and she felt so suddenly nauseated she was forced to lie back down.

Dawn will be coming soon, she decided. The camp will start stirring; I'll get Joseph and we'll make plans. It won't take so very much to organize another trek. We'll find George near Victoria-Nyanza or somewhere. Somewhere out there. Joseph will know. I'll take the girls, Eugenia told herself; we'll see Victoria Falls. They can ride; we'll bring the *syces;* I'll have to lie in the cart, of course, but James can . . . James can . . .

It was that name that undid her, that made her stop in the middle of her recitation and wrap herself so tightly in her own cold arms that she began to weep. Eugenia opened her mouth and thought she might be screaming. But no matter how many hot tears poured from her throat or how fiercely she clenched her eyes she couldn't erase the memory of her son's small body falling amid the plantain leaves. The leaves dripped; the trickle became a stream; the ground swelled into a spongy mass that turned blood-black while the stream crashed on through the clearing to fall to an ocean very far away.

"Oh Mother," she cried, "oh Mother, oh Mother. Oh James."

*T*HE GOOD OLD *S.Y.*
A L C E D O   *A G A I N*, George thought. Thank God. And about to set sail, too. Thank you, God, a second time. George hustled across his study, taking solace in the rows of bookshelves standing at parade-ground attention, the desk in apple pie order, the paperweights, the paneled walls and coffered ceiling: the feel and heft and consoling delight of mahogany and marble, burnished brass, scribed leather, and honest, big-as-life, spit-and-polish, unstinting American labor. Thank God, George kept repeating. Thank the good, good Lord. Near disaster, that little episode with Genie. A man can't be too careful, when it comes to his family. A man can't be vigilant enough. George looked around the room. "Yes, sir," he said aloud, "can't be careful enough. A family's a family. No replacing it, no indeedy."

From the wheelhouse came the high, thin whistle that was Captain Cosby's response to the harbormaster's all-clear signal. Better and better, George decided. That means the recoaling's completed, the fire-room gang's been rounded up, and the last of the dignitaries have been shuffled through the main saloon and back to the muddy streets of Mombasa. George could imagine their slithery, gray fingers, mold-spotted calling cards, and ingratiating "So sorry . . . Such a terrible shame about Madame's unfortunate accident. . . ."

In one ear, George told himself, and out the other. You put your right hand in. You put your right hand out. You put your right hand in and you shake it all about. . . . You do the hokey-pokey and you turn yourself around. . . .

"That's what it's all about!" George sang out the last line of the school yard song. He was in a rip-roaring mood. He was loaded for bear, happy as a pig in a freshwater pool.

"Next stop, the Seychelles Islands," he nearly shouted, "and this time nothing's going to stand in my way. This time I'm playing it safe, and as close to the vest as it comes. No one threatens George Axthelm's little brood while he draws a breath!" George liked the sound of his own voice. It had an authoritarian air like an all-men social gathering or the hallowed halls of privilege and wealth. It sounded like Philadelphia.

"And this little volume, too," George said as he picked up a book from his desk. "Damn lucky to find it on such short notice. And in Mombasa, too, of all places. Genie will be really tickled."

George traced the tiny gold ostrich embossed on the book's spine. "*The Story of an African Farm,* by Ralph Iron," he chuckled loudly. "Alias Olive Screiner, Dutch descendant, South African resident and London literary lion. Or lioness . . . as it were . . . Genie'll be better in no time. Just wait and see."

George imagined his wife in her deck chair, her long skirts arranged under a summer blanket, her hat tied with a gauzy veil, and the book, his gift, his humble offering, clasped in her excited fingers. "Oh, George!" she'd say. "How did you ever manage to find this? Why, I didn't think Mombasa even boasted a bookseller, let alone one dispensing such a questionable title!"

And the way she'd say "questionable" would show how perfect his gesture had been and how perfectly understood. "Not in a million years would I imagine your approving my reading a book like this! Not after all that gossip back home."

And George would answer, "Whatever gives you pleasure, my dear . . ." and let the rest of the sentence trail off because mystery can be quite seductive as hell.

"Whatever puts the roses back in my little wife's lovely cheeks," George echoed as he glanced at his desk, smiled, and ran his hands through his hair. Forty-two, he thought, I'm only forty-two; I've got a lifetime of marriage before me. "Your lovely cheeks . . ." he repeated.

George had the bad luck to speak those words aloud just as Beckmann opened the door. George hadn't heard the knock—if there'd been one. He'd been too engrossed in his daydream.

"Nice of you to care, George," Beckmann said. The joke lay like a lump. There was no mirth in Beckmann's eyes. "I didn't realize how pasty-faced I looked till all of you came galloping in from the veldt. The life of one of your father's faithful followers is never a party. Not for me the solar topee and twill riding britches, the picnic spread on the high plains grass."

"My wife is ill, Ogden. I'll thank you to remember that." George knew the phrases sounded automatic, that they gave him away as someone who's been caught with his mind where it shouldn't be.

"Oh, I do remember, George. I was there at the station when you came flying home," Beckmann answered. He was about to add, "With your tail between your legs," but thought better of it. George had enough problems at the moment, Beckmann decided, and if there was one thing he'd learned from his many years doing the Turk's dirty work, it was that even a weak man turns belligerent when cornered. A direct accusation can be lied to—it can be bullied, bluffed, and forgotten—but a suggestion rubs like a stone.

"I was the one who brought the carriages and the enclosed landau for our invalid." Beckmann was smiling. "Though I regret to say that I was not the stalwart lad who came roaring in from the bush, demanding the ship be prepared for the lady's arrival, ordering up a nursing station and restocked medicine chest. So sporting of Lieutenant Brown to do all of that for you, George. A man of action at all times."

George turned away from Beckmann and looked out the window. The harbor bristled with activity. Black-skinned people like so many spawning shad, skin, teeth, white-flecked fingernails, pink palms, and loose-jointed arms and shoulders wriggling in the sun: the sight made George sick. The light hurt his eyes and the movement caused his head to spin. For a few delicious moments he'd been returned to the comforts of Philadelphia; now he was back on his boat, a man lost in uncharted waters. George let the curtain fall shut. The African dust fell out in the air. The stewards aren't doing their jobs, he thought, but he knew he wouldn't reprimand them.

"You needed to see me, Ogden?" George returned to the room. It had taken on an entirely different personality; it might have been the reading room in a public library or a hotel lobby in a northern city.

"As I matter of fact, I did, George." Beckmann eased himself into a chair and reached for a cigar. He knew how to take his time.

"This may seem an inappropriate moment to discuss business—with your wife convalescing—but I assure you Eugenia's well cared for, and I seriously doubt you could get near her cabin anyway, what with the DuPlessises and young Lieutenant Brown swarming about night and day. I hope I merit such an exemplary nursing staff—even for a mild concussion." Beckmann studied his cigar, lit it, and inhaled deeply. It seemed as if the enjoyment of his first puff of smoke were the only thought in Beckmann's mind.

George knew better. "Say what you have to say, Ogden. I want to be on deck when we cast off. Cosby's already been given the all clear. I don't have all day."

"Indeed you don't, George," Beckmann answered. "The owner of a yacht is a very busy fellow."

George didn't bother to respond. He let the insult settle where it fell. There's a lot more where that one came from, he thought, no point in chasing down each one. George felt weary suddenly, enervated and limp. The picture of himself and Eugenia was flickering fainter and fainter.

"You interrupted with what I assumed to be important business, Ogden. Shouldn't we be discussing that and not my wife's malady?" George heard his own words after he'd said them. They had an echoey sound, as if the person who'd spoken them weren't real.

"We've had another message from Laneer Ivard, George." Beckmann played with the names and took another long puff of his cigar. "This cable was routed from Singapore. Obviously he doesn't trust the sultan's regime. He intimates that the place is full of spies. . . ."

"God damn it, Ogden!" George wanted to shout. "My wife is ill! Don't bother me with your piddling problems!" At that moment George hated Beckmann so vehemently he felt it would take nothing at all to pick up the poker lying beside the fire grate and bash the man's face to a pulp. It would feel good, George thought, a vindication for everyone slurred by those smarmy words: for poor Mrs. DuPlessis hovering over the sickbed, for Dr. DuPlessis, who fretted and blamed himself, for Eugenia, who, poor lamb, had apologized for spoiling their stay in Africa while they'd jounced the long way back down to the coast. Even for Lieutenant Brown. Though, all at once, George remembered he didn't like Brown much either.

I didn't cotton to the way he ordered that train from Nairobi, George told himself, or how he bossed the *ketito* servants about, or made them pack up the luggage. There was too much frenzy and too little concern for appearance. The function of a civilized man, George reminded himself, is to seem courteous in a careless world. The 'white man's burden' and all that. Brown doesn't understand that concept at all. He simply decided, in my absence, that the only place for Eugenia to recover was on the yacht and that was the end of that. Why, if our safari had come back from the bush any later, we might have found the whole kit and caboodle picked up and gone.

The memory rekindled something in George's brain. "I hope you're not inferring anything unseemly about my wife, Ogden," he said. Laneer Ivard and his cable ceased to exist.

"About Eugenia?" Beckmann couldn't believe how well his ploy was working. This becomes easier and easier, he told himself. George does my work for me.

"How could that be?" Beckmann asked.

"What you said. Genie and her. . . . Brown, you know . . . and Mrs. DuPlessis and the doctor . . ." George started to founder. He wanted to accuse Beckmann of not believing his wife's illness, or of insinuating that the attention of three good people was a sham. But that wasn't the true problem and George knew it.

"They're good souls, every one . . ." George insisted. "Why, if they hadn't pulled together back at the *ketito,* I don't know what—"

"You're quite right," Beckmann interrupted. "It's refreshing to witness devotion to one's work. To one's employer. Admirable. It is. You're absolutely correct. The doctor's an exemplary creature. His wife, as well. And I certainly never intended a slur on our young mercenary. Selfless duty, I'd call it. With rewards to be reaped in heaven itself."

George felt himself choking on his own spit. "What is it you wanted to see me about?"

"Laneer Ivard has wired that Mahomet Seh is—"

"Jesus God, Ogden! Don't you ever think about anything else? 'Laneer Ivard has wired that Mahomet Seh is getting restless about the arrival of the bloody rifles.' " Rage scalded George's throat; he felt as out of control as a chicken under a farmer's ax.

"We'll get to bloody Borneo when I bloody say so! They can't bloody start without us. No tickee, no laundry, remember that one, Ogden? We've got Brown. We've got a hold full of extra-special, extra-shiny Springfield A3, thirty cals. with plenty of shiny, little bullets, and they've got bloody nothing."

Beckmann let George's anger run itself out while he turned his attention to the ceiling. There were times on the yacht, when it was as still as it was at this moment, that Beckmann had an impression of never having traveled at all. It was the carved paneling, or the way the wood near the chandelier was gilded: There was something that resembled Linden Lodge so exactly that it tricked his mind into thinking it was home.

"A misunderstanding, I'm sure, George," Beckmann said when George stopped his tirade. "I merely mention the cable to suggest that this . . . how shall I put it? . . . this escapade in Africa has placed us behind schedule. Everyone—Eugenia's father, the elder Ivard, Laneer, even Mahomet Seh—is in his appointed place, waiting for the appointed—"

"And I say they're nobodies till we get there!" George's words jumped out in hot clots. "And furthermore, Laneer Ivard's got no bloody balls!

"You said so yourself, Ogden." George pretended not to see Beckmann's thin-lipped smile. There was too much self-satisfaction in it. "Way back in . . . in . . . anyway . . . before Madeira . . . Laneer's gone native, that's what you said." George wasn't sure his chronology was correct, but that wasn't important. What mattered was throwing Ogden's words right back in his smug, fat face. "I'm no dummy," George wanted to crow, "I can connive with the best of them."

"You told me Laneer was at the sway of whatever slim-hipped, dark-skinned body turned his head. Why, by the time we make it across the Indian Ocean, he may have decided to side with the current sultan or play footsy with the goddamned Dutch! The goddamned, bleeding Royal Dutch Petroleum Company! Or the Samuel brothers and goddamned, bloody Shell."

"I see your time in the bush has been most instructive," Beckmann answered. "It's given you an interesting way with words. I'm sure they'll be useful in the days ahead."

Eugenia opened her diary, closed it, opened it again, then shut it with a slap. Talking to the blank pages of a book wouldn't help. There were decisions to be made: Tell James. Don't tell James. Tell George? No, that was laughable.

Eugenia closed her eyes and tried to see the future, but black things kept slipping into her thoughts: shadows and boggy holes big enough to suck down a ship. It was difficult to concentrate with so many pit-falls to avoid; they bubbled and stirred like dark masses in a frozen lake. "They'll break with a crack if you skate too close," Eugenia heard her grandmother's warning, "then you'll tumble in and drown because you didn't have the common sense to stay away."

Philadelphia, Eugenia tried to reassure herself, we'll return to the house on Chestnut Street; the children will go back to school; I'll resume my afternoon box at the Academy of Music; George will do whatever it is that he does with his days, and then we'll see. Easy words, Eugenia rolled them into position and waited for direction, but her mind inadvertently became bundled up in household chores—ordering new draperies for the second-floor sitting room and rearranging the downstairs linen cupboards—till her thoughts jangled like the majordomo's keys, and she was left in a shrouded room sniffing camphor and cedar block and the boiled onion scent of gilt wash rubbed on the picture frames.

"Silverfish," Eugenia whispered, and Mrs. DuPlessis, who was in the act of opening the passageway door just the tiniest, the very tiniest crack, rolled her eyes heavenward as she squeezed herself into the patient's room.

"Oh my dear. I wouldn't worry about silverfish right now if I were you." Mrs. DuPlessis had taken on the square-edged cheer of a professional nurse. She made her mind up to tell Gustav about this newest delirium as she continued:

"It's a good idea to have something take your mind off your troubles, but I don't think we need fret over silverfish just yet. I'm sure Higgins has all our little insect pests on the move. Not many ships as tidy as our *Alcedo*!"

For a moment Eugenia was confused; she couldn't imagine how Mrs. DuPlessis had inserted herself into the china storage vault on Chestnut Street. Then she recognized her cabin and knew that every problem she'd been trying to deny was as true as day.

"And how's our little dizziness this afternoon?" Mrs. DuPlessis moved close. Lavender water and then something like the smell of a gutterless street moved with her. Tight clothes in need of a proper airing. The mistress of Chestnut Street made a mental note while her thoughts returned to an inventory of chamois bags, shelves lined with flannel, and plate rags boiled in milk and dried by the kitchen fire.

"We should put all the soup tureens and punch bowls in one corner," Eugenia was about to answer, but stopped herself in time. "Much better," she said instead. It was interesting to exist in two worlds, Eugenia thought; it was like playing a child's game. The goal was not getting caught.

"Actually the dizziness is almost all gone." That was a lie, but Eugenia was determined that no one guess the truth.

"These brain concussions can be dangerous things." Mrs. DuPlessis put a great deal of emphasis on the word *brain*. It became as blue and fleshy as an uncooked sausage. "Why, I remember one case of brain fever that Gustav treated at the university . . ."

"How are the children, Mrs. DuPlessis?" Eugenia asked. She didn't want to be rude, but she didn't think she could stand any more charnel house stories, and mentioning the children usually averted descriptions of illness and death. Eugenia sat up a little straighter in her pillows and fluffed the lace of her bed jacket over the coverlet. For that moment, she was in her cabin and nowhere else on earth.

"I told them to keep away till I called." Mrs. DuPlessis beamed and Eugenia could imagine how Paul and Jinx and even Lizzie had been bribed. Sweets were Mrs. DuPlessis's stock-in-trade. She was a regular

Mother Ginger with her brood: a broad-stomached lady whose volu-minous skirts concealed her children when danger threatened.

Eugenia smiled at the picture.

"Well, there's our lovely smile again!" Mrs. DuPlessis fairly chirped. "You do look much, much better. Thank the good Lord. I al-ways tell Gustav that I should have been a nurse. Any patient grows well in my care."

"What about James?" Eugenia wanted to ask suddenly. "Where is he? Why hasn't he been to see me?" Then she caught herself up short: he can't come to me now, she argued; it's not wise; it's not right. You know that, Eugenia. Don't ask stupid questions.

Eugenia turned her face into a pillow and felt tears as slick as a baby's bath. She didn't make a sound; she might have been suffocating in brine-soaked linen and down. She drew up her knees as if she could escape by turning huddled and small, by becoming insignificant as a pebble.

"Of course you miss your little ones!" Mrs. DuPlessis gushed. Eu-genia's sorrow filled the older lady with grieving remorse. They were her tears, too, her own loneliness, her barren yearning. Perhaps we shouldn't have been so strict, she told herself. The children are worried about their mother; that's only natural. And she about them, as is right. Perhaps Gustav is wrong. Perhaps Eugenia needs a touch of youthful exuberance. Women are put on this earth to bear children, af-ter all. That's why God created us.

"Paul's made you a marvelous drawing of the bull eland your hus-band shot on safari," Mrs. DuPlessis soothed as she shook out a tas-seled lamp shade and turned its rose quartz finial to catch the light. Pretty things help cheer a despondent breast, she recited to herself while the stone caught the glow of the mirror and cast a pink band onto Mrs. DuPlessis's chubby hand.

"The drawing is full of expression, especially about the eyes; they're really very sad and lifelike. He wanted to bring it in right away, but I persuaded him to wait till you were feeling more chipper. Now, I real-ize I was wrong."

Mrs. DuPlessis never hesitated; she considered herself a great judge of human nature, a psychic, like her sister, when it came to the trou-bles of a suffering soul. "The doctor was wrong, too," Mrs. DuPlessis insisted. "What you need is to see your children. A mother should never be without her babies."

Eugenia heard those words and thought her heart would burst. Why can't my worst fear be moths in the woolens? she thought. Or what I'll wear to the Governor's Ball or whether amber beads look dowdy on mignonette velvet. Why can't I go back to my simple life?

"And that is what you certainly are, my dear," Mrs. DuPlessis continued, "a born mother."

Ogden Beckmann was burning up with anger. His body shook and, for a moment, crossing the carpeted hall, walking stiffly toward his own cabin, he thought he might have a touch of fever. Dengue or malaria, something picked up from the insufferable air of this stifling port. Then he pushed aside the self-indulgent symptoms and realized that what caused his muscles to shiver and his bones to ache was nothing else but rage.

Who gave George permission to question my authority? he demanded. Or Brown the cheek to thumb his nose at convention? And what, in God's name, has happened to Eugenia?

Brown and Eugenia. Eugenia. Brown. Watch out, watch out, a voice whispered in his ear, but it couldn't or wouldn't go on.

"Brown and Eugenia, what?" Beckmann wanted to shout. "What have you seen?" But the voice slunk off with a nervous giggle. "I wanted her for myself," Beckmann needed to protest. But the voice had disappeared down an alley. Out of sight for the moment, but not gone. Definitely not gone.

"I'd better go out on deck," Beckmann said aloud, ignoring the voice's echo. "We should have cast off already."

Beckmann disturbed Henry and Ned chatting at the rail. "What are you two doing above decks?" he asked angrily. "I'll report you to Captain Cosby."

"We was just waiting to see the last line go free," Henry answered dutifully, then added a hasty "sir."

"I'll report you for insubordination."

Henry and Ned stared silently at their shoes and shuffled off in separate directions.

"Don't let me catch you up here again!" Beckmann shouted after their shabby figures.

Fat chance of that, thought the two boys. The man's got a bone in his craw; it's as plain as the nose on your face. He's got ants in his pants and a stick up his you-know-what.

I wanted her for myself, Beckmann's brain repeated.

"Tell us the names again, Dr. DuPlessis!" Paul jumped onto the lower rung of the railing and leaned out, waving to the thinning crowd. The ship was taking such an awfully long time to sail! The men at the ropes seemed to move in a pantomime of slow motion. "Hurry up!" Paul shouted to the world at large.

"Frigate and Platte, La Digue, Denis, Praslin, Mahe, Bird—"

"Bird!" Paul interrupted, laughing. He bounced against the rail like a ball on a rubber string.

"If you stop me, Paul, I may have to go back and start all over again," Dr. DuPlessis intoned.

Jinx nudged her brother in the ribs and they both laughed harder, then Mrs. DuPlessis picked up the joke and joined them.

"And Felicité . . . " Lizzie leaned as far forward as she dared and pronounced the word 'Feleesseetay' in an exaggeration of Dr. Du-Plessis's careful Belgian accent.

"Good for you, Lizabeth," he said. "Do you remember what it means?"

" 'Happiness or well-being,' " Lizzie quoted.

"Tell us some more funny names!" Paul swung back and forth. His blue sailor suit rubbed against the rail's chalky metal and grew white streaks like the stripes down the back of a baby deer.

"Paul," Mrs. DuPlessis warned, patting his small shoulder, but she was smiling broadly and Paul looked up at her and grinned in return.

"I won't fall, Mrs. DuPlessis," he said. "I promise."

"More names!" Jinx demanded. It seemed they'd been waiting for-ever for the *Alcedo* to leave. First there was all that coal to be loaded; a big black, gritty cloud that had huffed and puffed its way over the ship, forcing them inside till Dr. DuPlessis said it was safe to go back out on deck. "Black lung," he'd said severely. "That's what breathing coal dust gives you. We must stay inside till they finish shoveling our fuel."

Black Lung! Paul had thought that was an excellent pirate name; he'd run around the saloon shouting, "I'm Black Lung and this ship and all who sail in her are mine!"

But then they'd gotten onto the names of the Seychelles Islands (that's where they were going next—they were in the Indian Ocean) and that had become the new game. It was like playing "Memory" at the *ketito* before Mother's accident; Mrs. D. couldn't remember any-thing in proper order; she blurted out whichever name popped into her head first, so anyone following her had an easy time of it. There were ninety islands in all! They were learning them in groups (Dr. D.'s sug-gestion), so anyone with half a brain could win. And besides, the way Dr. D. did the lesson was much more fun than a class with Cousin Whit! (Lizzie, Paul, and Jinx would do anything to avoid resuming their "tutorials.")

"More names! More names!" Jinx and Paul began in unison.

"Curieuse, Aride, West Silver . . ."

"Long John Silver!" Paul shrieked.

"Paul! Hush!" Lizzie scolded; she was afraid of calling attention to their truancy. She was afraid Father would come in and say, "What? Not at lessons? But we're leaving port. The routine must be followed."

Dr. DuPlessis decided to ignore Paul's remark. ". . . Silhouette, Sainte Anne, Cerf . . ."

"And to think those islands were once the Garden of Eden . . ." Mrs. DuPlessis murmured; her voice was dreamy and faraway-sounding and Lizzie answered with an echoing "Yes."

Then both ladies, young and old, stared at the hills beyond Mombasa town as if they were seeing the Garden itself: lions lying down with lambs and birds with feathers so delicate that touching them was like brushing the deepest velvet or turning your hand in a summer breeze.

"Well, that's what General Gordon wrote, my dear," Dr. DuPlessis interrupted. "I don't believe it's a viewpoint accepted by theologians. Universally, that is."

Her husband's words could be confusing sometimes, so Mrs. DuPlessis decided to retort, "Well, if anyone should know Eden, that man would. Why, Gordon's seen all of India, I believe. As well as Africa. And they call him 'Chinese' Gordon back in England. So he obviously knows the cradles of civilization by heart."

"But Syria, my dear? Jerusalem? Beyrouth? Baalbek?"

"You can be so unromantic, Gustav!" Mrs. DuPlessis snorted, but her voice was gentle. "Can't we believe in a Garden of Eden?"

"Yes," Lizzie whispered, her eyes on a wondrous world.

"Eden! Eden!" Paul shouted in a singsong voice. "We're going to Eden. We'll eat dugong and capuchin. We'll dance until the night is green . . ." These were new words for Paul and he liked their sound. A dugong was a kind of walrus, Dr. DuPlessis had said, and a capuchin was a monkey.

"Oh, Paul! You can be so fractious sometimes!" Lizzie turned away from her little brother's antics while Dr. DuPlessis and his wife smiled in happy collusion and Jinx sighed to no one in particular, "When will we ever leave Africa?"

Eugenia didn't even want to touch the book George had brought her, let alone read it. *The Story of an African Farm*, by Ralph Iron: Eugenia looked at the gold ostrich etched on the book's spine; its feathers were fluffed in benign circles like a child's party dress, and its curving beak was the broad smile of an empty face.

Eugenia took her eyes off the gift, pulled the sheet toward her chin and slid further into her covers. Ostrich feathers, she thought, and marabou trim, peacock fans and hats made of the brown wing tips of Chinese pheasants; for a moment Eugenia felt so nauseated she was afraid she might be sick. Her stomach rolled over; her hands became greasy and sweat dripped from her neck. She ran her tongue over her lips; they were dry as tissue paper.

I didn't want this, Eugenia thought, and then was ashamed to find tears so close. I've got to stop this maudlin behavior, she told herself. I did this to myself, after all. I have no one else to blame.

But what does George's present mean? *The Story of an African Farm.* And all his stammering and bashfulness, the way he gurgled out the name of the book's heroine as if she's someone we both know. As if this Lyndall person is some ideal George sees in me. And Ralph Iron, too, what kind of name is that? Is "Iron" supposed to have a hidden meaning?

"I hate all books and betterment," Eugenia said aloud. "I hate lectures and hectoring. I hate thinking." But what do I want? she wondered. To go home? No, that's not it. Home's no different from my cabin on the yacht. You carry your troubles with you, like a turtle with its shell.

Eugenia decided to get out of bed, and as she put her feet toward the floor and her slippers she glared at George's gift as though it might hurtle through the air and bar her way.

An African farm, Eugenia repeated, what does it mean? Is George trying to admit something? Or are we supposed to become different people? living a simple, bucolic life? And why does it have to be Africa?

Or is the book a warning? Eugenia didn't want to think about the days at the *ketito* when she and James and the girls had created the closest resemblance to family happiness she'd ever known, but they were there just the same. Eugenia drove the memories from her thoughts.

Out of sight, out of mind, she told herself. Dwelling in the past makes the present more difficult. Besides, I have to remember that I'm a very lucky woman; I should count my blessings. There I was at the *ketito,* worried to death about Paul, and he came back without so much as a scratch. And think of all the needless fuss I caused!

And the girls, Eugenia continued, look how they're blooming. I have a perfectly lovely life. "If wishes were horses, beggars might ride." Remember what Gran always said.

This seemed the correct tone to take. Eugenia put on her dressing gown and began to brush her hair. One hundred strokes, she ordered, and raised her arm higher. Her shoulder was stiff from the fall; it ached to move it. Some dancing partner I'd make, she thought, and then immediately criticized her own foolishness.

When this trip is over, I'm going back to Philadelphia, Eugenia told herself. I'll be the person I'm supposed to be: a wife, a mother, a woman with a place in the world. I'm not going to give that up. Not for all the tea in China. My children come first. If I can't remember that, I'm nothing but dust in the street.

"But what about James?" The sound of her voice was startling. It was like a wail from another room. Eugenia put down her brush. She did this with utmost care, aligning brush and comb and mirror and buttonhook and shoehorn and pin tray till her eyes grew hot and full, and she lost sight of those objects and saw instead the azure-blue walls of her hotel bedroom in Port Said and the afternoon sun sidling through the jalousie slats and raking the blue with slabs of light that looked as solid as bricks made of gold. She wasn't alone in her bed, and she didn't have a care in the world.

The *Alcedo* left the port of Kilindini on Mombasa Island and headed east by north on a straight line across the Indian Ocean, the last great body of water before the Selats Kunda and Karimata opened the sluice of the South China Sea and the ship spilled on to Borneo and the lands beyond.

To George "the lands beyond" were Korea, Japan, Russia, and China. He was giving serious consideration to stopping at Port Arthur, entertaining Czar Nicholas, then visiting Shanghai and the imperial walled city in Peking. The oldest pine tree in the world was rumored to be found on an island near Japan, and it was said that one could still see coolies traveling across China packed in open boxcars like so much herded beef.

Those were tourist spectacles, events and sights to give the tales told round the home fires more excitement, more authenticity, and they were written in George's notebook as "possible excursions," jottings taken from authors and naturalists like Douglas Rannie, Carl Alfred Bock, or General C. G. Gordon himself, just as George had also built up a conscientious list of all the African animals he needed to "bag." Travel, he'd told himself, was a matter of accomplishing certain tasks.

In Borneo (George had noted) there were orangutan, or *maya,* as they were called locally; there were rhino, honey bear (but no tiger), *babirusa* pig, and *plandok,* a deer so small a hare could dwarf it. There were fish that walked and monkeys with long, red, human noses that the natives, with fine humor, had nicknamed "Dutchmen." All those creatures were described in George's journal under the heading "Sights Not to Miss." After the necessary episode with Brown, Mahomet Seh, and the Ivards, père et fils, George was planning a very special holiday.

He'd set it up in his mind already: a flotilla of sampans piercing the jungle waterways, the streak of headhunters glimpsed through the trees, the screech of macaws, the cobalt-blue flash of a kingfisher. He'd have a huge bamboo cage constructed by the local folk and they'd swing among the branches of nipa palms and casuarina, snaring all the kingfishers the cage would hold.

So, returning home, George could saunter into the Philadelphia Club or the Union League and casually mention, "Ah, yes, *alcedos*. Caught a few of them down Borneo way. Spot of bother they had, weathering the trip. Only four made it, but they're beautiful specimens, as blue as the Billiton sky. Couldn't have my ship come back without a few of her fine-feathered kin."

George had practiced that scene already. There'd be the disagreeable task of the rebellion in Sarawak to contend with first, of course. Probably a bit of a mess to tidy up after; things didn't always come off as planned. Even with the great Turk behind them.

But George hadn't bothered to rehearse those scenes. They'd be quickly done, he'd promised himself; and then, like pulling a tooth, the pain would be over and life could go on. On to the good, the important things: the garnering of anecdotes, the gathering of prizes.

In his yacht's wheelhouse, as Mombasa and the rest of the near-forgotten interior of British East Africa turned into a blob, then a blur, then a hazy whiff that resembled a cloud bank instead of honest, solid ground, George ordered Captain Cosby to hoist the auxiliary sails. "We'll start the nine hundred miles toward the Seychelles under steam and sail," he said. "Then we'll take on coal at the naval station there before heading to Borneo."

And then we'll be almost done, George thought. And almost home.

How many heads have you taken?
How many lovers have you had?

*L*ANEER IVARD thought the Dayak saying was ridiculous. It must be the *tuak* speaking, he told himself, that homemade alcohol they guzzle from bamboo cups. In all his years in Borneo, Laneer Ivard had never understood whether the motto was a compliment or an accusation. The number of heads strung across the rafters of a longhouse denoted virility and bravery. That part was easy, but the idea of a girl being extolled for her lewdness didn't seem wise in the least.

That and the fact that a marriageable girl was encouraged to sleep with any man of her choice. The sacred rite must mean very little, Laneer decided as he watched the prow of his boat cut through the turgid coastal water. Mangrove roots cut through the swamp silt; they looked gawky and thin like the knock-kneed legs of heron or the spindly calves of the goitered dancing master Laneer had been subjected to in his British public school. The man had had foul breath and gray-green teeth to match. Laneer would never forget him.

Laneer Ivard stared at the muddy water and wished the boat would move faster, which, of course, it failed to do. Of course, he'd have been given the slowest prau, he thought. It only made sense that he, the "rajah muda," the "crown prince," should be forced to swallow this humiliation along with everything else. By not taking the official yacht, he'd given the men at Pangalong Jetty in Kuching town something fresh to whisper over and a new way to show their contempt. Laneer felt like ordering the rowers to put more muscle into their strokes; he felt like screaming and screeching and leaping up and down, but that all took too much effort. Better leave well enough alone, he decided; better sit back in the shade and let the subhuman species do the only work it can.

If Sinen were here, Laneer tried to comfort himself, he could order the men to move faster. He could intimate that His Highness was displeased, that heads would roll if they didn't hurry. But Sinen wasn't there. Sinen was back in Ivartown, probably fast asleep. With his head slipping from the pillow and his mouth lying open so gently that only the closest and most loving inspection would detect his secret.

Laneer Ivard returned to his contemplation of marriage. Marriage in England, marriage among the Malays and Chinese and Dayaks. At least the native longhouse girls were allowed to call the whole thing off. A "bad dream" was enough of an excuse; it was considered an omen of evil afoot. The starchy, coarse-skinned, bone-encased women in London weren't given such an easy out.

But then neither were the men, Laneer thought, returning to a favorite topic. Imagine, just imagine, discovering that the female you'd forever bound yourself to could recklessly toss aside her titian curls, that her waist was not that of a wasp, and that she had more hair covering her body than her poor, misguided and misinformed husband grew on the top of his waggling head.

No, Sinen could not have come with me today, Laneer decided, jolting his thoughts to the present. I couldn't risk Mahomet Seh seeing him. I couldn't risk the place we're going. These are desperate men, these pirates, these Bajua, these *perempak*. These rebels. When they raided the town of Kudat on Maruda Bay, they left all the Chinese shopkeepers mutilated and dying or dead. I could not allow my Sinen to be seen by men like these.

"Mahomet Saleh. Mat Saleh. Mohammed Seh. What do I call you? These Malay names are so confusing," Laneer Ivard muttered peevishly as he twisted his neck, swiping at sweat with a handkerchief still scented with eau de cologne. What a miserably hot day, he thought. Why on earth did I agree to meet Seh here? The coast is nothing but one hellish stew pot. I feel I've been boiled alive.

The rebel only grunted his answer; he kept his eyes on the thick sago palm leaves, making certain his men were hiding the rajah muda's prau carefully enough. Even though the cove is sheltered, hidden from the rest of the Sarawak coastline, care must be taken at all times, the rebel told himself. And such a large prau for one passenger. If secrecy was the rajah muda's main concern, he should have chosen a smaller vessel, not the biggest he could find at Pangalong Jetty.

A Bugis warrior appeared beside the Malay rebel. His naked body was as squat and round as an orangutan's and as powerful. The Bugis stared at his master. The lack of movement in his empty face said: *The prau is hidden as you ordered.* It said: *Like you, I wonder how many others know about this meeting; His Highness may not like keeping secrets.*

"Well, you could at least bring me some tea," Laneer whined as he looked at the squalor around him. The landing was no more than a few square feet hacked out of the jungle. There were more insects than he cared to imagine; everything seemed to swill and swell on their slithery backs, and the noise of creatures traipsing through the bamboo and nipa palm was nearly deafening.

"That is, if you can even make tea in these primitive conditions. I'd expected a real camp, you know, when I agreed to this little get-together. A proper armed fort or something." Pirates, Laneer tried to console himself, seeking comfort with a bit of excitement; I'm finally getting to meet the real thing! Seh may be a rebel now, but he started life as his ancestors did, terrorizing the islands of the South China Sea. Pirates with knives in their mouths and gore on their faces! The dreaded *perempak.*

The thought was faintly thrilling; Laneer felt perked up, in spite of his physical discomfort. If my great-uncle James, and his pal, Sanford Raffles, could see me now, he gloated. Rid Borneo of pirates, indeed! They'd only succeeded in driving the criminals deeper into hiding. And it had taken the aid of the Royal Navy to do it! A fat lot of good those gunboats did. A lot of wasted shot, if you ask me, Laneer thought. And wasted English muscle!

"Look at me, Uncle Jim," Laneer wanted to shout, "your heir, the last of the glorious Ivard brood, about to have tea with the enemy, chatting about weather and sailing conditions with a man who'd as soon hang my head out to dry in a mangrove tree!"

The Malay rebel turned his back on Laneer's reverie. Some message had passed between the Bugis and himself, and he'd decided it was time to begin the climb into the jungle. Laneer was startled by their sudden movement, but he followed along, trotting like a roly-poly puppy, huffing and puffing as he rushed to keep up.

"I guess we're not going to be civilized, after all," he said. "Break bread . . . have a spot of tea . . . Or do you have a different camp? That little clearing does seem a bit small and ill equipped for a rebel force as large as yours is reputed to be."

Three Iban sailors joined the procession; Laneer recognized the tribe. Sea-Dayaks, their build was longer and leaner than the Bugis', but their strength was just as fearsome.

"That place wasn't private enough, I suppose, Mr. Seh?" Laneer called out as he jogged along. "Though remember, before you take me much further into the jungle I have to be back in Ivartown by nightfall. Whatever would anyone say if I were out all night?"

Laneer snickered loudly, "Why, just think, the sultan would give his eyeteeth to know where I was right now. The gossip about your encampment is all over the palace. . . ." The noise from his laugh riffled the greenery. For a moment there was no other sound, and Laneer was aware of his own voice dropping back through the jungle the way inappropriate and overloud words fall on a silent dinner party.

The Malay set his jaw but didn't answer, the Bugis gripped his spear tighter, while the Iban warriors continued to cut through the jungly green, severing the bamboo curtain with blows from their razor-sharp krisses.

"I say, slow down," Laneer squawked. "I'm not used to this dashing about through the foliage. *Ipo* trees and all that other poisonous stuff! Why, I can't even see a path. . . . If there is such a confounded thing."

The dense leaves closed quickly on the group, making them nearly invisible to one another. "Slow down, I say!" Laneer shrieked again. "I have no idea where we're going! Mr. Seh! I say, slow down, won't you?"

But the Malay didn't break his pace for a moment. He wound through the twisting vines and trunks like a serpent on a rat hunt; one moment his body was there, the next it was gone. And he did it all silently! He and the Bugis and Iban slithered on at an ever faster pace. Laneer couldn't believe his eyes.

Pitcher plant leaves and thorny creepers lunged at his body. His fine silk pongee suit was snagged and torn, his smooth face scratched, and his dusty-blond hair turned to a shamble of matted knots. The stripped canes of nipa palm whipped across the path and Laneer threw out his hands to protect himself till he saw how his fingers bled. "Slow down, Mr. Seh," he shouted. "Mr. Saleh. Mat, Mahomet . . . Whatever your confounded name is!"

No, he's not like a snake at all, Laneer decided, huffing and puffing and falling behind in spite of his efforts. He's more like a big mammal. Something muscley and tall with enormous shoulders and the kind of haunches that look like they're about to spring. A leopard, maybe, Laneer thought. "You look as mean as a leopard," he wanted to call, "and as dumb." But he didn't.

The group raced upward through the jungle. Light flashed on a naked back and then disappeared. There was green, then bright brown, then green again. Green tinged with black, with blue, with vermilion, and something paler than platinum or silver.

"Where in God's name are you taking me?" Laneer panted. "If I weren't a prince, I might be afraid you were dragging me into the jungle just to hack me to bits and take away my head," he giggled nervously.

"It's a lucky thing I'm rajah muda or I might really be afraid! I bet you could fetch a fancy price for my blond hair. It's an unusual color in the jungle, I'm told." Laneer tried another laugh, but the sound was hollow and false, and the single snort that echoed from the Malay and Bugis was less than reassuring.

"You might answer," Laneer complained. "It wouldn't kill you, you know. A little politesse. That's what's wrong with this country. No one has any manners."

Then the rebels started to climb in earnest. The mountain should have been cooler, but it wasn't. The air, if possible, was even steamier and more difficult to breathe, while the jungle grew, step by painful step, more terrifyingly impenetrable. At every turning, Laneer and his escort were thwarted by vines grown monstrous and fat. When the Iban or Bugis cut them, sap poured out like blood from a vein. And, oh, the smell was unbearable! Something seemed to be rotting underneath; the ground squished like sewer water and a new stench rose with each step.

"Nice place you've chosen for your camp, Mr. Seh," Laneer gibed with a gasp. Then a horrible thought occurred to him and he turned round to mark their path. It was gone: The cuts in the trees, the split bamboo, had disappeared. Where they'd come from, Laneer would never be able to remember, and where they were going was just as lost.

"Please," he suddenly cried out, "Mr. Seh. Saleh. Whatever your name is. Stop. I'm the rajah muda . . . my ancestors . . . my father . . . Let's go back to the clearing. . . . I've all the information you need right there. On the prau. It's all on the prau."

Laneer stumbled, then righted himself, only to fall again. "I don't know what you want . . ." he whispered frantically, clawing his way through the tangled roots, ". . . dragging me up here . . . But whatever it is, you may have it. I give you my word. Please, just let me go home. The Axthelms are . . . When they come you'll be . . . Beckmann . . . there's a man named Beckmann who . . ."

The Bugis and Iban raced ahead through the jungle. Tree trunks, leaves, and branches snapped shut behind them.

". . . They've promised the rifles . . . and whatever else you want!" Laneer felt tears start to stream down his face. ". . . I've got to be back by nightfall . . . remember? . . . Just tell me what you want!"

The Malay turned around only once. "I'm not Seh," he said. "Now keep quiet!"

The Turk started to cough again. Carl hated the sound; it grated on his nerves and he felt his father did it on purpose. No one should need to cough that much, Carl decided. It was vulgar and gross, a touch of the influenza or not. His father might have been a farmer or miner, hacking out his weary lungs, and the study at Linden Lodge had taken on the same seedy, worn-out aspect.

"I really think we'd better get the doctor to take a look at you, Father," Carl said firmly. His hands gripped the armrest of his chair; for the first time in his life he wondered how other sons managed. All of us are burdened with the old and infirm, he thought; rich or poor, they cling to power till their very last breath. They know that giving up control is as good as dying.

"Did you hear what I said, Father?" Carl repeated louder.

The Turk choked, then barked: "That's just what you'd like, isn't it, sonny boy! Get some quack to send me to a hospital! The only reason they build those places is so poor people don't muck up the streets while they're dying. You won't catch me entering one of those lice-infested holes. No, sir."

"They wash them down with carbolic acid," Carl countered automatically. "So they're not 'infested,' as you so delicately put it."

"But, of course, Father," Carl continued with as much force as he dared, "I would never recommend your entering a hospital. I merely suggested we get someone to look at that cough."

"Can't look at a cough, ninny!" the Turk sang out.

Oh, for God's sake, Carl thought; he's become an imbecile since he's been ill. He's like a spoiled baby, impossible to handle and vindictive to boot. But a quiet "I realize that, Father" was all Carl allowed himself to answer.

The Turk and his son stared at each other across the room. An autumn night that should have been festive with the anticipation of harvesttime, that should have been filled with bowls of hot walnuts and the sheen of new apples, was desolate and grim instead. The fire in the grate meant nothing. The study was bleak and bitter; even the smells of the brass lamps and tapestried pillows evoked illness and age, even the clock on the mantel ticked in a rhythm both feeble and frail.

How long have we been waiting for word from Beckmann? the Turk wondered suddenly. He knew he didn't dare ask; this little touch of grippe had taken more out of him than he cared to admit. Time and emotion were playing tricks on him. It seemed years since George and Eugenia had left, and the old man wanted, in the middle of that ridiculous and inopportune moment, to have the whole family gathered together again: the grandchildren playing in the garden, the joyful sounds of their happy, little games, Paul racing in to nestle in his grandfather's lap.

That's who I really miss, the old man thought; he's the only person in this miserable family who counts for anything. Paul, named after my own dead father, God rest him wherever he is. Can't say anything, of course, the Turk warned himself. Can't expose a soft heart or weak character. Not after all the lectures I landed on my sons' heads.

Trust no one, that's what I told them, your own family least of all. Everyone's out to get you, that's always been my motto. Everyone wants something. Find the need and pander to it. . . .

Maybe it's just this little malady, the Turk told himself, maybe that's why I seem to be preoccupied with dying. Everyone goes sooner or later, he reasoned, and I'm better off than most. The Turk looked around his study and tried to take heart, but the room had an unhealthy aroma, even to his old nostrils, and he sniffed it the way a wolf would examine a fouled cave, and then started to cough again.

My affairs are in order, the Turk assured himself. I've built an empire of money and power, and I'm certainly not afraid of a scene at the deathbed, choking out some painful words to a few tightfisted sharpies.

No, the old man repeated, it's just that I miss young Paul. It's as plain as the nose on your face. I'm not sick; I'm not dying; I just want my grandson back. I don't want him off in Borneo; why, anything could happen there. Children get all sorts of ailments in the tropics. They have insects that can bury themselves in your skin to lay their eggs; they've got worms that eat through the soles of your feet and eels in the water that kill with a quick, sidelong swoosh.

The old Turk's cough grew louder; it shook his weary frame, and rattled his ears and pinched, greasy cheeks. He'd never admit that the plan itself was causing concern, that he was beginning to doubt its safety.

"Where were we"—he shook his head angrily as if he could shake away worries as well—"before this idiot cough interrupted us? Carl, what was I saying?"

"Laneer Ivard, Seh, and the regime that will take over as soon as the current sultan is deposed," Carl answered warily.

There it was again, the Turk thought, that little lump of nameless fear! It clanked up and down in Carl's words. "Deposed" had the sound of the guillotine, and Carl was enjoying every moment. The Turk was suddenly aware that this son would never miss his younger brother. Or Eugenia. Or the children. The jungles of Borneo could swallow bodies whole for all Carl cared. For all any of them cared. Tony's not like that, though, the old man remembered. Tony turned out all right. Maybe it was because he was the eldest. More like his mother. Tony and Paul, the old man thought. They turned out all right.

"I thought we'd been through all that," the Turk complained.

"Before the *Alcedo* left. That's when we went through it, Father," Carl repeated. "But now George and the cargo are moving on to the Seychelles Islands. Word should be sent to Beckmann on Mahé. He should be given alternate plans. In case some part of the uprising fails. In case Brown can't carry it off. Or the Ivards lose their nerve.

"No matter what happens, Father, we cannot afford losing those coal seams. Or, as you so cannily suggested, the possibility of discovering fuel oil." Carl's voice had become didactic, but he wondered how much information was getting through. Sarcasm and anger seemed to have lost their effect. "Or perhaps you've forgotten our rivals out there? Marcus Samuel? The Nobels? I hear there may be some hookup between Nobel and the Samuel brothers' Shell Company. To say nothing of Royal Dutch."

"But surely that won't happen." The Turk roused himself. "Samuel is part of a syndicate and the Nobels are concentrated in Russia. Surely they can't stand in our way."

"Oh no?" Carl responded; he was beginning to enjoy himself. He let his words sink in. He could see his father's mind fidgeting with the names as if the skull were glass and the brain turning gears, like a clock. Nobel, Baku, Caspian Sea: Those were painted on one notched wheel. Another said: Marcus Samuel, Shell, and Royal Dutch Petroleum. The Rothschilds' BNITO was on a third, while the fourth spelled out: Petrol Gesellschaft—Germany.

"But those are . . ." the old man struggled. "What I mean is . . . we don't need . . . It's still too soon. . . . Those are experiments, really . . . Nobel's rigs . . . and Samuel is a syndicate made up of a group of lesser companies . . . heating oil . . . lamp oil . . . that sort of thing. . . . for God's sake, the Samuel brothers started as shell traders— purveyors of fancy marine collectibles—they're of no importance. . . ."

"The Shell tanker *Cowrie* traveled to London on liquid fuel! Ten thousand miles on liquid fuel. From Balikpapan to the mighty Thames. An experiment maybe, Father. But no secret."

The Turk glanced about the room as if hunting for spies. "No need to raise your voice, Carl . . ." he began.

"And here's another little tidbit." Carl was definitely in his element. I'll give the old goat something to cough over, he thought. I'll give him something to rattle his ancient bones.

"Just in case you continue to insist there's no cause for concern—" Carl paused again. He was definitely having a good time. He considered walking to the window or toward the desk, strolling about while his warnings hit home. Instead he stayed where he was. He wasn't adept at the dramatic pause—at least not yet.

"Ever heard of *Mei foo,* Father?"

The Turk didn't move; Carl hadn't expected him to. He'll play tough to the end, Carl realized. Well, two can learn this game.

"*Mei foo,* for your venerable information, Father, is the name the Chinese have given Standard Oil. It connotes an institution so large the sun never sets on it." Carl was enormously pleased. A grin spread over his beaky face.

"That's kerosene, you idiot!" the Turk roared. "That's kerosene Rockefeller's peddling out there to the Yellow Peril. Tin lamps with the stuff already in it; the company's sold hundreds of them, maybe thousands, but it's not the same thing at all! *Mei foo,* Carl. Better say: 'My fool'!" Laughter belched from the old man's mouth, then turned into a coughing attack, then a grinding gasp.

Carl wondered if he should pound the old man on the back, but he stood his ground instead.

"As you say, Father," he answered. "My fool."

Carl's clipped response cut the Turk's cough in mid hack. What else does my son know? the old man wondered. What other cards does he have up his paltry sleeves?

"So we won't worry about anyone else, Father. We'll be our own little world. The planet of Axthelm. The Nobels are only Swedes, after all, and the Rothschilds are Jews. What can they do?" Carl knew he had the upper hand, but he decided not to use it just yet.

"Though, if I may remind you, Father—as you, yourself, have said time and again—'leave nothing to chance.' That's why we've got to make doubly certain Beckmann has—"

"Beckmann . . . ?" The old man wavered, returned a used handkerchief to his pocket, and then retrieved another and equally soiled one. "Beckmann . . ."

Carl watched his father with disgust; the old fool was stalling for time; that was obvious.

"Beckmann," the Turk repeated slowly, then on a sudden inspiration blurted out: "Laneer Ivard."

"Jesus, Father!" Carl exploded. "What have we been discussing all this time? What are we working for? Goodwill? Love? A helping hand to those less fortunate?

"I thought this was about money. I thought that's why we were dragging the yacht halfway around the world. To control the coal seams. The coal seams and the future of fuel oil along the coast of North Borneo.

"No coal, no ships. Remember lecturing me on that!" Carl's voice had risen to a high-pitched scream, and the Turk had the vivid impression of having spilled a mug of warm milk or of having knocked a bowl of oatmeal off a table. He felt like a very small child.

"But surely Beckmann has been in touch with Laneer Ivard?" The old man suggested. It was all coming back into focus: Sarawak, Kuching, the Ivards, George and the yacht. Those other names Carl had thrown in were a mere test. That was all they'd been: a test of concentration. Or a smoke screen. Carl was definitely hiding something, but the Turk decided to play along. Sooner or later his son would trip over his own big feet.

"That's all sewn up, that situation," the Turk continued; his words were mild and affable. They allowed him to consider one thing while he said another. "It's in the bag, as it were."

"That's just the point, Father!" Carl shouted; frustration boggled his throat. "Our last letter from Laneer complained that he hadn't heard a word. Don't you remember my telling you that?"

"Well, Sir Charles Ivard then . . . Why can't he . . . ?" The Turk was suddenly aware of remembering nothing but holding Paul on his lap the afternoon the *Alcedo* had sailed. He tried to erase the picture, but it had a mind of its own. There was Paul; there was George's study and Beckmann near the window. The Turk could feel the little boy in his arms. He could see his small face: upturned and happy.

"God almighty, Father!" Carl choked out. The old man's lost it, he decided. He's turned into a milk-sodden baby, and I'll have to handle this entire situation on my own. Direct the operation in Borneo while I play nursemaid here at home.

"Sir Charles is only a figurehead, Father"—Carl's voice lacked true patience; it ground down the words as if squashing bugs—"as is Nicholas Paine, the Honorable Nicholas . . . Eugenia's father. . . . You remember him.

"They are there to keep the present sultan happy and unsuspecting. So he doesn't grow suspicious of Laneer or our Mr. Mahomet Seh. We've discussed this over and over!"

And over and over, Carl thought, ad nauseam. All the plots and clandestine meetings might as well have been children's games. Carl was truly angry. Angrier than he permitted himself to be.

"I'm not an idiot, Carl," the Turk finally answered. "And I'm not a baby. And I'm not too long in the tooth to hear you, so there's no need to shout. I know what we're doing out there. Don't underestimate me."

Reluctantly, the Turk put aside the memory of Paul, and as his words grew more measured, they became stronger. "My question is whether our involvement is enough to warrant the risk. This is a family we're sending there."

"Risk!" Carl almost shrieked. "Enough to warrant the risk? Why, if this comes off, we'll be able to control . . ."

"And if it doesn't?" the Turk's voice was slow and even.

"If it doesn't . . ." Carl began, then grew quiet.

Neither man moved. Each knew his own position, but neither could guess the other's. Carl might believe his father had grown hopelessly feeble and old, that he couldn't be trusted again. But he wasn't exactly sure.

And the Turk might feel bullied and buffaloed. He might feel Carl had succeeded in taking control, but there was still the fear that he hadn't. Or maybe fear that he had.

The old Turk decided to pick up the mantle again. "And if it doesn't . . . ?" he repeated.

"We both know the answer to that" was Carl's too hasty reply.

"Who are you then?" Laneer Ivard had fallen flat on his face. He didn't know if he'd been pushed or if he'd stumbled, but he decided to lie still as a possum. "Who are you?" he whispered again. "If you're not Seh, who are you?"

The jungle floor was grotesque. If the smell was bad while walking, it was worse lying down. Bloodworms as fat as fists slithered through fallen leaves, and insects with pointed, black wings tumbled after them. Laneer didn't dare move for fear of squashing the hellish lot: one group dense as a putrid pig's bladder, the other as sharp as a nail.

"Get up!" the Malay ordered. The Bugis and Iban stopped their headlong race and turned back. "Pick him up," the Malay told them, but the words were foreign to Laneer. "You'll have to carry him the rest of the way."

Laneer watched the Iban sailors' tattooed arms hoist him into the air. He decided to go limp; he'd turn as unresisting as a slug, then see how they liked it. The Bugis warrior stared at him and Laneer thought, He looks as though he's taking my measure; they're still cannibals, after all.

"Put me down!" Laneer moaned, and tried to squirm out of his slug-like posture.

"Will you walk?" the Malay asked.

"I can't!"

"Then you will be carried. Like a pig."

Laneer's feet and hands were bound together and slung from a pole.

"Please, just kill me here. There's money in the prau . . . some jewelry . . . It's all yours. Only don't make me go on like this."

"Who said anything about killing, Your Highness?" the Malay jeered. "I thought you wanted to see Mat Saleh."

The Turk watched his son. The clock on the mantel seemed to tick louder than ever and the noise jumbled the old man's thoughts.

Laneer Ivard, he recited in silence, a rebel called Mahomet Seh, a yacht with a hold full of Springfield A3s, Beckmann and a man he'd named Brown. Sir Charles and Nicholas Paine. . . . Then he got lost in rattling off other names: the Nobel family in Baku, the Samuel brothers, Standard Oil, Royal Dutch . . .

"What's your answer, Father?" Carl's voice broke the chain. "I can't go ahead until you tell me what to do."

"No," the Turk said distinctly, "that you could never do. None of you."

It seemed a lifetime that he'd been dragged through the jungle. It grew dark, and then it was deep night. Laneer drifted asleep and then woke. His dreams were like those in a fever. He'd pictured England, a flat on Cadogan Square, the rooms glowing and blue as if snow covered the floor, and then a smell as tempting as kippered herring or sardine toast or hot water bottles in a feather bed.

Laneer's wrists and feet ached; he swung back and forth on the pole, trussed like a roebuck or pig. Then there was light up ahead; the Malay whispered to the Bugis, the Bugis to the Iban.

The procession stopped and the Malay ran forward. Laneer heard him whistle. The answer was the call of a bird. Feet came running; people shouted. His litter was swung through the air. Torches shone in his face. Then he was thrown to the ground.

"My answer," the Turk repeated slowly, making up his mind to something, rediscovering something in himself and his family. "You know my answer." The words hissed like hot metal as they hit the night air. "My answer is what it always will be. What it always has been. We cable Beckmann. Instruct him . . . whatever's necessary . . . that if Laneer or Brown or the sultan fails us . . . you know the rest, don't you, Carl? Or you tell yourself you do.

"You think I'm old and infirm and you sit there licking your chops. 'It won't be long now,' you say. 'It'll all be mine soon enough.' But you've underestimated me. And so you have failed another test."

The old man swallowed; his throat felt dry and hot; he thought about Paul again and pictured his grandchildren playing in the garden or jumping off the wooden raft in the man-made lake. He'd give anything, he realized, if he could have them all there. He'd give anything he had.

"But don't you think for a moment," the Turk continued with effort, "don't you think that I can't carry on. That I've lost my nerve."

Laneer Ivard was cut free and the Malay pushed him erect. "Mat Saleh," he heard whispered. "Mahomet Saleh. Mohammed Seh. Mat Saleh. . . . Tuan, this is our rajah muda."

"*Senang sini,*" Laneer tried, but his tongue was too swollen to speak. "I am comfortable here," he wanted to say. "I am peaceful; please, let me rest."

"The rifles?" he heard. Then no more. The tall man continued to tower above him, but those were his only words.

"The Axthelms . . ." Laneer mumbled, ". . . the *Alcedo* . . . They're on . . ." Then his body sprawled in a heap and he said nothing more.

In his dream, Laneer heard the man speak once again. "*Selamat be-layar,*" he laughed loudly. "A good voyage." The sound must have been the only noise in the wide, green jungle.

TWENTY-ONE

*E*UGENIA WAS THINKING
about the smell of wisteria, or rather, she was actually smelling it as the vines trailed, thick with bees and violet as fox grapes, over the walls and roof of the gazebo at her grandmother's house. Even the close-fisted new leaves had a scent; they unrolled and curled upward, wafting waxy perfumes and the gurglings of a hundred gorging bees onto your head. The young leaves were hairy like cat's paws, and of a green so pale they might have been ice chips standing in a frozen puddle.

Eugenia couldn't shake the memory. It was all she could see of the afternoon. Her deck chair disappeared and the wicker-work tray, her books and letters and ink stand, the straw carpeting where the children had dawdled over their morning lessons, even the white rail and the virtuous line it maintained against the shameless shimmying waves.

"I am remembering the smell of wisteria," Eugenia wrote in her diary, then added a hasty "October 20, 1903—somewhere in the Indian Ocean, and my first day outside!"

In the garden of my grandmother's house in Philadelphia there was a small gazebo built more of wisteria than of wood. The vines were very old and gnarly and they twisted in and out of the building, over and up and around; when the plants were in blossom the place was engulfed in flower.

There were white flowers, and lavender, and purple as dark as night.

And they were filled with bees. Fat, happy bees with their bodies tucked so far inside each blossom you might miss them if you didn't look closely. Wisteria honey—there's a thought. I've never tasted it. Perhaps it's too sweet for human consumption—nectar for the gods.

Eugenia stopped writing. The description was all wrong. It wasn't what she'd intended to write; she wished she could rip out the page and start again. But that was her rule: what was written remained. That's why one must be careful, Eugenia reminded herself, hearing the prim bossiness of her aunt Sally Van Rensselaer's instructions: "One must plan ahead, my dear. Never write anything you'll be ashamed to read later."

"Or do," Eugenia added under her breath, then banished that tantalizing thought. She placed her diary squarely on the reading tray, picked up her pen, and turned to a fresh page. *Or do.* The words came back by themselves.

October 20, 1903, continued:

Linden Lodge is the Turk's country house. I'm not sure if the name is taken from the trees along the main drive or if was it was borrowed from "Unter den Linden," Kaiser Wilhelm's castle near Berlin. My father-in-law is enamored of all things German; I don't share his sentiments, but I don't mind the name of the house.

Eugenia paused again. That entry was no better. She read it over. "Think, Eugenia." She could hear her aunt Sally Van's and her grandmother's similar warning: "You must think before you leap." Eugenia returned to her diary.

"The Lodge" has a wisteria walk—a long, covered ramble from which to survey the Turk's estate: the man-made ponds flowing from one to another, the stand of rhododendron and the azaleas grouped in clusters near the trunks of the tall Dutch elms.

I mention spring plantings exclusively because the wisteria walk is visited only when those plants bloom. When the wisteria fades, the "Walk" is left to the gardeners, and we of the Axthelm family turn our attention to the rose garden and boxwood lanes that loop in mazelike circles around an ornamental fish pool.

My children, especially, have a fine time chasing along those lanes. At least, they did last year. I imagine Paul will still. Lizzie won't (she's far too grand and ladylike) and Jinx is caught on the fence.

Eugenia closed her diary with a bang. I might as well be writing a treatise on the flora of eastern Pennsylvania, she decided bitterly. What a description of a life. No emotion allowed. Eugenia let her fingers wander across the tray and its linen cover while she studied the waves, but neither hands nor eyes were where they seemed to be. She was back in her grandmother's sitting room, an eighteen-year-old planning to be married. She heard the clock in the downstairs hall sound five long gongs while she waited and waited for her grandmother's impromptu lecture to continue.

"Those difficult conjugal encounters"—that was the subject of the day, Eugenia remembered. It was to be my introduction to sexual passion. If passion is the correct term.

"What I always found best, Eugenia . . . what I preferred, that is"— her grandmother had placed a strange stress on the new word; Eugenia could still hear it—"was to make up the week's menus in my mind during those difficult conjugal encounters." Silence—a pause indicating enough said—then a change of tone that bustled with relief.

"I suggest you adopt a similar habit. Using one's memory can be very consoling. And, as you know, I've never liked idleness." And that had ended the lesson.

Then we turned to the far more important problem of planning a ladies' luncheon in my honor, Eugenia remembered. As my grandmother said, she didn't like idleness. Eugenia wondered briefly if the old lady had confused the word *idle* with *voluptuous,* if the tenor of her existence, her bustling activity, her fixation with rules and conduct, had been a way of staving off desire. "An active mind, Genie," she liked to admonish. "Don't let your thoughts lie fallow. That's where the devil does his work."

"Oh, Lord," Eugenia said aloud. The wicker tray shifted with a rustling crack and she heard Africa all over again: fields as fallow as any on earth, veldt and hills stretching unplowed and untamed as far as eyes and ears could travel. Eugenia could smell the high, wild grass and the oily density of leather boots. She reached out her hand and a larger and harder and warmer one reached back.

I suppose my grandmother wouldn't have approved one lick, Eugenia told herself. The thought made her smile. It also made her a little sad, and she wondered if, as two grown women, they would have brought comfort to each other.

Silver marks, Eugenia realized, good lace, which corner to bend on a calling card, and how to "turn the table": Those were the essential elements of my education. I was raised to be a wife and hostess as some people are trained for the diplomatic corps. I was taught French, a smattering of classical art, and an appreciation of certain kinds of music. None of them to be taken too seriously. Passion must keep its ugly distance.

But there was something in the smell of her grandmother's wisteria vines that returned, something potent and tragic as a ghost. Eugenia had a clear picture of herself; she was dressed in a white pinafore and the high-buttoned, black shoes of a nearly grown girl, and she sat in the gazebo pretending to read *Lorna Doone* while her heart blew about with the clusters of blossoms that draped the knotted vines and latticework walls and fell in clumps from the roof itself. The gazebo had reminded her of a drawing she'd seen: a watercolor picture of old Japan in which a woman with a face like the moon spread embroidered robes upon the floor and waited for her distant lover.

"Where are you, Eugenia?"

"Mmm?" Eugenia answered without thinking. She recognized James's voice, but couldn't for the life of her imagine what he was doing in her grandmother's garden.

"You seem a hundred miles away." Brown's words were soft. He bent toward her, and Eugenia had a sudden fear that this gesture would be noticed and misconstrued. I'm my grandmother's pupil, after all, Eugenia thought as she straightened herself in her chair, put her hand to her hat brim, and squinted upward through the sun: the image of a respectable Philadelphian.

"I'm not that much of an invalid," she said. "You needn't bend down. I don't need any more cosseting." Eugenia laughed as she spoke. The sound was polite. It said: *We are acquaintances only, two people meeting by chance.*

"It's the first time you've been out on deck since we sailed."

"And the first time I've seen you alone"; Brown didn't add that sentence. He knew it wasn't safe. The *ketito* seemed a long while ago. Brown stood erect and put his hands at his sides.

"I was remembering the scent of wisteria," Eugenia wanted to answer. "I was in my grandmother's garden, holding a book in my hand, not reading, just daydreaming—the way teenage girls do—and I was filled with such longing."

But that jumble of words brought another memory: the copper window screens at the *ketito,* and the first hint of daylight brushing their dusty sides. I was always alone by that hour, Eugenia realized, and I'd run my hand across the bare sheets, hoping to find James still there. It was a game I played while I stared at the green-brown screens and watched the light build. The sun was like an army on the march; you couldn't shut your eyes against it.

"Africa seems so long ago," Eugenia said instead. "We might never have stopped there at all." Her voice was quiet. "This could be the Mediterranean, I suppose. Or the Atlantic. The oceans begin to look alike, don't they?"

Eugenia turned her eyes to the water: the waves like a throng of people, a market day crowd gathered for a good time—a pinch here, a bartered kiss there, a roll in the hay and a couple of laughs. "The waves look as if they're having a wonderful time," Eugenia finally added.

Brown kept his hands at his sides, but it was an effort. The pillow cradling Eugenia's head and the loose strands of her hair, her shoulder in the sunlight, and her fingers curving lightly in her lap were all as tempting as gold. In a decisive movement, Brown clasped his hands behind his back.

The pose made Eugenia laugh in earnest, and she allowed herself to look directly into his eyes. Or she didn't allow it. Decision and impulse: She never knew which took precedence. Did you choose one path over another, or did you simply throw caution to the winds and hope for the best?

"I've missed you," Eugenia wanted to say. "I want you back."

It was fortunate she didn't speak, because George stepped forward at that moment. He'd been watching his wife and the young lieutenant, and although there was nothing improper in Brown's behavior, it made George decidedly uncomfortable. "Mooning about" is how George would have described Brown's posture. Making a nuisance of himself. The fellow can't give Genie a moment's peace, George grumbled to himself. Not his lookout how she's feeling. I'm grateful and all that for his know-how back there in Africa, but enough is enough. Genie should be allowed to get well on her own.

"I see you brought my little gift out on deck, my dear. Do hope you're enjoying it." George touched the book lying next to Eugenia's diary; he tried to be blustery and hale, but next to Brown he looked pale under his skin, as though he were dressed in rhinoceros hide.

"Oh, George! I didn't see you there!" Eugenia covered her surprise in forced cheer. "Yes. Yes, I am enjoying it." That was a lie. Eugenia hated *The Story of an African Farm,* and the girl Lyndall, and Waldo with his religious fervor, and the damned Germans and the way they brutalized the three children. In fact, there was nothing positive Eugenia could think to mention. "We fight our little battles alone; you yours, I mine." That was a line from the book that had stuck in her mind. It wasn't a pleasant conversation starter.

"Well, let me see what we have here." George picked up the blue and gold volume. "I must confess I haven't had a glance at it yet. Couldn't scare up this copy till close to departure time."

George laughed slightly, pleased with himself, with the afternoon, with his wife, who looked as delicate as a spring lamb. "Sent all over Mombasa town to find our author here—authoress—I should amend that. Excuse me, Genie. No slight intended to the gentler sex."

George wished Brown would get the message and back off. It seemed infernally impertinent of the fellow to stay so close. A husband and wife should be allowed their privacy, after all. The rough and ready days on safari were over and done. It was time to resume the demeanor of polite society again. Brown should go back where he belonged.

"Well, let's see. . . ." George paged through the book as he cleared his throat. Eugenia was afraid he intended to read the entire story aloud. He held the pages to the light with a show of empathy, then paused as if awaiting inspiration. He seemed proud enough to pop.

". . . Well, now, here's a passage: '. . . I am not in so great a hurry to put my neck beneath any man's foot; and I do not so greatly admire the crying of babies—' " George stopped in his tracks. There was so much silence it seemed the ship had lost momentum.

"Oh, I see . . ." George said finally, then closed the book with great care and held it in his hand, uncertain what to do with his gift. If the waves could have stopped to gawk, they would have.

". . . A bit thick, that," George continued with a small, choked voice, "wouldn't you say, Genie? I mean, is the entire . . . ?" George attempted an offhanded laugh. ". . . Well, I wouldn't have purchased it for you if I thought its message would prove unsettling. . . . And, of course . . . of course . . ." George stumbled over his words. He didn't look at his wife. ". . . What I mean to say is . . . well, crying babies and all that, Eugenia . . . what I mean is . . . I certainly never doubted your qualifications as a mother. . . ."

This was such a stab that Eugenia was sure she'd gasped aloud. You can be married, she realized, you can think your husband dull-witted and cruel, you can share such a paucity of speech and intent that you might as well be foreigners with no common tongue. But the fact is you are married. You know each other to your bones.

I should speak, Eugenia told herself, say something safe and chatty. But nothing brought forth the words.

"How long, sir, till we reach the Seychelles?" Brown decided enough was enough. A book was a book, after all; it was unimportant. If George had hurt feelings, too bad. Eugenia wasn't the one to blame.

"What's that? The Seychelles?" George looked surprised, as though he'd forgotten Brown was there.

"Our passage across the Indian Ocean, sir? To our next landfall. How long will it take?" George is a jellyfish, Brown told himself, and Beckmann's a dupe. The only man with any sense is ten thousand miles away.

"How long?" George repeated. He wished Brown would quit his wife's chair and give him some breathing room. He felt he was being scrutinized, or challenged, or something equally unpleasant. "Six or seven days, I believe. That's what Captain Cosby told me. It's a long stretch of water between Africa and the islands."

What gives this young pup the wherewithal to question me? George fumed. He should be off polishing brass or . . . well . . . busy. George couldn't think any further. Damn the man's eyes, he added. The thought created courage. "Any reason for the question, Lieutenant?"

Eugenia heard the change in her husband's tone. The pretense of civility was gone.

"None, sir. None at all. Just wondering when we'll be getting on to Borneo." Brown didn't budge from the side of Eugenia's chair. If anything, he seemed to move closer. Both men held their positions.

So that's the ploy, is it? George railed. Borneo, when will we get to bloody Borneo? Beckmann and Brown in cahoots. Show up old Georgie, make him look like an incompetent little bugger with no more brains than a monkey on a stick.

"I don't suppose the place will drift away without us," George answered. Jocular ease couldn't mask his warning.

"Why all this quibbling over Borneo?" Eugenia asked. She kept her voice bright and breezy, but she suddenly wished that both James and George would go away and leave her in peace. Borneo, business, currents, miles traveled, and schedules kept were games for boys to play. "You're it," they shouted. "I'm bigger; I'm faster. I win; you lose; you're dead." It was a meaningless shuffle.

"I'm tired," Eugenia said without waiting for her husband's response. "I'm going to my cabin. That spill in Africa must have taken more out of me than I thought. Or perhaps it's the unexpectedness of being out in the sun again." Neither man heard the irony in her voice.

Eugenia stood abruptly. She didn't wait for her husband's arm—or Brown's. She chose the side of her chair nearest James, because it was the closest path to the companionway door. There was no other motive in her decision.

Brown reached out to steady her, but Eugenia pushed him away. She didn't want to feel his fingers on her wrist, his hand on her elbow—or anything warm. She wanted cool sheets, an untouched pillow, and then something as uncomplicated as memory.

"I'll have a tray sent down for my dinner," she said without looking back, then added for the sake of the footsteps she knew would follow: "I'm all right. There's no need to see me down. I can look after myself. And don't send for Dr. DuPlessis." The anger Eugenia felt was intolerable. It was like hunger, prowling around in her stomach, knocking sense and decency flat. I hate myself, Eugenia realized all at once. I hate myself, and I hate both of them. I've allowed a terrible thing to happen.

Eugenia woke in total darkness. A woman in spite of myself, she thought. The words hadn't been part of her dream, but they'd stuck with her as though they'd been whispered intently by someone close by. "A woman in spite of myself," Eugenia said aloud. The phrase's potency was beginning to fade. Eugenia couldn't remember why she'd carried it out to her waking world.

The rest of the dream had been unspoken. It had consisted of snaky vines slithering in high circles and tinkling glass ornaments suspended among them like miniature bird cages in a florist's thicket. The glass shards blew together, producing sounds like phony laughter and prisms of color that bombarded everything with light. In her dream Eugenia had stood up rapidly and without warning, and she'd crashed her head in amongst the glass and greenery. A clanging protest and the sensation of splinters stroking her cheeks had followed from the dream to her pillow. The feeling was mesmerizing, tempting, and cold. Eugenia didn't dare turn her head.

She lay on her back, staring toward the ceiling, waiting for her eyes to adjust to the lack of light. The laughter could have been real, she thought, it could have been the children playing in the passageway. The possibility gave her solace; it was an ordinary, everyday occurrence unconcerned with fear or prescience or memory.

Eugenia turned on the lamp and glanced at the clock. Nearly one in the morning, she realized; my children are fast asleep. This information brought its own revelation. I didn't say prayers with them, Eugenia remembered; I didn't tuck them in. They went to bed attended by Prue, while I stayed in my cabin, dead to the world. The discovery gave Eugenia a sense of complete uselessness, as though she didn't exist in her own life. I'm as empty as a bowl without water, she thought, as a field after the sun has set.

But for some reason those words didn't make her sad; if anything, she felt exhilarated and lighter than air. Eugenia swung her feet to the floor and jumped out of bed. I can do anything I want, she decided. She had a childhood memory of desiring invisibility, of wanting to fly, swoop around, seen or unseen. But this new emotion was unconnected. It had nothing to do with escaping. It meant walking on the earth, full out and exposed; it meant that wherever she stood, she did so by her own choosing.

Eugenia looked at the room without bothering to light the other lamps. She felt rebellious, even a little mean. If we were back in Philadelphia, she thought, I'd get myself dressed, slip out the door, and hire a hansom cab to drive the rest of the night. Or I might vanish for a day or two, and then come home. Or I'd walk, all alone, down the center of Chestnut Street, and my shadow in the moonlight would be larger than the signposts, larger than the gas lamps, larger than the trees. When I reached a corner my shadow would pass ahead, and anyone approaching would shrink away in fear. My head would be clothed in a hood and my body in a mantle, but when I raised my arms, the garment would fall free and my arms would stretch the length of the city block, the length of the cobbled street; I'd embrace each shuttered window.

*E*UGENIA WAS MISTAKEN in thinking she was the only passenger awake in the first hours of October the twenty-first. Sitting in his cabin, still dressed in dinner clothes, Ogden Beckmann was a long way from sleep. He hadn't bothered to light the lamps, but the moon, jumping by fits and starts from thick cloud to thin, made stabbing passes at his windows. For a moment Beckmann, silent in his lounge chair, would be lighted as though by torch flame, then the moon would flick to the floor, to the bed, to a dresser drawer, grow bored, and rush away again. When it returned, it was with the same scramble and scurry; moonlight would fling itself onto Beckmann's face, onto one hand or one patent leather shoe, but finding no response, it would hurry off in search of a more receptive client.

Whores, Beckmann thought, all of them. The only movement he made was a spasmodic jerking of his foot. For some reason the moon never chose to examine that leg; the creaking leather may have scared it, or the agitated stamp. Beckmann's foot beat an angry tattoo, and the moon suddenly had better places to visit.

Whores, he repeated. Ogden Beckmann couldn't say for certain when he'd first become aware that Eugenia and Brown were lovers, but that morning on his way to examine the new charts on the bridge, when the revelation had stopped him cold in his tracks, he realized he'd known all along. All of a sudden the charts had become irrelevant, and Captain Cosby's recitation about landfalls and current movement turned innocuous as a mosquito's whine. After an appropriate interval, Beckmann had beat a retreat to his cabin, then spent the rest of the day trying to believe his lying heart.

I wanted her for myself, Beckmann kept repeating, but it wasn't the same sensation as the day they'd left Africa, when Eugenia had been bustled aboard, strapped to a litter and vulnerable as a drowning cat, or the evening in Port Said when Beckmann had felt Eugenia's sexuality cover him like a sheet on a hot night. It wasn't a glance across the table or leaning too close over a hand of piquet. Those had been fantasies, games he'd played with himself—like seeing how long he could go without water, riding a horse an extra five miles, or sitting so long at his desk that his feet went icy and numb. They were tricks for the mind to turn while it watched and waited, because Beckmann had believed all along that Eugenia would be his, that after Borneo or Korea, Port Arthur or Kobe, she'd finally smile and say: "Yes."

"Yes," Beckmann repeated. He couldn't help the word. Then he said "Whores" louder, but the epithet brought no relief. Beckmann's toes tapped faster and the rub and scrape of patent leather momentarily obliterated thought.

"Seeing is believing," Beckmann finally announced. The phrase plopped into the room as if another person had spoken. What Beckmann hoped was that his mind had guessed wrong. Seeing might not be believing, he told himself; it might dispel fears, instead of increase them.

But I won't spy for my own benefit, Beckmann assured himself; it will be for the good of the voyage, for the good of our mission. A liaison with Brown would ruin everything we've worked for. It would create an untenable situation, spoil months of preparation. Beckmann repeated the lies till he almost believed them. Till it wasn't the possibility of watching Eugenia's naked body that drove him out of his cabin and along the passageway toward the ship's hold. It wasn't to fuel his imagination or the frenzy he'd drag back to his own empty bed. It was for the good of the expedition, for the business in Borneo, for the Turk, for the Axthelm trust. Beckmann promised himself the same thing over and over as he crept through the dark corridor and down the stairs that shook under his body like a rope-bridge spanning a chasm.

"I came because I couldn't help myself." Eugenia's body swayed in the dim light. Her words weren't quite true, but they'd do. Eugenia had come to the hold because she could help herself. At that predawn hour when the ship seemed to be flying toward land faster than ever before, when Eugenia had woken to a dark and solitary cabin, stood on her bare toes, and waited for an epiphany, a visit to James had seemed completely in order.

The problem was speech. She and James had had romantic early mornings at the *ketito,* but time had been their friend there, circling them with forgiveness and encouragement. They'd been permitted to talk of anything at all, or nothing. They'd lazed through the long nights with life stories, dreams, bits of forgotten songs, till the sun had coughed apologetically and they'd been forced to go their separate ways.

"I don't think I remember the ship moving so fast. Captain Cosby must be making up for lost time. . . ." That wasn't what Eugenia had meant to say at all. The words presented horribly discordant pictures. The ship and Captain Cosby were pragmatic; mentioning them brought forth daylight and order, and turned the ship's hold into something grubby and deficient. "Making up for lost time" might as well have been "Let's get on with it; I haven't got all night." In any event, the words sounded suggestive and too brazen by far; they made Eugenia want to hang her head and cry.

"I'd forgotten how dark it is down here," Eugenia used a cheerier voice. "Like a fox's lair." She tried to look further into the hold, but shadows cut off her sight. Beyond the rim of the single lantern, the room edged away in blackness. I might as well make love in a cave, Eugenia thought. She didn't want to look at the floor, but couldn't stop herself. Leaving her cabin, she'd been happy and certain, but now, confronted with the reek of coal dust, the hiss of kerosene and its yellow glare, Eugenia felt suddenly bereft. She shifted her toes along the wooden planks; they were grainy with sand and the footsteps of too many people.

"But I like the ship's motion," Eugenia tried again. "It makes me feel as though I'm waltzing."

"It's a heavy sea," Brown answered. "That's what you feel." He wanted to reach over and touch her, but something held him back. "This part of the Indian Ocean can be very rough."

"I feel a little sick, too," Eugenia said hopefully, then immediately reneged. I can't tell James yet, she reasoned, then closed her mind to further question. I can't tell anyone.

"Once in a while. Not now, though. I'm fine now." The delivery was clinical; it shut off all need for help.

"This section of the Indian Ocean is famous for seasickness," Brown answered by rote. He remained beside the crates and didn't move.

Neither of them spoke after that; there seemed nothing more to say. Impervious, indifferent, or just plain selfish, the ship continued to rollick forward. Her timbers creaked and the waves dashed out a noisy response. Then spray from a thousand buckets of salty water tossed up a foamy chant while the wood and caulk and tar and steel of the *Alcedo*'s body shouted a resounding reply. *A ship needs to move,* it cried. *It needs water and wind and fire in its belly. It needs speed and an ocean with no sight of land.*

"I love that sound," Eugenia said finally.

"I've missed you" was all Brown answered.

It didn't take much for them to find each other then. Their clothes and hands and feet became part of the ship's rhythm. Brown slipped the eyelets from Eugenia's dressing gown and held her, and she pulled at a sleeve, a shirttail, and a belt buckle to hold him. It was a dance they did, a measured pattern whose movement their bodies had already discovered: a hand to a hip, a knee near a thigh, shoulder to shoulder, and shoulder by waist.

"You see," Eugenia said, turning her face to watch Brown. "I told you I'd be here. And I am."

She didn't allow herself to think about anything else: the voyage's end, Philadelphia, George's family, George himself, what future she'd make for herself and her children. Or who those children would be. Pretend those problems don't exist, she reasoned, and maybe they'll go away.

While Brown ignored his fears as well. He didn't say: "You think I'm one thing, but I'm not. I'm along for the ride because I was hired; I'm no more a guest than you." He didn't warn himself: This is what comes from daydreaming, taking your ease, forgetting your work. He didn't say: If you'd kept your eyes open . . . If you'd done what you were told . . .

"Here I am, as promised," Eugenia said again, and Brown answered, "You are so beautiful."

The sun wasn't yet up when Beckmann confronted Brown in the hold. "To think we trusted you," he said, rushing forward in such agitation that the bulk of his body crashed into one of the crates. "Why, George Axthelm will . . . when I tell him what . . ." Beckmann seemed impervious to the blow the crate had given him. He stepped aside as though only a minor obstacle had deterred him, and then started for Brown again.

". . . His own wife!" Beckmann shouted. "His own wife! And down here in the filth and slime. . . ." Beckmann was beside himself; he hadn't shaved; his cheeks were scabby and gray, and his black suit was limned with dank circles that could have been sweat or puddles of grease.

"I couldn't believe my own eyes! That poor, innocent young woman! A mother of three . . . How could you? . . ." Flecks of spit sizzled on Beckmann's chin as he struck his hand on his chest, once, twice, then a third time for good measure. The noise was as loud as a tree trunk toppling. Someone needs convincing, Brown told himself, but I don't think it's me.

"I couldn't believe my eyes . . . like a . . . like a . . ."

Brown didn't move a muscle. The idea of Beckmann lurking on the stairs was enough to make him lose control, but he held himself back. Not yet, he decided; not yet.

". . . And right there on the floor . . . like a sow in . . ." Beckmann stopped for breath; his face had turned livid red and pulpy, and his breathing was sharp and shallow. ". . . without even a shred of decency left . . . If it weren't for the rifles, Brown, I'd kill you myself. I would. Right now. With my bare hands if necessary. If it weren't for . . ." The words bubbled up like bile. Beckmann made a grab at a crate; his fingers were rigid as wire.

Brown said nothing. There wasn't any need. He'd taken Beckmann's measure; he knew what ailed the man, and he knew what to do. It was the idea of Eugenia that held him back: Eugenia reflected in Beckmann's eye, in George's, in his own. She blunted his resolve; she confused the issue.

Why did I weaken this time? Brown wondered. My rule's always been: Do the job and leave. Keep to yourself. Keep your counsel. Remember your place. Why did I believe things would be different this time?

". . . And what do you tell her, you miserable little piece of . . . in the midst of your fornication . . . what do you say?" Beckmann's words wheezed on in short gasps as if he were panting for air or a second chance. He grabbed his shirt collar and wrenched it loose; a gold and sapphire stud popped free, but Beckmann paid it no mind. He didn't even turn his head to follow the final plink.

"Do you whisper plots to take over the world . . . tell her you'll save her when the time comes . . . ? The dashing hero and all that bunkum . . . ? Well, let me tell you something . . ." Foam gathered at the corners of Beckmann's dry lips; he licked them and swallowed hard. "Let me tell you, sonny boy . . ."

"If you mean the job in Borneo," Brown interrupted quietly, "I don't mix business and pleasure."

But I did, didn't I? Brown told himself. I forgot why I was here. I allowed a fancy suit and pretty picture to turn my head. I lost track of who I am.

" 'Business and pleasure!' Aren't you the cool one. . . ." Beckmann clutched at another crate. He was losing ground and he knew it. Eugenia bobbed back and forth in his mind. Maybe she prefers Brown, he found himself thinking. Maybe I never had a chance. ". . . Aren't you the snappy gent!" Beckmann attacked again; he'd use the words he'd prepared if they killed him. "I hope you can maintain this demeanor in front of the lady's husband. . . . I hope when I go to him after breakfast that he'll understand why—"

"I wouldn't do that if I were you, Ogden," Brown said; his voice was quiet, but he was pleased with the advantage using Beckmann's first name gave him. The result was immediate, and it did Brown's heart good. A red-hot poker, he thought. "We both know George has nothing to do with this."

"Oh, George doesn't, does he? . . ." Beckmann's carefully acquired accent began to break apart. The letter r turned to mush in his throat; like cold porridge, it stuck halfway up, halfway down. Beckmann swallowed hard and pushed on. The king's own English be damned, he thought.

". . . Well, maybe you and Mistress Eugenia don't care about her husband, but you'll have second thoughts about the Turk . . ."

Brown had stopped paying attention to Beckmann's words. He was concentrating on the accent. He'd heard it before, but he couldn't place where. His first thought was the Caspian Sea. But unless it was the Nobels' compound at Baku, Brown knew the region was wrong. The sound was too European.

". . . And I'll wager she won't relish the old man discovering her wanton ways. Even if George doesn't mind . . . even if he's given up hope of controlling her . . . even if he's forsaken the conjugal bed. . . ."

"You're not making sense, Ogden," Brown answered. Beckmann's problems were too obvious to discuss.

"I'm not making sense!" Beckmann's scream was raspy with phlegm; vowels clogged his windpipe. He spit to clear his throat, then wiped his mouth with his sleeve. The entire pretense of Ogden Beckmann, courtier to the great, was finished. "You . . ." he said, ". . . you . . ."

Beckmann knew he was losing his grip. His memory jumped to the day he'd hired Brown, given him a name, for God's sake, given him a chance. Then Beckmann saw Eugenia: Eugenia arriving at the pier in Newport the morning of departure; Eugenia dressed in white with a veil that trailed her like feathers on the wind. Beckmann remembered that moment vividly because he'd stood transfixed at an upper window, his hand on the glass like a frozen claw. I stood there and did nothing, he told himself. It was a sickening revelation.

"... You ... you ..." Beckmann tried again. Defeat filled his chest; words were as hard to find as pullets' eggs. *I wanted her for myself,* Beckmann's soul screamed. *I wanted her for myself.* Then a burst of noise erupted: "... You jeopardize this entire business by sleeping with a ... with a whore and then insist—"

"Don't say that." Brown's voice was steely. For a moment Beckmann was stunned into silence.

"What shouldn't I say, Jimmy?" Beckmann heaved himself upright and yanked at his coat sleeves. His jaw clamped up and down; his tongue wagged, and his fingers worked over his pockets like locusts in a wheat field. Speaking the name revived him.

"Little Jimmy, works for a nickel ... What am I saying you don't like? That you're a hired boy ... here to teach a few fuzzy-wuzzies how to fire a gun? ... A toy that goes pop like a weasel. ..." Beckmann was beginning to feel much better; he imagined doing a dance: a sailor's jig with squeeze-box and pipe. He shuffled his feet and remembered his patent leather evening shoes. The shoes gave him stature. He was nearly his old self.

"... Or is it the 'business' you object to? You've gotten too high and mighty for a little rebellion, now that you're bedding a—"

"Don't say it, Beckmann."

"Is that what's making you so touchy? The name I'm calling your mistress?" Beckmann was on top of the world again, as full of spite as a boy skinning a cat. I beat out Brown, he told himself; Eugenia's mine by default. It doesn't matter how I get her, as long as I win in the end. Beckmann took a deep and satisfying breath. "You can't bear to hear Eugenia called a whore?"

Brown was on him before either man knew what happened. A blow to the ribs, another to the belly, a third to the center of the quivering jaw: Beckmann was down without raising a hand. Brown stood up. The hold was filled with a stench like death. Brown reached over and felt the neck pulse. Beckmann was unconscious but not dead. Not yet.

The body will have to be moved, Brown decided. I'll have to drag it out on deck and push it overboard. The scene took on a clear, hard edge. It was familiar: a simple task met head on.

Brown lifted Beckmann's feet; the body was awkward and heavy, and it rolled slightly, as if it had trouble adapting to this unfamiliar circumstance. Brown dragged Beckmann by the ankles, then by the arms, and finally by the coat collar. What a fortunate coincidence the man had a decent tailor, Brown thought briefly.

In the corridor Brown had to hurry; he couldn't chance being seen. But luck was with him; Beckmann had chosen the dark hour before dawn for his confrontation. From the corridor, the deck will be easy, Brown realized. And from the deck an imaginary stumble overboard is nothing. It will look like an accident. By the time anyone notices Beckmann is missing, the body will have disappeared. The ship will leave it behind like yesterday's garbage.

But there's no going back, Brown realized. This is the end to Eugenia, and a house with a hedge and a pony cart in the lane. It's the end to settling down, and a quiet life. I kill Beckmann and stay as I am. I kill Beckmann and the dream's finished. *But that's all it was,* another voice answered. *A dream. A tiger can't change its stripes and neither can you.* Wishes and horses, Brown remembered.

Brown pulled Beckmann's body through the upper companionway door and rolled it toward the deck rail. I'll have to make sure before I drop him overboard, he reminded himself; there can be no sudden resurrection for Mr. Ogden Beckmann, no miraculous tale of a drowning man rescued by a wandering steamer.

Brown pulled a piece of glass from a fold in his belt. Less than three inches long, it was honed to a dagger's point. It was an old trick: a sliver of glass in the heart; the wound it left was the size of a pinprick, while the body swallowed the weapon whole. Here's justice for Mr. Ogden Beckmann, Brown said silently.

He held up the blade; it was shiny and slim, almost pretty in the predawn light, like an icicle on a holly berry tree. Death can be as shrill as a pig-sticking, Brown thought, or as slow as a whistle on an empty hill; it can fly at you like a witch in torment or sit by your feet without saying a word.

He pushed the blade in; it felt like nothing at all, like a hoe in new loam, like a spoon in a cup of warm custard. He'd hoped it wouldn't be so easy this time. He'd hoped the act would have grown harder. But it was reflexive, finished without a backward thought. Brown pumped Beckmann's chest once to drive the point home.

Then he rolled the body over the ship's side. The sound it made as it hit the water was muffled by the noise of engines and the flurry of coloring waves. It was no more than a plink in a pond. Brown stood, dusted his knees, and waited for a moment, watching.

There are some things you never forget.

"*B*UT HOW COULD OGDEN have fallen overboard? Wouldn't someone have seen him? A night watch or something?" Eugenia stared into the waves; they looked as mean as faces suddenly. As far as her eye could see, there was this angry mob. The *Alcedo* seemed bucketed about and defenseless, no more protection than a governess cart and a frightened pony. It could have been one of the children, Eugenia thought, one of my children slipping between the rails, unseen and left in the water.

"Can't we go back and look?" Eugenia turned from her husband to Brown; she didn't bother with Captain Cosby. "Isn't that what usually . . . ?" But all three men presented a solid blue-clad front. Why is George dressed in that silly yachting outfit? Eugenia wondered suddenly. And today, of all days. The choice seemed inappropriate in the extreme. It's a costume, she told herself, that's all it is. The word made her angrier than it should have; Eugenia looked away from the three sets of righteous shoulders and glared at the waves again. One of my children, she repeated. The image wouldn't leave her alone.

George didn't answer his wife for a moment. There was a great deal to consider. First off, Ogden's disappearance: Was it foul play or an accident, and did it matter? And did he, George, care? Then came the murky question of blame or, at the very least, responsibility. Then there was the ticklish problem of Borneo, and what might or might not get bollixed up as a result of the man's untimely demise. George stared at the ocean; his expression was impossible to decipher. Really, he thought, it's more than any civilized man should be asked to consider before his morning kippers.

"We'd never find him," George said at last. He didn't dare look at his wife.

"If I may interject, sir. Ma'am." Captain Cosby's words were intended to soothe, though he was greatly troubled. In all his years he'd never lost a man overboard. And in the middle of a calm sea, he repeated to himself over and over; who'd ever heard of the like?

"If I may add my nautical expertise, Mrs. Axthelm, your husband is correct in his assessment. We'd never find Mr. Beckmann. Even if he were alive, we wouldn't have any . . ."

"Oh, how horrible!" Eugenia burst out. "Deserted out there! We might as well have pushed him in ourselves! How can we go on like this? What if it had been . . ." Eugenia realized she was dangerously close to tears. That's just what I need, she thought angrily, to cry over Ogden Beckmann. But Ogden could have been anything: a chair, a picnic basket, a sheaf of letter paper, laundry shears. Everything has a soul, she told herself; you don't forsake it because you're bored. Eugenia shook her head suddenly, and George and Captain Cosby blurred and ran together and James turned into a stick of wood. "What if one of the . . ."

George wished his wife would pull herself together. Her irrational fears left him powerless. It hadn't been one of the children, after all, and creating a melodrama served no useful purpose. She'd used the same hysterical behavior in Africa, and look where that had gotten them. Paul had been fine; he'd come back from safari a bigger, braver boy, while his mother languished in bed with concussion of the brain.

"Thank you, Captain. That will be all." George's words were firm. He shook himself back to the present. Beckmann was gone; there was nothing anyone could do. A nasty business, but a fact of life. If the man hadn't drowned first, sharks would finish the job. And if he managed to survive, the *Alcedo* would never find him. It would be like hunting up a needle in a haystack.

"What are you all trying to hide?" Eugenia couldn't help the words; they flew out of her mouth before she could stop them, but none of the men responded. They pursed their lips, curled their toes in their shoes, stared straight ahead, and prayed for the question to vanish.

"It's not a matter of hiding anything, Eugenia," George answered finally. "We are simply looking for an expedient solution to an unfortunate problem." That seemed as good a response as any. George wanted to keep his temper in check, though he felt sorely tried. Genie's histrionics were disconcerting, to say the least. "Thank you, Cosby," he repeated. "You've been most helpful."

"Very good, sir." Captain Cosby didn't leave, though he knew he'd been dismissed. "I'll be on the bridge if you need me."

In spite of his words, Cosby lingered; he wanted to add his theory of a solitary walk on a slippery deck, a little too much alcohol, a stumble, perhaps an accidental blow to the head, but he realized Mrs. Axthelm couldn't take further discussion. Death is no place for a woman, he told himself. A strong constitution is required in these matters, Cosby decided. The fairer sex is always the weaker vessel.

"Very good, sir. Ma'am." Captain Cosby made two stiff bows and walked off down the deck. He appeared to stand straighter and taller, as if, by dying, Beckmann had bestowed an honor on his ship.

Eugenia didn't bother to watch the captain leave; he was merely one blue figure disassociating itself from its twins. What are they hiding? she thought again. Then she remembered the night before: her empty cabin, the ship's hold, and the yellow light that had built a boundary for her thoughts. Where was I, she wondered, when Ogden fell overboard? Was I with James? Or tucked safely back in my quiet bed? Eugenia didn't dare look at the jeering waves or the ship's deck, which seemed, at the moment, as insignificant as celery seed. Nothing was safe if the ship shrugged off her duty. "We should be doing something," Eugenia insisted. She said the words for herself as much as for George.

This accusation was the last straw for George. It was bad enough to be charged with deceit, though where Genie had gotten that notion George couldn't guess, but on top of it all to have the label of ineffectuality leveled at his head . . . well, it was the final straw. George felt lumped in with Brown: a dismissible youth. It just wasn't fair.

"And that is exactly what I have been doing for the past hour, my dear." George's tone suggested mounting displeasure; he might have been a father confronting a very silly daughter. "I agree that this is a tragedy of the highest order, but I'm afraid wiser heads must prevail."

George reached for his wife's hand. Genie will come round eventually, he told himself. A little pat will put things right. But either Eugenia moved or the ship rolled and George's gesture fell on hollow air.

"We'll arrange a nice memorial service on the fantail," he said as he slipped his fingers back in his pocket. "I'm afraid it's all we can do."

George was aware of feeling quite a tangle of emotions, not the least of which was elation. The first sensation was of being a child let loose in a sweets shop. Then he felt a sort of terror, not at getting caught with his thumbs in the peppermint jar, but at being in the place all alone. Sarawak, he told himself. I've got to pull off the entire coup by myself. Beckmann's death was definitely a mixed bag.

George imagined storm clouds gathering on the home front: telegraph messages and ultimatums and a flurry of letters. That picture floated him along for a moment; he saw himself riding out the hurricane and saving the day, but then another thought burst into his brain. If removing Beckmann gives me a new lease on life, George wondered, who else might benefit?

"You haven't said anything yet, Lieutenant," George ordered. "Surely you have an opinion. Everyone else seems to. Including my pretty wife." The last words were intended as an admonition, but Eugenia seemed oblivious.

"I'm afraid I don't, sir," Brown answered. "Aside from the hours when we gathered formally, I didn't see much of Mr. Beckmann."

"Indeed." George recognized the lie, but was powerless to refute it. The lie was a reminder, after all, a warning that the job came first. "You didn't see Mr. Beckmann last night then?" he added. Asking questions made George feel he was in charge.

"Not after we gave up that game of cards. I believe that was when we retired. Whitney was there as well, and the doctor." Brown's answer was as smooth as cream.

"Retired." The word jolted Eugenia; it was so out of character for James. The idea of something concealed jumped into her brain again, though what George and James might conspire against her was beyond imagination.

"George," she said abruptly, "all this talk gets us nowhere. We should sail back and look for Ogden. That's all there is to it. Captain Cosby can steer the exact course. . . . He's got the necessary charts and instruments—"

"This isn't a garden path, my dear young lady. We can't follow a trail of bread crumbs." George chuckled indulgently; he wanted to smile at Brown over his wife's head, but the man might as well have been made of bricks.

"I'm not a child, George," Eugenia answered. "You needn't treat me as such."

"I'm sure Mr. Beckmann's out of his misery," Brown interrupted. His voice was quiet, and his body didn't move, but there was nothing languid about him. If activity is release or solace or peace, Brown was the opposite.

Eugenia stared at his face. The eyes were shrouded as if by fog. Eugenia thought they looked immensely cold; the blue didn't reflect her own face or the waves or the ship or the day; they were an entity all their own. "Out of his misery," she repeated silently, then realized: Of course. James has seen this kind of thing before: a ship in a storm, a friend swept away. I need to show my sympathy. That's what he's asking for.

"I imagine so," she answered. It seemed brutal not to touch him.

"Brown's right, Genie," George agreed in his good-natured, don't-you-worry-your-pretty-little-head voice. "Better if Ogden drowned right off."

Eugenia turned away from both men and studied the water, the blue and yellow expanse of Indian Ocean tides. This sea carries coconuts and tree trunks, she told herself, rattan husks, betel palm boughs and narwhal tusks—everyday objects from one land that create myths in another. In Africa, the princes prize the *coco de mer* as an antidote to poison, and they whisper dark secrets about subterranean forests no human eye has seen, while across the Indian Ocean, the poor little fruit is as common as dirt. Thus the narwhal's tusk becomes a unicorn's horn; it is reborn, renamed and worshiped as it never was at home. Ogden Beckmann could swim to the safety of an undiscovered island—his descendants could create a new race—or he could die.

Eugenia concentrated on the familiar sound of her husband's yacht moving through the water: the thrum of engines and the cut of salt spray. On July the twenty fifth we left Newport, she told herself. I was the last passenger on deck. I watched the coast of Rhode Island blur with Connecticut and New York till the entire North American continent was a wisp like smoke in an empty lane.

When the final sea gull departed, I looked forward, and never once looked back. I believed nothing could touch us, Eugenia realized; I believed we were invincible, that love would never die.

So Ogden Beckmann was given a brief memorial service on the fantail of the *Alcedo*. It was the sunny afternoon of October the twenty-third, a day of golden light and high clouds, with a breeziness that called to mind the best part of a northeastern seaside summer. Except for the black-clad figures and their shambling gaits, the yacht could have been cruising Block Island Sound, and there was a moment, for each passenger and each crew member, when that guilty revelation set upon them. It was the smell of the wind, or the slide of a shadow on a heated length of teak; it was the touch of brass warmed by the sun, the crisp tip-tap of a sailcloth awning, or the rattle and chime of a halyard shaking on a pole. If you closed your eyes, lifted your chin, and let the breeze drop like buttercups, you were home.

It was a difficult time for everyone. George, chagrined at his own pleasure, put on a long face and spouted pompous words about a life well lived. Brown covered his feelings in a facade of surprised disbelief, and Eugenia tried to wade through the lies and half truths cast up about her. In the midst of the maudlin speeches and droning prayers, she thought: A man's body was left in the sea; he may be dead or he may not; no one saw him fall.

It seemed to Eugenia that everyone—Captain Cosby, Mrs. Du-Plessis, the doctor, George, and even James—was hiding some secret about themselves, and the more righteous each became, the more distant she grew. Even her own children appeared facile in a mimicry of grief. Their tears were voluminous, but she couldn't understand for whom they were shed.

"Eternal Father! strong to save," they sang together.

> *Whose arm hath bound the restless wave,*
> *Who bidd'st the mighty ocean deep*
> *Its own appointed limits keep . . .*

None of us mean these words, Eugenia thought, none of us care. What was Beckmann but an odious, disagreeable presence? Why should we miss him now that he's gone? He wasn't much use alive. But her mind saw only a dark figure, sinking alone in a coal black night.

> *. . . Oh, hear us when we cry to Thee*
> *For those in peril on the sea! . . .*

The service finally ended and the group scattered in self-contained silence. Eugenia pulled off her hat, extricated its pins with a frown of either anger or concentration, and shook the long veil clear, but the netting snagged on a brooch, ripped, then waved in her face with a cloud full of lightning and hail. "I hate wearing black," Eugenia announced to no one in particular. She wished she could toss this particular hat overboard. Watching it lag behind and sink would be a relief. She crumpled the veil and handed the entire mess—hat, pins, and torn netting—to Olive, who waited, mum and fearful as always.

And I hate gloves as well, Eugenia decided while she went to work on the black kid cuffs. The buttons seemed infinitesimal, elusive and slippery as though someone had rolled them in oil. Eugenia realized her hands were shaking. She made a lunge for the gloves' fingertips, yanking so hard that she popped three wrist buttons before the wretched leather pulled loose. The gloves were then slapped into Olive's hands as if Eugenia never wanted to touch them again. Olive knew better than to speak; she retrieved the three lost pearls with a deft, quiet shoe.

Mrs. DuPlessis watched the entire scene: the problem of Eugenia's hat and the shameful abuse of the buttons. With or without gloves, Eugenia's hands were still trembling, and Mrs. DuPlessis noted this sign of weakness with satisfaction while she preened herself on her own inner fortitude. Not many people were as comfortable with death as Mrs. DuPlessis.

"You shouldn't say that, my dear," she cooed. "You look very well in the darker tones. I've always said so. Very discreet and modest. Quite the lady." Then Mrs. DuPlessis added her own gloves, veil, and hat to Olive's pile, fluffing the decorative feathers with a light, loving gesture. "Take my funereal kit down, too, Olive," she said. "There's a good girl."

Eugenia decided Mrs. DuPlessis had become insufferable, homey and pretentious at the same miserable time. Who else would pack mourning clothes for a pleasure cruise? Eugenia wondered. Who else would refer to them as a "funereal kit" and add a hat that resembled a crow fight at dusk. Fury stamped through Eugenia's chest and made mincemeat of her stomach. We might as well be sipping after supper cocoa, she realized, sitting in a lady's retiring room, discussing cooks and gardeners while our husbands finish their cigars. A man's body is adrift in the sea, sinking or swimming, dead or alive, and we feign relief at such a tidy end.

"Funerals are never easy," Mrs. DuPlessis sighed as she patted down her hair, then revived a limp curl with two stubby fingers. "But, my dear, we must endure them. A fact of life, as my dear Gustav says. A sad fact of life. Though it's a shame we couldn't have had a small orchestra. . . . A dirge is so moving when played on a cello . . . but, of course, we weren't prepared. . . ."

Eugenia hardly heard a word. In her mind Beckmann's body lazed upward toward the ocean's surface. Bubbles followed it, and the kind of light that gets trapped in ice. The body was naked and gray as a whale, and it hung at the edge of her memory with blubbery insinuation. I believed we were invincible, Eugenia repeated silently; I believed love would never die.

"Good of you to come up so quickly," George blurted out. He wasn't quite sure how to conduct this meeting with Brown. The man represented a confusion of class George couldn't quite comprehend. Brown is a hybrid, George told himself, looking for a simile that would make the situation easier; he is a botanical freak. But, a newly created specimen remains just that: a separate species. Brown may masquerade as one of us, but he can't change, George told himself. And a tiger can't change his stripes.

"Sit down, Brown. Cigar?"

"Thank you, sir, no."

"Glass of port? Something stronger?" This wasn't the right approach at all. The man wasn't his equal, after all. George hesitated again.

"No. Thank you. Sir." Brown's repetition of the title made George realize the man was equally uneasy. Brown was putting as much distance between the two of them as he could.

George cleared his throat, widened his stance, and clasped his hands, statesmanlike, behind his back. "The reason I called you up here, Brown," he said, "the reason I called you up here . . . well, did Ogden . . . did Mr. Beckmann call you Brown or . . . well, what I mean to say is . . . is there another name you prefer, a name Ogden . . . that is, Mr. . . ."

"Brown is fine. Sir."

"Good. Fine. Brown." George rattled off the words while he stalled for time. This is deuced difficult, he told himself. I don't know how much the blasted fellow knows, what Beckmann said about our involvement in Borneo, or if Brown only understands his assignment: Distribute the rifles, train Seh's men, then let them work the rebellion in their own fashion. George walked to his desk and stared down at a coastal chart of Sarawak, hoping his thoughts would settle those problems between them. He was beginning to wish he'd paid more heed to Ogden's lessons. The Ivard family and their peculiar intricacies, especially.

July the twenty-fifth, George remembered suddenly. And in this very room. Father, Beckmann . . . the day of departure . . . orders taken and promises given. What a long time ago it seems, George told himself. Here we are, halfway round the world, and it's only just getting on to winter at home. Summer weather here and a lifetime away, while in Philadelphia it's the dark days of autumn and the close of a year like all the rest.

"Seems a good while since we left home, doesn't it, Brown?" George said half to himself. "As if that stuff and nonsense along the way happened to someone else. As if we were different people. In Madeira, you know, and the Med . . . in Port Said . . ." George hesitated and glanced at the chart again; he'd lost his train of thought completely.

"I suppose I'm not making much sense," he added, trying to remember what it was he'd envisioned; he'd had a glimpse of something—an emotion or nervy-edged fact—and it had spoken lucidly to him, like a figure in a dream. It knew something he did not; it had enticed him, then disappeared. "Time is no more than a commodity, after all," George concluded, then rambled on:

"Where would we be without it, though? That's what I'd like to know. You can't argue with facts." George returned to the map and ran his fingers along the ridges that marked depth and shipping lanes and the powdery dots that meant unexplored coves. A navigational chart is a good thing, George told himself; it lets you know where you stand. Or sail.

"Sink or swim," George said. His hand drooped heavily on the paper; it felt clammy, as though it had fallen asleep.

Brown didn't speak; he knew George would get to the point sooner or later. Besides, Brown reminded himself, I don't have any pressing engagements; I can sit here all day if I want. The thought made him smile. He felt relaxed and completely at home. George would speak his piece, or he wouldn't. He'd stumble along like an old blind dog or tear off with a frightened yap. Brown knew who was in charge. He looked at the blue sky through the windows and felt the easy creak of his chair. Its leather smelled remarkably good.

George continued to stand hunched over his desk, studying Kuching and Sarawak, Pangalong, Pontianak, and all the other unpronounceable Malay names. The Turk with his study, his special cigars, and his imperious, biting hand seemed a million miles away. So this is what it's like to be on your own, George thought. This is what people call independence.

"Did you ever know your father, Brown?" George asked without looking up. "Not to look at, I mean. But to talk to?"

"You wanted to ask me about Beckmann" was Brown's only reply.

"At the risk of repeating myself . . . but what man does not . . . at the risk, Mr. Paine, of boring you once again with this amusing little tale . . . or fable, if you will . . ."

The Honorable Nicholas Paine tried to pay attention to the sultan of Sarawak's words, but he found himself nodding off, not sleeping exactly, but dreaming nonetheless. There was a woman in a filmy dress and she was surrounded by heavy green leaves, like Evangeline in the poem . . . a white dress and ivy . . . then sealing wax . . . and a fire no one could extinguish.

". . . though I credit it as true and not an apocryphal tale. . . . Am I boring you, Mr. Paine? . . ." The sultan ceased his recitation suddenly, and the palace in Kuching, Sarawak, turned as silent as a church.

The change of inflection startled the Honorable Nicholas. "No, no, sir . . . Your Highness. What I mean is . . ." Paine stammered, pulling himself forward on the silk cushions that covered a bolster gone sour and rank. Appearance is everything to these people, he thought, and immediately replaced his hands on his knees. Anything might be lurking in the grime below.

". . . Just so . . . just so . . ." The sultan returned to the gauzy trappings of his throne; he rubbed his back along the pillows like a honey bear scratching against a tree. The movement was euphoric. The sultan sighed deeply, then continued: "These folktales are . . ."

Where are Sir Charles and that weasel, Laneer? Paine wondered for what felt like the thousandth time. Where's that infernal Ridgeway, and why do I have to face this interminable interview alone? The sultan droned along, repeating the same phrases over and over and over again: ". . . the ship, *Hollandia*" . . . "the Dutch emperor . . ." Paine felt consigned to the ninth circle of Hell.

And the man's misconceptions are staggering, the Honorable Nicholas told himself, simply staggering. Since when do the Dutch have an emperor? Or perhaps the old coot's referring to the kaiser. Kaiser Willy . . . "Unter den Linden" . . . Paine found his thoughts drifting off again. His jaw sagged toward his chest, then jerked upright. Why did I have to come to Borneo in the first place? he quibbled. Why couldn't I have stayed in Manila? At that moment, all memory of Eugenia and George, their festive arrival, the great yacht pulling up the Sunghai Sarawak, the sultan and the Ivards and their lavish welcome fete, were wiped from his brain.

The Honorable Nicholas had been transported back to Cairo, then to the American legation in Dar es Salaam forty-odd years before . . . then he was basking in the charms of a female companion in a garden bower after the Boxing Day Ball . . .

"Hull down on the trail of rapture/In the wonder of the Sea." . . . Richard Hovey, now there's a poet for you! The lines from "The Sea Gipsy" rattled the old man's ears like a gong going off. The Honorable Nicholas came full awake.

It was October 26, 1903. The *Alcedo* should have been in Sarawak by now. The suddenness of this revelation was startling; Paine was yanked into the present, where he became acutely aware of the stench of his surroundings and his own position as scapegoat. I'm a miserable little sambar deer staked for a tiger hunt, Paine told himself, here because I have a pretty name; it's value by association. I'm dispatched to Borneo to be leapfrogged over and piggyback-ridden. Touch me and some of my fine old blue blood will squirt out and lead you toward salvation. The Honorable Nicholas cut short his diatribe; self-doubt never pays the milkman, he reminded himself.

It's all George's fault, Paine decided; he shouldn't have stopped so long in Africa, at least not after that debacle in Port Said. The yacht's a full two weeks late, maybe longer. And we're left sitting on needles. The Honorable Nicholas's thoughts became sharp as two tacks. Time's running thin, he realized. The sultan was promised rifles. If he wants to make hash of a few unarmed rebels, nothing's going to stand in his way.

A promise is a promise, after all, Paine recited inwardly. That's what makes the Brits successful colonists; they deliver the goods. . . . Paine's mind started to ramble again, but he pulled it back long enough to continue his deliberations: October the twenty-sixth, nineteen and three . . . the Turk made the deal, of course . . . through Ivard . . . Sir Charles, that is . . . my friend . . . not that buffoon, Laneer. . . . Laneer doesn't know his nose from his left shoe. He couldn't tell you if a rifle was pointing at him or a bongo tree.

Paine began drifting again. He sagged gently in his chair, an old man, frail as dried grass. His breathing became rhythmic, then shallow and slow. Coal deposits, he remembered . . . got to tell the Turk . . . good for the Axthelm Trust . . . But the Dutch are the problem . . . the Dutch and His Highness. . . . The *Alcedo*'s got to arrive . . .

Then Paine's thoughts turned green as a day in April; he was on a wide lawn dodging croquet balls that rolled from under a stand of elms. There was laughter, and the whack of mallets, the ping of metal, and more wooden missiles than you could shake a stick at. Paine's breaths became a full-fledged snore. Genie . . . water . . . boil the water . . . not safe for the children . . .

". . . I fear I am losing you, my dear Mr. Paine. . . ."

"Eh? What's that? What's that?" The Honorable Nicholas gaped, coughed, and slapped his arms against the chair cushions. "Not at all, Your Highness. Not at all."

". . . Not any of Aernout Lingen's description . . . ?" the sultan quizzed.

"Heard every word, Your Highness. Every word."

". . . The two white buffalo . . . ?"

"Know all about 'em."

". . . And the fifty dwarfs . . . ?"

"Dwarfs?" Paine quivered and blinked. Dwarfs, he thought. What was the old fox blithering about this time? Was Axthelm supposed to supply dwarfs as well as guns? Well, they might be good for a sneak attack, Paine told himself; rebel soldiers might not see them coming. . . . Besides, if Axthelm promised . . .

"... The fifty dwarfs that the previous sultan, my father, used to keep round him ..."

"I must have missed ..." Paine hesitated over the words. Time was certainly playing tricks. What did Axthelm's dwarf army have to do with the sultan's father?

"You Westerners turn a deaf ear to that which does not suit you." The sultan scratched his back on the pillows again; he lurched from side to side and his throne shook under him. "You ignore what you choose."

"Dwarfs, yes," Paine soothed; he felt horribly confused.

"Fifty!" the sultan shouted. "Fifty men with arms and legs bound fast from infancy, so all were made the same height and expression, like carvings in wood. The common people fought to have their babies chosen; it was a great honor. Such as your English boys going off to Eton or Harrow."

"Well, now, Your Highness ... I don't believe—" The Honorable Nicholas was about to protest but the sultan plunged on:

"My father kept two hundred wives and fifty dwarfs! Our palace rivaled any in Europe; there were more people living beneath these roofs than in many of your paltry, rock-pile towns. And jewels, too, and priceless silks and ivories. We had, before the Chinese, before you Western invaders tried to destroy us, wealth that would dazzle the eye. ..."

"I want my rifles, Paine!" the sultan roared suddenly, struggling to his feet while the glossy hangings of his throne enveloped him like a spider's web.

"I insist upon the guns! This Axthelm has promised me guns! And if I do not see them soon, I will be forced to return to my old benefactor, the Dutch nation, and take aid from their greedy hands! You will drive me to it! You know you will! This man Seh must, must, must be stopped!"

Brown had concluded his interview with George. It hadn't been satisfactory. Brown couldn't be sure what George knew, if he shared Beckmann's suspicions. Or had any of his own.

And he hadn't liked relegating Eugenia to the category of guilty secret, but it hadn't been possible to sit in George's study and not feel her presence between them. Brown forced his thoughts back to the job he'd been hired to do. There's safety in activity, he told himself.

Then he left the study behind, and started down the corridor. Borneo's my lookout, Brown decided. Beckmann was the mastermind, or some faceless man in Philadelphia. But George knows nothing. His answers about Seh and our rendezvous were naive or stupid or both; on top of that he's consumed with an also-ran family named Ivard. Brown steadied his thoughts. George's problems have nothing to do with me, he decided. Seh will be waiting; that's all that counts.

Brown came to the stairs that led to the lower level and sleeping cabins; he'd be passing Eugenia's room in a moment, but he wouldn't allow himself to stop. His face took on the opaque expression Eugenia had noticed the morning Beckmann died. There was no reading Brown's thoughts; what feelings he had, leaving Eugenia's door, he kept to himself.

Seh will be waiting, Brown told himself inwardly. He'll signal the *Alcedo* to move in close to land, that it's safe to unload. But we'll have to be quick about it; we can't risk discovery. The sultan must remain in the dark.

Brown reached the stair to the ship's hold. I'll be safe down here, he decided. I'll have a few hours to put my thoughts in order, come up with a schedule for the arms delivery and a backup routine if Seh fails to show, or if I'm captured. I need to create a plan that's watertight. I'm dealing with savages, after all, and the last thing the Axthelms want is their name involved. Seh's rebellion must appear autonomous: local politics, nothing more. An unnoticed squib in an outdated newspaper.

But Eugenia was there in the dark recess of the doorway, and she interrupted his thoughts.

"James," she whispered, keeping her eyes on the corridor, "may I speak to you?" It took Brown a moment to remember who she was and why she knew his name.

They stood on either side of the white crates and looked as flat as paper in comparison. The boxes seemed the only things living in the dark room; they were proud and painted and huge, and Eugenia and Brown were like cutout figures, propped up and fooling no one.

"But I don't understand, James," Eugenia said again. "Why do you think George knows?"

"Just a hunch," Brown answered. That seemed the safest lie: Your husband knows; we've got to end this. It was a straightforward and inarguable statement, but it hadn't worked. Eugenia had tossed the words aside. "Why?" she'd kept asking, as if persistence paid off.

But she also believes in bravery, Brown told himself, and decency and a fair deal for the poor. She thinks the good are rewarded in heaven. Faith, Hope, and Charity. "I told you, Eugenia," he repeated. "It's a hunch."

Brown couldn't think of another answer; he looked at the crates and promised himself that Eugenia would never guess the truth, that she'd never know what the boxes contained. His hand dusted one white surface, and he stopped in mid-movement as if the hand might betray him.

"But wouldn't he say something?" Eugenia continued. "To me at least?" Her thoughts were whirling around, lighting on one thing, then another. She watched Brown's hand on the box, and she glanced at his face. It looked entirely different: square and thick and stubborn, as if he had something he wouldn't release. It wasn't a face she remembered.

"I don't know what your husband's capable of." Brown stared at the crates. He couldn't say Eugenia's name. Or George's. Get this over with, he told himself. Do the job and get out. She returns to Philadelphia; you disappear in the jungle.

"But . . . after that awful discovery about Ogden . . . I'm sure he would have . . ." Eugenia felt as if she were running for her life, tumbling headlong without time to pant or cry. "Look at me," she wanted to scream. "Tell me you love me. Hold me. Take me back." But then something stopped even those emotions, and replaced them with rigidity or stoicism or a void like the holes in her dreams. ". . . which you do of your own free election . . ." Eugenia remembered.

"You have to trust me, Eugenia." Brown's throat went tight and hard, and no more words came out. I don't have to do this, he thought. I could quit. Jump ship, tell George: "I've changed my mind. You can take your money and burn it for all I care." And maybe, Brown reasoned, that would be for the best. He might forget this silly scheme. Stand up to his father. Become a man.

Eugenia watched the changes filter across Brown's face. There was a moment when she felt a pang of hope, then realized she'd been defeated. "I do trust you, James," she said, but while the vow was still in her mouth she knew it was a lie.

When we get home, Eugenia tried to reason, when James and I are on our own. . . . The comforting phrases fell where they stood. As far as the eye could see there was nothing but row after tall, black row of questions.

"I'll go now," she said. Her voice was steady, but it took concentration. The sound of the words were more important than their meaning. "You seem preoccupied. . . . I guess with Sarawak so close, there must be a lot of work to do on this machinery"—Eugenia glanced at the crates and forced a smile—"all these ore-smelting mechanisms. . . . I don't know much about it . . . but I'm sure with—" She'd been about to say "with Beckmann gone."

". . . Well, I'm sure George will be . . . and my father . . ." There was nothing to add that wasn't a reminder of how trapped they both were. "Impossible," Eugenia might have been saying. "This is impossible."

Brown heard "Borneo" and "George" and was reminded, though it wasn't necessary, of exactly where he stood.

"Yes, you'd better," he answered.

The *Alcedo* took on more coal at Port Victoria, Mahé Island, as planned. There were no shore excursions. The children, under the watchful eye of Prue and Whitney, were sent to exercise on the dock, but the rest of the adults stayed on board. General Gordon's Garden of Eden was ignored. The group was quiet, as if bracing for a fight.

Within a day, the ship was ready to depart. Captain Cosby unrolled the maritime chart that would take the yacht along the channel that cut through the reefs surrounding the islands. The entire eastern side of Mahé was fringed with coral, and Cosby would be glad to get the *Alcedo* clear of the deadly stuff. So without further ado, the lines were cast off, and the *Alcedo* moved ahead while the Seychelles Islands fell behind. They disappeared in greenery and the senseless, tangled mist of all islands. The Morne Seychellois, the Trois Frères: soon even those two peaks were no more than a smattering of gray clouds swirling over the open sea.

TWENTY-FOUR

*L*IZZIE WAS ON DECK. She'd put as much distance between herself and her brother and sister as she could, but she could still hear their voices—if not the exact words of the geography game they were playing with Cousin Whitney. She'd been excused from the lesson because she could recite the places backward and forward. As if anyone cares about some silly names, Lizzie told herself. She stared at the water. It had been five days since the *Alcedo* had left Port Victoria, and now they had to go to a place called Borneo because Father had some important work there. For the first time since the voyage began, Lizzie wondered if they were ever going home. She put her hands on the rail and glared at the cuffs of her blue and white middy blouse.

I look just like a baby, she thought, all dressed up like Jinx, and Paul in his dumb little sailor's suit. We must look unbelievably stupid: a gaggle of newborn geese. There was a high-pitched garble of words from the open-air classroom. "Continent," Lizzie heard, followed by: "Is an island a continent?"; "Is Borneo?"

Feather-brained nitwits, Lizzie decided. She moved further down the deck. Borneo! she thought as she ground her shoe's untied lace into the deck floor. What's so whizzer about Borneo? Who wants to visit a sultan or a palace anyway?

Lizzie pulled a pencil from her pocket and began to run it along the rail stanchions; the tap-pop-plip sound it made was fun to listen to, and you could make the rhythm go faster or slower or even louder if you wanted. Lizzie was mesmerized by the game, then suddenly realized it made her look juvenile and ignorant. It was the kind of thing Jinx would do to get attention.

Lizzie dropped the pencil overboard and wondered if a fish might grab it by mistake, but nothing happened; the pencil sank, and a few dirty waves washed over the place where it had fallen, then the ship moved on. Lucky fish, Lizzie thought; I guess they'd die if they ate a pencil. "Lead poisoning," Mrs. D. would say.

Lizzie looked toward the foredeck; there was no one there; all the chairs were empty. She glanced back at the aft deck, but it contained only Whit, Jinx, and Paul, sitting in a schoolroom circle. They look like circus dogs with their paws wiggling in the air, Lizzie thought. Yap, yap, yarp. "But that's not fair, Cousin Whit." Jinx's peevish complaint drifted forward. Yap, yap, yip, Lizzie repeated to herself.

What does Jinx know about "fair"? Lizzie wondered suddenly. She thinks "fair" is an extra cup of cocoa, or staying up a half hour later, or "fair" is winning at Parcheesi. She's as dumb as they come.

Lizzie decided to move to the other side of the ship so she wouldn't have to listen to any further inanity—*inanity* was a favorite word that day—then she decided her lessons were completely finished for the day. And if Mother punishes me for leaving early, I'll simply lie, Lizzie told herself. I'll say I forgot. Who's going to punish me? God?

That concept seemed highly amusing; Lizzie imagined the church on Rittenhouse Square and the stained-glass windows with pictures of saints milling around Jesus. Lizzie imagined herself struck down by a bolt of lightning hurled by an infuriated saint. Or maybe Jesus' shepherd's crook would fly out of a window and pierce her heart. Lizzie pictured herself dying in her family's pew: the crook still protruding from her chest while she gasped a futile confession and her hands clawed the prayer books as if attempting to reveal a deep, dark secret. Her death would be long and agonized, and everyone would weep copious tears and beg her to recover, while she gave up her tragic ghost with a thin, brave smile. "Oh, Lizzie!" they'd mourn. "My daughter!"; "My sister!"; "My dearest child." It would serve them right!

Lizzie crossed the middle of the deck; she passed the ring toss net slapping against its poles, the chair cushions that smelled of sunshine and salt, the companionway door with its polished porthole, and the newly varnished games cupboard that was as shiny as ice. Lizzie ignored every one of those cozy signs of shipboard life; if anything, they made her more angry. Her feet stomped along. Engine steam billowed up, down, then raced across the wood's surface like terrier puppies; Lizzie tromped right through them. What would be fair, she thought, would be to go home right now. Forget Borneo and Korea and all those other places, sail across the Pacific, get on a train in San Francisco, and go back to Philadelphia. That would be fair.

The windward side of the yacht was much breezier than the leeward. Before she could reach the rail, Lizzie's navy serge skirt slammed against her knees and her blouse filled up like a balloon. She backtracked to the games chest to put her clothes in order; she hoped no one had seen her shirt front flapping about. I look like Mrs. DuPlessis, Lizzie thought. All bust and corset and fat belly. She yanked the middy blouse into place, wrenched the bows into globular pendants, and flattened her collar with a slap. If I can't dress like an adult, she said with her gestures, then I'll look like an idiotic, simpering kid.

Rebecca of Sunnybrook Farm, Lizzie remembered as she worked on her clothes. Little Miss Wonderful with her parasol and smoked pearl buttons and that sappy, goody-good hat. No wonder Jinx is enthralled with that stupid book; it's exactly the kind of vacuous nonsense a child her age would enjoy.

" 'Sunday Thoughts' " by Rebecca Rowena Randall," Lizzie quoted, half to herself and half for the benefit of whatever fish might be choking up fragments of lead and pencil. *Bitter* was the term she would have used in describing her tone. Or *sarcastic:* That word worked equally well. So did *cynical* which had the added advantage of making one person old and wise, and another childish and shallow. " 'Sunday Thoughts':

> *"This house is dark and dull and drear*
> *No light doth shine from far and near . . .*
> *My guardian angel is asleep*
> *At least he doth no vigil keep . . .*
> *Then give me back my lonely farm*
> *Where none alive did wish me harm . . ."*

Lizzie made a face as if she'd tasted something repulsively gooey; she sucked in her cheeks, pursed her lips, and turned her eyes into slits. "Who cares about a brick house or some out-of-the-way place like Riverboro! 'It was shelter for the little family at Sunnybrook.' Pooh!"

Lizzie threw herself onto the teak deck; the wood felt warm and inviting, and she stretched her blue-stockinged legs straight out in front of her and let the heat bubble through her calves and ankles while she leaned her back into a sunny wall. I'm thirteen years old, Lizzie told herself, not a ten-year-old baby like Jinx. In March, I'll be fourteen, and that's only five months away. Not even five months, she realized, because it's almost November now.

Fourteen, Lizzie thought. The number was magic; it dazzled with wondrous images: dresses covered in silver beads and hats of marabou feathers, satin-heeled shoes with buckles of nacre and jet. "Fourteen," she repeated aloud, then lolled her head against the wall and pondered the terrible fate that had placed her, a young lady of substantial age and hidden beauty, on a boat bumbling through the Indian Ocean. Heading for Borneo, of all heathen places! "I shouldn't be here at all," Lizzie nearly moaned. I should be in Philadelphia, attending dancing class and girls' school and parties for young ladies. I should be preparing for my debut year, speaking French, learning how to "pour" and practicing my curtsy in a court gown and train. The knowledge of how cruel life had become was unbearable; it caused Lizzie to clamp her eyes shut till they hurt and toss her head till it banged into the wall. "It just isn't fair," she whispered over and over again.

"Are you all right, Liz . . . Miss . . . Miss . . . Miss Lizzie." Henry looked down, worried, though unsure how to address the young lady. Mealtimes had their rules; teatime was the same; Higgins said you must "never speak to your betters without employing an appropriate title." The problem was that Henry couldn't forget how much freedom he'd had in Port Said, and what good friends he and Ned and the Axthelm children had been, so he often nearly said plain "Lizzie" by mistake. And sometimes he caught himself about to talk without using her name at all, as if he were family almost, or a friend. At those moments Henry realized he was probably the stupidest boy in the world.

"Miss Lizzie?" Henry repeated. He didn't know whether to sit on the deck beside her or continue to stand, bent forward at a halfhearted angle. Henry felt horribly tall, waving around like a scarecrow on a stick while his trouser legs flapped in the breeze like a couple of discarded feed bags. He forced himself to stay where he was. You'll be taking liberties, he recited to himself, if you sit without being asked. And remember what Higgins says about "taking liberties."

Lizzie didn't want to open her eyes. For a moment she imagined that keeping her eyelids clenched would made the voice disappear. What a disaster, she told herself. Why do these things always happen to me? Why couldn't Henry have stayed where he belonged? Lizzie's anger at appearing less than a mature, nearly-fourteen-year-old young lady turned to rage at Henry.

"What is it?" she snapped. "Did my mother's cousin tell you to fetch me back to my lessons?" She didn't grace Henry with a name, or Whitney either, for that matter. She was as aloof as could be. "Minion," she might have been sneering. "Vassal"; "You shall suffer when my father, the emperor, hears of this insubordination." Lizzie piled up walls of defenses as if they were wooden blocks.

"If he did send you, I'm not going."

"No, he didn't . . . I mean, Mr. Whitney didn't . . ." Henry faltered. "Miss . . . Lizzie . . ." He added the respectful titles, dragging them out piece by piece like treasures in a box. "I saw you bang your head, that's all. Miss . . . Lizzie. . . ."

"I didn't bang my head. It's a form of exercise," Lizzie answered. Her lips shriveled into a purple line, and she opened her eyes the tiniest crack as if concentrating on some planet only she had the wisdom to see. "It's an exercise to clear the brain. It promotes intelligence. That's how much you know!"

Lizzie banged her head again. The noise was louder this time, loud enough to startle her; Lizzie felt the wall shiver behind her, and wondered briefly if she'd damaged the bones in her skull.

"Ouch," Henry answered for her, nearly stumbling over his two large feet as he bent over involuntarily. "That sounded like it hurt. Miss." Henry remembered to add the title just in the nick of time.

"Well, it didn't," Lizzie answered. There were tears in her eyes, but she couldn't have said where they'd come from. They weren't caused by the pain in her head; that much was certain. Lizzie threw herself against the wall again, and this time the blow forced her to grip her skirt with both hands.

"I think you're far and away smart enough, Lizzie," Henry said desperately, forgetting the title entirely. "You shouldn't go banging your head like that. You'll get ill. Look what happened to your . . ."

"Miss," Lizzie corrected in the meanest voice she could find, then she pulled herself to her feet and attempted a regal and outraged stance. Her skirt was crumpled; her blouse had stuck to her back, and her head felt as though rats had built a nest in her brain, but Lizzie didn't care. Life is awful, she told herself. It's cruel and unfair and I hate every last minute of it.

Then without meaning to, she blurted: "I wish we could go home, Henry. Go home and be ordinary people . . . Have friends, go for walks in the park, feed the ducks . . . Don't you want to go home? Henry? Don't you?" Lizzie looked up at Henry and her face was red and shiny, and her eyes were filled with tears.

Henry didn't answer; he looked at his friend, took a step toward her, but was stopped by the sudden appearance of Eugenia stepping through the companionway door.

"Liz?" Eugenia said. "Lizzie? What on earth . . . ?" Eugenia took in the entire scene, registered what she thought she'd seen, and stepped briskly between her daughter and the unfortunate Henry. "Don't you have work below decks?" Eugenia demanded. Her voice was like rock salt splattering a window.

"Ma'am," Henry answered. "Yes, ma'am." He told himself he should go, that he'd been all but ordered to leave, but two difficulties held him back: one way was the desire to clear his good name—Mrs. Axthelm had definitely gotten the wrong impression—and the second was concern over Lizzie herself. She seemed awfully upset, Henry thought, and lonely, too. As lonely as he was. The two problems were not necessarily listed in that order.

"Yes, ma'am," Henry repeated, but he didn't move.

All sorts of bombastic phrases filled Eugenia's mind. "Now see here, young man," she imagined saying. "I won't have you behaving improperly with my daughter; we'll have no more of this; run along, and don't let me catch you mooning about again." I've become my grandmother, Eugenia realized with a jolt. A rule-ridden matron from Philadelphia. The transformation was shocking.

Fortunately Lizzie saved her mother from embarrassing them both with the words she knew were imminent; Lizzie shot a quick look at Henry from behind her mother's back. The look said: *Go. Please. I'm fine. Please.* Henry had no choice but to acquiesce; he walked away, knowing he was being measured and found lacking with every ungainly step. He damned his shoes and his trousers and especially the cuffs of his jacket, which crept higher and exposed more bony, red wrist with every galumphing stride. Mother and daughter were left alone.

What have I done wrong? Eugenia asked herself. Is George right? Am I a bad influence? Have I failed to see my daughter growing up? Have I been too absorbed in my own puny needs? Eugenia rattled off the questions but was incapable of answering even one.

"Lizzie . . . dear . . ." Eugenia finally began; she didn't know what words would follow; she was acting on the hope that age brings wisdom, and love: understanding. But Lizzie interrupted with an angry "I don't see why I can't have friends."

"But friends, Liz—." Eugenia was about to add: "of your own class," but stopped herself in time. That's the key, though, isn't it? Eugenia decided. The realization made her feel heavy and old and completely alone.

That's the message I've been taught to impart, Eugenia thought; that's what I memorized along with French and art and social graces: that there are people you cannot choose for friendship or for love, that there are boundaries you can never cross.

"If we were at home, I'd have friends," Lizzie insisted. The rage in her daughter's voice took Eugenia off guard. She felt knocked in the chest, as if a thief had attacked her in an alley.

"But you're not home," Eugenia answered; her tone was equally unpleasant.

It wasn't what Eugenia had wanted to say; she wanted to be consoling and kind, a mother who would put her arm round her daughter's frail shoulder and lead her toward the safer path. But those phrases were nowhere in sight, and Eugenia was left speaking someone else's mind.

"I hate this ship," Lizzie wailed suddenly. "And I hate being on it. And I hate lessons with a tutor who's really a cousin and I hate Paul and Jinx being so smarmy. And I never get to see you, and we've got to be good all the time and wear these stupid clothes and watch Mrs. DuPlessis waddle around like an old, fat hen, and Father's taking us to someplace awful and I don't know why . . ."

The list was far from complete, but Eugenia stopped her daughter with words that jumped in her mouth from out of the blue. "You are a girl, Lizzie," she said, "and because you are female, you do what you're told. Do you understand?" The sound of Eugenia's voice took on an odd ring as if someone else were speaking. "You never complain. You never get ill. You never grow tired . . ."

Eugenia forgot Lizzie entirely; the advice was for herself. "You never cave in," she said. "You never give up."

Lizzie glared at her mother; nothing she said made sense. "That's you, Mother!" she managed after a moment. "That's you! That isn't me."

George was in his study, pouring himself a whiskey and soda. Lately it seemed all he was capable of. He felt enervated and afraid. The ship kept pushing on; every day it was closer to Borneo.

"Soon we'll be in sight of Sumatra and the Selat Sunda," George said aloud, then tried to forget the names as soon as he'd spoken them. "Soon we'll pass the beacon at Tanjong Datu. . . . Soon we'll see Sarawak . . ."

George didn't hear Eugenia's knock at his door, and he didn't hear her enter. At that moment, his concentration had shifted away from his predicament to a stealthy observation of the decanter in his hand. He was trying to weigh the difficulties of pouring an extra splash of whiskey against the enormous task of putting the bottle down.

"George?" Eugenia said from the door. "George," she repeated louder.

George turned slowly around. "Ah, didn't hear your knock, my dear," he said; he looked like a frog who'd sat too long in the sun.

"I knocked twice," Eugenia dared him. "Then I walked in."

"Ah," George said. He gave the word the same weight he gave the whiskey bottle. "Walked in . . ." he said.

"I need to talk to you, George," Eugenia insisted. She sat in a chair, crossed her ankles, clasped her hands together, and stared at her husband's face.

George blinked a crooked smile and decided to put both glass and decanter back on the table. "What can I do for you, my dear? Not happy? Sea too rough? Isn't the chef providing . . . ?"

"George!" Eugenia leaned forward; her fingers gripped each other as hard as they could. She was afraid they'd fly off in all directions. "What are we doing? Where are we going?"

"Doing? . . ." George repeated studiously.

"Doing. Going. They mean the same thing," Eugenia interrupted. Her jaw was tight.

"Why, we're on our way to Borneo, my dear. That's where we're going." George had a momentary sensation of dizziness, so he stayed still till the feeling passed. A little too much of the hair of the dog, he told himself. Or not enough. The thought was as clubby as a private joke. George relaxed into a smile. "Should be only a few more days. Captain Cosby says . . ."

Eugenia wasn't listening. She'd come to ask a question and she wasn't about to be put off by her husband's routine and roundabout blither. She looked at the sweaty smile, the queasy lips, and the hand that drifted irresolutely between chair and table top. "To us," she insisted. "What is happening to us? To the children, to this family?"

"To us?"

"You're not a parrot, George! Don't repeat everything I say." Eugenia felt as if the bottom of her chair had fallen through, as if her legs weren't her own, as if she were weightless and pinned in place.

"To the children, then . . ." George wondered if he could build that phrase into a toast of some kind: Stand, toss liquor into his glass, then drain it with a flourish.

"You can't be as obtuse as you seem, George." Eugenia's tone was startling. George didn't think he'd ever heard anything so venomous. He gawked at his wife, but she met his gaze. For a moment neither of them spoke; finally it was Eugenia who backed down. You can't fight air, she told herself, or fog or a rainy day. Anger racketed around inside her; it surged up her spine into her throat and shook every finger. What's the use? she told herself. What's the use? Without intending to, her hand shot forward toward the armrest, but it missed its mark and rattled a small table laden with ivory miniatures, which then tipped, rolled, and went flying.

"Damn those things!" Eugenia said. Her words were high and fierce. She might have been choking on them.

"Netsukes," George corrected automatically. When danger threatens, he told himself, the safest place is the most familiar. "They're Japanese. . . ."

"I don't care what they're called!" Eugenia hurled herself out of the chair. It's like being married to a jellyfish, she thought, or an octopus or a frost-bitten fly. She glared at the carpet; it was littered with tiny ivory dogs and pigs and dragons and toads. They looked stupid and forlorn and as helpless as new milk; Eugenia imagined crushing them to bits. Tiny black eyes glanced up in fear, and outstretched claws and bunchy necks.

"What I am saying, George, is what has happened between us? I feel as if everyone on the ship has died. Not just Ogden. I feel none of us are in this world anymore. We walk around avoiding each other. We say: 'Excuse me'; 'Lovely weather'; 'So good of you to ask.' We say nothing at all! Even the children know something's wrong."

Eugenia stopped; she knew she was wasting herself on muzzy questions. Why can't I say what I feel? she wondered. Why can't I tell him what's on my mind? Frustration and self-loathing walked hand in hand down a garden path. What's the use of blaming George? Eugenia asked herself. Lizzie's anger is meant for me. I'm the one who's failed.

"But weren't the children playing about this morning . . . ?" George blinked through the haze of his memory, and tried to picture exactly when it was he'd last seen the children. It must have been this morning . . . hadn't he been out on deck with them? . . . or surely last night . . . ?

". . . I know I heard them somewhere . . . sounded very happy, too . . . shouldn't think the Ogden business was affecting them in the . . ."

"Jesus, God, George!" Eugenia exploded. "Have you ever listened to yourself?" There was the jellyfish feeling again; something cold and wet and heavy with indecision clung to her like a cape. There was nowhere to turn without a clammy tentacle oozing down over her shoulders; if she freed a hand, she lost an elbow; if she stretched her neck into the open, her legs were swallowed whole.

"Isn't there something you want to tell me?" she blurted out. "Or ask? Don't you have something to say?"

There, Eugenia told herself. Said. Done. And I'm glad. I don't care what he does. He can berate me. Threaten. Anything. We can't live like this; that's certain. Eugenia's promises were brave; they rose in her chest and heated her cheeks.

This was the moment George had been dreading. Ever since they'd left Newport he'd worried over the rifles and Eugenia. Not that there was anything inherently wrong in a cargo of weapons, he'd constantly reminded himself. It was just that a woman's sensitive spirit might recoil from the job he'd agreed to do. And Genie was no exception; George had known that all along.

She'd insist they turn the ship around or dump the things overboard or make some equally outlandish suggestion. Then she'd create all sorts of fuss about the Turk and a plot and her own father's part, and, on top of that, demand explanations. Whenever George imagined this confrontaion, his wife's angry questions became more and more unreasonable and harder to assuage; just remembering those fictions made him shudder.

"There's nothing to say, Eugenia," George decided to answer. He felt he'd come this far, and he might as well see the thing through. "I don't know what you're talking about. I've nothing to ask. Or tell." Good, George told himself, a lie smooth as lemon sherbet. George began to feel better; his head started to clear, and a pleasant sensation, like a long restful snooze, gave him encouragement.

"I don't really know what's gotten you so upset, my dear. I, for one, haven't noticed any change in our guests. I know your feminine nature is more sensitive than mine, but I certainly haven't detected . . . I mean, even in the kiddies' routine, there doesn't seem anything out of the . . ." Lying is a piece of cake, George told himself; I can say anything I want. Anything in God's blue moon.

". . . Ogden's unfortunate demise was only an accident, after all, regrettable as every misfortune, I agree. But, don't you feel . . . well, not to sound cavalier, Genie . . . but don't you think that death . . . in this instance, only, of course . . . might be looked upon as a not unimportant lesson? . . ."

George was aware that his wife was staring at him. She was standing as still as stone; her mouth was open and a frown made gashes above her eyebrows. She looked worn and faded, as if she'd spent a lifetime in hard work. Has she seen through the lie, George wondered suddenly. Does she know? Can that fool Brown have told her? Or Ogden? Could Ogden have . . . ?

Eugenia decided she didn't believe any of her husband's excuses. If he's waiting till we sail home to confront me with James, I'll be ready, she promised herself. If he needs the entire Axthelm clan to back him up, well, two can play at this game. Eugenia found herself standing straighter; she had a sensation of peace, a settling in of wisdom and resolve.

George misread every sign: His wife's silence was humbleness; her proud stance, faith in his good judgment. ". . . So you just run along back to your cabin," he clucked, "and don't worry that pretty little head about what people think. . . ." George felt better and better and better, as buoyant, almost, as he'd felt the afternoon he'd decided to go off on safari in Africa.

". . . We're all of us adults, Genie, quite capable of caring for our-selves. . . .We can feel sorrow for poor old Ogden, certainly. But some things can't be helped. . . . And you know, Genie, business, a certain kind of business, must be left to gentlemen who understand. . . ." George felt like wriggling into a dance. It's working, he told himself; she's following it hook, line, and sinker!

". . . So you just toddle along back to your little room and think about how much fun we're going to have in Borneo. You'll see your fa-ther again. Won't that be nice? . . ."

The comforting words poured out of George's mouth. It's going to be fine, he told himself: Brown delivers the rifles to Seh, the rebellion comes off without a hitch, Sir Charles Ivard assumes power, and the coal fields belong to the Axthelms. Beckmann's no longer needed, George recited inwardly, because I can handle this one myself.

"As you can see, Mrs. Axthelm . . . Master Paul . . . Miss Jinx . . . Mr. Whitney . . ." Captain Cosby continued with his daily geography les-son, moving his finger along the nautical chart with loving precision. The afternoon was pleasant, the quiet hour before teatime as unruffled and peaceful as always. Captain Cosby insisted on routine.

". . . we've had to sail north to catch the tail end of the southeast trade winds before dropping down to nose our way through the Selat Sunda and the Zutphen Islands. . . ."

Eugenia listened to the captain's words while she watched his hand trace a path across the chart. There's nothing in his world that can't be explained, she told herself. Everything has its place; everything has its reason. Eugenia was glad she'd decided to join her children's visit to the wheelhouse.

". . . Now you may be asking [though no one had] why the *Alcedo*, a steam yacht under power, should need trade winds to see her through. . . ." Captain Cosby paused to wait for the excited response he felt his question deserved. When none came, he proceeded with un-flagging enthusiasm: "That's because of a simple rule every good seafarer knows by heart: Keep the wind at your back. Coal-fired engines or no."

"And if there's a storm on the horizon," Eugenia silently recited another of the captain's maxims, "which you can neither hide from nor outrun, then batten down the hatches and ride it out. Batten down and don't let a surprise wave take you amidships." Paul can repeat that lesson verbatim, Eugenia remembered as she looked across the chart table at her son's eager face, then at Jinx and her frown of studious concentration. Lizzie's place at the table was conspicuously empty. She believes there are no more lessons to learn, Eugenia realized.

". . . Now there's a funny name: Zutphen. . . ." Captain Cosby hummed the word as he alternately glanced from the chart to the three-sided window, a habit that kept the ocean in sight at all times. ". . . It's in the Java Sea. We should be seeing Sumatra any moment, as well. Did Mr. Whitney tell you children about the island of Sumatra?

"It belongs to the Dutch people, you know. All of the southern coast of Borneo belongs to Holland . . . Buitenzorg, now that's a typically Dutch name . . . and Soerabaija . . . See here, Master Paul, Miss Jinx. . . ." Captain Cosby fingered the corner of the topmost chart, while Eugenia wondered what sorts of words she could use to repair her rift with Lizzie.

Words or gestures, Eugenia thought, how do you mend what you don't understand? How do you help another person when you're lost yourself? Eugenia stared through the window; the ship's bow drove forward in a knife-straight line, tossing waves aside like soft butter. It gave the impression that the *Alcedo* and not the captain had determined its own course. I've lived a life devoid of choices, Eugenia told herself; either I failed to recognize them or I followed the easiest path. I've been guided by ignorance or fear. It's time to change.

". . . British Admiralty, these nautical maps . . ." Captain Cosby continued, while Eugenia considered what a soothing voice he had. "I am the captain of my soul," Eugenia thought, "the master of my fate . . ."

". . . That includes the charts of Dutch-controlled land, as well. . . . And each one has a different number. . . . See here, Master Paul, Miss Jinx . . . ?" Captain Cosby bent down tenderly; his hand on the chart might have been a caress to a newborn. ". . . This one of the Selat Sunda was executed under the superintendence of a Rear Admiral Sir W.J.L. Wharton. You see his name? It's down here in the corner." Both children strained forward. "It must have been exciting to be one of the first men to explore these waters, don't you think, Master Paul? In spite of the pirates, that is. . . . Imagine all the . . ."

Eugenia watched the scene, but her thoughts began to drift. George, she thought suddenly, George is hiding something. I'm sure of it. And James, too. . . . But the idea of James having anything to conceal was too disturbing to consider. It would be like having an enemy in your house, an enemy inside yourself.

". . . Now this place . . . that's called Pulau Sumur. . . . You see, back when this area was first charted, the old Admiralty decided to use the real Malay names, so they wrote them down the way they heard them. . . . Except, of course, if the colony was British. . . . That's Billiton Island over there, and Ivartown here. . . . Ivartown's named for a Scotsman called Ivard. . . ."

Eugenia looked at the ship's polished wheel, at the brass fittings all neat and shiny, at the straightedges, calipers, sextants, and glasses, and tried to make sense of what her thoughts kept repeating. She listened to the slip-slap of rope rubbing wood, the distant grind of metal and oil, and the whirring breath of coal fires and steam. This ship knows something I don't, she thought. It's seen something I've missed.

". . . And here's Sarawak, where we'll be going. . . . That's on chart number 2106, Borneo Northwest Coast. . . ." Captain Cosby was so intent on his lesson that he didn't notice the second mate standing in the open door. The mate cleared his throat once, took two steps into the room, and then spoke to the captain in a whisper. Four childish and excited eyes watched the mate leave, then stared at the captain. It was as if their lesson were coming to life. Paul and Jinx were convinced they were on the brink of discovering a brand-new world.

"The watch has just spotted Kandang Balak," Captain Cosby announced with a wink to the children, "which means we won't travel up into the Telok Betong Roads, but we'll be passing close enough. There should be quite a few interesting ships. It's a major route, and you children will have a nice view of the Dutch East Indies. They say you can smell the spices from the plantations all the way out to sea. . . . And you, Master Paul . . . you'll win a prize if you can name all the varieties of vessels we encounter. . . ."

"Me, too!" burst in Jinx. "I get a prize, too!"

"But what about Borneo?" Eugenia interrupted. She felt a need to get on with it, all of a sudden, get to the heart of the matter, and her voice was abrupt with impatience. "How long till Sarawak and Kuching?" There was something about those names, something she almost remembered.

Captain Cosby might have been a ship himself; the change in course didn't slow or distract him in the least. If he felt perturbed at shifting direction, he made no sign. "We'll be traveling north along the coast," he answered. "Lieutenant Brown informed me that your husband wants to pass close to a point of land on the—"

"But how long till Kuching?" Eugenia persisted. There it was again, a name with an echo like a gong: It wasn't the metallurgy business or her father joining them or a visit to a sultan. It was something she'd heard months ago at Linden Lodge. Kuching. Sarawak. Kuching. And another name, too, a man's name, a foreign one.

"Two days, I should think, Mrs. Axthelm. That is, if we keep up this much steam and the currents don't turn fluky. . . . We've got to stop at Tanjong Datu, first, as I started to say. Your husband wants—"

But Eugenia stopped Captain Cosby without hearing any more. "Thank you for your time, Captain." The words tumbled out in a rush. "It's been a most informative lesson. But we won't keep you any longer. Paul? Jinx? Come along, children." Without waiting for Cosby's reply, Eugenia hustled her family from the wheelhouse.

Captain Cosby glanced at the topmost chart while Eugenia and the children hurried down the steps. All anyone asks, he told himself, is where we're going, not how; when we'll arrive in a certain place, not whether we'll be in one piece. The workings of a ship are taken for granted as if it were a locomotive or a motorcar, something you walk away from when there's trouble. No one understands that this is water we're traveling on, that storms and tides and hidden rocks dictate the path. They merely look at a name on a map and say: "There! That's the spot for me. That's where I want to go."

Automatically Captain Cosby listened to the sound his ship made as it drove through the water; he sniffed coal smoke and the pleasant, greasy scent of churning engines; he felt the ship's wheel shimmy under his hand and reassured himself that the *Alcedo* was proceeding properly. It was his habit to use all his senses: Hearing was vital on a foggy night; smell, imperative in the dark; and the touch of a vessel running beneath your feet said more about an engine room than any amount of tinkering over metal casings.

Where, Cosby repeated to himself, and when; that's all anyone cares about. Even Lieutenant Brown, our naval officer, who should know better by far. What was the first question out of his mouth the other night? "When will we pass the light beacon at Tanjong Datu?"

Remembering the scene made Cosby angry all over again. Impertinent beggar, he told himself. First the man requests a private visit to the bridge, next he tells me no one else can be present, then he goes all hush-hush and military and finally ends up dithering like any landlubber: "How close can we get to the beach? What's our chance for an obscure night?"

And the blasted fellow stared at the high- and low-water marks as if reading tea leaves in a cup, Cosby told himself. Any fool knows you can't divine the future by adding up numbers on a chart.

"We'll do it here," he finally says, then out and out orders me, captain of this vessel and a great many others before her, not to mark the spot! That's what he says! His very words: "Don't mark it. Just remember the place." Cosby felt heat swell his neck; his collar was tight; sweat chafed in puddles where it stood. He considered loosening a stud, then decided the sensation did him good. Cosby was enjoying his moment of fury.

"Just remember the place," he says! "Pirate Bay. Aptly named, don't you think?" Aptly named, I should say so! The veins in Captain Cosby's throat were fat and blue and his face appeared to have doubled in size. His scalp was prickly as electricity; he ran his hand through his hair and realized it was standing on end.

Then the blighted man has the gall to go on about a "royal excise tax" and the need to unload our cargo before we reach Kuching. "What do I care about an excise tax?" Cosby wanted to shout. "What do I care about some sultan's money-grubbing scheme? I've got a ship to run!"

I can't be making unscheduled stops, loading native praus with crates of machinery, and then letting them scoot off into the jungle! And at night, on top of everything else? Without a moon? In water that's reef lined or full of mangrove swamps or worse? Brown's lost his bloody marbles!

Cosby was breathing with difficulty; he opened a window for air, but the breeze was sickly and warm. Sweat puddles turned to rivers under his collar, inside his elbows, and cascaded down his chest into his belt. Don't let the fellow rile you, Cosby told himself. You saw Mr. Axthelm's orders; it's his idea, after all. If he wants to save a few pennies by discharging the crates early, that's his lookout. You were hired to captain a yacht, not run a business.

Besides, we'll either reach Brown's precious Tanjong Datu before daylight fades tomorrow or we won't. There's nothing to do but wait.

For the rest of that day and the next, Eugenia wasn't able to get a moment alone with Brown. She defied her better judgment and went to find him in the hold; she waited for him on deck, but he never appeared. He dined alone at luncheon, and at dinner was distant and polite, then he made his excuses and said that tomorrow would be another early day: ". . . So much to do before the arrival in Kuching.

Mr. and Mrs. Axthelm will understand, I'm sure. . . ." Brown never once looked at Eugenia.

Now it was close to midnight and Eugenia was alone on deck. The ship had passed the beacon at Tanjong Datu near dusk. Jinx, Paul, Prue, and the DuPlessises had lined the rail and shouted loud and enthusiastic choruses of "Borneo! Borneo!" but Eugenia, beside her children, had kept silent. She'd watched the green of the jungle come so close she'd thought they'd suffocate in it. Then the anchors were dropped with a hollow splash and the engines backed to make sure the coral or rock would hold. When the engines fell idle, the explorers deserted the deck and went inside.

Eugenia had been the last to leave the rail; she'd waited until the final streak of wispy, blue light was extinguished, or perhaps it had been swallowed whole by the jungle's blackness. The land had loomed nearer then, and air that knew only leaf mold and stagnant water and the hollow trunks of vine-encrusted trees enveloped the ship. It was the scent of that air that had finally driven Eugenia inside. She'd felt she'd been buried alive.

Midnight, Eugenia thought again as she paced the motionless deck. My children are nestled safe in their beds; the DuPlessises, my husband, the entire ship is off in dreamland; the engines are lulled and the anchors deep asleep in a fishy ooze. The *Alcedo,* at rest, was an eerie creature; it reminded Eugenia of a slumbering dragon. She hardly allowed herself to breathe.

There was a sound from the shore like a squealing pig, another like the wail of a bird or a monkey; something broke branches with a snap and something else screamed and fell. The shriek was so human it made Eugenia jump. She looked toward land, but there was nothing to see; the lack of color and shape was resolute, as though defying her efforts with a test of will, as though the darkness were human.

Tomorrow we reach Kuching, Eugenia told herself. Tomorrow we sail up the Sunghai Sarawak and moor in front of the royal palace. My father will be there: my father and Sir Charles Ivard and his son, Laneer, the rajah muda, and the great sultan of Sarawak himself. We will be civil; we will curtsy and bow; we will act suitably impressed and impressive, and say nothing at all. Eugenia stared at the land again, but it wasn't giving up any secrets. We will be polite, because that's all we know.

Suddenly there were lights at the shoreline. Or Eugenia thought they came from the shoreline; with the night so dark it was impossible to judge. The lights could have been from land or they could have been a boat bobbing up and down in the inky bay. Eugenia walked toward the bow, feeling her way along the rail hand over hand over hand. Puffs of hot air circled her face like taunts from an invisible person.

Then there were voices: faint, whispered grunts followed by the distinct sound of an oar in a wave. Not an oar striking water, but the drip-drip as it draws back and hesitates. Eugenia pulled away from the rail and stood still; for some reason she felt she shouldn't be seen.

"Here. You can tie up here." The words were spoken somewhere on the *Alcedo*'s aft deck, and they had the hiss of wind slipping between sails.

A mumble of recognition followed by something that sounded like *"Sela-mat ting-gal."*

"A happy stay ashore. I intend just that," the voice on deck laughed in answer, and Eugenia realized it was James. She felt frightened all of a sudden; instead of stepping forward and showing herself, she pulled further into darkness. But it's James, she told herself. Why should I be afraid? Besides, this is my husband's ship; I'm taking a midnight stroll; I couldn't sleep: I have a hundred reasons for being here. But she couldn't bring herself to move.

The boat mooring alongside the *Alcedo* was full of men. Eugenia could hear breathing and a slipshod shuffle as each shipped an oar. The men waited; they didn't come aboard.

"Easy with that." James's voice was louder. Something heavy was handed over the edge. Eugenia didn't dare turn. With a corner of her eye, she caught the shadow of a man and crate stretched out over the waves. A lantern has been lighted at the stern, she realized, but I'm well ahead of it; I'm as good as invisible. She moved to the rail and looked down.

The light wavered on the water; the color it spread was oily as candle wax; it slithered past one wave and made a mustard-colored puddle of another. A native prau bobbed in one of the pools as crates from the *Alcedo*'s hold were loaded onto it. Eugenia recognized the boxes immediately; they were the ones that contained George's machinery: the smelting equipment for the ore-mining company. What was happening made no sense.

"Sela-mat bela-yar," Brown said while another crate swung onto the prau's deck. Eugenia couldn't see him, though she heard his voice clearly; she could picture the way his tongue slipped over the sounds and the smile he'd have on his face. It was a memory of waking in the late afternoon, of blue shutters, a floor as hot as fire, the slither of wet sheets, and the gurgling, cozy sounds of a long day ending.

Then all at once there was George's voice: strained, high-pitched, almost unrecognizable, but Eugenia knew it immediately.

"Got them all off, Lieutenant?" he asked; he seemed to run out of air as he spoke, as if he were panting or had lost his way.

"All that we'd agreed to, sir."

"Get going then. Can't risk being discovered here. The sultan's boys could be anywhere."

James didn't answer, and Eugenia guessed that George had left. He doesn't want the men in the prau to see him, she realized, or learn his identity. Then she heard James climb down the rope and land on the prau's deck; his feet sounded stealthy as a cat's on warm sand.

Why this secrecy? Eugenia wondered. Surely, it's in George's best interests to follow his father's plans. Or did the Turk tell him to leave the machinery here? And if he does, how will it get to Kuching?

She leaned against the rail silently repeating the questions. She remembered talking to George and she pictured her last moments with James. I thought I was the center of both men's lives, Eugenia told herself. I thought their anger was rivalry for me. But maybe I was wrong.

She stretched out over the water and tried to count how many crates were in the prau before it eased its way from the *Alcedo*'s side. The boat inched forward; the oars slipped into place and the lantern swung in a bobbing circle. Orange light covered the waves and sent shadows of men, boxes, oars, spears, knives, and ropes spiraling across the night.

Eugenia stared at the faces as they strained to pull the boat toward shore. They were intent and fierce; all the light of home and hearth and children had left their eyes. Eugenia saw James standing above them; he had his back to her, but he turned one last time to look at the ship. She saw his face and, in that brief moment, he recognized hers as well.

*T*HE PALACE AT *K*UCHING was in turmoil. Today the Axthelms would arrive. Today the *Alcedo* would steam her majestic path through the mud of the Sunghai Sarawak to sit at the foot of the sultan's garden, as peaceable and quiet as a newborn lamb. Today was the moment everyone had prayed for. Everyone, the world! The people of Kuching felt the eyes of the universe were on them. For weeks they'd fattened pheasants, combed the hillsides for wild boar, hacked to pieces the largest, the fattest, sharks, and dug up buried jars of "thousand-year" eggs. They'd worked till their knuckles had turned red, till they'd dropped and slept where they'd fallen, till the maize crop had gone dusty and infants had cried at the sight of their mothers' faces. The Axthelms were on their way; the *Alcedo* was coming! If the rose-hued coconut meat turned slimy green, if the *satay* and *ketupat* went sour or the *tahu goreng* and *gula melaka* were transformed into vermin-filled mush, if the dancers forgot their steps or the musicians their notes, if the royal white peacocks were carted off one by one by crocodiles and drowned, it was the will of the gods: The sultan's servants, his princes, his peoples, his countrymen, had done their collective best.

Sir Charles and Laneer Ivard hurried through the palace compound, each sent (by the sultan) on a separate mission, while the Honorable Nicholas Paine was summoned away from his task (making a banner of welcome for his son-in-law and daughter) to sit at the sultan's side and soothe the frazzled, regal nerves.

In his palace apartment, the Honorable Nicholas accepted the summons like a death knell. He glared at Ridgeway as though the interruption had been his secretary's doing, then tossed the banner at the traitor's feet. "Judas Iscariot!" the Honorable Nicholas muttered under his breath, then ordered loudly: "Finish the damn thing for me!" The Honorable Nicholas was in a foul humor; the sultan's continuous and singsong demands had begun to pall. First the man had wanted a banner in English, then he'd decided a Malay translation would be "quite jolly" (that flag was to be painted on silk by the rajah muda, Laneer Ivard), then he'd changed his mind (banners were considered "insubstantial"), then he'd shifted back again ("It is a festival, after all, and festivals call for flimsy things!"). Heaven knew what whim would follow. If the sultan couldn't keep his Western henchmen busy proving their "willing obedience," he was a miserable man.

"I've got to go quiet one of His Majesty's little 'tremors,'" Paine sputtered. "Assure him all over again that George has the rifles and that he'll deliver them posthaste." Paine had given up hiding anything from Ridgeway. He'd guessed that his secretary had known all along about the rifles in the *Alcedo*'s hold: the rifles that were to be given over to the sultan, the rifles that would quell a rebellious Mahomet Seh and force a grateful sultan to return the favor. Guns for coal deposits: a tidy little exchange. Whenever Paine felt peevish with his post, he consoled himself by recounting the neatness of his mission.

And with no danger or risk involved! That was the pleasant part; the Axthelm name would remain unsullied. Paine (with Ridgeway in constant attendance) had been over and over the matter with Sir Charles Ivard. Eight crates of rifles didn't seem an exorbitant price for a fortune in coal or the power that ownership implied. Any eastbound ship passing on to the Philippine Islands would stop in Borneo to refuel. The Turk's farsighted maneuvering was brilliant. You've got to hand it to the old weasel, Paine told himself; Rome wasn't built in a day, but that's because Turk Axthelm wasn't in charge.

"Finish the damn banner, Ridgeway," the Honorable Nicholas barked again, "and then see if you can scare up our good friend Laneer, the esteemed rajah muda, and tell him to shake a leg with his translation. I don't want to be the fellow His Majesty blames when we can't unfurl the golden welcome."

Paine hurried off. As he passed through the corridor he felt tremendously relieved. Today was the last day he'd have to deal with the sultan or that spoiled brat, Laneer. Today he was living in palace apartments, but tomorrow the venerable father-in-law of the great George Axthelm would be on board the *Alcedo*, basking in glory and a job well done. And, of course, Genie would be there, too. Can't over-look that! And the kiddies: mustn't forget the kiddies!

As the old man's footsteps slapped away down the hall, Ridgeway made a face of disgust and picked up the fallen banner. It was hard to tell which angered him more: laboring as a seamstress or thinking about Laneer. Ridgeway didn't like the rajah muda any more than Paine did; in fact, he didn't trust him in the slightest. But in spite of keeping his eyes wide open and doling out quite a few well-placed bribes, he hadn't been able to discover anything unusual about the man. The Honorable Nicholas's secretary was left with the conclusion that Laneer kept a powerful secret police. In a country full of spies it was a risky move. Ridgeway lifted the banner and wondered just what Laneer Kinloch Ivard was up to.

Laneer Ivard was in a tailspin. An absolute tailspin. That's exactly how he would have described his state of mind. He felt like a dog whose tail had been tied with firecrackers. Whenever he tried to bite one off it burst in his mouth while the remaining ones scorched his skin. Laneer felt like racing through the sultan's palace, yelping and howling for mercy. Woof! Woof! Yipe! then a nice, cooling plunge in the lily pond. Laneer pictured himself bobbing to the surface, covered in duckweed and leaves the size of tortoise shells. He wouldn't look dignified, but he'd be a far happier man.

The problem, as usual, was Mahomet Seh, or Mat Saleh, or what-ever his heathen name was. But Laneer knew he had to wait for Ogden Beckmann and the *Alcedo*'s arrival before he could safely deal with the rebel chief. Beckmann will have the answer to this ticklish situation, Laneer told himself. He'll know how to handle this "surprise" of the sultan's; he'll know what to say.

Laneer tried to calm himself; he took long, slow breaths; he stretched his hands in front of him and willed them not to shake. Beck-mann will be here soon, he said over and over, and I'll dump this whole mess in his capable lap. I didn't get involved in this nasty, little plot to have it blow up in my face.

Laneer circled his apartments in the palace; they were hotter than Hades, but he couldn't sit still. He tried one chair, then jumped to an-other, then the next and the next, and on to the windows (which had no view and emitted a foul odor like water left standing in a chrysan-themum jar—in spite of his complaints, in spite of his rank, for the good Lord's sake!). Laneer's mind spun around like the gears in a cuckoo clock. I'm not going to witness any "public executions of rebel soldiers," he told himself. I'm not going to allow myself to be dragged into this little "spectacle" of the sultan's. The whole idea is preposterous: murders staged for an American family; I'm sure that's the last thing they'd want to see. (It wouldn't top my list, that's for certain!) And with rifles they supply themselves! With weapons stored in the belly of their boat! It's too absurd. Well, I won't be along for the ride, and that's final.

Laneer paced up and down; the grass matting covering the floor felt like a wet sponge under his feet; it squelched and squeaked and then crackled as some doomed insect met its maker. "Stupid man!" Laneer said aloud (he meant the sultan). "Content with only eight cases of Axthelm rifles. I promised the same amount to Seh, and he's only a pirate! A *perempak!* A Bajua! A nothing! The sultan should have held out for more. But what do you expect? Honestly, the mind reels at the lack of intellect in these people. I don't know why we waste our time.

"But I definitely will not witness those executions!" Laneer interrupted his own monologue as if shouting down another person. "No one can make me. I'm not going up on that hill to watch Mahomet Seh's men being blown to bits with Axthelm rifles. Why, what would happen if Seh found out I was there? I'd be in a pickle, then, I tell you. Worse than a pickle: I'd be up to my scorched little ears in a stew pot! With a tribe full of savages drooling over their spoons!

"I promise guns to help Seh's war against the sultan, and meanwhile the selfsame model blows the captured rebels to smithereens! That looks just fine, doesn't it? Why, that looks Jim Dandy!

"And me in the audience? Grinning from ear to ear while I stand beside that pompous ass of a sultan? I won't do it, I tell you. I won't be a party to it. I won't go up on that hill tomorrow. Not for all the tea in China! If I do and Seh gets wind of it, well, we know what happens then. I'm marked as a traitor and my life's not worth a handful of toffee.

"I won't go, I tell you. I absolutely and positively refuse." Laneer felt he was losing his mind; he wanted to tear at his hair and rub fire ash on his cheeks. He glared at his feet jittering over the floor and tried to slow his steps; he put one set of toes down, then an instep, then a heel, then followed the same rhythm with the other foot.

"Beckmann," he whispered. "Beckmann will know what to do. I'll wait for Beckmann. I won't utter a word. When the sultan speaks, I'll just smile. When he mentions how pleased he is to receive rifles from the Axthelm boat, I'll grin like a Cheshire cheese.

"Or cat . . . or whatever it is. . . ." Laneer was suddenly aware of the sound of his own voice and he leapt backward as if the noise were on fire. *Palace walls have ears,* his mind shouted a warning. *Suppose you've been overheard?*

"Sinen!" Laneer screamed in panic. "Sinen, where are you?" Without waiting for an answer, Laneer Kinloch Ivard, rajah muda, gave his order. "Go down by the river, Sinen. Send word as soon as you see the American ship. There's a man named Mr. Ogden Beckmann who's coming especially to visit me. He's come a very long way, and I must be the first man to greet him."

All morning the *Alcedo* had been bombarded with native craft. The slow turns of the Sunghai Sarawak were dangerous at any time, but today they were teeming with boats; there seemed hardly room for water as well. Sampans collided with the yacht's sides, and praus filled with babies and chickens and dogs crashed into each other as they fought to get near. Boys with knives in their teeth tried to clamber aboard; parents shouted and held up squalling infants or goats or sea turtles gulping at air: Everything was considered marketable, and every price open to discussion. Reasonable discussion, too!

"Murah! Murah, tidak mahal!" Cheap! Cheap, not expensive! Eugenia, at the rail beside George, needed no translation; the way the words were screamed conveyed their meaning. For a moment husband and wife were silent. So this is Borneo, Eugenia thought, this is the place we've been longing to see. This is why we left Philadelphia.

Each family paddled closer than it dared; one sampan outmaneuvered another, and in the smallest space of a second, every living thing on board was offered for sale. Clenched fists shook with the strain of holding aloft both animal and child while hope twisted every face. Even the babies, Eugenia thought, even the babies are frantic with need. Then the first boat was driven off and another crammed into its place:

"Berapa? . . . Tunggu sekejap!" How much you pay? . . . Wait! Come back!

"Encik! . . . Puan! . . . Murah! Murah! . . ." Mister! . . . Missus! . . . Cheap! Cheap! . . .

Eugenia wrenched her eyes away from the river and looked at her husband again. "But I still don't understand," she shouted above the roar. "Why didn't you tell me about this excise tax before?"

George didn't turn as he answered his wife. He'd decided that his family should stand near the rail for the two-hour passage up the river, that the pose would enhance the image of visiting royalty, and he didn't want to mar it now, not with the palace so close: not after all his efforts. So he waved to the throng with a stately greeting and spoke through a ready-made smile:

"Didn't think it necessary, my dear. Taxes are taxes. They shouldn't worry a pretty head." George's glance fell on the sea turtles. Terrapin stew, he told himself. Now that would make a welcome change. I must remind the chef to purchase some tortoise meat. George waved again, then in a fit of European largess, tossed a few coins over the side. The squalling became worse; it was like a tidal bore or a hurricane or a tornado on a hot afternoon. Bodies dived into the water, dugout canoes upset, chickens plunged beneath the waves, but the coins were retrieved: every last one of them. George smiled and held both palms upward, facing out. The pale skin was empty; the crowd moaned regret, and the *Alcedo* pushed on.

"But won't the sultan find out you sent equipment ashore last night?" Eugenia leaned very near her husband. It was so hard to hear in this din and the question seemed crucial. She glued her eyes to the tree line and didn't let them sink back to the frenzy of the overturned boats.

"Not if we don't tell him." George was amazed at how simple lying had become. The only difficulty was in remembering the details. The rest, the embellishment, was mere gravy. Gravy and spuds and green peas in their pods. Another note for the chef, George reminded himself, fresh peas with a hint of spearmint leaf.

"And I trust we none of us will tell him, my dear," George added serenely. "After all, it's for the good of the company. No point in paying taxes till we've done a bit of work. Callused hands, and all that." The smile that delivered the homily was blissful.

"But won't the sultan hear about Lieutenant Brown?" Eugenia insisted. She kept her expression pleasant, gazed toward the land, put her "best foot forward" as George had insisted, but her heart wasn't in it. All of a sudden Eugenia missed Beckmann. He would have advised against this, she told herself; he would have told George that his plan is full of holes. Excise tax or no.

"A strange white man out in the jungle?" Eugenia continued. "Won't the sultan wonder why you put him ashore? Won't that be the first question out of his mouth?" We'll be sent packing, Eugenia realized. We'll be ordered to retrace our route down this miserable river, and there will be no one to help us. This hungry mob won't be so humble then.

"The sultan won't know what's happening until it's too late." George's sunny face turned momentarily cruel, then he remembered his pose. His cheeks turned shiny with complaisance; they reminded Eugenia of sugared grapes: sweet, watery, and of no consequence.

"So, don't you worry your pretty little head, my dear," George added. "I have it all under control.

"Now, you go get the children. I believe they're near the stern with your cousin, Whit, and our dear Prudence. Pangalong Jetty should be coming into sight any moment and we all want to be together for our grand entrance. We want to be seen at our best. Best foot forward, my dear. Don't forget. Tell the kiddies, too. We represent the Axthelm name . . ."

But before his wife could hurry off, George took her hand and clasped it. "Genie," he intoned while his expression grew actorish and grave, "I've done something. . . . Something that I believe will . . ." George stopped and allowed himself a view of the stands of mangrove, banana, and bamboo, the smoke rising from jungle cookfires, and the brown bodies that lined every curve in the river. He took a breath, sighed, lifted his chin, and continued:

". . . Something, Genie, that will make you very proud . . ." The words were hesitant and grand at the same time; it was exactly the effect George had hoped for, though it made Eugenia want to pull herself free. Her hand seemed caught in a snare: a bird net or a badger trap. She couldn't imagine what her husband was talking about; she couldn't imagine being proud of him, or loving him either. She couldn't picture the day ahead: the dignitaries bowing and scraping or her father arriving with a show of studied concern. It was a spectacle to watch, not join: a pantomime or operetta. All that concerned Eugenia was where James had gone and why. "I'll get the children" was all she answered.

There were cymbals clashing as the yacht hove into sight at Pangalong Jetty: cymbals, gongs, drums, and serunai trumpets raised in a terrible chorus. The gamelan players were doing their best to accommodate the inharmonious strains of the Americans' native song, but it wasn't easy. They'd decided to overcome the tune's obvious flaws with flourishes from gong and trumpet: In their hands the National Anthem became a dirge that floated over the palace grounds, the Sunghai Sarawak, and into the hills.

The Honorable Nicholas Paine stood on a bright green lawn that faced the jetty; flanking him were the rajah, Sir Charles Ivard, and the rajah muda, Laneer Kinloch Ivard. The rest of the crowd spilling behind the three men were members of the sultan's retinue. The Axthelms' arrival was a state visit: Every minor functionary or tribal prince had been granted a position on the palace grounds according to his rank. Ridgeway had been edged nearer to the back, however, because, as the local princes told themselves, the man was only a scribe, while his master, old and venerable-looking though he might be, had no official title—therefore the scribe must be inferior. As the yacht inched forward, the princes slipped forward; soon they created a glued-together block. If one fell into the river, the others would follow, and they'd take Ridgeway, Paine, and the Ivards with them.

It was only after the *Alcedo*'s ropes had been flung ashore and made fast that the sultan and his seven-year-old-son began their entrance from the palace gates. They'd observed the yacht's progress from windows hidden in the harem, because, though the sultan didn't want to seem overanxious, he needed to time his appearance perfectly. The sultan was a man who understood the fickle workings of power: how important a mere moment might be. When the yacht's ropes were tied to Sarawak soil, the sultan's wait was over.

He and his son advanced slowly and created a procession all their own. An umbrella of rose-colored silk stretched above their heads; tassels of parrot green and braided ribbons of scarlet, gold, and magenta cascaded behind them. As father and son marched toward the river, and the men supporting the silk canopy hurried to keep pace, the cloth shimmered and danced about. It caught the sun and seemed to swell. Then the bamboo poles shook and the umbrella billowed to life. The two monarchs didn't utter a sound, though their bearers hissed indignant orders:

"*Belok ke kanan!*" ; "*Belok ke kiri!*" ; "*Jalan terus!* . . ." Turn right! Turn left! Go straight! . . . The bearers might have been gnats or haze filling sleepy eyes; the sultan was oblivious. He kept his own pace, and his boy, counting steps in his head, followed suit.

They walked toward the *Alcedo*'s bow while their subjects kowtowed and groveled, clearing a human path for their illustrious leader and his heir, the young boy who would, this day, bear witness to his father's greatness.

Eugenia watched the scene with fascination but very little comprehension. *So this is Borneo,* her mind kept repeating, but it wouldn't go any further. Kuching, Sarawak, North Borneo: They were names to recite, nothing more. Without understanding her role and with no desire to examine her emotions, Eugenia fell back on form. She behaved as she'd been raised to behave. George had instructed her to stand with the children at the mid-ship rail and not move until he called her. George had told her to stay in one spot and call as little attention to herself as possible; he wasn't sure which Moslem customs the sultan observed, and he didn't know whether Eugenia would be welcome in the palace or if she and the girls would be relegated to the harem. George didn't want to make any gaffes; he'd repeated that warning over and over. He wanted the day to go just right. Eugenia stayed put, and did as she'd been told.

At the moment, George stood at the rail as well, but he kept his back to his wife as he watched the sultan and his bearers stroll slowly across the lawn and then down toward the jetty. He couldn't make up his mind about his wife and children. Moslem customs, he told himself, require certain courtesies. For instance: Do I present my wife or do I leave her behind? Or do I pretend she doesn't exist? And what about Jinx and Lizzie? And Paul? Indecision gnawed at George's stomach; he thought about terrapin stew, then *haricots financière* and potatoes *duchesse,* then about how green the palace grounds looked. They're laid out like European lawns, George told himself, recognizing the similarity in an instant. He pictured rowing matches and suppers under white canopies, and oysters on the half shell and prawns in lemon butter.

Then, like a bolt from the blue, George realized the sultan had a child by his side. Oh, my! George thought, and made his decision. He whispered an order and Paul was produced. The little boy stood beside his father. Two fathers, two sons: mirror images in grandeur.

George and Paul started off down the gangway. With every step, their strides grew more assured, till they stood on terra firma, face to face with the sultan and his son. Eugenia watched her husband bow and fall on one knee, while Paul tried to imitate his father and the sultan laughed, reached a jewel-encrusted hand to her son's face, and raised it from the ground. We've crowned ourselves king and queen, Eugenia thought, but we're like children pretending; we haven't made enough rules for this game. We're waiting to see how the other person plays. The Ivards are waiting, my father's waiting, and George is rocking on his heels while the sultan strokes the air with rubied fingers.

The sultan laughed again and this was taken as another sign; there was a stir on the dock as everyone began to speak at once. An effusive welcome gushed upward from the crowd. Eugenia caught her name repeated over and over: "my daughter"; "my wife"; "Mrs. Axthelm"; "Madame Axthelm." She guessed it was time to disembark, but George gave no notice of his wife and daughters. With only his profile showing, he looked as though he'd forgotten the existence of the ship and the rest of his family. Paul was the only one he remembered: Paul waiting under his father's heavy hand, Paul eyeing the sultan's son while the weight on his shoulder grew as painful as lead. Self-conscious terror, Eugenia realized. I tell him he's a big boy, but he's still only a baby.

Then for reasons all his own, the sultan decided to proceed back up the hill to the palace. He grinned, fluttered his hands and elbows in several directions at once, then turned on his heel while the bearers scurried to catch him. They look like Maypole revelers who've forgotten the step, Eugenia thought. She wanted to laugh at the improvised dance but knew she couldn't. Instead she put her arms around her daughters and tried to play her part. This too shall pass, she reminded herself. We won't be stuck in this country forever.

Then George was flying back up the gangway with a breathless "We've done it, Genie! He was absolutely charming! Not at all like Brown led me to expect"—George ignored his mistake and rushed ahead—"and he's planning a little entertainment for the men tomorrow . . . the sultan, that is. . . . You ladies are to rest up in a pavilion he's concocted specially while the men attend a 'modest show.' . . .

"Those are his own words—a 'modest show'! Isn't that just like royalty?" George wanted to gloss over the fact that the entertainment was to be an all-male event and that he'd consented to have Paul join them, in spite of Brown's warnings to stay aboard no matter what. But the man didn't know beans, George told himself. The sultan was an absolute delight! And every inch a monarch!

"My own son will, of course, accompany us," the great man had said. "I should think you would wish your heir with you as well. These boys are never too young to witness nobility."

George didn't know what the sultan was planning, but he was certain it would be charming and he was equally certain Eugenia wouldn't approve. At the very least a "gentlemen only" show sounded improper, and if Eugenia put her foot down, there was bound to be a row. And now that he was on his own, George told himself, now that Brown and Beckmann were no longer hounding him, he needed to prove who was boss. If he chose to involve his son in the sultan's magnanimous plans, well, he'd just dare anyone to stop him! Danger, indeed! Why the fellow was a gentleman! They'd be safe as peach pie in his hands.

George raced ahead with his description of the sultan's immeasurable goodness while he stood at the mid-ship rail and continued to nod and wave for the benefit of the crowds on shore. A hand was raised, the chin lowered; it was a drill that couldn't be altered: The jaw jutted forward in gratitude and the hand was clasped to the breast.

George didn't bother to tell his wife about the crates of rifles the retainers had wanted to carry off immediately, and he didn't mention Mahomet Seh, whom the sultan had referred to in a sudden snarl as a "vicious murderer." Those little twists of character were foibles Genie would never understand. Why, if she knew about the rifles, George reflected, breaking into an indulgent smile, she might refuse to let anyone go ashore at all! Women could be so fainthearted. Look at Africa! Look at what a fuss she'd made about the safari!

"And, Genie, His Majesty has invited all three children to sleep in the palace tonight! What do you think of those apples? With Prue, of course," George added quickly. "I insisted on that. Knew you'd want me to. Can't have the little nippers without their nanny.

"What do you say, ladies?" George turned to his daughters. "Won't that be something? Sleeping in a royal castle?" As he smiled at Lizzie, he lifted his hand in the air again and waved to the adoring crowd. It was an imperious, negligent gesture; George had learned how to be a king.

"They can't go," Eugenia said. She felt she was being sucked down a drain; water swirled faster and faster; she couldn't hold her head above it. "Not without me," she added. "They can't go ashore without me."

"Oh, Mother!" Lizzie, Jinx, and Paul protested in unison while George joined them with: "Please?" All four voices wheedled, stretching the vowels into diphthongs the size of a pony's stall.

"What about water?" Eugenia demanded. "Or mosquitoes? Are there beds in the palace fit to sleep on?" Eugenia didn't look at her children's faces; she knew she was the ogre, the spoiler of happy times, the fussbudget who should have stayed at home, but something kept telling her not to believe her husband. Something said: *We're in too deep; we're in way over our heads.*

"What does my father think about this change of plans?" Eugenia finally added; this was her last line of defense, but she knew George would see through the strategy. "I thought we'd see him first off. That he'd be coming on board. That we'd be staying on the yacht together."

"My dear. My dear," George chuckled as he gave Paul another conspiratorial nod. "Business before pleasure. You know the schoolroom rules. You'll see your father tomorrow. There will be plenty of time for family reunions then. We men must work today."

George couldn't risk saying more. Stick to the practiced story, he told himself, repeat the salient facts: a metallurgy company, cases of machinery to separate antimony and melt ore, the Honorable Nicholas and Rajah Ivard on hand to make the new company run smoothly. Genie knows that tale, George reminded himself, no point in frightening her with the truth just yet; there'll be time for her to show her delighted surprise later.

For a moment, George allowed himself to imagine that happy event: Eugenia overwhelmed by his cleverness, gushing about bravery and avowing misty-eyed devotion. Later, George reminded himself again.

We'll have time for this later. Then he repeated his silent totem: It will keep. George pulled himself back to reality.

"Come along, kiddies," he announced with a bang. "Let's get ready to visit the sultan's palace. You'll pack up your best togs and off you'll toddle with Mistress Prue. . . ."

"I'll go as well, George," Eugenia interrupted. She knew she'd lost, that she had no resources left, that there was no argument worth pursuing. "If the children are staying on shore, then so am I. If the sultan doesn't approve, well, that's too bad."

Mahomet Seh, Lieutenant Brown, the Bugis second in command, and the Iban tribesmen hurried through the darkening jungle. They were racing against time. The executions of rebel soldiers had been rescheduled; they'd been supposed to take place later in the month, but the sultan had changed his mind. (A "royal prerogative," he'd declared in a hasty decree.) The sultan had decided to put on a "spectacle in honor of our foreign guests"; as "a special Malay treat, we will dispatch prisoners before an adoring throng." As soon as the *Alcedo* arrived in Kuching, that plan would be put in motion. Brown guessed the yacht was already there, that she'd arrived that morning, or possibly early that afternoon. Now it was approaching evening, which meant the executions would take place the next day. There was no time to lose.

Seh and his men, with Brown as their teacher, traversed trails no foreign eye could have discovered; they scrambled up streams, crawled along hillsides crumbly with mud, balanced on tree trunks crossing a chasm, and braced themselves, clasped arm in arm in arm, to ford a swollen river. A lot of jungle separated the beacon at Tanjong Datu from Kuching town.

Training the rebels had proven more difficult than Brown had imagined. And he'd been told he'd have more time: two weeks at the minimum. That had been the original scheme: unload the rifles, work with the men, and when he and Seh thought they were ready, march on Kuching town. The rebellion was to appear spontaneous, self-contained, a tribal war; the *Alcedo* would play no part; she'd be long gone down the coast. But the sultan's decree had changed all that.

Teaching was accelerated, a lot of it accomplished on the move, but the rod bayonet was regarded with suspicion, if not downright disgust; Seh's men couldn't grasp the concept of running the bayonet forward, then fastening it with a catch, or conversely, when not in use, of sliding it back to lie within the fore end of the stock. *What good is a bayonet,* the men's stubborn faces said, *if it doesn't act like a spear? And what good is a spear if you leave it at home? How will your enemies know you if you don't come properly armed?* The idea of sheathing the bright new knives was as laughable as ignoring a dream, as absurd as living in peace, as futile as loving your neighbor.

Every time Brown inspected the rebels' new weapons, he found bayonets jutting out at sickening angles. He and Seh repeated the drill over and over—"Bayonet forward, catch, release, return"—while Brown pictured the men who'd first designed the rifle. I'll bet they didn't imagine this crowd would end up with Springfield A3s, he told himself; I'll bet if they knew, they'd rush headlong into the Massachusetts hills.

"No! It's bayonet forward," Brown would order, "then catch, then release and return. Return, I said! *Belakang!* Return!" While the man would calmly slip his bayonet forward, catch it, pause for a moment, admiring his handiwork, then instead of replacing it alongside the stock, he'd stab the thing into the ground or a tree or a nest of vines or a rock till it broke in two. Then he'd raise the barrel, sight along it, and squeeze the trigger. The sound of the rifle's retort always delighted the rebels. For a moment, they'd be all smiles, swaggering with a grin toward their comrades, chuckling and pointing at the sky. It was a big joke, the gun going off, and the men would stare upward as if waiting for a flock of birds to fall down: plucked and clean and maybe even cooked and warm—a feast on the jungle floor. Then Brown's student would remember the broken bayonet and toss the Springfield to the ground.

Fortunately there was a surplus of rifles; ruined ones were discarded. The jungle would cover them the same way it twisted around the Dayak heads hanging in the longhouse rafters, Brown thought. Besides, what does it matter where Turk Axthelm's "gifts" end up? I was told to deliver the weapons and train the men; after that my handsome salary and I are on our own.

Brown glanced backward along the path Seh and the Bugis had chosen. A new rifle might be difficult for the rebel soldiers to understand, but staying in file and moving in level silence was something they learned in their bones.

Ahead of Brown, almost within sight of a mangrove swamp near the water's edge, Mahomet Seh stopped and indicated it was time to cut inland again. They'd reached the mouth of the Sunghai Santubang, the smaller tributary of the Sunghai Sarawak that flowed through Kuching, and they couldn't risk being seen by the sultan's patrol. The few villages dotting the nearby mountains would welcome Seh and his men. They were old allies. Seh and the Bugis started uphill.

"Selamat tinggal," Lieutenant Brown called in a whisper.

The Bugis only grunted—he resented Brown's authority—but Seh laughed. "Yes, Mr. Brown," he said, "it is, as you say. 'A good stay ashore.' Your sense of direction is good. Most white men get lost in the jungle, but you have not erred once. Not even in the dark."

Brown decided not to answer. This was no time for small talk; they had to be in place on the hill above the town long before the sultan's soldiers arrived. Surprise was everything.

The way inland became increasingly difficult to follow; very few tribesmen chose this route and jungle paths were swallowed quickly. Vines tripped the unwary; a hand reaching for balance could grab a poisonous pit viper by mistake, or the foothold you thought was firm could tumble you down a mountain. The trick, Brown knew, was not to panic. Being lost in the jungle was no different from being lost anywhere. Once you established a sense of place, you could live for weeks or even years before hacking your way free. The jungle held the necessary tools for survival: drinking water in bamboo stems; ti plants, fiddleheads, and lotus lily to provide nourishment when game was scarce.

Brown automatically marked the route Seh followed and wondered what the *Alcedo* must look like to the villagers at the river's muddy edge. He almost wished he could be there to witness the natives' astonished surprise, but then he realized Eugenia would be on deck. Don't think about her, he told himself. The past is the past. It's better off forgotten.

At least she and the children will be on board when the shooting starts, Brown reminded himself. I made certain of that. I warned George not to let them leave the ship. I told him the yacht would be the only safe place when we start our work.

After we've finished on the hill, things should return to normal fairly quickly, Brown decided; the majority of the sultan's army will turn tail or switch allegiance, while the few stragglers that rally round their deposed king will be disposed of. Brown pictured Seh and his Bugis and their form of retribution; "disposed" didn't describe Seh's methods by half. That's why Seh's insisting on the hilltop, Brown realized; he doesn't dare fight near town; he can't risk frightening his new subjects. He won't look like a savior if they see him in action.

Brown watched the men ahead of him; their footing was sure, they could maneuver the jungle climb at a half run or a lope, and they seemed tireless. God is on their side, Brown told himself, or a god. That's what they believe. At least that's what Seh tells me. I hope he's right. If he's not, and they're in it for profit, then Kuching will end up in cinders. Pirates don't care; they like tangible assets. Good intentions are as worthless as paper hats.

Brown denied the voice that said: *You're no different. You're here be-cause you've been paid. You take the money and run like the rest.* But I don't burn houses, he reasoned; I don't kill children and I don't drag their mothers into the dust. *Oh, don't you?* the voice spat back, but Brown wouldn't listen.

At least Eugenia and the children will be aboard the *Alcedo*, he promised. Whatever happens, they'll be safe.

Mrs. DuPlessis puffed and wheezed and strained to loosen her corset stays. The heat and steamy muck that passed for air in the sultan's "ladies' and children's pavilion" was too much to bear! Certainly it was! No dignified daughter of American soil should have to put up with this nonsense. "I don't see how you stand it, Eugenia," Mrs. Du-Plessis announced fiercely. Her corset ribbons had become a web of tangles, a veritable sin-ridden trap! Mrs. DuPlessis clenched them in her fingers, but nothing would untie the knots. If the good lady had al-lowed herself to curse, this would have been an excellent moment. "I believe these things are the work of the devil," she added with the ve-hemence of a fallen angel.

"Mmmm . . ." Eugenia answered, but her mind wasn't on Mrs. Du-Plessis or her problems. She was concentrating on a list of necessities they'd need for the night: mosquito netting, incense sticks to drive away insects, clean sheets (plenty of clean sheets), water decent enough to wash in and clean enough to drink. Eugenia stared around her at the ladies' pavilion and tried to imagine how she'd make it into a home for her children. An enormous round room crammed with all manner of European beds, pillows, bolsters, settees, mahogany tables, ottomans, and footstools, but missing a single partition—it looked like a giant ballroom converted to a dormitory, like housing for a refugee prince or an army of occupation bunked down in a castle. The crystal chandelier draped in gauze and dangling in the center of the ceiling only heightened the impression. Eugenia had been told the gauze protected the prisms and candles from the swallowlike birds that zoomed through every open window and door, but the covering meant the candles were useless. The chandelier was a pretty object bought to impress; efficiency was not the issue. Neither was light.

"This was constructed especially for us?" Eugenia asked without turning to look at Mrs. DuPlessis. In answer, Eugenia heard only grunts and then the loud pop that meant a hook and eye had exploded. "All this work for us?" she repeated. "I can't believe it."

Eugenia left Mrs. DuPlessis to her corset as she explored the room. No American or Frenchman or German or Italian would have dared build this, she decided, it's more Victorian than the queen herself. It's as if the sultan saw a drawing of an Englishwoman's bedroom, and decided to magnify it fifteen times. One wardrobe wasn't good enough for His Highness, oh no: There had to be eleven, and twenty chaises, and fifteen looking glasses, and as for end tables, the more the merrier. And we won't mention sewing tables or cut-glass bibelots or yards and yards and yards of lace. If Windsor Castle had a harem, this would be it. That thought amused Eugenia for a moment; she imagined stiff-necked Englishwomen collapsing on satin pillows in poor imitations of voluptuous poses.

Then she wondered again how this strange building would become a haven for her family, how she could protect her children in a room that obviously harbored scorpions and snakes, where the overstuffed furniture was suspect, the wardrobes were as dangerous as rat traps, and the glassless windows were an open invitation to anything that walked or slithered by. Worrying about her family, Eugenia found herself suddenly lighthearted. A challenge is a wonderful thing, she decided. You toss away your everyday cares, roll up your sleeves, and get to work. In her mind, Eugenia was already rearranging beds, moving them away from the windows and placing them in a circle near the chandelier. Not under it, though, she reminded herself. Who knows what might squirm out of that thing at night?

"Like a wagon train," Eugenia said to herself. "Only the beds will face out instead of in, and we won't have a fire." The thought made her smile.

"What's that, my dear?" Mrs. DuPlessis gasped. She'd finally managed to loosen half of her corset, but her face was red as strained beets and the careful coiffure she'd arranged in honor of the royal visit had become a lopsided bundle of frizzled brown moss; it looked like an abandoned bird's nest sitting on a telegraph pole.

Eugenia felt sudden compassion. Would my own mother have been like this woman, she wondered, or would she have been like me? Would I be taking care of her now or . . . ? The rest of the question was too ridiculous to pursue. I wouldn't know what to do if the tables were turned, Eugenia told herself, if Mrs. DuPlessis said: "Now, dear, you've worried enough. I'm going to take over from here on. You just sit still, have a nice cup of tea, and Prue and I will arrange everything. I don't want you to lift another finger." The picture was tempting; it made Eugenia momentarily sad.

"I'm sorry, Mrs. DuPlessis"—Eugenia put as much kindness into her voice as she could—"I didn't hear you. I was reorganizing the beds in my mind . . ."

"I was talking about the heat, my dear," Mrs. DuPlessis whimpered as she sank into a gooey mattress. A puff of something that smelled like decomposing cabbage rose as Mrs. DuPlessis sat, and she looked as pained as a princess finding a pea. "I don't know how you can put up with it . . . and you're still fully clothed as well. . . . Take my advice, my dear, shift into your nighttime garb. . . . It's just us girls here, after all . . . with the men all off. . . ." The speech ended in a whine; it was the first time, since her marriage, that Mrs. DuPlessis had been parted from her husband and she didn't like it one little bit.

"I don't know why we adults couldn't have stayed on board," Mrs. DuPlessis added. "The children would have been fine here with . . ."

"Because I won't be separated from them." Eugenia's anger flashed up; she wanted to say more, but stopped herself. Words spoken in anger . . . she recited to herself. I've got to remember Mrs. DuPlessis means well, that she came ashore out of concern for me. She followed us out of the goodness of her heart. She would have stayed on board if she was selfish.

All the same, Mrs. DuPlessis's grumblings were beginning to pall. The children and I would have had a better time alone, Eugenia decided; we could have pretended we were camping out; we would have read silly stories and laughed. This would have been an adventure, not an endurance test.

"I'm going to see how the girls are doing in the wash house," Eugenia said; separating herself from Mrs. DuPlessis, even for a few minutes, would be an enormous relief.

"But I'll be all alone." Mrs. DuPlessis's voice was the scarcest whimper.

"Paul and Olive are right next door in the cook house." Eugenia heard a snuffling intake of breath as she started toward the wash house door. "You're right," she could have said, "a lady's maid and a boy of five don't offer much protection," but some mean instinct held her back. Something inside Eugenia made her decide: I've enough to do.

The bathhouse was full of splashing. In Malay fashion, there were no tubs; floating on your back in warm water was unheard of. The proper way to wash was to douse yourself with cool water supplied by an enormous earthenware urn that had a small dipping cup attached to a cord. This method suited Jinx to a tee. At first she'd thought that she'd have to crawl inside the four-foot-high jars, that she'd have to take her bath standing up, but one of the sultan's wives (Jinx guessed the country had a lot of queens) had shown her what to do.

There'd been many gestures used in the description, and Prue and

Lizzie had looked thoroughly confused while two more queens (there were five in the room) had giggled behind their hands and then gotten into the act as well. Pretty soon everyone knew how to take a Malay shower-bath and the room became slick as the jungle floor. Water sluiced over everything. The five queens, in their cloth of gold sarongs, were soaked; Prue, in her starched white pinafore, was soaked. Water dripped from the ceiling, guzzled down the room's three drains, sloshed over the edges of the jars, and rained from the walls in ripply sheets. And to make the event even more fun, a family of frogs had appeared from behind one of the big jars and the mother, father, and baby frogs were having a bath as well.

Jinx was in the middle of their jumping excitement when her mother walked through the door. "Look!" she shouted, bounding up and down on her naked feet while her wet hair streamed down her naked back. "They've got frogs living inside the house. The queens say they only show themselves when someone takes a bath. They like showers, too." Jinx didn't bother to look at her mother.

". . . *Ayer* is the word for water," she continued. "The queens told us. And *nama* means name. . . ."

"And *apa* means what? . . ." Lizzie joined in. Eugenia was relieved to see her elder daughter so happy. Her discontent seemed to have vanished completely. It's because she can't decide who she is, Eugenia thought; she's partly a child and partly an adult, and not wholly comfortable in either world.

". . . And if you want to say: 'What is that thing called?' " Lizzie added quickly before Jinx had a chance, "you say: *Apa nama?*"

At another time Eugenia would have corrected her daughter; she would have said, " 'One says,' darling, not 'You say,' " but Eugenia still felt tenuous with Lizzie. Their fight hadn't been the ordinary mother-daughter squabble; there were too many secrets withheld.

"It looks as if you two are having a wonderful time." Eugenia smiled. That seemed a safe enough statement.

"Want to see something funny, Mother?" Jinx had grown tired of playing with the frogs; she'd decided to make a soap frosting for her body, lather it all around, and then toss great gobs of it on the ceiling. "Watch what happens to the queens when I say this word.

"*Rimau!*" Jinx yelled, and the sultan's ladies reacted with an elaborate shudder and squeal, then started to giggle furiously. Their response was obviously old hat.

"They do that every time," Jinx boasted, sharing the joke. "You're not supposed to say the word for 'tiger' in this country. It's very bad luck. You have to say: 'His Lordship' or 'The old gentleman'; that's what tigers like. If you say *rimau,* they come and eat you up!"

The ladies jumped again, indulging the children, then fell silent and began to nudge each other. "The mother is here," they were telling each other. "It is time for us to leave."

The bathhouse grew quiet as the ladies departed. Prue stepped forward with Turkish towels brought from the yacht, with dressing gowns and hairbrushes and bedroom slippers, and the brisk job of preparing for bed was begun. Jinx submitted her head to a towel, then a hairbrush, then put her arm in a readied sleeve and slid her feet into waiting slippers. The movements were routine, practiced every night (without the frogs, of course), and Jinx might have been a doll turned round and round as its owner changed its clothes.

"The queens said tomorrow we'll go see the tame monkeys fetching coconuts," Jinx said as the neck of her nightgown was fastened. "And some fish that crawl out of the water and up into trees so they can blink at you."

"It sounds as if you've been having quite a conversation," Eugenia said as she held up a small hand mirror for Lizzie, then caught her daughter's eyes watching and gave her a tentative smile. Lizzie's mouth didn't return the smile; it remained clamped in a stubborn line, but her eyes brightened, and Eugenia decided that small victory was enough.

"Don't you want to know how the monkeys do it?" Jinx demanded.

"Do what, darling?" Eugenia asked. She couldn't remember a thing Jinx had said; she was thinking about Lizzie, trying to find words of understanding. I'm the mother, Eugenia told herself; I should know what to do. It's up to me to help my children. It's up to me to show them how to live.

"Prue, go find Paul and settle him in. I'll finish up here," Eugenia said. Then she thought, Every night since Lizzie was a baby I've been doing the same thing: First teeth are brushed, then baths are taken, and before bedtime, stories are read, then it's prayers, good night kisses and sheets tucked over sleepy shoulders. This is what you give your children: this solidity, this sense that the world is a cozy and loving place. These are the moments they never forget.

"Pick coconuts! The monkeys pick coconuts!" Jinx was exasperated. She'd been ready for what seemed like hours, but there were Mother and Lizzie dawdling the night away. Just like they always did! Paul was usually the first, she, Jinx, a close second, but Lizzie was always a zillion times slower! And Mother let her get away with it! Every single night!

Eugenia looked at her younger daughter, standing shotgun straight and full of fire, and all of a sudden the world seemed as small and comforting as it did to her daughter. I'm the mother, Eugenia decided, and if I don't know what I'm doing, well, I'll make it up as I go along.

"And how do these monkeys pick coconuts, madam?" She laughed as she bundled all the wet towels into a ball, tossed it in a corner, then reached for her daughter's hands and tucked them safely against her elbows.

"Well, you have to get a special kind of monkey . . . one without a tail . . . and you tie a rope around his waist . . ." Jinx's description continued as the three started back toward the pavilion. The night had become solid black, though no cooler; it was as warm as midday and twice as damp. Eugenia looked at the lighted pavilion windows and saw fruit bats swooping in front of the light. Their wings were as large as hawks' wings and they beat the air with a whir and a whimpering moan. She could smell jasmine, too, and something sweeter, a scent that appeared and then vanished. When she thought she recognized the flower, the scent disappeared. It taunted her memory; something lay on the surface of her mind, but it faded as soon as a new wind blew.

". . . then you say 'Hijau' if you want coconuts for milk, and 'Kuning' if you want them for curry. The monkeys know lots of words. . . ." Jinx chattered away at her mother's side, slid her fingers down till they clasped Eugenia's, and swung their two hands back and forth. Lizzie removed herself, and her body either said *That's a baby's game* or *I wanted to play, too.*

"What a lot you've learned," Eugenia answered her younger daughter. "I'm sure Cousin Whitney will be impressed."

Lizzie said nothing, but Eugenia could feel her close by. She was walking in step, a separate being but not so very far off.

". . . well, you see the way it works, Mother," Jinx continued, "is that the monkeys know the difference in the shells of the coconuts, or the husks or whatever you call them, and they only bring back what you ask for. . . ."

Eugenia let the words thread through the night; she imagined them weaving into the trees: ribbons of thought waiting to be plucked from the branches, pressed flat, reread and relived.

". . . And guess what else, Mother? There are crocodiles thirty feet long. That's as big as our living room at home . . . and we're going to see those, too. The queens said—" Jinx suddenly stopped her recitation. "Don't you just love it here, Mother?" she said. "Don't you just wish we could stay forever?"

Eugenia was dreaming about her mother. Not her mother as she'd last seen her—a young woman with a young child—but as an older lady, a lady who'd aged, a lady born in the 1830s who was still alive in 1903. She was talking to Eugenia, to her grown daughter, and although Eugenia couldn't understand the words, she knew they were pleasant: a comfortable chat in a kitchen newly painted, but without dishes in the glass-paneled cupboards or rag rugs on the fresh-scrubbed floor.

It wasn't the house Eugenia had grown up in, the place she'd last seen her mother alive; it was a smaller house, sunnier, happy the way only tiny homes can be, and Eugenia had the impression her mother had just arrived. A lilac branch lay beside a speckled pitcher, a knife in place of flower shears, and a small green spider exploring its sudden change of abode. I brought the flowers, Eugenia thought. In my haste I broke a bough from the nearest tree.

Her mother's hair was very white, but she was still slender and as beautiful as ever. Even her hands were lovely; they hadn't aged at all, and the tips of her fingers were as round as they'd always been. The "artistic soul." Eugenia remembered her mother's adage: square-edged fingers meant a "practical being." And a practical being was decidedly inferior to one with a "free and loving heart."

Eugenia's mother toyed with her wedding band and another ring Eugenia had loved as a child: two hearts clasped like baby fists—the gold as pink as rose petals and nearly as transparent. That ring had a long history. Even as a little girl, Eugenia had known that. It could be traced back through four generations of women. Eugenia stared at the hearts, came awake only long enough to wonder where the ring had disappeared to, then returned to sleep and the kitchen.

Her mother was bustling back and forth from a tin-topped table to a Welsh cupboard, sipping tea, adding a sliver of lemon and the smallest amount of sugar crystal, while she made out a list of chores she wanted her daughter to do. There was a buzz in the room of gossip, contentment, and trust.

Eugenia woke; the laughter faded and her mother's face, the clink of saucers, and a smell as full of hope as fresh varnish, whitewash, and paint. Nothing remained of the kitchen except that sense of completion: a bond of wordless love. But returning to the world of sleeping men, Eugenia had one brief glimmer, an image sharp as day: Her mother was alive. Then she was back in Kuching, in a damp, musty bed, and her mother was somewhere else.

Eugenia lay still and listened to the sounds of her children sleeping: Paul with his short, even puffs, Jinx with her snorts and mumbles, and Lizzie talking to some imaginary soul who understood her. Then there was Mrs. DuPlessis with her fearsome snoring and Prue and Olive as quiet as two mice. The entire ladies' and children's pavilion was awash in sleep. Eugenia tried to retrieve her dream, but it scattered like sand.

Suddenly there was a scream. It came from the jungle or the river-bank or somewhere near town and it went on and on and on; the noise seemed to last forever and Eugenia felt as though it were walking, by half inches, up her spine. Then the scream gurgled and choked as if drowning, gasped for air, and ceased. The silence it left was absolute, as if every insect, animal, fish, bird, and human on the face of the planet had died. Eugenia slipped off her sheet and tiptoed to a window. The darkness was lessening, stirring in an eyelid's flutter out of night. Eugenia guessed that dawn lay just over the horizon.

Then there was another scream; Eugenia stayed at the window and listened. The sound followed the same pattern: a wail that grew louder and louder as it rose in terror and despair, then a gurgle, a gasp, an-other gurgle that seemed to squelch liquid, then the same awful si-lence. Eugenia looked back at the sleeping room, but the beds lay in dreamland. Stretched Malay fashion around rattan bolsters, the "Dutch wives" intended to keep their bodies cool, Mrs. DuPlessis, Lizzie, Jinx, and Paul were impervious.

Another wail started; Eugenia wished she could close her ears. Someone is enduring terrible torture, she thought. But even as those words came to mind she realized it wasn't someone; it was something. The sound was animal, not human. Pigs, she told herself; they're killing pigs. Eugenia looked out the window; there was nothing to see. But this is a Moslem country, she reminded herself; Moslems don't butcher pigs. Then she remembered Dr. DuPlessis and his lectures about the Chinese population: "the backbone of the country," the "hard-working people, without whom Borneo would sink into 'a slough of despond.' " "Notwithstanding the Dutch and English, of course," he'd added.

The pig slaughter continued while Eugenia wondered why people made the choices they did: her father's work as a diplomat and George's desire to make the old Turk proud. She thought about Rajah Ivard and his son, Laneer, the sultan and his own small son, and finally about James and his disappearance into the jungle. Why are we here? Eugenia asked herself suddenly. What are we doing in this place? We've sailed halfway around the world and all I know is that pigs die before breakfast.

She stared at the jungle and then in the direction of the harbor. The pig butchery ended finally, and the predawn air filled with different sounds; there were cheeps and chortles, squeals, rasping croaks and a high-pitched, nasal whine of a lizard advancing on its insect prey, and suddenly in the branches of two separate trees, an extraordinary light:

something like fire blinking in one and an answering glow in the other. One light turned on; the other turned off. One grew bolder and advanced; the other followed suit. They were sending messages from tree to tree.

"Fireflies," Eugenia said aloud. "Firefly armies . . . 'ignorant armies clashing by night' . . . 'Dover Beach' . . . how does that poem go?

" '. . . Ah, love,' " she began, " 'let us be true'

> "To one another! for the world, which seems
> To lie before us like a land of dreams,
> So various, so beautiful, so new,
> Hath really neither joy, nor love, nor light,"

Something forced Eugenia to stop momentarily; it was a sensation like pity or sorrow, and it sat on her chest till she shook it off:

> "Nor certitude, nor peace, nor help for pain;
> And we are here as on a darkling plain
> Swept with confused alarms of struggle and flight,
> Where ignorant armies clash by night."

" 'Nor certitude, nor peace, nor help for pain . . .' " Eugenia repeated, then added the first line from the Browning poem: " 'You know we French stormed Ratisbon. . . .' "

TWENTY-SIX

L

IKE ALL NIGHT WAN-DERERS, Eugenia had returned to bed just before dawn. Now it was full, bright daylight, but she was still fast asleep. Outside the pavilion, encroaching on the palace grounds like fog, were the sounds of a jungle town greeting the day: cookfires simmering with a fizzle and snap, children shouting, tethered goats bleating and cocks and hens in dusty competition. Eugenia didn't move. If she heard the noise, it became part of her dream; she carried the sounds wherever she went. The whoop of a rooster on a longhouse roof was easy to translate to another time, another country; the chime of temple bells was harder. Eugenia lay on her bed with her eyes closed, and took it all in. She hardly moved.

The Malay servant, waiting by the lady Axthelm's side, hoped and prayed that her hovering presence might remind the dreamer to stir out of dreamland. Custom forbade the girl to wake the sleeper: to do so was to risk separating the soul from the body; any sudden noise might frighten the traveling spirit, might cause it to depart and the deserted body to shrivel and die. A soul on its nightly voyage must find its home undisturbed in the morning. The servant repeated those warnings to herself again and again.

But the two girl children were already up—and the older lady; and the boy long since gone with his father and His Highness, the sultan. And now there was this new problem: a strange messenger from the white ship, and nothing to do but wait till the lady Axthelm's eyes drifted back to earth. The servant stared and stared and begged her gods to allow the soul a swift return.

When Eugenia did open her eyes, she hadn't the slightest idea where she was. She saw a room so vast it looked like a railroad terminal, a crystal chandelier with carved drops as fat as grapefruit, and a girl in a green and orange sarong standing near her feet. The girl was holding a tray with a blue pot placed square in its center; there was steam coming out of the spout. Tea, Eugenia thought, morning tea: how lovely. She stretched her arms, wriggled her feet under the sheets, then remembered: We're in the palace in Kuching; there's some kind of festival today. George is going, and Paul, but we ladies have been kindly requested to cool our heels at home. A Moslem country is a Moslem country. Entertainment is for gentlemen alone.

"Are my daughters—?" Eugenia began, but the serving girl turned goggle-eyed, then pointed her chin toward the door and said something unintelligible. I should have paid more attention to Jinx's lessons last night, Eugenia told herself. The moist heat of the room seemed thicker than it had been the night before. Living in Sarawak must be like soaking in a perpetually hot and oily bath, Eugenia decided as she sat up. Her linen gown was stuck to her back as though with paste, and puddles of water had formed under her knees.

At that moment Jinx came running in. "Thank heavens you're up, Mother!" she yelled; her voice was proud and excited. "Henry's here. He says he has something to tell you. He's talking to Liz right now." Jinx threw herself on her mother's bed and began to inspect the breakfast tray.

Oh, no, Eugenia thought, another scene. All of a sudden she didn't want to get up at all. She wanted to go back to sleep and start the morning over again. "Ignorant armies," she remembered suddenly, but transposing the poem to daylight hours dissolved its intent and made her smile instead. " 'Where ignorant armies clash by night,' " Eugenia recited. Henry, like all problems, faded with sunlight.

"Mother," Jinx reminded, "you promised."

"It doesn't matter," Eugenia answered. "You're too young to understand. And anyway, you don't appreciate the better things in life." There was nothing vengeful in either voice; mother and daughter were playing a game.

"I just don't like all those silly poems," Jinx answered as she stretched herself across her mother's mattress; the tray bounced when she settled in place. *"Apa nama?"* Jinx asked the serving girl while trying to peer into the steamy pot.

"*Teh*," The girl answered, then added, "*Cawan*," when Jinx pointed at the cup.

"*Apa nama?*" Jinx repeated, lifting the dome off a closed dish.

"*Gula melaka*," the servant said.

"Oh, Mother," Jinx wailed as she plopped the lid back in place, "you're so lucky! You get a big dish of tapioca pudding. We only had small ones for our breakfast, and it's so good! It's got something like molasses mixed in. Paul said the *gula*—that's what we called it— looked like frogs' eggs, and Mrs. DuPlessis got mad at him and said he'd end up a heathen.

"We ate out on the veranda because Prue said we mustn't disturb you. She said we must let you sleep as long as you like. That you're on holiday, too. . . ."

Eugenia sipped her tea while her daughter talked. It had the scent and taste of jasmine flowers, and Eugenia decided she was the most fortunate woman in the world.

". . . And there were these three brown birds perched on the edge of our table, and they began to eat crumbs from Liz's hand . . . then one hopped over and stood right on my plate. . . . It was bigger than a sparrow, I think, though I don't quite remember sparrows' sizes, and it looked me up and down and had this very curious—"

"Did Henry say what he wanted?" Eugenia interrupted gently; she tasted the *gula melaka*, then returned the spoon to the plate.

"No." Jinx jumped off the bed, spun around once in indecision, then headed for the door. "But it's important." Jinx was almost out of sight. "He looks frightfully serious. Liz thinks so, too. That's why she's talking to him. Because he looks so sad. You really have to get up sometime, you know, Mother."

Eugenia sighed, closed her heart to laziness and irresponsibility, then decided to forgo the dubious pleasure of eating tapioca pudding for breakfast. She motioned for the serving girl to remove the tray, put on her dressing gown, and walked out onto the pavilion veranda. A mother is a mother, she told herself. Above and beyond anything else she might be.

Henry was immediately in front of her. *Frightfully* is a good word, Eugenia thought, that's how I would have described him, too. She wrapped the cords of her dressing gown tighter. Girding for battle, she told herself, but the phrase had lost its humor. "Yes?" Eugenia said. "What is it, Henry?"

"It's . . . it's . . . the gentlemen's enlightenment . . ." Henry stammered. He'd never felt so tongue-tied in his life. He'd come to the ladies' pavilion on a mission, but waiting on the veranda and seeing Miss Lizzie again had turned his resolve to cold mutton soup. Henry felt he was no more than a wavery bit of gelatin left in the bottom of a pot.

"*Entertainment?*" Eugenia corrected. "Is that the word you want?" Dampness rolled down her shoulders and arms; her skin felt as though spiders were building a home; and all she could think of was her bathtub on board: bubbly water, lavender soap, a sponge for her knees and a brush for her back.

"That's it, ma'am," Henry garbled. "*Entertainment.* That's the one." He looked down the veranda for a sign of encouragement or escape, and finding none, let his shoulders collapse in a curve.

Eugenia studied the boy. Gangly, seventeen or thereabouts, a spotty face, red eyes, redder hands, feet as big as flippers, hair uncombed: What does Lizzie see in him? she wondered.

"And just what is it, Henry," Eugenia asked, "that you'd like to tell me about the entertainment His Majesty, the sultan, has arranged for the gentlemen? What is important enough to wake me?" If I don't sound exactly like my grandmother, no one does, Eugenia told herself. I might as well be dressed in black ruching with a cameo brooch at my throat.

"Oh, ma'am." Henry yelped, "Higgins warned me not to say nothing. . . ." The boy can't even speak proper English, Eugenia realized. The discovery made her weaken momentarily; pity swamped her and lassitude, like too much love, sucked at her chest. Then another emotion took hold; Eugenia stiffened her spine; impatience bubbled like sweat. "Get on with it," she wanted to order. "I can't help your backstairs squabbles."

". . . He said I'd catch it if I blabbed, and I didn't mean to watch them, ma'am, honest, I didn't . . . I wasn't spying or nothing . . . God's truth! You've got to believe me. . . .

"I was just on my way down to see what shakes Ned was up to . . . if he wanted to set up some fish poles down by the stern, you know . . . these waters is so full of fish they keep bumping each other into the air, and some of them has wings, like, so when they get knocked about they flitter like squirrels at home . . . the ones with those little webs in their paws—"

"What did you see, Henry?" Eugenia demanded. She noticed Lizzie and Jinx creeping forward; they'd kept a respectful distance, staying at the other end of the veranda, but curiosity drew them closer. Eugenia waved her daughters away with one quick gesture; she felt cross as a bear.

I haven't eaten a decent meal since yesterday, she realized. I've been forced to sleep in a dormitory, in a bed that smells like a cave. I dream useless dreams about forgotten creatures, then spend the rest of the night listening to the slaughter of God knows how many wretched pigs. Finally I'm served custard and molasses instead of a proper breakfast, and now this boy is sniveling over some servants' quarrel and asking me to intercede because my daughter's taken a fancy to him!

"What did you see, Henry?" Eugenia insisted again, but she needn't have bothered with her demands. Fear had driven Henry to the pavilion; he didn't heed the tone of his mistress's voice; he didn't notice Lizzie's warning glances or see the sentences stacked against him. Henry had come ashore against all sound judgment, against hope for betterment or even a fair deal. He was on the veranda because he'd seen something that had scared the living daylights out of him.

"Guns, ma'am!" Henry exploded. "The sultan's men, they was taking guns from our ship!"

"But Higgins was there," Eugenia prompted. Her voice was civil, but just barely. "You just said so yourself. Higgins wouldn't allow untoward behavior." Eugenia felt a prickling of fear, but turned it against Henry. How dare he disturb us here? she fumed; how dare he come ashore and scare us with suppositions and rumors and back-stabbing servant-boy tricks?

"He was, ma'am. Higgins was. But Master George, he wasn't. And I didn't mean to watch them, ma'am, really I didn't . . ." The red rims of Henry's eyes made him look like a flinching puppy. Eugenia felt like shaking him till he whimpered.

"Never mind all that, Henry," she ordered. "What do you mean 'Master George wasn't'? My husband doesn't oversee everything that happens on board." Eugenia pounded out the words, but another voice whispered that Henry was correct—that George should have been present.

"That's just it, ma'am! I don't know. . . . It all seemed so sneaky-like . . . old Higgins handing off a bunch of brand-new guns to some bloody heathen—beg your pardon, ma'am, I don't mean no disrespect to His Highness and all—but all those big boxes in the hold of the ship . . . ?" Henry stopped in time to see Lizzie staring at him. She couldn't hear what he was saying, but she could see the worry on his face.

"What is Mother saying?" she mouthed; Lizzie tried to move forward, but Jinx held her in place.

Henry dragged his eyes back to Eugenia. ". . . All those big boxes, ma'am . . . ?" he repeated. ". . . The ones the Lieutenant had to watch out for? They all contain rifles, ma'am. Every last one of them. Rifles . . . ammunition . . . that's what Higgins was passing off to the heathen. . . . They're not machinery at all. . . . The Lieutenant, he took some, too. . . ."

"That's a very tall tale, Henry!" Eugenia spit out, then continued with a more reasonable "I witnessed the men unloading a few of the crates of machinery myself, before we docked here . . . the night we passed the light beacon at Tanjong Datu. It was done to avoid an excise tax. The decision had nothing to do with—"

"Oh, no, ma'am, it wasn't no tall tale." Henry was white-faced but staunch. "And it wasn't machinery, neither, ma'am. It was guns, sure as sure. That's what I heard old Higgins telling the mate. He said Mr. Brown's off in the jungle with them savages, and that when he and the sultan's boys get together, there'll be hell to pay. . . ."

"Be quiet, Henry!" Eugenia's voice sliced the air. She couldn't think, she couldn't plan, she couldn't get to the bottom of this absurd story, and Henry's panicky ramblings only made things worse. "When Mr. Axthelm returns, he'll set the matter straight. I'm sure there's some reasonable explanation for—"

"There ain't no time, ma'am! Higgins, he told the mate the sultan's planning some executions this morning. He's going to conk some poor old prisoners he's got molting away. . . ."

Eugenia turned away from Henry so abruptly he might have been water. She marched into the pavilion and shouted for Prue and the girls to follow her. A "Gentleman's Entertainment," she told herself: rifles for the sultan, rifles in the jungle with James. Executions. None of it made any sense, but the words kept repeating themselves: *machinery, my father, the Ivards, the sultan.* Eugenia couldn't see a connection, but she knew it was there.

Or maybe it isn't, she reminded herself as she ripped off her dressing gown and stepped into the same white shirtwaist dress she'd worn the night before. The dress was still soggy with bathwater; mildew spots had begun to creep down the sleeves and bodice, but Eugenia didn't notice; she slid her hands through the lace cuffs and began to fasten the skirt. Maybe there's no connection at all, she thought; maybe this is a random list, a few names thrown into a hat for an overactive imagination to conjure into catastrophe. Maybe it's pure coincidence.

Eugenia considered that question as she finished getting dressed. She was operating on two levels. One was her mind: counting names, weighing chance against a systematic plot, searching her memory for clues. The other was her body: putting on clothes, moving forward in an orderly and purposeful fashion. The two existed side by side, but there was no exchange of information. The body moved by rote—first came the stockings, then the shoes—while the mind grabbed intuition, sound, sight, half-heard phrases, and flung them about like letters stored in a chest.

Then the reasonable side of Eugenia's brain spoke up. *George would never put his family in danger,* it said. *He wants the best for us; he loves us, after all.* While the emotional side answered: *Where have you been? When are you going to come to your senses?*

Reason parried: *But James loves me; he wouldn't be involved in any-thing underhanded?* While emotion interrupted with a long, hard laugh: *Use your noggin,* it gloated. *Wake up!*

Eugenia decided to ignore both voices. The only important thing was to find Paul. The rest could be sorted out later. Guns or machinery: There was a logical explanation somewhere; there always was.

"Prue," Eugenia demanded, "where did my husband say he was taking Paul?"

"Why, off to the 'gentlemen's entertainment,' miss." Prue was startled by her mistress's voice; she seemed like a different person.

Eugenia laced up her walking shoes; she didn't look at Prue as she spoke: "Which way did they go?"

"Why, miss, I don't really remember. . . . It was a while ago, and I was . . ." Prue started to tidy away Eugenia's dressing gown and turn the bed linens to air, but a sudden "Well, think!" stopped her in her tracks. The dressing gown dropped in a heap.

"I . . ." Prue faltered, "I don't . . ." while Eugenia stood up with an angry "Never mind. What time was it?"

"Oh, early, miss!" Prue was glad to find a question she could answer. "Way before you woke up. Mr. George, he said not to wake you. . . ."

Before Prue could finish, Eugenia had hurried through the door. Lizzie and Jinx watched their mother leave, feeling like castaways stranded on a beach. They didn't say a word.

As Eugenia reached the veranda, she turned with a final order. "I want all of you back on the boat right away. Mrs. DuPlessis, Prue, Olive! Leave these things. We'll send for them later. I'm going to find Paul and set things right. And Lizzie and Jinx, no questions. Just do as you're told!"

While Prue simultaneously remembered where the men had gone. "Up on the hill, miss," she called. "That's where the entertainment's taking place. Jalan, I think they called it."

The way up Jalan Hill was snaky with vines. George had to stop constantly to free a foot or hand. He looked back at the others, at old Mr.

Paine and Sir Charles Ivard, young Whitney and Ridgeway, and wondered how they managed to look so unencumbered; even the sultan, despite his baggage of royal krisses, headdress, and robes, appeared unhurried and relaxed. Laneer Ivard was the only man who seemed upset by the climb; he snatched at the vines as if he wanted to eat them, and pushed aside the royal bearers to tear at the vegetation himself.

"I can't believe you're going ahead with it!" Laneer muttered as he finally came abreast of George. "We can't be seen there! The sultan means to go ahead with the executions right away! Seh will—"

But Laneer was forced to drop behind before he could say more. The path was too narrow for two, and the sultan didn't condone conversation in which he had no part; general chat was the order of the day: something the entire column could share. Laneer lurked in single file and waited for another chance to speak his piece.

George watched Laneer shrink into the bushes; he was becoming increasingly concerned that Laneer Kinloch Ivard, rajah muda and heir to his father's title, was off his rocker. Executions, indeed! The sultan would never permit such a thing—especially in front of guests. George didn't understand all the hysteria about Seh, or Laneer's insistence on discussing Ogden Beckmann and the plot to overthrow the sultan. Out in the open, too! Under the man's very nose. Laneer may think these Malays have an inferior brain capacity, George told himself, but it's our rajah muda who's missing his marbles.

George struggled to keep in step with the column while he considered this unfortunate discovery. It was unsettling, to say the least. Here he was, forced to trust a man with a brain like a squashed pea while his other so-called advisers were two dodderers hardly worth their weight in salt. George's mind tumbled over these problems as he continued to climb the hill. His solar topee chafed, then squeaked in his ears and beat a tattoo on his forehead while the hat's sweatband seeped water like a shredding sponge. Plus the fact that his boots kicked up a thicket of rancid vegetation whenever he lifted them! George wanted to pull out his handkerchief and fan himself; he wanted a drink of cold water and a seat on a pine-covered mountaintop in Maine. But you can't have that, he told himself, you can't let up, or show weakness of any kind. You're the boy what's in charge; George repeated that promise over and over and over again.

This is my party, after all. Old Georgie Porgie pudding and pie. I'm the fellow what's handling the Axthelm concerns. It's me and no one else. I dispense a few rifles in a day or two, let the sultan play with his toys, then wait for Brown to arrive and the regime to quietly topple.

A foolproof scheme if I ever saw one, and Ogden Beckmann, for all

Laneer's gabble, was no more than a minor player. George indulged in some well-deserved pride; there'll be plenty of thanks when this little gambit is over, he soothed. Plenty of gratitude while a few snooty souls eat their share of crow. "Georgie Porgie pudding and pie/ Kissed the girls and made them cry . . ."

Laneer's voice interrupted George's thoughts again and he stared at the rajah muda as if he were a flat-eared rodent. "We can't go up there!" Laneer was hissing: "It's death if we do. I know Seh! I've been with him in the jungle. I know the man, I tell you! . . ."

"My dear, Laneer," the sultan shouted down from the head of the procession, "is there something you wish to share with us?" He laughed loudly at his own joke; his belly wobbled and his jeweled turban seemed to quiver on his head as beams of light struck a ruby, then an emerald, then a row of sapphires encased in gold.

The sultan snapped his fingers and wiggled his wrists as he included his courtiers in the jest; he was going to be indulgent with young Laneer this afternoon. The sultan didn't want anything to spoil the show he'd arranged for Mr. George Axthelm. His honored guest must want to see the new rifles at work: the new Springfield A3s, the prisoners shattering like sticks, the ill-conceived rebellion going up in smoke, and that pesky Mahomet Seh tied in ropes like a hog. It was going to be a most enjoyable afternoon, the sultan assured himself, a most enjoyable day!

"Nothing to share, then, Laneer?" the sultan laughed again, and the rest of the group immediately imitated him—even old Paine and the elder Ivard. George heard them catch the sultan's attempted joke and pass it to young Whitney, who then repeated it to Dr. DuPlessis. Soon the entire jungle shook with false mirth. Raspy intakes of breath were substituted for true amusement; the royal column sounded like a hospital full of tubercular patients.

"No, I have nothing to share," Laneer muttered, and the group guffawed even louder. Everything was amusing when one walked with the sultan! His retainers passed the witticisms back and forth between them; they wouldn't stop till His Highness dropped another pearl. "Nothing to share" became their talisman: "Nothing," one would say, and another would answer, "Share." "Nothing" . . . "Share" . . . "Nothing" . . . "Share" . . . The line up Jalan Hill was doubled over in forced laughter while George continued his ditty: "When the boys came out to play/ Georgie Porgie ran away . . ."

While the native princes, their retinues, Sir Charles, Ridgeway, Dr. DuPlessis, Whitney, and the Honorable Nicholas kept the sultan's lame jokes alive, Laneer Ivard came to a sudden and sensible conclusion: He would not go to the clearing. Seh was waiting there—Seh with his terrible Bugis and fearsome Iban, knives in their teeth and guns in their callused hands—Seh waiting to swoop down as if on pet rabbits in a cage. The sultan didn't recognize the trap because he believed what he wanted, because he was a stupid man, educated with puffery and empty phrases: a blockhead, a numskull, and a fraud of a king. The sultan decreed that an appropriate spectacle for a white guest was gunning down a handful of rebels; he didn't know the real target was himself.

Laneer stood to one side of the trail and bent low to the ground in an imitation of overwhelming nausea. He knew the sultan couldn't tolerate illness, that he had a terror of infection.

The procession came to a halt as the sultan called out, "Too much *nasi padang,* I fear, for our good friend the rajah muda. Overfeasting is never healthful, Laneer. We have warned you many times on this sticky issue." There was another laugh, followed by sycophantic echoes, but the trick worked; Laneer was allowed to go free.

The rest of the procession sidestepped him gingerly as the sultan clapped his hands as a sign for the parade to continue. Nothing was going to spoil his fun; he'd see to young Mr. Ivard when they returned to the palace—rajah muda though he might be. The sultan settled his wrath, remembered the prisoners huddled on the hill, and smiled.

Laneer waited till the jungle swallowed the ridiculous group, till the last Western boots kicked up the last scorpions and the glassy snakes slithered back to their churned-up mud, till the Durian trunks stopped wriggling and the glossy bamboo ceased rattling and the sultan's fatuous whine was overcome by the screech of a black cockatoo, then he bolted down the hill.

Eugenia ripped aside the vines. Every twist in the trail seemed harder than the one before. She didn't know which way the hillside clearing lay, but she knew to travel upward. Thorny tendrils and leaves ripped her dress, snagged her hair, and slashed her hands and arms, but she pushed on. If Henry's right about guns and executions, and if Paul has to witness some poor natives being shot, I will never forgive George, she promised. I'll shoot him myself. I will. Anger made her hurry, but speed made the jungle harder to fight. Every tree, every vine, every dog-sized leaf, seemed to have fingers that grabbed her and spikes that stuck her; it was as if they were human, as if they were impeding her progress on purpose. Eugenia looked at her sleeves; they were torn and stained with blood. When we get back to the ship, she promised herself, I'm going to yank off this dress and toss it overboard. I never want to see it again.

Suddenly there was a noise up ahead, a loud crashing as if a huge animal were hurtling downhill. Eugenia shrank into the thicket and waited. The noise continued; saplings snapped in half; branches broke in two. Eugenia froze and imagined tigers. She pictured bloody faces and snarling mouths; she closed her eyes tight. *Rimau,* she thought; no wonder the sultan's ladies jump at the word.

Paul was getting tired; it seemed forever they'd been walking up the hill. He was hot and thirsty. He wanted to see the surprise the sultan had promised. His Highness hadn't told anyone what it was yet, but Paul was imagining a circus. He knew the palace had a zoo; Dr. Du-Plessis and Grandfather Paine had told him so. Paul thought they might sit on long benches and eat lemon ice and watch all sorts of comical things. There might be a trained bear or an ape in a turban. Or an orangutan with funny, long orange hair. Or a proboscis monkey with a fat, red nose.

Paul trudged along. He didn't dare take his father's hand; he knew he was too big for that nonsense, but all the same he wished he could. Then he thought about his mother and his sisters, and wished he were back with them; he could be playing a game on the boat or listening to a story or tossing bread to the dolphins with Jinx. Paul's trousers began to feel as if ants were making a nest inside the legs; his shirt collar rubbed; there were black bugs swarming under his hat brim, and his tongue, when he rubbed it against his cheek, was as dry as a pair of shoes.

Suddenly Paul remembered fruit punch and swimming in Grandfather Axthelm's pond, and Linden Lodge and the maze made of clipped bushes, and the sound of the big clock in the hall and the smell of the stone walls after a summer rain. He thought about Christmastime and the knights' armor standing at attention in Grandfather A.'s front hall. Then he remembered snow and tobogganing with his cousins and cocoa after, and a bath in a tub so big you could swim in it. And warm pajamas and falling asleep while more snow fell and the sky got blue and the hills turned white as stars. Paul walked up Jalan Hill beside his father, but what he saw and heard was his bedroom in Linden Lodge, the big panes of glass growing frosted on the inside while under the covers, he discovered a warm spot for his toes, peeped into the dark room, and could hardly wait for morning.

Eugenia's tiger turned out to be Laneer Ivard. The man was quivering with fear: He hardly took time to stop. "Oh, you frightened me so!" he screeched. "I didn't see you till I nearly crashed into you. You should have called out or something. Warned me at least! I might have died of fright!"

Eugenia didn't have time to respond. Laneer was off down the path almost before she knew what had happened. "Fly! Fly, before it's too late!" his departing body squealed. "They're in the trees, waiting like panthers. They've got sharp, pointy teeth. You can't risk being seen there! The whole thing's become one big, bloody and godforsaken mess! Get out while you can!"

"What is? Who is?" Eugenia called after him, but Laneer had disappeared.

"Seh," a voice called back, then there was nothing: no leaf motion, no bird calls, no slide of jungly ooze. Laneer Kinloch Ivard was as good as asleep in his palace rooms.

Mahomet Seh, Eugenia thought. That was the name she finally remembered.

The Honorable Nicholas was becoming increasingly perturbed. Surely young Paul shouldn't witness an execution, he thought. If, in actual fact, that was the sultan's intention. Surely no child should be present. Not even the young crown prince. If, and there was always that consoling "if," that was indeed the sultan's plan.

But it's so hard to gauge these Orientals, Paine considered, so difficult to find a common thread. To show the soles of one's feet is believed to be the very height of impropriety, but a public beheading or a prisoner garroted to death in a village square: That is civilized behavior. Civilized behavior in an uncivilized world: Paine returned to the familiar phrases that made the day acceptable. Diplomacy, he thought, is the art of melding two worlds into one. It takes tact and a certain laxity of morals. Turning a blind eye. Trusting in a higher wisdom or, at least, divine intervention.

The immediate problem was Paul, of course. Paul and the sultan's young heir. The Honorable Nicholas decided to speak to his son-in-law about it at the very next opportunity. George should be apprised of the sultan's little quirks, the Honorable Nicholas told himself. When His Highness says execution, he just might mean it. And, really, with these people, Paine remembered, one should never take unnecessary chances.

They were almost near the top of the mountain, almost at the clearing! Paul could see a flood of light up ahead on the path; it was bright, yellow light, the kind you get on a sunny afternoon when nap time is over, and when, more than anything in the world, you want to be outside playing with the bigger children, climbing trees with them or building forts out of sheets and laundry line and blankets pilfered from the linen cupboard. Paul felt revived; the long march was over! He might have been standing in the window of his room at Grandfather A.'s house, yanking on his clothes while he watched his cousins tumbling over the wide lawn—he was that excited, that anxious to be part of the game.

A circus, Paul told himself. I bet it's a circus! Or a zoo. A zoo would be nice, too. Especially if there were tigers! Or leopards in long cages, pacing around and flicking their tails through the bars. Or maybe an elephant to ride. A baby elephant just for me! Paul pulled himself straighter and walked a little faster. If there was going to be a circus— or a zoo—he wanted to be first. He looked at the sultan's son just ahead of him on the trail. The boy had been ordered to turn around to wait for his young guest. Paul guessed he was a prince; he was equipped with all sorts of fancy weapons: a bow and arrow in a red and black sheath on his back, two daggers stuck crosswise in his belt, and a silver-handled sword on his hip. But he didn't look happy with his getup; he looked terribly serious—angry, almost, as if waiting for a five-year-old baby was beneath him. Paul decided the prince was too spoiled to know how lucky he was, and that if he, Paul, had that sort of arsenal, he'd be beaming from head to foot. Imagine going out to play in a real soldier suit with real armor and knives made of gold! And a hat with jewels all over it like Ali Baba and his Forty Thieves! Paul looked at the clothes and the boy and grinned, but the young prince glared at the ground.

Lieutenant Brown and Mahomet Seh were in place on the hilltop. They watched the sultan's group begin to straggle into the clearing. Brown was surprised to see George and several other men in European clothes. Damn it to hell, he thought. Can't the man do anything right? I told him to stay on the boat. I told him this was no place for his games. And dragging the others along, too . . . there's Whitney and Dr. DuPlessis. . . . George is a complete idiot, Brown told himself angrily. If he's brought Eugenia, I'll murder him myself.

Brown turned to the rebel leader. "I didn't expect the white men," he said carefully. "They mustn't be harmed. Tell your men."

"As you wish," Seh answered, but Brown didn't like the tone. It lacked commitment. It lacked good faith. It lacked honesty. Seh has nothing to lose, Brown remembered.

"Listen to me, Seh," he said. "If even one of those men gets as much as a scratch, you'll answer to me. I know tricks that would make your hair stand on end. With or without a headhunter's ax. My work may be finished, but I'm still here. Remember that."

Brown looked at the entire fiasco one final time; there were white men in white suits, brown men in silks, brown men in rags, in leopard skins, in uniforms, or nothing at all. He lifted his eyes from the clearing. Get it over with, he thought; finish the job and get out.

"Almost time," Brown said.

He never saw Paul. He wasn't looking for him, and not in the farthest reaches of his imagination, would he have expected to find the little boy on the hilltop. Paul was with his mother; that's all Brown knew. He was where he should be. He was safe. George might have been the world's worst blunderer, but at least he loved his children.

Brown let his eyes travel over the men he'd trained as they crouched on the hilltop. Each man held his rifle; each was poised and ready. Brown's instructions had taken. He turned his back on the clearing.

Seh, Mahomet Seh. The name shouted itself in Eugenia's head as she ran. She knew she'd heard it before. It was what she'd been trying to remember. Suddenly everything came clear. Seh was the rebel leader the Turk had mentioned long ago in Philadelphia. George, the Turk, Beckmann: Each one knew the name. And if Laneer Ivard was right, then Seh was waiting for the sultan in the clearing. Waiting to leap from the trees. Like panthers, Laneer had said.

Eugenia forced the picture from her mind. Paul's with them, she told herself; my son's up there, too. She tore through the jungle. Her hands were bloody; her face was scratched. *Paul's in the clearing,* her mind shouted. *Paul's on the hill.*

"I say, old man." The Honorable Nicholas sidled over to his son-in-law. He didn't want His Highness to get wind of their defection, but, by God, it didn't seem right for a tyke like Paul to see a man gunned down. Or men. Paine had noticed quite a few rebel prisoners waiting under heavy guard.

Must be twenty, at least, he thought. And a sorry lot indeed. Regular ragamuffins. The Honorable Nicholas looked over at the guard, spiffily done up for this festive occasion, new rifles and all, and the sergeant major with a leopard skin cape. No extravagance spared. The sultan was going ahead with it: sure as curtains. His soldiers would execute the prisoners right in this clearing. In front of his guests. It was as plain as the nose on your face.

"I say, old man . . ." Paine started again.

George didn't quite get it. He heard what old Paine was saying, but wasn't sure what the words meant. Surely the sultan hadn't dragged them all the way up here for some kind of Far Eastern shoot-out, George told himself. Surely that was some kind of Malay joke or a poor translation of a local custom; execution could mean anything. A plan could be executed. Laws could be executed, or a piece of music or a portrait painted on commission. And what was a sultan if not the ultimate executive? And executives needed to execute decisions.

His Highness would get his new guns soon enough, George decided. What more did he want? Then it would be only a matter of the white folks biding their time till Brown arrived on the scene. A few days, at most, George promised himself. Then they'd wave bye-bye and sail home. Sail home in glory. To the comforts of the Corinthian Yacht Club and a few rousing toasts at the bar.

All the same, George decided not to venture too far into the clearing. If men were going to be shot, he didn't want Paul to witness the spectacle. George shielded his son from view and hemmed and hawed while he tried to follow Paine's halting words.

In his private enclosure at the head of the clearing, the sultan had finished talking to his sergeant major. Everything was in perfect readiness. Everything had been done according to his exact and demanding specifications and to his complete satisfaction, but his most honored guest, Mr. George Axthelm, the man to whom he owed everything, continued to hesitate near the jungle path, deep in discussion with his father-in-law and his wife's cousin, Mr. Whitney Caldwell.

The sultan graced George with a regal but demanding wave. The wave said, *We await you. Come here! There's more important work ahead,* but George treated the gesture as if it were no more than a friendly greeting and smiled and nodded in reply. Miffed, the sultan decided to proceed in spite of his guest's rude behavior. Perhaps a sudden, loud retort is more dramatic, he told himself. More imperious, more forceful. Perhaps Mr. Axthelm needs to be taken by surprise. When he sees the first prisoner drop, he'll change his mind. They'll all change their minds. They'll be dumbfounded and speechless. I am Sultan of Sarawak, after all.

The sultan motioned to one of his retainers that his young heir should be placed beside him, then he slowly raised his right arm as a signal to his troops' commander. The soldiers obeyed the order immediately; they hoisted their Springfield A3s, tucked in their chins, and sighted along the barrels.

It was the sign Mahomet Seh had been watching for, too. He looked at the captured men, stretched in a shivering line, and thought: We'll be able to save some of our comrades. Some, but not all. The rest will be sacrificed. But a sacrifice is good for the business of rebellion.

Seh had been surprised to see the sultan bring his heir. A mere child watching men die as if they were no more than the puppet images of Wak Long or Pa'Dogah, he told himself. It was unthinkable, inexcusable. The sultan's heartlessness was as staggering as it was legendary. But, Seh decided, if the father takes the son, it is the will of Allah. If the child dies, it is the father's doing.

Seh motioned to his men. They crept forward like cats in a shadow.

Eugenia had just reached the edge of the clearing when the shooting started. She was so startled by the noise that at first she looked toward the trees to see what was making all the racket. There were men swarming down on all sides. The jungle behind the clearing was full of naked, running bodies. They looked like brown beetles dropping from trees, like howler monkeys, like toads with human legs. Eugenia watched the sultan's soldiers turn in rapid dismay; she heard their screams of fear, and for a moment she forgot to look for her child.

There was confusion everywhere. A few soldiers pushed past her; desperate to regain the safety of the path, they nearly trampled her in their haste. But the rest of the sultan's men were trapped in the center of a wide-open space. Trapped and turning in slow, wild-eyed circles. Their guns dangled uselessly, and their shields and spears dropped to the ground. The men were pinned in place.

Eugenia saw the soldiers fall. Blood covered everything: the grassy hillocks, the stones, the wood slats of the sultan's private enclosure. While she watched, the sultan was shot; his abdomen exploded in a swirl of red, which he covered with his hands as he crumpled. Then a tall man leapt into the enclosure and kicked the dying body. More men poured into the clearing; the sultan's troops were slaughtered while they crawled, whimpering, for cover; native princes were clubbed to death with the butt end of rifles and the sultan's young son was stabbed through the heart, then his body was heaped on his father's. Eugenia watched the child's turban roll free; the weight of its jewels carried it in a looping circle across the grass.

"Paul!" Eugenia screamed. "Paul!" Her legs finally started to move, and she struggled toward the clearing.

Then suddenly George was running toward her. Through the smoke and yellow-gray haze, Eugenia could see him clearly. He ran past Sir Charles Ivard and her father, past Dr. DuPlessis and Whitney. He was stumbling, tripping and crying, and Paul was in his arms.

Eugenia raced to meet them. Paul turned to his mother. He looked terrified but unharmed, and she reached out her arms to take him, intending never again to let him go, never to let anger come near him, never to let evil or hurt touch his young face again.

But one final shot rang out. It wasn't fired by anyone in particular or at anyone special, it was an exuberant display, perhaps, proclaiming the strife over, the battle done, and it rose from the mass of living and dead men the way a song might, or a shout of reckless triumph. But that one last shot hit Paul just as his mother took him in her arms. It burst into his small head as he passed between his parents' hands and his body grew stiff as it spun toward the blow.

Flesh showered Eugenia's face; blood splattered her shoulder and sleeve. Clots of hair seemed suddenly everywhere: tumbling through the air, clinging to the branches of trees, dusting her arms and hands, and drying on her shoes. Eugenia tried to move; she wanted to shield her son. She succeeded only in turning her head.

Paul's face was gone, cut in half, shattered: One eye and his nose had vanished, and pulpy stuff like brains or muscle or thought tumbled out of the hole. It poured over Eugenia's cheeks as she cradled her child. It slithered over her lips: a sticky, hot goo. It was wet and it tasted like salt.

Eugenia ran for the path, clutching Paul's head and holding his body so close to her own they might have been one. She wanted to get back to the ship, fit the pieces of her son back together, find the eye socket, the slivered skull, and rebuild them like bricks. She wanted to take away the fear she'd seen in her child's startled eyes, but she couldn't. Paul was dead; he'd been killed in an instant.

TWENTY-SEVEN

*E*UGENIA SAT AT HER DESK, but no words came. Out of habit she'd opened her diary, but the blank page gathered dust; there was no help there. "You know we French stormed Ratisbon . . ." Eugenia thought. That phrase was someone else's sentiment, someone else's discovery.

> *. . . On a little mound, Napoleon*
> *Stood on our storming-day;*

I should take off my dress, Eugenia told herself, but she didn't make a move. I should have it cleaned, too. It's covered with stains and mud from the jungle. And torn. Olive could mend it, though, bleach out the spots, replace the lace; she's a wonder at repairs.

But the white shirtwaist Eugenia had worn in Kuching remained stuck to her skin: the bodice liver colored and stiff as cardboard, the sleeves hard as tree bark. When I stand up, Eugenia promised herself, that's what I'm going to do. When I leave this chair, that's what I'll do first. When my feet start to work again.

Outside the cabin windows, the *Alcedo* found her bearings in the open sea, tossed the coast of Borneo behind, and headed for the deepest water she could find. *It's good to be home,* the ship seemed to say. *It's good to feel salt waves beneath me again.* The yacht shivered, rattled her timbers, and bellowed with pleasure. Eugenia heard nothing.

Instead she stretched her hands forward and looked at her cuffs. They were flecked with brown, with bits of flesh, with hair. Her hands were splotchy, too, and under her fingernails were black lines of blood. If I take off this dress, she wondered, what will I wear?

"You know we French stormed Ratisbon . . ." Eugenia repeated silently. Then she stared at her neat little desk top. It was the same as yesterday, the same as last week, or a month ago. There were her books in their proper place. There was her pen, her paper, the photographs of her three children's faces: the silver freshly polished, the glass wiped clean.

I could open the closet and choose a new frock, Eugenia argued. I could bathe, wash my hair, call Olive. I could stand up. Lie in bed. I could go out on deck and take a brisk walk. . . .

You know we French stormed Ratisbon:
A mile or so away, . . .

In the passageway there was a scurry and whisper. They're bringing another tray, Eugenia realized, as if I'd want to eat. My son is dead. What good is food?

"Genie?" The name came through the closed door. "Genie? It's your father." The words sounded miles away, read not spoken—or recited badly like some hammy actor in a stagy play. Eugenia couldn't decide if it was worse to lie to yourself or to others. When you delude yourself, she wondered, does the rest automatically follow?

"Genie, dear. You must come out. Eat something, you know. Or take a healthful stroll in the fresh air. . . . We're way out at sea, now. . . . Not a trace of land, so you wouldn't have to . . . you wouldn't have to . . ." The rehearsed chat faltered; Eugenia's father was ill equipped for his role.

". . . Besides, Genie, you haven't had a bite in well over twenty-four hours. . . . And we need your help, don't you know. Poor George is . . . well . . . he's beside himself, really, carrying on and so forth. . . . We can't get him to . . ." If there was more to the speech, it was lost on the listener.

Poor George, Eugenia repeated to herself, poor George. Drunk as a skunk with a shipload of worried attendants. Blaming himself for the death of his son. My heart bleeds! He wanted to escape scot-free, I suppose. He wanted to walk away with his hands lily white and a smile on his face. And now he expects our pity!

Twenty-four hours, Eugenia thought again. One day. Yesterday morning we were in Kuching. In the afternoon we sailed. It's afternoon now, I think . . . and another day. Or it's morning and the day after that. I should get up. I should change. But Eugenia stayed in her chair.

Time passed. There were more mutterings in the passageway: Mrs. Du-Plessis was gooey, Dr. DuPlessis reasoning; even Whit put in a brief appearance at the far side of the door. Then her father returned saying something about "a funeral service," about its being "a mere formality . . . a few hymns, a prayer or two, nothing too taxing. . . . With the heat and all, Genie . . . can't delay forever . . . poor little fellow won't keep. . . . Thirty hours, don't you know, is a . . ."

Next came: ". . . . You can have other children, Genie. . . . You're luckier than most. . . . You'll see. . . . And George can . . . well, you and George will. . . ."

Eugenia put her hand on her stomach and felt it heave. Revulsion, nausea, new life: What did it matter? Sins of omission, she told herself, or sins of commission. If you see something and look the other way, or you never see it at all, are you any less to blame? If you allow yourself to be guided by ignorance or fear, if you let the easy path seduce you, do you free yourself of guilt?

Eugenia stood up, pushed the chair away, and lifted her hands from the desk. It was time to change her clothes. She started with the cuff buttons, but they were stuck to the fabric and difficult to manipulate. A dark crust flaked off on her fingers, and when she went to work on the sleeves, the remaining white fabric was streaked with rust-red stripes.

I'll take off this dress, she promised, then I'll put it away. I won't let Olive fix it or clean it. I'll hide it in the top of my closet and no one, but me, will see it again.

In her chemise and ripped stockings, Eugenia found a large Kashmiri shawl, spread it on the floor, and placed the dress in its center. Then she folded the sleeves, the skirt, and the bodice into smaller and smaller squares.

> . . . Out 'twixt the battery-smokes there flew
> A rider, bound on bound
> Full galloping; nor bridle drew
> Until he reached the mound.

Eugenia continued her work; her movements were gentle but orderly, and the poem kept pace.

> . . . By just his horse's mane, a boy;
> You hardly could suspect . . .

Eugenia rolled the parcel into a smooth, flat bundle, doubling it back on itself, again and again and again, then she tied it with a sash of sky-blue linen, and stored it in the highest reaches of her closet. That's all I have left of Paul, she thought, and simultaneously remembered the poem's terrible last line.

When her mother came into her cabin, Lizzie was amazed to see a green silk evening dress, and she blurted out her surprise without meaning to. "But those are dinner clothes, Mother!" she said, then added a sad little "You look beautiful, though."

Eugenia heard the wistfulness in her elder daughter's voice. "You will too, darling," she said. "Everything comes in its proper time. You'll be grown up before you know it."

That wasn't what Eugenia had come to say. And she hadn't meant to put on a dinner dress, either. It had merely been the first thing her hand had fallen on after she'd put away the shirtwaist she'd worn in Kuching.

Eugenia sat on Lizzie's bed, gazed at the orderly comfort of the room, listened to the peaceful tick of the porcelain clock and the gentle lull of waves beneath the portholes. Outside the sky was as blue as ever, and the reflection it and the water sent washing into the white room, across the ceiling and dancing over the tidy desks, the dressers, the beds, and the chairs was the same as it had been months before. Paul could have been next door in his own cabin, or he could have been out on deck with Whit or running anywhere through the large and welcoming ship. If you close your mind to reason, Eugenia thought, you can believe anything you want.

She drew in a decisive breath, settled her hands in her lap, and began: "Lizzie . . ." Eugenia said, then realized she had no idea where her words would carry her. It was the first time she'd spoken to her children without a plan, without a lecture or lesson in mind.

"I know these past two days have been difficult. . . ." Eugenia hesitated again, ". . . And that you and your sister must have felt frightened, and I'm sure lonely and deserted, too. . . ." Eugenia stopped; the words were a terrible weight. "Difficult isn't a very good description, is it? For what we all feel?"

Lizzie wanted to say something kind, but she couldn't think what. Her mother's fancy clothes made her uneasy. So did this strange, quiet speech. Mother seemed like a different person. Before Paul died, she never would have worn an evening frock in daytime. Or come into her daughters' cabin and huddled like a visitor on the edge of the bed. The transformation made Lizzie feel jumpy and scared; she was afraid she might cry at any moment. So she sat icy still, and didn't blink her eyes.

"... For what we feel ..." Eugenia repeated, then pulled herself together and continued in a louder voice:

"... And I'm as much to blame as anyone. More perhaps, because I ..." The words trailed off again. Because I what? Eugenia asked herself. Because I'm better than other people? a more loving parent? That thought nearly undid her. Never let yourself be guided by ignorance or fear, she reminded herself. The phrase brought a measure of solace.

"... But we have to stick together, Liz. ..." Eugenia's words came easier. They were said for her daughter and not for herself. "... We three: you, your sister, and I. We have to stick together because we love each other. Because we're a family ..."

What about Father? Lizzie wanted to protest. Doesn't he count? Isn't he sad, too? Won't he miss Paul just as much as we do? Confusion made Lizzie angry. Her face turned red and she bit at her lips.

Eugenia looked at her daughter. What passed between them was a recognition of place. *I am your mother,* Eugenia's face and body said, while Lizzie's answered: *I know and I want to trust you, but I'm not sure I can.*

"I realize you're worried about your father, Lizzie." Eugenia's voice was soft. "I know you haven't seen him, and I'm sure there've been all sorts of ..." Rumors? Eugenia thought. Gossip? What do I say to help my child? Does she know that her father's been drunk in his cabin ever since Paul died? that even the stewards don't want to go near him? that he spends his few waking hours shouting incomprehensibly and flinging objects at the walls?

"... all sorts of frightening talk. ...

"But what I want to say, Liz, is that we are, each one of us, responsible for what we do: I am, you are, and your father as well. If we make mistakes, we are the only ones who can set things straight. I think you know that already. You've had squabbles with your sister—baby squabbles, they must seem now—but you're the only ones who can patch things up. I can't intervene, or Prue, or anyone else.

"Our lives are our own. Do you understand what I'm saying?"

"Yes," Lizzie answered. She had the most sickening feeling all of a sudden. She knew exactly what her mother was going to say next. "Aren't we going back to Philadelphia?" she asked.

It took Eugenia a moment to answer her daughter, not because she was undecided or hadn't framed her response, but because Lizzie's perception was so acute. Mother and daughter regarded each other and neither looked away.

"No," Eugenia said, "we're not." Then she added, "You are a brave girl, and I love you with all my heart."

• • •

When Eugenia opened the door to George's study, he was in a momentary lull, slumped in a chair like a worn-out bear, his head pitched forward on his chest, his legs sprawled and his arms in a heap. The room smelled of urine, vomit, and rot and there was no table, no lamp, no bookshelf or painting, left untouched. Every surface had a scar. Tossed books dotted the floor; straight chairs had tumbled; the walls were speckled with holes; and broken glass lay crumpled in dirty, wet piles. Eugenia waded through the wreckage; she lifted her skirts and kicked her way clear. "George," she demanded. "Wake up."

Her husband came to with a moan. "Didn't see them . . ." he said. ". . . Didn't know . . . thought Father . . ." Or words that sounded similar. The voice was as thick as damp fur. "Father . . ." George repeated. The word could have been *father* or *farther* or *fodder.*

"George," Eugenia repeated. There was not one ounce of pity in her. "Sit up and listen."

George complied immediately. As best he could, at any rate. An order was a thing he'd never been able to refuse, and, in his mind somewhere, there was his father calling him to attention. Or it might have been angels. Angels coming to forgive him. An angel in a green robe with hair fluted like a lady's. George remembered that his son was dead, that the fault had been his and that his only hope was redemption.

"Angel," he repeated. "Here." Then he slapped his knees together and scrunched backward in his seat. The cushion was wet as a puddle. "Here I go," he added, then flung his hands through the air. They landed with a plop on his lap.

"It's Eugenia, George." Anger made Eugenia still as stone. At another time she might have confused the emotion with serenity or peace; she might have thought: How reasonable I've become. But this sensation had nothing to do with tranquillity. "I want you to wake up and listen."

"Awake . . . awake . . . awake . . ." George chirped, then he flopped his head backward and eyed his wife. "Looking lovely, my dear. . . . Special occasions always . . . though, green . . . green dress . . . thought black more appropriate . . ."

Eugenia didn't listen. "I've instructed Captain Cosby to put me and the girls ashore on Billiton Island," she said.

"Going . . . ?" George asked, then blinked, trying to remember what shore excursion he was missing today.

"We will remain there until the fortnightly packet comes from Singapore."

"Singa . . ." George echoed. He was searching his memory, but he was certain the place hadn't been on the itinerary. Not the last time he looked, anyway.

"Singapore, George!" Impatience stomped through Eugenia's throat. "The yacht is not going there. I am. I am going to Singapore without you. And I'm taking the girls."

"Taking the . . . ?" Fog began to clear in George's brain. Or it lifted long enough for him to see shapes: ideas in the mist, or reason.

"The girls. Your daughters. Lizzie and Jinx. I am taking them off this boat, and I'm not coming back. We are leaving, George. I am leaving you. The girls are going with me.

"Most likely we will settle in Shanghai, though," Eugenia added after a moment. "In China. I've heard there is a large European settlement there. English, French, and so on." The details of her plan lined up in a row. Eugenia drew comfort from repeating them. "It's a cosmopolitan place. There's a school for English-speaking children."

It took a while for this information to sink in. It wasn't that Eugenia hadn't been succinct enough or that her voice lacked precision; it was George's lack of belief that turned him frog-faced and panting. "Leaving . . ." he gulped, ". . . leaving . . ."

There was nothing for Eugenia to add. She stood her ground, and tried not to look at the room: the shredded curtains, the ruined carpet, the hunting prints dangling on their wires. Did I ever believe in this voyage? she wondered. Did I think a change of place would save my marriage? It was so hard to remember. The young woman who'd walked on board the *Alcedo* might as well have been a child of ten.

". . . The girls . . . ?" George asked. The truth was beginning to settle.

"I've told Lizzie," Eugenia answered.

This seemed a terrible blow. George's shoulders slumped, and his chin collapsed. Little Liz, he thought through the rain and gloom of his brain: Little Liz, just like a picture. He remembered Madeira all of a sudden and Lizzie dressed like a Spanish lady; she was wrapped in a rose-colored shawl, with her hair piled on a tortoiseshell comb. George blinked his eyes. Tears or something milklike and warm squelched on his cheeks.

"Not going . . . Philadelphia . . . ?" he muttered. It was his last feeble try.

"No," Eugenia answered. She said the word slowly, as if she were thinking something through as she spoke. "I will never set foot in Philadelphia again."

• • •

For Paul's funeral, Captain Cosby had brought the ship round so it faced into the oncoming wind and tide. He knew it was necessary for the yacht to move forward immediately after the service ended, that the weighted body must slide from the open-ended coffin and sink quickly from sight. But it was equally important for the engines to idle during the burial prayers, for the *Alcedo* to have, at least, an illusion of compassion and peace. Captain Cosby wanted to spare the family any unnecessary grief. He also knew that all arrangements were his responsibility. No one on board, with the exception of Mrs. Axthelm, seemed capable of action. But, of course, you couldn't have a mother plan her own child's funeral. It would be inappropriate, to say the least.

Captain Cosby instructed the mate to go to full steam following a nod from the deck, then he picked up his *Book of Common Prayer* from the wheelhouse desk and carried it aft toward the stern. He was there in advance of the mourners. He needed to make sure everything was ready: the small, cloth-draped coffin and the white-suited sailors who would tip it over the rail.

Captain Cosby adjusted the placement of the standing desk they'd use as a pulpit, then he ordered a table brought out from the main saloon and had Paul's small coffin set on it, then finally told Higgins to find two sprays of greenery and enough black ribbon to create several large bows. As an afterthought, he had nine dining chairs carried out as well. This was an emotional time, the captain reasoned. Fainting was not unheard of, especially among the weaker sex. When all was in readiness, Captain Cosby sent for the family.

Eugenia was the first on deck. She had Lizzie and Jinx right behind her, but her body, hesitating in the doorway, blocked their view momentarily and she had the scene to herself. A pulpit, an altar, a coffin covered with a white pall, funeral wreaths, and nine dining chairs grouped in a semicircle. Chairs? Eugenia wondered. Chairs from the dining saloon? It was all her mind could take in. She registered what she saw, and moved forward into the light.

The girls followed, then Dr. DuPlessis supporting his whimpering wife, then Prue, then Whit, and finally the Honorable Nicholas hovering near George. Eugenia walked to the makeshift sanctuary. She refused to sit. Instead she took Jinx's hand, and then Lizzie's and placed the girls beside her: Jinx at her right, Lizzie at her left. With that spare movement completed, Eugenia stood straight and still. The others could stand or sink or collapse; it was no concern of hers.

There was some consternation over Eugenia's decision, but in the end, the entire party followed her example and stayed on their feet with their backs turned reluctantly to the chairs. They maintained the same wavering line they'd used in entering the deck, though George edged his way closer to the rail. He thought he might need some extra support.

After George and the Honorable Nicholas had found an acceptable spot, Captain Cosby opened his prayer book and began to read from "The Order for the Burial of the Dead":

" 'I am the resurrection and the life, saith the Lord: he that believeth in me, though he were dead, yet shall he live; and whosoever liveth and believeth in me shall never die . . . ' "

Captain Cosby's voice filled the air; it seemed to echo as though rattling through a large, empty tunnel. Even the funnel smoke never sounded like that, Eugenia thought, even the wind in a storm. She wondered what the difference was: a man reading or the air whistling. Then she decided that the man's voice was devoid of life, while the wind had purpose; it had a road to travel.

" '. . . For I am a stranger with thee, and a sojourner . . . ' "

"A sojourner," Eugenia repeated silently. Then she clasped her daughters' shoulders and drew them as close as she dared. With the gentle rise, fall, and sideways spread of the *Alcedo*'s deck, the three became one person. Eugenia felt Jinx's body, and Lizzie's; they pressed against her hip to thigh, and when she shifted her feet for support, her daughters moved theirs as well.

" '. . . thou art God from everlasting, and world without end.

Thou turnest man to destruction . . . ' "

Suddenly Eugenia was aware of a total lack of natural sound; the waves didn't rustle and the wind didn't play among the stanchions or set the guy wires whining. And there were no birds chattering overhead. Where are the sea gulls? she wondered. Didn't they follow us from shore? Doesn't Borneo have sea gulls? Eugenia looked at the sky; it was speckless, cloudless, and colored with a blue both merciless and opaque. It was like plaster and stone and paint.

" '. . . For since by man came death, by man came also the resurrection of the dead . . . ' "

The service went on and on. Eugenia thought it lasted hours, or days. She heard the words; she tried to take them in, but they ended up sounding hollow and unreal. Captain Cosby stopped for a while and Dr. DuPlessis took his place. Eugenia had the impression he was talking about Paul, saying something about him as a child and a friend. At any rate, he wasn't reading from the prayer book. Or he didn't seem to be reading. Then the doctor left the pulpit and Captain Cosby returned.

Eugenia imagined she'd been frozen in place. With her girls so close, she couldn't move, but then she didn't really want to. The three were stuck together; one couldn't fall if the others held fast.

What other events took place in this spot? Eugenia wondered. Then she remembered the shooting match, the ship dead in the water, and the night she'd found her way down to the hold. For a moment Eugenia shut her eyes, but the blue sky was still there and the shroud with a white so pristine and flawless it scorched the back of her eyelids.

" '. . . O teach us to number our days: that we may apply our hearts unto wisdom . . .' " The word filtered through for a moment; Eugenia turned it over in her brain. She looked at it, examined it, and tried to comprehend its meaning.

Then, without warning, they were opening hymnals and singing:

"The strife is o'er, the battle done,
The victory of life is won . . ."

Eugenia guessed the hymn had been her father's choice; he'd always been partial to the facile sentiments of Eastertide. Adversity and dominion. The triumph of good sense. Eugenia didn't look at him. She didn't look at George either.

". . . The three sad days are quickly sped,
He rises glorious from the dead: . . ."

Eugenia sang as loudly as she could; she sang till her voice filled her being, till it drowned sorrow and doubt and fear, till it carried over the waves in a strong and determined line.

"From death's dread sting Thy servants free . . ."

The other voices followed Eugenia's: Lizzie and Jinx, melding into their mother's, Mrs. DuPlessis weeping copious, noisy tears, Dr. Du-Plessis frowning as if memorizing a medical text, and the Honorable Nicholas hovering, hesitant and unsure, at George's sickly side.

"That we may live and sing to Thee. . . ."

The song rang out for miles and miles and miles. When the last human voice sounded the last note of " 'Alleluia!' " the air took up the refrain, and "Alleluia" seemed to blow about the ship, whip past the funnel, roll up and down and forward and back, while the waves picked up the noise, and the *Alcedo* began to throb. Then the shout disappeared in a burst like a shell exploding. Silence returned, thicker than before: You couldn't shake it out of your ears if you tried. Captain Cosby resumed his place, opened his prayer book to another page, and began to read again:

" 'Man, that is born of woman, hath but a short time to live, and is full of misery. He cometh up, and is cut down . . .' "

Eugenia ceased listening at that point. She'd had enough. My son is dead, she thought. What good are words or hymns or consoling phrases? I had a child I called Paul; I read to him, soothed him, held him when he was sick. I touched his face when he slept. I knew him better than I know myself, and loved him a hundred times more.

Captain Cosby droned on for a while, then Eugenia's father shuffled forward and garbled something about "Paul, my only grandson . . ." while George tried to reach the makeshift pulpit and failed. Barely holding himself upright, he retreated to the rail and stared at the water as if he wanted blood. Eugenia felt Lizzie and Jinx stir under her hands. She looked at her husband as if she'd never seen him before. Or she looked through him as though he had vanished from the earth.

Then it was Captain Cosby's turn again: " 'Almighty and ever-living God,' " he said, " 'we yield unto thee most high praise and hearty thanks for the wonderful grace and virtue declared in all thy saints . . .' "

"High praise" and "hearty thanks," Eugenia thought. Those words have no place here. "Wonderful grace and virtue": Why should I praise God when my son is dead?

Eugenia gazed at the water. Families, I thought the waves were once, she remembered. Cousins and aunts and uncles, grandfathers, mothers, and children, tossing their loving lives toward a sunny sky. I thought we hovered in the midst of them, acknowledged as the same: a clan of like-minded folk.

" '. . . We therefore commit this body to the deep . . .' "

Eugenia was torn between listening and not; she felt her daughters stiffen and knew her own body did the same.

Captain Cosby paused as the sailors raised Paul's coffin.

" '. . . looking for the general Resurrection, and the life of the world to come . . .' "

The captain sprinkled seawater on the coffin's white shroud, and the cloth turned blotchy and gray as the damp spots swelled and spread. Eugenia watched them; they grew dark and stuck fast to the wood. A first taste of salt, she thought.

The sailors raised the coffin, carried it to the ship's rail, steadied it momentarily, then tipped the open end toward the sea. The body was weighted, Eugenia had known it would be: the small, mummy-wrapped package so carefully surrounded with stones, no hopeful limb could escape. But what astonished her was how quickly Paul's body slid from the box. The coffin was tilted and her child plummeted feet-first to the waves.

He was there on deck one moment, covered in a soft blanket, asleep in the hot, groggy sun, and then he was gone. Water swirled forward to cover the hole his small body had left; the place turned brine-green, then as clear as rock crystal, then silvery blue as new foam filled the void. Finally it was a white as soft as snow.

Eugenia tried to mark her son's grave, but the waves looked all alike; they stretched out forever, one sea melding into the next, around and around the earth, one hundred times if you could. A thousand. A billion, or ten. For as long as the earth turned, you'd never see the same spot again. Paul had been there and now he was gone.

This is what Eugenia wrote in her diary:

Paul is gone. It is October, near the end of the month, I think. The day doesn't matter. We held a funeral service on deck—on the fantail

The line stopped there. Hesitating only a moment, Eugenia started again. She was determined to see this thing through:

I tried to listen to the words, but my concentration wavered. I think everyone was kind. I didn't really notice. George was unwell. I couldn't have cared less.

She stopped again, aware of the ticking of her clock, the familiar noise of the ship, the waves, the engines humming, and her own heart beating:

No. What I mean is this: The whole funeral was stupid. Stupid and a waste. They all are, I suppose.

No one knows what another person feels. No one cares in the end. We are all of us alone. We do the best we can—some of us. The rest are ignorant or lazy or frightened or selfish. I have been all those things, so I know. I have done every bad thing I can imagine.

Eugenia ripped the page forward. The activity served as a reminder. She dipped the pen into the inkwell, waited with the nib poised in the air, waited too long, then was forced to re-ink it. When she continued, her strokes looked different:

I think about James sometimes. I think about where he is. I can't conceive of his death, but it must be a possibility. This is difficult to write. I don't know if I can say more. We were so happy, for a while

There was another pause as Eugenia tried to bury all memory:

The girls and I will continue on to Shanghai via Singapore and Billiton Island. Most likely as soon as the scheduled packet arrives. Captain Cosby thinks there is a fortnightly sailing. No one knows me in Shanghai. I will have the baby there. There are European doctors, and a European settlement—many nationalities, in fact. Russians, as well. We can do as we wish and live as we see fit. No one need know our history. I'm not sure what I'll tell the girls when the time comes. I suppose as little as possible.

I used to believe God would help me—or that good won out in the end. I thought fairness was returned in kind. But I don't understand why Paul had to die, and I don't know how I'll continue

Again the page was left unfinished; Eugenia nearly tore it in half in her haste to move on; then she began her final entry:

Never let yourself be guided by ignorance or fear.
Never let the brightest light be your only beacon, or the easy path seduce you.
You have the ability to choose for yourself, and you must embrace that responsibility, because it is hard won.
That's what I want to teach my daughters.

Then Eugenia wrote out the whole of the Robert Browning poem, "Incident of the French Camp." When she reached the last line, she hesitated only a moment.

You know we French stormed Ratisbon:
A mile or so away,
On a little mound, Napoleon
Stood on our storming-day;
With neck out-thrust, you fancy how,
Legs wide, arms locked behind,
As if to balance the prone brow,
Oppressive with its mind.

Just as perhaps he mused, "My plans
That soar, to earth may fall,
Let once my army-leader Lannes
Waver at yonder wall,"—
Out 'twixt the battery-smokes there flew
A rider, bound on bound
Full galloping; nor bridle drew
Until he reached the mound.

Then off there flung in smiling joy
And held himself erect
By just his horse's mane, a boy;
You hardly could suspect
(So tight he kept his lips compressed,
Scarce any blood came through),
You looked twice ere you saw his breast
Was all but shot in two.

"Well," cried he, "Emperor, by God's grace
We've got you Ratisbon!
The Marshal's in the market-place,
And you'll be there anon
To see your flag-bird flap his vans
Where I, to heart's desire,
Perched him!" The chief's eye flashed; his plans
Soared up again like fire.

The chief's eye flashed, but presently
Softened itself, as sheathes
A film the mother eagle's eye
When her bruised eaglet breathes:
"You're wounded!" "Nay," his soldier's pride
Touched to the quick, he said,
"I'm killed, sire!" And his chief beside,
Smiling, the boy fell dead.

Eugenia put down her pen, blotted the wet page, closed her diary, and replaced it with great care in its niche in her desk. Then she tidied up the inkwell, put her pen in a drawer, and stood up. There is a final moment for everything, she thought.

When the *Alcedo* entered the harbor at the English settlement on Billiton Island, Eugenia was ready. The trunks containing her clothes and the girls' were piled neatly on deck. It hadn't been so very hard; Eugenia had Prue's help and Olive's: Packing to leave was a matter of neat, uncomplicated movement. Saying her good-byes had been equally easy.

Eugenia had faltered only once, and that had been with the DuPlessises. Her father had presented no problem. There was a handshake and averting of eyes; very little was said. Eugenia decided that was for the best; whatever emotions might or might not exist were better forgotten. Then George had refused to forsake his cabin, and, again, Eugenia felt his behavior was acceptable. Or simpler to deal with.

After Captain Cosby dispatched a mate to inform her that landfall in Billiton was imminent, Eugenia walked to the foredeck rail with her daughters and watched the *Alcedo* pull closer and closer to the pier. The ramshackle pilings and tilting quay didn't look strong enough to take the ship's weight and rapid advancement, but Eugenia knew they would. Or they wouldn't. And then she and the girls and Prue would descend to the lighter and row slowly ashore. Minor obstacles had become unimportant. We will sleep where we find a bed, she thought; we will move when we need. Nothing will bind us except our own desires. We are as free as hawks in a garden. Our lives are our own. Eugenia turned her attention to the town.

It was a small place, as orderly as a village. There was only one street and that one embraced the entire bay; Eugenia could see the whole of it quite clearly; it was stalwart where there were houses and grassy where there were none, and Eugenia thought: We'll have a fine time walking here.

The day was blue and very fair; the breeze, a mixture of ocean and mountain air, was fresh and clean as a day in May, and Eugenia lifted her face to it and smiled. Jinx and Lizzie moved closer to their mother; her mood infected them and they unconsciously reached for her hands. "You are brave girls," Eugenia started to say. "You are fearless and strong," but she knew it wasn't time yet. They'd learn those lessons later. Eugenia held her daughters tight and watched the ship reach land.

POSTSCRIPT

On July 10, 1905, the steam yacht *Alcedo* returned to Philadelphia after an arduous trip around Cape Horn and up the coast of South America. Captain Cosby and a skeleton crew were the only people aboard; George Axthelm, the Honorable Nicholas Paine, Dr. and Mrs. DuPlessis, Whitney Caldwell, and all extraneous deck crew, stewards, chefs, and maids had been put ashore in San Francisco prior to the grueling Pacific/Atlantic passage.

Following extensive refurbishment of all private and public rooms, the *Alcedo* was left riding at anchor in the Frith and Company boat yard. A decision to sell her was never finalized. Neither was she used, though a minimum staff was maintained at all times. The ship's long white hull and imposing size became a fixture of the Philadelphia harbor, and finally an oddity.

When the United States entered World War I on April 6, 1917, the yacht was commandeered by the Navy and refitted for use as a troop ship. During her third transatlantic run the *Alcedo* was attacked by a German battle cruiser near Faial in the Azores and sunk.